PERILOUS AWAKENING

Loedicia lay by the campfire asleep, immersed in a dream she never wanted to leave. In it she was with Roth Chapman, the husband who had won her after so long a brutal struggle. He was caressing her slowly, skillfully, bringing her toward the all-dissolving intoxication of desire.

Then she realized it was not a dream. Opening her eyes, she saw the handsome, ruthless face of De-Mosse Gervaise, the frontier scout who was legendary both for his feats of courage and his conquests in love. Already his hand was beneath her buckskin shirt, his fingers moving gently, stroking her nipples until they stood in firm peaks.

She knew what was happening now, but even as her tongue formed a protest, her hungering flesh mocked her feeble words. . . .

THE WILD STORMS OF HEAVEN

Watch for *DEFY THE SAVAGE WINDS*, the fourth novel in this bestselling Signet series.

The
WILD STORMS OF HEAVEN

JUNE LUND SHIPLETT

A *Sequel* to
THE RAGING WINDS
OF HEAVEN
and
REAP THE
BITTER WINDS

A SIGNET BOOK

To the memory of my beloved parents,
Gladys and Arthur Lund.
I wish they could have lived to see it.

SIGNET
Published by the Penguin Group
Penguin Books USA Inc., 375 Hudson Street,
New York, New York 10014, U.S.A.
Penguin Books Ltd, 27 Wrights Lane,
London W8 5TZ, England
Penguin Books Australia Ltd, Ringwood,
Victoria, Australia
Penguin Books Canada Ltd, 10 Alcorn Avenue,
Toronto, Ontario, Canada M4V 3B2
Penguin Books (N.Z.) Ltd, 182–190 Wairau Road,
Auckland 10, New Zealand

Penguin Books Ltd, Registered Offices:
Harmondsworth, Middlesex, England

Published by Signet, an imprint of New American Library,
a division of Penguin Books USA Inc.

First Printing, February, 1980
17 16 15 14 13 12 11 10 9

This first chapter of this book appeared in *Reap the Bitter Winds*,
the second volume of the trilogy.

 REGISTERED TRADEMARK—MARCA REGISTRADA

Printed in the United States of America

BOOKS ARE AVAILABLE AT QUANTITY DISCOUNTS WHEN USED TO PROMOTE PRODUCTS OR SERVICES.
FOR INFORMATION PLEASE WRITE TO PREMIUM MARKETING DIVISION, PENGUIN BOOKS USA INC., 375
HUDSON STREET, NEW YORK, NEW YORK 10014.

Loedicia

1

Moonlight crept into the shadowy folds of the furled sails and made strange patterns take shape like ghosts through the rigging, as a full breeze gently rocked the ship. The night was warm and humid, the scent of magnolias from the plantations along Port Royal Sound filled the air with their sweet fragrance, and below the quarterdeck, in one of the cabins, two figures lay pressed close in a narrow bunk, unmindful of the heat or the late hour.

Roth stirred, feeling Loedicia's softness against him, and once more he was aroused. She was life to him, and he could hardly believe that after all these years she would finally be his again. In the morning he'd have the young man who captained the ship—the one they called Beau—he'd have him perform the ceremony making her Mrs. Roth Chapman, then he'd take her to the Château on the banks of the Broad River, his home, where she belonged, and this time it would be forever.

Loedicia moved as he stirred against her and she nestled even closer in his arms. She hadn't really been asleep, only dozing. Her body was too alive for sleep, her senses too keen. She was content in his arms, yet so aware of him. She felt his bare skin next to her, the soft hairs on his chest brushing her face as she turned her body all the way toward him, snuggling close.

Nineteen years earlier she had married Roth, thinking her first husband, Quinn Locke, was dead; then Quinn had miraculously turned up alive barely two months after the nuptials, making her second marriage void. But she had become pregnant before Quinn's return and had given Roth a son. A son her first husband had resented and almost grown to hate over the years. Quinn saw the boy as a symbol of the love between Loedicia and Roth that had never died. Although Loedicia had loved her husband fiercely, she'd loved Roth too and had always kept a special place in her heart for him. The tortuous years between her brief marriage to Roth and the present had been wrought with anguish as she'd tried to rationalize her feelings for the two men, but now Quinn was dead. He'd been killed by a bullet intended for Roth's son. The son Quinn had thought at one time was his but against whom he had turned as the child grew and he realized the truth. With Quinn's death a part of Loedicia had died too. A part that could never be replaced. Yet at the same time, a new peace was born within her. She'd given Quinn her love unashamedly from the depths of her heart, putting all else aside, but now, her love was free again. Free to be given to Roth.

Roth's arms moved up her back, his lips pressing against her forehead. "Are you awake?" he asked, whispering in the dimly lit cabin, and she sighed.

"I haven't really been asleep."

He held her closer, paying little heed to the sweat that stuck to their bodies, only conscious of his need for her. "Sometimes I think I'm dreaming," he said as his hand moved down over her hip, feeling its velvet smoothness, and she lifted her head lazily, her violet eyes gazing into his handsome face, and she reached up slowly, touching the slight frost at his temples that made him look even more attractive, running her hand through his dark, almost black hair.

"You told me once you never wanted to see me again," she whispered softly, and he frowned.

"Did I say that?"

"Emphatically."

"That's because I couldn't have you."

"And now?"

"I'll never let you go," and he kissed her deeply, letting his hands caress her once more, bringing her to life.

Suddenly she felt his muscles tense, and his hand stopped on her breast, caressing it hesitantly as he became distracted. "Did you hear anything?" he asked softly, his lips against hers, and she stared into his dark eyes, wanting only to kiss him again, but instead she listened, straining her ears.

"Only the waves," she replied, but he jerked his head suddenly, looking at the ceiling.

"Listen!" he cautioned, and she tuned her ears toward the ceiling of the small cabin.

4

Now she could hear scuffling noises, soft but firm, on deck. "Could it be morning?"

He shook his head. "It couldn't be later than two or three."

"Then who?"

Suddenly there was a knock on the cabin door, and Roth sitrred, startled. He reluctantly took his arms from about her and slid from the small bunk, slipping into his underwear and breeches, and hurried to the door as she pulled up the lone blanket to cover herself.

He unlocked the door and opened it hesitantly until he saw his son's worried face. The boy was eighteen now. No longer a boy, but a young man far older than his years, and for Roth, looking at him was like looking into a mirror. He had the same dark hair and dark eyes. So dark it was hard to see their true color.

"What is it?" he asked, whispering, and Heath frowned.

Heath was second mate on the *Golden Eagle*, a French privateer, at the moment anchored off the coast of Port Royal disguised as the *White Dolphin*, a merchant ship.

"Beau wants to see you above deck," Heath said softly. "It's urgent," and his face reddened. He'd met his father for the first time only the day before, and although he'd warmed to him, the thought that he was spending the night with his mother in the cabin without having the convenience of a marriage ceremony embarrassed him. Mothers weren't supposed to do things like that. But then, his mother was different. She was beautiful and unpredictable, and he'd seen more than one man look at her with hungry eyes.

"I'll be right up," Roth said, and closed the door as Heath turned away; then he walked back to where Loedicia waited. He dropped down, sitting beside her on the bunk. "I don't know what's happened," he said. "But Beau wants me on deck. I shouldn't be too long." He leaned over, kissing her long and hard, hating to leave her like this.

She watched him leave the cabin barefoot and shirtless, and she sighed contentedly.

Heath was waiting at the end of the passage, and Roth followed, feeling the warm breeze as he stepped on deck. Beau was at the rail in much the same attire as Roth, only he was staring toward shore, a grim look on his swarthy face.

"What is it?" asked Roth as he addressed the younger man, and Beau straightened, nodding off beyond the jib.

Roth followed the motion of his head until his eyes distinctly made out the outline of a ship some four or five hundred yards away. It was silhouetted in the moonlight, the rigging gaunt, like picked-over bones, with the sails furled.

"British," stated Roth, and he turned back to Beau. "How long has it been there?"

"Long enough to send a boat in to shore."

"In the middle of the night?"

"They called from shore a few minutes ago, and insist on coming aboard."

Roth frowned. He was certain he knew the ship. Only yesterday morning he'd been in Beaufort with its captain signing some papers the captain had brought to him from his businesses in England. Roth lived in Port Royal, owned a shipyard in Beaufort, a shipping company in Charleston, and still ran the shipping and shipbuilding companies his father had left him in England. He continued frowning as he glanced at Beau.

"You think they're suspicious?"

"I know they are. Why else would they want to come aboard?"

"They can't touch you in these waters."

Beau sneered. "May I ask who's to stop them?" and Roth flushed.

Beau was right. There wasn't an American ship in sight, not even a merchant. They were looking at a British ship in American waters without any jurisdiction, but the fact that the whole British Navy was looking for Beau made him uneasy. If the British captain learned the truth, he'd overlook protocol, apologize to the Americans later, and Beau and Heath would hang for sure.

"I'll go talk to them," suggested Roth. "Maybe we're wrong assuming they're suspicious of who you really are. I know the British captain. Maybe I can talk him out of wanting to come aboard."

Beau's eyes relaxed momentarily as he quietly gave orders for the men to get a boat ready and Roth headed back to the cabin.

"I have to go ashore for a few minutes," he explained to Loedicia as he stood below in the cabin a few minutes later, putting on his shirt and boots. "There's a British ship lying off the port bow with a nose for trouble, and I think her captain's smarter than we think. He wants to send out a boarding party."

She raised up on her elbows, watching him, then sat the rest of the way up as he talked.

He leaned over the bed, and she laughed as he pulled her

6

into his arms, his body warming her. "I wish they hadn't disturbed us."

"I know," she answered.

"I love you."

Her eyes shone. "I love you too," and he kissed her sensuously, his mouth devouring her, reluctant to leave, hating to be away from her even for a short time.

"I'd better go before he sends Heath back down," he said as he released her and left the cabin.

Men were scurrying about in the darkness as he reached the deck, and Beau was fully dressed now as he waited next to the rope ladder. The longboat was already in the water, bobbing up and down like a cork, and Roth stopped, glancing over the side.

"I'd better go alone," he said as he saw a man waiting for him in the small boat, and Beau looked at him sharply. "Under the circumstances, I think it's best, just in case," and Beau stared at him a minute, then agreed, so the man in the boat climbed back aboard and Roth started over the side, confident it was nothing to worry about and praying he was right.

On shore, Captain Horace Marlin paced the small dock, then stopped, looking abruptly at the three sailors standing a few feet from him. All three had been aboard a frigate captured by Captain Beau Thunder a little over a year earlier, but they had managed to escape from the French prison they'd been thrown into. On returning to England, they'd been reassigned and were now part of the captain's crew.

"I hope you three are right about this," the captain said as he faced them. "I don't relish instigating an international incident, then finding out we were wrong."

All three men stood patiently as the captain fussed about, glancing at the rest of the men he'd brought to shore with him; then finally the sailor in the middle spoke.

"We couldn't be mistaken, sir," he said. "I'd know the lines of the *Golden Eagle* anywhere. She rides different in the water. There's just something about the ship. Once you see it, you never forget it. That is, if you're a sailor and know your ships. I'll swear that ship's the *Golden Eagle*."

The captain straightened, then glanced toward the ship again, in time to see a small boat leave its side and head for shore, and he scowled. "Now, who the devil could that be?" he said, and reached next to him where his aide stood, and asked for his spyglass.

One man was silhouetted in the boat, and he was rowing

toward them. But it was too dark to see who it was. The captain kept his eye on the small boat all the way in until it was just a few yards away; then he cursed softly as he recognized Roth Chapman.

Roth swung the boat into the pier and called out, "Tie up!" then he tossed the rope to a sailor standing near the edge, and when the boat was secure, he climbed ashore. "Are you insane?" he began as he faced the captain, his face dark with anger. "It's three in the morning! What the hell are you trying to do, anyway?"

The captain blustered, licking his lips. He'd had no idea Roth Chapman was aboard the ship, and he was as startled to see him now as he would have been to see the King of England. "Mr. Chapman!" he exclaimed, and his face reddened. "I had no idea."

"Surely you've an explanation," snapped Roth, and the captain flushed.

God damn! Now what could he do? This was probably one of Roth's private ships. Roth was not only one of the richest men in England and America, but a close friend of the King of England and grandson of the late Earl of Cumberland, and a privileged guest in British society, even though he'd chosen to live in America. But yet . . . the men were so determined, all three of them. He glanced at them quickly, then back to Roth.

"I have three sailors over there, sir," he said formidably, "who were once part of the crew of a ship captured by the notorious Captain Thunder. All three, I'm afraid, claim that the ship you just left is his ship, the *Golden Eagle*."

Roth's eyes narrowed, and he turned, looking at the three men. The pier was dark and their faces were hard to read. He turned back to the captain. "And when did they come to this conclusion?" he asked.

"Two of them work night watch, the other's the cook."

"Night watch? You mean they've only seen the ship in the dark, yet they think they can identify it?"

"They're good sailors," explained Captain Marlin. "They know their ships."

"Not as well as they should," said Roth. "That ship is the *White Dolphin* out of Jamaica."

"Excuse me, Captain," interrupted the sailor in the middle, and the captain turned to him, his face still flushed.

"Well?"

"Sir," the man began, "the *Golden Eagle* has a scroll design along the side, hiding its gun ports when they're not in

8

use, her jib boom is extra long, and she doesn't carry a figurehead. I realize it's dark, but I suggest you look through your spyglass."

The captain still held the glass in his hand, and he frowned, then put it to his eye. He took his time scrutinizing the ship, the glass moving across every inch as it lay quiet in the water. He scanned the jib, his eyes taking in its length, then moved to where there should be a figurehead; there was none. He moved the glass to the side, where the faint outline of a scroll design was visible in the moonlight, then back again toward the jib, just to make sure before taking it from his eye.

He turned to Roth, his eyes wary. If this was the *Golden Eagle*, what the hell was Roth Chapman doing aboard? And if it wasn't the *Golden Eagle*, why did it fit the description?

"I think we'll take a look aboard anyway," he said, his curiosity aroused. "It shouldn't do any harm."

Roth's jaw set angrily. Of all the luck. He glanced toward the ship. He could barely make out figures moving about on her deck, and he bit his lip. If Captain Marlin and his crew set foot on board, anything could happen and probably would, because Beau wouldn't give in without a fight. Beau was three-quarters Indian, although he looked like his French grandfather, but Heath said he could be savage at times, and Loedicia and Heath would be right in the middle of it.

"Captain," said Roth stubbornly, trying to argue him out of it as the captain and his men began heading for their boats, "these are American waters. You can't just board any ship you want because you think something's wrong," and the captain stopped, looking about him at the quiet night.

There wasn't another man on the dock except his sailors, and not another ship in sight. "Mr. Chapman, sir," he said, pretending politeness, "I don't give a damn what waters I'm in. I've been hunting that bastard for months. If that ship isn't the *Golden Eagle*, I want to know why she fits the description my men have given me, and if she is the *Golden Eagle*, I intend to take her, American waters or no American waters!" He eyed Roth suspiciously. "And if she is the *Golden Eagle*, sir," he stated boldly, "I'd sure like to know what the hell you were doing aboard her," and Roth's face went white as the captain turned and continued getting into the boat with his men.

Now what could he do? Beau had been doing him a favor bringing Loedicia to him, and now look at the mess he was in.

9

The captain stopped and turned, looking at him. "Are you coming with us, sir?" he asked, and Roth hesitated as he stared at the captain. It was so dark he could barely see his face, but he didn't like what he saw. Captain Marlin was a crusty old goat who'd been on the seas too long for his own good and was too used to having his own way, and he liked nothing better than a battle to prove his worth.

"I'll take the boat I came ashore in," he answered, and climbed into the longboat by himself, his hair bristling at the captain's arrogance. He had to think of something by the time they reached the ship, but as he swung out from the pier behind the captain's two longboats, he realized they were leaving him behind, and he tried to row faster.

Suddenly he heard a shout from the captain's boat and glanced up, his oars stopping in midair as he gazed across the water at the *Golden Eagle*. He watched, fascinated, as the sails began to unfurl one by one, and slowly, luxuriously caught in the night breeze; with a creak and groan the *Golden Eagle* heaved forward and began moving, inching across the water. And as each new sail unfurled, his heart beat all the faster and he sat still in the boat, holding tightly to the oars, a sickening feeling in the pit of his stomach as the ship picked up speed. Loedicia was still on the ship, and here he was in this goddamn boat!

His eyes followed it as it moved through the water, each new sail that unfurled lengthening the distance between them.

"Row toward the *Fortress*," yelled Captain Marlin, seeing his prize begin slipping from his hands, and the British longboats turned in the water, heading for the sleeping man-of-war, increasing their speed as the captain shouted angrily.

Roth cursed as he sat helplessly in the drifting boat, watching the *Golden Eagle* slowly melt into the darkness; then he turned his head, watching as the longboats reached the British man-of-war and the ship came to life. Within a few minutes sails were unfurling, the anchor had been weighed, and she began moving slowly forward.

Roth watched solemnly, his hands still clenching the oars as the ship moved along in the dead of night, giving chase to the *Golden Eagle* until it too disappeared from sight.

For a long time he sat motionless, staring off into the darkness that surrounded him, hearing only the gentle lap of the water hitting against the side of the boat, his heart not wanting to believe what had just happened.

The night was exceptionally quiet now, not another soul in sight, and he cursed disgustedly as he dipped the oars back in the water and began turning the small boat toward shore. He was angry, upset, and frustrated. Of all the stupid things to happen. He shouldn't have stayed the night. He should have gathered Dicia and her baggage together and taken her back to the Château last night when he'd first arrived, but he'd been so thrilled at being with her again that nothing else had mattered.

He should have remembered that Captain Marlin and the *Fortress* were at Beaufort, but he hadn't dreamed they'd set sail before Beau could leave, and besides, who would think anyone would recognize the *Golden Eagle* in her disguise? Heath had explained that they'd used it successfully dozens of times when they were in neutral ports.

Roth maneuvered the small longboat in at the dock, tied up, and climbed ashore, standing alone in the darkness, the breeze ruffling his hair. He took a deep breath, then turned abruptly and headed for the livery where he'd left the horses earlier in the evening.

His son, Heath, Heath's half-sister, Rebel, and Rebel's husband, Brandon Avery, the Duke of Bourland, had ridden inland early in the day to fetch him, and he and Heath had come back alone, leaving Rebel and her husband at the Château. They were there now, waiting for him to bring Loedicia back.

No lights were on in the livery, it being almost four in the morning by now, as he stood deciding what to do, then walked up and began pounding on the door.

It was some minutes before the bleary-eyed stableman swung the door open and held the lantern up to stare at him.

"What the devil . . . Mr. Chapman!" He rubbed his eyes, then blinked. "Somethin' wrong, sir?" he asked, and Roth stepped inside, not offering an explanation.

"I need my horse, Tom," he said, and headed for the stall where the horses he and Heath had used were bedded down for the night. He searched about, finding the saddle, and began saddling the horse quickly as the man stared sleepy-eyed.

"It ain't even light out," Tom protested, but Roth paid little attention as he finished saddling one horse, then went to the other.

When both horses were saddled, he walked them outside, Tom shuffling behind in his nightshirt, and the last Tom saw of him and the two horses was their backsides as they headed inland.

"Now, if that don't beat all," he exclaimed, shaking his head; then he shuffled back inside, wondering what had happened to the young man who'd been with Mr. Chapman earlier.

He set the lantern down and blew it out, then went to the window at the back of the room he kept next to the horses' stalls, and he leaned over, looking out. The back of the livery overlooked the water, and he squinted as he gazed out over the sound. There was nothing in sight, only the faint moonlight on the empty water, and he wondered where the boat was that Mr. Chapman had rowed to earlier that evening. Oh, well. He shrugged, stretching lazily, then scratched his stomach. 'Tweren't none of his business anyway, and he crawled back into bed.

Roth slowed the horses to a walk as he left the sleeping town of Port Royal behind. What was the use of tiring the horses when there wasn't a damn thing he could do? By now Beau Dante, known to the British Navy and his crew alike as Captain Thunder, was probably past Hilton Head, heading out to sea.

He thought over events of the past few hours. He'd been in the fields at his plantation yesterday afternoon, seeing how things were progressing, when he'd caught a glimpse of a carriage coming up the drive to the house. He'd left the field on horseback and ridden to the house to discover Heath, Rebel, and the duke. He'd met Rebel and the duke in London the year before, and as he rode along now, he thought back to those days.

He'd been on a business trip to Portsmouth, England, and had had to ride into London for an audience with the king and some of his naval advisers when he'd run into Loedicia, her husband, Quinn, and their two children, Rebel, a beautiful girl almost nineteen, and Teak, a tall strapping blond boy of fourteen who looked every bit of eighteen and was the image of his father.

He remembered seeing Loedicia for the first time after so many years of separation. He'd come to a ball given by the Duchess of Bourland, Brandon Avery's aunt, her first ball since the death of her husband the year before, and he'd found himself staring across the ballroom floor directly into Loedicia's warm violet eyes, and the same yearning sensations had flooded through him that he'd felt twenty years before when he'd first fallen in love with her. He'd tried to forget her over the years, but Loedicia wasn't a woman any man could easily forget, especially after having once been married to her. She was a sensuous woman, beautiful and earthy, with dark curly hair, violet eyes, and a natural warmth that always thrilled him, and he'd never been able to find a woman to take her place in his heart.

Years before, when they both thought her husband, Quinn, had been killed by Indians, Roth had married her, supposedly to keep Lord Kendall Varrick, Quinn's cousin, from marrying her. She'd been betrothed to Lord Varrick before running away and marrying Quinn, but she was deathly afraid of the man. When Kendall learned of Quinn's death, he'd been determined to get her back, and she'd turned to Roth.

At first her feelings for him had been mixed, Roth knew, because she'd loved her husband very much. But shortly before Quinn's unexpected return, she'd given herself to him, loving him as she once had Quinn. Then Quinn had returned, and he'd lost her.

It had been both an agony and an ecstasy to see her again in London, for he'd learned, from her own lips, that, unknown to him, she'd given him a son, Heath, and because of this her life with Quinn had been less than ideal.

London had been a fiasco in more ways than one, and as he rode along now, with the sky beginning to lighten to dawn, he remembered another dawn when he'd held Loedicia in his arms and she'd confessed her love for him. It had been at a small inn on the English downs.

Quinn had been thrown into prison by the then Earl of Locksley, Lord Elton Chaucer, whose title Quinn had put claim to. He'd been arrested on a trumped-up charge of murdering Kendall Varrick almost twenty years before, when in actuality, although no one but Roth and Quinn knew it, Loedicia had shot Lord Varrick, trying to save Quinn's life. Loedicia knew that Roth was the only one beside herself who knew the truth, and he could save Quinn because he was a friend of the king, and King George would believe him. Unfortunately, however, Quinn and Roth had almost come to blows when Roth had lost his head and kissed Loedicia at a lawn party and been caught by Quinn. The only thing that kept Roth from accepting Quinn's challenge at the time was his inability to hurt Dicia any more than he already had. So when Quinn ordered him to leave London and never see her again, he'd complied, but then there she was in the salon at his home in Portsmouth begging his help, and how could he refuse? She'd come all the way alone to plead with him. What was he to do?

They'd been caught in a storm on the way back to London from Portsmouth and been forced to take shelter in a small

13

inn, and it was a night so vivid, even now he could close his eyes and see her sitting looking at him with her warm eyes. Her body soft and wanting, begging him to love her. It was as if the years between had never been, and he'd died a thousand deaths when morning came.

He remembered the look on her face that morning when she'd realized it was time to go, and he thought of what she must be feeling now. After all these years they were finally free to love, and suddenly this. . . .

There were tears of frustration in his eyes and an ache in his heart as he felt the first tender rays of the warm sun in his face and smelled the fresh morning air. She should be here by his side, enjoying it with him—not miles away.

When he reached the Château it was shortly before ten, and although he should have been tired from lack of sleep, the anger and frustration of losing her again refused to let his eyes close. He turned the horses over to Jacob, the stableman, a big black he'd bought when he'd first come to the state three years before. Jacob had worked his price off and was now his own man and stayed on working for wages. Paying wages to a Negro was a practice Roth was condemned for by many of his neighbors, but a practice that pleased him.

Jacob rubbed the horses' noses as Roth handed him the reins, and he frowned at the sadness in Roth's eyes, but he didn't say anything, only watched, shaking his head as Roth headed for the house, where work still progressed.

Roth stopped for a minute and stared at the place, listening to the hammering and sawing, watching everyone scurrying about trying to get things done. The Château wasn't finished yet. When he'd bought the land, he put in indigo and put up a small place to live. The indigo crop had been good that first year, convincing him to stay, so now he was going ahead with the manor house, and this year they had in a crop of cotton. Last year a gentleman named Eli Whitney had made a machine he called a cotton gin that took the seeds from the cotton so much faster than could be done by hand that cotton had begun to flow on the market, and Roth was taking advantage of it. He'd even sunk money into a cotton mill he was having built along the Broad River at the back of the property, not far from the wharf.

He sighed as he looked at the house in its half-finished stage. He'd told Dicia all about it last night as she lay in his arms, and he'd been pleased at the prospect of showing it to her this morning and letting her help with the finished product.

He swore softly and exhaled disgustedly as he started toward the house, then saw Rebel standing in the doorway watching him, a puzzled look on her face. She was a beautiful young woman, looking much like her mother, with big violet eyes but with hair the color of faded dandelions, as her father had had. Quinn had been a strikingly handsome man, tall and blue-eyed. A renegade by all rights. A backwoodsman and Indian fighter who was also an English earl, a title he managed to claim while he was in England. Roth had liked him, and that was strange too. He should have hated him. But he was the kind of man a person couldn't help but admire. He'd been a violent man in some ways, and Rebel had inherited some of his wild rebelliousness. Her name fit her well.

She stepped out onto the veranda, the spring wind blowing her long flaxen hair. "Where's mother?" she asked, frowning as he approached, and he stopped, his eyes darkening.

"She's on the *Golden Eagle* somewhere out to sea by now," he explained, and took her arm, turning her toward the door. "Come inside and I'll explain."

He ushered her to the drawing room, sparse with furniture and minus a carpet, and made her sit and listen while he told her what had happened. She could tell how distraught he was as he finished.

"Maybe they'll head back in when it gets dark again," she said.

"Not a chance. If I know Captain Marlin, he'll make sure he haunts the waters off Hilton Head, unless he catches them, and in that case I hate to think what might happen. He had two other ships waiting for him off Hilton Head, and the *Golden Eagle*'s no match for three ships."

Reb bit her lip. He was right. The *Golden Eagle* was heavily armed, but three ships against one . . . It'd be a slaughter. "They won't catch them," she said confidently as she stared at Roth. "The *Eagle*'s the fastest ship afloat. I know. She'll get away."

"Then what?" asked Roth. "They won't dare try to even sneak back in."

She stood up. "But these are American waters. They have no right to lay in wait for them."

"That's what I told the captain of the *Fortress*, but he ignored it." He walked over and stood looking out the huge bay window that overlooked the river and the bottomland. "I'll tell you what's going to happen. If the *Golden Eagle* gets away, the *Fortress* will turn tail and come back to the sound

15

with its sister ships in tow. They'll spread themselves around the area, faking repairs or business or some such, and lay in wait for the *Eagle*, and who's to force the issue?"

"Aren't there any American ships around at all?"

"Private merchants at Beaufort and a few in the sound toward Hilton Head, but they won't chance an incident that could have international repercussions." He turned to face her. "And to top it all off, Captain Marlin's going to ask for an explanation from me, and what do I tell him? That my son is Captain Thunder's first mate?" He took a deep breath. "My shipbuilding firms in England supply the British fleet. My shipping companies deliver arms to the British Army. My father was the fourth son of the Earl of Cumberland, and King George considers me a friend, and I'm supposed to tell them that my son is fighting on the side of France? The situation's awkward, to say the least."

Rebel's face reddened. "I'm sorry," she said regretfully. "We shouldn't have come," but his eyes softened as he looked at her.

"Nonsense! If you hadn't come . . . Rebel, I love your mother very much."

"But now we've gotten you in a mess."

"I'll get out of it somehow."

"Get out of what?" asked a voice from the doorway, and they both turned to face Brandon Avery, the Duke of Bourland, Rebel's husband of only a few weeks. He was tawny-haired, with gold-flecked brown eyes. Handsome in a foppish way, his appearance elegant.

Roth hadn't gotten to know him too well while in London, but what he did know he disliked. The man had never done him any harm, but his attitude left much to be desired. He was arrogant, as if he looked down his nose at everyone, and Roth wondered what a girl like Rebel could see in him. Heath explained that they'd been married aboard the *Golden Eagle* with its captain officiating, but Heath seemed none too pleased with his half-sister's choice of a husband.

"I'd have sworn she and Beau were in love," he'd told his father as they'd ridden toward the *Golden Eagle* the noon before. "But then, I never could tell what either Reb or Beau was thinking, and they're both so damn stubborn. I think she married Brandon just so she could be a duchess and to spite Beau." Roth remembered Heath's words now as he glanced first at Rebel, then to the tawny-haired man standing in the doorway.

"We had an unfortunate encounter with a British man-of-war," he stated. "I'm afraid the *Golden Eagle*'s miles out to sea by now, and Loedicia's still on it." He explained the whole incident, and the duke watched Rebel closely as Roth talked.

When Roth finished, there was a slight twitch at the corner of the duke's mouth and his eyes looked amused.

"You think it's funny?" asked Rebel angrily, and now he actually smiled a vicious smile.

"I hope they catch the bastard and hang him!" he stated boldly, and Roth's face darkened as Rebel snapped back.

"My mother's on that ship, and my brother!"

"Nobody'll hurt your mother, Reb, don't worry," he answered. "If I know the countess as well as I think I do, she can talk her way out of anything, but I'm sorry, Reb . . . Heath may be your brother, but he's just as guilty of crimes against the crown as Captain Thunder is, and I'm afraid I have no love for either man."

"You're talking about my son, sir!" said Roth as he stared at Brandon, but the duke never flinched.

"I realize that, sir," he answered, "so perhaps under the circumstances it might be best if I rode to the nearest town to inquire about lodgings for myself and my wife until we can find a ship heading for the Indies and we can finish the journey to Grenada that Captain Thunder so inconveniently interrupted. After all, I do still have my post as governor there to think of."

Roth glanced quickly at Rebel. Her face was flushed with anger as she looked at her husband, and he sensed rather than saw the disgust she felt, and he felt sorry for her.

"On the contrary," he said sternly, not wanting to hurt her any more than he felt she'd already been hurt. "I said the two of you were welcome here, and I don't go back on my word."

Brandon glanced about at the unfinished room devoid of the comfortable furnishings he was used to, then cocked his head back, listening to the sounds of the hammers as the men worked outside. "I'm not really sure I want to stay," he ventured, sighing. "I hadn't realized when you suggested it last night that the incessant noise and confusion would get on my nerves so," and Rebel glanced at him quickly, her eyes narrowing.

"A little noise won't hurt you."

"I detest it," he said haughtily, and he glanced around the room at the bare walls and at the floor without a carpet and she knew what he was thinking, but he'd better not say it. He'd said enough last night after Roth and Heath had left.

He'd confirmed to her his dislike of living in what he called crude circumstances, with the house only partway finished, and he also disliked the familiarity of the servants, who were all black. "Blacks have only one place in life," he said as they'd prepared for bed. "If this were my plantation, they'd be in the fields, not the house. I feel uneasy with them around," and Rebel had learned another facet of her husband's complicated personality. One that hadn't come to light before, and one she didn't like. She stared at him now, praying he wouldn't say anything further.

"I'm sorry the noise disturbs you, your Grace," apologized Roth stiffly, his eyes still dark with anger at the man's insolence, "but I'm afraid the work has to be done. As I said, you're welcome to stay, as you wish, whatever suits you," and he sighed. "Now, if you two don't mind, I'm going to order a bath and clean up, then take the ship out and see what I can learn."

"You have a ship?" asked Rebel.

"Down on the river. She's a small three-master, specially made. I can't catch up to them, they've got too much of a head start, but I can meet the *Fortress* if she tries to come in."

Reb stepped forward anxiously. "May I go with you, Roth . . . please? I can't just sit here and wait."

He looked at Brandon. "And you?"

"Anything would be better than this," he said, and he closed his eyes, listening to the hammering, as Rebel glanced quickly at Roth, her eyes apologizing.

An hour later they boarded Roth's private ship, the *Interlude*. The Château overlooked the Broad River, and a pier had been built to accommodate the ship. She was a trim vessel, but with extra sails fore and aft, and narrower than her contemporaries.

Roth had given orders, and the crew was waiting to shove off the minute they stepped aboard. Rebel was surprised to hear Roth shouting orders.

"You captain your own ship?" she asked.

"When I can. And I work in my own fields when I get the chance, and I guess I do a lot of other things most folks wouldn't approve of," he answered, his eyes wandering to Brandon, who was standing away from them against the rail looking up at the sails as they unfurled.

"The man who drove us out here yesterday was telling us," she said. "It seems you don't believe in owning slaves, either."

"Oh, I own them. For a while, that is. I buy them, then set

a wage for them and let them work off their sale price. When they've paid me back for my initial investment, they have a choice of staying and working here at the Château or leaving. Most of them stay." He turned and headed for the wheel, while she followed, and Brandon's eyes left the sails, watching them from the railing.

"You don't believe in slavery?" she asked.

"Do you?"

"No."

"But your husband does."

She looked uncomfortable. "Yes," she murmured; then her head went up stubbornly. "But it doesn't matter."

He turned to her, looking deep into her eyes as she stood beside him, and she blushed under his scrutiny. "You don't have to apologize to me, Reb," he said softly. "What your husband does or doesn't do is none of my business . . . unless he intends to cause trouble for Heath," he added. "Then it matters very much."

Her eyes fell; then she glanced furtively toward Brandon, and back again to Roth, her lips trembling. "When we arrived yesterday, I was so happy for you and Heath," she said softly. "I love my brother dearly, and he's been so upset since he learned the truth about you being his father. I was pleased that he'd finally found you, but now . . . Brandon says he's going to inform the King of England and anyone else who'll listen that Heath's your son, and he doesn't believe that you and Mother were married once. He thinks Heath is the result of an affair."

Roth's forehead wrinkled into a frown.

"Especially because of my father's reaction to you when we were in England," she explained.

Roth took the wheel from his helmsman, and as the sails caught the wind, he maneuvered the ship out into the river. They talked, and he listened intently to Rebel's revealing conversation.

"Brandon hates Heath and Beau," she went on. "I think he hates them because of the kind of men they are." Her eyes came alive, watching ahead as the ship moved downstream. "You met Beau," she said. "He's a dynamic person. He commands his men out of respect, not fear, something Brandon wishes he could do. And there's a warmth and sincerity about Heath that draws people to him." She turned to look at Roth, watching the way he handled the wheel, his face determined. "Something he inherited from you," she added, and he looked pleased.

"I wish I'd had a chance to get to know Heath better," he said as he watched the river ahead, turning the wheel slightly to catch the swifter current; then he glanced over at her. "He told me that he and Beau Dante grew up together at Fort Locke," he said, and her eyes narrowed as she glanced quickly toward her husband, who was still standing at the rail, then back to Roth again.

"Shhh . . ." she cautioned, putting a finger to her lips. "Brandon doesn't know Beau's real last name. All he knows is that he's Captain Thunder—Beau Thunder, as his crew calls him. Someday he intends to quit privateering for the French and settle down and become respectable, and the fewer people who know his real name the better."

"Heath said he's the son of an Indian chief."

"His father is Telak, chief of the Tuscarora at Fort Locke, but he's one-quarter French. His mother is one of Telak's four wives, and her father was a Frenchman." She turned again and watched as the ship cleared the mouth of the river and moved into the sound. "Fort Locke is on the shores of Lake Erie by the Ashtabula River, and we all grew up there together, even my brother Teak, who's still back in England. My parents treated Beau almost like a son. Mother was very partial to him, and they even sent him to a school in Philadelphia."

Roth watched Rebel's eyes as she talked of Beau. They were alive and warm, her face glowing. Heath was right: she was in love with him. He glanced quickly at Brandon, who had left the rail and was walking toward them, and he wondered. If she was in love with Beau, why the hell had she married Brandon?

Brandon stretched, then walked over, putting an arm about Rebel's waist possessively, and Roth saw her stiffen at his touch. "Your ship seems quite sound, sir," he said, addressing Roth. "Why do you have to stop at Hilton Head? We could perhaps scout the coast."

"It's a big ocean," answered Roth as he maneuvered through the sound, which at the moment was dotted with small fishing boats. "We could miss them too easily. I don't know if the *Golden Eagle* would have headed out to sea, or north, or toward the gulf. We could end up on a wild-goose chase."

They reached Hilton Head, furled the sails, and dropped anchor a few hundred yards offshore, where they couldn't miss a ship approaching from any direction. The afternoon was hot but windy as they settled down to wait.

Three American merchant ships passed into the sound, and two moved out, one sailing north, the other south, but the *Interlude* still held its position. There was food and drink aboard, and to while away the time they played whist in Roth's cabin. But his mind wasn't on the whist game. Too much had happened since yesterday, and he excused himself time after time to pace the deck, watching the horizon.

It was well after dark when they finally gave up and weighed anchor, heading back for the Château, and later, in their bedroom, as Rebel and Brandon prepared for bed, Brandon stared at Rebel hard, watching her brush her long flaxen hair.

"How can you like the man after what he did to your father?" he finally said as he slipped into his nightshirt, and she stopped the brush halfway down her hair, staring at her reflection in the mirror.

"I don't expect you to understand," she answered, then continued brushing. "You don't believe anything I've told you about Roth and my mother anyway, so how can I expect you to understand?"

He frowned as he walked over and stood behind her, looking down at her hair. It was burnished gold in the candlelight. She was a sensuous woman, her whole body, every movement, every gesture a natural invitation, yet he was sure she was unaware of it. Sometimes his desire for her nearly drove him mad, but she was still edgy and held herself back. If she'd just let herself go . . . just once. They'd been married only a few weeks, true, but by now she should have come out of her shell.

She was wearing an emerald-green satin dressing gown, and he reached out, pulling it off her shoulder, the strap on her nightgown moving with it; then he leaned down, kissing her velvet skin, and he felt her muscles stiffen beneath his lips.

"Why do you do that?" he asked angrily, and she tried to laugh it off.

"Do what?"

"You know very well what I mean. Every time I touch you, you tense up, as if you can't stand it."

"Don't be silly, Bran," she exclaimed as she set the hairbrush down and stood up, walking toward the bed, pulling the shoulder of her dressing gown back up. "I'm just tired. It's been a long day and I've got a headache, that's all."

"You've had quite a few headaches since we've been married, haven't you, Reb?" he said as he stared at her. "Last night, the night before, the night before that."

"I can't help it . . . really . . . my time of the month was due a week ago and it's not here yet. Maybe that's what's wrong . . . I don't know."

She glanced back at him furtively as she stood beside the bed, and she saw the expression in his eyes suddenly change as he stared at her, and he scowled.

"You think . . . already?"

"I don't know . . . I'm not sure yet." Her voice was strained. The thought of carrying his child sickened her. She stared ahead at the picture on the wall opposite the bed, not even seeing it, her mind miles away. Why had she ever married him? Why? Her mother had warned her. She'd been right. You couldn't pretend love. For a while you could put on a good show, but deep inside, you knew. It was always there. She hated his hands on her, and every time he claimed his right as her husband, she cringed beneath him, hating the feel of his body against hers. His lovemaking, as he arrogantly called it, was a one-sided affair with no thought to her needs or wants. It didn't really matter, though, because no matter what he did, it couldn't arouse her enough to make her want him. She'd thought it would be so easy. What a fool she'd been.

Brandon walked over to her and took her by the shoulders, turning her to face him. "Why didn't you tell me?" he asked. "I had no idea."

"I'm not sure," she said hesitantly, her face flushed. "It may be nothing. It might start any day."

"And if it doesn't?"

She shrugged. "Then I guess I'm pregnant."

His hands dropped from her shoulders. "You don't seem too happy about it."

"Am I supposed to be?"

"Most women would be pleased to give their husbands a son."

She flicked the hair back over her shoulder belligerently. "Do I have to be like most women?" she asked, and his eyes shifted over her, to the outline of her full breasts concealed by her dressing gown, then to her throat, soft and smooth above them, and up to the stubborn tilt of her chin and the sensuous depth in her eyes.

"That you'll never be," he answered emphatically. "But don't you want children?"

She bit her lip; then her mouth closed stubbornly. "I didn't want them now," she said softly. "Not now." Nor ever, she thought. Not your children, anyway.

She turned from him and walked to the window that overlooked the river at the back of the house and closed her eyes, ignoring Brandon, who was watching her curiously, and all she could see were a pair of green eyes beneath a crop of black wavy hair, the lips smiling at her cynically from his bronzed face. Why couldn't she forget Beau Dante? He'd done nothing but break her heart from the moment she'd become aware of him. How many times those eyes had haunted her over the past few years. Eyes that could stir her like no others. Was it any wonder she succumbed to him? She thought back to that night. The night before her wedding. She'd been unable to sleep, and had gone up on the deck of the *Golden Eagle*, watching the stars, wondering if maybe she'd made a mistake by saying she'd marry Brandon. But then, she'd promised herself that she was going to be a duchess. Besides, she'd vowed never to give her heart to anyone ever again. That no man was ever going to make a fool of her as Beau had before, when he'd mocked her protests of love and left Fort Locke three years before. She'd been young then, yes, but not too young to know what her heart was telling her, and as she stood by the rail that night, she'd been more vulnerable than she'd ever been before. Maybe that's why Beau's arms had looked so inviting. Maybe that's why, when he found her on deck alone, she'd melted against him without any inhibitions. And when he'd carried her to his cabin and made love to her, she'd given herself to him shamelessly. How was she to know as she lay beneath him, surrendering to him, that he had no intentions of marrying her?

"You're an earl's daughter and I'm an Indian with a price on my head," he'd said afterward, shattering her illusions, and a tear rolled down her cheek now as she remembered the ache in her heart the next day as she and Brandon had stood on the deck of the *Golden Eagle* and Beau had said the words that had made her Brandon's wife.

Brandon watched her now from across the room. The rigid stance, apparent preoccupation, then he saw her tremble slightly. "What's the matter?" he asked sharply as he shortened the distance between them, but she shook her head.

"It's nothing," she answered, her voice breaking as she continued to stare out the window.

"It's that Indian, isn't it?" he said savagely, his eyes blazing, but she shook her head, still refusing to face him.

23

"No!"

He reached out and spun her around. "Don't lie to me!" His eyes flashed angrily. "Something was going on between you two on board ship, wasn't it? I saw it. I'm not stupid. Don't think I didn't see the looks that passed between you!"

There were tears at the corners of her eyes, but she lifted her chin stubbornly.

"What is he to you?" he cried as he stared at her, but she didn't answer.

She couldn't, because she didn't know herself. She hated Beau for what he'd done to her. For giving her a taste of heaven, then plunging her into the hell she'd found in Brandon's arms. Yet she couldn't forget him. She'd never forget him.

"I asked you," he said again viciously. "What is he to you?" and she inhaled quickly, holding back tears.

"He's nothing," she said softly, breathlessly, but his eyes narrowed.

"Then it's time you remembered this," he said heatedly, and reached out, pulling her into his arms. "You're mine, Reb, only mine, do you understand?" he said passionately. "Even if he wanted you, he could never have you . . . your my wife now . . . mine!" and his mouth crushed down on hers brutally, bruising her lips; then he picked her up, heading for the bed.

"Brandon, no," she pleaded, her mouth still hurting from his kiss. "Not tonight, please, Bran. I don't want it tonight. I don't feel good, please," but he paid her no heed as he dropped her on the bed, ripping the dressing gown open against her violent protests. "Stop, Bran!" she cried, her heart pounding as she tried to keep him from taking her nightgown off, but it only infuriated him more, and he ripped the wrapper and nightgown from her.

"You've said no for the last time, Reb!" he snarled as he threw the clothing aside, then stared down at her as she cowered naked on the bed. "I'm through trying to humor you. I married you because I wanted you, because I had to have you. You do things to me, and by God I'm going to have you whenever I want, do you understand?" and Rebel gulped back the tears, wanting to die as she saw the bulge beneath his nightshirt; then he quickly pulled the nightshirt off and was on the bed with her.

"Brandon, please," she begged tearfully, "not tonight . . . please," but he grabbed her hair, his eyes darkening, and she winced.

24

"Tonight and any other night," he answered hotly, his face flushed, eyes frenzied with his desire for her. "And if you fight me, that's all the better, my love," he whispered. "It only makes the taking all the better," and Rebel groaned agonizingly against him as he forced his way into her. He took her savagely, against her will, and that night she learned another shocking facet to her husband's character. Brandon Avery, the Duke of Bourland, and newly appointed governor of the island of Grenada in the West Indies, was not beyond raping a woman, even his wife, and enjoying it immensely, while down the hall in the master bedroom, Roth stood by the open French doors of the balcony that overlooked the river, unaware of the misery to which Rebel was being subjected. He stared off into the star-filled night, praying that Captain Marlin and his ships had been unable to catch the *Golden Eagle*, and wondering what the hell he was going to do about the whole damn mess in the morning.

2

The afternoon sky was overcast, waves rolling the ship haphazardly, with the wind pushing hard against the sails. The temperature had dropped drastically overnight, and now Beau stood at the rail, his green eyes darkening as he watched the three ships still dogging along in their wake.

"If we can just keep this pace until nightfall," he said to Heath, who stood at his elbow, "we can put in at the island. It's been a good three weeks since we took on stores in San Salvador, and the food and water's getting low."

"Jacques St. Alban?" asked Heath, and Beau nodded. Jacques St. Alban was a French agent living on a small island off the coast of Georgia, from where he often replenished the supplies of French ships caught in the area, and more than once Heath and Beau had taken advantage of his services. Heath wasn't sure Beau's idea was a good one. "But they'll get ahead of us," he said.

"That's what I'm hoping for. If we can lose them at the sound and head back up the coast, we can sneak back into

Port Royal long enough to deposit your mother with Roth, then head for Martinique. They'll be halfway to the gulf before they discover we're not ahead of them."

"If it works."

"And why wouldn't it?"

Heath shrugged. "I don't know . . . it just seems . . . This whole thing has been a fiasco right from the start," he said disgustedly. "Who would have dreamed my sister would be engaged to the man we'd decided to capture? Why didn't the French agents in England mention her when they sent back their reports? Now we don't have him, my father's dead . . ."

"You said Quinn wasn't your father."

"Well"—Heath flushed—"you know what I mean. And now Mother and my real father are separated again. All we really have is half a crew in Martinique waiting to be picked up with whatever money they managed to get for what was left of the ship and prisoners, which probably isn't much, since we had to turn the biggest fish loose, our disguise is shot to hell, and we've got half the British Navy after us."

"Three ships."

"Three ships, six ships . . . hell! What does it matter how many, as long as it's more than one! We're no match for two ships, let alone three."

"That's why I intend to lose them."

"And if you can't?"

"I'll outrun them."

"To where?"

"Martinique."

"If the wind holds."

Beau glanced at the sky. "It will." Then he turned as Loedicia and Lizette approached.

Lizette had been Loedicia's close friend since twenty years before, when they'd first met in the wilderness at Fort Locke. Her husband had been Quinn's lieutenant, and when he was killed in the revolution, she'd stayed on, acting as mother hen to the Locke family, and Loedicia had insisted she accompany them to England. When Heath, Rebel, and the duke had left the ship in Port Royal to find Roth, Lizette had stayed on board with Loedicia, trying to persuade her not to be so stubborn. Now she stood beside Loedicia, her eyes mirroring concern.

"I see they're no closer, *mon ami*," she said as she took a brief look back at the three specks on the horizon.

"Thank God," said Heath. "Beau wants to be far enough ahead by nightfall to lose them."

"We didn't lose them last night," reminded Loedicia, pulling her cloak about her against the chill wind that was whipping the deck.

"That's because I didn't try," answered Beau. "But tonight we should be halfway down the coast of Georgia. I've a friend there. He's helped us before, he'll help us again."

"A French agent?" asked Lizette, who'd been born and raised in France.

"A good one," answered Beau, and Loedicia frowned.

"In America?"

"Mother," said Heath, "America is full of Frenchmen who are still loyal to France."

"And Englishmen still loyal to England," she answered.

"And Americans who are loyal to neither side," added Beau. "So when we leave the island, you'll forget where you've been," he said to them, and Loedicia studied him intently.

"Why do you fight for the French?" she asked, and Beau's eyes darkened.

"My grandfather was French, or have you forgotten?"

"But Heath's grandfather was English."

"And it seems his father still is," said Beau.

"Nonsense," she retorted. "His only interest in England is the businesses he's inherited from his father. He's an American now, and has been since the war."

"Money has a way of distorting loyalties," said Beau. "But I hope you're right, for all our sakes."

Heath glanced at Beau. "What do you mean by that?"

"I just hope there aren't more British ships waiting at Port Royal when we sneak back in."

"He'd never do that! He's my father!"

Beau looked at Loedicia. "You can trust him?" he asked, and her eyes softened.

"With my life."

"That's what you're doing," he said, scowling, "trusting him with your life, because if we go back in there and bump into any of the British Navy and they recognize us again, it'll be a bloody mess. I won't give up without a fight."

"You don't know Roth," she answered. "He'd never do anything that would harm Heath or myself in any way, regardless of what might happen to himself."

Beau studied her thoughtfully for a minute as the wind whipped her dark hair about her face. She and her daughter, Rebel, were so much alike except for the coloring of their hair, and every time he looked at her he was reminded of who he'd given up; he cursed bitterly to himself at the thought of Rebel, and his face darkened to match his eyes.

"I only met the man once, Countess," he said, "but I'll take your word for it." He glanced back toward the ships following them, and Loedicia frowned.

"Why do you insist on calling me Countess?" she asked. He'd been calling her Countess since she'd come aboard ship. "It used to be Mrs. Locke," and he turned back to her.

"That's what you are now, isn't it, ma'am, a countess?" he said. "Your husband was an earl?"

"But he was Colonel Locke to you, Beau."

There was a cold indifference in Beau's eyes. "That was a long time ago," he answered curtly, his jaw tightening. "Now, if you'll excuse me, ma'am, I've things to attend to," and he bowed politely and walked away.

Loedicia glanced at Heath, whose eyes followed Beau as he headed for the other side of the ship. "What's the matter with him, Heath?" she asked. "He's changed so," and Heath sighed.

"He's in love with Reb," he answered abruptly, and Loedicia stared at him dumbfounded; then slowly her eyes moved to where Beau stood talking to one of his men.

She should have guessed it. The looks that had passed between the two in spite of Rebel's marriage to Brandon. "Does Rebel know?" she asked breathlessly, and Heath shook his head.

"I don't know. He won't even talk about it since her marriage."

"But he talked about it before?"

Heath blushed. "Not really. Not in so many words. But I've seen it ever since the day we left Fort Locke three years ago and he lingered on the trail to say good-bye to her. There've been times he's mentioned her over the years . . . and I've seen the look on his face, but now he tries to act like she doesn't even exist."

Loedicia turned from Heath and stared at Beau. He wasn't yet twenty-five, but he had the bearing of a man much older, and he was handsome as the devil, with dark hair and dark green eyes, but he seemed a hard man. Stern, rarely smiling, and sometimes Loedicia could almost see the savage in him, and she wondered if Rebel had been aware of Beau's feelings.

"I told you years ago he looked at her *avec passion, ma petite*," reminded Lizette. "But don't worry. She's married to Le Duc now, and it is the end."

Loedicia sighed. "Is it, Lizette?" she asked. "I wonder," and she turned to look at Heath, remembering when she thought her marriage to Quinn had been the ultimate climax to her life. Instead it had been a prelude to twenty years of mixed emotions when her heart found little peace.

By nightfall it had started to rain a misty drizzle, like thick fog. The *Golden Eagle* had kept well ahead of the three British men-of-war and was hugging the coastline so far ahead of them that it was only a matter of guesswork as to whether they were still being followed.

Heath was above deck with the helmsman, while Beau sat at the table in his cabin working on his map, navigating every mile; then suddenly, shortly before midnight, Beau threw down the pen and bolted for the door, grabbing his coat and hat. It was wet and dark as pitch as he stepped on deck and made his way to the wheel. Heath was soaked to the skin, his eyes squinting against the fine rain that beaded his face.

"Send the order to douse all lights," Beau said abruptly as he took the wheel from the helmsman, and Heath moved to the bell. Its eerie tolling echoed through the rain-drenched ship, and seconds later complete darkness followed its knell.

Beau steered straight ahead for another ten minutes, Heath checking the instruments at various intervals and marking the hand lead, keeping him posted; then slowly he moved the wheel, turning the ship about, heading west.

"My God it's dark!" he said as the rain sprayed his face. "If they follow us in this, they're better seamen than I thought," and he held his course steady.

Heath and the helmsman watched from Beau's side now, and Heath wiped the spyglass each time after scanning the horizon, giving Beau a report as they went. The wind had increased, pushing full sails, and it whipped against the silent ship as they moved stealthily through the water.

"Do you see anything yet?" asked Beau, and Heath frowned.

"Nothing," and they kept steady on their course. Then Heath saw it and held the glass harder against his eye. "Land!" he finally sighed, and Beau exhaled. "The Devil's Horns," acknowledged Heath enthusiastically, and Beau smiled, pleased as he called to his soaked men scattered about the deck awaiting orders.

"Cut sail!" he yelled, and the ship suddenly came to life.

Within half an hour's time the big ship crept into the sound and dropped anchor a few hundred feet offshore of a small island, and Beau began breaking out the longboats.

Sleep had eluded Loedicia and Lizette. They were too keyed up, and they stood at the rail, capes pulled about them, watching Beau and Heath disappear over the side and head for shore in the drizzling rain.

"We could have picked a better night," said Heath as the longboats left the ship behind, and Beau laughed cynically as the rough waters tossed the boats about.

"Going soft on me?" he asked.

"Jesus, we'll be lucky if we don't end up with the fevers in this mess."

"Don't complain," admonished Beau. "This mess, as you call it, could keep them from finding us," and Heath said he hoped so, because the way things seemed to be going lately, he wouldn't be surprised if they'd followed them right on in.

"You're getting to be a pessimist," said Beau, and Heath shrugged as he looked off toward the shore, shrouded in darkness, and shook his head skeptically.

The three longboats beached on shore, men tumbling from them covering the wet sand; then Beau stood on the beach, looking about, getting his bearings as the men crowded around him. "Left," he said heartily, pointing in that direction, and they started off through a grove of beech trees, making their way inland. About fifty yards from the boats Beau grinned as the outlines of buildings forced their way through the dark, rainy night.

The house was small, shuttered and dark, not a soul about, but it didn't slow Beau down. He was used to arriving at odd hours and knew what to expect. A vigorous knock and a shout, and in minutes a light went on, then another, and as they waited, the door slowly opened.

"*Sacrebleu!*" came a soft voice in surprise, and the door swung open wide.

The men poured into the small room, filling it as the man greeting them smiled sleepily. "*Mon Dieu, mon ami,*" the tall bearded man exclaimed sarcastically, "you arrive at the most convenient hours," and he closed the door behind them. He was almost a head taller than Heath and Beau, his hair and beard a sandy red, with big warm gray eyes and an infectious smile. He walked over and called into one of the back rooms, and a young woman emerged a few minutes later, her calico dress pulled on hurriedly, her feet bare, pulling her long auburn hair back, tying a raveled ribbon about it. Her eyes were pale blue and her skin exceptionally fair. She wasn't a beauty, but she was as warm and friendly as her husband,

30

and a bit on the plump side since the birth of their second child last spring.

She eyed them sleepily, her smile warm. "You must always wake us in the wee hours?" she asked as she finished tying the ribbon, then smoothed her hands down her dress, and Beau apologized.

"Unfortunately, Marie, I never seem to need help in the daytime," he said, then quickly explained the situation.

When he had finished, the big man stood up and nodded to his wife. "Give them something to scare off the chill," he said as he headed for the door. "I'll get the men," and he grabbed a coat and hat as he went out.

Marie turned to a curtain behind her and pulled it aside, revealing a shelf with several jugs lining it. She reached up and took one down, handing it to Beau; then she headed for the cupboard.

"No need for glasses," said Beau as he uncorked the jug and whiffed its contents. "We can all take our one swig right out of the jug," and he met with protests and groans from the wet, bedraggled crew. He straightened sternly, his face sober, like granite, eyes darkening, his easy manner gone, and he stopped their chatter with one long hard look. "We stay sober," he said roughly to the men, "every last mother's son of you. We'll have time to celebrate when we get out of this mess, and I mean one swig. Right now we need clear heads and strong backs." The men's grumbling reluctantly stopped.

Beau lifted the jug to his lips and took a long, hard swallow of its contents, then tried to take a breath as he handed the jug to Heath. By God, it was strong. The pale amber liquid burned all the way down, hitting his stomach like a ball of fire, burning his mouth, making his eyes water. He shook his head and exhaled vigorously.

"Good God, what the hell did he put in it this time?" he asked, gasping, and Marie's lazy eyes twinkled.

"The same as always, *mon ami*," she answered, smiling. "You are just gone so long you forget."

He had forgotten. He shook his head as he watched Heath trying to swallow the foul-tasting brew; then he felt a warmth penetrating every nerve in his body, and he was suddenly no longer cold. The stuff was potent as all hell, and he grinned back at Marie as the jug was passed around the room and the men took their turns, arguing over who was taking longer swigs than they were entitled to.

Marie sat down at the table with Heath and Beau. "It has been a long time," she said, her eyes questioning as the muffled noise of the men arguing over the jug almost drowned out her soft voice, and Beau nodded.

"We left Paris three weeks before Christmas."

"You are going back?"

"We're heading for Martinique to pick up the rest of the crew as soon as we make another attempt to drop Heath's mother and her friend off at Port Royal."

They continued talking while the men emptied the jug. When Jacques returned, he had three men with him.

"I sent one of my men to the end of the island to keep watch in case your unwanted friends discover your deception," he said as he stood in the doorway waiting for them to join him, the water dripping from him onto the bare wood floor.

Financially, Jacques and Marie were none too well off. But they were in love, and it mattered little whether there were shoes for their feet or rugs for their floor as long as there was food in their mouths, a roof over their heads, and a soft bed to make love in. Jacques's work for his native land was a work of conscience rather than love or money, for he still had brothers in France, and he felt it his duty to help. The pay he received for his services was merely a token.

As the men handed the jug back to Marie and filed out the door following Jacques's men, Jacques laid a hand on Beau's shoulder. "I have a favor to ask of you, *mon capitain*," he said, detaining him, and Beau hesitated, looking deeply into the man's soft gray eyes.

Heath stood at Beau's elbow, knowing full well the scene to be played next.

Beau watched his men disappear toward the warehouses, then nodded. "And . . . ?" he asked.

Jacques smiled as he glanced inside, motioning with his head toward Marie, who disappeared into one of the back rooms. "When you leave Port Royal, I know it's asking much, and with the British onto you, it will be dangerous, but I have a message for Philippe."

Beau frowned. "New Orleans?"

"I can't send it cross-country, there's no one to go. My carrier broke his leg last week. Besides"—he shrugged—"you can go faster by sea. Even if I could find someone, it would take forever."

"We shouldn't go into New Orleans. We shouldn't even fly the *White Dolphin*," suggested Heath from Beau's side. "And if we fly the *Golden Eagle*, we could run into the British on the way."

"The Spanish are feuding with England at the moment, *mon ami*, and you will discover British ships are scarce in the gulf. Besides, you could become something else."

"What?"

He shrugged. "Perhaps I have a flag about, I'll look." His eyes bored into Heath's. "This message must be delivered," he said. "It's imperative," and as he finished the sentence, Marie entered the room once more and walked over, handing him a large white envelope. He held it between his fingers, holding it dangling toward Heath. "The French need Orleans," he said decisively. "In here is a plan by which they can crush Spain's hold on the city, but it must be put in the right hands."

"We take it to Philippe?" asked Beau, and Jacques's mouth tilted at the corners.

"*Oui.*"

Beau didn't like it. His men were waiting in Martinique, and it'd be hell avoiding the British; yet . . . if he could sneak into the Mississippi sound, past the channels, and into Lake Borgne under cover of darkness, he could anchor in one of the coves and go ashore. It was risky. The Spanish had no love for the French and were wary of Americans, but they could chance it. He frowned as he turned to Heath. "What say, shall we take one more chance on the *White Dolphin?*" he asked, and Heath shrugged, then nodded, and Beau plucked the letter from Jacques's hand.

"There's ten thousand in gold to share when that letter reaches Philippe," Jacques said furtively, and Beau shoved it in the inside pocket of his coat.

"Then we wouldn't want to lose it, would we, my friend?" he said, and they were smiling as Marie watched them step into the darkness outside.

The rain continued to plague them for the remainder of the night as the three longboats ferried supplies to the boat anchored offshore, and the hours seemed to drag as the night wore on.

Loedicia and Lizette finally had succumbed to sleep in their cabin, literally exhausted, unaware of each new boat-load pulled alongside and the staples were brought on board. Boxes of coffee, tea, barrels of flour, sugar, salt, dried fruit and vegetables, dried and smoked meat, and several boxes of gunpowder for the crew.

By dawn the rain had stopped and the last boat was on shore, loaded, ready to shove off. Beau stood beside it, feet planted firmly in the sand, shaking hands with Jacques while damp, misty clouds sifted up from the water like gray tendrils, devouring the daylight that was rapidly approaching. He glanced toward the ship nestling in the unsettling fog. It looked forlorn as it gently rocked on the water. His farewell to Jacques was quick and abrupt, and he was beginning to follow Heath and his men into the longboat, ready to shove off, when the sound of a horse's hooves jerked his head up, and all the men looked as a shout rang out from the woods beyond the warehouse.

Beau hefted his leg back onto the wet sand at the edge of the water and stood beside Jacques, waiting for the rider to reach them.

The horseman was young, perhaps sixteen, his clothes hanging on him, wet and sopping, hat plastered on his dark head, his broad face screwed into a breathless scowl.

"Three ships," he gasped as he reined in, his horse's hooves throwing sand at their feet. "They should be well into the sound by now." He took a deep breath, then went on. "I rode as fast as I could."

"British?" asked Beau, and he nodded.

"Aye, Captain. Looks like the blighters what's on your tail."

Beau cursed. "Damn!" he muttered, and glanced quickly off in the direction from where they'd entered the sound; then he turned, looking ahead into the fog farther in toward the coastline. "We'll have to sneak out the back way, around the island," he said quietly, and straightened his shoulders.

Both men quickly shook hands again, and Jacques helped them shove off as the fog began to thicken. Beau strained against the side of the boat, then leaped in and watched as the men struck the oars, and the beach was soon shrouded and lost from view behind them. Alert now, he fixed his attention on the ship lying in wait, wondering if there was time to clear the island before the men-of-war sailed in.

The wind that had almost taken its last breath when the rain stopped had started to kick up again, and he thanked God as he saw the fog begin to swirl like smoke clearing a chimney on a cold winter day. He needed wind and lots of it if he was to make his bid for freedom. Damn the British anyway.

His eyes were seething as he climbed on deck and began shouting orders.

Below deck in her cabin, Loedicia stirred, awakened by the sounds of the rigging as the sails unfurled, slapping in the wind. Each new creak and groan was louder than the one be-

34

fore, and she felt the heaving of the ship as it began to move. She slipped from the bunk and grabbed for her wrapper, shoving her arms quickly into the sleeves, tightening the sash; then she put on her cloak, pulling it close about her, shoving her feet into a pair of slippers.

When she reached the deck, the ship was completely surrounded by a blanket of thick fog, so thick she could barely see Beau at the wheel. Moving forward, she made her way to him, feeling the dampness of the fog that swirled at her feet and snatched at her clothes.

"My God, are you trying to leave in this?" she asked anxiously. "It's thicker than anything I've ever seen."

Beau didn't look at her. He was too busy trying to navigate. "I had no choice," he answered angrily. "Somehow they caught on to us. I only hope the fog slows them down enough until we can get out of here."

"There's another way out?"

"Around the island, but it's close to the shoreline and tricky. Rocks and a sandbar, and I hope to God we don't get hung up."

Leodicia frowned as she saw the expression on his face; then she turned as Heath approached and both men stood talking, almost oblivious of her presence.

The big ship moved slowly forward through the heavy fog, with only enough sail to keep her inching along. Beau trusted the wheel to no one. He'd had to use this way out before, but only once, and fortunately at that time he'd been at the helm, and he prayed he'd remember his settings.

The men grew exceptionally silent as the ship slithered through the water, and even Beau held his breath from time to time, the fog swirling like thick smoke obstructing his view, and once he felt the ship scrape bottom, but she continued moving.

It was over an hour later when the fog began to lift, the water deepened with whitecaps, and Heath and Beau both smiled. The open sea greeted them, the first struggling rays of the sun steaming the fog from the water, and the gray mantle of dawn began to fade into pale yellow. With a sigh of relief Beau called for full sail and the ship headed out once more into the turbulent waters of the Atlantic. Unfortunately, however, the British were not far behind. They'd navigated the narrow straits well and emerged from the fog a short time later, like leeches, determined to hang on.

Loedicia had dressed hurriedly, and now she stood on deck, soaking in the warmth of the morning sun as it dried up the previous day's rain. The temperature had climbed in the past few hours and the weather was turning balmy again, with a rough sea whitecapping, hitting the ship in protest as they plunged through at top speed. She turned, watching the three ships in the distance. The chase had been going on all morning, and still the British were no closer, but could they keep up this speed? And what of Roth?

Her eyes misted as she stared across the horizon, and there was an ache in her breast that wouldn't be stilled. Beau'd said a few minutes ago, when she'd asked him, that if they could lose the three British ships, they were heading for a place called New Orleans, a city she'd only vaguely heard of, and there was no way now to try to get back to Port Royal. Not with the British so close behind. And even if they lost them, they'd probably haunt Port Royal Sound, just waiting for them to return.

She closed her eyes, feeling the sun and wind in her face, listening to the constant creak of the ship, and she could see Roth's face before her and it was torture to know he wasn't there to touch. For the first time in almost twenty years she could love him freely, without feeling guilty, and now he was gone, snatched away again, leaving her empty and alone. She clenched her fists stubbornly.

"But I won't give in," she whispered aloud, the wind stealing her words as she spoke. "I won't give up Roth . . . ever. Somehow I'll find a way back to him." She raised her eyes toward heaven, and tears glistened, then rolled down her cheeks. "You took Quinn from me, God, but I won't let you keep Roth from me, do you hear? I won't . . . I won't," and she bit her lip, then hung her head. "Please," she begged, humbly this time, her voice a whisper, "don't do this, God, not Roth too. Let us be together," and for a long time she stood at the rail alone, her eyes steady on the horizon, her heart in her throat, praying.

For the better part of a week they managed to stay ahead of the three vessels, God knows how. The wind stayed good, the nights clear, and during that time only a few stray ships were sighted, most of them Spanish, some Dutch and Portuguese. Each day Beau held his breath as he watched the sky, waiting for the telltale signs that could becalm his ship, putting an end to their run, and deliver them into the hands of the enemy, but each day he breathed a sigh as the weather held firm, and with determination they rode a steady course along the coast of the Spanish-held Florida territories.

They were two days from the keys, and it was early afternoon. Beau was watching the sky, frowning, his torso bare to the hot sun, his jaw set firm as his eyes moved to the sails, beginning to droop as the wind began to die. Then suddenly a shout broke his concentration, and he turned abruptly as Heath approached.

"Four ships off the starboard bow," Heath informed him, "and by the way things have been going this trip, they're probably all British," but Beau only glared at him as he snatched the spyglass from his hand and put it to his eye.

They were still too far away, but maybe . . . Beau watched, entranced, his mouth held firm. Suddenly he broke into a wide grin, and Heath scowled. "Take a look at that, my friend," said Beau, laughing as he handed him back the spyglass, and Heath sighed with relief as he stared through it.

Four French frigates were bearing down on them under a blue cloud-scattered sky, and at the moment they looked like heaven.

"Run up the *Golden Eagle*," said Beau jovially as he took the spyglass from Heath and put it to his eye again, and Heath grinned, heading for the mizzenmast.

All hands stood on deck as the French frigates sailed close. They passed within calling distance of each other, and Beau felt at ease for the first time in days as he shouted across to the captain of the lead ship, who happened to be a friend, informing him of the enemy astern. And as the frigates turned the chase back onto the hunters, the British ships heaved about in the water, trying to break away, and the last the *Golden Eagle* saw of them, they were heading out toward the open sea with the frigates in hot pursuit, and five days later, the *Golden Eagle* slipped quietly into a small cove in Lake Borgne, just outside of New Orleans, with the *White Dolphin* flying again from her mizzenmast.

The night was exceptionally dark as they dropped anchor and broke out one of the longboats. Loedicia and Lizette watched impatiently as Heath and Beau, dressed in dark clothes, climbed over the side of the ship.

"I don't know why I can't go with them," complained Dicia to Lizette as they watched the two men row toward shore. "I'm so tired of this ship. Our feet haven't been on land since we left England six months ago," and Lizette shook her head.

"Be patient, *ma petite*. Perhaps when they return."

Loedicia sighed wistfully. "When they return . . ." Then her eyes flashed angrily. "When they return, they'll head for Martinique. Heath said Beau only came here to deliver a message to someone." She clenched her fists. "I can't go to Martinique. I want to go back to Port Royal."

"But we can't . . . at least not on the *Golden Eagle*. The British will be watching. If we could find another ship. Perhaps Heath and Beau will think of something."

Loedicia's heart sank. They had to think of something. They had to. She moved slowly along the rail, feeling the warm night breeze on her face. She stared off toward shore, but Heath and Beau were out of sight already, and she felt the faint movement of the ship beneath her feet as it drifted, anchored in the lagoon. How good it would be to be on dry land for a change. To feel solid earth and smell the trees and flowers, and suddenly she wondered what was happening at home.

Home! Fort Locke! She'd tried not to think of it since Quinn's death, but now the sober thought came to her. Someone would have to let them know at the fort. Somehow, someone would have to tell them of Quinn's death at sea, because they'd be waiting for his return. He'd promised to go back, a promise he'd meant to keep. She closed her eyes, trying to visualize the house by the lake where she'd spent so many years with Quinn, raising their children, and the fort beside it with the Indian village spread out beyond. She'd loved it at Fort Locke in spite of the dangers. It had been home, and she hadn't wanted to leave. She remembered last year when she'd sat on her horse, wearing buckskins, and looked out over Lake Erie for the last time, then turned to look at the log house. She'd had a premonition that she'd never see it again, and now . . .

Her thoughts wandered again to Roth. She missed him terribly. Her love for him had been a puzzle to her over the years. She knew she loved him, but if anyone had asked her why, it would have been hard to answer. The same way it had been with Quinn. The love was just there without her even asking or wanting it to be. At one time in her life, if someone had told her it was impossible to love two men at the same time, with the same violent passion, she'd have agreed, but not anymore. She knew now that it was possible, but she also knew the heartache it could bring.

She shook her head, but that was over. She glanced about at the crew and the ship and the night. If she could only reach him . . . She needed him, and stubborn tears welled up in her eyes.

Heath took a deep breath as he and Beau beached the boat, hiding it in some bushes, then stood surveying the beach. It was early evening, with no moon as yet to light their way, but they'd been here before and knew where to go. Sand gave beneath their feet as they trudged toward an embankment and scrambled up, then set out toward a small settlement about a mile inland.

Philippe Pignolet lived in a group of cottages in the bayou, but worked in New Orleans as a gardener for a wealthy Spaniard. More than once over the past two years Heath and Beau had visited his meager home, delivering their dangerous cargo, then slipped quietly away again.

They moved through the swamps, cautious and alert, skirting the marshes, then approached the cottages casually. Dim lights shone from inside them, but it was early, and some of Philippe's neighbors were still out enjoying the warm night air, and they glanced furtively a few times as Heath and Beau sauntered down the road and to the back door of the small cottage where Philippe lived with his wife.

The door was left open to the warm night air, and Beau stuck his head in, frowning. "Philippe, Genevieve?" and he knocked quietly as he called, startling a dark-haired woman who stood at a table in the center of the room, flour up to her elbows and a rolling pin in her hand.

She was a pretty woman. Her hair was like ebony, her skin dark, with flashing blue eyes that stared at the two of them in surprise as the back of her hand flew to her forehead and she set the rolling pin down hurriedly, sighing. *"Mon Dieu,* you scare me half out of my wits, you two," she murmured soflty as she lowered her hand again, then began wiping the flour from her hands on a towel slung on the back of a chair.

The kitchen was small and cozy, with a bare floor, calico curtains, and a well-scrubbed look. Genevieve Pignolet was in her middle thirties, childless, but always seemed content helping others. Philippe often argued that she gave too much of herself to her friends. There wasn't a person in the small village, man, woman, or child, who hadn't accepted her ministrations at some time or another with an attack of gout, stomach pains, or fever. She was better than a doctor, and her breads and delicate pastries had filled more than one empty stomach. Now, however, as Heath and Beau watched her, she looked sad, and there were tears in her eyes as she stood watching them enter the modest kitchen.

She sniffed in, as if trying to keep from crying, then motioned toward the chairs and asked them to sit down, as if they'd just dropped in for a casual visit. It had been almost a year since she'd seen the two men, yet she acted as if it had been only yesterday and brought out mugs of cider and pastries, offering them as Beau and Heath glanced at each other dubiously.

"What is it?" Beau finally asked as he accepted the mug of cider from her. "What's happened? What's wrong?" and he saw her swallow hard, her eyes misty. He and Heath had spent almost two weeks here once and had gotten to know the woman well.

She bit her lips as she handed Heath his mug of cider, then set the pastries at the end of the table where they were sitting. "You have come for Philippe, *oui*," she said, making it more of a statement than a question. "But Philippe is not here." She hesitated; then: "Philippe is dead," she murmured softly, and both of them stared at her, the cooling mugs of cider all but forgotten. "He and a friend went to the city one night over a month ago, and when they returned his friend was dragging him. They had both been beaten, and Philippe had been stabbed. He died in my arms."

They were stunned. Philippe had been a strong man, and it would have taken more than one man to get the best of him. "I'm sorry," said Beau huskily, and she smiled wanly.

"It is over now, M'sieur Beau," she said, her voice strained. "The worst of the crying is over. Although so many times I think of him and it starts again." She shrugged as if to shake off the melancholy that was waiting to engulf her, then walked toward the door, standing to stare out for a moment into the night. Suddenly, after a few moments, she turned abruptly. "But so much, *que será, será*, it was the will of God."

Beau looked at Heath, then back to Genevieve. He hated to question her at a time like this, but he still had a letter to deliver. His head tilted back, and he cleared his throat. "Genevieve," he said, trying not to sound too callous, "I know it doesn't seem the right time, but it's very important."

Her blue eyes stared at him intently.

"Did he manage to say anything to you before he died? Anything about his contacts, who he went to see in New Orleans?" and she frowned.

Philippe had told her so little about his activities. He'd always said the less she knew, the better, for her own safety. But that last night he'd whispered a name, and she answered Beau hesitantly.

"He was barely conscious, and I don't think he even knew he was home," she answered. "But he kept repeating one name over and over again, DeMosse Gervaise."

"That's all?" asked Beau. "Just the name?"

"*Oui*, just the name." She used her hands, expressing herself fluently, as did most Cajuns. "I don't know what it means, *m'sieurs*. Maybe he was the contact . . . maybe he killed Philippe . . . I don't know. But whatever, it is the only thing he said before he died."

Beau frowned as he stared at the mug of cider, then finished the last of it. "Have you any idea who M'sieur Gervaise might be?"

She nodded. "*Oui.*" Her hands flew again nervously. "After Philippe was buried, I send his friend to the city to find out." She walked to the other end of the table and began rolling and kneading the pastry dough again. "M'sieur Gervaise is staying at the home of Barón de Carondelet."

"He's the governor!" exclaimed Beau, and she nodded.

"*Oui.*"

"You're sure he said DeMosse Gervaise?"

Her eyes filled with tears again as she poked and prodded, taking out her frustration on the rich pastry dough. "I could not be mistaken, *m'sieurs*," she answered softly. "I was listening close, hoping he would know I was there . . . wanting him to call my name . . . I am sure he said only one thing, DeMosse Gervaise."

They stayed for a while longer, and she let them look through Philippe's personal things, but it was no help. There was no clue as to the gentleman's significance and why Philippe should call his name so fervently. When they finally left, making their way back through the bayou, it was quite late.

"What do we do now?" asked Heath as they left the cottage and village behind.

"We go to New Orleans, I guess," answered Beau. "But we don't go tonight." His eyes shifted across the horizon as the tilt of a crescent moon began to top the moss-laden cypress trees. "We sail into New Orleans tomorrow morning." Then he glanced at Heath. "How's your Spanish?"

"*Muy bien, mi amigo*," Heath answered, "but I hope the French frigates chased those British far enough away, or we'll have the devil to pay." Then he glanced quickly at Beau, frowning. "By the way, how do you intend to dock in New Orleans and keep Mother from going ashore? You know her temper, and I had a hell of a time talking her into staying aboard tonight."

Beau scowled as they skirted a boggy pond, following a narrow strip of dry ground that rimmed it. "I forgot about your mother . . ." He worked his way toward the hill overlooking the beach and stood gazing toward the small lagoon where the *Golden Eagle* nestled comfortably, barely visible in the faint moonlight.

What could they do with Loedicia? As Heath said, she was an unpredictable commodity. He'd seen her defy her husband more than once at Fort Locke when she was determined to do something. And if she made up her mind to go ashore in New Orleans, she'd go ashore, even if she had to swim. She and Rebel, two peas in a pod, and for a moment he thought of Reb's flaxen hair and violet eyes and there was an ache inside him. God! How he missed her. He remembered her eyes filled with anger, then softening to a warm caress, her soft body beneath his, surrendering to him lovingly, and his loins began to throb. Quickly he shoved the thought aside, concentrating on the moment at hand. Right now her mother was the problem, and he sighed.

"I think I have a solution," he said as he turned to Heath. "That is, if she'll go along with it, and it'll keep her mind off Roth. Come on," and he motioned for Heath to follow him as he headed down to the beach and to the waiting ship.

The next morning, shortly after sunup, the *Golden Eagle*, still flying the flag of the *White Dolphin*, sailed into the harbor at New Orleans and dropped anchor at the Place d'Armes with her holds full of cargo and an anxious crew. Beau's swarthy good looks enhanced his simple captain's uniform with its big gold buttons and shiny braid, and beside him stood Heath, resplendent in tight-fitting black velvet pants and Spanish bolero with crimson and silver trim; his hat sported a white feather, and across his shoulders was slung a black cape lined with red satin.

Loedicia had fussed over Heath proudly as they'd helped him into the suit that had been rolled up in a drawer in his cabin, letting it out here and there, making sure Lizette had managed to remove all the wrinkles, and now, as Loedicia gazed at his tanned face, the dark curly hair just above the collar framing his black eyes, with a hint of ringlets at the ears, she sighed.

"What a handsome son I have," she whispered to Lizette as they stood watching the activity. "He's filled out so in the past few years, and there's a way about him . . . like his father . . . but sometimes, when I realize he's my son and I see him grown into such a man, I feel so old."

Lizette shook her head. "But *non, ma petite*. You are not old," she said as she studied her friend. "You do not even have one gray hair, as I have. Your hair is black like the day we met. And your figure is still that of a girl."

Loedicia looked down at herself, straightening the waist-coat of her suit. The weather was hot, and she was sweltering in the gold silk traveling suit she had on, with its long sleeves and high black velvet collar. She was sure it made her look old and matronly, but in reality, with the small straw hat perched atop her head, she looked quite young.

At thirty-nine, Loedicia was still strikingly beautiful, with a natural warmth and vitality that made her seem years young-er. Her husband had often remarked that even when her hair turned gray her heart would still be young. She was earthy and sensuous, with warm violet eyes. The kind of woman men covet and women envy, yet there was nothing preten-tious about her. Besides English and French, she spoke Iroquois fluently, having lived among Indians during the eighteen years of her marriage to Quinn, and spoke Hindi, having been raised in India. She rode bareback, could shoot a squirrel at fifty paces, or a man if need be, skin a deer, clean a rifle, and tan hides, yet could make herself at home in the most sedate drawing room.

She hadn't known it at the time, but it was her varied life-style that convinced Beau to engage her in their escapade, and now, as she watched the gangplank being secured and glanced quickly at Lizette, dressed in her proper gray dress with its white collar and cuffs, befitting an abigail, her stom-ach began to flutter wildly.

Beau had insisted it would be so easy. She would be her-self, the Countess of Locksley, but the rest would all be pure fabrication. The story was that she'd been visiting friends in Madrid, and unfortunately her husband, an English earl, had been killed in a duel by a hot-blooded Spaniard who'd lost his heart to her. He too, however, had been mortally wounded in the duel, and to escape the scandal, she'd left Spain hurriedly on the first ship sailing from the harbor. With her had come her maid and the young son of her host, who was to escort her to New Orleans and see she met the right people. The *Golden Eagle*, flying the flag of the *White Dolphin*, had been to Spain many times during its voyages, and Beau had met Barón de Carondelet's best friend, Fernando de Varga. Heath, with his dark curly hair, dark eyes, and suntan, was to masquerade as Don Diego de Varga, nephew of Fernando, a young man the governor had heard of but never seen.

"We've heard Fernando de Varga speak of his nephew of-ten," said Beau as he explained the details to Loedicia. "He's noted for his carousing and conquests with the ladies, so perhaps we can pretend that he got carried away with his amours and found it necessary to leave Spain rather hurriedly with a recommendation to look up his uncle's old friend in New Orleans."

It sounded simple enough, but would it be? Loedicia spoke French fluently, but knew no Spanish, and her knowledge of Madrid was appalling. Her only knowledge of Spain was learned from books while teaching her children when they were young because there was no one else at the fort to teach them.

"Double-talk," suggested Beau when she complained. "You're glib enough to sidestep positive questioning. Be vague. You're a woman. They won't expect you to have a brain, only to look beautiful," and Loedicia glared at him.

"I hope that's not your opinion, young man," she challenged, and he looked hurt.

"Would I be asking you to help if I didn't think you had brains?" he said, and continued instructing her on her mission.

She and Heath were to gain entrance to the governor's house and establish themselves as his guests, at which time she was to flirt with and learn what she could about DeMosse Gervaise, who Genevieve informed them was an elusive bachelor in his early forties.

"Who probably hates women," commented Loedicia at the time, but here she was now, getting ready to embark with Heath, who was smiling and offering her his hand, while Beau stood by eyeing her solemnly, his eyes showing their amusement at her anxiety.

"There's nothing to worry about, Mother," whispered Heath as she set her hand on his arm and he began escorting her from the ship, with Beau ahead of them and Lizette trailing behind. "Just remember to call me Diego, and I'll call you *la condesa* and you'll do fine."

She swallowed hard and held her head high as she began descending, her eyes scanning the wharf, her stomach tied in knots, because although he said not to worry, the venture was a dangerous one and they could easily forfeit their lives if discovered. A myriad of faces, like one big blur, stared at her as they reached the levee and Beau called for a carriage, then escorted them through the crowd to stand by one of the buildings, waiting for one to pull up.

"Now, remember," reminded Beau softly to Heath, "I'll be

at the monkey-wrench corner at Royal and Canal streets every night around ten waiting for a report."

Loedicia looked at him, her eyes searching his face, her heart in her mouth. "What if they won't let us in?" she asked breathlessly.

"They will," he assured her. "One look at you, Countess, and the door will open wide," and she shivered as she wondered if she'd ever see Roth again.

She fought back her fears as the carriage pulled up. She had to put Roth out of her thoughts, for a while anyway. There was nothing she could do. She needed him badly, but for now her needs would have to wait. Right now Heath and Beau needed her, and she had no time to be selfish. Besides, Roth was miles away and there was no way to get to him. She straightened her skirt on the seat as she sat down, with Lizette at her side, and her chin set stubbornly. By God, she'd make it. She promised Heath and Beau. She'd be the best damn scarlet lady New Orleans had ever seen.

3

Loedicia and Lizette were intrigued with New Orleans, but the stench was worse than Philadelphia. The conduits, beneath wood sidewalks called banquettes, that carried the garbage and refuse to the swamps and Lake Pontchartrain, were often clogged, and as a result the garbage lay seasoning until a heavy downpour flushed it away. Unfortunately it had been some days since the last rain, and they had to hold handkerchiefs over their noses to soften the odor.

The houses were mostly brick and stucco, two stories with tiled roofs, balconies encased in wrought iron, and high walls hiding the courtyards from their view. The shops were varied, some even selling voodoo charms, so Heath said.

As they rode along, Heath spoke in French, trying to explain some of the voodoo to them. "See the powdered brick on some of the doorsteps?" he asked, and they both nodded. "They expect it to keep the evil spirits and ghosts away," he said. "Then there's the gris-gris. Some are just charms for good luck, but some . . . they set a white candle in the center of a cross made with salt and place coins at the end of each of the cross's arms. Placed on the steps of a house it's like putting a curse on the people inside."

"That's witchcraft," exclaimed Lizette, and Heath agreed.

"Zombies, charms, love potions, goofer dust, curses—they're all a part of New Orleans," he said.

Loedicia eyed him dubiously. "What is goofer dust?"

"Dirt from a grave. Any grave. It's supposed to have magic powers."

"I think your voodoo queens and Telak's shaman have something in common," she asserted, and he shook his head and glanced quickly at the driver, who he knew was listening, and lapsed into English, lowering his voice, hoping the man wouldn't overhear. "Don't let Beau hear you say that," he said to his mother. "He's sensitive enough about his father."

She frowned, whispering back, "You mean he's ashamed of Telak because he's an Indian?"

Heath hesitated. "No, not exactly ashamed, but . . . have you ever wondered what it's like for him?"

She studied Heath seriously as he went on.

"He looks white, Spanish perhaps, or just deeply sun-tanned, and he feels white inside, but he's three-quarters Indian."

"Is that why he never let Reb know how he feels?"

"I think he did let her know."

"Oh?" Loedicia's eyebrows raised as Heath and Lizette both glanced again at the driver, to let him know his curiosity about their conversation was unwanted, and the man straightened immediately, gluing his eyes to the dusty road ahead, and Heath continued, in French this time.

"Just before we went ashore back in Port Royal, Rebel disappeared below to check out the cabin, and Beau disappeared below deck at the same time. When he came back on deck, there was something . . . I couldn't put my finger on it. His eyes looked hard, as if he was hurting inside, and when she came up, she'd been crying. Oh, she tried to hide it, but I've known Reb long enough to know when she was fighting her feelings. I just wish to hell she hadn't married Brandon, that's all."

"Well, she did," stated Dicia as she saw the driver lean toward them again, trying to hear. "Now, suppose you tell me more about this city, which, as I look around, looks less and less like a city."

It was true. They were already out of the Vieux Carré and were riding along the Mississippi river front, and a few minutes later the carriage turned into a drive and through the gates, up to a magnificent house, its red-tiled roof gleaming in the sun, its stucco walls reflecting the heat of the morning from inside the high walls that surrounded it.

To Heath, driving through New Orleans had been almost like driving through Spain itself. Since the fire in 1788, the Spaniards had rebuilt the city, ignoring its French heritage and all that seemed to be missing now were the bull ring and the Inquisition. Although he'd heard the latter was secretly being practiced; and for a moment, as he stared at the governor's house, he had misgivings about involving his mother in all this. But as the carriage stopped before the heavy oak door and he stepped down, waiting for her to alight, he knew Beau had been right. If anyone could discover whose side M'sieur Gervaise was on, she could, and he smiled, holding out his hand for her.

When the door was opened, Loedicia was amazed to hear Heath's command of the Spanish language, and although she knew nothing of what was said, she assumed it was effective, because the servant who answered the door, a mulatto wearing sandals, white pants, and a red shirt, with a number of beads about his neck, gave them no argument.

They were escorted into a sitting room, where they sat on a plush velvet sofa with heavily carved mahogany legs and arms, waiting for the servant to appear again with someone.

"You're sure this Governor Carondelet has never met Don Diego?" whispered Dicia as the three of them sat side by side, and he nodded, a finger to his lips, motioning for her and Lizette to be quiet.

"Sometimes the walls have ears," he warned, and she straightened, looking about, and frowned weakly at Lizette beside her.

What on earth was she doing here, anyway? A woman of her age playing spy. Spy? She was a spy. At least as far as the Spanish were concerned, she'd be considered one if caught. My God! It had sounded so easy when Beau had first mentioned it. Now her stomach was full of butterflies and her legs felt like jelly. Maybe she should have refused. But then . . . She glanced at Heath again. He looked every bit the young Spaniard, his dark eyes searching the room, and she knew that in spite of the danger, she'd done the right thing.

She was brought back to the moment at hand by an abrupt cough as a man stepped through the beaded curtains that separated the sitting room from the rest of the house, and she glanced toward him, directly into a pair of hard brown eyes that were looking her over intently from above a very masculine clipped beard and mustache the exact burnt-honey color of his gold-streaked hair.

Heath stood up, bowing elaborately, his hat in front of him at his waist, and he began speaking in Spanish. She caught the words "Don Diego de Varga," "La Condesa de Locksley," "Lizette" and *"inglesa,"* but the rest was all a jumble to her.

Heath and the man spoke back and forth for a few minutes more in Spanish and she heard the gentleman mention Barón de Carondelet while he was talking; then the man's eyes looked directly at Lizette, seeming to dismiss her as unimportant, and rested instead on Loedicia as he addressed Heath again.

"Sí," answered Heath, smiling, then lapsed into French as he introduced her. "Ah, Condesa, may I introduce to you M'sieur DeMosse Gervaise, houseguest and good friend of his excellency Barón de Carondelet. M'sieur Gervaise, La Condesa de Locksley and her abigail, Madame Lizette De-Bouchard," and M'sieur Gervaise bowed deeply as his eyes met hers, after merely nodding slightly toward Lizette, who bobbed a quick aknowledgment with her head.

He looked like a hard man, unfriendly. Yet Loedicia could tell by the way he gazed at her and held his hand out for her that he was impressed.

His mouth felt warm and firm, the mustache scratching her lightly as he kissed her hand, but the hand that held hers was anything but soft. The skin on his fingers was tough and callused in spots, belying the elegant clothes he wore and the impression he gave of being an aristocrat who let others do the work for him. The lack of softness to his hands would have escaped the eye of most casual observers, but Loedicia had lived too many years with Quinn, learning to judge men by the little things they did and didn't do, said and didn't say.

"M'sieur Gervaise," she acknowledged, smiling brilliantly, her violet eyes masked to what she was thinking. "I am pleased. Most pleased," and he released her hand as Heath spoke.

"La Condesa speaks no Spanish, I'm sorry to say," he apologized for her in French. "But her French is excellent, her English superb."

"Then shall we converse in English?" asked M'sieur Gervaise as fluently in English as he'd spoken in French and Spanish, with only a slight accent, and Dicia was surprised.

"It would please me," she said. "Fortunately, while I was

in Spain, my hosts were generous enough to speak only French or English when I was present." Her eyes twinkled. "Unless they had a secret, however; then I'm afraid they were quite safe using their native tongue. Señor de Varga and his family served me well as interpreters if the occasion arose, but I must say I believe I prefer English. The tongue gets less twisted."

The man's eyes followed her face solemnly as she spoke, and she could feel her hands, now resting in her lap, growing damper by the minute with perspiration as he scrutinized her.

"I explained to the young gentleman that his excellency, Barón de Carondelet, and his family are due back at any moment," he said. "They spent the night at a friend's home where there was a ball last evening. It was late, but I came back anyway. They stayed, preferring to return after breakfast this morning. They should be here shortly, and I'm sure the governor will be pleased to finally meet his dear friend's only nephew," and he glanced at Heath, who straightened proudly.

"Don Diego has assured me," she said, "as did his uncle, that Barón de Carondelet would be able to arrange a place for me to stay. It's rather embarrassing, but I feel I can't return to England as yet."

"Señor de Varga has explained that your husband is dead, Countess, but you're not in mourning?" he asked.

She looked at Lizette in dismay, then glanced down at her yellow suit. Fool! She'd forgotten. She did have one black dress, she could have worn it, but no, she had to wear the deep yellow. "I'm afraid I left Madrid in such haste that I neglected to purchase mourning clothes, and my wardrobe consists of only one black dress, *m'sieur*," she answered sweetly. "Unfortunately, there are no dressmakers on the high seas."

Gervaise's words accepted her explanation, but his eyes rejected it as he looked first at her, then Lizette, then back to her. Damn! He was suspicious. Maybe now was the time to throw out the bait. She was just starting to open her mouth when a commotion from the hallway beyond the beaded curtains caught their attention, and Monsieur Gervaise moved toward it, greeting a man as he stepped through. They spoke in Spanish, and from the little Dicia could understand, it was obvious Monsieur Gervaise was explaining to his host their presence in the sitting room.

She tried not to stare at the man, but although he was rather short and stout, his hair graying, he was an impressive figure, even after a night of merriment. In his early forties, he was impeccably dressed in a gray suit embroidered with delicate silver and black roses, his lace-trimmed shirt decorated with a small black tie about the neck, and he walked leisurely across the room as he continued talking to DeMosse Gervaise in Spanish; then he halted in front of her and nodded his dark head.

"La Condesa de Locksley, is it?" he asked, and she nodded her head in return, extending her hand toward him. He took it hesitantly, his eyes questioning as he bent to kiss it, then dropped it abruptly, nodded to Lizette, "Madame DeBouchard," then turned to Heath and spoke once more in Spanish.

Loedicia could feel DeMosse Gervaise's eyes on her as she watched the governor, and she felt uncomfortable; then the governor turned to her and spoke in French.

"Since you know so little of my native tongue, Condesa, and unfortunately I am rather a bumbler in your language, may you and I speak French?" he asked, and Loedicia nodded.

"*Oui, m'sieur,*" she answered, and he turned his attention again to Heath.

"So you are the nephew Fernando always talked about," he said in Spanish, and Heath frowned.

"Talked about, your excellency?" he questioned, and the governor's face reddened slightly.

"Shall we say discussed?"

"If I know my uncle, sir, he undoubtedly complained," answered Heath. "He's forgotten what it is to be young and virile," and the governor looked Heath over, scowling.

"Your uncle told me one day your sins would catch up with you, young man. Is that why you left Spain?" he asked bluntly, and Heath straightened, his handsome face chagrined.

"You hurt me, your excellency," he answered indignantly, laying his hand over his heart, then gesturing flippantly with the same hand. "May I just say that I felt it best for all concerned to take a little . . . shall we say, holiday."

"And the *condesa*? M'sieur Gervaise said she's a widow. Have you expanded your affections to include older women now?"

Heath was somewhat taken aback. He'd heard that the governor was outspoken. For once rumor was right. "Ah, but no, your excellency," he answered as he looked at his mother, who was watching them curiously, wishing she could understand their conversation. "The *condesa*"—she understood that. They were talking of her, and she watched the governor's face as Heath continued, "She and her husband, the late Earl of Locksley, were guests in my father's house." His eyes widened. "You have no doubt heard of my cousin Sebastián?"

The governor shook his head and looked at DeMosse Gervaise; then both shook their heads.

"No," he said. "I have not."

Heath sighed and rolled his eyes. "You think I chase the ladies? I am a timid mouse compared to him. Don Sebastián is my mother's cousin on her mother's side, once removed. He had pledged his heart and soul to all the ladies, and actually given it to none, then he took one look at *la condesa*, here, and lost his heart for the first time in his life." He glanced at his mother, who was watching them, her violet eyes alert, lips parted as if waiting for a clue to the gist of the conversation, and he vowed she looked more beautiful at the moment than he'd remembered her being. "Unfortunately, the earl didn't appreciate Sebastián's amorous attentions toward his wife," he went on. "A duel was fought, and the poor earl was killed instantly. Don Sebastián died two days later, declaring his undying love for *la condesa*." His eyes pleaded convincingly, expressing his mortification as he spoke to the governor. "The scandal was too much. She had to get away, but to go back to England was beyond enduring, so it was decided she come here, and since"—he cleared his throat—"since at the time my love life was getting slightly out of hand, I was chosen to escort her." He straightened, his broad shoulders straining the bolero jacket at the seams. "We were hoping you would be able to recommend a place for her to stay."

Barón de Carondelet sighed as Heath finished his recital and he glanced at Loedicia.

Her face reddened as she realized they had been talking of her and that Heath must have told the governor the tale they'd concocted.

The governor, tuned to the actions and manners of a lady of quality, was impressed. He had no way of knowing that the blush was not because she was ashamed of the scandal, but because she was embarrassed lying to them. Regardless, the blush worked and the governor's eyes softened.

"My dear *condesa*," he said to her in French, "Señor de Varga has delicately divulged your circumstances to us, and I wish to convey my deepest regrets for your untimely experience. You will excuse my countryman for what he's done, but at times we express our emotions rather passionately," and she smiled wanly, her hand at her throat in feigned distress. "It would be gracious of you and Señor de Varga," he continued, "if you would accept the hospitality of my house for as long as you care to stay, and Madame De-Bouchard may stay with you," and he made a brief nod toward Lizette, who had listened stoically to the whole conversation, liking none of it. "I'm sure my family will be ever so pleased," and Loedicia's stomach relaxed, but her expression never changed.

"Barón de Carondelet, you are too kind," she answered, "but I did not expect . . . If there is an inn . . ."

"Condesa, the inns in New Orleans aren't worthy of your presence," he stated. "There will be no argument. You are to stay here," and it was done.

That morning they settled into the governor's house, met his wife and daughter, and their masquerade began in earnest.

Lizette stood in the bedroom a short time later and shook her head as she began unpacking Loedicia's clothes. "Gervaise is too glib and his eyes look at you too much," she spouted hurriedly as she laid some of Loedicia's underthings in the armoire, then began hanging up her dresses. "I don't like it."

"But that's just the point, Lizette," she argued. "Beau wanted him to notice me."

"Like that?" she asked, shocked. "His eyes do all but rape you, *ma petite*, and what of Roth? You have forgotten him so soon?"

Loedicia's eyes saddened, and she walked to the balcony overlooking the beautiful courtyard below, where water from a fountain cascaded into a pool and oleanders with their leathery leaves and array of white and deep rose blossoms grew abundantly, and she sighed. "I'll never forget Roth," she whispered softly. "And somehow, some way, I'm going back to him, Lizette," she said stubbornly. "And if making eyes at this M'sieur Gervaise will hasten that day, then I'll make eyes at him."

Lizette's lips tightened. "He is a dangerous man."

"I know." She had seen it herself during their luncheon. "It shows in his eyes," she agreed. "But if he's the man Beau and Heath are looking for . . . what else am I to do, Lizette? I can't swim back to Port Royal," and Lizette shrugged.

"I don't know, *ma petite*, but I'm afraid for you to get

mixed up with this one. He is cold and calculating, and I am afraid for you."

Loedicia turned from the balcony and stared at her friend. "Poor Lizette, always worrying about me, never yourself. And I'm always dragging you into some kind of danger."

"For myself I don't care, *ma petite*, but I promised Quinn I'd take care of you. How can I do that when you won't listen?" She threw up her hands and shook her head. "*Mon Dieu!* If we are caught, have you no idea what will happen?"

Dicia shivered and suddenly felt cold. "I know only too well, Lizette." Then she seemed to shake herself as if brushing the ugly thoughts aside. "But we won't be caught. Besides, what could they charge me with? Impersonating myself? After all, I am the Countess of Locksley and my husband is dead."

Lizette sighed, exasperated. "I see it does no good to try to make you come to your senses before you get any deeper, *ma petite*, but just how do you expect to learn anything? You can't go about saying 'troubled horizons' to everyone just to see what they'll do. They'll think you're crazy."

"No. But I can let the passwords drop at the first opportunity during our conversation, when everyone's present, then let him come to me, if he's the one." She stepped back to the window and stared down once more into the courtyard.

Her opportunity didn't come as soon as she thought, however. The barón's wife, Doña Mariá Concepción, monopolized her time, enjoying her company, taking her to teas, socials, and dinner engagements, and DeMosse Gervaise sauntered about in the background, watching her, but never giving her an opportunity to approach him alone.

It was three days later when her opportunity finally arose. The barón was having dinner guests, and she was seated next to Heath, who'd been placed opposite the governor's young dark-haired daughter. She was pretty, her eyes strangely blue, and her skin fair for a Spaniard's.

"A throwback from her father's Irish ancestry," remarked DeMosse, who sat on Loedicia's other side.

The barón's mother had been the daughter of an Irish peer, and Heath, true to the character he was playing, flirted with the girl outrageously all evening, his eyes and words caressing her across the table. At times Loedicia wasn't quite sure it was all an act. If he was merely playing a part, he was doing it extremely well. Loedicia had had no idea he was so well-versed with the ladies, but since their arrival he'd been the most charming cavalier, and the barón's daughter, as well as all the other ladies present, was simply swooning with delight.

It was during the course of the dinner conversation that Dicia found an opportunity to use the passwords Beau had given her. The barón was complaining of the Spanish courts and their inane handling of the American frontier and of a possible English invasion from Canada into the northern territories of Louisiana, and most of all France's preoccupation with wanting to control New Orleans.

"You'd think with one full-scale war already in progress they'd leave well enough alone," he exclaimed in French, so that even Loedicia understood. "But *non*, they try to undermine my people and even send spies to try my patience."

"It seems you have many 'troubled horizons,'" Loedicia said as she lifted her wineglass, trying to keep her hand steady. "It sounds like it would almost be too much for one man to handle alone," and he looked at her sharply.

"It wouldn't be if they'd let me handle things my way," he announced, and glanced at his other guests, continuing his disparagement of the situation as if he'd forgotten she'd even spoken, but it was later in the evening when she discovered her words had borne fruit.

After dinner, they'd retired to the music room, where the governor's daughter, María Felipa, entertained them with her prowess on the pianoforte; then they'd been escorted to the theater, where they enjoyed the performance of M'sieur Louis Tabary and his sensational group of young actors and actresses who had fled from a murderous Negro uprising in the French West Indies and had captured New Orleans' heart.

Loedicia had seen a few plays in London, but nothing like this. The performances were unique, their repertory varied, and she found herself forgetting for a few moments everything but the stage before her. It was as the applause died and they began to leave that Monsieur Gervaise took her arm.

"And now, Condesa," he said firmly, as his fingers pressed into her bare flesh. "Let me tell you about my . . . troubled horizons."

She glanced at him apprehensively. He was smiling wickedly, and his eyes traveled to the low décolleté of the red satin dress she wore, then up to her eyes that studied him.

"The red clashes with them," he said softly, and she looked puzzled. "With your eyes," he explained. "You would look exquisite in yellow or violet, but you should never wear red, my dear. Not with eyes like that," and she blushed.

"I do believe you're flirting with me, *m'sieur*," she said, but he ignored her remark.

"Perhaps you'll let me escort you home, Condesa," he offered as the others walked ahead of them. "Their carriage is already overcrowded," and she remembered that he had ridden to the theater by himself, driving his own carriage. "The others are going on to join a house party at the home of one of the governor's friends. I'm sure you'd find it dull and boring."

"Oh, would I?" she asked, and his fingers tightened on her arm.

"Decidedly. Besides"—his voice lowered only for her ears—"I think we have something of importance to discuss."

They were speaking in English now, while all about them was a murmuring mixture of Spanish and French. DeMosse offered his apologies to the barón for himself and Loedicia, and Loedicia could feel the barón's eyes staring at her as DeMosse settled her into his carriage, then climbed up beside her. She glanced quickly at Heath, who was beside the barón, his arm entwined in María Felipa's, and he nodded his approval to her as the carriage lurched forward.

Neither of them spoke for some time; then DeMosse cleared his throat. "There are no troubled horizons where men are free," he said as they left the city behind; then he asked curtly, "Where is Philippe?" and he headed the buggy toward the river.

"Philippe?" She tried to look surprised.

"Come now, Countess," he said sternly, his face showing none of the usual charm it had earlier at the theater. "The pretense is over. You didn't drop those passwords accidentally. Where is Philippe?"

She turned to him now, her face sober, all flirtatious affectations gone. "He's dead," she said boldly, and saw him frown.

"And the letter?"

"We have it."

"Good."

"But how do we know you're to be trusted?" she said. "After all, living in the governor's house . . ."

"What better way to keep informed?" he answered. "And I did know the rest of the password, which proves I'm Philippe's contact," and he moved the carriage off the road, stopping beneath a cypress tree, securing the reins, then turned to her. "I'll be leaving here the day after tomorrow," he said quietly, letting the import of his words sink in. "I must have the letter before I go. My friends up north are waiting for it."

"Your friends?"

"I'm not in this by myself, Countess, remember?" he said abruptly. "Or are you really a countess?"

"I am."

He smiled, a hard smile. "But your husband's not dead."

"On the contrary. My husband is very dead."

His eyes softened. "I see." His arm went up to the back of the carriage seat, brushing against the black lace that trimmed her dress sleeves. He tried to look into her eyes in the darkness, but all he could see was their vague outline. "How did you get mixed up in this?" he asked, and she turned away from him, looking out toward the river.

"Let's say I'm helping out a friend."

"The friend must be very dear to you. If the barón ever suspected, your life would be worth very little."

"And you?"

He shrugged. "I like living dangerously."

She cocked her head as she studied him. He was a good-looking man, rugged beneath an exterior of pretended softness and gentlemanly charm, but there was a violence in his eyes that reminded her of many of the men who'd stopped at Fort Locke over the years. They talked of death and killing as casually as women spoke of children, and with almost the same reverence.

"Where's the letter?" he asked as she stared at him.

"I don't have it."

"Who does?"

"I can't tell you. Not yet. I have to have someone else's permission."

He sighed. "This friend of yours, it's the Spaniard? The young man, Diego de Varga?"

"No."

"No?"

"No. He's merely a means to an end." She didn't want him to know Heath's true identity. The less he knew, the better, at least for now, until they were sure. "Someone else has the letter."

"Your abigail?"

"Lizette? Good heavens no. Lizette came along because I couldn't get rid of her even if I'd wanted. We're dear friends. She promised my husband before he died that she'd look after me, and she's just stubborn enough to do it, no matter what it entails." She shifted in the seat and straightened her skirt, then glanced at him from under her dark lashes. "I'll arrange a meeting," she said. "It's too late tonight. Can you delay your departure one day?"

"No."

"Oh!"

"The morning after tomorrow, I leave for the mouth of the Yazoo River. There's a man waiting there to meet me, the baron's business. Then I wait for another man and pick up another message. I'll give him the letter and head for Philadelphia with the message he gives me. The men will wait there only so long, and the baron's man has probably been there a month already."

"The baron knows you're going?"

"He thinks I'm picking up a message from one of his men and taking it to Philadelphia, which I am, but I'm also running my own line for France."

"You're playing both sides!" she said disgustedly. "Don't you have any scruples?"

"Where money is concerned, my dear Countess, there are no scruples," he answered.

She stared at him, her violet eyes questioning. "Just who are you?" she asked, puzzled, and his eyes grew intent on her face.

"Why do you ask?"

"You're not a French gentleman of leisure, that I know," she said. "Your hands are callused. The hands of a man who's done hard labor. And the way you carry yourself . . . your eyes never miss a thing. No, M'sieur Gervaise, you're not the charming casual Frenchman you pretend to be."

"Would it surprise you to discover I'm the son of a marquis?"

Her eyebrows raised.

"Unfortunately, my father loved gambling and died in debtors' prison, with my mother at his side. I was born in the Bastille." He hesitated. "Doesn't that shock you?"

"No." She shook her head. "In the life I've led, M'sieur Gervaise, it takes more than that to shock me. But how is it you're free?"

"A grandmother with a soft heart. When my father died, my grandparents paid for my mother's and my release, but my grandfather had little love for me, nor did my stepfather after my mother's remarriage. As soon as I was able, I left, heading for America."

"And you've been on the move ever since?"

"I light here and there."

"And how did you meet the baron?"

"Let's say I was in the right place at the right time."

"That's not an explanation," she said.

He hesitated a moment, then looked at her intently. "I saved his life shortly after his arrival in New Orleans some years ago when some cutthroats attacked the carriage he was riding in. He invited me home for dinner and we became friends. When he learned of my knowledge of the frontier I soon became a courier for him, and because he's never learned otherwise, he trusts me implicitly."

"But your sympathies are with France?"

He straightened as he stared at her. "My sympathies are where I can make the most money, Countess. You should realize that."

"I thought as much." She took a deep breath. It made her nervous to have him stare at her like this. "Tell me, this Yazoo River, where is it?"

"North some three hundred miles on the Mississippi."

"And from there you go to Philadelphia?"

"You've been to Philadelphia?"

She didn't answer; her mind was suddenly alert, her nerves tingling as a new wave of thought filtered through her. "M'sieur Gervaise," she asked hesitantly, letting her thoughts take wing, "have you ever been to South Carolina?"

"South Carolina?"

"Port Royal, to be exact."

"Can't say that I have."

"Do you think you could find it?"

"Is it near Charleston?"

"South of Charleston."

His eyes darkened. "I could find it. Why?"

She turned to look out over the river, and bit her lip, then faced him again, her body trembling over her sudden decision, and she took a deep breath. "I'll pay you two thousand dollars in American gold to take me to Port Royal," she answered firmly, and he whistled in surprise. "You said you went where the money was, and it won't be that much out of your way. In fact, after you leave me, you can take a ship from Charleston and reach Philadelphia sooner."

He was flabbergasted. "Do you realize what you're asking?" he said in disbelief, and she sighed.

"I'm asking you to take me to Port Royal."

"Through some of the wildest territory east of the Mississippi."

She laughed lightly. "M'sieur Gervaise, I have been through country so wild we had to cut our way through the underbrush. I can ride with or without a saddle if need be, and shoot a rifle as well as any man."

He studied her, seeing the determined set to her chin, and her abilities were no surprise, but to go cross-country . . . "That's not the point," he finally said. "It's a long trail for a man, let alone a woman."

"I'm not as fragile as I may look, sir," she answered, and he shook his head, then turned, staring off toward the river. He turned back to her suddenly.

"Why not sail to Port Royal?"

"Because I've had nothing but water beneath me for over six months already, and I'm sick and tired of it." She lowered her eyes. "Besides, I haven't found a ship anywhere in New Orleans that's willing to take me for any amount of money. They're all headed for either England, Europe, or the Caribbean, and no one wants to go out of his way."

"And you want to go to Port Royal."

Her voice was tremulous. "I have to."

"Why?"

She glanced at him quickly, her eyes narrowing.

"I merely asked why," he said, and she pursed her lips, wondering if she should tell him the truth.

"I was supposed to be married to a man who's at present living in Port Royal," she said. "Unfortunately, there was an untimely incident and we were separated."

His voice lowered. "I should have known." His fingers began to play with a lock of her hair as he stared at her in the shadows of the cypress tree. "May I ask his name?"

"Chapman, Roth Chapman."

"The Roth Chapman?"

She was surprised. "You know him?"

"I've heard of him. I hear he's on his way to being one of the wealthiest men in the world, with England's help."

"That's not fair! He can't help it if his father left him an inheritance in England."

"But he'd never think of selling it, would he?"

"You don't like him," she said, hearing the animosity in his voice.

"I don't even know the man, but I hate any man with that much money." Then his eyes softened. "Besides, who wouldn't envy the man you'd be willing to track halfway across the country to marry?"

"You're trying to flatter me again."

"On the contrary. I'm merely being truthful. You're a beautiful, sensuous woman."

She flushed self-consciously. "Will you take me or not?" she asked, trying to put his mind back on the subject at hand, and he stroked the short, clipped beard that accentuated his hard chin line, then brushed a finger lightly over his mustache.

"Two thousand?"

"In advance."

His eyes stopped on hers.

"It'd be stupid for me to try to carry that much money with me without your knowing it, so I'll just take it along. When we reach Port Royal, it's yours."

He smiled cynically. "You mean Mr. Chapman wouldn't be willing to reimburse me?"

"I wouldn't ask him," she answered. "But will you take me?"

He hesitated, looking her over carefully. She was an enigma, and he'd never met anyone quite like her. A titled lady who could ride, shoot, and play spy. He wondered what other accomplishments she might have. And who was the mysterious friend she was working for? If not the young Spaniard Diego, then who? And if Diego wasn't taking Philippe's place, where did he fit into the picture? The whole affair was intriguing . . . and after all, two thousand dollars was two thousand dollars . . . and it wasn't really that far out of his way, he argued with himself. Besides, it might prove interesting.

"You'll have to leave most of your trunks behind," he finally said.

"I know."

"And what will you tell the baron?"

"I don't know." She frowned. "I'll think of something."

"What?"

She bristled, irritated. "I don't know."

His eyes brightened. "I could think of something."

She looked at him suspiciously. His eyes were gleaming. "I'm sure you could," she said, then turned toward the road and stared as a carriage approached and passed without seeing them in the darkness. She turned back to DeMosse. What could she tell them? Women didn't go wandering into the wilderness with men they hardly knew, leaving everything behind, without a good reason, and she couldn't tell the baron her true reason, or all their lives would be in jeopardy. She could wait and sail. Yet this was her chance. She might not be able to persuade a ship's captain to take her to Port Royal, at least not for months and months, or perhaps never.

If she didn't go now, who knows when she'd ever see Roth again? Heath and Beau were headed for Martinique, then France. "All right, what should I tell them?" she asked, unable to think of anything at the moment.

"We could run away together."

"Run away?"

"We fell madly in love . . ."

"In five days? Oh, come now, M'sieur Gervaise, not even the governor is that naive and stupid."

He grinned, and his hand went to her shoulder, caressing the back of her neck. "I thought maybe we could make it look believable."

She tensed, her body stiffening. "I'm afraid not, m'sieur," she answered softly, staring into his hard, arrogant eyes. "Love is one thing at which I pretend quite badly."

His fingers continued caressing her neck, and strangely, it felt good. She frowned.

"What's the matter?" he asked.

"Nothing."

"I thought perhaps you'd changed your mind." His voice deepened. "Or maybe you need some help," and he leaned toward her, only to be stopped as she pressed her hands against his chest.

"Not that kind of help," she answered firmly. "Surely you've got a better suggestion."

His jaw tightened as he stared at her; then his hand reluctantly returned to the back of the seat. "There is one alternative," he said. "There's an English couple, Sir Charles Pomfrey and his wife. They've bought land up the river a ways at a place called Baton Rouge. We could pretend you've discovered they're old friends and you've decided to pay them a visit until you're ready to return to England."

"Does the baron know the Pomfreys?"

"Slightly."

"But you know them well?"

"Quite well. I intend to stop in and say hello on the way."

"You think he'll believe us?"

"The Pomfreys are friendly people. I think he'll believe us."

"How far is this Baton Rouge?"

"About a hundred miles upriver."

"You go by boat?"

"We'll take a keel boat as far as Baton Rouge, then cut out from there on horseback."

She thought it over for a few seconds. "That's a much better suggestion than your first," she said, but he smiled wickedly.

"Everyone to his own taste," he said. She frowned as he went on, "But tell me, is there any way you can set up a meeting with this friend of yours for tomorrow morning?"

"I don't know." She frowned. "Señor de Varga is to meet him tomorrow evening at a designated spot. I doubt if he'll be able to reach him before that time."

"And there's no way you can contact him?"

She thought for a minute, wondering what Heath would do when he discovered her plans, and wondering if maybe he could slip down to the docks to see Beau early in the morning. "I'll try," she answered hesitantly. "I don't know . . . but I'll try."

He nodded. "Good, then since everything's taken care of, I presume we can enjoy the rest of the evening," and he leaned forward once more, his arms engulfing her, but again her hands held him back.

"You seem to forget rather easily that there's another man," she whispered as he stared at her, but he didn't seem daunted.

"But he's miles away, *chérie*," he said, and his brown eyes looked deeply into hers. "What he doesn't know won't hurt him."

"But it'll hurt me."

He continued to stare, his mouth twitching reluctantly only inches from hers; then he shrugged. "As you wish," he said, and his arms dropped from about her. He plucked the reins up and in seconds the carriage was back on the road and he began describing the Pomfreys to her.

They made plans as they rode, and that evening while Lizette helped Loedicia prepare for bed, she listened quietly to Loedicia's plans, then exploded with all her French fervor. But her protests and admonitions were unable to make Loedicia change her mind.

"Very well, then *ma petite*," Lizette finally surrendered. "But I go with you," and Dicia knew there was no use trying to argue her out of it. Any argument she might put up would fall on deaf ears. One was as stubborn as the other. If she went to Port Royal, Lizette would be right on her heels.

4

                       nd

Loedicia was a little apprehensive as the carriage pulled
away from the house and headed down the long drive, but
there was no turning back now. The baron had believed her
story and cautioned DeMosse to take good care of her on the
way to Baton Rouge, inviting her back for a stay whenever
she was in town again, and she felt guilty about the lies.

Heath was the one that worried her. He'd argued inces-
santly last night over her decision, but had finally given in to
her because he knew that when she made up her mind about
something as important as this was to her, she could be as
stubborn as a mule. He had two consolations however:
Lizette was going along, and they were picking up another
man the other side of Baton Rouge. A man, both he and
Beau had heard, who was one of the best backwoodsmen in
the territory.

Heath had managed to contact Beau early the day before
and arranged for a meeting last night that had turned out
well, although Beau was wary of DeMosse.

"There's something about the man," he told Heath as they
watched DeMosse and Loedicia walking toward the carriage
that had brought them to the rendezvous. "I bet he'd sell his
soul for the right money, and probably has already," and
Heath agreed.

But he was their only contact. The letter was turned over,
and ten thousand in gold was loaded aboard the *Golden
Eagle* before dawn that morning. Now Loedicia waved to
Heath, who stood beside the governor, frowning as they
drove off. Heath had informed the governor that since the
condesa was in good hands, he'd decided to visit the Florida
territories, which he'd heard were beyond description, and
he'd be sailing in a day or two, but in reality he and Beau
were sailing to Mobile, dropping off Jacques's share of the
gold with an agent who'd take it the rest of the way, since the
water off the coast of Georgia would be crawling with British

ships, then they were heading for Martinique to pick up the rest of the crew.

A frightening shudder went through Loedicia as she watched the image of her son fade in the distance, and her fingers tightened in her lap, but she was on her way to Roth now, and that's all that mattered.

They were deposited a short time later, bag and baggage, at the river front, where Loedicia had her first encounter with the Mississippi. DeMosse explained that its name came from the Indian words "Meact Chassipi," meaning "ancient father of waters." Loedicia'd sailed the big ships, canoed on the lake, and ridden rafts, but never in her life had she experienced the likes of a keelboat.

It was close to seventy feet long and perhaps eighteen feet in the beam and almost five feet deep. Pointed in bow and stern alike, roofed over to protect the passengers, it was a large floating cabin with a narrow gangway on each side, the length of the boat.

As they stepped aboard, following their baggage, Loedicia glanced at Lizette, who was wrinkling her nose in distaste at the crew, whose crude remarks as they boarded the cumbersome vessel brought a sharp reprimand from DeMosse that surprised Loedicia by its results.

"Remember, ma petite, this was your idea," remarked Lizette as they were led inside the boat, where a table and chairs graced the main room. There were two other rooms for sleeping, one for ladies and one for the men, with feather tickings spread about the planking, and not a bed in sight. The cargo was carried below in a makeshift hold into which Loedicia's largest trunks also disappeared.

There were boxes and benches about the main room, and DeMosse gestured toward them. "If you ladies will have a seat, we'll be shoving off in about half an hour," he said as Loedicia eyed him curiously.

"This is it?" she asked, and he looked amused.

"You don't like it?"

She shrugged. He was waiting for her to complain, and she knew it; then he could say she asked for it. Well, she wouldn't give him the satisfaction.

"Naturally I don't like it," she answered firmly, "but I guess it'll have to do," and she pulled off her hat, removed her gloves, and began to make herself at home as best she could.

Their departure was accompanied by a round of rousing

cheers and catcalls from shore as they cast off and the men poled into midstream, the boat slowly moving upriver.

The men who handled the keelboat were rough and hard, their hands callused, muscles bulging beneath well-worn clothes, and the man who barked the orders was the worst of the lot, and with reason. He had to be strong enough to take on any man that might try to cross him, and this took a special breed.

"They're a cross between an alligator and a horse," explained DeMosse that evening as he and Loedicia stood in the warm night air on the gangway, leaning against the shelter watching the stars as the boat slowly moved upriver.

She glanced toward the stern, where their captain stood tall in the moonlight, battered hat jammed square on his head as he studied the shoreline. Then, as she watched, he stretched lazily, said something to the man at the tiller, and disappeared inside the shelter.

Loedicia, Lizette, and DeMosse were the only passengers on the boat so far, and now, with most of the crew except the polers settling down for the night, it was exceptionally quiet. The river was beautiful, with the moon on it turning the trees on the banks to silver.

"Quite a contrast to this afternoon, isn't it?" DeMosse said as he gazed into the warm night, then watched as the polers walked past them, their weight against the long poles as they poled from bow to stern, and she agreed.

The daylight hours had been filled with yelling, cursing, and utter chaos as the men poled, walking in rhythm.

When it was too deep to pole, but the current was slight, oars suddenly appeared and the men laid muscle to them, heaving them in and out of the water while the captain kept time; then there were times it was so shallow he cursed liberally, scraping the bottom more than once as poles stuck in the silt. At night, however, like this, it seemed so calm and serene. But the hardest part was yet to come, as Loedicia learned the next afternoon, when they pulled closer to shore and secured the towrope tied to the top of the keelboat's mast, which stuck some thirty feet into the air. Now the backbreaking work began.

The current was strong, and poles were useless, so the ropes, some thousand feet or more, were braced onto the men's shoulders as they walked the riverbank, and by sheer strength the men literally towed the boat, inching it forward a few feet at a time against the current. Loedicia watched in awe as the men pulled against the weight of the boat, and suddenly she had a new respect for these crude, burly men. God, they were strong.

Sometimes, when the current was so strong the boat made no headway at all, even with all hands at the ropes, one of the men would work his way upriver, tie the line to a tree, then the crew would steady themselves on the deck of the boat and gather in the line, moving the boat on again.

The procedure was tedious and slow, a back-breaking job, and Loedicia was surprised when DeMosse joined the crew, straining his muscles with the best of them. At times the foliage was so dense on shore that they had to cut their way through as they moved along the bank, but it didn't seem to dampen their spirits. They laughed and cursed and fought the same as ever, each man trying to prove his worth as the boat inched along.

Two weeks and some weary but beautiful winding miles behind them, the keelboat pulled into the dock at Baton Rouge, and DeMosse, his clipped beard now grown a good half-inch longer, frowned as Loedicia and Lizette waited beside him for the boat to tie up.

He knew Loedicia had enjoyed the trip in spite of the hardships, but then, who wouldn't enjoy the Mississippi? She was a proud river.

"Sorry we're here already?" he asked as the men brought their baggage up from below and Loedicia and Lizette took a good look around.

The keelboat had brought much-needed supplies to the settlement that boasted some shabby buildings, a grist mill, a church, the usual inns and stores. It was a close-knit town, the inns catering to the river trade, the flatboats hauling produce from the surrounding countryside to New Orleans. Loedicia had seen towns like it dozens of times, carved from the wilderness and nurtured by the greed of their inhabitants.

"And where do the Pomfreys live?" she asked as she held out her hand, letting him help her climb ashore.

"About two miles due east."

"We walk?"

He helped Lizette ashore, then grinned, his teeth showing exceptionally white against the suntan he'd acquired in the past few days and against his darkening beard. "I think I can probably find a wagon to take us," he answered as he motioned for one of the men to hand him the last of the baggage; then he turned again to the ladies. "I'll escort you to the Redbird Inn. It's the other side of the waterfront, and you can wait there while I get a wagon."

The Redbird Inn was clean, its floors scrubbed white, its tables covered with gingham cloths, its proprietor only too anxious to serve them an evening meal of boiled beef and cabbage with plenty of potatoes, new young peas from the garden out back, and fresh strawberries picked from the nearby woods. It was fancy fare after the mush, dried vegetables, and heavily smoked meat that was served on the keelboat. They'd picked up three other passengers on the way, all of them men, and Loedicia was glad DeMosse was along. His constant attention to their welfare discouraged any false notions that the ladies might invite their friendship, and they had disappeared quickly on their arrival in Baton Rouge.

All in all, the trip had been a good one. Slow, but enjoyable, and now Loedicia and Lizette ate their evening meal talking over the adventure while they waited impatiently for DeMosse.

The wagon he hired was driven by a Cajun up from New Orleans, and his skill with the team was anything but proficient. Loedicia swore he hit every bump and rut in the makeshift road, but then, as DeMosse explained, there were few wagons for hire, so there was little choice.

They pulled into the long drive to the Pomfreys' at dark, and DeMosse sighed as he helped the ladies alight. Lights were just beginning to flicker in the house, set comfortably in the midst of some giant oaks, and the warmth they gave to the windows was inviting as they strode up to the door. Tonight they'd sleep in soft beds, for the large house had ample room for visitors.

Sir Charles Pomfrey and his wife were perfect hosts, and unlike the tall tale told to the baron in New Orleans, DeMosse told them the truth as far as he knew it. The Countess of Locksley had hired him to take her to Port Royal in the Carolinas, where her future husband awaited.

"You mean you're not frightened to travel through such wild country?" asked Sir Charles's plump wife, Effie, over a glass of claret in the drawing room before they retired.

Loedicia smiled, reassuring her. "I've been in danger hundreds of times over the years," she said, "and I always managed to survive."

"But the frontier . . . the Indians."

Loedicia's violet eyes warmed to the woman's fear. "I'll be fine, I assure you. Besides, M'sieur Gervaise has promised to take the least-dangerous route."

"There is no least-dangerous route," said the portly Sir Charles as he glanced quickly at DeMosse. "Unless, of course, he means avoiding the Natchez Trace altogether."

"I do," answered DeMosse. "We're going on to Fort No-galles, then move east, crossing the Natchez, but staying as far from it as possible. There's an old Indian trail that goes all the way to the Savannah River. I was that way once about six or seven years ago. It shouldn't be too hard to find."

"I wish you luck," offered Sir Charles. "Even at that, it's no place for a woman," but Loedicia wasn't to be dissuaded, and for the next few days arrangements were made as swiftly as possible.

DeMosse bought three horses, three pack mules, and enough supplies to last a good three months, but the surprise was the day they left, when Loedicia and Lizette greeted him wearing their buckskins.

His eyes looked them over curiously, scrutinizing every line as Loedicia fastened the bundle of clothing she'd managed to salvage from her trunks onto her pack mule, then faced him, demanding a rifle.

"A rifle?" he asked, surprised, but she held her ground.

"A rifle," she affirmed. "If you think I'm going without a rifle, you're sadly mistaken."

He glanced down at the knife in its sheath at her waist, and his eyes narrowed. "That's right, you did say you knew how to use one, didn't you?" he said.

"And I also said a lot of other things which were true, M'sieur Gervaise," she stated. "So if you'll find me a rifle and powder, we can be on our way."

He stared down at her slight figure clad in the buckskins. Then his eyes moved to her hauntingly beautiful face. She'd told him little about herself on the trip upriver. In fact, all he still knew was what she'd told him the night she'd hired him, and he wondered where a titled British lady would acquire buckskins that were apparently well-used.

"These are yours?" he asked, flicking his finger against the fringed collar of her shirt.

"They're mine," she answered. "I didn't say I was always a countess, m'sieur," she said evasively. "Now, if you'll just get me a rifle . . ."

He promised to stop by town and pick one up on the way, so when the three mules were all packed and their good-byes and thanks said to the Pomfreys, they started toward town, where DeMosse bought her a Kentucky rifle and some powder; then as the few people at the river front that morning watched in awe, commenting back and forth, the trio started upriver, disappearing into the wilderness.

Lizette still hated riding, but for Loedicia's sake she'd tackle anything. She had blisters before they'd gone even a half day's ride, and Loedicia forfeited one of her quilted dressing gowns from the bundle of clothes she'd brought along. It was ripped into heavy pads to cover Lizette's seat, and every time Loedicia glanced her way as she trailed behind them, she felt a pang of guilt. After all, Lizette wouldn't even be here if it weren't for her.

With time however, the blisters healed and became calluses, and Lizette tolerated the ride, beginning to enjoy somewhat the luxuriant scenery along the river.

DeMosse knew the land well, pointing out landmarks along the way and explaining some of the river's history. It was a glorious land, and occasionally they left the river, going cross-country, picking the river up again farther on, but each mile brought a sadness to Loedicia's eyes as she remembered the trek east she and Quinn had made just a little over a year ago. So much could happen in a year. One could live a lifetime in so few months.

She tried not to think of the past, and clung to the future, but that too was vague. It all hinged on a great deal of ifs, the most important being if she could make it to Port Royal. After their short stay at the Pomfreys' and talk of the Indians, she wasn't quite as confident.

She glanced at DeMosse, ahead of her, as she rode pulling the pack mule behind her. DeMosse Gervaise was a strange man. He'd shaved his beard and mustache off while they were at the Pomfreys', explaining that with the weather getting hotter it was a liability, and Loedicia studied his face now as they rode. His jawline was square and sharp, his mouth a little too broad, but the combination, with his gold-and-green-flecked brown eyes, was pleasing. He looked far different without the clipped beard and mustache. The genteel ladies'-man look about him was gone, but Loedicia wasn't sure she liked what was revealed. He was an attractive man, but there was a hard core to him, a ruthlessness and to-hell-with-it attitude that sometimes reminded her of Quinn. He could yell at her when she did something wrong, with the same mercilessness Quinn had often shown, but there was one thing lacking. Never once did he ever apologize if he was in the wrong, or try to make up for his temper.

They made camp late and broke camp early, and at night, as Dicia lay beneath the stars and open sky, she'd ache for Roth and wonder what he was doing, and if he was searching for her. But then, where could he search? Oh, God, how she missed him, and she thought back to England and to that night in the inn. She'd fought her feelings for him for so long, so many years, yet she had wanted him so badly that when their love for each other finally drove them beyond caring, beyond any guilt they might have had, she'd lived a wild rapture of ecstasy she'd never forget, and it was with her yet as she lay in his arms on the *Golden Eagle,* but now the torment of being without him was almost unbearable. She loved him so, and she shivered involuntarily, begging God to hasten the day when they could be together, because she knew she was needing him more and more as the days went on.

It took five days of constant riding from sunup to sunset to reach Fort Nogalles, where the Yazoo River flowed into the Mississippi, and they rode in early one afternoon to the stares of the men. There were no white women at Nogalles, only a few squaws, and the sight of white women this far north was a godsend to men starved for the sight of them, so it was no wonder that both women were treated royally. But the fort commander expressed his doubts as to their trip being a wise one.

He spoke only in Spanish, so Loedicia heard it secondhand from DeMosse. It displeased her just the same. Almost everyone at the fort spoke Spanish, and it frustrated her because she never knew what they were talking about, so the fact that they stayed only one day met with her wholehearted approval.

They left the fort early in the morning, heading east, their supplies replenished and a good night's sleep behind them. The day was cool for the first part of June, and the scent of mock orange mingled with the smell of the river water as they left it behind.

They had ridden perhaps three miles when DeMosse reined up and motioned for them to pull up at the side of the trail.

"What is it?" asked Dicia, her eyes alert, ears strained; then she heard the call of a night heron, out-of-place at this hour of the day. It seemed to come from their left, and DeMosse raised his hand to his mouth, answering back with the call of a night hawk. In minutes the brush rustled, then scattered as a man approached them, his buckskins loose over his lanky frame, his gray-flecked brown hair growing down the side of his cheek, stopping just short of the chin. He grinned, his tanned face framing a set of steely gray eyes beneath bushy brows, and a set of teeth that made him look all mouth.

"Well, where the hell you been?" he greeted DeMosse boisterously, and they shook hands, DeMosse grinning back.

"Buttering up the governor and keeping company with the ladies," he answered, and the tall man eyed Loedicia and Lizette, his forehead creasing into a deep frown.

"What the hell you doin' with them out here?" he asked, and DeMosse explained as simply as he knew how, filling him in on the details, but omitting the price Loedicia was paying him.

"Dammit all, DeMosse, I ain't keen on goin' cross-country, and you know it," he explained. "Last time, I almost lost my scalp," and he reached up, running his hand through the salt-and-pepper hair that topped his head, but there was no arguing with DeMosse.

He introduced Loedicia and Lizette to Jess Willoughby, then handed Jess the letter Beau had turned over, and Jess disappeared once more into the woods with a promise to catch up to them in an hour's time. True to his word, he came lumbering into view, leading his horse behind him, a little over an hour's ride farther along the trail. The letter was on its way upriver again, and DeMosse could rest a little easier. Jess mounted and reined in beside DeMosse.

"Where did you say this countess is from?" he asked furtively as he took a quick glance back at Loedicia, who was riding her horse with ease, and DeMosse frowned.

"Well, she says she's from England, but I have a feeling there's more to the Countess of Locksley than meets the eye. She's far too at home on horseback."

Jess glanced back at Lizette. "That maid of hers sure ain't," he said, chuckling as he watched Lizette's impromptu version of how not to ride a horse. "You really mean to take them to South Carolina?"

"That's what the ladies are paying me for."

Jess ran a finger across his long straight nose. "Hmmm. I gave Billie the letter, and he's on his way north, but what of these?" he asked, putting his hand on the inside pocket of his buckskin shirt, where a small leather packet was tucked away. "Genet failed, but we can't. If we get these papers through to Philadelphia, it'll open up a door for France right into Louisiana. Washington won't dare ignore what's going on out in the territory. He's trying to stay neutral, but dammit, the British are only biding their time. They intend to have a good line of forts all along the Mississippi, and if we don't stop them now, they'll be trying to take the states back, you watch and see. There'll be war again before long, unless

71

something's done. The redcoats never did like losin' that one." He touched his hand again to the packet. "Yes, sir, DeMosse, these we gotta get through," and DeMosse dug his horse a bit harder in the ribs as they moved up an incline, the trees towering overhead like a canopy of green above them, with only rare rays of sunlight streaming through.

"Jess, why are you fighting for France?" he asked casually as they rode along, and Jess shrugged.

"Money. Why?"

"Just curious." He patted his horse's neck, then looked at his friend. They'd covered a lot of miles together off and on over the years, but they'd never really been close. Most of the time it was a matter of necessity, and besides, they were both on the same side, the side with the most money at the moment. Jess was as greedy as he was, and if he went along, he'd want half of the two thousand. He could send him to Philadelphia alone, but if he did that, Jess would collect both their shares, and he'd probably never see him again for another year, and by that time his share would be gone. Oh, Jess would have some damn excuse about why he let it trickle away.

He straighened in the saddle and glanced toward Jess. "I suppose you want a cut," he finally said, and Jess studied him hard.

"It's either that or I go to Philly on my own."

DeMosse glanced back at Loedicia, her hair picking up the few scarce sunbeams that seeped through from overhead, and it shone iridescent like the feathers on a raven. She tilted her head up as she rode along, watching a squirrel playfully cavorting in the trees, and her profile caught in the sunlight. God, she was beautiful, like a painting. To have a woman like that would be sheer heaven. She was alive, vivid. More woman than he'd seen in years. Maybe that's why he'd taken the job. Not the money so much, although it was an incentive, but the thought of traveling with her was intriguing. He'd met dozens of women, but the minute he'd laid eyes on her he'd felt the vibrations deep inside. She was a special breed of woman, the kind a man didn't run across every day, and he wondered what Roth Chapman had that made her willing to risk her life to reach him, yet, at the same time, he wondered if maybe he could change her mind before they reached Port Royal. It was worth a try. She was fascinating.

"All right. She's up for a thousand," he lied, with no thought to cheating his friend, "so that makes five hundred apiece. I don't like sharing it, but I have no choice. It's that or lose my whole commission on the Philadelphia deal, and I don't intend to do that."

Jess grinned, not realizing he was being cheated. "Thought you'd see reason," he said as he took a deep breath, inhaling the fresh air; then he glanced back toward Loedicia. "Got eyes on the countess, ain'tcha?"

"So what?"

"Just statin' facts."

"Well, keep it to yourself," he snapped, then turned his horse, reining back toward Loedicia, who was having trouble with her mule. "Pull harder," he said as he called to her across the stream of water the mule was balking at, but the stubborn animal hung back, snorting and bellowing at the small, bubbling trickle that crossed his path.

"I am pulling," she yelled forcefully, "but the damn thing won't budge." She slid from her horse, waded the stream, and moved to the back of the mule, shoving against his flank, but he was planted solid. Walking around to his front, she stood staring the wretched thing in the face. This was the first time he'd done this since they'd left Baton Rouge. All the miles of forest, and he had to pick this particular spot.

DeMosse rode back across the trickling stream and dismounted. "What made him stop?"

She shrugged. "Who knows!"

"Well, he can't just stand there."

"I know that." She glared at him angrily. "You have any ideas?"

He motioned toward Lizette, who was patiently waiting for Loedicia's mule to move. "Go around," he said as he gestured. "Maybe if he sees you moving into the water, he might get the idea."

Lizette dug her heels lightly into her horse's ribs and moved him forward, her mule walking docilely behind. Her mule stepped into the water without so much as a glance toward Loedicia's mule, and Loedicia looked disgusted.

"Now, why couldn't mine have done that?" She grabbed the rope again and began pulling, but he still wouldn't budge.

DeMosse was beside Loedicia, and he reached out, taking her hand, removing the rope from it, then stood staring down at her. "Let's go for a walk," he said, and she stared at him perplexed.

"A walk?"

"Sometimes mules don't like being pushed. Let him relax." He gestured upstream. "We could walk a short way." He

73

turned to Jess. "You and Lizette can keep on the trail, go slow, we'll catch up."

Lizette glanced quickly at Loedicia. She didn't like leaving her alone with DeMosse. In fact, on the whole trip so far she'd managed to keep them from being alone together as much as possible, but now with Jess along . . . She didn't like DeMosse. As a man, he was handsome and charming enough, but there was something about him and the way he looked at Dicia. But she had no alternative now, and rode on, following Jess up the trail.

Loedicia and DeMosse tethered their horses to a small sapling beside the stream, securing the mule's rope to the ring at the side of Loedicia's saddle; then they started sauntering upstream, leaving the animal by himself.

"And just what are we supposed to do on this walk?" she asked as she kicked a small pebble into the stream, then reached over and picked a wild daisy.

"Talk."

She looked at him skeptically. "About what?"

"I think it's time you told me who you really are."

"I'm the Countess of Locksley," she answered, but he disagreed.

"You're more than that."

"I guess so . . . yes."

"What?"

"My husband claimed the title not quite a year ago," she explained as she began picking the petals off the daisy, dropping them as they went. "Before that we lived on the frontier here in America. He was what you'd consider yourself, I guess, a backwoodsman and adventurer."

"And an English earl?"

"Why not?"

"But you didn't always live on the frontier."

"I was an English lady, born and raised in India, if you must know." She glanced back toward the mule, and stopped, watching him. While they'd been talking, he'd moved over away from the stream and was nuzzling against her horse. "I think our ruse has worked," she said, motioning with her head, and he glanced back, smiling, then took her arm, turning her about as they talked, and they retraced their steps slowly so as not to give the mule any new ideas.

This time the animal forded the stream without any trouble at all, and when they joined Lizette and Jess farther on, DeMosse made a remark about mules being as unpredictable as women, which didn't set well with Loedicia, and she let him have a taste of her temper as they rode along.

The rest of the day was uneventful, and they camped some thirty miles from Fort Nogalles.

The second day out, in late afternoon, they crossed the Natchez Trace that led up into the Ohio Valley; then they headed deeper into the wilderness. At times the underbrush was so dense they had to cut their way through, making a trail, and vines wrapped the treetops, almost suffocating them in a canopy of mottled green that made it seem like they were riding through perpetual twilight.

For the next few days they struggled through what seemed like endless forests with only an occasional meadow or small stream. The terrain was wild, untamed, and there were times Loedicia would have sworn they were lost, but when she mentioned it to DeMosse, he just grinned maddeningly.

Finally, one evening shortly before dusk, they were looking for a place to camp and maneuvered their mounts around some wild elderberry bushes and up the side of a small, rock-covered slope, when DeMosse sighed.

"There," he said, stretching his arm in the darkening twilight as they reached the top, and he pointed beyond them. Loedicia stared in awe.

Ahead of them, nestled between rolling hills, was a virgin river, its grass-covered banks sloping gently to the water's edge, where trees clung tenaciously, holding onto the ground with gnarled roots as the river rushed past, and the pink rays of the darkening sky above it sent a faint glow playing through the branches of the trees and dancing on the water.

"It's beautiful," Loedicia sighed as she stared.

"It's the Tombigbee," said DeMosse, "and we're right where I figured we'd be." He gave his horse a nudge in the ribs, and the others followed him down the slope to the water's edge. "We'll cross tonight and camp on the other side," he said as they rode. "If we'd ended up downriver about ten miles farther, it would have been too wide and deep to cross, and ten miles upriver would have given us two rivers to cross instead of one. As it is, about twenty miles farther there's another river about the size of this one, if we hit it in the right spot, that is, and beyond that some fifteen miles are the mountains and more rivers, with about four hundred miles to go."

"It's that far?" Loedicia exclaimed as she drew rein beside the water and stared into its shallow bottom that was only about two to three feet deep in this particular spot.

"I told you, *ma petite*," said Lizette, nudging her horse between Loedicia and DeMosse, "it would not be easy. It took us weeks on the water, it will take us months in this godforsaken land."

"Not months, Lizette," said DeMosse, "but if nothing happens, we should reach South Carolina about the middle of July or later."

"And what are you afraid might happen, M'sieur Gervaise?" asked Lizette.

"Indians." He shrugged. "Who knows? We've been quiet so far, and it's a big country. They may not even know we're passing through."

"If they do?" asked Dicia.

"There might be a speck of trouble. It all depends on whether they're Choctaw, Creek, or Cherokee."

They crossed the river and set up camp on the opposite bank. Jess and Lizette had been like a pair of antagonistic bears the whole trip so far. Always at each other, sniping and sarcastic, and the fact that Jess found Lizette attractive helped her mood even less. She was determined not to let him look too inviting, even though he was the only other man for miles around besides DeMosse. Sometimes his good humor and twinkling eyes were too much for her, however, and she'd succumb to his charm, talking with him and laughing spontaneously, her anger at his stubborn antics of earlier in the day all but forgotten.

Loedicia stood now beneath a tree near the edge of the river and glanced back toward camp, watching the two of them arguing over the best way to cook the fish Jess and DeMosse had caught for supper. Jess wanted to bake them in wild grape leaves, and Lizette wanted hers skewered and roasted. Loedicia had watched them since Fort Nogalles. There was something intimate about the way they fought and laughed, the way lovers would, and she wondered how long it would be before they discovered it themselves.

She turned from them and walked closer to the edge of the water. It was dark now, the moon not up yet, and the light from the fire, where Lizette and Jess knelt, cast flickering shadows into the darkness, but the night was warm and full of the scent of fresh water and wildflowers that blanketed the riverbank. She thought of the long trail behind them and the long trail ahead, and suddenly her thoughts froze as DeMosse spoke from behind her.

"Thinking of Mr. Money?" he asked cynically, and she turned about slowly, her eyes hostile.

"That's nasty."

"I guess I'm just nasty by nature." He stared at her intently. "But you were thinking of him, weren't you?"

"And if I was?"

He inhaled, eyeing her skeptically, his face shadowed in the darkness. "You know," he said as he stepped forward and stood beside her on the riverbank, "I've been trying to put two and two together ever since we left New Orleans, and I never seem to come up with four."

Her eyes narrowed. "How's that?"

"You said your husband became an earl less than a year ago, and I heard you and Lizette talking about spending last Christmas in England with your family. Now I know it takes at least three months to sail from England to America, and you confessed that your husband wasn't really killed in a duel but buried at sea, so tell me, my dear Countess," he continued, "just how is it you're headed for Port Royal to marry another man so soon after your husband's demise?"

She frowned, and her eyes fell, avoiding his. Maybe it was time he learned the truth. He'd probably guess it anyway the minute he laid eyes on Roth after seeing Heath. They were too much alike.

"It's a strange story," she answered.

"I'm listening."

"All right. I guess you have a right to know." She looked out over the water again, listening to its gentle flow as it slipped against the rocks and tree roots, wearing away the dirt that held its banks. "My husband and I had been married only a short time when we were in an Indian attack and I thought he was killed. Roth Chapman and I thought we were the only survivors. I knew I was pregnant, and he helped me travel cross-country from Sandusky Bay to Philadelphia, where my daughter, Rebel, was born. Shortly after, when she was about a month old, I married Roth. Then two months later, my husband suddenly arrived in Philadelphia. His supposed death had all been a big mistake. I returned to the frontier with him, and Roth went on his way. Nine months later, however, I had a son, Roth's son. We didn't realize it until the boy grew up. The young man you saw at the baron's house masquerading as Diego de Varga is really my son Heath."

"Roth's son?"

"Yes"—her voice lowered—"Roth's son. My first husband was killed a few months ago saving Heath's life. I won't go into the details, it's too long a story. But we ran into Roth in

77

England and . . . well, when my husband was dying, he made Heath promise to take me to Roth."

"Then that's the only reason you're going? Because of a promise to a dead man?"

She whirled on him, her violet eyes alive with passion. "No! That's not it at all." Her voice lowered. "I'm in love with Roth. I always have been."

"With Roth . . . and your husband?"

"I loved him too."

He stared at her, the darkness obscuring part of her face, making her look more like a painting than flesh and blood. "You were in love with both of them?"

She lowered her eyes and looked back toward the river. "Unfortunately, yes. And although I was happy with my husband, I could never put Roth completely out of my thoughts, and our marriage suffered because of it. My husband was a jealous man. He hated what happened, and he almost grew to hate Heath." She exhaled, straightening her shoulders. "I have another son, too. He was born four years after my husband and I were reunited," she confessed, her voice vibrating. "Teak's still in England. He's younger, only he wanted to stay there and go to Oxford." Her voice saddened. "He doesn't even know his father's dead yet." She turned toward him again, tears in her eyes for the first time since he'd met her. "He's the new Earl of Locksley, and he doesn't even know it," she said softly; then she turned back again toward the river.

She stood with her back to him, the flickering light from the fire dancing in her dark hair, and he felt warm and strange inside. What was it about this woman that aroused him? He'd had dozens of women over the years, even a duchess, but never had he met a woman who could just look at him and stir the fire in him like she could. From the moment she'd stepped into the governor's sitting room his loins had tingled at the prospect of taking her, yet she wasn't a woman to idly use, then throw aside. She was made for special attention, for loving and caressing.

His voice deepened. "You're still in love with Chapman?"

"Yes."

"How do you know? It's been so many years."

"Not really. I told you we ran into him in London."

"For how long? A few weeks, days?"

She shook her head, her back still to him. "It doesn't matter how long, I know."

"Maybe you're kidding yourself. Maybe what you see in

him is only what you want to see. . . . What kind of a man is he? He may have changed over the years."

"No!" She closed her eyes, and suddenly her body trembled as she remembered being in Roth's arms, feeling his body against hers, looking into his eyes, warm with love. "No!" she said again, and sighed. "Roth could never change. Not for me."

He leaned over her shoulder. "How can you be sure?" he said, his lips caressing her ear, and suddenly a shiver went down her spine, exploding in her loins, and she whirled around, startled at the reaction. "You see," he whispered softly, his eyes devouring her, "he's not the only one who can make you feel." He reached out, gently cupping her face in his hand, staring into her eyes. "I could make you love, Loedicia." His finger caressed her cheekbone intimately. "Every woman wants love."

"I know," she answered, her voice tremulous. "That's why I'm going to Roth."

His hand dropped abruptly. "Damn Roth!" he blurted, his eyes crackling dangerously. "He's not here. I am."

"So that makes it all right, I suppose!"

He grabbed her shoulders, and she stared into his brown eyes, usually cold and hard, now warm with passion, and at the sensuous mouth beneath them.

"Is anything worthwhile ever cut-and-dried, Loedicia?" he whispered huskily as he stared at her. "Do you always judge your feelings by whether they're right or wrong? Don't you ever just feel?" His eyes searched hers as his deep voice caressed her senses. "You need me, I know. I've watched you . . . the gestures . . . the little things . . . you need a man's arms. Loedicia, you need love, you know you do."

She felt strange, totally unstrung. His voice warmed her deep inside, and his hands on her shoulders almost hurt, yet the sensation was pleasing. Why? She wasn't in love with him, she knew, but he was tall and rugged and the masculine smell of him whetted her senses.

"How long can you hold out, *ma chérie*," he went on, softly pleading. "Your body is not dead. Not to this," and his right hand moved from her shoulder to the soft flesh of her neck, and his fingers stroked the nape of her neck sensuously.

Hot tingling sensations shot down her spine, melting into every nerve in her body, weakening her knees, and she couldn't move. She couldn't even cry out; she could only stare at him transfixed.

"There is fire in you, *ma petite*," he said, his slight French accent filtering into his voice, which was barely a whisper. "You were made to be loved."

She swallowed hard, fighting her body's unwanted response to him. "Loved, not used, sir," she finally managed to gasp breathlessly, finding her voice again, but having it almost strangle in her throat. "There's a difference," and her eyes bored into his stubbornly. "You, sir, would merely use me, and when it was over . . . No. When I give myself to a man, it's more than a convenience. More than an animal instinct. I won't be used!"

His mouth tightened at the corners as he stared at her in the darkness, the faint firelight dancing in her eyes. Then the finger that had been caressing her cheek moved down across her lips, and he felt her tremble. God, how he wanted her. His body was on fire. But he wouldn't force her. Not Loedicia. He'd never forced a woman yet. Never had to, and he wasn't about to start now. She'd give in, just like all the others. There were a lot of miles ahead of them. Lonely miles.

His mouth softened again, and his eyes caressed her face. "I never use a woman, Loedicia," he whispered passionately, his fingers tracing her jawline intimately. "I fulfill her. No woman has ever lain beneath me and felt used, only satisfied."

"Well, this woman won't!" she gasped, deliberately forcing her body to ignore its wanton desires. "I'll never lie beneath you satisfied or otherwise, DeMosse Gervaise," and she tore herself from his hands, thrusting her head up stubbornly, and began walking back toward the fire, where Lizette and Jess were laughing over Lizette's attempts at cooking the fish.

Every step she took was torture. Her body had betrayed her, and now, even now, her knees wobbled beneath her buckskin breeches and her hands trembled. She walked directly to her bedroll and silently dropped to the ground, staring into the fire. My God, what was she doing in this wilderness, anyway? She'd been a fool to come. She should have listened to Lizette.

The bedroll was crumpled beneath her, and she changed her position, straightening it, then glanced into the shadows by the river, where DeMosse still stood leaning against a tree. She could see the silhouette of his tall, muscular frame, and her body began to ache all over. Was it possible to love one man and want another, even though you had no love for him? The ache in her loins grew worse, and she turned her head, staring at the fire, begging her body to forget what DeMosse's hands had kindled when they'd caressed her.

As she stared into the flames, her mind twisted first this way, then that, until she was totally confused. Only once before had this ever happened to her. Quinn had been in Boston on a business trip that took almost three months, and she'd begun to miss him terribly. The children were young yet and kept her busy during the day, but the big bed was lonely at night, and she'd lie for hours wanting him, her body aching for him. Sometimes on those nights she even thought of Roth, remembering the short months they'd spent together, but the memory of those nights only made her ache all the more.

It always happened when Quinn was gone from the fort any length of time, but before, she'd managed to get through it without any ill effects. This time, however, had been different. A group of men had come down from Albany, heading west, and had stopped at the fort for a few days, as most travelers did. If Quinn had been home, they'd have supped at the Lockes' table, but in his absence the men, four in all, stayed at the fort, taking their meals with the men.

It was at the fort one afternoon that Loedicia literally bumped into their leader, a tall, good-looking man with dark piercing eyes and a ready smile. She'd been to see Captain Holmes and was leaving his office as the man entered, and they collided very ungraciously. She was thrown backward, but before she could lose her balance altogether, his hands were on her to steady her, and she found herself looking up into a pair of fascinating eyes that seemed to burn their way right into her very soul and brought a warm, tingling sensation deep in her loins. By the time they had both apologized and she'd left the fort, she was flushed and unnerved, her calm composure completely rattled.

Twice more that day she'd accidentally run into him, and each time her reaction to him had been the same, and it frightened her. Their eyes would meet, and it was as if a silent invitation passed between them. An invitation to a dormant passion that lay deep within them both. A passion founded, not on love, but on a physical magnetism that vibrated between them.

Unable to rationalize her feelings, she'd retreated to the house and stayed away from the fort until the men were gone. Quinn had come home the evening after their departure, and she'd welcomed his arms, shoving the incident aside, and only now, after all these years, had she remembered it. She hadn't loved the man. She'd barely known his name, yet there was something about him that had stirred her. The way DeMosse was stirring her now. She felt like a traitor to Roth. Yet, as she glanced once more toward the river, in time to see DeMosse heading back toward the fire, she wondered what it would be like to feel once more the rapture of a man's arms.

Angrily she shut her eyes and turned away, pretending to ignore him as she finished straightening her bedroll, then joined Lizette and Jess on their side of the fire.

That evening she had a hard time getting to sleep, and for the next few days as they traveled through the dense woodland, she was even more aware of DeMosse than she had been before. She noted the familiar stance he had, legs apart, arms akimbo, that reminded her somewhat of Quinn, and the arrogant thrust of his head when he wanted his own way. And she could feel his eyes on her constantly, caressing, inviting, pleading.

They'd left the Black Warrior River far behind and were now in the foothills of the Appalachians. Mountains stretched high ahead on the horizon, and DeMosse picked a campsite not far from a small mountain stream where dense trees obscured them. They made evening preparations as usual and settled down for the night in the small grove, the sounds of the forest lulling them to sleep.

It was that time just before dawn when the gray mists of morning slowly began edging the night away and the small glen was still shrouded in an enveloping darkness. Loedicia stirred uncomfortably on the hard ground, her body only half-awake, her eyes still closed. She'd had a terrible time falling asleep last night. Her mind had wandered over a thousand memories and stirred a dozen new ones, and now it was as if the thoughts still haunted her. She'd been dreaming that she was with Roth. That he was caressing her, his hands on her breasts, his face close to hers, and she could feel his breath warm on her cheek.

She rolled all the way over onto her back languorously, her mind clouded and half-asleep. The dream had been so real. Then suddenly she held her breath and swallowed hard as the hair at the nape of her neck bristled. It was real. The hand on her breast was warm and firm. She could feel it, kneading, fondling sensuously, and she let out a soft cry as her eyes flew open and she stared up into DeMosse's face, only inches from hers.

He lay on his stomach beside her, leaning over to look down at her, his body pressed close to hers, his hand beneath her buckskin shirt. "Good morning," he whispered lazily, and she felt her body tingle, every nerve alive, responding to his touch.

"No!" she begged, trying unsuccessfully to move away from him. "You're not being fair . . . you're taking advantage . . . I'm not awake," but his fingers moved gently, caressing her nipples until they stood in firm peaks.

He ignored her protests as he argued with her, his hands talking for him, while across the fire from them Jess too was awake, only he wasn't listening to DeMosse and Loedicia. He was listening to another sound that had filtered through the darkness from beyond where the horses were tied.

Without making a sound, and still flat on his belly, Jess inched forward along the ground in the darkness, away from the fire, moving toward the cover of a large bush, pulling himself beneath its branches. He lay with the leaves covering his body and glanced back quickly toward the few glowing embers, he could faintly see Loedicia still protesting and DeMosse still urging; then he began inching forward again, still on the ground, his hands feeling ahead into the fading darkness.

He was some thirty or forty feet from the fire when he pulled up short, rolling next to a fallen log, pressing his body as close to it as possible, and he held his breath. Not ten feet to his right, partially hidden among the trees, were two Cherokee.

Pale shadows were beginning to lift now, melting the darkness away, and he could see their scalp locks, like stiff brush atop their heads, silhouetted against the wakening sky. He glanced quickly toward camp in the early light of dawn, and as he saw the faint outline of DeMosse's head lowering to meet Loedicia's, the air was rent by a shrill cry that made his hair stand on end, and the Indians broke from the woods.

DeMosse had no time to even try to reach his knife. They were on him as he started to kiss Loedicia, and he drew his lips hurriedly from hers, rolling away, both feet instantly drawn to his chest, meeting his first attacker with a force that threw the Indian back half a dozen feet in surprise.

Loedicia, shocked by the first onslaught, rolled onto her stomach as DeMosse's legs recoiled, and she began scrambling to her feet, trying to get clear as he tried to spring forward, but DeMosse never got off the ground. They were on him in seconds, four men using full force, muscles taut, pinning him in the grass, where he fought like a madman, twisting and turning from side to side, trying to break their grip. Every muscle in his long, hard body came into play, but it was no use. There were too many, and in minutes he lay cursing, a moccasined foot at his throat, his face beaded with sweat, eyes flashing angrily.

Meanwhile, Loedicia'd been trying to gain her feet unsuccessfully, slipping awkwardly on the dewy grass, and she let out a shriek as one of them, a tall brave, his face contorted with rage, managed to grab her by the hair, pulling her off balance, and she fell, sprawling on the ground on her back. She kicked and scratched, but it did little good as he fought her, rolling her over, and thrusting her arms behind her, binding her wrists with thin strips of leather.

This done, he yanked her savagely to her feet, while her eyes blazed at him, and he dragged her, fighting all the way, back to the fire, pushing her against DeMosse, who by now was standing stoically, his arms behind his back, strips of leather not only circling his wrists, but tied from one leg to the other, giving him just enough distance to move at an awkward hobble, and beside him stood Lizette, her face white, eyes still heavy with sleep. She'd been sound asleep when they'd grabbed her, only seconds before, and even now, for a minute, she thought she wasn't fully awake and it was all a nightmare. But when she felt the pain in her shoulders where her arms were forced behind her, and the burning flesh where the rawhide strips cut into her wrists, she knew it was real, and tears began to fall slowly down her face. Tears of anger and frustration.

Three Indians stood guard on the three captives, hovering over them as the rest of the Indians began looking about the camp, looting the pack mules, and gathering the horses together, and Jess, hidden some yards away in the bushes, slowly rose to a half-crouch as he watched. It wouldn't take them any time at all to miss him, and he knew it. There were four horses and four bedrolls, and they'd probably been watching them for days. If he was going to get away, it had to be now or never.

He took one last long look at Lizette, Loedicia, and DeMosse standing reluctantly by the dying campfire surrounded by close to a dozen Cherokee braves, with no chance to escape. Then, as the first rays of the morning sun tipped the horizon, turning it into a sea of pink gold, he set off in a zigzag pattern, plunging into the forest, where he disappeared from sight.

5

Charleston, South Carolina, June 1794

Even the temperature didn't seem to cooperate anymore. It was hotter than blazes, and the whole city was feeling it. Roth impatiently paced back and forth in his office, stopping now and then to gaze out the huge window that overlooked the harbor again, counting the ships anchored there, making sure there were none he'd missed since morning.

Three weeks! It had been three damn weeks since Beau had weighed anchor and sailed from Port Royal Sound, and there wasn't a trace of the *Golden Eagle* or HMS *Fortress,* for that matter. Not a word, not a sign. Where the devil could they be? He'd questioned every ship that had pulled into the harbor, but the answers were always the same, nothing! If only he had something to go on. They could have blown each other out of the water, for all he knew.

His shirt sleeves were rolled up against the heat, and he loosened the collar of his ruffled shirt, opening it at the throat, taking a deep breath, then wiped the sweat from his forehead with his handkerchief as he heard the bell above his office door jingle abruptly. He turned, expecting to see one of the men from the shop with papers for him to sign, but instead, his eyes opened wide as he stared into the face of the last person in the world he'd expected to walk through his office door.

Rachel Grantham stood directly inside the door, smiling at him, her hazel eyes pleased at the startled expression on his face; then she shut the door deftly behind her, the skirts of her emerald-green watered silk swishing as she walked toward him.

"You don't look very happy, love," she cooed softly as she stopped in front of him, fingering the small beaded bag in her hands, tilting her head up so the hat that was perched atop her chestnut curls looked like it was ready to take off on its own. "What's the matter? Aren't you glad to see me?"

He straightened his shoulders firmly, the shock of her abrupt appearance over, but its effects still lingering. "I thought you were in England."

She sighed, looking wistfully out the window, her hands fluttering to her breast. "After Brandon left, life became rather dull," she complained petulantly. "Bourland Hall was bad enough after Jules's death, but have you ever wondered what it would be like to live in a house that size all by yourself? I wanted some excitement, a change." She eyed him curiously, taking in his slightly disheveled appearance. "I didn't think you'd mind."

He stared at her intently for a minute, then turned away, his dark eyes brooding. Rachel Grantham was Brandon Avery's aunt by marriage. Her husband had been the former Duke of Bourland, from whom Rebel's husband, Brandon, had inherited his title, and Roth had known her for years, having grown up together in Portsmouth, England, their family estates side by side. In fact, it was at Rachel's first ball after the duke's death that Loedicia had stepped back into his life after an absence of almost twenty years, and it was with Rachel that Loedicia's husband, Quinn, had committed an infidelity that had driven Loedicia back into his arms that night at the inn, although Rachel wasn't aware that Roth knew about her indiscretion. But at the moment he cared less whether she was here or not, and his face showed it.

"You have a place to stay?" he asked, trying to be polite, and she eyed him expectantly.

"I was planning to stay at your place, dear," she answered. "You did invite me, you know. Of course, it was some time ago, but I was sure the invitation was still open. It is, isn't it?"

His mouth tightened and his dark eyes glared at her, resenting her intrusion. "Rachel, you've . . . well, you've come at a bad time," he confessed, trying not to sound too put out, and he walked over to his desk, moving behind it, pretending to sort the papers on it into neat piles as he talked. "There's . . ." He straightened, looked directly at her. "Quinn's dead, Rachel," he said abruptly, and saw her mouth fall open in surprise; then he went on. "Loedicia was here, and we were planning to get married, but the ship she was on . . . it sailed . . . I don't know where she is." He exhaled disgustedly. "You just shouldn't have come, that's all!"

Her startled eyes narrowed as she stared at him, trying to sort out what he was saying. "What are you talking about?"

she asked, moving slowly toward his desk. "What do you mean, Quinn's dead and you're going to marry Loedicia?"

"Just what I said. Quinn was killed and buried at sea. Loedicia's son Heath brought her here, and we were going to get married, but that night a British ship dropped anchor and Beau was scared off—"

"Now, just a minute. . . . Who's Beau?"

Roth explained about Beau and the *Golden Eagle* and tried to fill in his story to make it more coherent, but there were still gaps that didn't make sense, still explanations left unsaid, and she stared at him in disbelief.

"You . . . and Loedicia?"

"But I don't know where she is. I don't even know where to start looking for her." He left the desk and moved back to the window, staring out again at the boats in the harbor. "I've been frantic for three weeks wondering what could have happened. I was a fool. I should have taken her off the *Golden Eagle* right away, and I'd have her here with me now." His eyes grew misty, close to tears, and Rachel was surprised.

"She means that much to you?"

"Wasn't it obvious in London?"

"That you were quite smitten, yes, but I had no idea the most eligible bachelor on both continents was willing to give up his freedom for a woman from the backwoods, and another man's wife to boot. Why, she even speaks some heathen Indian language."

"And French and Hindi," he added, "and she can ride like the wind and survive off the land, and she probably shot almost as many men in the war for independence as I did." He turned to face her. "So what does that have to do with my loving her?"

Rachel shrugged. "Nothing, really, I guess. I just thought you'd prefer a woman a bit more genteel, more feminine. A woman with charm and finesse. I thought that little escapade in England was just a lark."

"I prefer a woman of flesh and blood, not powder and paint. Besides," he said, "I think it's my business who I marry."

She reddened. "Oh, of course it is." Her eyes lingered on him. "But there will be dozens of eyebrows raised."

"Not if I can't find her," he stated bluntly, and at that moment the door opened and one of the draftsman from the outer office came in with some sketches for him to okay, and Rachel stood to one side watching until he was finished.

Roth was still extremely handsome and virile for a man of

forty-six; his dark hair, with only a bare trace of gray at the temples, framed a rugged face with expressive eyes, dark and compelling. He stood with his back to her, and she noticed the muscles that rippled beneath the silk shirt he wore and the broad shoulders they extended across. Every movement he made was graceful, like a sleek panther, exact and deliberate, and the fact that Loedicia's absence could shake him enough to make him almost cry was a shock.

Roth had escorted some of the most attractive women about over the years, including herself, but she'd never known him to be serious about anyone. He seemed to tire of women easily, spending as little time with them as possible, and even his friends wondered sometimes why he treated women so casually. A pretty face and a well-turned ankle rarely captured his attention, and now she was beginning to realize why. How long had he been in love with another man's wife?

Roth approved the draftsman's sketches, suggesting a few minor changes here and there, then sent the man out and turned once more to Rachel.

"I'm staying at my town house here in Charleston," he said calmly, his earlier irritability subdued. "Both Brandon and Rebel are there at the moment, and I guess you're welcome too, but it would have been better if I'd had some warning. I'm afraid I'm not very good company lately."

"You're serious about all this, aren't you?" she said, and his jaw set stubbornly.

"I've never been more serious about anything before in my life." He began rolling down his sleeves and buttoning them, then walked to the coat rack, retrieving his black velvet frock coat from its hook, shrugging into it, then grabbed his hat. "We might as well go out to the house now," he suggested as he reached for the doorknob. "We can send someone for your baggage later. Is it at the dock?"

She hesitated, looking at him sheepishly as he opened the door to escort her out. "My trunks are at the Château in Port Royal," she answered. "I went there first. All I brought with me to Charleston is one small trunk, and it's in the outer office."

"Why the devil did you go to Port Royal?" he asked, and her eyes met his.

"How was I to know you wouldn't be there? Besides"—she tilted her head flirtatiously—"I didn't think you'd mind."

"Apparently there are a lot of things you didn't think I'd mind," he said disgustedly, and ushered her through the door.

"Well, come on, let's go," and he closed the door firmly behind them.

Roth's town house was a disappointment to Rachel. There were only five bedrooms, a drawing room, library and den, dining room, music room, and the kitchen with servants' quarters, and it was anything but ostentatious as far as her taste was concerned. She thought with Roth's money his house should resemble Bourland Hall in London; instead it fronted onto the street with only a short walk to the door and a small patch of grass barely large enough for a few flowers. There were no stables, and his horses and all the carriages were boarded around the corner in a livery.

As they entered the house, Rachel easily noted the lack of frills. There were few pictures on the walls, or decorations of any kind, and the furniture was bought for comfort rather than beauty, although Roth did have excellent taste.

It needs a woman's touch, she thought as she reluctantly handed her hat to the young girl who'd answered the door. The girl couldn't be more than fifteen or so, and although her skin was light, her hair was coarse, like black matted wool, and her features, except for slightly generous lips, were delicate, with lovely pale blue eyes.

Until reaching South Carolina, Rachel had come in contact with few blacks, and this was her first encounter with a quadroon. "That girl," she said to Roth as he led her into the drawing room, "she looks black, yet . . ."

"Her mother was a mulatto whose father was white, and her father was white too. She's what's known as a quadroon," and Rachel's nose wrinkled in distaste. "Some plantation owners as well as their overseers think little of using women slaves for their own pleasures," he explained.

"Oh . . . how could they touch them?" She shuddered. "How could a man put his hands on those black ugly creatures?"

Roth frowned. "Some Negro women are quite beautiful, Rachel. Besides, there are some men who don't care, as long as she's got a body."

"It's disgusting!"

"Oh, I agree, but not for the same reasons as you do, I'm afraid. I don't think any man has any right to own, let alone force himself on, any woman, be she black, yellow, red, or white."

"But you have slaves at the Château. I saw them."

"Not slaves, Rachel, men and women. Bought on the auction block, true, but they work for me for wages until they're free, and I've never touched one of the women, nor has my overseer."

"You set them free? Those black savages?"

"Watch your tongue, Rachel my dear," he cautioned as he looked behind her. "One of them is standing in the doorway now, and I believe he's trying to get my attention."

She whirled about to face a very tall, lean Negro of comparatively light frame dressed in a gray suit and white wig, but whose cold eyes regarded her bitterly from his dark face.

"You wanted me, Joseph?" asked Roth, and the man nodded as he addressed Roth.

"The duchess said as how if it was you arrived home, would you join them in the gardens? A gentleman arrived only minutes ago who's been anxious to see you."

He nodded and took Rachel's arm. "Shall we, Duchess," and she went along, watching the extremely tall bewigged black man out of the corner of her eye, shuddering at the large nose and thick lips that sneered at her as she followed beside Roth.

"Joseph was the son of a Watusi war chief before his capture at the age of twelve," explained Roth, noting her curiosity, as they walked through the large rooms toward the back. "He's going to the Century Fellowship School for free Negroes here in Charleston, and plans to be a cabinetmaker someday. He works for me to help finance his studies and finish paying off his initial cost, and he's saving every extra cent he can, doing odd jobs for people on his days off. He's already a skilled craftsman in the trade, and he's only twenty-four. I bought him three years ago from a man who said he was incorrigible. They were ready to cut off his foot for his third attempt at an escape. I talked his owner into selling him to me instead. He's invaluable. Practically runs the house while I'm away, and I think he's taken a fancy to Delilah, the young lady who took your hat at the door."

"You mean he has the freedom of the place when you're not here?"

"And he hasn't let me down in the three years he's been here."

"You're too naive, Roth," she said. "Why, he could turn on you at any time."

Roth grinned. "He won't," and he gestured through the French doors that led into the garden, and it wasn't only Rebel and Brandon whose eyes opened in shock as they saw him escort Rachel out, but Roth's mouth fell as he stared at Captain Horace Marlin, late from his Majesty's ship the

90

Fortress, who stood beside Brandon, hat in hand, face scrunched into one of the fiercest scowls Roth had seen for some time.

"My God, Captain!" exclaimed Roth as he stared at the man's none-too-clean uniform. "Where the devil have you been, and how'd you get here?"

"What's left of the *Fortress* sailed into Charleston but an hour ago, Mr. Chapman," the captain answered, his bloodshot eyes blazing. "I've barely kept her afloat. We've been chased halfway across the ocean by four French frigates, and by God, the only thing that saved us was a storm, blew up from the Indies, almost like a hurricane, it was. Lost my two escort ships to the Frenchies too. As soon as we cleared the storm, I headed back to see if that stinking privateer was still slinking about. I was just about to ask the duke and duchess here if they knew anything about it," and Rebel glanced quickly at Roth, her eyes frightened.

Roth offered the captain one of the wrought-iron chairs as he tried to sort things out in his mind. He must have been so addled by Rachel's sudden appearance that he'd missed seeing the ship in the harbor when he'd looked out the office window. He turned to offer Rachel a seat too, but she'd already settled herself next to Brandon on the marble bench beside the walk and was in animated conversation, bemoaning the events that had kept Brandon from reaching Grenada.

"Don't worry," Roth heard Brandon telling Rachel. "I still intend to go. I'm trying to find a ship now to take us," and Roth glanced at him quickly, frowning, then turned back to the captain.

"What happened to the ship you were chasing?" asked Roth, his mind on one thing, Loedicia.

"It was the *Golden Eagle*, Mr. Chapman, it had to be," announced the captain gruffly. "She's the only thing that could have moved that fast in the water."

"But what happened to her?"

"First of all, I want to know why you were aboard."

"To hell with why I was aboard. This is America, Captain, and I don't have to account to you or anyone else as to why I was aboard."

The captain's eyes narrowed. "Mr. Chapman, might I remind you of your obligations to his Majesty? I realize you're no longer an English citizen, but you do own property in England and deal with our government extensively. It could be embarrassing for you."

"And just what do you intend to tell his Majesty?"

"That from all appearances you seem to be friends with one of England's bitterest enemies, Captain Thunder. A man who's sold his allegiance to the French and his soul along with it."

"Why stop there?" interrupted Brandon sarcastically from the marble bench where Rachel sat on one side of him and Rebel on the other. "Why not tell him the real truth. That Captain Thunder's first mate, Heath, is none other than Roth Chapman's own son."

Rebel's face paled. "Brandon!"

"Well, it's the truth."

Rachel gasped as she stared at Roth, and the captain's eyes hardened.

"Is that true, Mr. Chapman?" he asked forcefully.

Roth didn't answer. Instead he sighed. "May I ask again, what happened to the ship?" he said, and the captain's mouth twitched nervously.

"Is he your son?"

"Yes!"

The captain stared at him, his eyes unreadable; then he took a deep breath. "The last I saw of it, they were close to the tip of Spain's Florida territories. Probably made their way to the keys, or Havana or Jamaica, or maybe even into the gulf, New Orleans, Mobile, Mexico. But I can't head that way. Spain's having a set-to at the moment with us, and our ships are staying clear of Spanish ports. I guess they're squabbling over that Louisiana territory again."

Roth hadn't listened any further than New Orleans. He should have thought of it before, but New Orleans was Spanish. Still, Heath had mentioned having been to New Orleans a few times . . .

"Was that your only interest in the *Golden Eagle*?" asked the captain as he continued staring at Roth, who was gazing out across the lawn at the magnolia trees in bloom behind the rose garden, their sweet fragrance floating to him on the gentle breeze, reminding him of the night he stayed aboard the *Golden Eagle* and held Loedicia in his arms. The scent of magnolias had been strong in the air that night.

"No, that isn't my only interest in the *Golden Eagle*," he answered softly, turning back to face the captain, his dark eyes brooding. "The woman I intend to marry was aboard that ship, the mother of my son."

"I'm sorry." The captain's face reddened as he cleared his throat. "I didn't mean to pry into personal matters, sir," he said. "I came back here because I thought perhaps they'd doubled back."

"They haven't!"

The captain stood. "Then I guess I'd best be going. But I'm afraid I'll have to warn you, sir," he said, his face stern, unfriendly, "the king will hear about this whole bloody mess, and if I ever lay my sights on the *Golden Eagle* again, I'll blow her clean out of the water regardless who's aboard. Do I make myself clear?"

"Quite!" retorted Roth.

"Then I'll not keep you longer." He bid the ladies goodbye and bowed to the duke, then turned to leave.

"I say," said Brandon, stopping the captain as he started into the house, "are you going straight to England, Captain," he asked, "or is there a chance you could take us to Grenada? I was to have been there weeks ago. I'm the new governor, and . . ." he began to tell the captain the story as they disappeared into the house, and Rebel stood up, watching them go, her eyes cold and unfeeling.

"How can he do that to you?" she exclaimed as she watched her husband following the captain inside. "How could he be so cruel?"

Rachel stood too, glancing quickly at Rebel, noting the bitter droop to her mouth that hadn't been there when she was in London, and the hard look to her eyes. "Roth told me you and Brandon were married now, Rebel," she said. "I thought surely by now you'd have discovered what the true Brandon Avery was like."

Rebel bit her lip as she looked at the duchess, then turned back to Roth. "I'm sorry, Roth," she said, laying her hand on his arm. "He's still angry over everything that's happened, I know, but that doesn't give him a right to do what he did."

Roth put his hand over Rebel's as it rested on his arm, then glanced down at the young woman. She looked so much like her mother that he felt a physical pain in his chest at the resemblance. "It's not your fault, Reb," he said, trying to reassure her. "Brandon has little regard for the feelings of others as long as it furthers his own ambitions, and he'll never change. Compassion is not one of his virtues."

"But he had no right to mention Heath."

He lifted her hand from his arm and held it between both of his as he looked at her. She was so unhappy, he knew, but there was nothing he could do about it. Whatever else, she was Brandon's wife. "He really did no harm, Reb," he assured her. "It would have come out in the open anyway.

Things like this have a way of coming to light. I'm not ashamed of Heath or my feelings for your mother, I just wish Brandon didn't try to make it all sound so casual and degrading. There was nothing wrong with what happened between your mother and myself. The only thing wrong with it is when people try to make it something it's not."

Rachel sauntered toward him as he held Rebel's hands, looking down at her. "Roth, aren't you being somewhat impractical?" she said, and he looked over at her. "There's nothing right about having an affair with a married woman. If this gets out, you could be ruined socially."

Rebel's hard eyes blazed as she turned quickly to the duchess. "He didn't have an affair with my mother," she blurted savagely. "They were married!"

"Married?" She laughed bitterly. "Don't be ridiculous."

"It's true," stated Roth as he dropped Rebel's hands. "We both thought Quinn was dead. When he showed up alive, she went back to him."

"At least that's what they're telling everyone," retorted Brandon boldly from the French doors as he joined them again. "It makes for a nice story. Quaint, but not very plausible."

"Believe what you want," said Roth.

"I intend to," answered the duke, then looked at his wife. "Thank God we don't have to accept his hospitality any longer." He sighed. "Captain Marlin has consented to escort us to Barbados, and we can get a ship from there to Grenada. He'd take us all the way, but he has a commitment to return to London."

Rebel's eyes mirrored her thoughts, and Roth wished there was something he could do for her, but she was the duke's wife and was bound to him. "We can't go yet," she protested, her face pale. "We haven't found Mother yet."

"I'm sure wherever your mother is, she can take care of herself," he insisted, glancing quickly at Roth, who disliked his insinuation. "The captain said they're doing some repairs today, and working through the night, and they'll be leaving first thing in the morning, so we can have the servants start packing now. We'll stay shipboard tonight."

"But I don't want to go!"

Brandon's eyes leveled on hers. "It isn't what you want that counts, my dear," he retorted. "We're going, and it's all settled."

"Still giving orders, Bran?" interrupted Rachel. "You always were good at it," and he shot her a quick glance.

He and Rachel had been far more than just aunt and nephew before Rebel had come on the scene. Rachel was only a few years older than Brandon and had been much younger than his uncle. The affair, culminating after the death of his uncle, however, had been more one of convenience rather than affection, and Rachel had been moved very little by their parting of the ways.

Brandon straightened arrogantly as he studied his aunt, remembering the nights they'd spent together in savage surrender, then he looked at his wife, her cold violet eyes masking an equally cold, passionless body. Not once since their marriage had she given herself to him willingly. Her surrender had been a duty, void of emotion, and he knew it, but someday, someday he'd bring the fire and passion to the surface. Someday she'd beg for him. . . .

"I'll see to the servants," he said ungraciously, then addressed Roth. "I realize you meant well, Mr. Chapman," he stated vindictively, "although I resented having to accept your charity, but now, since I no longer have the need for it, I'll confess that your country is one of the most crude environments for a man to have to live in, and I'll be pleased to leave it behind. It will be a pleasure to be back among people who show proper respect to the nobility, and although I hate to be beholden, I guess it's only proper that I thank you for your hospitality to my wife and myself, such as it was."

Roth stared at the young man, who was a good fifteen years his junior, and his eyes narrowed. "Your unusual offer of thanks is accepted, your Grace," he said coldly, his body straightening to a height enabling him to look down on Brandon, "but I would equally assure you, if it hadn't been for the fact that Rebel is Loedicia's daughter, you'd never set a foot on any of my property, whether in Port Royal or otherwise. In fact, if it hadn't been for Rebel, I believe you'd have found yourself languishing in some French prison, or better yet, perhaps even dead. You should consider yourself lucky."

"Not lucky," answered Brandon, his brown eyes sparkling ironically. "If a man's smart enough, he can make his own luck," and he addressed Rebel. "Shall we see to the packing, my dear? I'm sure Rachel and your future stepfather won't mind. They can discuss their childhood together. You did know they lived side by side in Portsmouth, and I believe at one time she had hopes they'd marry someday," and Rebel glanced quickly back at Roth and Rachel as Brandon led her into the house, continuing to ramble about the relationship.

"So what now?" asked Rachel, looking at Roth's disconcerting face while he listened to Brandon's tirade as he disappeared into the house. "What are your plans?"

"I'm going after Loedicia."

"You're . . . ?" Her eyes widened. "But where? You have no idea where she is."

His eyes suddenly came alive, and his face looked younger, more animated. "I have an idea," he said simply. "At least now I know where to start," and he turned, staring once again at the magnolias, breathing in their sweet fragrance, "but I'll have to return to Port Royal first. I'll send your trunks back to Charleston with one of my men, and I'm sure you can find a ship back to England."

"But I don't want to go back to England."

"Well, I'm afraid I won't be at the Château, Rachel, and it'd be ridiculous for you to come with me."

"Don't be absurd." She shrugged. "I'll keep myself company."

"It wouldn't work." His irritability with her was surfacing again. "If you want to go to Port Royal, I'm afraid I can't stop you," he conceded as he saw the stubbornness rising in her eyes, "but if you must know the truth, I won't have you at the Château. I'm not bringing Loedicia back there, only to have her discover you've taken up residence. Not after what you did to her in London."

"What do you mean, what I did to her in London?" she asked warily.

"Don't think I don't know," he said. "I know all about your escapade with Quinn the night of the Duke of Umbridge's lawn party. You're lucky Loedicia didn't kill you when she found you in bed with her husband."

Her face reddened. "She told you?"

His voice lowered. "Yes, she told me, and I suggest that by the time I return with Loedicia you've found it convenient to return to London. There's nothing for you here in America." He straightened, his dark eyes regarding her intently. "You can ride back as far as Beaufort with me, and one of my men can come up with your things. You can take the next ship back to England from there. Now, if you'll excuse me, I have some matters to discuss with Joseph before he announces dinner," and he left her standing alone on the lawn amidst the camellias, azaleas, jasmine, and the ruby-red trumpet vine that covered the iron fence beyond the magnolia trees.

Her eyes followed him intently as he disappeared into the drawing room, and her generous bosom rose and fell agitatedly beneath the green silk of her gown. He was fluffing her off. Roth Chapman, of all people, and for what? That violet-eyed bitch! Pretending to be so self-righteous when all the time she'd given birth to another man's son. No wonder Quinn had hated Roth. No wonder sparks had flown whenever the two men met. Back to England, ha!

She turned on her heel, heading for the house, and entered, walking through the drawing room into the hall to look for the little servant girl, Delilah, so she could find her trunk and change for dinner, and there was a fierce look of determination on her face. She didn't intend to be sent packing like some unwanted relative. Not anymore.

She was almost fourteen years younger than Roth, and she'd been a girl of only eight or nine when he'd joined the army, but after the war for independence, when his father had become ill and he'd come back to Portsmouth, she'd no longer been too young, she'd been all of seventeen, and he'd noticed her then, all right. She'd made him notice, and he'd said nothing about having been married to anyone. He'd escorted her to many a soiree, and if her parents hadn't arranged her marriage to Jules Grantham, the Duke of Bourland, she'd been hoping she might have a chance with Roth. But the son of the fourth son of an earl, even if his grandfather was the Earl of Cumberland, wasn't exactly the catch of the year, and besides, he seemed to have no intention of asking for her hand. Marriage seemed to be the farthest thing from his mind. So she married the duke like a dutiful daughter, yet kept her friendship with Roth alive over the years, and whenever he came to England, she and her husband had both entertained him as an old friend. Yet she'd often wondered what it would be like if that friendship had become something more, and she smiled to herself as she continued looking for Delilah.

Roth had finished giving Joseph his instructions, and turned at the end of the upstairs hall in time to see Brandon leave the room he and Rebel shared and go downstairs. He dismissed Joseph and walked down the hall, knocking softly on the door to the couple's room.

Rebel opened it, and he saw immediately she'd been crying. She let him in, then went back to gather up the last pieces of her accessories set about the room, the tortoiseshell hairbrush from the dresser and the small music box Roth told her had belonged to her mother years before, when she'd been his wife, and she set them gently in her portmanteau.

"Are you going to try to find her?" she asked hesitantly, trying to hold back the tears, and he nodded.

"Don't let Brandon know, but I'm heading for New Orleans. The day Heath and I rode back to the *Golden Eagle* he'd told me that he and Beau had friends there. At least it's someplace to look. It's better than staying here jumping at shadows and nearly going crazy every time a ship sails into the harbor. I can't even keep my mind on my work."

"I wish I could go with you."

He reached out and took her hands in his, then pulled her into his arms, smoothing her hair as he held her. "I remember bouncing you on my knee when you were such a little thing," he said huskily. "You were such a beautiful little girl . . . like my own daughter. It broke my heart to see you and your mother leave. You looked up at me with those big violet eyes of yours, your little hand wrapped around my finger, and I . . ." He hesitated, his voice breaking. "I wish you were my daughter, Reb . . . I wish—"

Suddenly the door flew open and Brandon stood on the threshold, staring at them, his eyes glazed with anger, his nostrils flaring dangerously. "Take your hands off my wife," he cried, his voice vibrating dangerously, and both of them whirled toward him as Roth's arms slackened and Rebel took a step backward.

"What on earth . . . what's the matter with you?" she cried as Brandon took a step toward them, his face livid, and suddenly she began to laugh, almost hysterically. "You think . . . Roth . . . ? Oh, Brandon! You're sick!" she cried, her eyes hostile. "Roth was a father to me once. He bounced me on his knees and sang to me when I was a tiny baby."

"But you're not a baby now, Reb, are you? You're a woman," Brandon accused viciously, his eyes like burning coals, "and except for the color of your hair, you're the image of your mother. I'll not have him using you for a substitute."

"A substitute?" Her voice rang a pitch too high. "A substitute? Good God, Brandon, how perverted can you get? He was merely giving me a fatherly hug. If he'd wanted to do more, he had three weeks to do it in, and he's never so much as touched me."

"Well, he won't get the chance again, either," he stated arrogantly. "We're leaving. Our bags are at the door, and the carriage should be out front by now. I'm just thankful we hadn't unpacked all our things and there was so little to repack."

Roth stepped aside as Brandon pushed between them, retrieving his wife's hat and gloves from the bed, handing them to her, then took his hat from the dresser and grabbed her portmanteau from the vanity bench.

"I hope to God, sir, that I never have the occasion to venture into this rebellious country of yours again," he said as he grabbed Rebel's arm and headed her toward the door, "and by all that's holy, I hope that in his good time Captain Marlin will make good his boast and wipe the *Golden Eagle* from the seas, sending that devil who commands her to hell, where he belongs. And as far as your hospitality goes—"

"As far as his hospitality goes," interrupted Rebel, angrily wrenching her arm from her husband's grasp and running back to throw her arms about Roth's neck to hug him, "I thank him with all my heart," and she whispered in his ear as his head bent down to her, "Write to me, Roth, and tell me when you find Mother." Then she let go as Brandon grabbed her arm furiously and pulled her out the door behind him, while Roth stood shaking his head.

If only he was her father he'd show that arrogant son of a bitch a thing or two, but he wasn't, and instead he walked to the head of the stairs and watched them leave, his heart heavy in his chest.

The next morning he and Rachel left for Port Royal, traveling by coach-and-four. The road between Charleston and Beaufort wound through miles of marshland where they often bogged down and it took all the driver's skill to pull them clear, and there were numerous ferries to cross, slowing them down even more. What could have taken a day and a half if Roth could have traveled alone on horseback took two days by coach, staying at inns along the way that made Rachel turn up her nose in disgust. To her, they were crude and inconvenient, everyone having to eat in the same room, with no private parlors, and the linens smelled musty, like the very air itself in the swamps.

When she had journeyed from the Château to Charleston the first time she'd insisted Roth's driver bypass the swamps, and although it had taken two days longer, the inns had been better and the ride more comfortable, but Roth was in a hurry, and Rachel's comfort was the farthest thing from his mind. He cared little whether she liked the dark swamps with moss hanging heavy from the cypress and oak, or the mosquitoes that made it necessary to sleep beneath nettings at night. He hadn't asked her to come, and he hadn't asked her to stay, and her very presence irritated him.

When they finally reached Beaufort, he made arrangements

for her passage on a ship back to England, settled her in an inn to wait, and promised to send her trunks up from the Château as soon as possible, and that way she wouldn't have the added inconvenience of traveling to the Château and back.

"You might even enjoy some sightseeing while you're waiting," he advised her as he settled her in her room. "There's St. Helena's Church and the remains of the arsenal, and there are some beautiful gardens."

"Oh, I just love flower gardens," she said sarcastically as she gazed about the room he'd acquired for her. It was rather pleasant, if you called a parlor and bedroom luxury, but her meals would have to be taken downstairs with the other guests, and the thought was nauseating.

He opened the window to let in the fresh air, and looked at her, frowning. "So you don't like it. So why did you come in the first place? That was three years ago I asked you and Jules to come over. You might have known things would have changed since then. There's a ship on its way up from Jamaica, due here in two days, and you can sail back to your precious England, where they'll treat you with the respect a dowager duchess deserves. I'm afraid here in America titles such as yours have little influence on people. Now, if your husband had been a senator, congressman, governor . . . But nobility? That went out with the revolution, my dear." He walked toward the door, and she protested.

"You're leaving me here, just like that, without even introducing me to anyone?"

His eyes mocked her. "Now, Duchess, since when did you ever need an introduction? *Au revoir*," and he opened the door, closing it quietly behind his strong frame as she stared after him.

She reached up slowly, removing her hat, her thoughts starting to work rapidly as she stared at the closed door in front of her; then she walked to the window and looked down at the street below.

Roth's tall figure disappeared once more into the coach-and-four, and she dug the hatpin deep into the small velvet hat she held in her hands, her hazel eyes glinting wickedly as she watched the coach move down the street and out of sight around the corner of a building; then her eyes moved along the street and stopped.

"We'll just see who goes back to England, Mr. Roth Chapman," she whispered silently to herself. "We'll just see," and her eyes fell on a sign above a small shop across the street, and she smiled to herself as she removed the pin from her hat again, stuck the hat on her head, and deftly set the pin back again in place. Then, smiling, her face aglow, she left the room, heading down the stairs, and by the time she was halfway across the street to the office building, she was humming a gay tune to herself, her anger at Roth not completely forgotten, only simmering beneath her casual appearance of gaiety, but going back to England was the farthest thing from her mind.

6

It took Roth a whole day to stock enough provisions on board the *Interlude* to last until he reached New Orleans. He hired some extra men and left with a full crew on a beautiful June morning with the sun a hazy ball of fire coming up over the horizon and the weather hot and muggy. He stood on the deck, letting his helmsman, Casey, take the wheel as he watched the Château disappear in the distance. Casey was a redheaded Irishman who looked like one big freckle, with a ready grin and eyes the color of the ocean before a storm. He'd been Roth's mate and helmsman since he'd first built the *Interlude*, and was his closest friend next to Silas.

The men were still working on the house, and he'd given Silas instructions to keep them at it while he was gone. The stables were almost completed, and they were waiting for glass for the windows on the north wing of the house, and the chandelier for the foyer was to be shipped from Charleston any day, along with the wallpaper for the rooms which had been on order for months.

"Maybe it'll look more like a home by the time I get back," he'd said to Silas Morgan, shaking his hand as he left him in charge. Morgan had been under his command during part of the war and had stayed with him when he'd left. He was friend, overseer, helped with the bookwork, and ran the place during Roth's frequent trips abroad.

Silas was the opposite of Casey—sedate and serious, rarely smiling, his muscular frame moving about the place with a quiet efficiency, his brown eyes and square, stubbornly set jaw putting up with little nonsense. He was a just, fair man, a few years older than Roth, and now he'd take over again without so much as a fuss, running the house and the crops as he'd done dozens of times before. He was an octoroon, although few knew it. He had little of Casey's ready wit, but he did have a way with people, persuading the field hands and workers to put in a good day's work far easier than a whip or cat-o'-nine-tails would have done, and consequently Roth's crops were in and flourishing by the time he set sail, and he knew he could look forward to another good crop this year and that everything was in good hands.

But Roth's heart was heavy as the *Interlude* moved into midstream and he walked over to take the wheel from Casey. He was taking a chance. There was every reason to think they went to New Orleans, yet they could have easily set out for Martinique, where Heath said they'd left part of the crew.

The *Interlude* sailed down the Broad River, the sleek ship, faster than its contemporaries, reaching the sound in record time, and Roth heaved a sigh as they cleared the sound, passing Hilton Head, and broke into the open sea. It felt good doing something for a change instead of having to sit about wondering.

Three days out, they hit a squall that threw them off course, but by afternoon of the next day they were back again, hugging the coast, passing old Spanish galleons, French frigates, and a few Dutch ships, heading toward the keys.

They maneuvered their way through the keys and into the gulf, where they were becalmed for two days, the hot sun beating on them relentlessly as Roth both cursed and prayed as he paced the deck, watching the pale sky for a sign of change. Finally, the third morning the sky began to deepen to an azure blue and a wind stirred the sails, gently at first, barely visible to the naked eye, and every hand held his breath. Then shortly before noon a cheer went up as the sails filled and the sky once more came to life and the ship slowly began to move. They were on their way again, and finally, the first week in July, the *Interlude* sailed into New Orleans with Casey at the helm and Roth at the rail taking in the city as they dropped anchor. Roth had never been to New Orleans, although he'd heard a great deal about the city and its governor, who was literally making it into a fortress. He could see the walls being built as they sailed in. The city would be impenetrable before long. Governor Carondelet was going to make sure that no one would take New Orleans from him by force; that was certain. He breathed a sigh and stood at the top of the gangplank, straightening his blue velvet frock coat, setting his hat on his head of dark wavy hair at a rakish angle. So now where did he start?

"Shall I go with you?" asked Casey as he approached his captain, but Roth shook his head.

"This one's on my own, Casey," he said. "I don't really know where to start first, but I hear they have a police system in New Orleans equal to none, so I guess I'll start there," and half an hour later he was at the office of the Alcalde de Barrio having an interview with the commissioner of police, who didn't remember the *White Dolphin*, but who remembered the so gorgeous *condesa* who was seen frequently, for a few days that is, accompanied by the governor's friend Monsieur DeMosse Gervaise. But when asked of the *condesa's* whereabouts, he merely shrugged, advising Roth to inquire of His Excellency Barón de Carondelet, so it was a short time later, toward late afternoon, that a carriage carrying Roth pulled through the gates and made its way to the door of the governor's home.

Roth took in his surroundings curiously, the thick walls with scrubby sago palms and the sweet scent of jasmine and oleander saturating the hot afternoon, and his eyes flickered quickly over the sandal-footed servant who opened the door for him, his white pants topped by a red shirt at the waist with a braided cord.

The dark-skinned man stared at Roth rather incongruously, as did the gentleman into whose presence he escorted him, and Roth frowned as the man introduced himself.

The man was seated behind a desk in what was evidently the library, and his dark eyes, sifting over him, made Roth somewhat uncomfortable. "I am Francisco Luis Hector, Barón de Carondelet, governor of Louisiana," the man announced as he stood. "And you, sir?"

"Roth Chapman, American, sir," he said, realizing the barón's English was not too articulate.

"American?" The barón frowned as he leaned forward and looked more closely at Roth, and now Roth felt even more uneasy. "Strange," exclaimed the barón, rubbing his chin thoughtfully. "You resemble remarkably a young man who escorted La Condesa de Locksley here from Spain about a month or so ago. In fact, I'd say the resemblance is very striking. Too striking to be coincidence."

"Then she was here?" asked Roth. "The commissioner of police was right?"

The governor's eyes hardened. "You know *la condesa?*"

Roth was almost ready to blurt out the truth; then suddenly something in the way the governor looked at him put him on guard, and he decided to tread softly. "I know the countess, yes."

"And the young man. The one who looks enough like you to be your son, this young scalawag, Don Diego de Varga, you know him, too?"

Roth's eyes narrowed as the governor spoke. Don Diego de Varga? What was Heath up to? All right. He'd play along, but he'd move cautiously. "What's he done?" he asked hesitantly, trying not to look too bewildered, and the governor shrugged.

"Nothing, really, just stolen my daughter's heart, then left as unconcerned as if she hadn't existed." The governor's fingers tightened about a letter opener he was fondling in his hands. "From all rumor says, however, and because I know his uncle, Fernando de Varga, and have heard him speak of the young man, it's typical I guess. But it would please me to know why you look so much alike, *señor*."

Roth mulled the governor's words about in his head. For some reason Heath had been posing as a Spaniard, and if so, he couldn't possibly tell the governor the truth. Heath had hinted that his connections in New Orleans were French, so obviously his reason for being in the city had nothing to do with merely finding a place to hide from the British, and from the look on Barón de Carondelet's face, Loedicia was right in the center of the whole mess. Now it was up to him to ferret out what the hell they were up to without getting himself arrested for being a French spy.

"I believe I can explain satisfactorily, your Excellency," he said casually, "but may I ask first if they told you anything about the countess?" He had to know what they were bandying about.

"Ah, *sí*, indeed they did"—he shook his head—"and I feel sorry for the unfortunate lady. To think that a countryman of mine would shamefully duel over another man's wife. *Madre Dios!* And that he killed the earl instead of merely wounding him—bah! It was probably well Diego's cousin, this Sebastián, whoever he is, did die from his wounds. The whole episode was sordid, to say the least. I can't blame *la condesa* for wanting to leave Madrid as soon as possible, but I do think they could have chosen a better traveling companion to send with her than young de Varga. Such an eye for the ladies, that one. *La condesa* was fortunate he did not seem attracted to older women."

Roth's brain struggled with the information the governor had just thrown at him, and a picture began to take shape. He did some fast thinking and began some equally fast talking. He cleared his throat and tried to look embarrassed if that was possible, hoping the governor had never been familiar with his name. On introducing himself, the governor had given no indication of ever having heard it before. His embarrassment looked genuine, and the governor's eyes narrowed as Roth finished clearing his throat. "I should have realized," he said, acting very disconcerted, his handsome face chagrined. "I'm afraid Diego has stretched the truth somewhat, your Excellency." His hands twisted nervously as he straightened his coat. "He did not tell you the whole truth. You see, I, *señor*, am Rothford Sebastián Chapman at your service," and his eyes met the barón's steadily in the boldest lie he'd ever told in his life.

The barón's mouth fell as he stared at Roth dumbfounded; then he slowly sank into a chair. "Sebastián? But . . . but they said you were dead . . . and you're an Englishman . . . an American!"

"My father was an Englishman, my mother Spanish. Most of my mother's family calls me Sebastián. Actually I'm Diego's mother's cousin. Her mother and mine were sisters, hence the resemblance."

"But . . . you killed the Earl of Locksley?" The barón was flabbergasted.

Roth's chin thrust out defiantly. "He deserved killing, the arrogant bastard!" Then he glanced quickly at the barón. "Excuse the language, your Excellency," he apologized, "but the whole situation's rather unnerving."

The barón's face was pale. "Go on," he urged weakly, his voice revealing his astonishment, "finish, *señor*. I would hear the truth. If truth it is."

Roth's face reddened as he cleared his throat again and inhaled, the breadth of his shoulders becoming even more pronounced, his dark eyes more intent. "I have met many women in my life, your Excellency," he began huskily, "many women, and for me the sport has been worth the chase . . . for a while, that is." He glanced at the baron surreptitiously. "I'm sure you know what I mean."

The barón continued frowning as he stared at Roth, not saying a word.

"Then, while in London on a holiday I met Loedicia, the countess." His eyes grew warm as he spoke her name, and it was no wonder, as much as he truly loved her. "Never before have I met nor shall I ever again meet anyone to compare with her." His head tilted back, and he looked off across the room to a painting hanging on the opposite wall. It was a landscape, beautifully done. The artist was evidently a master. "Like this," he said, strolling toward the painting. "It's one of a kind. The beauty, the grace." He turned back toward the barón. "For the first time in my life I met a woman I couldn't say good-bye to." Then his face hardened. "But unfortunately she was . . ." He walked to the barón's desk and leaned across it, his eyes blazing. "Do you know what kind of a man the earl was? Did she tell you?" he asked.

The barón shook his head hurriedly, his eyes curiously alive. "No."

"I thought as much. Even now she tries to cover for him. Why is it women hate to admit mistakes where their hearts are concerned?" He straightened again and walked to the window, gazing out into the courtyard at the back of the house, tracing the gnarled, twisted trunk of the oleander as it nestled againts the courtyard wall. "He was a beast," he went on. "She was rarely out of his sight, and he ordered her about as if she were a slave." He turned and glanced back quickly. "A woman like that!" Then he looked back out the window again. "She was alive, vibrant, and he tried to smother her under his vicious arrogance, but it didn't work. Instead, she bloomed like an orchid, exotic, exciting. I fell in love with her the moment we met." He looked again at the barón. "And much to my surprise, she returned my feelings."

He watched the barón's face closely to see what effect his last words were having on the man.

"She told you this?" he asked. "You had assignations with her?"

Roth walked over and leaned across the desk again, his eyes pleading. "There were circumstances when we happened to be alone, unplanned of course, but we knew, both of us, that it was no casual relationship."

"And her husband?"

Roth's eyes narrowed as he straightened, beginning to enjoy the ruse he was perpetrating. The ridiculous look on the barón's face was reward enough, and if the game were not such a deadly one, he could have laughed. Instead, he inhaled, visibly incited.

"The earl saw what was happening and took his wife to Europe, but I followed."

Barón de Carondelet frowned. "*La condesa* encouraged you?"

"The earl was ten years older than she. When they'd first married, perhaps . . ." Roth threw up his hands. "Perhaps she did love him in her own way, once." He nodded. "Yes, I'd say she loved him like anyone loves something they become accustomed to over the years, but it was not the love a woman like Loedicia should have."

"You followed them to Madrid?"

His eyes fell as if he suddenly felt penitent. "I had no choice. She became my life, the reason for my existence."

"And her husband called you out."

"We were caught alone in rather an embarrassing situation, and the results were inevitable. I tried only to wound him, because I was afraid if I killed him, she'd never forgive me, but as always, something went wrong." He turned hurriedly and walked back to the window. "I have to get her back, your Excellency," he said, his voice deep with emotion. "I tried to explain that I didn't mean to kill him, but she wouldn't listen. She's headstrong and stubborn at times."

The barón sighed, then stood up, his face puzzled. "But why did they tell me you were dead?"

Roth twisted around so he could see the barón's face. "She probably thinks I am dead." He reached up toward his left shoulder and touched himself gingerly, indicating he'd been hurt, pretending there was a wound beneath his coat. "The wound is almost healed now. The last she saw of me, I was almost dead. Actually, they didn't expect me to live, and I guess perhaps Diego's family felt it best to let her think I was dead—that way the affair was ended. But I won't let it end." He turned back to the window and stood staring out once more into the courtyard. "I've traced her to your home, your Excellency," he said softly, then turned. "I must know where she is."

The barón's eyes studied Roth shrewdly. The story was plausible, and both *la condesa* and Don Diego were reticent about speaking of the earl or Sebastián . . . yet, the manner in which *la condesa* suddenly decided to visit friends in Baton Rouge and gone off with DeMosse . . . could it be that since she thought her lover dead she'd found another so soon? But the man before him seemed sincere . . . He sighed, bewildered. "I don't know what to say, Señor Chapman. If your story is true, what you did was unforgivable."

"Let her be the judge of that."

"But to kill a man so you can take his wife?"

"I didn't want to kill him. I didn't even want to take her from him. I just wanted to be near her, but now . . . my God, sir . . . now I can be with her and make her my wife. I'm not a young man anymore. The rest of my life is too precious to be wasted. But first I must find her. If you know where she is . . . ?"

"You'll go after her?"

"I'll go after her."

Barón de Carondelet smiled cynically as he remembered the way DeMosse Gervaise had looked at *la condesa,* and he wondered if perhaps the man before him was not the first to suffer the results of this woman's indiscretions. No matter, it was none of his affair anymore, but it would certainly be interesting to see what happened when the two met face to face. The woman was dangerously attractive; perhaps others had even fought over her. DeMosse and this Sebastián would be well-matched. Yes, he'd love to be there.

"She has gone to Baton Rouge," he informed him. "A friend of mine, M'sieur DeMosse Gervaise, escorted her there. They journeyed up the river by keelboat."

"How long ago?"

"Somewhere onto two weeks ago. She was to visit old friends, Sir Charles Pomfrey and his wife. They have a plantation there."

Roth sighed gratefully. "I see." Then he hesitated briefly as the governor stared at him. "I must thank your Excellency," he said humbly, his eyes steady on the governor's face, "and may I ask you to try to understand without condemning. To live without Loedicia's love is merely to exist, and I am tired of just existing."

The governor straightened as he looked Roth over again from head to toe, taking in the highly polished boots, made of the best leather, his breeches soft white doeskin, the velvet coat fitting him like a glove. His dark hair was barely frosted at the temples, and the handsome face complemented his suave charm. Yes, he could see why *la condesa* could be swept off her feet by such a man, but he knew DeMosse Gervaise well when it came to women, and he wondered which man *la condesa* would prefer, and it amused him to think that perhaps DeMosse had delayed his journey upriver long enough to spend some time with her. Ah, well, what were women for anyway but for men to admire and fight over?

Being polite, he invited Roth to dinner, but was just as pleased when he declined, and by the time Roth returned to the *Interlude*, it was only to inform Casey that he'd be gone several days.

"You need help?" asked Casey, and Roth shook his head.

"I need you here. If there's any question or any trouble, take her out awhile. It shouldn't take me more than four days up and four back. Give me a week and a half at the most."

"And then?"

"Hell, I don't know. Send someone to look for me, I guess."

"You're sure she's there?"

"That's what the barón said." He headed for the cabin, peeling his coat off as he went, Casey at his heels. He had flung a bundle at Casey as he'd boarded, and when they reached the cabin, he took it from him, unwrapping it, holding up a pair of buckskin pants, fringed shirt, and moccasins.

Casey scowled skeptically. "You know what you're doing, Captain?" he asked gingerly, and Roth frowned.

It had been years since he'd tackled the wilderness alone. Not since the war, when General Washington sent him south for a while to join Francis Marion and learn all he could, hoping the same tactics could be employed in the North. Actually, it was the months he'd spent with the Swamp Fox, as General Marion was called, that influenced his decision to settle in the South. He'd fallen in love with the land, an untamed paradise where a man could feel a part of the earth itself, but it had been a long time since he'd faced it alone. Usually Jacob or Casey or someone was along, but this time it had to be different, and he didn't really care.

Fortunately, he hadn't let the years creep up on him idly like some men, and had kept in shape, his muscles still as firm as they were ten years before, his stomach muscles flat, as he slipped from his fancy clothes and donned the buckskins, tucking the shirt in at his waist while Casey stood watching.

From a desk drawer beside his bed he took a pistol and knife, shoving the knife into a sheath in his belt, stuffing the pistol in the top of his buckskin breeches; then he strolled across the cabin and took a rifle and powder horn off the wall rack, checking it over carefully. It hadn't been fired for some time, not for necessity, anyway. Occasionally he'd practiced with it, just to keep it and himself in shape. He slung it over his shoulder, then reached into another drawer for a small leather pouch that jingled as he held it up.

"I think you're crazy," said Casey. "How many years has it

been since you rode like that? Why don't you take a keel-boat?"

"Too slow. Those damn things are all right coming down-river, but I haven't seen one yet that can move upriver faster than a man on horseback." He fastened the pouch about his neck with the long leather lacings, then let it rest inside his shirt against his bare skin, just above his waist. "I've already bought horse, saddle, and supplies," he said as he tucked the pouch close against his ribs. "If I get started now, I've got about three to four hours of daylight left."

"But you ain't familiar with this country."

"All I have to do is follow the river."

Casey wasn't any too happy. For years Roth never went out of his way when it came to females, now suddenly he had an itch in his pants so bad he was worse than a dog after a bitch in heat, and he wondered just what this woman was like that she could hold a man like Roth Chapman to her for all these years. It wasn't just the bond of the son they shared and the fact that she'd once been his wife. It was more than that, much more, and he could see it in Roth's face.

"Quit frowning," said Roth as he headed for the door. "I'll be all right, but before I go, in case there's any trouble of any kind with the authorities in any way, and you have to pull out and stay out, head for the delta." Casey shut the door behind them, and Roth strode down the companionway toward the stairs with Casey in tow. "Drop anchor off the Main Pass in one of the coves and wait for me. I'll find you."

"That's all swamp. You can't survive in there on your own."

"I rode with the Swamp Fox, remember?" he reminded him as they ascended the stairs to the quarterdeck.

Casey was peeved. "But you didn't have no lady with you then."

Roth smiled as he thought of Loedicia. "I know."

"But you can't bring no lady through them swamps."

Roth stopped and turned to stare at Casey, at the worried look on his face; then he put his hand affectionately on the man's shoulder. "Casey," he said slowly, "the lady I'm bring-ing back with me will probably be able to give me a few pointers on swamp survival. You just don't know her." His eyes shone alive, warm. "Wait'll you meet her, my friend," he whispered softly. "Just wait'll you meet her," and Casey shook his head as Roth bid him good-bye, and he watched him, the rifle slung over his shoulder, walking hurriedly down the gangplank.

Roth had been riding for over two days and was well over halfway to Baton Rouge. The horse he'd bought was a roan gelding that took his commands easily and attached himself to Roth quickly. They rode the banks of the twisting, turning Mississippi, but Roth had never ridden this land before, so he stayed close to the river instead of shortcutting from bend to bend. He was losing precious time, but making up for it when the land was flat enough to let his horse out.

He'd passed keelboats inching upriver, and flatboats and keelboats coming downriver, floating gently in some places and crashing so fast in others they took anything in their path, including two Indians in a canoe with a catch of furs earlier in the afternoon. Watching from shore, half-hidden among the trees, Roth saw the Indians swim ashore, then stand shaking their fists at the careening keelboat as it disappeared out of sight around the bend, a gale of laughter floating in its wake, and he shook his head. Survival. Even on the river it was who could survive.

He nudged his horse a bit harder now in the growing darkness and moved on, looking for a place to bed down, remembering another time of survival years before when he and Loedicia had trekked cross-country after the Indian attack, believing Quinn dead, their guide a stoically quiet half-breed incongruously named Joe Roaring Mountain. It had been winter then, bitter cold, yet they'd survived, and Rebel was born the night they'd ridden into Philadelphia. Strange how a man's life can change so over the years, jumping from one emotion to another, from sadness to happiness, then dragged to the depths of despair again.

The Mississippi River was wide and unpredictable, flowing like a sedate lady at times, then sometimes thundering with a violence that was frightening. Especially after a rain. But tonight it was warm and balmy, and as evening shadows began settling about him, he stopped and dismounted in a shady spot, screened from prying eyes on the trail above him by an overhang of rock, yet with a soft bed of moss to lie on and a patch of grass for the horse to graze. He didn't build a fire, but ate what was left of the rabbit he'd shot and cooked that afternoon, and broke a few pieces off what was left of the loaf of dark bread he'd brought along, washing it down with warm water from the flask tied to his saddle; then he lay down a few feet from the edge of the river, leaning on one elbow, listening to the sounds it made as it moved toward the sea.

It had rained the day before, and the muddy water still

carried broken branches and other telltale debris with it, and he watched, fascinated, as complete darkness slowly descended; then he saw the lights from a flatboat as it drifted by, and he stretched, leaning back onto the ground, his arms beneath his head, gazing up at the sky overhead, staring off into the dark night until one by one the stars began to emerge, and he sighed.

Twenty years ago, when Loedicia had ridden back into the wilderness with Quinn, his life had all but ended. He frowned as he thought of all the medals and decorations he'd received for gallantry in action during the war. Hell, it wasn't gallantry. After she'd left, he just hadn't cared whether he'd lived or died and had volunteered and taken chances no sane man would, yet he'd come out alive.

Now, as he remembered holding her in his arms aboard the *Golden Eagle* back in Port Royal, he thanked God for giving her back to him. He loved her so much. He closed his eyes, his body trembling as he saw her violet eyes before him, the curves of her body as she lay on the bed in the cabin inviting him to take her. His fingers moved slightly beneath his head, and he could almost feel her skin beneath his hands, awakening his desires again.

He opened his eyes quickly, aroused by his thoughts of her, and continued staring into the star-filled sky. It wasn't only his physical need for her that drove him. It was everything about her. The soft way she laughed. The way her eyes warmed when she looked at him, danced devilishly when she was teasing, then glowed like fire when she was angered. Everything about her, every gesture, every motion was a balm to his heart.

Many times over the years, after he'd lost her, he'd tried to find someone who could purge his heart of wanting and needing her, but she'd buried her love deep inside him, so deep that other women left him empty. He breathed in deeply, smelling the earthy smell of the water a few feet away, shutting his eyes once more to think of her, and slowly fell asleep.

As Roth rode slowly into Baton Rouge, scowling at its raw exterior, the noonday sun was hot, the weather muggy, and sweat clung to his skin like he'd been rubbed in bear grease. There was a fight in progress somewhere along the docks, and the aggressive noise of the crowd that had gathered made him wary.

His horse slowed as he neared an inn, and he reined up, looking it over while he stayed astride. The place didn't look any too friendly, but then neither did he. He'd managed to grow a stubble on the way up, and he scratched his chin. Better get rid of it first. He couldn't have her see him like this, and he dismounted, leading his horse to the hitch rail in front of the Redbird Inn.

It was cooler as he stepped inside, but just as muggy, and the innkeeper's eyes glared at him warily when he said all he wanted was a place to get some soap and a good clean shave, but the man obliged, leading him to a room in back, handing him a washbasin, water, towel, and soap; then Roth saw the man's eyes warm admiringly as Roth began shaving with his knife.

"Know anyone around here named Pomfrey?" asked Roth as the man watched him shave, his gray eyes curious beneath the bushy gray brows, for the man standing in front of him shaving, although dressed like a backwoodsman, had the airs and breeding of a gentleman, with a soft articulate speech seldom found in the wilderness.

"Sir Charles Pomfrey," he answered, leaning against the door frame as he watched. "Lives about three miles due east. You know him?"

"I know a lady who's staying with the Pomfreys," he said, but the man frowned.

"Ain't no lady there, 'ceptin' Sir Charles's wife, Effie."

Roth stopped for a second, the knife midway in a downward stroke on his cheek, and he stared into the mirror, looking toward the man; then he shrugged and went on. "You probably didn't know about her," he said, but the man's gray eyes shone stubbornly, and his thick lips pursed.

"There ain't no lady there," he repeated with determination. "I knows everybody within twenty miles, 'ceptin' Injuns, that is. Ain't no lady at the Pomfrey's. Not no more there ain't, anyway."

Roth's knife dropped from his clean-shaven cheek and he wiped the soap from his face, his eyes questioning. "What do you mean, not anymore?"

The man studied Roth for a minute, sizing him up as Roth still held the knife in his hand, wiping the blade on the towel. He didn't look like a man who'd need much persuasion to cut somebody's throat at the moment. and when their eyes met, he obliged him with an answer.

"There was a lady 'bout a month, three weeks ago. Two ladies, in fact, one was French. They come up here with DeMosse Gervaise and went out to the Pomfreys' place, but a couple days later all three, DeMosse and the two ladies, headed upriver toward Fort Nogalles, wearin' buckskins and ridin' horses with a pack mule apiece."

The innkeeper saw Roth's hands tighten viciously on the towel as he handed it back to him and sheathed his knife; then Roth reached inside his shirt extracting a few coins from his pouch. "Here," he said coldly, "for the shave," and he reached for his rifle, his face suddenly dark and foreboding, slinging the rifle over his shoulder. "Now, if you'll tell me which way it is to the Pomfreys', I'll be much obliged." The man glanced down at the coins in his hand, then nodded.

There was a physical ache in Roth's chest sometime later as he left the Pomfreys and headed back toward Baton Rouge, the happiness he'd known only hours before shattered by what he'd just heard. His heart was heavy and he was on the verge of exploding. Why hadn't it occurred to him before? He'd been so intent on finding her, so wrapped up in his own dreams. When the barón had spoken of DeMosse Gervaise, he'd paid little attention, but now, as he rode along . . . what was it Sir Charles's wife had called the man, a handsome devil? And Sir Charles himself had laughed about the man's prowess with the ladies, and both had called him a scoundrel and an adventurer, a man with few scruples. This was the man who was escorting Loedicia across miles of wilderness? She was trying to get back to him, and he loved her all the more for it, but the little fool. The crazy little fool! She'd put her life in the hands of a man like that. What was she thinking of?

He shuddered as he rode along, figuring the weeks they'd been gone, knowing there was nothing for him to do now but head back to Port Royal and hope and pray that for once in his life DeMosse Gervaise would keep to his bargain and deliver her safe and sound. Suddenly he cursed. Dammit! Damn the whole rotten mess! He'd been so sure, and tears welled up in his eyes. He'd been so long without her, so long, and he let out a cry of anguish. Oh, God, he prayed, thrusting his head back until the lump in his throat felt like it would suffocate him. Why? Why? And he spurred his horse viciously, back to Baton Rouge, down to the wharves, to the keelboats and the loud, uncouth men who ran them, to the first boat he came to, and as he led his horse aboard, he felt as wild and untamed and angry as he looked, and there was a fire in his eyes that stopped any questions before they started, and as the keelboat left the shore, careening down the Mississippi, he felt like a man riding the tail end of a hurricane, lost and alone.

Casey blinked hard and glanced twice as he saw Roth coming up the gangplank, and he knew instinctively that something was wrong. Roth's normally friendly face was frozen into a stubborn look of defiance, his buckskins were filthy, and he looked like a man ready to tear the world apart with his bare hands. And most of all, he was alone.

"Don't you dare ask where she is," he shouted to Casey downstairs in the cabin as he stripped from the dirty buckskins, throwing them at the man, then began washing off some of the grime of the past few days, the cool water from the basin making him shiver in the heat of the hot New Orleans afternoon.

"I didn't ask a thing," retorted Casey. "Not a thing, Captain," he said as he watched Roth's anger frustrating his every move.

"Good!" stated Roth as he finished washing, then began pulling on his clothes. "Because I'll tell you where she is, that stubborn ornery female," and his eyes were misty. "She's traveling cross-country on her way to Port Royal. Straight across all that wilderness. Miles and miles of it, and do you know who's with her?" he asked, knowing full well Casey didn't know, and answering his own question. "A man named DeMosse Gervaise." He eyed Casey, his dark eyes even darker as he sat down to put on his boots. "Do you know who DeMosse Gervaise is? Well, I found out that too! Ask any keelboatman on the Mississippi about DeMosse Gervaise. Ask any lady in New Orleans about DeMosse Gervaise, ask any husband in Louisiana about DeMosse Gervaise! He probably couldn't wait to get her out in the wilderness alone. By hell, when I get ahold of her, doing a dumb, stupid thing like that . . ."

Casey had never seen Roth in such a state. It was unreal.

"Of all the foolish . . ." Suddenly he stopped his ranting as he finished pulling on his boots, and stood up again, staring at Casey, who'd stood quietly by listening to his tirade, and his shoulders slumped wearily. "If anything happens to her, Casey, I'll never forgive myself," he said softly, shaking his head. "The little fool . . . I'm not yelling at you, Casey, I'm just upset. I was going to bring her back. We'd be together again, and now it starts all over again."

Casey swallowed hard, his freckled face determined. "We can be home in a week," he suggested softly. "She's ready to sail now. Just give the word," and for the first time in days Roth felt less alone.

"Just pray she's there when we get there," he said, heading

115

for the cabin door; then he turned to look at the redheaded sailor at his heels. "Thanks, Casey," he said, and tried to smile.

Casey smiled back. "Full sail?" he asked, and Roth grinned broadly as he straightened, his anger subdued, replaced once more by anticipation.

"Full sail," he confirmed, and within minutes the crew was rounded up and the *Interlude* sailed out of New Orleans back into the gulf.

They were some three days out of New Orleans, the wind brisk, the sea a deep azure blue, with only an occasional cloud hanging low in the sky. Roth stood at the rail, letting Casey take the helm. The sea air filled his lungs, and the sun on his face felt good, but his heart still bore the scars of disappointment and his mind still argued his unrest. He thought over everything the Pomfreys had told him, then remembered the look in Governor Carondelet's eyes when he'd told of DeMosse Gervaise, and he remembered too the reputation that followed the man's name whenever it was mentioned along the Mississippi, and he frowned.

He was jealous, dammit. And he was afraid, and a tightness filled his chest. He'd lost her to Quinn once; could he lose her to this man? If Gervaise tried to take advantage of her loneliness . . . She was so vulnerable. Her very presence cried out "Love me," and what man could resist her violet eyes and sensual mouth? She was so alive and vital. A woman that needed loving like a cat needs to be petted, but not just someone to sleep with. She needed someone to love her, and there was a difference, a difference he knew better than anyone else, but would she recognize it? Sometimes people's emotions played funny tricks on them.

He closed his eyes and exhaled, feeling the slight salt spray on his face as they hit the waves; then he turned abruptly, opening his eyes as a shout went up from the crow's nest.

"What is it?" he hollered, and the man leaned down, cupping his mouth to be heard better.

"There's a ship off the starboard, can't see her colors, too far away yet."

Roth walked to the jib and alerted Casey as he went by. Then, "Let me know as soon as you're sure," he called up, putting his hand over his eyes to shade them, yanking the spyglass from the waistline of his pants.

He scanned the horizon with the glass, picking up a small dot, a speck on the horizon, approaching fast; then suddenly he straightened as the ship drew closer and closer, its sails opened to the wind, its colors riding high in the breeze.

"She's the *Golden Eagle*," shouted the man from the crow's nest, resting his spyglass atop his knee as he leaned down, and Roth's eyes lit up in surprise as he focused the top of the ship's mizzenmast into view.

It was the *Golden Eagle!* Her trim lines pulled into view, sails open full, and he sighed. "Pull up alongside her, Casey," he shouted. "Let her see who we are," and he stood at the rail watching and waiting as the ships drew closer.

Beau and Heath were side by side on the deck of the *Golden Eagle,* their eyes squinting in the sunlight as they approached the smaller ship, maneuvering broadside, some distance away yet.

"She's a strange one," said Heath as he shaded his eyes. "Got the lines of an assault ship and the sails of a square-rigger, with an extra sail fore and aft, but she's not as big," and Beau frowned.

"American, I'd guess. Special made. Somebody's toy."

"Easy pickin's," said one of the men who'd gathered behind Beau, but Beau frowned.

"If she's British, yes, but not American. We're not on their list of favorite people, but we aren't enemies yet either, and I don't intend to start now." He turned to one of the men behind him. "Tell them to lay one across her bow when we get in range, but I don't want a hit." He turned to Heath, his dark eyes amused. "That should bring her up short."

The distance between the two ships was quickly disappearing as the *Eagle* heaved about in the water and made a sweep, her fast sails increasing her speed, and her captain wondered why the other ship had cut sail and lay easy prey; then suddenly Roth froze as the echo of an exploding shot drifted across the space between them and he saw a splash just beyond the jib boom and the *Golden Eagle* moved broadside, but too far away to even yell.

"The hell . . . he's firing on us," Roth blurted in surprise, then smiled sheepishly as he realized Beau had no idea who they were. He hadn't even mentioned owning the *Interlude* to Heath. "Strke a white flag!" he called to his men as they continued drifting, most of their sails furled, and the *Golden Eagle* circled them, coming back again for another broadside, this time closer; then he turned to Casey, a grin on his face. "You're about to meet my son, Casey," he announced proudly as he straightened, broadening his shoulders, and stared out at the ship continuing to bear down on them as the white flag was hoisted. "Unless they don't see the white flag," he retorted, then moved to the rail again, his hand waving vigorously in greeting as the ship once more narrowed the space between them and pulled up alongside, but this time so close he could count the men on board. "Cut more sail!" he called to the men above in the rigging. "And move her in closer," he yelled to Casey as the *Golden Eagle* rode the waves, so close now he could see the men's faces, and he laughed heartily at the astonished look on Beau's face.

"What the hell are you doing out here?" hollered Beau, as his men stared restlessly.

Roth yelled back, "Looking for you and Loedicia!"

Beau glanced quickly at Heath, then back across the water to Roth.

"We left her in New Orleans!"

"I know." He glanced quickly at Heath, his dark eyes intense, then back to Beau. "Where are you headed?"

"Mobile!" Beau shouted across the water, and Roth turned to Casey.

"We're going to Mobile, Casey," he said, then looked back across at Beau. "We'll follow you in," he yelled, and Beau acknowledged, then turned to Heath beside him.

"I have a feeling your father knows about your mother's hare-brained heroics," he said as he motioned toward one of his men, "and I have a distinct feeling he doesn't like it." He gave the man orders for full sail, then looked once more at Heath. "And I wonder just how you're going to explain to him why you didn't stop her from doing such a damn-fool thing, and I have a feeling you'd better start thinking up some good answers." He strolled away, leaving Heath standing on deck, staring across at the *Interlude* as its sails once more began to unfurl, and two days later, toward evening, both ships dropped anchor in the harbor at Mobile.

"How the hell could I stop her?" Heath complained a short while later as they sat around the table at the Crow's Nest Tavern, talking over a mug of ale. "You lived with Mother long enough to know that when she makes up her mind to do something, she'll do it regardless."

Roth frowned. Heath was right. She was stubborn, but usually used her head.

"Besides," added Beau, "we weren't about to sail back into Port Royal. We figured to stay as far away as possible."

"That's what's so ridiculous," said Roth. "There wasn't another British ship within miles of Port Royal, not even in Charleston, until Captain Marlin sailed into Charleston three weeks later. You could have sailed in and out again without any trouble at all."

Beau's eyes hardened. "But the odds were against it."

"I know, I know." Roth nodded. "It's just . . . it was such a stupid thing for her to do. She should have known I'd come after her as soon as I found out where she was."

"Which could have been never," added Heath. "She knew we were heading for Martinique, which was even farther away and it was too dangerous for her in New Orleans under the circumstances. Besides"—he studied his father carefully—"she was anxious to get back to you."

Roth's eyes settled on Heath, and his mouth tightened at the corners. "And this DeMosse Gervaise . . . you met him, Heath, what kind of a man is he?" he asked, and Heath frowned as he glanced quickly at Beau, who was nursing his mug of ale; then he looked back at his father. Evidently Roth knew something of DeMosse Gervaise or he wouldn't be asking, but he hated to tell him the truth. He looked uncomfortable.

"He's just a man . . ." He shrugged. "A French agent, really . . ." But Roth wasn't satisfied.

They spent the next hour arguing over what the man was, then expounding on what they'd do if he didn't show up in Port Royal, and reminiscing about the circumstances and coincidence that had brought them together again; Beau and Heath thought Roth's tale to the governor was uproariously funny. Roth was halfway through telling them of Rebel and Brandon's uncalled-for departure and Rachel's untimely appearance when the door to the tavern opened and three men lumbered in, trying to look nonchalant.

The tavern was far enough from the docks not to be too crowded, yet close enough to be one of the first places most men coming downriver hit first, and the man in the middle looked worn and tired, as if he'd just arrived at the end of a long journey. Everyone in the tavern stared as his two companions solicitously seated him at a table close by, ordering a mug of ale from the buxom serving girl; then everyone went back to what he was doing.

"But I tell you they're probably dead by now," the man in the middle was saying breathlessly, his face weary yet excited as he tried to keep his voice low, but Roth, Beau, and Heath could hear every word, and they stared at each other curiously as the man went on, "The last I saw of them, they was surrounded by Cherokee. . . . They didn't have no chance, not one in a million, and they was tied hand and foot. God!" he said, sighing. "I'm exhausted. I been runnin' for days."

"But that don't mean they're dead," countered one of his companions. "If the Indians had them tied, they didn't plan on killing them."

"Not right away," the man in the middle said, his gray eyes, bloodshot from loss of sleep, following the serving girl as she brought his ale and he took a big relaxing swig. "They usually like to roast them first, a little at a time."

The one on the other side scowled. "Don't be so gruesome."

"I ain't gruesome. I just know Injuns, that's all. They hang them up by the heels over a slow fire, then poke them with sticks when they start to blister."

The one on the other side looked pale as Roth and Heath glanced at Beau, seeing the stubborn tightness about his mouth as the man described the Indian torture.

"Shut up, Jess," said the one on the other side. "We don't need any descriptions." He watched anxiously as the man in the middle, the one he'd called Jess, sipped his ale. "I suppose he had the papers with him," he said, and Jess set down his mug.

"*Had* is right. Those papers will never reach Jefferson now, and you can kiss DeMosse Gervaise good-bye, too."

At the mention of the name, Roth's head snapped to attention, and all three glanced quickly at the trio of men. The man named Jess was dressed in dirty buckskins, his graying hair rumpled and wet with sweat, but the other two were neatly dressed, one in a suit of deep blue broadcloth, the other in black, and they looked more like businessmen.

Heath started to stand up, but Roth reached out, grabbing his arm, signaling him to stay put. "Shhh," he warned, "don't let them know we heard just yet," and they looked away again, pretending to be engrossed in their own conversation, and the men continued talking low, trying to keep from being overheard, but their voices still carried across the small space between the tables.

"If I know DeMosse, he's probably talked his way loose already," said the man in black, who seemed to be more in command of the situation, but the one named Jess smiled cynically.

"Don't bet on it. DeMosse has crossed just as many Injuns as white men. It all depends on whose camp they take 'em to."

"You said he had women with him."

"Two. They was payin' him a thousand dollars in gold to take them to South Carolina."

"The greedy bastard!" The man in black spat his words out. "If he'd tend to what he's bein' paid for . . . but no, dangle enough money in front of his nose and he'd do anything. . . . With those papers lost, we don't have a chance of persuading the President to interfere." His face was rigid, his eyes angry. "This means we're still on our own. Washington won't act without proof. . . . Damn DeMosse anyway. I told Tom Jefferson's man he couldn't be trusted any further than the smell of gold would take him. A thousand dollars—he was getting five times that much for this job."

Jess's eyes twinkled mischievously, now that the ale had cooled him. "But you didn't see the lady."

"Probably some quadroon or doxy from New Orleans."

"On the contrary." Jess finished his ale off in one big gulp and wiped any excess from his mouth. "She was a countess . . . prettiest thing you ever seen, specially in them buckskins. She had DeMosse nearly bustin' his britches to get at her."

Roth's eyes darkened as they listened, and this time it was Beau who grabbed Roth's arm, keeping him from jumping to his feet.

"Let me handle it," Beau said softly, his voice deep and resonant as he stood up, and the three men at the other table glanced up quickly as Beau stood up and walked toward them. "Excuse me, gentlemen," said Beau as he swaggered up to their table, "but I couldn't help overhearing part of your conversation, and I'd say you had a few troubled horizons, am I right?" and he emphasized the passwords.

The man in black squinted, his dark blue eyes wary. He was perhaps in his fifties, his face gaunt, the suit he wore hanging on his thin body, and his hair was quite gray. The man in blue was younger, more solidly built, his hair a dishwater color, with long sideburns almost meeting at the point of his chin, and dark brown eyes that glanced quickly at the buckskin-clad man who sat between them, wondering what he was going to do; yet it was the man in black who spoke.

"There are no troubled horizons where men are free. Who are you?" he asked Beau, his eyes wary, and Beau leaned closer, as if bowing.

"I'm Captain Thunder, sir," he answered low enough for their ears only. "I sail the *Golden Eagle* for France."

"By God," said Jess under his breath, and he grinned broadly. "You ain't!"

The man in black studied Beau carefully, noting the black hair and deep bronzed skin, green eyes that resembled fiery emeralds, and his casual air of importance. "I'd say he's telling the truth," he said, and stared at Beau intently, "but I was expecting you two days ago, Captain," he said, and Beau straightened.

"The wind isn't always at its best, Mr. Minette," he said. "You are Mr. Antoine Minette, am I right?"

"I am."

Jess was puzzled and glanced at Antoine Minette.

"I've been waiting for Captain Thunder to arrive," Minette explained. "We were to meet here two days ago, and I've been watching for him every night. That's why I sent word for you to meet me here, Jess." He turned to Beau. "I received word that Mr. Willoughby was at the outskirts of town with news of the utmost importance."

"And that is?" asked Beau.

"That the whole thing has gone wrong." Mr. Minette flinched, his deep-set eyes watering as if he were about to cry. "Another agent was carrying papers to Philadelphia to present to Thomas Jefferson, proof that the British outposts in the west are not strictly in the fur-trading business . . . proof that the British are merely biding their time while they smuggle guns, ammunition, and supplies into Louisiana territory and farther west, and when the time is right, they'll try to take back what they lost in the war, but now . . . the man who carried those papers is probably dead, and with him went the end of our hopes of talking the United States into entering the war on the side of France. Mr. Jefferson is on our side, but without proof to use as a persuader . . ." He shook his head. "And it would take another year or more to gather the evidence again."

"This agent you speak of, is it DeMosse Gervaise?"

"You know him?"

Beau didn't elaborate. "I know him," he stated, "and I know the Countess of Locksley, who, I believe, from overhearing your conversation, was with him, and also her friend Lizette DeBouchard." He looked at Jess Willoughby, and his dark green eyes were frighteningly alert. "Did I hear you right, sir," he asked, "were they captured by Indians?"

Jess glanced furtively toward Heath and Roth, who were still seated at the other table, quietly listening, and Beau knew what he wanted. He motioned for the two to join them.

"Let me introduce my friends," he said as they stood next

122

to the table. "My first mate, Heath, and his father, Mr. Chapman. Roth, Heath, M'sieur Minette."

"And Jess Willoughby," said Jess as he stood up, shaking their hands vigorously, "and this here's Mr. Tutwiler," he offered, pointing his thumb next to him, toward the younger man in the blue suit, who seemed reluctant to accept the introduction. He was new to intrigue of this sort and afraid of his shadow, and he wasn't quite sure whether he trusted these three or not.

Mr. Minette questioned Beau. "They know why you're here?" he asked, motioning toward Roth and Heath, and Beau assured him there was nothing to worry about, they were absolutely trustworthy, and the three sat opposite them at the table.

"Now, Mr. Willoughby," asked Beau, "tell us exactly what happened," and Jess told the story of their capture, describing colorfully his journey downriver alone afterward.

As Jess talked and they all listened quietly, Beau sat calmly, tracing the outline of a pine knot in the top of the table with his finger, his face unreadable. Then, as Jess finished, he stopped and looked up, his finger resting on the pine knot.

"Doesn't it seem strange to you, Mr. Willoughby," he said, his eyes narrowing, "that the Cherokee took them captive? Ordinarily Indians kill and scalp rather than taking prisoners, unless they need slaves, that is, but the Cherokee had to have been deeper into Southern territory than they ordinarily would have been, and it doesn't seem possible they'd drag slaves that far back to their main camp. Captives would be a burden to them."

Jess frowned. "You know," he said, pointing a finger at Beau, "I got to thinking about that." He raised his hand, calling the serving girl to bring them all another round of ale. "That ain't like them Cherokee at all, not at all," he finished as the girl walked away.

"Precisely," confirmed Beau.

"They ain't got no use for three captives"—his eyes brightened—" 'lessen they know who they are, that is," he said, and turned to Minette. "You think maybe somebody paid them Cherokee to stop DeMosse from gettin' through?"

Antoine Minette looked doubtful. "It's possible," he said hesitantly, "but . . . I don't know . . . How would they know he was heading that way instead of taking the Natchez Trace? I didn't even know. Nobody knew except DeMosse, yourself, and the ladies."

"He left from Fort Nogalles," answered Roth, remembering his talk with the Pomfreys at Baton Rouge. "Perhaps someone there overheard them."

"How do you know he left from Fort Nogalles?" asked Jess quickly as he looked at Roth suspiciously, and Roth's face reddened.

"My interest isn't in M'sieur Gervaise, Mr. Willoughby," Roth said softly, easing the man's hostility. "My only interest is in locating the Countess of Locksley. I traced her as far as Baton Rouge and was told they were headed from there to Fort Nogalles, and from there they were heading for South Carolina. She was on her way to see me, sir," he explained. "We were to be married," and Jess's eyes fixed stiffly on Roth.

So this was the man she was traveling all those miles to see. The man DeMosse was hoping to make her forget. He looked Roth over more carefully, noting his solidly handsome face, the dark penetrating eyes and firm mouth, and his face reddened in return as he remembered a few minutes ago telling Mr. Minette that DeMosse had his eye on the countess.

"Chapman . . . that's right," Jess said, and he nodded slowly, remembering, and his gray eyes lit with recognition. "Roth Chapman, that was the name." He shook his head. "Well, I'll tell you, Mr. Chapman, sir," he said, his voice sincere, "you sure got yourself some lady there," and his eyes warmed admiringly. "Yes, sir, you sure do," and Roth frowned as the serving girl brought them their round of drinks.

"I had a lady, Mr. Willoughby," Roth corrected softly, and they understood as he continued. "Now, just where did you say you were when you were attacked?" and Jess gulped a swig of ale, then answered.

"We was just past the Black Warrior River, about twenty-five miles west of the Cahaba River, near the foothills of the Appalachians, south of the Cumberland Range."

"Think you could find it again?"

Jess glanced at Beau, then Heath, who hadn't spoken a word, but who'd been watching him intently, then back to Roth. "You want me to go back up there?"

"We'll go with you, of course." Roth turned to Heath, who nodded, then Beau. "You will go, won't you, Beau?" he asked, and Beau hesitated as Jess laughed scornfully.

"A sea captain and his mate in the backwoods? I ain't goin' back up there with a bunch of tenderfeet who don't know their ass from a hole in the ground."

Beau's eyes looked amused as he studied Roth's face; then he looked at Jess and spoke to him in Iroquois.

Jess's eyes bugged out as he listened; then: "Well, god-damn, if that don't beat all!" he exclaimed, dumbfounded, but Beau only smiled smugly.

"You understood me?" he asked Jess, and Jess nodded.

"You're damn well right I understood you."

Beau motioned with his head toward Roth and Heath. "If you don't go with us, we'll go ourselves," he said, knowing he couldn't desert his friends. "But it'd be easier and we'd be much obliged if you'd come along."

Mr. Minette put his hand on Jess's shoulder. "Perhaps you should," he suggested, his voice taking on a new urgency. "Perhaps you should, Jess." His eyes hardened. "Perhaps . . . there's a chance the papers may still be intact. Sometimes Indians can be pretty shrewd. They might know what they've got ahold of and hang on to them."

Jess took another swig of ale, then licked his lips, wiping his mouth on the back of his hand as Antoine Minette went on.

"If you could locate them and find those papers and take them on to Philadelphia . . ."

"And if the papers are gone?"

"Then at least we tried." Mr. Minette's eyes narrowed shrewdly. "Remember, Jess, there's five thousand dollars waiting in Philadelphia for the man who gets those papers through. Five thousand dollars," and he held up his hand with the fingers spread apart. "And it doesn't have to be M'sieur Gervaise who brings them in."

Jess scowled. "But if the papers ain't there? If the Injuns burned them along with DeMosse . . . ?"

"Will two thousand in gold compensate you, Mr. Willoughby?" asked Roth, leaning close to the man so he wouldn't misunderstand what he was offering, "because that's what I'll pay you to take us to the spot where they were captured, and I'll give it to you in advance. You can leave it here in Mobile for when you return. Of course, if the papers are there, you'll make seven thousand instead of two thousand, but either way, you win. We can go alone, but this isn't our part of the country. With you along it'll be easier."

Jess studied the three men intently, then made up his mind. It was a good bargain. "All right, gents, I'll go," he said. "But we use horses, travel light, and move fast, and I only hope we're not risking our fool necks for nothing," and Roth assured him it wasn't for nothing.

Roth had to know whether Loedicia was still alive or dead, and the thought that she might be dead, that he might never see her again, ate at his insides and he felt sick as he watched Beau transact his business with Antoine Minette, and they made plans to leave early the next morning; then they all left the tavern to go back to their ships and get things ready. But Roth was curious as they stepped into the sultry evening air, and he turned to Beau as Jess Willoughby and the other two men disappeared down the street.

"Just what did you tell that man back there that made his eyes bug out when you spoke to him in what I assume was Indian?" he asked as they walked back toward the ships, and Beau glanced over at Heath, who grinned broadly, then answered for Beau.

"He told him, in Iroquois, that no one called the chief of the Tuscarora's son Wild Thunder a tenderfoot, but that if he told his companions Beau was an Indian, he'd not only hang him by the heels and roast him, but strip the skin from his body inch by inch while he was roasting," and Roth glanced at Beau, startled.

Beau shrugged, his dark eyes unreadable. "It served its purpose," he stated boldly; then his eyes looked amused as he saw the strange look on Roth's face, and he smiled, a rather wicked smile. "But don't worry, Mr. Chapman," he assured him very seriously, "it's been a long time since I've roasted anybody alive," and he glanced quickly at Heath, who seemed to be enjoying his father's uncertainty; then they both burst out laughing, and Roth sighed with relief as he realized Beau had been teasing him. Yet, there was something about this young captain, something hard and almost unfeeling, something cold and he wondered as they continued toward the wharves if perhaps there wasn't still much of the savage in Beau Dante; and the next morning, late, as they headed upriver on horseback, to where the Tombigbee and Alabama rivers joined, he was glad for the opportunity to get to know his son and this friend of his better. If he could do this, if he could turn his heart to Heath and get to know him, if they didn't find Loedicia, if she no longer lived, then she could live for him in their son, and at least part of life would still be worth something again.

7

Except for the mumbling voices of the Indians, the small clearing was quiet, as if the early-morning chatter of the birds had ceased by some strange instinct when the Indians attacked, and Loedicia watched warily as the Indians searched for Jess, moving stealthily through the underbrush and trees surrounding the small camp, and she wondered herself what had happened to him. They knew he'd been there, but he'd disappeared. How? His bedroll was empty, his horse still tethered with the others, but there was no sign of him.

After almost an hour of vain searching, during which time their pack mules were ransacked and her and Lizette's clothes scattered about the clearing by laughing braves who thought even her beautiful gold ball dress was funny, the Indians reconnoitered, and one, a tall, stoic brave who was obviously their leader, stood before them, hands on hips, his painted face sneering at them in self-satisfaction.

He reached out suddenly and grasped Loedicia's chin, his bronzed fingers hurting her flesh as he tilted her head in the early-morning light to see her eyes, and he grimaced. "Yes, she is the one," he said in Cherokee to his companions, who surrounded them. "I was not wrong," and Loedicia's eyes hardened as he released her chin, and she thrust her head back, staring at him defiantly.

"I am what one?" she asked suddenly in the man's own language, surprising them and DeMosse, who'd had no idea she knew what the man was even saying, and looked at her sharply.

"See," said the brave, his chest expanding as he smiled broadly, "who but the squaw of Yellow Hair would know what the Cherokee says?" and the braves about him nodded, mumbling among themselves, and Loedicia had a strange feeling that maybe now, after hearing his little speech, she knew why they'd been captured instead of killed, and so did DeMosse.

"But plenty of people can speak Cherokee, including me,"

127

said DeMosse boldly in Cherokee, questioning the brave's remark, "so what makes you think she's the wife of Yellow Hair?" and the Indian smiled.

"I have seen the wife of Yellow Hair before," he answered. "It was many seasons ago when I accompanied some of our elders to the land of the great waters to talk with our brothers from the north. We visited many tribes, one being the Okswego Tuscarora, whose Chief Telakonquinaga has pledged his allegiance to Yellow Hair. Their village lies next to Fort Locke, which is named after Yellow Hair, and although he was gone, she was there. I remember well when she came to the lodge of Telakonquinaga to greet us in her husband's absence. Who could forget a woman with eyes like the violets on the hillside in spring and hair that shone like an Indian maid's yet curled like the glory vine curls as it clings to its neighbor? Yes, she is the wife of Yellow Hair," and DeMosse turned, studying Loedicia's face.

Her hair was disheveled from her tussle with the Indian who'd caught her, her eyes were glaring angrily, and there were dirt smudges on her cheeks, but her face had a strength and purpose to it that was missing from that of the average woman.

"Locke . . . Locksley," he whispered in English, as if to himself. "The Countess of Locksley . . . Quinn Locke, Yellow Hair, as I've heard the Indians call him. You never did speak his name, only spoke of him as the earl—he's your husband?"

There were suddenly tears in her eyes. "He was my husband," she said softly. "He's dead now. Everything I told you that night by the river is true. All I neglected to tell you was his name."

The Indian listened for a minute, puzzled, unable to understand their English, then spoke, cutting them off abruptly.

"Enough!" he yelled angrily. "You will cease talking," and he looked at DeMosse more purposefully now, his eyes intent on his face; then the Cherokee's eyes narrowed shrewdly. "You," he said, looking directly at DeMosse, "you speak our tongue. Perhaps . . ." He cocked his head, looking him over from head to toe, the tall muscular frame, broad shoulders, and he paused, then nodded. "Yes . . . it could be," he continued in Iroquois, "where the squaw of Yellow Hair is, so there should be Yellow Hair."

"Don't be ridiculous," said Loedicia as she realized that the Cherokee had some strange notion maybe DeMosse was

Quinn. "He's not Yellow Hair. He doesn't even look like Yellow Hair."

"He is as tall, and his hair has the sun in it," and she glanced quickly at DeMosse, realizing for the first time how much the sun had bleached his hair. It was almost as blond as Quinn's had been.

She sighed, disgusted. "But Yellow Hair has blue eyes. This man's eyes are brown. He is M'sieur DeMosse Gervaise. He's not Yellow Hair. Yellow Hair is dead."

The Indian stiffened, and his face lost its smugness as his eyes narrowed viciously. "Yellow Hair is not dead. If he were dead, all the tribes would know," he stated dramatically, but she wouldn't listen.

"He is. He was killed when we were sailing across the great water from the land that's far away," she tried to explain. "Yellow Hair is no more," but the Indian shook his head slowly, indicating he didn't believe her. "What do you think I'm doing here?" she pleaded. "If Yellow Hair were alive, would I be here?"

"Yes, if Yellow Hair was here also," he said, and looked once more at DeMosse, as Lizette turned to Loedicia.

"He'll never believe you, *ma petite*," she said in English. "It's useless to argue."

"But he has to believe me."

"Why? Maybe it's best he thinks Quinn's alive. *Mon Dieu*, if he's convinced he's dead . . ." Her eyebrows raised quizzically. "After all, he must have a special reason for capturing you . . . at least we're all still alive. If you convince him Quinn's dead, who knows what he might do with us."

Loedicia frowned as she stared at her friend. Maybe she was right. Ordinarily they'd be dead by now, their scalps hanging from the Cherokee's war belt, but they weren't. For some reason, these breechclouted Indians with their painted faces and colorful feathers sticking from their scalp locks wanted Yellow Hair's wife alive, and the Cherokee's voice interrupted Loedicia's thoughts.

"You will not talk in your own language anymore," he said again, his eyes blazing, his head held erect as he stared at them. "I cannot understand what you say. You will speak the language I speak or you will not speak at all," and he turned, looking at the men around him. "Gather their horses and we will return to the camp of Bleeding Fox. He will know the truth," he said, and as he turned to walk away, hands grabbed them, shoving them after him, and their long trek began.

They were made to walk while the Indians took turns riding their horses, and DeMosse's legs stayed hobbled, so it was even doubly hard for him to move. Loedicia marveled that he could move at all, especially when the rawhide rubbed his ankles raw and they bled with every step, yet he never uttered a sound of pain. Like Quinn, she thought. The stubbornness of a man who'll endure anything rather than be called a coward, and although some of the things he did angered her, for this she had to admire him.

At night they were fastened together and usually tied about the trunk of a tree, and it was then they'd whisper back and forth in English so their captor, who they learned was called Howling Wind, wouldn't hear them and threaten to cut out their tongues, as he'd threatened once already.

Their first night from camp, exhausted from their forced march, Loedicia leaned her head back against the rough bark of the huge oak they were tied to and sighed wearily.

"I'm sorry," whispered DeMosse, the first time he'd apologized for anything since they'd left New Orleans. "If I'd been on watch as I should have been, they wouldn't have gotten the jump on us. But there'd been no sign."

She closed her eyes, remembering those moments just before the Indian attack when DeMosse had lain above her, his eyes looking into hers, his hands on her breasts, then his lips had lowered to touch hers.

"They'd have come anyway," she answered huskily, trying to forget the fever the touch of his lips had aroused in her body. "What matter is it who's at fault?"

He grimaced as he moved his feet to a better position and felt the blood, slippery against the leather that held his ankles imprisoned. "I'm still sorry," he said in the darkness. "Not for what I did, but for my lousy timing," and she almost smiled.

It was just like him. He wasn't apologizing for trying to take advantage of her, but for doing it at the wrong time, allowing them to get caught, and she wondered what would have happened if the Indians hadn't come, and it frightened her almost more than the predicament they were in.

For the next three days they walked until their legs felt as if they no longer belonged to their bodies, and each day the constant movement would break open the scabs about their wrists and about DeMosse's ankles that had formed during the night, and they were fed barely enough to keep them alive. The only time their arms were untied was when they stopped to relieve themselves, but even then eyes were on them all the time, afraid they'd make a break for the woods, and Loedicia cringed, trying to hold back as long as she could, but she had to survive.

Lizette was the one Loedicia worried about. She was older by almost eight years and had always lived a more sedentary life, never really becoming a part of the wilderness that had been her home, and her very nature fought against what was happening to them, making it even harder for her.

Then, on the fourth day, they moved into what DeMosse said were the mountains of the Cumberland Plateau, heading northeast, and he didn't like it. Up ahead lay the heart of the Cherokee nation at a place the Cherokee called Chattahoochee.

But they didn't go all the way to Chattahoochee. After almost a week of constant moving, they followed a trail between two mountain passes, then came upon a lake, its banks dotted with log huts, the flatland beyond it planted with corn and vegetables, the hills beyond covered with soft pine. There was a gentle slope where they approached the village, and as a storm brewed in the distance, they moved down it, the Indians pushing their prisoners ahead of them, and were greeted by a milling crowd of men, women, and children.

Dark clouds were scattering across the late-afternoon sky, and deep peals of thunder rumbled threateningly as the three of them staggered wearily into the Indian camp, herded hurriedly on by Howling Wind and his braves. They were hardly able to stand, their clothes filthy, lips swollen from lack of water.

Loedicia stumbled, glancing furtively at DeMosse, who was directly in front of her. His ankles were bleeding again, and she winced as one of the Indian women, an old wrinkled squaw with half-rotted teeth, picked up a stick and leaned close, driving it into his ribs. Then it began.

A small boy beside her heaved a rock, then two more, one hitting her on the side of the cheek, and she could feel the bruising crunch. Then two women on the other side of her grabbed at her long dark hair, yanking it mercilessly, almost pulling her off balance, and hitting at her face while she tried to pull away, only to bump into Lizette behind her, who was being thrown from side to side by vicious blows rained at her head.

Loedicia was furious, but there was nothing she could do except duck, trying to hide from the blows, as more and more of them joined the first tormentors and the crowd enlarged.

Then suddenly Howling Wind straightened in the saddle, his face rigid, and he quickly spurred his horse forward until it was next to Loedicia, right in the middle of the confusion. "Stop!" he cried, his voice thundering at them savagely, as he raised his arm in alarm, fending a stone off his elbow. "Stop! These are my prisoners," and the voices dropped around him, hands stopping in midair as the crowd stared. He took a deep breath as he looked about, gazing arrogantly into the crowd; then he singled out one young man over all the others. "Go tell my brother Chief Bleeding Fox that I would have counsel with him, Strange Wolf," he said firmly, his voice loud enough for all to hear. "Tell him that I have prisoners of great importance and desire that all should come to the meeting lodge." Then he turned to the woman who'd dealt the first blow. "And you, old woman," he said, "you and the others"—and he looked over the crowd—"you will hold your sticks and stones from this moment until I shall tell you otherwise. These are my prisoners and I wish no harm to come to them. If they die, they will be of no further use to me," and his eyes relaxed knowingly, warming at the secret thoughts that crept into his heart, and the people began to back away slowly, reluctantly, wondering why he'd stopped them and cheated them out of their fun. What could possibly be so special about these three bedraggled prisoners?

Howling Wind watched in silence, his face stern as they moved back, the sticks and stones they had planned to use on the prisoners dropping slowly from their hands, their faces puzzled; then he sighed. They were disappointed, he knew, but he had no choice. He wanted the prisoners alive, not dead or dying. He turned to his men, singling out three of them, motioning them forward.

"Take them to the meeting lodge," he ordered smugly, pointing to the prisoners, "and I will follow shortly," and he watched, pleased with himself as they were herded off again, this time toward the center of the village, where the meeting lodge stood.

Loedicia lay quietly on the floor of the huge hut. The constant bloodcurdling whoops of the Indians, coupled with the savage beat of the drums that had started half an hour ago when they'd been dragged here, was deafening, and she wished she could cover her ears to block it out, but her hands were still tied behind her back as were DeMosse's and Lizette's.

She closed her eyes, listening to the erratic rhythm of the drums, marking the beats, knowing what they were saying.

Quinn had taught her how to read their messages when they lay awake at night in their house near Fort Locke and listened to Telak's drums far into the night. But these drums were different. They weren't hundreds of yards away, they were less than a hundred feet, and their pulsating rhythm pounded in her head until it hurt. They were telling any Indian within earshot that the squaw of Yellow Hair now belonged to the Cherokee.

Loedicia's body was numb, and she could hardly feel anything anymore. Her eyes had become accustomed to the inside of the lodge, lit only by the light from the three huge fires sunk in its floor, and now she opened them again, shaking her head to clear it, and looked about, realizing that close to three hundred men and women had crowded in and were now staring at them, their faces like a hazy blur before her.

Her eyes moved from their faces to the rafters high overhead, then down again to the crowd, where they focused, resting uneasily on a lone figure that moved forward and stood only a few feet away, looking down at them. He was young for a chief, but the numerous colorful feathers dangling haphazardly from his scalp lock and the robe he wore designated him as one. His bare chest and arms were adorned with silver medallions and bracelets, and his fierce black eyes, painted at the corners with vermilion and outlined with white stripes, studied the three of them coldly; then he turned to Howling Wind, who approached from the other side of the lodge, the crowd moving back to let him pass, new painted streaks added to the war paint that already decorated his face.

The Indian chief, who stood before them, was impressive as he turned to greet Howling Wind. "Speak," he said to Howling Wind when they had finished their greeting, his deep guttural voice matching his far-from-handsome face. "I would hear now what you have to say," and the muscles in his arms rippled powerfully as he nodded unsmiling to Howling Wind, who stepped to one side so the people could also hear.

Howling Wind planted his feet firmly on the dirt floor, straightening arrogantly, then began. "Two seasons ago," he said loudly, almost yelling so all could hear, "we sent men north asking Thayendanegea to join us in our war against the white man. Even then we knew that the general the white man calls Wayne, the one some of our brothers to the north refer to as Strong Wind, was building forts along the big river Ohio. Even then he was preparing to drive us and the Shawnee and all our other brothers from our homes, to take what is ours, but when we asked for help, Thayendanegea mocked our braves, calling them old women, saying they did not know how to fight. That we were inferior to the Mohawk and Seneca. But now we can show him otherwise," and he looked at the prisoners, then back to his brother. "Who is it that has the squaw of the enemy of Thayendanegea? Is it Thayendanegea? No! It is the Cherokee. We who were called weak old women have done what he has been unable to do. We have captured the squaw of Yellow Hair, his fiercest enemy"—his voice rose—"and perhaps even Yellow Hair himself!" There was a loud gasp from the crowd, and mumbling, as Bleeding Fox lifted his hand for silence.

"Be still . . . I would learn what Howling Wind has said," he shouted, and Howling Wind continued as he walked over and stood closer to the prisoners.

His listeners were on edge now, their eyes anxious. He reached down, grabbing Loedicia by the hair, forcing her to face his chief, his hand twisting in her dark matted curls, almost pulling her from the ground. "This is the squaw of Yellow Hair!" he stated proudly. "I saw her many seasons ago, and I remember, but so you will not take my word alone, I call on Dark Morning and Straight Pine to be my witnesses, for they were also among our brothers when we visited the camp of Telakonquinaga, chief of the Okswego Tuscarora," and as he finished speaking, the chief motioned behind him and two warriors made their way through the crowd, then stood staring down at Loedicia's defiant face as Howling Wind continued holding her head in his viselike grip.

Both men looked her over carefully as she gritted her teeth, her eyes blazing, the bruise on her cheek beginning to swell; then they agreed with Howling Wind. She was indeed the squaw of Yellow Hair, and Howling Wind released her head violently, letting her fall to the dirt floor, some strands of her dark hair still clinging to his damp hand; then he stepped over in front of DeMosse and stood staring down at DeMosse's bloody ankles. Howling Wind only smiled as he turned his attention toward DeMosse's face.

"This one was with Yellow Hair's squaw," he began, then turned again toward his chief. "Where the woman is, so there too should be her mate. He is tall, as is Yellow Hair, his strength that of many men, and his hair is as gold, like the sun as it shines from the sky. But since I have never seen Yellow Hair, I will let my brother Chief Bleeding Fox judge who this man is to be," and he crossed his arms, waiting stoically for his chief's answer, hoping it would be the right one.

Bleeding Fox stepped closer, and DeMosse watched as he moved toward him gracefully, with the ease of a panther parading about its kill, cocking his head this way, then that as he looked him over carefully. He stopped barely a foot from DeMosse and stared down into his face, and his eyes hardened. "Who does he say he is?" he asked his brother, but Howling Wind shook his head.

"He has not said. Yellow Hair's squaw calls him a name, DeMosse, but I say he is Yellow Hair."

"I have heard it said that Yellow Hair has eyes the color of chicory blooming on the hillside," said Bleeding Fox.

"But do we know this to be true?" Howling Wind was willing to argue. "Have any of us seen Yellow Hair? No!" and the crowd mumbled, all of them shaking their heads as he went on. "We have heard many tales about him from our brothers of the north . . . that he can change himself into the animals of the forest to stalk his enemies, that he can walk on water, even when the ice is not upon it, that arrows can pass through his body. They have let us believe that he is not an ordinary man, yet is not his squaw an ordinary woman? Can she not bleed?" He reached down and grabbed Loedicia by the shoulders, forcing her to turn so the chief could see where the rawhide had bitten into her flesh, and she winced, biting her lip as he moved her wrists back and forth, opening the scabs again; then he watched triumphantly as the blood from the raw sores coated the rawhide strips that held them, some of it dripping onto the dirt floor.

He pushed her aside again, then straightened, his eyes narrowing shrewdly. "We have heard that the white man has a strange custom," he continued as he addressed his chief. "Before taking a woman, he presses his mouth to hers in what is known as a kiss. It is a sign of affection, meaning that he cares for the woman." Howling Wind stopped for a moment to look about him at the people listening intently, and he was pleased as he went on. "When our warriors swooped down upon these three," he informed them triumphantly, gesturing toward the prisoners, "the man Yellow Hair's squaw insists is named DeMosse was performing this act with the squaw of Yellow Hair while she lay on the ground beneath him," and once more he raised his head triumphantly and there was a murmuring in the crowd, but he gave them no time to doubt as he went on, "Who but Yellow Hair himself would be preparing to take this woman? I say this is Yellow Hair," and he pointed to DeMosse, "and I say that we should take Yellow Hair and his squaw to Thayendanegea to show him that we are not weak. That we are as strong and powerful as the mighty Mohawk and the much-feared Seneca." He clenched his fist, holding it tightly in front of him. "That these prisoners shall be his if he will but join us in driving the white man from our land!" and he shouted the last words, stirring a violent roar from the onlookers.

Bleeding Fox stared at his brother, then looked at the three people trussed up before him, the anxious shouts of the people ringing in his ears. If this was truly Yellow Hair, Thayendanegea would be pleased. For too many seasons Thayendanegea and Yellow Hair had been enemies, and if Thayendanegea would agree to join them . . . Even now the drums had informed them that General Wayne, who had made his march into their territory, settling at the Maunee near the great lake Okswego, was preparing to make war against the Shawnee. If he was successful, the Cherokee would be next, unless they showed the white-eyes their strength. With Thayendanegea and his friends as their allies, they would be invincible. The plan was a good one.

He stepped closer to Loedicia and commanded his brother to turn her once more to face him, then addressed her. "Does my brother Howling Wind speak the truth?" he asked solemnly as he stared at her. "Was this man putting his mouth to yours at the moment my warriors attacked?" but Loedicia only frowned, her lips held tight.

Wouldn't he like an answer? But he wasn't about to get one. She stared back at him, her eyes flashing, and tried to lick her parched lips, to moisten them just a little, but her swollen tongue felt rough and dry as it caressed them; then she shut her mouth tight again.

"Speak woman," he ordered, but she still said nothing, and he realized she wasn't going to, and suddenly his hand flew out savagely, catching the side of her head, throwing her sideways, and for a minute everything went black as she hit the ground hard, her forehead in the dirt.

She lay quietly, stunned for a moment, then opened her eyes hesitantly, everything before her blurring as she tried to focus them, remembering what had happened, and painful tears streaked her face, but she wouldn't give in. She couldn't, and she lay still.

Bleeding Fox held his breath, his nostrils flaring as he clenched the hand that had struck her into a fist, tightening it until the knuckles were white, but instead of hitting her again, he turned to DeMosse. There were other ways. "The woman would rather die, I think, than admit the truth," he said viciously to DeMosse, his fist clenching and unclenching effectively. "But I think you perhaps will be wiser. Unless, of course, you would wish the squaw of Yellow Hair to arrive at Thayendanegea's camp without the use of her arms and legs. It would be a simple matter to render them useless yet keep her alive, and no trouble at all. In fact, our women are disappointed that they were denied the pleasure that always accompanies new arrivals," and his eyes narrowed until they were barely slits in his face. "Now! I would have all the truth," he demanded angrily. "I would know, did you kiss this woman and are you Yellow Hair?" and DeMosse's eyes moved from the chief to where Loedicia lay, breathing heavily, her face still against the dirt floor.

If he said no, she didn't have a chance. The Indian would keep at her until they confessed what he wanted to be the truth; but if he agreed . . . What the hell! What did it matter who they thought he was anyway? He frowned, making up his mind.

"Yes!" he blurted gruffly, the words grating from his parched throat, and Bleeding Fox looked at him warily. "Yes, I kissed her," DeMosse confessed hesitantly, hoping she'd understand, "I kissed her and was ready to take her," and he glanced quickly at Lizette, whose eyes were now on him, her mouth open to speak, but the warning look stopped her. "It's no use," he said. "Howling Wind is right. I am Quinn Locke. I am he who is known as Yellow Hair," and he turned quickly to Loedicia, who was now trying to sit up in protest.

"No, DeMosse!" she yelled weakly. "No . . ." But his mouth set stubbornly as he looked once more at Bleeding Fox.

"So now you know," he said belligerently, "so now can we have done with this farce?" And he tried to hold his head steady, showing them he wasn't afraid. "Take me to Thayendanegea if you think you can, but remember, the Tuscarora are my friends. If they learn of it, you won't live to face Thayendanegea. I spit on Thayendanegea and I spit on you!" and he wallowed his tongue from side to side in his mouth, gathering what precious saliva he could and deliberately spit in the dirt, barely missing Bleeding Fox's feet.

Bleeding Fox stood motionless for a moment, then looked down at the wet spot where the spittle had missed his toe, and he grunted angrily. "So be it!" he snarled through clenched teeth, his lips quivering with fury, yet pleased with DeMosse's confession. "So let Thayendanegea then wreak his vengeance upon your bones," and he turned to Howling

Wind. "You have done well, Howling Wind," he praised his brother, breathing heavily, anger invading his whole body at DeMosse's insolent gesture; then he glanced quickly at Lizette, who was frowning as she watched DeMosse. "But first, so we know all, I would ask, who is she?" and Howling Wind whirled, staring at Lizette, who turned from DeMosse to face him.

Her graying hair was straggling against her cheeks, and fire blazed from her eyes as she stared back at them, trying to hold onto her courage, and Howling Wind looked lost for a moment. By the Great Spirit, who was she? The question was a good one. One Howling Wind didn't know the answer to, because they hadn't told him. All he knew was that they called her Lizette and she and Yellow Hair's squaw seemed to be friends, but he couldn't be made to look like a fool in front of the others. "She is a friend of Yellow Hair's, and as such, perhaps she too will be valuable to Thayendanegea," he said, catching at anything to make himself look good. "She can also speak our tongue and has the fire of Yellow Hair's squaw in her soul. I felt it best to bring her along," and he straightened defensively as his eyes met his brother's and he challenged him, warning him not to make light of his decision in front of everyone; then he gazed about, daring anyone to suggest he should have done otherwise, and Bleeding Fox turned from him, studying Lizette, noting the hatred in her eyes instead of the fear that usually dwelled in the eyes of the paleface women, and he exhaled, nodding.

"So be it," he said, and turned from her, walking away to stand before his people. "This is what I say," he shouted for all to hear. "We will let no one know what we are doing, for even now there are cowards among the Cherokee who I have heard are on their way to the white man's city to put their hands to another treaty the white man will only break. Their treaties are as forked as their tongues, their lies a drink we can no longer swallow." He turned, facing his brother once more, laying his hand on his shoulder. "Howling Wind, you will pick twenty of our bravest warriors and leave when the sun rises," he said. "You will take these three captives and go to Fort Niagara and tell Thayendanegea that the Cherokee is as powerful as the Mohawk." He paused, turning once more to the crowd, raising his hand from Howling Wind's shoulder, clenching his fist angrily. "This time we ask him not to help us, but to join us, and when he is with us," he stated, and his voice rose in volume, intense, angry, "when our tribes have become as one, we will spill the blood of the white man from

138

the borders of the Niagara," and he gestured dramatically, his arm sweeping wide, "south to the land of the Creek!" With his last words he folded his arms on his chest, raising himself to full height, and the lodge exploded in a myriad of war whoops that vibrated through its timbers and filled Loedicia's heart with dread, the drums that had been ominously silent once more beginning to beat, but this time they told no one of the plans that had been made, only that the camp of Bleeding Fox was celebrating.

Loedicia lay with her head sideways, the back of it on the dirt floor, staring across at DeMosse as the Indians began filing slowly out of the lodge, their anger kindled by the chief's fiery speech, their spirits high in spite of the rain that had started to fall. DeMosse was only a few feet from her, his hands and feet still tied, and although she knew he must be close to exhaustion and in far more pain than she was, there was a strength about him that pleased her. He looked toward her, and their eyes met.

"You're a fool," she whispered to him hoarsely in English as the last of the braves moved past, showing their contempt by spitting on his blood-soaked feet. "What happens when they reach Thayendanegea and he tells them you're not Quinn?"

He half-smiled. "They'll probably torture and kill DeMosse Gervaise. Either way, Thayendanegea will be satisfied," he said. "He knows who I am. In fact, he'd like nothing better than to get his hands on me. We've crossed paths off and on over the years, and he has little love for me, since we're on opposite sides. But at least this way we have a chance. From what you've told me, I gather no one at Fort Locke knows yet of Colonel Locke's death, am I right?"

"Yes."

He kept his voice low, barely a whisper. "Then if they heard that the Cherokee had captured both of you, there's a good chance his men might try a rescue."

"But how will they find out? The drums have quit talking."

"They may have talked enough when we first arrived."

She frowned and glanced quickly toward Howling Wind and Bleeding Fox, who were both some distance away talking with a group of warriors. DeMosse was right. Earlier in the day the drums had boasted of her capture, but the message had been a short one. "And if they didn't?" she asked.

"That's the chance we'll have to take." DeMosse was lying sideways, his big frame twisted with his legs bent and his head at an awkward angle as he looked at her. "Besides, they wanted me to be Quinn Locke so badly they could taste it," he added slowly as he tried to stretch closer to her, "so who am I to disappoint them? At least it's keeping me alive for a while longer and in comparatively good health." He winced as the blood oozed again from his ankles, and he bit back the pain it brought. "They'll save us for Thayendanegea now for sure," he said. "These Indians probably never heard of DeMosse Gervaise, so there'd be no reason to keep me alive. But they certainly have heard of your late husband."

"You're crazy," she whispered as she averted her eyes from him, watching Howling Wind turn toward them; then she lowered her voice even more. "These Indians weren't all that fond of Quinn," she cautioned. "They could be hard on you."

"I'll live through it."

"You know, sometimes you do remind me of Quinn," she confessed, trying to smile as her eyes met his again. "You have the same arrogant, cocksure attitude he always had," and he smiled back, his dried, cracked lips hurting with the effort.

"Is that a compliment?"

"Hardly."

"Too bad," he quipped, "I could use a compliment. Right about now my confidence is down to nil."

She moved her head, trying to get more comfortable. "Aren't you ever serious?" she asked, settling her head firmly again, more to the side, and he sighed.

"Only when I have to be," and suddenly their conversation was abruptly stopped by Howling Wind.

They hadn't heard him approach, but now he stood over them, looking down. "You will not talk in your language," he ordered angrily, his eyes blazing. "Only in my tongue will you talk," and DeMosse sneered.

"Then I guess I'm through talking for a while," he said, and Loedicia saw Howling Wind's eyes narrow, but was unable to warn DeMosse as the warrior's moccasined foot dug into his back in a swift kick.

"Yellow Hair will discover that the Indian is not faint of heart," Howling Wind said boldly as he kicked DeMosse again. "We do not become weak in the stomach at the sight of our enemies' blood flowing, so it would be wise to do as we command or you could claim the same fate Bleeding Fox was ready to render upon your squaw. It would be just as easy."

"What," asked DeMosse breathlessly, his ribs hurting like hell, "and spoil Thayendanegea's fun? He'd kill you for that,"

140

and Howling Wind's face hardened deviously as he thought over DeMosse's words.

Yellow Hair was trying to act brave and unconcerned. His words were caustic, meant to arouse anger, and at any other time Howling Wind would have killed him, but he was also right, and the face of Joseph Brant, known to the Indians as Thayendanegea, surged before him and he remembered what Strong Wind's soldiers could do if they were not stopped. He would leave him to Thayendanegea, and he clenched his teeth, holding back his vengeance, then straightened haughtily.

"We will see how much the white man laughs and makes merry when the skin is peeled from his body inch by inch and each member cut away piece by piece until all that is left are the bones to dry in the sun," he said, and this time it was Howling Wind's turn to smile. "I have heard it said Thayendanegea is an expert at keeping men alive to feel the power of his vengeance," and Loedicia moaned, knowing he spoke the truth.

Thayendanegea had been educated by white men, in white men's schools, and was given the commission of captain in the British Army, but he had no qualms about how he treated his enemies and was skilled at torturing them, keeping them barely above the realm of the unconscious so they'd feel every thrust of pain he applied. She'd heard Quinn discuss him many times, and the thought sickened her.

"Your woman mourns already," said Howling Wind as he glanced at Loedicia, hearing the sound that escaped her throat, and his voice hardened. "I will watch rejoicing when the blade of Thayendanegea cuts down the roots that furnish life to you," he said, "for when this happens, I know that then Thayendanegea will truly be our brother and the white men will be driven from our lands," and he lifted his hand, motioning toward the two men who'd identified Loedicia earlier, and another man he'd singled out of the crowd, and ordered them to take the prisoners to one of the other lodges.

They were dragged unceremoniously to their feet, pushed outside, and this time deposited in a smaller lodge a few yards away, where they spent a restless night listening to the storm outside, without benefit of supper, a fact DeMosse attributed to his too-active tongue and cursed himself, regretting the pain it was causing Loedicia and Lizette.

The next morning they were shaken awake and fed a gruel of hot corn mush and berries, then dragged from the hut to stand before the circle of painted warriors. The storm had

141

wet the ground heavily during the night, and now the sun coming up over the treetops made everything glisten wet and slick.

Howling Wind paraded back and forth in front of them like a strutting peacock, the feathers on his scalp lock bobbing in the early-morning air as he walked; then suddenly he stopped and motioned to his men, and DeMosse was pulled from between them and pushed up before him. Howling Wind studied him for a minute, his face impassive; then he reached out, turning him around, and cut the leather that bound his wrists, then bent over, doing the same to his ankles.

DeMosse stood for a moment in disbelief, his back still to Howling Wind as he touched his wrists slowly, peeling the rawhide from them; then he turned around as Howling Wind signaled his men, who cut the rawhide binding the wrists of the two women also, and DeMosse frowned.

"Why?" he asked, puzzled, as he tried to rub some circulation back into his freed hands, and Howling Wind sneered sardonically.

"We have many leagues to travel," he said, "and it is easier if you ride. Now you will mount," and he motioned with his hand as three braves walked up guiding their own horses, their saddles still on them.

Once on the horse's back however, DeMosse's hands were again tied, in front of him this time, and secured to a ring in the saddle, and his ankles were tied to the stirrups, giving him enough room for movement, but not enough for freedom. Then strong lead ropes were fastened to his horse's halter instead of reins, and Howling Wind inspected him, satisfied.

DeMosse turned and looked behind him at Loedicia seated atop her horse, and he winced. They had just begun to tie her wrists, and he watched the rawhide once more cut into the bloody scabs and saw the pain in her eyes; then he continued watching while her ankles were tied to the stirrups.

She thrust her head up defiantly as Dark Morning finished tying down her ankle, then moved to the left side, and her eyes caught DeMosse's unexpectedly. He sat motionless, staring at her, looking directly into her eyes, and his body flushed inside. What was she trying to say? Her eyes looked strange, intimate.

Loedicia felt his eyes on her, accusing. If she hadn't talked him into taking her to South Carolina, they wouldn't be here. But then, if he hadn't tried to seduce her, they might have gotten away. Damn him anyway! Now his expression was

142

changing. Why did he have to look at her like that, as if . . . as if he cared?

Lizette sat rigid on her horse's back and watched the look that passed between Loedicia and DeMosse, and she didn't like it. It was not strange that DeMosse was able to pass himself off as Quinn so easily, because he was a man much like Quinn. A fact that she knew had become apparent to Dicia too. But he was also a man who took what he wanted of life, regardless of the consequences, and unlike Quinn, he gave little in return. He was the kind of man who would break a woman's heart without asking permission first, and Lizette was afraid for Loedicia, because she knew she was vulnerable, especially now, and she dreaded the close proximity of the long ride they had ahead of them.

She glanced quickly away from Loedicia and flinched as the leather tightened about her own ankle, then was secured to the stirrup, giving her only enough freedom to ride without breaking her ankle, yet not enough to leave the horse of her own free will. Her eyes rested on the Indian who was performing the task. He wasn't quite as tall as Howling Wind and he was leaner, with a deep scar across his forehead into which he'd put some sort of yellow concoction, then lined it with vermilion. Howling Wind had called him Many Scars, and now, as he finished and turned, walking away toward his own horse, she could understand why. There were at least six other large, deep scars on his body; each he had proudly filled with the same yellow paint and lined with vermilion, and the effect was grotesque.

When they were all tied down and the sun was well up over the horizon, the drums once more began their rhythmic beating, and Howling Wind's braves lined their horses up, ready to depart. Bleeding Fox stood beside Howling Wind's horse, then raised his hand, and again the drums stopped as the men, women, and children crowded about, staring eagerly.

"For this day we have waited long," Bleeding Fox began, his voice ringing through the village. "Some of our tribe at Chattahoochee are content to take crumbs thrown to us by the white-eyes, who have broken every treaty they have set their hand to. But we are not fools, and they and Thayendanegea shall know this. The Cherokee are mighty and powerful and the Great Spirit has put his blessing upon us by setting his hand against Yellow Hair and his squaw. So now may the Great Spirit journey with Howling Wind and our braves to the land of the Niagara, and may their journey be

143

fruitful." He turned to Howling Wind. "Hold your head high, my brother," he said haughtily, "and let them know that the Cherokee are as mighty as the Mohawk, and may the Great Spirit guide you on your journey and protect you from all our enemies."

His hand moved upward, and Howling Wind's hand moved down to clasp his wrist, and the words were sealed; then Bleeding Fox stepped back out of the way.

"Hai-yee-ah!" Howling Wind yelled, and his voice carried to the treetops, still wet with last night's rain, his hand raised in a forward gesture, motioning them to follow, and he dug his horse in the ribs and moved out, the procession slowly following. They passed the meeting lodge, moving on between log houses, then across a meadow to a path north of the one where they'd entered the valley the day before, moving out onto the trail, heading past the planted fields, the three prisoners safely in tow. The warriors surrounding them were bare-chested to the morning sun, their fringed buckskins rolled up into a small bundle and slung across their horses' backs in case of bad weather, and Bleeding Fox watched them disappear, a smile on his face; then he turned and walked back to his lodge.

Loedicia was uncomfortable in the saddle tied down like this. The rawhide was rubbing her shins, and she knew before long they'd be raw and sore too, but at least it beat walking. She glanced down at her horse's head, watching it toss restlessly in front of her as Dark Morning held the lead rope, guiding it. Horses were rare yet on the frontier, the Indians acquiring them any way they could, yet every warrior this morning was mounted. They'd probably used almost every horse in camp in a gesture to show their strength to Joseph Brant. The more horses a tribe had, the more powerful its medicine, and how was Brant to know whether these were their only horses or not? Chief Bleeding Fox was shrewd.

The first day took them some twenty miles from the village, where they made camp next to a small stream. Much to their surprise, although they were guarded so closely they could breathe on their captors, they were allowed freedom during meals, the first night dining on rabbit and squirrel the Indians had shot during the day. But they were still instructed to speak only Cherokee, a practice they adhered to reluctantly, but complied with under the threat of Howling Wind's sadistic vengeance. Howling Wind's temper was short, and he seemed to enjoy picking on DeMosse, as Loedicia had warned, and more than once, as the days went on, he was disciplined for not eating fast enough or talking too much or taking too long to relieve himself, since two guards were needed when they disappeared behind the bushes to perform the latter.

The second afternoon on the trail, when DeMosse could take it no longer and complained about the ladies having to suffer the same indignity he did when they relieved themselves, by having two guards watching them, Howling Wind not only had the straps about his ankles tightened, making his ride the rest of the afternoon even more difficult, but after refusing him food that evening, had him hung by his arms from a high tree branch all night with his feet just tiptoeing the ground, then taunted him, spitting in his face every time he went by.

But in a way, even though it felt like his arms would be torn from their sockets, DeMosse was pleased. Howling Wind's vengeance was far from satisfied. He would have loved to beat him, or cut him, or break his bones, but he knew he didn't dare. Thayendanegea would think little of a half-dead gift. No. He had to turn Yellow Hair over to him without his body bearing any marks of abuse or torture, so he was forced to do only that which would leave no ill effects, and DeMosse knew it was killing Howling Wind inside, and it made what DeMosse did have to suffer easier to bear.

They moved steadily northward, skirting the main village of Chattahoochee, and a few days later crossed a river DeMosse told them that evening was called the Tennessee; then they followed along another river he called the Sequatchie, which led through the mountain valley for some miles, leaving it again as they moved into the Cumberland Gap.

Each day seemed to grow hotter under the July sun, and the trail they followed was rough and overgrown. At night bugs and mosquitoes plagued them while they tried to sleep tied in their awkward positions, and during the day they sweltered.

Two days after leaving the Cumberland, the scout Howling Wind always sent ahead brought back news of a party of Shawnee ahead on the trail about a half-hour's ride, so Howling Wind, with four warriors to help him, left the main trail with the prisoners in tow, leaving Dark Morning in charge, instructing him to approach the Shawnee in peace and tell them that they were on their way north on a special mission concerning the welfare of all the tribes, but to say nothing of the prisoners. Since they wore no war paint, they would probably be believed, even though the Shawnee and Cherokee were far from being friends. With the white man invading the frontier in increasing numbers, they were fighting less among one another, so their chances were good on being believed and it was the truth. Not all the truth, but the truth, and Loedicia glanced back at Dark Morning as another Indian pulled her horse from the trail and they headed into the thicket.

Howling Wind wasn't dumb. He knew that if they all left the trail and the Shawnee found their horses' tracks, they'd try to find out who it was and follow them, and their secret would be out. But by leaving most of the warriors on the trail to greet the Shawnee, they'd have no suspicion that others had left, and they'd go on their way without getting suspicious.

His ruse worked, and an hour later they merged on the trail again, and once more Howling Wind sent his scout ahead.

The same ruse was perpetrated often in the next few days as they moved deeper into Shawnee territory, and occasionally they heard the drums from some village close by, and Howling Wind would listen, then move again, often leaving the trail to avoid the village.

One afternoon, a few days after a rainstorm that had blinded them, forcing them to seek shelter in some caves, they moved up the Scioto River toward Painted Creek, following the winding river, and Loedicia sat stiffly in the saddle, staring ahead at Howling Wind. For the past few minutes the sound of distant drums had invaded the warm afternoon air, and she had paid little attention at first. Now her ears pricked up and she listened intently, realizing Howling Wind was listening too. They continued moving, the horses slowly picking their way through the tangled growth covering the ground, and she cocked her head, making sure there'd been no mistake.

She glanced ahead at DeMosse and saw his head tilt sideways and knew he was listening too, and that evening as they ate supper, he confirmed what they all had heard.

The drums had told them that a few weeks before, the Shawnee, under the leadership of Chief Blue Jacket, had attacked General Wayne's army at Fort Recovery, and although the battle had ended in the Indians' defeat, it had given the white man a lesson he could understand. The Indian would not leave his lands without a fight, and Blue Jacket was sending out invitations far and wide for his red brothers to join him, regardless of what tribe they belonged to.

"What village is closest?" Loedicia asked DeMosse that evening as she talked quickly, trying to eat at the same time, because it was a habit of Howling Wind's to stop them from eating if he thought they were talking too long, and she was starved.

DeMosse licked his fingers, then used them to wipe from his long growth of unkempt beard the dripping juice of the half-raw piece of venison he was eating, as he answered. "We just left the Scioto and we're heading north." He frowned as he took a bearing on the setting sun. "I'd say the drums must have come from Cornstalks Village. It's closer to the Scioto, about a half-day's ride from here."

She watched his face as she juggled the hot meat in her hands, then took a bite, savoring the taste of the venison as she flicked it back and forth with her tongue, cooling it. His beard was filthy, streaked with the leftovers of past meals, dirt clinging to the crow's-feet at the corners of his eyes, and dust lay close along the edge of his hairline. His streaked blond hair, down to his shoulders now, was straggly and greasy, and the hand that reached up and pushed it out of his face was black with grime. He looked very little like the dapper Frenchman she'd first met in Governor Carondelet's home, except for his eyes. They were still alert, intense, and there were always gold flecks dancing in them when he looked at her.

"Reading drums comes in handy, doesn't it?" he said, and she flushed, realizing she and Lizette looked as bad as he did. Their hair was filthy, clothes dirty. Howling Wind refused to let them bathe, and she wrinkled her nostrils, thinking of the stench that probably clung to them.

"*Mon ami,*" asked Lizette from beside Loedicia, her body weary as she sat cross-legged, wiping the juice from her fingers onto her leggings, "do you think the drums told the truth when they said the British had promised to help Blue Jacket?" and DeMosse frowned.

"I doubt it. They've been promising to help them for years, but the only Indians who've ever received their help have been the Mohawk, and that's because Joseph Brant has kept them out of American territory in the past few years. If the British throw their hand in now, there'll be an all-out war with the United States, and they don't want that. Not yet. They have work to do first." He was eating fast, like the rest of them, as he talked, his hands helping his teeth tear the meat from its bones. "Remember the morning we were captured, when Howling Wind found that packet of papers in my inside shirt pocket and strewed them on what was left of the campfire, watching them burn?" he asked, and they both nodded as they went on eating. "Those papers were to go to Thomas Jefferson, who was to use them to talk President Washington into joining the French and their war on England. They're arming their forts and trading posts on the frontier, the ones they were to have given up in the treaty of Eighty-three, and those papers were the proof. Now they're gone, but believe me, the British aren't satisfied with the way things are, and they'd like nothing better than to take back what was once theirs. They aren't ready yet, however, so, no, I doubt very much they'll jeopardize what they're going to need in the future to please a few savage Indians who are bound to lose in the long run anyway. General Wayne has over two thousand soldiers out there—" Suddenly DeMosse was cut short as Howling Wind, who'd been standing behind them listening, stepped forward.

"And we have over two thousand braves," he boasted angrily. "Captain Pipe, Tecumseh, Red Pole, Black Wolf, Lame Hawk, Captain Johnny, and Blackfoot. All their warriors will join Blue Jacket as we plan to do. Your General Wayne is far outnumbered. His forts will fall before our vengeance and when Thayendanegea joins us, the redcoats will have no choice but to join us also. Then we will watch what happens."

DeMosse smiled cynically. "Should be interesting," he said. "Wonder if I'll be around to see it?" He watched curiously as Howling Wind's eyes narrowed, wondering if he was getting ready to inflict one of his special treats on him for being insolent, but evidently he hadn't been angered enough. All he did was glare at them, then turn and walk away, and Loedicia sighed.

DeMosse finished eating and leaned back, relaxing, his eyes still on Loedicia as she ate. Even with her face covered with dirt and grime she was exciting. There was an earthy quality about her that intrigued him. At night, trussed up as they always were, he'd shut his eyes and think of her, and sleep always came more easily.

He watched her now, wondering why she hadn't told him who she really was from the start. Surely she'd know that he'd have heard of Quinn. His name was as well-known along the northern frontier as Daniel Boone's was along the Kentucky River, but she'd referred to him only as the earl.

He studied her, remembering the way the sun had made her hair shine like a raven's feathers. Now it was dull with dirt and grime. But her eyes were alive and animated as she talked to Lizette, and he remembered how they always danced dangerously when she was angry, and most of all, as he clenched his hand, he could almost feel her full breast as he'd held it beneath his fingers and caressed it that morning while he looked deep into her eyes, drowning in them. God! She was the most tantalizing woman he'd met in years, and he sighed as he sat back up; then he glanced at Howling Wind, who was also staring at Loedicia from a short distance away, and he frowned as he read the look on the Indian's face.

Howling Wind's eyes looked closed as he leaned against the tree, but they weren't. They watched Loedicia furtively, every move she made, every gesture. She was fuller in the breast than most squaws, yet her waist was small, giving her a fragile appearance. She was anything but fragile, however, and he knew it. More than once since he'd captured her he'd wondered what it would be like to feel her body beneath him, and the only thing that had kept him from taking her so far was the vow he'd made before he'd left.

He had dedicated his body to the Great Spirit, as had all the other warriors, vowing to forsake the pleasures of women until their mission was accomplished, a vow he now cursed having made. Ordinarily white women appalled him with their pale eyes and light skin, but this woman was different. She was exciting, and just to look at her made his manhood rise. His eyes dropped from her abruptly as he realized what was happening, and he turned away, strolling off, trying to put her out of his mind, unaware that DeMosse's eyes followed him curiously as he disappeared alone among the trees.

The next few days stayed warm, with only a slight shower to slow them down. They crossed the Hocking River and camped on the shores of the Great Buffalo Swamp, crossing the Licking River two days later and heading for the Tuscarawas. At the Tuscarawas River, near Killbuck Creek, where they crossed, they bypassed a huge village of Delaware without any trouble at all, then narrowly missed being spotted a few days later when they stayed too close to the trail and almost ran into a band of young braves out hunting.

By now, Howling Wind's frustrated desires were becoming harder and harder for him to control. He'd go to sleep at night and dream about the white woman. She'd be bathing in a pool in his dream, the clear water up to her shoulders;

then, at the sight of him approaching, she'd stand up, raising her arms toward him, and he'd die a little inside at the golden glow of her skin, the firm lift of her breasts. But every time he tried to reach out and touch her, the face of Thayendanegea would suddenly appear before him, shutting her out, and he'd wake up in a cold sweat, his loins aching. The dream was real. Too real, and he'd find himself staring at her hungrily, wondering if her naked body really did look as beautiful as it did in his dream.

They'd been traveling for weeks now and were well past the Chautauqua Lake into Seneca country heading north toward Niagara. Howling Wind had been taking his frustrations out on DeMosse more and more lately as the weeks passed, and it irritated him, because more than once, after he'd been watching the white squaw Yellow Hair called Loedicia, he'd find Yellow Hair staring at him curiously, his eyes filled with hatred, and it bothered him. He had a feeling Yellow Hair knew what he wanted, and Howling Wind knew it was the one thing Yellow Hair wouldn't be able to face. Yet he could do nothing. To break his vow now might ruin his mission, destroying his people, and consequently, because he couldn't have what he wanted from the woman, he took it out on her mate, thinking up new, unusual torments like staking him out all night in the cold rain and at other times forcing him to stay awake all night when everyone else was asleep, by fastening him to a tree with a leather rope about his neck, his toes barely touching the ground. If he relaxed to sleep the leather tightened and choked him, so he had no choice but to stay awake.

Thus it was that Howling Wind stood early one evening shortly before sundown watching Loedicia. The weather was extremely hot and she had finished eating and was fanning her buckskin shirt at the waist to let in some air while she talked to Yellow Hair, and he saw the white man's eyes drop to the low neckline of her fringed buckskin shirt where her breasts divided voluptuously, and his eyes narrowed. He had been trying to think of some way to get even with Yellow Hair, and the idea that had just crossed his mind was a fascinating one, and he smiled cynically to himself as he straightened, then strolled over toward the fire.

His piercing eyes looked the three of them over deliberately as he approached; then he raised a hand, motioning toward Dark Morning, who had just finished eating.

Loedicia watched Howling Wind warily as his eyes moved back to stare at her.

"Bring Yellow Hair's squaw," he ordered Dark Morning boldly, and she drew back as Dark Morning stepped toward her.

"What are you going to do?" she asked hesitantly, leaning away from Dark Morning, but Howling Wind didn't answer as Dark Morning reached out and grabbed her arm, pulling her to her feet, and shoved her toward Howling Wind.

Howling Wind turned, walking toward the river, where the horses were drinking, his back straight as a ramrod, while Dark Morning pushed her reluctantly after him.

The river was some yards away through the trees, and Loedicia didn't like it. DeMosse had warned her that Howling Wind had ideas about her. The only thing he couldn't understand was why he hadn't done something about it, until he'd learned from one of the other braves that they'd taken a vow to the Great Spirit before leaving and that none of them were to take a woman until their mission was over, a fact that at the moment Loedicia wasn't sure she believed as Howling Wind stopped next to the water's edge and turned, staring at her.

"Take off your clothes," he said calmly, and she gasped.

"Why?"

"In a few days we reach Niagara, and I wish to present a clean gift to Thayendanegea," he explained, but Loedicia eyed him suspiciously, not knowing whether to believe him or not, then glanced behind her at Dark Morning, who was watching Howling Wind curiously.

"I said take off your clothes!" he ordered more firmly. "And do not try to escape, for Dark Morning and I will be watching," and he crossed his arms, waiting.

Loedicia's face reddened, and she set her feet stubbornly in the sandy soil at the river's edge, anger rising in her eyes, and she shook her head. "No, I will not take off my clothes," she stated boldly, her hands clenched as she pulled them closer to her side. "And no one will take them off me, either, without a fight!"

Howling Wind's eyes tightened and his face went rigid. "You will take off your clothes," he shouted arrogantly, his nostrils flaring passionately as he uncrossed his arms and grabbed her by the shoulders, "or I'll do it for you," but he hadn't counted on her temper.

She reached up as he grabbed her, her jagged fingernails slicing down the side of his face, leaving deep gashes, and her knee, kicking out viciously, almost caught him hard in the groin, hitting his thigh as he moved sideways. Releasing her shoulders quickly, he grabbed her wrists this time, holding them to keep her nails from his face, his hands like iron bands about them, and he put pressure on, bending her backward, forcing her to the ground, fighting her all the way, her feet kicking out at him as she went down, her voice breathless.

"Get your stinking hands off me!" she screamed as she hit the ground hard, but instead, he spread her arms over her head, holding her wrists against the damp ground, and she panted desperately, thrashing from side to side to break his hold, but he was too strong.

"Take her feet!" he yelled to Dark Morning, who had been standing behind Loedicia in a quandary, reluctant to become a part of what was happening, but he couldn't ignore Howling Wind's command, and stepped forward, trying to grab her flailing feet as she whipped them back and forth, hitting him at random in the face, the head, pushing at his nose, digging against his ears. But she was no match for him, and in minutes he had her legs pinned to the ground by the ankles, and he looked at Howling Wind for instructions.

"What do I do now?" he asked, breathing heavily, knowing little of what was going on in Howling Wind's mind, and Howling Wind snarled.

"You will pull the leggings from her body," he said, panting, his eyes wildly intense, but Loedicia had other ideas.

"If he lets go, I'll kick," she gasped through clenched teeth, and Howling Wind glared down into her face as she lay beneath him; then he bared his teeth as an animal would and his hand tightened on her left wrist, bringing it over to meet her right wrist, holding them both down with one hand, and his breath flew at her in a savage grunt as he raised his free hand.

"You will not be awake to protest!" he stated viciously, and she gasped as she saw his fist heading for the side of her head, then felt the sickening crunch as it hit and the world spun around in a thousand pieces, until suddenly there was nothing left to feel or remember, only a black void, disrupted occasionally by a smattering of light that tried to reach out to her, but never quite materialized.

She had no idea how long she'd been unconscious, but it felt like an eternity. Her first sensation of awareness was the feel of water against her bare legs, cold, chilling water that made her shiver involuntarily. She shook her head, trying to clear it as she realized the water was getting deeper; then an empty feeling gripped the pit of her stomach and she felt the hands, like a vise, holding her arms. They were carrying her into the water, one on each side of her, and she was naked. Without warning, her head flew back and she let out an agonizing shriek.

"No!" she yelled, her voice echoing through the woods beyond the water. "You can't, not like this, I won't let you!" and she tried to fight, but the blow on the head had weakened her and it was as futile as a butterfly trying to fight a hawk.

They shoved her forward, submerging her head in water, then dragged her to the surface again, a sputtering bedraggled mess, but she still wouldn't give in. She fought them, thrashing out wildly, kicking, screaming, scratching, biting, until she could no longer move on her own; then over and over again they plunged her into the cool, dark water until she thought she'd drown; then, when her cries of protest had become so weak they were barely a hoarse mumble, and she thought she was about to collapse into oblivion, they began dragging her back to shore.

She knew they were moving because she could feel the water pushing against her body, but she could feel nothing else except bitter numbness. They pulled her from the water to the bank and started to let go, then tightened their grip again as she began to sink limply to the ground, and they held her steady.

She could tell her feet were on solid ground again because she could feel the rough stones and sand scraping them as they lifted her a little higher and began carrying her forward again, away from the river, her feet dangling uselessly. She tried to concentrate, to stand, to make her legs do what she wanted them to do, but it was as if they weren't even attached to her body anymore, and she groaned miserably.

They carried her by the arms, one on each side, dragging her farther off, away from the camp, and there was nothing she could do about it. She was so weak she couldn't even raise her arm to protest when they finally stopped in front of a huge tree and Howling Wind shoved her limply into Dark Morning's arms, startling the warrior.

"Hold her a moment," he said, and Dark Morning stared down at the half-conscious woman in his arms, feeling her bare flesh against his hands, pressed against his body, and he frowned, looking up at Howling Wind, who had taken the lasso strapped to the belt of his breechclout and was making a loop of it.

"What are you doing?" he finally asked, getting up enough

courage to question his leader, and Howling Wind glanced at him, his eyes darkening. He didn't like being questioned.

"Since Yellow Hair seems to enjoy the punishment I have meted out to him for his insolence," he answered as he reached down and grabbed Loedicia's wrist, fastening the loop about it, "I will give him a punishment that will not be quite so desirable, nor so easy to ignore," and Dark Morning's eyes grew wary.

"But our vow?" he questioned.

"What of the vow?"

"If we touch this woman, our mission will fail."

Howling Wind smiled wickedly, reassuring him. "We will not touch her," he said, his voice deadly, "but neither will Yellow Hair, and that will be a pleasure to see. Now, bring her to the tree," and Dark Morning helped him as they pushed her back against the tree, pulling the rope around the trunk to fasten it on the other wrist so she was securely tied; then they did the same to her ankles, letting her feet barely touch the ground, but tying her legs so they were in a spreading position and she was unable to move and could only hang wearily.

Howling Wind stepped back, surveying their handiwork, and he took a deep breath. The tree they'd spread-eagled her to was set in a shaft of late-afternoon sunlight that fell on her body, turning it into creamy gold. Her breasts were firm, high, her hips well-rounded, and the dark hair, which hung forward now, almost covering her face as her head drooped, was curling riotously as water dripped from it.

He looked her over slowly, feeling his blood growing hot as his eyes flicked across her shapely thighs stretched open to him; then, afraid of giving himself away, he turned quickly to Dark Morning.

"Come!" he said sharply, his voice breaking huskily. "Follow me," and he spun about rapidly, heading back toward camp with Dark Morning at his heels.

DeMosse had heard Loedicia's cries and had tried to reach her, his big frame stopped in its rescue attempt by six warriors who'd wrestled him to the ground and were now panting and out of breath as they secured the ropes on him once more, and he knew his erratic plunge against them in an attempt to reach Loedicia would probably cost him the freedom of his hands and feet at supper for the rest of the trip, but he didn't care. Her agonized cries had inflamed him. They were pitiful cries, like those of a wounded animal.

Howling Wind stepped forward, standing directly in front

of DeMosse, who was trussed up on the ground next to the fire, and he sneered arrogantly as he looked him over. "Yellow Hair wishes to see his squaw, am I right?" he asked pretentiously, and DeMosse growled from deep in his throat.

"What have you done to her?"

"What have I done to her?" Howling Wind's eyes taunted, his tongue crisp and abusive as he looked about at his warriors standing in the small clearing. "I have decided to give you a treat, O Great Yellow Hair," he answered sarcastically. "It has been many moons since you have enjoyed the pleasures of your woman's body, I know, so I have arranged for you to refresh your memory, lest you forget. Of course, I can't free your hands, and I'm afraid she also must be restrained, but perhaps you will enjoy the occasion to some extent. Bring him!" he commanded, his eyes narrowing viciously, and some of the warriors reached down, dragging DeMosse to his feet, and shoved him after Howling Wind and Dark Morning, who were already headed back through the trees toward where Loedicia was tied.

DeMosse was so angry he could hardly breathe, and he clenched his teeth tightly to keep from yelling at the top of his lungs. His feet shuffled forward belligerently, and he was pushed first by one hand, then another, until suddenly, as he stumbled against a small oak tree, he glanced up quickly, realizing Howling Wind was no longer in front of him. Instead, there was an old maple tree, and his eyes widened, his mouth going dry as he stared straight ahead at Loedicia's naked body silhouetted against its bark, leather ropes holding her up.

He stopped, breathing heavily, leaning against the oak tree, letting it support him, feeling its rough bark against his cheek as he stared transfixed, unable to take his eyes from her. God, what a sight! Her dark hair was wet, flung back from her face that was lifted as if in prayer, and her eyes were shut, her face pale like chiseled marble, but her body, caught in the glow of the setting sun, was ripe and voluptuous, every curve flowing gracefully together in a symmetry that made his heart start pounding, the blood come rushing to his head. What on earth was this madman doing to him?

He straightened awkwardly, swallowing hard, and started to turn, but was stopped by Howling Wind, who'd moved to his side, so close his breath was on DeMosse's ear.

"Don't look away," the Indian whispered furtively, his eyes flashing. "Look at her," and he reached out, grabbing DeMosse's head, holding it steady so he had no choice.

DeMosse wanted to shut his eyes, but couldn't; he was fascinated, and there was a lump in his throat. If only he could help her. If only he could take that soft, warm body down and draw it close in his arms and show it pleasure instead of pain, and he cursed softly to himself as Howling Wind's voice fell once more on his ears, taunting maliciously.

"How long has it been, Yellow Hair?" he asked, knowing he'd get no answer. "How many moons since you held your woman beneath you and drove your manhood home? How long since your mouth covered hers and your hands warmed her body?"

DeMosse went cold inside, then hot, his body unconsciously responding to the taunts as his eyes caressed each curve, each line, resting for what seemed like an eternity on the patch of soft, curling hair between her thighs; then suddenly Loedicia moaned and his eyes moved upward, abruptly stopping at her face. She was staring at him now, her lips pleading, her eyes open.

"No, DeMosse," she groaned hoarsely, her voice stark, unreal. "Don't do this to me," she begged, but he was helpless.

There was nothing he could do. Howling Wind had made sure of that. God, what was the Indian trying to accomplish, anyway? Why? His body was on fire, and he trembled clear to his toes, his loins beginning to ache with a wild passionate ache that hurt. Then suddenly it dawned on him. Howling Wind wanted her. He wanted her so badly it hurt, just like DeMosse was hurting now, and having to deny his body what it craved was an unbearable torture. Now he understood. Howling Wind wanted Yellow Hair to suffer the same torture he was going through. He would dangle her in front of her husband until his desire was so strong it cried for release; then he'd deny him. Only he thought he was doing it to Yellow Hair. He thought he was bringing back memories to a man who would remember, but instead he was whetting the appetite of a man who had longed for what lay before him as much as Howling Wind himself did, and it was just as devastating.

Loedicia turned her eyes from DeMosse, leaning her head back against the bark on the tree, staring up into its branches. Her body felt strange, as if it didn't belong to her, as if it were a thing apart from her head and her thoughts. She wasn't beaten. He could embarrass and humiliate her all he wanted, but she'd never give in. Not as long as there was a breath in her body. This would be over soon. It had to be over soon. She flushed and her face reddened as she felt

DeMosse's eyes sifting over her and heard Howling Wind mumbling in his ear again.

"What was it like, Yellow Hair?" Howling Wind murmured effectively. "Was her blood hot? Do you remember what it was to put your body to hers, to let her touch your manhood and make it swell with pride?" and DeMosse groaned, breaking out in a cold sweat, his body shaking as the bulge in his pants grew tighter and he felt himself begin to leak.

The man was mad, utterly mad! He tried to shut his eyes, but they wouldn't let him. He wanted to blot out the anguish the sight of her brought him, because although he cursed Howling Wind for what he was doing to her, and hated him for it, he couldn't deny that he wanted her as much as the Indian, and for the same reason.

Howling Wind kept his vicious little game up until the shadows beneath the trees lengthened and the sky grew dark and DeMosse felt as if his body was ready to explode. Then as abruptly as he'd started, he straightened, turning toward Dark Morning and the other warriors who'd been standing to one side watching.

His eyes were wild, glassy, and his lips trembled as he spoke, but it was too dark for the warriors to see closely. DeMosse saw it, however, and he felt sick. In trying to arouse him and drive him to the verge of madness, Howling Wind had driven himself too far.

"You will take Yellow Hair back to the fire," he said tremulously, trying to keep his voice from shaking. "I alone will handle the woman, get her clothed and back to camp," and DeMosse glanced toward the warriors, who began slowly to converge on him in the quickly growing darkness.

Dark Morning seemed reluctant to move, however, and his voice was low as he spoke. "I helped you with the white woman earlier, I can help you now, Howling Wind," he offered, but Howling Wind declined.

"I said I will do it alone," he answered, and DeMosse, who was being hustled away, moved closer to Dark Morning and got a good look at the Indian's face. He was staring at Howling Wind with a suspicious look on his face. "I said I will take care of the woman alone," repeated Howling Wind as Dark Morning hesitated; then the Indian turned reluctantly, following the rest of the warriors and DeMosse, glancing back now and then behind him, until Howling Wind and the woman were lost in the darkness.

Howling Wind kept his back to the woman, his breathing

157

unsteady, hands shaking. He couldn't stand it anymore. His body cried for release until he shuddered. He watched the camp, his eyes on Dark Morning, who moved into the firelight, and he sighed. Now he and the white woman were hidden in the darkness of the woods. No one would know, and he turned slowly.

Loedicia was tired and afraid. The night air had brought cooling relief to her body, but had also brought bloodthirsty mosquitoes that were tormenting her unmercifully. She had withstood the humiliating ordeal Howling Wind had put her through, God knows how, but Howling Wind's words as he goaded DeMosse haunted her like an ugly nightmare and she remembered the agonized look on DeMosse's face as he tried to fight against the natural instincts of his body. There was no denying the lust in DeMosse's eyes as he was forced to look at her, but there was something else there too, a warmth and sensitivity. He wanted her, but not in the same way Howling Wind did, and for this she was thankful.

She glanced at the Indian's vague form as he stepped closer in the darkness. She could just barely make out his face, and she swallowed hard at the look on it, cringing beneath his stare.

He bent down, untying her ankles, pulling the rope from around the tree, and she hung limply, the ropes still about her wrists holding her up. This done, he set his huge hand firmly at her waist, spreading his fingers out over her skin, holding her body in place against the tree trunk while he loosened the ropes from her wrists and let them fall, and her hands dropped limply to her sides.

He stared into her face for a minute, then removed his hand, stepping back away from her, letting her try to stand on her own, but she couldn't. Without anything to hold her up, she slid to the ground like a rag doll, her legs like jelly beneath her, her back scraping the tree trunk on the way down, and she ended up sprawled in the grass at the foot of the tree at his feet. He looked down at her as she tried to move, trying to get up, trying to force enough strength into her arms to raise herself.

What was the matter? Why wouldn't her arms and legs move? She had to get up. She couldn't just lie here like this. She tried to pull herself from the ground and managed to move a few inches, but the effort was too much and she collapsed reluctantly into the cool grass, staring up at Howling Wind, who glanced quickly back toward camp, his eyes alert, watching. Something about the way he stood bothered her and made her uneasy.

He was standing rigid, every muscle in his body taut, like a fine wire being stretched to its limit; then his arms moved furtively and she glanced down his lean body and saw him shove the breechclout aside, and her mouth went dry.

Oh, God, no! He wouldn't! He couldn't! He had taken a vow. He wouldn't dare touch her. He wouldn't! She had to scream, let them know what he was going to do, but as she tried to move, opening her mouth to yell, he was suddenly beside her, his hand clamped over her mouth, his eager voice filling her ears.

"You will not cry out or I will kill you," he whispered hurriedly, his fingers hurting her mouth as he pressed her head to the ground, and his other hand touched her body, beginning to move down it feverishly, searching, probing between her legs, then trying to push and lift her thighs to receive him.

She moaned beneath him, gathering all the strength she could muster, but it wasn't enough, and tears filled her eyes as she felt his strong hands part her thighs wide, and with a savage grunt he moved over her and entered, thrusting forward hard, and she wanted to die. His hand loosened on her mouth as he worked feverishly above her, but it didn't matter. Nothing mattered but the ugly feel of him inside her, and she turned her head, shutting her eyes, sobbing softly to herself as the noise of his rutting grated on her ears. Then suddenly, as quickly as he started, he thrust forward hard, letting out a sharp muffled cry, and she knew it was over as he shook spasmodically, stopping deep inside her; then he leaned forward, trembling breathlessly, his face so close to hers she could feel his breath on her cheek. She swallowed hard, biting her lip to keep from crying out.

"You are much woman!" he whispered gruffly against her cheek, and she felt sick inside.

"Get off me!" she gasped through clenched teeth, her whole body incensed over what he'd done. "If you're through, get off me!" and he grunted, pulling away, slipping from her.

He stood up, putting his breechclout back into place as he took a quick glance back toward camp to make sure he hadn't been observed; then he relaxed and sighed, looking down at her, his dark, piercing eyes studying the body of the woman who had made him feel like this. He felt alive, warm. The ache, gone from his loins, was replaced by a blissful feeling of content.

He reached down and grabbed her by the arm, trying to

pull her to her feet, but she was too weak, so instead he reached down, and to Loedicia's surprise, lifted her into his arms, then stood up, heading back toward the river.

He had raped her savagely, without feeling, but now as he walked, carrying her, with her head lolling weakly against his chest, she was puzzled. He was almost gentle, and she began to cry again, tears streaming down her face. He had no right to be gentle. She hated him, hated the feel of his bare skin against her as he walked, hated everything about him. His pawing hands, his leering face. She didn't want him to be gentle. She wanted to scratch his eyes, tear at his ugly scalp lock, and spit in his face, but all she could do was lie in his arms, frustrated, her body warm against his as he carried her back to the river.

He set her down easily on a patch of grass beside her pile of clothes, then knelt before her on one knee. "I will help you put them on," he said softly, picking up her leggings, but she shook her head angrily, sniffing back the sobs.

"No!" she exclaimed, her voice a low, raspy protest. "No!" and she swallowed hard, breathing deeply, and moved her hand, reaching it out feebly toward him, and her hand closed on the leggings, grasping them desperately. "I'll put them on myself," and he let go, letting them drop, and she dragged them to her, wadding them up, holding them against her breasts, the anger she felt for him beginning to bring a new feeling of strength back into her body. Her shoulders drooped forward as she hugged the leggings, resting, recouping her strength, and all the while he stooped across from her, one knee on the ground, waiting.

Any minute she expected him to lash out and hit her for being too slow, but all he did was watch, his dark eyes studying her intently.

Finally she sighed, relieved as she felt her muscles begin to respond, and she moved wearily, one eye on Howling Wind, the other on what she was doing as she shuffled about clumsily on the ground, trying to pull on the leggings. He reached out as if to help her.

"Keep your dirty hands off me!" she spit out bitterly, and he shrugged, sitting back again on his heel, resting his arm across his knee as he watched. "Do you have to watch me?" she asked breathlessly, her body beginning to surge with life again as energy began to flow once more through her.

She rested for a few minutes again, then stood up gingerly, swaying a bit as she tried to steady herself and pull the leggings the rest of the way up at the same time. Her legs were wobbly, but she managed to pull them on all the way, fastening the waist, then started to reach for the shirt, almost falling on her face.

Howling Wind sprang forward and caught her, his arms circling her, and her flesh crawled at his touch.

"Don't!" she cried angrily, trying to wrench herself free, her eyes blazing as she stared at him wide-eyed. "Let me go!" and he obliged, straightening her first, putting the shirt in her hands, and she cringed, her face filled with loathing. "I hate you," she murmured softly. "I hate you," and she lifted the shirt, pulling it down over her head, panting from the effort. "You're nothing but an animal!" and she reached down slowly, picking up her moccasins.

He straightened, taking a deep breath, his face a vague blur in the darkness that surrounded them as she slipped on her moccasins. "I am a man," he answered, correcting her, then continued. "But before we return, I must make it clear that you will tell no one what I have done. If you do, I will deny it, telling them you try to make trouble. Do you understand?"

She stared at him. Oh, she understood, all right. It was her word against his, and what did it matter anyway if they did believe her? Who would punish him? He was the chief's brother. Her eyes narrowed. "I thought you made a vow," she said bitterly, and he frowned.

"It is none of your business what I did. I will do as I wish."

"So I see," she said, then let her hands fall to her sides, lifting her chin defiantly. "The others have to keep their vows, but the great Howling Wind is exempt, is that it?" she taunted angrily. "Did the Great Spirit tell you you didn't have to keep your vow, or did he give you a special dispensation or something?" and he took a step toward her, looking down into her face.

"You are right," he said huskily, his voice filled with emotion. "I should not have touched you, but I did, and now it is over." His voice deepened. "We will return to camp, lest I be tempted again," and she trembled.

He wouldn't, not again, and he saw the hesitation in her eyes.

"Do not push me too far, white woman," he said abruptly. "Once a vow is broken, there is no reason to continue to keep it, is there?" and she bit her lip, her eyes staring into his, and she swallowed hard.

"If you touch me again, I'll kill you," she warned fearfully. "Somehow, some way, I'll kill you," and he smiled smugly.

"Perhaps," he retorted. "Perhaps you will, then again, maybe I deserve it," and she frowned, taken by surprise.

"Wh-what do you mean?"

"As I said before, I am a man, not an animal, white woman. I have feelings, as you do, and maybe tonight for the first time I discovered that there is more to taking a woman than mounting her and spilling my seed. Your body has satisfied me like no other has ever done, and although I took you with anger and force, afterward, when the pleasure of your body filled me, I did not want to leave you. I wanted to stay with you and give you the pleasure I had received, but you would not let me. I have never felt this way before, and it puzzles me. Maybe it is the Great Spirit's way of punishing me for breaking my vow, I don't know, but I do know that if I take you again it will not be as it was tonight. You will not be forced. I will not hurt you. I will take you slowly, giving you the same pleasure you have given me," and she stared at him dumbfounded.

"I don't believe it," she exclaimed slowly, incredulously, as she gazed at him. "I just don't believe it. You think that after what you've done tonight I'd willingly let you take me again? You're insane! The only way you'll ever take me again, my brave warrior, is by force, do you understand?" Her voice lowered bitterly. "If you think a few tender words are going to make me forget what you've done to me, you're sadly mistaken. You're still the same man who humiliated and defiled me, and nothing you do or say will ever stop me from hating you!" Tears sprang to her eyes. Tears of anger and frustration. "The sooner we get to Niagara, the better," she said defensively. "I'd rather die a slow death beneath the knife of Thayendanegea than a slow death beneath the body of Howling Wind. Do you understand?" and his eyes narrowed.

"I do not like your words," he said solemnly.

"And I don't like what you did to me!"

His eyes flashed angrily as he stared at her. "We will return to camp," he said abruptly, straightening to full height, "and you will say nothing," and once more he was the same Howling Wind she was used to as he reached out, grabbing her arm and turning her toward camp.

He had given her a chance. He had offered and been rejected. He would forget the moments of tenderness he had felt for this woman. He would no longer be weak, and his eyes were once more hard and cold as he followed her back to the campfire and ordered Dark Morning to tie her hands and feet; then he moved off by himself, ignoring the heated looks he was getting from DeMosse, and moved to the other side of the fire and settled down. Tonight he would sleep well. There was no ache in his loins, no sweat on his brow. He was content, and he closed his eyes. Two more days and they'd reach the Niagara.

8

The air was thick with mosquitoes as the four horsemen made their way through the dense foliage, brushing aside limbs as they rode. Roth reached up and felt his chin. He'd been trying to keep himself clean-shaven, but the heat and humidity were doing their best to fight him, and he felt the dark stubble that was covering his face again.

"How much farther?" he asked as he let go his chin and called to the man ahead, and Jess turned in the saddle as he continued moving.

"About half a day's ride!"

Roth settled back and sighed. It had been over two weeks since Loedicia's capture, and his hopes were at a low ebb. They'd been moving as fast as possible, but the forests were so thick and dense, the trails so overgrown. It was going to take weeks to find her. That is, if she was still alive.

He glanced up ahead as Jess ducked, moving out from the tangle of trees into a small clearing where soft field grass carpeted the floor, with tiny wildflowers perking their heads up now and then.

Beyond the meadow was a line of hills resting in the early-afternoon sun, and Jess headed toward them with the other three close behind, maneuvering his horse into a pass that ran between the last two hills, and for the rest of the afternoon they rode along side by side in fairly open terrain.

It was late afternoon when the four of them disappeared again into a labyrinth of green trees and vines, still heading northeast; then suddenly, after about an hour's ride, Jess drew up and stopped, taking his bearings.

"Through here," he said, pointing off to his right, and they followed him again through a screen of trees into a small clearing.

Roth held his breath as he slowly moved his horse forward, then reined in, staring at the mess. It was still there. Rain had soaked it, wind had scattered it, and the sun parched it, but it was there.

Women's clothes were scattered from one end of the small clearing to the other, and Roth cursed softly to himself as he slid from his horse and stood looking around. He reached down and picked up what was left of the gold dress, staring at it, frowning, then crumpled it in his hand.

"The Cherokee don't have no use for pretty dresses," said Jess as he dismounted, standing beside Roth; then Jess moved over to the cold remains of what was once the fire, bending down to pick up a piece of paper.

"What is it?" asked Beau, bending forward, leaning one elbow on the front of his saddle, and Jess looked up.

"I think it's what's left of the papers DeMosse was carrying," he said as he unfolded it, then glanced down.

He was right. There were bits and pieces of words on the charred paper. Not enough to make sense, but enough to identify them. He bent over, picking up some more pieces, unfolding them and studying them, then shook his head, letting them flutter from his fingers, back to the ground. "Five thousand dollars shot to hell just like that," he said as he watched the charred bits of paper land on the cold ashes of the dead fire.

Beau got off his horse, followed closely by Heath, and they began to study the area, circling it, checking for footprints, but there were none, the weather having obliterated them.

"But there's one thing," said Heath as he pointed a short distance away to where the remains of horse droppings lay on the ground.

Beau stepped past the droppings and over a log at the edge of the clearing, then stood staring off into the woods. There were a number of broken branches on the underbrush, some trampled ferns just starting to come back to life, and a few rocks disturbed from their resting place. He moved farther on, seeing small signs here and there.

"They went this way," he yelled back toward the clearing, and Jess laughed.

"Sure as hell beats me how a man who can catch a trail that easy ended up on a sailing ship," he said, and Beau's head jerked up as he glanced at him. Jess hadn't questioned Beau's identity on the trip so far, but now his curiosity had gotten the best of him. "How is it the son of an Indian chief prefers to sail a privateer for the French, anyway?" he asked.

Beau retraced his steps back to the clearing. "My grandfather was a Frenchman, Jess," he answered slowly.

"That explains part of it," said Jess, "but you was raised Injun, had to be. Forgive an old man's curiosity, son, but I've been wonderin' all the way up here and ain't had the nerve to ask—how come you seem more white man than Injun?"

Beau frowned, as if he didn't want to answer, then shrugged. "I went to school in Philadelphia. Colonel Locke and his wife sent me."

"Colonel Locke?" Jess was puzzled. "You mean Quinn Locke, the man the Injuns call Yellow Hair?"

"That's right."

Jess scowled, his mind working fast. "You said you was the son of a Tuscarora chief—you Telakonquinaga's son?"

"That's right."

"Holy Jesus!" Jess scratched his head. "I met that one. You got a pa to be proud of, son."

Beau's face reddened and he looked uncomfortable.

"What's the matter, ain't you proud of him?"

"Jess, I think it'd be best to drop the subject," said Heath as he stepped up beside Beau, and Jess studied Beau for a second, then laughed.

"So it's that way, huh? Well, don't worry, son," he said, "there's lotsa fellas don't see eye to eye with their pas, you know. Why'd you think I took to the trail? I was seventeen when I lit out from home. Been in the woods ever since. Ain't nothin' to be ashamed of."

"He gets along fine with his father," stated Heath, irritated with Jess's probing, but Jess wouldn't let the subject drop.

"Then if it ain't that . . ." Suddenly he half-frowned, his gray eyes wrinkling at the corners. "That's it, ain't it?" he exclaimed, then tried to reassure Beau. "It's 'cause you're part Injun. Hell, son, don't let bein' part Injun bother you. There's lotsa good men got Injun blood."

"I'm not part Indian, Jess," said Beau, his eyes darkening. "I'm three-quarters Indian. There's a difference. My father's got four wives and between them there are eighteen children, including myself, and all of them look Indian except me. So don't try telling me it doesn't matter. I've had to live with it, you haven't. At least as Captain Thunder no one has to know what I am and I don't have to account to anyone but myself, and for Christ's sake," he complained as he looked at the older man, "will you quit calling me 'son.' It's irritating as all hell. Call me 'Captain,' or 'Beau,' or anything but 'son.' "

Jess grinned sheepishly as his eyes met the younger man's. "Sorry, son . . . I mean, Beau," he corrected himself, "I'll try to remember." Then his face grew more serious as he turned to Roth. "Seen enough?" he asked as Roth, who'd been poking through the scattered clothing and boxes, approached him, and Roth nodded.

"Any ideas where they took them?" he asked.

"Could be. Cherokee don't generally move this far south. There's a big spread of them up at Chattahoochee. Most likely come down from there. But I can't figure out why they'd take them prisoner and not scalp 'em right here. Don't make sense."

Beau frowned. It didn't make sense, unless . . . "Would the Cherokee be working for the British?" he asked. "Mr. Minette said it was a possibility," but Jess shook his head.

"Hell, he don't know nothin' bout Injuns." His face reddened as Beau's eyes hardened, and he hesitated, then went on. "In the first place, the Cherokee are too far from the British. Now, if it was the Shawnee, Miami, or one of them, I'd say yes. But the Cherokee are too far east, and then, them papers . . ." He nodded his head toward the charred remains in the fire. "If the British had hired the Cherokee to find DeMosse and stop him, they would have been instructed to bring back any papers that were found. No." He scratched his head. "I think it's something else."

"Could they have found out who my mother was?" asked Heath suddenly. "Would that have made a difference?"

"Your mother?" Jess laughed, shaking his head. "Hardly, lad," he said. "Now, what the hell use would they have for an English countess?" and he stopped laughing suddenly as Roth, Heath, and Beau exchanged knowing glances.

"She is a countess, ain't she?" he asked. "She said she was a countess, and you said . . ." He glanced quickly at Roth.

"I said she's the woman I'm planning to marry," he said softly, "the mother of my son, and she is a countess, but she's also the widow of Colonel Quinn Locke, the man you said the Indians called Yellow Hair. Would that make a difference?" and he saw the shocked expression on Jess's face.

"She's . . . ?" He stared at them, then swallowed hard. "You mean I was . . . I was riding with Quinn's wife and I didn't even know it?"

"You knew him?" asked Heath.

"Off and on over the years I did, sure. I bumped into him

here and there. We was always on the same side. Fought with him in a few frontier battles during the war. Rode with him that time we almost caught Joseph Brant, chasing him clear back to the Niagara. Quinn wanted me to stop by the fort afterward, but I headed east instead. Never did meet his wife. Remember him talkin' about her, though." He looked at Heath, his eyes questioning, then glanced at Roth, and Roth knew what he was thinking.

"It's not like that at all," Roth said, not wanting him to misunderstand. "I married her when we both thought Quinn had been killed. A natural mistake, but a rather unfortunate one for her. He showed up later alive, but the damage had already been done."

"I'm the damage," said Heath.

Roth scowled. "I didn't mean it that way."

Heath smiled at his father. "I know," he said, "but Quinn felt that way." He looked at Jess. "I was raised as Quinn Locke's son, Jess," he explained. "Beau and I grew up together, and the 'damage' wasn't discovered until I began to look like my real father."

"Well, I'll be damned," said Jess. "You never know, do you?" He straightened, looking about the clearing as he scowled. "That could explain things," he said, "but I don't know why they'd have a reason for taking her if Quinn's dead."

"Few people know he's dead except us," explained Heath. "That might make a difference."

Jess scratched his chin as he stared across the clearing at the clothing and other debris scattered about, and he sighed. "It could be." He pondered. "But then . . . oh, hell, it don't really make sense. Most of the Cherokee want peace, except a few like Great Oak and Bleeding Fox. Yet, maybe . . ."

"Maybe what?" asked Beau.

Jess's hand dropped from his chin. "I don't know how much you know of what's goin' on in the Northwest Territory," he said, "but General Wayne's got forts built all along the Ohio River and all the way to the Little Miami, right under the nose of the British, and I've heard rumor that Fort Presque Isle, Fort Locke, Fort Pitt, and the others are all going to throw in their hand when the big push starts. They want the Injuns to sign a treaty to move their boundary from the Ohio farther west, and if I know the Injuns, they ain't gonna do it. Now, if the Injuns knew who the lady was and thought they could hold her hostage to keep Fort Locke out of it . . . it'd be one less enemy to fight, and it's in a strategic spot if Brant and the British decided to join in."

"But how could the Cherokee, who've never seen my mother, know who she was?" asked Heath, and Beau put his hand on Heath's arm.

"Jess may be right, Heath," he offered. "I just thought. The summer before you and I left Fort Locke, I remember a group of Cherokee stopping at the fort to powwow with my father. The colonel wasn't there, so your mother greeted them as usual in his place. They could have seen her then and remembered." His eyes shone, amused. "Let's face it, Heath," he went on, "your mother's a woman not easily forgotten, even by Indians," and Heath's face reddened beneath his dark curling hair.

Why did Beau have to keep reminding him? It was hard enough having a mother who looked like Loedicia did; did he have to rub it in? Why couldn't she be like other mothers, plump and matronly?

"Do you know how to get to this Chatta . . . whatever it is?" Roth asked Jess, trying to spare Heath's embarrassment.

"I think rather than head right for Chattahoochee we better follow the trail Beau spotted off there," he said, pointing behind Beau and Heath. "I have a feeling the chiefs at Chattahoochee aren't in on this. If we lose the trail, then we'll head for Bleeding Fox first. He's just south of Chattachoochee about forty miles, and if she ain't there we can circle up east toward Great Oak's camp, pulling back around to Chattachoochee if we have to, but they may have left a good trail. I don't think they was expectin' to be followed," and he headed toward his horse. "Shall we mount up, gents, we've got about three or four hours' ridin' before dark hits us," and they followed him to their horses, taking one last look at the small clearing before heading out.

Jess asked Beau to take the lead, since his eyes seemed to be a bit better at spotting the trail, but even then the going was slow, and there were times Beau was sure he'd lost it, then sighed as he picked it up again.

"It seems to be fresher now," he said one afternoon some days later as he saw the outline of a hoofprint across a fallen leaf. "I imagine the Cherokee are riding and making their prisoners walk. That gives us an advantage. We're all on horses and can make better time," and it was some three days later that Jess stopped them on the top of a small rise, early one morning, and pointed ahead to what looked like an open trail between two large hills dense with pine.

"Through that pass is Chief Bleeding Fox's village," he said as he maneuvered his horse so he was hidden more by the underbrush, then cautioned them to do the same, and Roth saw why.

As they watched, a group of some eight Cherokee made their way through the pass, scouting the trees and hills ahead, moving cautiously. They were all on foot, and the morning mists, still lingering in the low pass, swirled about them and upward, melting into the sun that was topping the horizon. They watched the warriors circle the base of the hill, then head northward, eyes alert for game or anything else that might be around, then Roth looked at Jess.

"What now?"

"Now we decide. Do we all go in, or just one of us?"

"I go in," said Beau, and they all turned to look at him.

"Why you?" asked Jess.

"Because I have a breechclout with me, and now that you mention Bleeding Fox, I remember his brother Howling Wind was with the elders that stopped at my father's village that day. We spent a whole afternoon together. It was four years ago, but I think he'll remember."

Jess rubbed his chin as he stared at Beau, then nodded. "You're probably right. Bleeding Fox hates white men, and it'd give him pleasure to get his hands on us, but tell me," he said, dropping his hand to the reins once more, "what kind of a story you plan to tell them?"

"It all depends on whether Mrs. Locke is alive or dead," he said, and saw Roth grimace. He reached in his saddlebag and pulled out a breechclout, then slipped from his horse. "Excuse me, gentlemen, while I change," he said, and darted behind some bushes. A few minutes later he reappeared carrying his buckskins, rolling them into a ball. "I could probably have worn the buckskins," he said as he wrapped them tighter, "but they don't have the same effect."

"They certainly don't," said Roth, surprised at the transformation.

The breechclout he wore was beaded with intricate designs and fringed, barely covering him, with his sheath and knife at his waist, and he wore a different pair of moccasins with the same beading on them. His chest was bare, but as they watched, he reached in his saddlebag and pulled out a huge medallion on a chain, setting it around his neck; then he took a conglomeration of feathers out and straightened them, fastening them in the top of his hair.

"Ordinarily most Tuscaroras have a round scalp lock

directly on top of their head, opposed to the lengthwise one of the Cherokee," he explained to Roth as he fastened the feathers and beaded band down securely. "But my father always let me wear my hair the white man's way. Colonel Locke's influence, I presume. Howling Wind should remember it."

Roth gestured to his attire, his face puzzled. "Are all these significant?" he asked, and Beau glanced at him in surprise, forgetting for a moment that Roth had spent most of his years in the East.

"The clothes, no. The medallion, yes. Without it I'm only another Indian," he answered. "With it, I'm the son of a Tuscarora chief."

Roth frowned. "I hate having you go in there alone," he said. "I feel like a coward staying out here."

"Don't," said Jess. "Beau's right. We'd only be signing our death warrants if we went in there. This way we have a chance to learn what's what."

"And if she's alive in there?" asked Roth.

"Then the lad'll keep his eyes open on the lay of things and we'll figure a way to get her out."

Beau looked at Jess, annoyed. "Jess," he said disgustedly, "will you quit referring to me as a lad? I'm a grown man with a ship of my own and a crew of bloodthirsty privateers, and I could string you up by the ears if I had a mind to," and Jess laughed.

"Oh, hell, Beau, maybe you can trick them swashbucklers you sail with into thinkin' you're hard as nails, mean as hell, and made of stone, and maybe you look like a ferocious savage in that getup, but you can't fool an old backwoodsman like me. No sirree. And don't you go worryin' if I forget and call you 'lad' or 'son' once't in a while. I don't mean nothin' by it, I just got a poor memory, that's all. And at my age everybody downside of thirty's a young'un," and Beau couldn't help it. He broke into a slow grin.

"There, what'd I tell you," said Jess, and Beau straightened his coup belt, turned, taking the saddle from his horse, then leaped easily onto his back.

"You're an ornery old coot, Jess Willoughby," Beau said as he bent over and reached almost to the ground from the horse's back and grabbed his rifle where it hung on the saddle and hefted it over his shoulder, then straightened, grabbing his horse's reins. "But just you and Heath take care of Roth here while I'm gone, you hear me, so if she is in there she has something left to come back to. And don't worry if I'm in there a couple of days or more. It may take a while," and he tipped his hand to his forehead in a farewell gesture, then dug his horse in the ribs and disappeared among the trees.

"He's a strange one, that young man," said Jess as Beau disappeared from sight. "But I guess I'd be a strange one too if I had to live with what he has to live with."

Heath retrieved Beau's saddle, deposited it in front of him on his horse; then the other two mounted and they turned their horses about and made for a good spot to sit down and stay put.

Beau moved easily with the horse, making his way down the well-worn path to the village. It'd been three years since he'd had a breechclout on, and it felt strange to be a part of it all again. How different the land was from the water. How different the bark huts spread out before him from the cities of the world he had been to.

He saw a movement near one of the huts some distance away as he rode along, then another, and as he drew closer the path was lined with men, women, and children staring at him curiously. He reined in as a tall warrior who looked more impressive than the others stood in his path.

"I wish to see your chief, Bleeding Fox," he said in their own language as he spoke from the horse's back.

"Wait here," he said, and Beau crossed his hands in front of him, waiting while the man turned and walked off.

The others were quiet, just staring at him, mumbling among themselves, but Beau didn't mind. He watched straight ahead to where the man had disappeared, then sighed a few minutes later as he returned.

"Chief Bleeding Fox will see you," he said as he approached. "Come." Then he turned, walking back the way he had come, with Beau, still on his horse, following close at his heels. They stopped before a log hut and Beau dismounted.

"In here," the Cherokee said, and motioned ahead of him.

Beau entered the hut and squinted, adjusting his eyes to the dim light inside. A large Indian sat cross-legged on the floor, smoking his pipe, his face unsmiling, eyes curiously alive. He took the pipe from his mouth and spoke.

"And what does the son of a Tuscarora chief want in the camp of the Cherokee?" he asked solemnly, and Beau straightened, flexing his chest muscles, showing his strength.

"I am Wild Thunder, son of Telakonquinaga, chief of the Okswego Tuscarora," he said as he watched the startled expression in the man's eyes. "I would ask if the chief's brother Howling Wind is in the village. I met him some time ago in my father's camp and at that time I expressed a wish to leave the north country and he suggested I join the Cherokee in driving the white man from our lands."

Bleeding Fox was staring at him dumbfounded, the pipe completely forgotten.

"Now that Colonel Locke is dead," Beau went on, "my father has consented to let me choose the road I would walk without interference, and I choose to fight against the white-eyes," and he watched Bleeding Fox trying to compose himself.

The Indian set the pipe aside, his face darkening. "What is this you say of Yellow Hair?" he asked abruptly, and Beau tried to feign bewilderment.

"Yellow Hair?" he asked, and Bleeding Fox stood up.

"You said Yellow Hair is dead. This cannot be so."

Beau scowled. "But it is so. He and his squaw went to England, and on their return their ship was fired on by what the white man calls privateers. Quinn Locke was killed and his woman disappeared. Word of this reached our village some time ago from the white man's chief in the city they call Philadelphia."

"But that can't be," stated Bleeding Fox, his voice shaking. "If he is not Yellow Hair . . . who is he?"

"Who is who?" asked Beau.

Bleeding Fox stood perfectly still for a long time, staring toward the open door of the hut; then he turned slowly and looked at Beau. "Howling Wind is on his way north to Thayendanegea with Yellow Hair's squaw and a man who claims he is Yellow Hair," he said angrily. "He is to trade them to Thayendanegea for his support in our war against the white-eyes. But if he is not Yellow Hair . . ."

"Who did she say he is?" asked Beau, trying to look upset.

"She called him by a name, DeMosse." He clenched his fist. "But he said he was Yellow Hair."

Beau was pleased, yet troubled. At least they were alive, but it would take some doing to catch up to them.

"When did he leave?" asked Beau, and Bleeding Fox's dark eyes studied him hard for a minute, but he didn't speak. "Perhaps I could overtake him and let him know the truth," explained Beau. "I would not wish my friend Howling Wind to be made a fool by Thayendanegea."

Bleeding Fox continued thinking things over; then: "We will use the drums," he said.

"The drums? Do you want the whole northwest to know Howling Wind has been a fool?" asked Beau. "If I leave now and move fast, I can catch up to him if you will tell me the trail he took and when he left."

Bleeding Fox still wasn't convinced. He was uneasy. After all, what if this was a trick, too. This young man, although wearing the clothes of a chief's son, did not look Indian. "You are sure of what you say?" he asked suspiciously.

Beau puffed his chest out, looking disgruntled, his face rigid, green eyes staring directly into the eyes of the man before him. "You would question the word of Wild Thunder?" he asked boldly. "I am the son of a chief. My word is true. I came here as a friend."

"And how can I be sure you are as you claim?" Bleeding Fox asked. "You do not look like an Indian, though you speak like one and wear the clothes of a chief's son."

"Where else would I get the clothes of a chief's son but from my father?" he replied.

"You say you are from Fort Locke. Then how is it you did not meet Howling Wind on the trail?"

Beau thought quickly. It was obvious that Howling Wind, hauling prisoners, would take the shortest route. "I took the shore trail and came down the Sandusky," he answered, and Bleeding Fox nodded.

"Howling Wind went through the Buffalo Swamp to the Chautauqua." He shook his head. "But it still seems strange this man would claim to be Yellow Hair."

"If he hadn't claimed to be Yellow Hair, what would you have done to him?"

"We would have killed him."

"Isn't that enough reason to claim he is someone he is not, to keep himself alive?"

"Your words make sense," answered Bleeding Fox. "But I do not like them."

"Nor do I like what has happened. My horse is fast. Perhaps I can reach him in time."

"They left six moons ago with twenty of our warriors. You will leave tomorrow with two of my braves to accompany you—that is, if you are who you say you are," and Beau's eyes narrowed. Now what did he have in mind?

Bleeding Fox walked to the door of the hut and whispered something to the Indian who had brought Beau to him, then walked back to Beau. "There is a warrior here who was with Howling Wind and Dark Morning when they accompanied some of the elders from Chattahoochee north to your father's camp," he said arrogantly. "If Straight Pine recognizes you

173

as Wild Thunder, then you shall leave at dawn and he will go with you along with White Wolf."

"And if he happens to have forgotten me after four years?"

Bleeding Fox smiled. "Then as a chief's son you will not be afraid to prove yourself," and Beau tried not to let the expression in his face change as his mouth went dry.

He'd seen more than one man die proving himself at his father's hands, and he wondered what Bleeding Fox would have planned for him. Whatever it was, it wouldn't be pleasant, and for the first time in his life he was glad he had been raised an Indian, because he knew he could live through whatever lay ahead.

He was fortunate, however. Straight Pine not only remembered him, but remembered that he had been one of his father's favored sons, sitting at the council fire with him while he talked with the elders.

"Something we were not allowed to do," Straight Pine said jealously. "I remember Howling Wind pointing out to me that Wild Thunder sat at his father's right hand, indicating he would be chief at his father's death."

"This is true?" asked Bleeding Fox, and Beau's face reddened.

It was true. His father had discussed it with him many times, but how was he to make his father understand? How could he lead a tribe of people he wasn't really a part of?

"Yes, it was true once," he replied. "But I'm afraid it is no more. If I were to go back now, I would probably find my brother Two Crows sitting at my father's right hand," and what he said, he felt, was the truth. By now his father would know he had no intention of returning, and for a moment the thought hurt.

Bleeding Fox was pleased with Straight Pine's words and made his apology to Beau for doubting him, then called everyone together to honor their visitor, telling them of the white man's deception and the part Wild Thunder would play in ending it, and the rest of the day was spent entertaining him with horse racing, games, and dancing, with a huge feast setting the mood for a hot, breathless night.

Beau licked the venison from his fingers and tasted the roast corn, newly peeled from its husk, savoring the flavor as he thought of Roth, Jess, and Heath sitting somewhere in the woods, pulling on jerky with only the mosquitoes for company. The feast was topped off with a plum pudding thick with nuts, and corn popped white and frothy then saturated in honey to nibble on while the dancers performed.

The food was good, but he ate sparingly, knowing too much food after the sparse fare he'd had on the trail would give him a stomachache. He glanced about as he finished eating, taking in the scene before him. How familiar it was. All too familiar, and he felt a gnawing anger inside him. He'd left all this behind, and now here he was right in the middle of it again. Then he thought of Loedicia and straightened stoically. She was Heath's and Rebel's mother, but she'd been like a mother to him so many times, and he almost smiled as he thought of Heath. How often Heath had complained that his mother didn't act like a mother. If only he knew how fortuante he was to have her for a mother; then, thinking of Loedicia made him think of Rebel, and he sighed. That was behind him. It was no more, yet he couldn't forget her. He'd never forget her. How did you forget someone you loved so much?

Suddenly he stirred as the drums began beating, their beat driving deep into his memory, and he tensed. He hated those drums. Hated the memories they brought back, but he couldn't let it show on his face. Instead, he looked pleased, turning toward Bleeding Fox.

The man was sitting next to him, his head bobbing to the beat of the drums, and he smiled back at Beau, then lifted his hand, motioning for the dancers to begin.

Beau had seen this same scene a thousand times as he grew up. Men and women stomping the ground to the savage beat of the drum, losing themselves in the rhythm until their surroundings had no existence beyond the labyrinth of their minds. It was insanity to him. The drums had never had a meaning for him, even when he was very young. When he'd been forced to dance to their rhythm it had been an alien act. Now, as he watched the dancers, listening to their weird cries of ecstasy, angry at their nonsensical childlike actions, seething inside, he noticed one dancer who seemed different from the others.

Her movements were more stilted, less abandoned, and her eyes continually sought him out as she danced about the fire with the others. She was young, perhaps not yet seventeen, and there was the hint of a smile about her mouth whenever her eyes met his.

He glanced quickly at the other dancers; not one of them even knew he existed anymore, so engrossed were they in the frantic beat of the drums. As she moved to this side of the fire again, her eyes still sought his and her arms moved over her head gracefully. The tilt came again to the corners of her mouth as she swayed, then let her body dip to the beat, continuing on.

He was curious, and watched her, his forehead creased into a frown; then suddenly a thought swept over him, and he felt a strange, sickening feeling inside as he remembered, and he turned toward Bleeding Fox reluctantly, seeing the smile that still lit his face, and he knew he was right. There was no need to even ask about her.

After a while the drums stopped and the dancers with them, each in a different grotesque pose. All except the young woman he'd been watching. She knelt prostrate now before him, her arms stretched out as if paying him homage, her head bowed low at his feet.

"Take her," said Bleeding Fox as Beau turned to him. "She is yours. A virgin to send you on your journey, to bring you luck that you may reach Howling Wind before it is too late," and Beau looked down, staring at the girl. He'd been right. She was his for the night, and he didn't want her.

She lifted her head and looked directly at him, her dark sloe eyes intent on his face. For an Indian she was prettier than average. The bridge of her nose smaller than most, her face almost heart-shaped.

"You are disappointed?" asked Bleeding Fox, seeing the look on Beau's face that he was having a hard time trying to conceal.

"No . . . not at all," Beau answered, saving the situation. "I am very pleased, only surprised that you see fit to present me with a maiden so lovely," and Bleeding Fox smiled as the girl rose from the ground, sitting back on her heels.

Beau knew what was expected of him next, so he stood up, holding his hand out to her. She put her hand in his and stood up. She was short, like Rebel, barely reaching his shoulder, but there the resemblance stopped.

"I will show you to your lodgings," she said shyly, her voice soft and melodious, and Beau glanced quickly at Bleeding Fox, then back to the girl.

"Could we take a walk down by the lake first?" he asked, wanting to delay what he knew was expected of him, and thinking of no other way.

She smiled. "If you wish."

They moved from the circle of warriors, who were still unwinding from their frenzied dance, and strolled along between the lodges and on down to the path that led through the trees to the lake. The moon was up now, its silvery light making a mirror of the water as they approached, turning the trees on its banks to a wonderland of silver. Neither of them had spoken as they walked the long path to the lake, but now finally Beau broke the silence.

"What do they call you?" he asked, and she swallowed, her voice timid.

"I am Gray Dawn."

"You came into the world in the morning?"

She smiled at him shyly. "Yes, and you during a storm. Is that not so?"

He turned and looked down at her, but this time her eyes fell before his. "Yes," he said, "I was born during a storm."

He studied her for a minute, her eyes still staring downward, her face shadowed. She was frightened. He was sure of it, and now that he was closer, she looked even younger than he'd thought. God, it was hot tonight! The air was still, not a breeze stirring. He looked out over the water.

"Do you swim in the lake?" he asked abruptly, and she nodded.

"Oh, yes." Her eyes raised to his once more. "Do you wish to swim?"

"I wish to swim," he said. "The night is very warm and I would cool off before we go to your lodge," and he stepped quickly to the water's edge, unfastened the band of feathers from his head, dropping them on the ground, then stepped in, wading out to his knees, where he plunged in headfirst, feeling the cool water caress his body. He swam a few strokes, then surfaced, standing up, glad to feel the bottom of the lake beneath his feet. The water was a little over waist-deep, and he wiped the hair from his eyes, then looked toward shore. His heart skipped a beat as his eyes fell on the girl silhouetted in the moonlight.

She was stark naked, her clothes back on the bank, and she was up to her knees already in the water as she waded toward him. Then, with the ease of an otter she was in the water, swimming, her arms moving with even strokes. She drew up to him and stood up facing him, water dripping from her face.

"I too was hot," was all she said, but the invitation was there in her voice, and as he watched, she flipped backward in the water, the moonlight playing down her body, across her full young breasts, giving a hint of her young curves just before she disappeared beneath the surface.

He plunged in after her, and for the next few minutes they

177

swam side by side, cavorting in the water like children, splashing one another and laughing; then suddenly he stood up and watched her swim toward him, and something stirred inside him.

She was no longer an Indian maiden swimming toward him, she was Rebel, and this wasn't some lonely lake in the middle of nowhere, it was the shores of Lake Erie, and he sighed, his memory bringing it all back to him. He felt his heart start pounding, the blood beginning to race in his veins.

Gray Dawn burst forward out of the water, her arms raised above her head, water dripping from her rosy nipples, and he let out a sharp cry as he grabbed her, pulling her toward him. He flung her up, cradling her in his arms, and urgently moved toward shore, while she lay passively, staring at the intense look on his face. He stepped ashore and moved to a spot screened from the world by low-hanging bushes and laid her gently in the grass, and his hand moved, cupping her breast. The nipple hardened as he stroked it gently; then his hand moved, open, across her flat stomach, to the patch of hair below it, and his fingers kneaded her urgently.

"I am frightened," the girl whispered softly from out of the darkness that surrounded them, and suddenly he froze, his fingers still on her, and his voice was husky.

"I'm sorry. I didn't mean to frighten you," he said, and moved his hand, resting it on her hip, smoothing the skin beneath it.

"I have never had a man," she said, and he nodded.

"I know."

"But it is my wish to please you," and he turned away from her, looking out of the darkened shadows to where the lake was bathed in moonlight.

How like her. It was what she'd been taught, as were all Indian women. She was there to please him. What of her pleasure? He turned back, looking down into her face, barely visible in the darkness.

"And how about your pleasure?" he asked softly. "Don't you want anything from tonight, or are you content to lie here unconcerned and let me do what I will?"

Gray Dawn was puzzled. She had never heard her brothers or the other men of the village speaking of pleasing their mates. And the women. Most of them hated when their husbands bedded them. It was the duty the women did to please them. But now this warrior . . . he wanted to know if he could please her.

"Do you really mean what you say?" she asked timidly,

and his hand moved up her hip, gently caressing her stomach, to her breast, and he leaned over, his tongue on the end of her nipple, touching it lovingly, and she sighed, feeling strange sensations tingling through her.

"Does that please you?" he asked, and she felt her body grow warm inside.

"Oh, yes."

"And what else would you have me do to please you?"

She reached out and touched his face. She had noted the deep green of his eyes earlier. "You have lived near the white-eyes for a long time, have you not?" she asked.

"Yes."

"You know their ways?"

"Yes."

"Then you will know what they do." She hesitated, then went on. "When Howling Wind brought the man who said he was Yellow Hair and his woman to us, he said there is an act the white man performs before he takes a woman," she whispered passionately. "He said the man puts his mouth to the woman's mouth, and it is called kissing. He said the white man was doing this to Yellow Hair's squaw when they attacked, and that's why he was sure he was her mate. I have never before heard of this kissing. It would please me if you would show me what it is like," she finished, and he let her words sink in.

DeMosse was kissing Loedicia? How could that . . . ? Momentarily he forgot the girl beneath him as he thought of Roth.

"That's all right, you don't have to," Gray Dawn was saying as he shook himself back to what he was doing, and he sighed.

"Oh . . . no, Gray Dawn," he apologized, "I was thinking of something else. I'd be pleased to show you what a kiss is," and he bent down, his mouth touching hers, and his hand moved once more on her breast. He had to go through with it. If she was still a virgin when morning came, he'd be laughed out of the village and she'd be shamed among her tribe for not pleasing him.

Her mouth was soft beneath his, unmoving at first; then his tongue moved out, touching her lips lightly, and he felt her respond. His hand stroked more firmly and his mouth sipped at hers deeply, over and over again, until she moaned beneath him.

His mouth eased on hers ever so slightly. "What do you

think of the white man's kiss?" he said against her lips, and her arms went about his neck, her body arching upward.

"Do what you will to me, Wild Thunder," she whispered, her body on fire. "I am no longer afraid," and he reached down, slipping the breechclout off, and he moved over her, caught in the throes of the passion he'd been denying himself for so long, and he made love to her as if she were Rebel, wanting her to be Rebel, and it wasn't until afterward as he lay above her and felt her hands stroking the muscles of his back that he remembered she wasn't Rebel, and he let out a hoarse sob as he slipped from her body, and lay on his back in the grass beside her, staring out into the night that was now filled with stars.

Gray Dawn lay beside him, her body still tingling wildly from his passionate lovemaking, and she too stared up at the star-filled sky, and she was puzzled.

"Wild Thunder?" she asked breathlessly, her voice trembling. "Why do not the women of the village willingly enjoy pleasing their mates?" she asked innocently, and suddenly he realized what he'd done.

In his eagerness to try to capture what he'd once had with Rebel, he'd made love to her, not as an Indian made love, quickly, for his own pleasure, but as a white man makes love, not only for his own pleasure, but to please his mate, and he cursed softly to himself. How could he make her understand? What a fool he'd been.

She raised up and looked down into his face, her eyes warm and languid. "You have kissed as the white man has before, haven't you?" she asked, and he nodded.

"Yes."

"I like it."

He reached up, putting his hand in her dark hair, pulling her mouth down to his. "So do I," he said, and kissed her again, the warmth of her kiss running through him. "You'll have to teach the warriors of the village to kiss you like this," he said, but she shook her head.

"They will not."

"How can you be sure?"

"I know." Her eyes looked deeply into his again as she studied him. "They are not like you," she said softly. "You have white man's blood in your veins."

He tensed, his hand still in her hair. "What makes you say that?"

"Your eyes, they are green. Besides, you did not hurt me when you took me, as the warriors hurt my friends. But don't worry. I will tell no one of your white blood. If you had wanted them to know, you would have told them." She smiled as her finger touched his bare chest, making circles on it. "Would you like to stay here tonight rather than going to the lodge?" she asked, and he smiled back.

"Why not?" and she bent down, kissing him again, and his arms went around her as he tried to forget a mane of flowing blond hair and violet eyes that made his heart ache and tore him apart inside.

He woke the next morning to her whisper in his ear. "It will soon be light," she said. "You are to leave at dawn," and he opened his eyes and looked at her small face nestled in the crook of his arm. He started to move, to put on his breechclout, covering himself, but she stopped him. "Please, before you go," she pleaded, her young voice caressing his ear, "kiss me once more and let me feel you inside me," and he frowned.

My God, what had he done? She'd never be satisfied with these selfish warriors again. He should have left well enough alone.

She reached down and touched him, and he groaned, feeling himself begin to harden. The sky was still dark enough, gray shadows hanging among the trees. What difference did it make? And he pulled her to him, kissing her again, bringing his body back to surging life once more.

Later, as Beau stood next to his horse, preparing to leave, with Straight Pine and White Wolf at his side, Bleeding Fox stood before him wishing him well; then: "Did Gray Dawn please you?" he asked matter-of-factly, as they prepared to mount, and Beau nodded, trying not to blush as he gazed out at the crowd standing around them, singling out Gray Dawn's sloe eyes as they stared longingly at him.

"She pleased me far more than I expected," he said, and saw her smile proudly as he turned and mounted, and he smiled back. His words had sealed her honor, and now the only thing she'd worry about would be trying to convince the man who claimed her that kissing and taking a woman the white man's way was better.

He whirled his horse, and the three riders moved off between the huts, past the vegetable fields, and into the pass that led between the hills. As they moved along, making their way along the worn trail, Beau prayed his ruse would work. He'd discovered that because few white men ever ventured this far, they kept no guards on the pass between the hills, and the warriors that had left yesterday morning had been heading on a week's journey to Chattahoochee to learn the sentiments of the Cherokee there regarding the white man's bid for peace.

He let Straight Pine be first out of the pass, White Wolf second, and he brought up the rear. As he moved past a large gnarled tree and into the open, he reined up, his face rigid as he looked directly toward the hill where he knew his three friends were waiting.

"Wait!" he called to Straight Pine, his voice eager, eyes intent on the hill, and both warriors turned, moving their mounts in close.

"What is it?" asked Straight Pine, and Beau pointed toward the hill.

"I saw something move up there." He pointed about halfway up. "I'm sure it was a man."

Straight Pine frowned. "I saw nothing." He looked at White Wolf. "And you?"

White Wolf was short, stocky, a white streak at the front of his scalp lock, his dark eyes slanted more than most, while Straight Pine was typical, with his flat nose and wide mouth.

"I saw nothing," answered White Wolf.

"Well, I did," insisted Beau. "If you want to wait here, I'll take a quick look."

Both Indians shrugged as they settled back on their horses.

"Go right ahead," said Straight Pine, "we'll wait for you here," and Beau nodded.

It took him less than ten minutes to locate Roth, Jess, and Heath, but as he rode into the clearing where they were waiting, he cautioned them quickly to stay put on the ground without moving, and he stayed on his horse, moving first this way, then that, back and forth among the trees as he talked, pretending to be looking for someone or something.

All three men stayed motionless in the shadows as Beau rode back and forth, giving them instructions, trying to keep the back of his head toward the warriors down at the pass so they wouldn't see he was talking; then finally he dug his horse in the ribs and turned, cantering back down the hill.

"I guess I'm seeing things," he said as he joined his companions. "Let's go," and they circled the foot of the hill, heading up the trail.

Jess laughed as they watched the three horsemen disappear up ahead; then he slapped his hat on his head as he reached for his horse's reins and untied them from the small tree where he'd been tethered. "Didn't I tell you that lad was smart?" he said to Roth as he pulled his horse around and mounted, then watched as Roth and Heath both got into the saddle. "He had one chance in a million to pull this off."

"And yet you let him go in there," exclaimed Roth. "You knew they might kill him!"

"Hell's fire, they might kill us too if we don't hush up and hightail it out of here," he replied. "You heard the lad. There's four of us and two of them, and they'll be sleepin' heavy when they camp tonight, and that should be far enough up the trail from Bleedin' Fox's village that he won't get wise. If we was to kill them two here, so close, the buzzards would lead Bleedin' Fox to 'em afore we got over the next hill. No sirree, the lad's right, so let's go," and they moved out slow and easy, following the trail the three horsemen up ahead left.

Beau was pleased. They'd traveled almost thirty miles since sunup and were moving faster than he'd expected. He just hoped Jess, Roth, and Heath could keep up. Their horses had already come a long piece and weren't any too fresh after only a day's rest. The horses his companions were riding were fresh and young, enjoying the fast pace they were forced to keep.

They camped in a wooded area when dark came, and it must have been close to morning when Beau heard Heath's signal from behind him, then heard Jess across the fire in the shadows, and Roth's signal from his left. Beau lay on his side as far from the fire as possible, and he looked furtively at his two companions. They seemed to be sleeping quite peacefully, but you could never tell about an Indian.

Then suddenly, as Jess stepped forward into the firelight, Beau saw Straight Pine move, his hand gripping the knife at his waist, but he didn't get a chance to use it as the shot from Jess's rifle hit him in the chest. The noise brought White Wolf up onto his haunches, his eyes wild, hands groping for his knife, but he was too slow as Roth's knife embedded itself deep in his throat, and his fingers clawed at it while he stared at Beau, who was slowly rising from the ground. Then White Wolf shuddered and fell next to the glowing embers of the fire.

Roth stepped the rest of the way out of the shadows and stared at the two Indians on the ground, and he frowned. "I don't think anyone ever gets used to killing, do they?" he said softly, and Jess shrugged.

"Guess they don't, Roth," he replied soberly. "White man or red man, they die the same way, hard," and Roth shuddered as he leaned over and retrieved his knife.

"Well, let's bury them then and get on with it," he said, wiping his knife blade in the grass to clean it; then he straightened, and Jess, obeying Roth's orders, reached into the pile of rubble he carried with him on his horse, pulling out a small shovel, and moved off from the fire and began digging.

"Well, Beau, what did you learn back there?" asked Roth, slinging his rifle back on his shoulder and sheathing his knife. All Beau had done when he'd talked to them in the clearing that morning was to give them instructions for the ambush.

"They'd been there, all right," he said as he moved to Heath's horse and took down his saddle, then went to his own horse, took the small bundle that was his rolled-up buckskins off it, and set the saddle in place, tightening the cinch, then unwrapped his buckskins as he talked. "But they're on their way to Niagara now. Howling Wind thinks DeMosse is Quinn, and he's turning them over to Joseph Brant, hoping to bribe him into joining them."

"What the hell ever made them think he was Quinn?" asked Roth, and Beau turned abruptly, ducking behind a tree, not just so they couldn't watch him change, but to keep Roth from seeing the uncomfortable look on his face.

He couldn't possibly tell him what Gray Dawn had told him. What if Roth came all this way for her, and she no longer wanted him? Well, he wasn't about to add to any doubts Roth might already have, and he stuck his head out from around the tree as he slipped from his breechclout.

"He told them he was Yellow Hair," he answered as he put on his buckskins. "It was a smart move. It kept him alive. I told Bleeding Fox that DeMosse wasn't Yellow Hair, and he went livid. If DeMosse had told him who he really was and convinced him of it, he'd have been a dead man on the spot." He pulled the buckskin shirt over his head and stepped from behind the tree.

"You told them Quinn was dead?" asked Roth.

"That's right."

"And he believed you, just like that?"

"Not quite that easily, but the important thing is, he believed me." He motioned to the two dead Indians. "We were on our way to try to catch Howling Wind before he reaches Joseph Brant. I gave Bleeding Fox a tale about knowing a shortcut that would bring me out north of the Alleghenies, where I'd have a chance to catch up with him if we moved fast. He fell for it."

Heath frowned. "How much head start do they have?"

"Six days, but they're moving slow."

"Six days is a long time."

"It's been a long time since I've been in that country," said Roth. "Is there a chance we could make it?"

Heath hung his head. "Not a chance."

"But we can reach Fort Locke," answered Beau. He straightened his shoulders, glad to get out of the breechclout. "As soon as Brant gets a look at DeMosse, he'll know it's not Quinn, and I'm sure Mrs. Locke will be able to convince him Quinn's dead. With his enemy dead there'll be no reason for him to do anything to his wife. In spite of the fact he's an Indian, he's supposed to be a Christian of sorts; he'll probably be willing to send her packing with anyone who shows up to take her. By that time maybe we can be there with a few of my father's warriors to take her off his hands."

"You're sure?" asked Roth.

"Hell, he ain't sure of anythin'," yelled Jess breathlessly as he leaned on his shovel, tired from the digging, "but it's a damn good idea and beats tryin' to break our necks chasin' the wind," and he stood up, sticking the end of the shovel in the ground. "I say we do like the lad says and head for Fort Locke. Now, how about one of you younger gents helpin' relieve on the shovel for a while," he said as he stepped back toward the fire, wiping the sweat from his brow, "and let an old man take a rest," and he settled down beneath a tree as Heath walked over and took hold of the shovel handle. "As I said," Jess jawed at them as he settled back, "it beats chasin' the wind."

Fort Locke still seemed so far away.

9

It was the middle of August, hot and dry, as the small band of Cherokee rode into the fort at Niagara. They had reached a Mohawk village the night before and were led in by one of the British army scouts, an Indian the men at the fort called Chauncey, but who referred to himself as Red

Fox. He was dressed half-Indian, half-redcoat, with a face mean enough to part your hair.

Most of the soldiers, gathered around watching the procession move in, gave it only a quick glance at first; then their heads jerked up curiously as they realized two white women were in the procession, and a white man with a huge bushy beard that made him look like a grizzly, and they were tied to their horses.

"What do you suppose it is?" asked one soldier as he sat on the steps of one of the buildings cleaning his rifle, and the other grinned.

"Probably settlers gettin' too close." He spat on the ground as he watched.

"Maybe," said the other, "but it don't look like no ordinary escort bringin' them in," and he was right.

Howling Wind sat tall on his horse, new paint on his face to make him look more frightening, and he stayed mounted as their guide dismounted and went into the adjutant's office to tell him of the visitors.

A few minutes later the door opened and Red Fox strolled out, followed by a large gruff man in uniform, his face blustery as he stared.

"What is it you want here?" he asked Howling Wind in Iroquois, and the Indian frowned at the man's tone. He was a white man and he'd rather spit on him, but he was a friend of Thayendanegea's.

"I am told you can reach Thayendanegea," he said stiffly. "I wish a council with him," and the big man in the red coat with the shiny buttons nodded.

"I can reach Thayendanegea, yes," he said. "What is it you wish of him?"

Howling Wind's eyes narrowed. "I will tell Thayendanegea."

The soldier looked at his scout, then motioned for him to come to one side. "What do you think of all this, Chauncey?" he asked the Indian in English, and Red Fox grunted.

"Cherokee come long way. I would send for Thayendanegea."

The soldier straightened, his protruding stomach pulling at the buttons on the vest he wore beneath his coat. "All right, but take these people out while I send one of my men for him." He glanced at the prisoners, noting that the woman in the middle seemed cleaner and in better condition than the other two, and wondered who the hell they were. Oh, well, what did it matter? It didn't pay to interfere with these sav-

186

ages. He'd learned that years ago, and he shrugged, walking back into the building.

"The redcoat chief say you camp outside fort while he send man for Thayendanegea," Red Fox told Howling Wind as he mounted his horse, then turned it back toward the gates. "Come!" and he led them from the fort to a spot some mile and a half away, where they made camp.

Loedicia sat quietly astride her horse, her thoughts wandering as she wondered what Roth was doing. So much time had gone by and so much had happened. She shuddered as she came back to reality and watched Howling Wind dismount, then set his horse to graze. He glanced her way, his eyes sifting over her casually, and her face reddened. Since the night he'd raped her his attitude toward her had been strange. At times he'd been solicitous, almost kind, yet at others he seemed unusually harsh, and sometimes she'd discover him staring at her, his eyes so intense she felt as if she was stark naked before him again, and it frightened her.

When they'd returned to the camp that evening and her hands and feet had once more been tied for the night, Howling Wind had gone off by himself—to try to appease the Great Spirit for breaking his vow, she assumed, but now she wasn't so sure. She had the strange feeling now that the vow was broken he'd become reckless in his thoughts, and it bothered her. What was it he'd said that night? Once a vow's been broken . . .

She moved, trying to get into a better position in the saddle, then stopped abruptly as Howling Wind walked over to DeMosse, staring into his face. He motioned for two of his men, and they walked over, untying DeMosse, pulling him from the horse; then they dragged him by the arms across the clearing to a couple of small trees near the edge, and she watched angrily as they tied him between the two trees with his arms stretched as far as they'd go. He could stand, but he could go nowhere, and he didn't dare relax or his arms felt like they'd pull out of their sockets.

She frowned as she watched. DeMosse had lost weight since their capture, as had she, and his scraggly beard made him look gaunt. He raised his eyes and looked at her as they finished fastening his wrists, and she blushed, looking quickly away. She still couldn't face his eyes, not after what had happened. Not after what he had seen. He'd had no right to see her naked, and he had known. He had seen the haunted look in her eyes when Howling Wind had brought her back, and he had known she'd been raped. Even though she'd denied it, he'd known.

She could feel his eyes on her yet as the same two warriors came over and untied her, pulling her from the saddle; then, obeying Howling Wind's orders, they tied her hands and feet together and shoved her to the ground. She rolled over as they walked away, and she watched as they did the same with Lizette; then she glanced again at DeMosse, this time her eyes lifting to his, not turning away, and she was startled. He was staring at her passionately, his eyes ruthlessly alive, and she trembled. Why did he do that? Why did he look at her like that? He had no right, and she stared at him for a moment, fascinated, then closed her eyes and turned her head quickly away.

Howling Wind was restless. They'd waited all night, all morning, and half of the afternoon, and still no sign of Thayendanegea. Then suddenly, as he was about ready to ride to the fort once more, he heard the sound of horses and stood up, frozen to the spot as a large group of riders appeared, the man leading them gazing at the warriors in the camp haughtily as they rode in.

He rode his horse next to the fire, then stopped as he looked about. "Who is it that wishes to speak to Thayendanegea?" he asked as he settled back on his horse, and Howling Wind stepped forward.

"It is I," he answered steadily. "My name is Howling Wind. I have been sent by Bleeding Fox of the Chattahoochee Cherokee to bring Thayendanegea a gift that will make his heart sing," and he straightened his shoulders proudly as Thayendanegea studied him.

Thayendanegea was no longer young. His looks were marred by lines of age, his broad face wrinkled, the light in his eyes dimmed, but the muscles beneath the scarlet cloak he wore were still impressive and they rippled as he shifted on the horse's back and addressed Howling Wind. "And what is this gift you have brought, and why have you brought it?" he asked, and Howling Wind was disconcerted. Thayendanegea was showing his contempt for the Cherokee by remaining on his horse.

He tried not to show his anger at the insult. "When the Cherokee were here many seasons ago, we asked the Mohawk to aid us in driving the white man from our lands," he said. "At that time the great Chief Thayendanegea said we were as old women and could not fight. When you see the gift I have brought, you will no longer think us weak and will be glad to join us in our battle," and Thayendanegea's eyebrows raised.

He dismounted, the large band of warriors with him also dismounting, and they stood waiting. "Well?" he asked, and Howling Wind's eyes shone.

He turned toward DeMosse, his back straight as a poker, and strolled across the clearing to where he was stretched between the two trees, securely bound, and he stood before him gesturing. "Behold, Thayendanegea," he said to the man who'd followed closely behind him, "your enemy Yellow Hair," and Thayendanegea's eyes narrowed as he looked from Howling Wind to the prisoner, then back to Howling Wind.

"You think he is Yellow Hair?" asked Thayendanegea, and Howling Wind's eyes grew wary.

"He has said he is Yellow Hair," he said firmly, and Thayendanegea laughed, nodding his head.

"Ah, yes. He would lie to save his neck," he said, his mouth twisting into a sneer. "He is not Yellow Hair, Cherokee. He is DeMosse Gervaise, agent of the French."

Howling Wind's eyes were hostile. "You are sure?" he asked, dumbfounded, his belly filling with anger as Thayendanegea nodded.

"I am sure. Quinn Locke's hair is the color of the corn just as it ripens," he said slowly, "and his eyes are the color of the sky in summer. I have seen him many times. I have also met DeMosse Gervaise before, and even with the beard, I would know him."

DeMosse stared at Joseph Brant, a slight smile at the corners of his mouth. "We meet again, Mr. Brant," he said mockingly, insolence hiding the fear that tugged at him. Joseph Brant's eyes narrowed until they were barely slits in his wide face.

"Yes, we meet again, M'sieur Gervaise," he answered. "I wonder if you will elude me so readily this time," and he turned to Howling Wind. "I thank you for your gift, Howling Wind," he said. "It is not Yellow Hair, but the man you have brought me will suffice. I have had a score to settle with him for a long time, as have my friends the British. He will be welcome as a gift, but I must decline the offer to join you—"

"Wait!" said Howling Wind, interrupting him, trying to save face, and he moved to Loedicia, who lay on the ground watching them, her face pale. "You say that is not Yellow Hair, and perhaps you are right, but this is the squaw of Yellow Hair, for I have seen her and know it to be so," and he reached down, pulling Loedicia to her feet, holding her in front of him.

Thayendanegea walked toward Howling Wind slowly, his eyes on the woman who faced him. He looked her over as he approached, his hands tossing the red cloak behind his shoulders, the feathers in his scalp lock dangling at an odd angle.

He stopped in front of her, and his hand went under her chin. It was growing late, and the afternoon sun had begun to sink. He studied her face, noting the dark curly hair and violet eyes; then he spoke.

"Are you Yellow Hair's squaw?" he asked calmly, and she hesitated.

"Yes," she finally said stubbornly, "yes, I'm Quinn Locke's wife, or rather, I was, but he's dead now," and Joseph Brant's eyes showed surprise.

"Dead?"

"Yes. We went to England, where he claimed the title of earl that had been stolen from him when he was a boy, and on our way home he was killed when a French privateer captured the ship we were on. My husband's body lies at the bottom of the ocean now." Tears welled up in her eyes. "I tried to tell the Cherokee, but they wouldn't listen," she cried. "All of this has been for nothing," and he stared at her as if sifting her story over in his mind.

"Oh, I don't think it has exactly been for nothing," said a voice from behind Thayendanegea, and Loedicia froze, her heart in her mouth as the warriors behind the Mohawk chief stepped back to let a tall red-haired man through, a broad, satisfied smile spread across his face. She hadn't noticed him when they'd ridden in. Her eyes had been on Joseph Brant, but now she trembled.

The last time she had seen Elton Chaucer was in England, and he'd been wearing blue satin, lace, and velvet, his clothes the epitome of the well-dressed English lord. Now he wore black pants tucked into dusty riding boots, a fringed frontier shirt, with a black cape about his shoulders and a black hat in one hand. His cold, pale blue eyes smiled viciously as he looked at her, then turned to Thayendanegea.

"If you don't mind, Joseph, I would say the lady is telling the truth," he said. "I happen to know both her and her husband, and I also know he was in England, because it was my title and lands he put claim to. Unfortunately, because of her husband's disclosures to the king, I was unable to stay around for the earl marshal's decision, but I'm sure she'd be calling herself a countess by now. If she says her husband is dead, he's undoubtedly dead, otherwise he'd be with her."

Loedicia's face reddened. "How did you get here?" she gasped in English. "What are you doing here?" His eyes darkened as he answered her in English.

"I am here because your husband learned of my smuggling activities and made it impossible for me to stay in England any longer, my dear lady," he stated angrily. "My wife and both sons died from sickness on the way over because we had to sail on a ship that wasn't fit to carry pigs, while you sat back in London and enjoyed what had been mine. You've forgotten, haven't you, that my cousin Lord Varrick left me title to all his lands when he died? Fortunately, it included land not far from here, where I've been living the past year. I believe they're the same lands he was to have brought you to as a bride twenty years ago, am I right?" He smiled as he saw the look on her face. "Ah . . . I know I'm right." He turned to Thayendanegea and spoke once more in Iroquois. "Friend Joseph, may I have a word with you?" he asked, and Joseph Brant frowned. "In private, if you don't mind," he went on, and the Indian chief shrugged, following him to a spot a short distance away, where they talked back and forth energetically, pointing to Lizette at one time, then back to Loedicia; then Elton Chaucer's eyes gleamed.

He and Thayendanegea returned to Howling Wind, and Thayendanegea raised his hand. "Hear me, Howling Wind," he said. "The gifts you have brought, I accept in friendship, but that is all that can be between the Cherokee and the Mohawk. My friends the British are here at Niagara, and it is here I must stay. I have no quarrel as yet with the white-eyes to the south, so I will not raise a hand against them until the day my friends the British can join me. I accept your gifts with all good faith, but you must tell your leaders that I refuse once more to join them against the general they call Strong Wind," and he crossed his arms, staring at Howling Wind, who was fuming.

Loedicia saw Dark Morning look quickly at Howling Wind, and she drew in a quick breath. There was blood in his eyes, and she knew why. His eyes had followed Howling Wind accusingly since the night he'd raped her, and now she knew Dark Morning was blaming their leader for the failure of their mission, and no logic would ever change his mind. Dark Morning was certain Howling Wind had broken his vow, and Howling Wind was a doomed man in the angry warrior's eyes. Loedicia winced as she felt Howling Wind's hands grip her arms hard from behind and hold her in front of him.

"Since the great Chief Thayendanegea has no use for the gift of Yellow Hair's squaw," said Howling Wind, his voice unsteady, "and since he has refused the offer of the Cherokee, may the Cherokee ask that this woman be returned to them to face the wrath of Bleeding Fox for helping perpetrate this deception?" But Thayendanegea shook his head.

"The gift has been accepted already, Howling Wind," he said, smiling, "and I in turn have decided to give her to someone as a gift. I'm sure it would please the spirit of Yellow Hair to know that his squaw will take the place of the wife my friend Elton Chaucer lost. The wife who died because of him," and Loedicia gasped.

"No!" she cried, her face white as Elton stared at her hungrily. "No . . . please . . . you can't! Thayendanegea, please don't turn me over to him . . . please!" Her voice rose in the small clearing, her eyes wide in horror, and she felt Howling Wind's hands tighten on her arms.

"She is mine!" Howling Wind shouted angrily as he stepped backward, pulling her with him, his arm holding her against him, and she forced her head around to look up at him, startled. He held her tightly, his arm about her waist, lifting her from the ground as he began backing toward the edge of the clearing. "She's mine, and no one else will have her!" he shouted; then suddenly a shot rang out, and she heard a sickening thud and the warrior's arms loosened about her and she fell forward to the ground, his body sprawled on top of her, pinning her down.

Dark Morning walked over, the smoking rifle still in his hand, and pulled the body of Howling Wind off Loedicia, his face filled with contempt. He reached down and pulled her from the ground, then straightened angrily. "Here, take the white woman," he said bitterly, shoving her into the arms of the man with the red hair. "Take both of the white women, we have no further use of them." Then he walked over to the rest of the Cherokee warriors, who were staring at him stoically, their eyes on Howling Wind's body.

Dark Morning motioned for them to mount their horses; then he too mounted and turned toward Thayendanegea. "Howling Wind was weak," he said, his eyes hard and cold. "The white woman bewitched him. But we are not weak or bewitched. The Cherokee does not need your help, Thayendanegea, and no more will we ask it," he said. "We return now to our village, to Chief Bleeding Fox, and will tell him

192

all that has transpired; then we shall join Blue Jacket in the west, and this I vow to the Great Spirit, that we will not rest until all the white men in our lands are dead." He turned for a moment, staring at Loedicia. "And this vow shall not be broken. We will not fail!" and he whirled his horse about and left the clearing, his warriors following, the body of Howling Wind left behind as a sign of their further contempt for what he'd done.

Thayendanegea strolled over and put his heel on Howling Wind's body, then gave it a shove and rolled it over, and Loedicia winced. There was a hole in the center of his forehead, where the shot had entered, and his face, now lifeless, looked sad and almost boyish.

She started to twist, trying to free herself from Elton's arm that was holding her like a vise.

"You're a lively one, I'll say that for you," he said in English as he lifted her feet from the ground and walked over, depositing her on her stomach sideways across the back of his horse. "I got a good look at you in the salon at the duchess's house that night, you know," he said as he came around to where her head was and lifted it, looking into her eyes. "I knew then you were something special, but I never dreamed you'd be dropped right in my lap one day. How fortunate it was for me that I happened to be visiting Joseph and was ready to leave for home at the time the runner from the fort arrived," and he dropped her head hard, walking back toward Thayendanegea.

The Indian had turned from the body of Howling Wind and was staring now at DeMosse as Elton ordered his men to get Lizette mounted, then walked over to him.

Elton might have been a handsome man except for the lines of debauchery that mapped his face and the greedy look in his eyes. "What will you do with this one?" he asked in Iroquois as he motioned with his head toward DeMosse, who was staring at Loedicia, and Joseph Brant smiled.

"First I will have him whipped," he said matter-of-factly, "then tomorrow we will take him to the fort and let the general question him. When he is through with him, we shall build a big fire, and perhaps then we will find out just how brave the white man is," and Elton shuddered. He'd seen these Indians at work, and he felt rather sorry for Monsieur Gervaise; but then, being sorry for people never got him anywhere. He held out his hand toward the Indian.

"Well, Joseph, good-bye," he said gruffly, his eyes moving to where Loedicia hung across his horse. "The gift will be greatly appreciated." He shook hands firmly, then turned toward his horse, and the last thing Loedicia remembered hearing as they left the clearing was the crack of a whip as it fell across DeMosse's back, but not a sound from DeMosse.

Her head was pounding, her stomach sore, and she was sure she had a few cracked ribs. They'd been riding for what seemed like hours, but she knew it couldn't have been too long, because it was still light out.

There were two men with Elton. Seneca, and one carried Lizette across his horse the same way Loedicia was being carried, and a couple of times Loedicia looked back to see her body hanging limp, and tears welled up in her eyes. Oh, God, would this nightmare never end?

They rode hours longer. It was well past dark and must have been close to midnight when they finally stopped. Loedicia's heart was in her throat. All the while they rode, Elton kept leaning over, telling her what he had planned for her, and she wanted to die. The thought of his hands on her made her sick with loathing.

He dismounted, then pulled her off after him, his hands pawing her all the way down. He turned to the two Seneca, and she could see in the moonlight that Lizette was on her feet, weary and tired, but still alive.

"We'll build a fire first," he said, and she wondered what he meant by "first."

He grabbed her about the waist and picked her up, carrying her to the foot of a tree, where he set her down, then moved about setting a fire. One of the Seneca set Lizette down next to her, and Loedicia was relieved.

"Are you all right, Lizette?" she asked, and tears flooded Lizette's eyes.

"*Oui*, I am all right, *ma petite*," she said slowly, her voice strained, "but I fear for you. This man is a worse savage than Howling Wind. I saw it in his eyes back in England. He is cruel, and I wish to God there was some way for it to end without your getting hurt."

Tears glistened in Loedicia's eyes. "You have suffered so much, Lizette, and all because of me . . . because of my stubborn foolishness."

Lizette shook her head. Her ribs hurt so badly, she was sure one was broken, or maybe more, from the way the horse had carried her, and there was a bad pain in her chest whenever she tried to breathe or speak. "I am here because I promised Quinn," she said slowly. "I loved both of you very much and I still love you. I would give my life if it were possible, if it meant your freedom," and now the tears gushed freely from Loedicia's eyes and she leaned her head over against her friend, finding a small bit of comfort from the feel of her so close.

"Oh, Lizette, Lizette," she cried mournfully, her body trembling, "how did this happen? The world was so good once. How did I end up here?" but Lizette had no time to answer as Elton stepped next to them and reached down, pulling Loedicia to her feet; then he cut the ropes that bound her ankles.

One of the Seneca came over for Lizette at the same time, cutting the ropes on her ankles, and the two women were ushered to the fire, where a rabbit was cooking slowly over a spit.

"Rather late to be eating," said Elton as he reached out and turned the spit, letting the juice drop onto the fire, where it sizzled, "but I wanted to put as many miles between us and the fort as I could. Thayendanegea has a nasty way of turning Indian giver if he's given too much time to think, and I sure don't want him trying to take you back." His eyes moved to Loedicia's face, and the hatred in her eyes only seemed to amuse him, so she looked away, staring into the fire, trying to think of Roth, praying that somehow, some way, in spite of all this mess, she'd be able to see him just once before she died.

When the rabbit was finished, Elton cut the bonds on their wrists and let them eat, his eyes resting on Loedicia, making it almost impossible for her to swallow.

She was uneasy. They'd finished the food a few minutes before, but Lizette hadn't kept hers down, and there'd been a tinge of blood at the corner of her mouth after she'd vomited.

"She's sick," Loedicia complained to Elton. "Can't you let her go? Can't you have them take her somewhere where there's help?"

He shrugged. "Not a doctor within miles," he said. "Besides, she isn't all that sick. Now, are you, Frenchie?" he asked, and reached out, tweaking Lizette's cheek.

"You're insane," cried Loedicia. "Anyone can tell she's ready to swoon," but he only laughed and grabbed Loedicia's wrist.

The two Seneca were watching him furtively, as if waiting for something, and suddenly he nodded. They stood up, then reached down and grabbed Lizette, pulling her to her feet.

"What are they doing?" Loedicia cried as she tried to wrench her hand free from his grip, but he held her firm.

195

"I promised them some fun," he said, leaning forward, his lips touching her ear. "Only I told them to take her where I wouldn't have to hear, because I was going to be busy myself," and Loedicia let out a scream of agony as Lizette's eyes widened in horror and they began to drag her away from the fire, while she shrieked, and begged, and tried vainly to fight them off.

"No!" Loedicia screamed. "No! My God, you can't!" she yelled, half-crying, trying to reach out to her. "Lizette! Lizette!" but he held her fast, his hand all but crushing her wrist. "You can't! You can't!" she screamed, and whirled on him, beating on him with her free hand. "Not Lizette! Not Lizette! You can't," and suddenly she stopped beating on him and she stared into his cold blue eyes, his bright red hair catching the light from the flames in the fire, making him look like the devil incarnate, and she couldn't talk for a minute, her voice frozen in her throat. "Oh, my God!" she finally gasped breathlessly. "Tell them to leave her alone," she begged. "Tell them to leave her alone!"

"Don't be silly," he said, his voice low and suggestive. "She's just learning how the Seneca like to use a woman, that's all," and she knew what was happening as she heard a low moan and a half-cry. "Now it's our turn," said Elton as he pulled her toward him, and his arms went about her awkwardly, holding her tightly. She turned her face, looking up into his eyes and her eyes spat fire.

"Don't you dare try it!" she warned angrily, her eyes wild, face livid. "You so much as get that thing near me and you'll wish you hadn't!"

His eyes narrowed, and for the first time since he'd accepted her from Joseph Brant he didn't find her anger amusing. His hands moved down her sides and he grabbed both her arms, pinning them behind her back. She tried to break away, kicking and twisting, anything to throw him off, but he was a big man and her strength was no match for his.

He forced her to the ground, almost breaking her arm to do it, and tears of frustration rolled down her cheeks. He looked down into her face, the firelight making a pattern of soft shadows on it, and he felt himself hardening all the more. God! She was exciting, sensuous. He had to get out of these clothes and get down to business before he began to leak all over himself.

He reached across her, over her head, and grabbed the ropes, still where he'd tossed them when he untied her hands, and he began to tie her again, with her hands behind her;

hen he rolled her onto her back, looking into her face again. He reached to his waistline and loosened his pants, dropping them slowly, and she shuddered at the sight of his swollen manhood; then suddenly a strange look crossed his face, a look of disbelief, and as she watched, he tried to reach to his back, as if to grab something, and as quickly, his knees buckled and he sank to the ground facedown, his body just missing hers, and she saw the knife protruding from his back.

She stared, fascinated, then looked up uneasily as a figure loomed out of the shadows, and she was unable to believe her eyes.

DeMosse's brown eyes scowled above the huge scraggly beard as he knelt down and retrieved his knife, wiping it off in the grass, then pushed Elton Chaucer's body aside and looked down at Loedicia. Reaching down, he turned her over and cut the ropes on her wrists, then sheathed his knife.

She sat up slowly and stared at him incredulously, noting the open wounds on his bare arms where the whip had reached as it tore into his bare back, and she reached out, touching one, and partially dried blood clung to her finger.

"It is you," she said, bewildered, and he nodded.

"I'm not the only French agent in Niagara," he explained briefly. "I have friends all over, and one of them gave me a ride in this direction. But come on, we have to hurry."

"What?"

"We have to gather up all their food and weapons; then we're going to tie their bodies on their horses and set them running. It'll throw anyone following off our trail."

She stirred eagerly, then stopped, staring at him. "Lizette! I forgot, we have to get Lizette!" she cried, and started to move in the direction the Seneca had dragged her, but he reached out, grabbing her arm, stopping her.

"Wait! No, *chérie*," he whispered huskily. "Lizette won't be coming with us anymore." She froze, motionless, then turned to look at him, staring. "But neither will the ones who killed her."

"No . . ." She shook her head. "You're wrong," she cried, her voice breaking. "You're wrong! You have to be wrong. Lizette has to be alive . . . she has to be . . . she has to be alive. Oh, God, DeMosse, say they didn't kill her!" She grabbed his bare flesh, her fingers digging into him. "Tell me they didn't kill her, DeMosse . . . please!" she screamed hysterically. "Tell me they didn't kill her!" but he shook his head, and suddenly she felt weak, and sick, and alone.

What was the use of going on? It was too much, and now

197

this. What was the use of anything anymore? Everything she loved was being destroyed. First Quinn, now Lizette. And what of Roth? It had been so long. Was she losing him too? Was there anything left for her? She let out a moan, tears streaming down her face. In the weeks since their capture, she'd tried not to think of Roth, but now that's all she could think of. She wanted him so badly. Wanted him to touch her and hold her and love her and take the pain away, and she began to cry hysterically, her body aching, convulsing in deep sobs.

DeMosse grabbed her shoulders and shook her. "Dicia, Dicia, *chérie*, for God's sake snap out of it!" he yelled and shook her hard, his voice trying to bring her back, but it did little good. "You can't break now, *chérie*, not now," he cried. "Not after coming so far. You can't . . ." But the tears wouldn't stop, they just kept coming.

He shook her again anxiously, waiting for the blank expression on her face to change, but it didn't. Then he did the only thing he knew to do, and pulled her into his arms, his mouth covering hers, and he kissed her long and hard, his mouth stopping her sobs, and slowly, as the seconds went by, her lips began to move beneath his, kissing him back eagerly. She clung to him as if she were drowning; then suddenly her mouth drew away from his, tears still resting on her cheeks, but her eyes were once more alive, this time embarrassed. She turned away from him.

"You'll be all right?" he said, relaxed now that she had calmed down.

"Yes," and his arms dropped from about her.

"Good, then let's get done with it and get out of here," he said. "I want to be as far from here as possible by morning." She sniffed in, wiping her nose and wet eyes on the sleeve of her buckskins.

They worked fast, gathering the small amount of food left, shoving it into one of the saddlebags, then took all the powder and two of the rifles.

"One for you and one for me," he said as he set them aside, and she paused. "You did say you knew how to shoot one," he reminded, and she nodded.

He found a shirt for himself to wear when his wounds healed and put it with the saddlebags; then he set to work.

They pulled Elton Chaucer's pants back on him, trying not to get any blood on them; then Loedicia walked his horse over and helped DeMosse lift him on, tying him crossways across the saddle, as Elton had tied her. This done, Loedicia brought the other two horses while DeMosse went after the Seneca, and she helped heft them onto their horses, tying them down. One's throat was slit, the other had a neat slice across his belly and another in his chest, and he had evidently been in the middle of his horrible handiwork when DeMosse caught him unawares, for his breech clout was off.

DeMosse made no comment except to tie it back on haphazardly; then they hefted him to the horse.

"What of Lizette?" asked Loedicia hesitantly, tears near her eyes again as he secured the second Indian, and he frowned.

"We can't give her a decent burial, and I don't want them to find her or what's left of her," he answered, then straightened, taking a swipe at his beard. "There's one thing . . . there's a pond a few feet from where they killed her. Knowing Lizette, I think she'd rather have a watery grave than be left to be eaten by scavengers," and tears flooded once more into Loedicia's eyes, running down her cheeks.

"Oh, God, DeMosse, poor Lizette," she cried softly. "What have I done to Lizette?"

He took her by the shoulders, holding her steady, looking deep into her eyes. "You didn't do anything to her, *chérie*," he whispered softly, "they did," and he motioned behind him to the dead Indians tied to the horses, and she understood.

"My poor, dear Lizette," she whispered softly, and he let her cry quietly, getting it out of her system as he moved into the shadows where she knew Lizette had been taken.

He found three large rocks and put one beneath her buckskin shirt, the other two in her breeches. Her body was already getting cold, and he tried to be impartial as he worked deftly. Then, taking some rope he'd brought with him, he tied it around her body, tying the rocks inside her clothes. This done, he rolled the body to the edge of the pond and pushed it quietly in, grimacing as he watched it sink from sight in the dark water; then he straightened, his grim work done, and returned to where Loedicia stood.

He began lining the horses up, and she questioned him, wiping away her tears.

"Why aren't we taking the horses? They'd be faster."

He stepped back, his hand raised, and turned to her. "Because they're too easy to track," he said, and his hand came down, hitting the first horse, sending it off in an easterly direction, and in a few seconds the other two followed. "I know horses move faster, but people move lighter," he said as he walked over and picked up the bag filled with food, stuffing the shirt inside, and slung it over his shoulder, then reached for the rifles and powder. "Moccasined feet don't dig into the earth or chip telltale scratches on rock," he went on. "Here," and he threw her one of the rifles and a horn of powder. "With luck, they'll keep chasing those horses for the next five miles and never know when we parted company," and he kicked at the fire, stamping it out gingerly, then scattered the remains among the leaves and twigs on the ground.

"Ready?" he asked as he finally turned and looked at her, and she straightened, her chin thrust out stubbornly, hefting the rifle over her shoulder.

"Ready," she said, and when he turned his back to her again, she followed him from the clearing, looking back only once, with tears in her eyes, then watching the outline of the man moving ahead of her with a determined look on her face.

Dawn found them almost fifteen miles away, heading southwest, moving faster than what she'd imagined. The long ride north, using a variety of muscles not used before because they'd been tied down, helped rather than hindered them and after their long night's tramp they were tired and exhausted, but not unduly sore.

Shortly before the sun began stirring, they found a wild plum tree and gorged until Loedicia was sure she'd end up with a stomachache, but the dry cornmeal they gagged down helped lessen the reaction they would have had to the not-quite-ripe plums, and Loedicia gritted her teeth together, crunching the small corn grains between them as she watched DeMosse.

"It feels like I've eaten dirt," she said to DeMosse as he stood with his hands on his hips, taking in the terrain. It was getting light, and he didn't want to travel in the daylight. They could be spotted too easily. He looked off toward the right, studying the hills, looking at one hill in particular.

"What is it?" she asked, trying to get the bits of cornmeal out from between her teeth, and he frowned.

"If I'm not mistaken, I think I've found a place to hole up," he said, and straightened the rifle on his shoulder, hefting the bag of food up beside it.

The hill was about a quarter of a mile away, with a stream at its foot, and they knelt down, using their hands as cups, and took a long drink before going on.

DeMosse stood at the bottom of the hill and pointed about halfway up, where a rock formation perched precariously, then pointed out a mass of honeysuckle vines near its edge.

"There's a cave up there behind those vines," he said as he studied it. "I'm sure of it, but it'll be a hard climb. Think you can make it?"

"If you can, I can," she said, and he smiled.

"Good," and he took her hand, helping her, and they worked their way up the hill. It was steeper than it had looked from a distance, and both of them breathed a sigh of relief as they reached the small cave behind the honeysuckle, and collapsed inside. They were safe. For a while at least, anyway.

It was almost dark hours later when DeMosse shook her awake. The heat of the day had warmed the cave, and she wiped the sweat from her brow with her sleeve as she sat up. They ate more of the plums DeMosse had brought with him, with another couple mouthfuls of dry cornmeal, then emerged from the cave as the sun once more faded from sight.

The night air was warm and balmy, filled with mosquitoes, but she didn't complain. It was just nice being alive and free again, and she had DeMosse to thank for that. They found the stream once more, and this time she bathed his back and arms and spread the juice of some leaves she'd picked on the cuts; then they took a long cool drink and moved on.

They walked for two, maybe three more nights, always at night. Loedicia would take care of his cuts before they'd start out, and by the fourth day he could wear the shirt he'd taken from Elton Chaucer's saddlebags. They were dirty and tired, eating what they could find growing wild. It was in the middle of the fourth night, the moon only a bare crescent in the sky when they reached the lake.

Loedicia heard it first. They were tramping through what felt like swamp grass, yet the ground was dry enough, and suddenly she stopped. "DeMosse?"

He turned and glanced back, stopping on the trail ahead of her.

"Listen!" she called softly. "Listen, DeMosse," and she put her hand to her ear, leaning forward, straining.

Then he heard it too, and his face broke into a grin. "My God, woman, you know how long I've been waiting for that sound?" he asked, and she smiled back as he gestured. "Come on!"

She could hardly keep up with him as they raced over what was left of the dried-up swamp, then felt the sand beneath their feet, still warm from the day's sun. Then she stopped, watching, amused, as DeMosse threw his rifle and powder aside and ran, splashing into the water, diving under, coming up dripping wet.

"Come on in, the water's fine," he said as he felt it caress his skin, letting it cool him all over, taking the shirt from his healing wounds, and she set down her rifle and powder too, then slowly waded into the water, letting it creep up her legs, over her body, until it felt like heaven.

The water was exceptionally calm as it lapped gently against the sand, barely making waves, and it felt clean and cool. She ducked her head under, holding her breath, rubbing her hair and scalp, trying to get at least a little bit clean, the best she could do without soap; then she glanced toward DeMosse, puzzled.

He was about ten feet from her and she could see the shadow of his arm moving in and out against his head; then his hand skimmed the water and he'd go at it again; then she realized. He had cut his straggly beard and was shaving it off, and she laughed.

"How on earth will I ever recognize you now?" she said as he worked at it, and he growled, pretending to be ferocious.

"By my big white teeth, I presume, *chérie*," he said, and she frowned.

He'd started calling her *chérie* that first night, and he was still doing it. She wanted to tell him to stop, but it seemed to come to him so naturally.

They wasted almost half an hour's precious time in the lake because it felt so good, then moved on, this time following the shoreline, walking right at the very edge so their footprints would be washed away. And although DeMosse was sure they weren't being followed anymore, he didn't want to take a chance, so as dawn began to break on the horizon, he moved inland and found a spot at the edge of a meadow where wild grape vines hung low, clinging to some chokecherry trees, and he lifted them as he would a curtain, motioning for her to get in.

She took the rifle from her back, threw it in, then ducked inside, and he handed her his rifle, then climbed in after her, letting the vines fall back into place. The grape leaves were close together, making a perfect screen, shading them from the sun and the outside world.

Loedicia sat for a moment, taking a deep breath; then she lay back relaxed, feeling the dampness on her back where the buckskins were still partly wet. "The weather's beautiful, isn't it?" she murmured as she watched a small patch of sunlight creep into the shadowy bower high above her head, and DeMosse nodded.

"I like the warm weather."

"Me too." She closed her eyes, feeling suddenly lazy, remembering the summer mornings she used to swim in the lake with Quinn and the evenings they'd sit on the veranda and watch the sunsets. Then she remembered her last night with Roth on the *Golden Eagle*, when the world had been so rich and full again, and Roth's face swam before her, more vivid than ever before, and she felt a stirring inside, a pleasurable need that had almost been brutally forced from her when Howling Wind had ravaged her. Suddenly her body was alive again, and a throbbing sensation warmed her, and she unconsciously moved her hips, remembering Roth's lovemaking, trying once more to capture the memory of him.

DeMosse turned and glanced down at her when she moved. Her eyes opened, then widened, startled, as she stared up at him, transfixed.

She hadn't meant to move. It had been spontaneous, and she had forgotten DeMosse was there, but now she felt warm and weak inside as he stared at her.

He leaned over, his eyes looking into hers, and she couldn't breathe, she was suffocating; then he bent down and his mouth touched hers, and it was as if her whole body was on fire. His lips sipped at hers hungrily; then his hand moved beneath her buckskin shirt and she felt it gently caress her nipple, making it harden.

She was weak and dizzy, her body aroused, and fighting seemed useless, especially since what he was doing to her felt so good. His lips left her mouth, and he kissed her neck, nibbling at her ear, his hand moving to her other breast, and she sighed. "DeMosse, you mustn't," she whispered halfheartedly, her head spinning, and he answered by kissing her again, this time deeply, sensuously, his tongue parting her lips, and she moaned beneath him. Then his hand moved down and she felt it between her legs. Her eyes closed reluctantly, savoring the feel of his fingers as they stroked her; then suddenly everything was wrong. The face that floated before her wasn't DeMosse's, it was Roth's, and in that moment she knew what was wrong.

"No," she whispered, pushing his head up, licking her lips where his mouth had caressed them. "No, DeMosse, it won't work. I can't," she said, and his hand moved, his fingers still fondling her, sending sweet sensations through her loins, and

203

she sighed. "You're not Roth, DeMosse!" she gasped breathlessly.

"I don't have to be," he whispered. "Don't you realize that? I can bring you the same thing he can. I can give you the same sweet release. Let me make love to you, *chérie*," but she shook her head.

"No . . ." Her eyes stared up into his, and there was no warmth or love in his eyes, only a wild, sensuous desire. "You don't understand, do you?" she went on. "What you could give me isn't what I want. What I want is Roth, not you. Oh, yes, I could get the same feeling, but when it was over you'd still be DeMosse and I'd still be Loedicia, only I'd be a very unhappy Loedicia."

His hand moved from between her legs up to her waist, and he leaned closer against her, holding her body to him. "You want me, Loedicia, I know you do," he said. "You love it when I touch you, when I kiss you . . . your body's crying for what I can give you," but she shook her head.

"My body's crying desperately for what Roth can give it, DeMosse," she whispered urgently. "It wouldn't be fair to you or to myself to let you be a substitute, because afterward I'd be ashamed for using you."

With her eyes open and her head spinning like this, looking at him made the reality of his nearness almost overwhelming. Her body craved a man's touch, its natural desires aroused to fever pitch, and it would be so easy to give in, but she also needed love, and there was no love in what she felt now. No love in the eyes that looked down into hers. What she was feeling right now was only lustful desire, and she turned her head, fighting against it. She reached down, pulling his hand from beneath her buckskins, her body trembling at its loss.

"I can take you by force," he said as he stared down at her.

"I know you can, but it wouldn't be the same, would it?"

"It doesn't matter to you that I might need you?"

"Yes, it matters," she said. "It matters very much, but it still doesn't change things."

"You're being stubborn."

"How?"

He reached up and ran his finger from temple to chin; then his hand covered her throat sensuously. "You know you're going to give in to me before we reach Fort Locke anyway, *chérie*, don't you, so why not now?" he said, and she smiled.

He was so sure of himself. He just didn't understand. How

could she explain? "It can never be, DeMosse, not between you and me, not ever," she said. "I'm attracted to you, yes, but that's as far as it goes. There'll never be anything between us," and he stared at her, his brown eyes curiously uncertain; then he smiled.

"Have it your way," he whispered softly. "But the day will come, *chérie*, when you can't take it anymore, when you beg me to make love to you, wait and see," and he let go of her and sat up, then stretched and lay down, his back to her, and he tried to still the ache in his loins.

Every day that went by brought her a new awareness of DeMosse. The things he talked about, the things he did. The way he looked at her when he touched her hand helping her over rocks or up hills. And often he'd pull her into his arms unexpectedly and kiss her long and hard, only to be rebuffed firmly. And in the daytime, when they rested, he'd tease her, nuzzling and kissing the back of her neck sensuously when she turned her back to him or slept on her stomach, and when she slept on her back she'd wake up to find his mouth covering hers, his lips warm and inviting, and it was driving her mad, because she couldn't really hate him.

He could have forced the issue and raped her easily, but he didn't. Instead, as they traveled, moving farther down the shoreline, closer and closer to Fort Locke, he just kept at her, doing everything he could to weaken her defenses and make her beg him to take her.

They'd been traveling for a week, and it was almost dawn as they walked side by side, turning a bend in the shoreline, and suddenly Loedicia stopped. She stood for a moment, motionless, as the first rays of dawn began filtering over the horizon; then she let out a sigh of relief.

"Oh, God!" she cried, her voice dancing with excitement. "We're almost there," and she moved forward a few steps, looking first this way, then that, recognizing the lay of the land and the beach. "I've been here dozens of times," she exclaimed. "Fort Locke's not a half day's walk away," and she covered her face with her hand and tears rolled down her cheeks.

"Hey, you're not supposed to cry," he said, but she couldn't help it, and late that afternoon when they topped the last hill and she saw her log house nestled at the edge of the sand with the willow trees sighing overhead, and the fort standing tall and strong with the bark huts of the Tuscarora beyond it, the tears flooded her eyes once more, and she half-stumbled, half-ran across the sand, dragging DeMosse with her by the hand.

She stopped abruptly at the steps to the veranda and stood for a moment squeezing his hand, her eyes shut. She wanted to go in, yet she didn't. There were so many memories in there. Quinn and the children. Tears floated gently down her cheeks, and she dropped his hand, then stepped onto the porch, her hands shaking. She stepped to the door and walked inside, and the whole world tumbled in around her as Sepia, her round body smothered in a calico dress, looked up from her sewing and almost let it drop in her lap.

"No . . . oh, no . . ." the woman cried as she stood up slowly, as if in a daze, setting the sewing aside; then she walked over gingerly and took a good look, shaking her head as if she didn't really believe it. "It is you . . . it is really you." She beamed happily and began to cry as she reached out and hugged Loedicia, then straightened, shaking her head. "Come," she said, her eyes wet with tears, ignoring DeMosse. "Come sit. I take care of you," and Loedicia glanced at DeMosse, smiling through the tears, as Sepia, her bronzed face beaming, led her to a chair and made her sit down.

"I'm all right, Sepia," she assured the Indian woman as she relaxed for the first time in months, wiping the tears away with the back of her hand. "I'm all right. But I want you to do me a favor."

"Anything," the Indian woman said anxiously, and Loedicia sniffed in.

"Go to the fort and tell Major Holmes I'm here," she instructed her. "Tell him I have to see him here at once, it's very important. Will you do that right away?" and Sepia nodded, all smiles, wiping her face with her apron, then hesitated a minute, looking at DeMosse before she disappeared out the door.

Loedicia stood up and looked about the room, and it seemed strange with its crude log furniture and Indian rugs. This was where she'd spent almost twenty years with Quinn. There were good memories and bad. She glanced at DeMosse, whom she'd forgotten for a few moments. He was giving the place a good once-over, testing the beams, strolling over curiously and looking into the other rooms. She pushed her tears aside and stood watching him for some time; then: "Just what on earth are you doing?" she asked, puzzled, and he grinned.

"Seeing how I like the place."

"Oh?"

He walked over and stood in front of her, then reached out, pulling her close in his arms, his voice lowering suggestively. "Why not, Loedicia?" he whispered. "I like the place. We could make it here, you and I. I could take up where Quinn left off. We could have all this, just like you had before, only more." His eyes shone. "I could build an empire here, and with you beside me, who knows where it would lead?"

She frowned, studying his face, fighting the ache that was surfacing inside her at his touch. Why couldn't he leave her alone? "It won't work, DeMosse," she whispered huskily. "Please, it won't work, not in any way, shape, or form. I'm just not in love with you," and she pushed him away, turning her back.

"How do you know? How do you know you're not in love with me?" he asked angrily, his eyes darkening. "Have you ever given yourself a chance to find out? You said I reminded you of Quinn. If so, then why can't you be in love with me as you were with him?"

"Because," she burst out, finally admitting the truth she'd been keeping, even from herself, and there was a sob in her voice, "because you're too much like him, yet not enough like him!" and her eyes filled with tears. "You have all of his faults, DeMosse, and few of his virtues. You'd swindle your best friend out of his last cent if it meant you could reach the top, and you know it. And you wouldn't be content to run this fort like Quinn did. You want money and the power you think it can bring." She sniffed in, her eyes saddened because she had begun to like him more than she should. "And you wouldn't be satisfied with me, either, DeMosse," she went on. "Oh, for a while, yes, but when the opportunity came, you'd follow the first pretty face that came along. That's just the way you are, and you'll never change. You're not the type. You think I haven't watched you? Well, I have. I loved Quinn even with his faults, because he was a man of virtue. I love you as a friend. We've shared so much together, but I'm not in love with you."

He leaned close to her ear. "Why not? Why can't you be?" he whispered passionately, but she stepped away, moving to the doorway, stepping out onto the veranda. He followed her, and his hands settled on her shoulders, pulling her back against him; then they moved down to her waist, lifting her buckskin shirt to caress the bare flesh, making her shiver. "Why can't you, *chérie?*" he pleaded, his lips caressing her neck, sending chills down her spine. "Besides, what does love have to do with a man and woman wanting and needing each other? It wouldn't be the first time, nor the last. Let me make love to you, Loedicia. I want you so . . . we could stay here, just the two of us . . ."

He kept on pleading passionately as she fought against him, her body warm and weak with longing; then suddenly, as she stared toward the lane that came up from the fort, her knees trembled, her pulses racing, and she didn't hear his words anymore; they began to fade into nothingness, like a hodgepodge without meaning, and she stared across the sand and grass, her heart singing in her breast.

It was him . . . it was! There was Sepia, and Major Holmes, and . . .

Her eyes slowly filled with tears as a new strength flooded her body, and a joyous cry wrenched itself from deep inside her as she tore herself from DeMosse's startled hands, his words faltering as she stumbled off the end of the veranda and began running down the lane, her hair flying, feet barely touching the ground.

Roth shortened the distance between them with long, running strides, and she flew into his outstretched arms, collapsing with ecstasy, her heart exploding inside her as she felt him warm and solid against her, and she raised her mouth to his, tears streaming down her face. She clung to him, kissing his mouth, his eyes, his cheeks, smothering his face with kisses, her heart filled with rapture, and he kissed her back, both of them oblivious of Telak, Major Holmes, and Sepia watching them in wonder while Jess grinned, Beau looked relieved, and Heath blushed quite red under his tan.

Loedicia was weak all over, her voice breathless as she drew her head back and looked up into Roth's face as he held her off the ground, his arms about her. "Where did you come from?" she gasped ecstatically, her eyes alive with wonder. "My God, I thought I'd never see you again," and he kissed her again, softly this time, his eyes on hers intimately as their lips met, and Major Holmes cleared his throat.

Loedicia swallowed hard, then drew her head back and turned to the major as Roth set her back on the ground, and she blushed as she held Roth's hand in both of hers, the touch of his fingers against hers making her tremble; then she let go his hand and threw her arms about Heath's neck, and he held her tightly, trying not to let his embarrassment at her unladylike behavior show. She reached out, and Beau grabbed her hand, squeezing it hard, and she smiled at Jess, wondering how on earth he'd managed it; then she moved back as close to Roth as she could, and he put his arm about her waist, holding her tightly against him.

"They got here early this morning," explained Major Holmes, his ruddy complexion redder than usual.

"Then you know about Quinn?"

He nodded as Roth's arms tightened. "We were getting Telak's men ready to go after you when Sepia came running down to the fort." The major still stared at her. "I still can't believe everything that's happened. It's all been such a shock."

"Maybe we'd better go back up to the house," she suggested; then she looked at Roth. "There's someone there I want you to meet. If it weren't for him, I'd probably be dead by now," and Roth glanced toward the house to a lone figure standing motionless on the veranda, staring at them, his eyes intent on Roth's face.

DeMosse frowned. So this was the man Loedicia was in love with. He watched them approach, and his jaw tightened self-consciously. The man was tall and ruggedly handsome. Dark hair with slight frost at the temples, dark eyes, and he walked like a man with a purpose, confident and impressive. Then, as they stopped in front of him, DeMosse saw Loedicia look up at Roth, and in that one look went a thousand words of love. She'd never looked at him that way. He glanced at Roth's face. He was answering her back with an intimate gaze that seemed to electrify the air between them, and suddenly DeMosse knew what she had meant. What he felt for Loedicia was nothing like what this man felt for her. He desired her. His body craved her, but Roth's soul was a part of her, and there was no need for words between them. The physical need they had for each other was only a part of it.

He put out his hand reluctantly as she introduced them, his eyes studying Roth for some flaw, but he saw none. The man's smile was warm and affably disconcerting, his handshake firm as he thanked him for saving her life. Then he saw it, the one thing that made Roth less a god and more a man like himself. As their eyes met, he saw the pain in Roth's eyes. The pain of not knowing what might have happened between himself and Loedicia during their days and nights alone together, and the thought pleased him, and he smiled as he turned to greet his old friend Jess.

The next few hours were spent relating tales, until the whole story was finally pieced together; then the men went back to the fort to clean up while Loedicia soaked in a tub and changed clothes. Sepia had kept the house ready for their return at a moment's notice, and Loedicia took a plain gray linen dress from the clothes press, pulling it on over her head. She stared at herself in the mirror. It was the first dress she'd had on since leaving Baton Rouge. Let's see, how long ago was that? Roth said it was near the end of August.

She frowned, thinking of DeMosse. There were times she had come so close to giving in to him. Moments when the future seemed so far away and the present so vital, and it frightened her. She finished fixing her hair, then went back to the kitchen, where Sepia was cooking supper, and was surprised to find DeMosse standing in the kitchen waiting.

She stood for a long moment looking at him. "I'm sorry, DeMosse," she said softly, and he half-smiled.

"Not as sorry as I am."

"There's always another woman around the corner."

"Not like you," he answered. "There'll never be anyone quite like you. You know that, don't you?" His half-smile faded. "But I guess you're right, *chérie*. I'm a rather restless sort. Besides, I saw the way it was between you two today. I guess I can't blame you."

There were tears at the corners of her eyes, and she couldn't exactly understand why, except she had become fond of DeMosse. You couldn't help being close to someone with whom you had been thrown together so intimately for so long, but she knew it wasn't love. Not love the way she needed it.

"I just wanted to make sure everything's all right with you now," he said, and she smiled.

"It is."

"Good. Then I'll get on with my life . . . there's still a lot of world out there."

That night they all sat at a table on the veranda eating, and as the setting sun dipped down over the lake, they made their plans. General Wayne had beaten the Indians at a place called Fallen Timbers only a few days before, and they were already talking of peace treaties. Traveling now, explained the major, would be less dangerous. During the evening Jess persuaded DeMosse to join him on a trek west, since they had nothing better to do; then they'd head back to Mobile to pick up the two thousand dollars Roth had left there for him, and as darkness began to descend, they pushed back their chairs and relaxed, thanking Sepia for their full stomachs.

Loedicia bit her lip, feeling empty inside as the men sat down on the steps of the veranda talking, and she looked at

Roth longingly, her eyes intent on his face. She knew Major Holmes would expect him to go back to the fort with the other men when they left, but she didn't want him to leave. They hadn't had one minute alone together since she'd arrived. She had to see him alone, and somehow he seemed to sense it.

"Loedicia?" he asked suddenly, his voice vibrating emotionally as he stood up at the top of the steps. "Loedicia, will you take a walk down to the lake with me before we return to the fort?" he asked, not caring anymore about proprieties, and she smiled.

"I'd be glad to," she said breathlessly and he walked over, holding out his arm, and she took it eagerly, holding it very tightly, but only he was aware of it as she excused herself from her other guests and they strolled slowly across the sand, everyone's eyes on them.

"I can't leave you tonight," he said softly as they walked along, knowing the others were watching them. "They're going to expect me to go back to the fort with them when they leave, and I can't."

"If you do, I'll never forgive you," she said, and he stopped, looking down at her face, shadowed in the balmy warm night that surrounded them.

"I can just say to hell with them," he said recklessly, his eyes dark and compelling, and she felt warm deep inside. "After all, they ought to know by now how we feel about each other."

Her eyes were filled with love as she looked at him. "Roth, before you do," she whispered, "I want you to know two things. First," she said unsteadily, "an Indian named Howling Wind raped me one night." She felt his hand tighten on hers. "I'm all right now," she assured him, "I've been raped before, remember? But it's still humiliating and loathsome." She took a deep breath. "Second, I know it's been worrying you, although you haven't said a thing, but I never gave myself to DeMosse. He wanted me to, and he tried to break me down, because he knew I was vulnerable, and I have to admit there were moments when I almost let my physical needs overrule my heart, but I couldn't. The only love I have to give anymore is for you, and without love the whole thing is meaningless."

He stared at her for a minute, then took her face between his two hands, and he leaned over, kissing her softly, lovingly on the mouth; then, to her surprise, he reached down and picked her up, swinging her into his arms, cradling her against him as he turned toward the house.

"Wha . . . what are you doing?" she asked, startled.

"Well, my love," he explained as he started back toward the log house with her in his arms, "since I've been living the life of a celibate the past few months, and since no one has made proper love to you since the last time we were together on the *Golden Eagle*, then I'd say we're both long overdue!" She stared at him wide-eyed, her face flushed as he reached the steps and mounted them easily. The men scattered, giving him room. Then, as he reached the door, he turned, still holding her tightly against him, and looked at all the faces turned toward him, their eyes bewildered.

"Excuse me, gentlemen," he said quite casually; then he glanced at Loedicia's flushed face, and her arms went around his neck as he turned back to face the men. "But with or without your good wishes, kind sirs, my future wife and I are going to bed. Good night!" They all stared, dumbfounded. Sepia, who was still clearing the table, dropped a cup that shattered in a dozen pieces, and Roth whirled, disappearing through the doorway into the house with Loedicia snuggled contentedly in his arms.

He went directly to the bedroom, stood Loedicia in front of him, turning her around while he unfastened her dress and stripped it and her underclothing from her, then sat her on the edge of the bed while he pulled off his shirt and pants. He knelt in front of her and took her face between both his hands as he had on the beach.

"You're shameful," she whispered softly, an impish smile playing at the corners of her mouth as he looked at her.

"I know, Dicia, my love, I know," he whispered softly. "I have never loved anyone in this whole wide world except you. I intend to spend the rest of my life proving it, and I mean to start now." As he kissed her, they fell back on the bed and she gave herself to him passionately, making up for all the months they'd been apart, while outside, Heath walked off by himself, trying to understand what made his mother do the things she did. Beau and his father continued arguing over Beau's decision to leave again, and DeMosse and Jess slipped quietly into the night, deciding not to wait until morning to start west. Sepia joined Major Holmes in a nightcap they both sorely needed.

Rebel

10

The sweet scent of exotic blossoms rich with perfume floated through the open doors that led to the balcony of Rebel's bedroom in the huge stucco house that was the home of the governor of Grenada. Rebel lifted her tired body from the chair and waddled across the floor, her swollen belly forcing the graceful lines from the way she once walked.

She stood near the edge of the open French doors and gazed down over the harbor of St. George, to the palm trees and crystal blue water with its boats bobbing on it here and there, and the lush green tropical forests that surrounded it. She hated it. Hated the sight of it. Always the same, never changing. She was the only thing that ever changed, and she glanced down at her grotesque figure and put her hand on its hard melonlike surface, pressing hard.

"I hate you!" she whispered viciously to herself as she stared at her stomach showing vaguely beneath the sheer nightgown she wore. "I never wanted you. I never wanted his children. Why did you have to come?" Then she burst into tears and stood leaning breathlessly against the doorjamb, crying.

But what good did it do to cry? She couldn't change things. She had made a mistake, a big one, and there was no way to change it. She sighed, wiping the tears from her eyes, and moved back across the floor wearily. She sat back down on the chaise longue where she'd been resting. She wouldn't dress, not yet. It was still early.

She leaned back and pulled the folds of her pale blue peignoir about her, trying to cover herself so she wouldn't have to see and could try to pretend it wasn't there while she read the letter one more time.

It had arrived the day before, and she almost knew it by heart already. She reached onto the table and picked it up, unfolding it as the tears filled her eyes. Then she wiped them away and began reading aloud. "My dearest daughter," it began, "this is the first chance I have had to write to you since our arrival home. Home being the Château, which Roth has told me would surprise and please you, now that it is completed. We arrived two days ago and were married yesterday morning in the chapel here, and I'm happier now than I have been for so long. I know you want to know what happened, and it is such a long story, dear, but I will try my best to tell it in as few words as possible." That was like Mother, she mused, then went on. "When we sailed out of Port Royal Sound, Beau had every intention of returning, but circumstances prevented it, and we ended up in a place called New Orleans."

She stopped reading, skimming by this part. She couldn't stand to read about Beau again, and she picked it up farther on, reading to herself the part about DeMosse Gervaise and the Cherokee and of Joseph Brant, and her mother's encounter with Elton Chaucer again, and Lizette's death; then she began aloud again, mumbling at first. "When we finally arrived at Fort Locke, imagine my joy at seeing Roth once more. He, Beau, Heath, and the man who had been with DeMosse and me when the Cherokee jumped our camp (I mentioned him earlier), Jess Willoughby—well, the four of them had arrived that véry morning on their way to rescue me. I wish I could tell you truly what it meant to me to have Roth there. I love him so. We stayed two days longer, although DeMosse and Jess left that evening, heading west somewhere. DeMosse is rather a restless man, somewhat like your father was, only worse." It was as if she read some extra meaning there, but she couldn't grasp it, then shrugged and went on. "I know it will surprise you, but on the way back, Roth and I found a delightful little orphaned girl in a Delaware village. She's half-Indian and half-white, and we call her Ann. She's five years old, and so lovely. We couldn't leave her, so brought her home with us, and she's going to fit in so well, I know. Already she has learned enough English to get along with the servants. She's such a bright child, and we are going to make her ours legally."

Rebel's eyes wandered down the page again, stopping at a sentence that bothered her, and she read it aloud again, letting it sift through her mind. "I know I shouldn't feel this way, dear, but only one thing mars our arrival. Brandon's

Aunt Rachel has bought the property next to the Château and moved in. I know it's probably petty of me, but I never liked the woman, and I dislike her living so close. However, there's nothing I can do, so will have to make the most of it."

Her eyes moved ahead again on the paper as she continued reading. "It feels strange to know I'm to become a grandmother, dear, and I'm glad you told Roth before you left. I only wish you could have left under happier circumstances (he told me what happened); however, my love is with you. I only wish I could be with you when the time comes, to make it easier for you. Roth was with me when you came into the world, and it helped. I can only hope that Brandon understands and will stay by your side to help, and please say hello to him for me. Well, that's all I can think of for now, my dear. I've written to your brother in England and to Mr. Briggs, informing them that Teak is now the new Earl of Locksley, and of my marriage, so have no worries there. Write when you can, and remember our love is with you always. Your loving mother, Loedicia."

Rebel stared at the signature and bit her lip, then folded the letter again and put it down. If her mother could endure what she'd been put through . . .

"I'm as strong as she is," she whispered to herself, then looked again at her swollen stomach and moved quickly from the chaise longue, hurrying to the armoire, where she opened the door wide, gazing at the beautiful array of clothes spread before her; then suddenly her face went white as a pain hit her, almost taking her breath away.

She stood motionless for a minute, then exhaled as the pain let up. She must have moved off the chaise too quickly. She'd have to watch that. She reached out, riffling through the clothes, and picked out a soft, full dress of deep turquoise, full and flowing, like the native women wore when they were pregnant, and she tossed it aside on a chair, then walked to the door, calling the maid.

"Cristabel! Cristabel!" she called from the door. "Have them set up my water." She heard an answering call from the hall, then walked to the vanity, lifting the lid of the jewel box. She reached in, fingering the necklaces inside. The Bourland family diamonds had been left back in England, where they'd be safer, but Brandon had bought her others, and she picked up a small delicate necklace of diamonds and aquamarines made to look like dainty flowers, with earrings to match. But instead of taking them, she picked up a necklace of white seashells strung together by Cristabel, and she smiled as she looked at it, then set it aside with the dress.

Cristabel knocked on the door when the bathwater was ready, and Rebel followed her down the hall, refusing to take the young girl's arm for assistance, trying to prove to herself that the cumbersome monstrosity pushing out in front of her didn't make her an invalid.

Cristabel only shook her head as she watched her mistress from behind struggling to walk gracefully. Lord, she was gonna have a big one, that's for sure. Cristabel was young, not more than sixteen, and short, with spindly legs and an underdeveloped bust, but a rosy smile that spread all over her dark-skinned face. Brandon didn't like her presence in the house, but Rebel had insisted, so he'd let her remain with a warning for her to stay out of his way.

The previous governor had had only Negro servants in the house, but Brandon refused, using slaves only in the yard and to drive the carriages. He'd sold the household slaves and hired white servants to replace them, a gesture that was watched closely by everyone on the island.

Rebel squeezed into the tub and relaxed, trying not to look at herself, and asked Cristabel if any more ships had arrived from America, but the girl shook her head. Then suddenly there it was again, the pain in her back, and Rebel's face went white. Cristabel stared as Rebel let out a cry.

"What is it, ma'am?" she asked, her eyes wide, and Rebel grabbed the edge of the copper tub, hanging on hard. Then, as suddenly as it had started, the pain was gone.

"It's nothing," she said, relaxing again. "Only a stitch in my back," but Cristabel shook her head.

"No, ma'am, that ain't no stitch," she offered thoughtfully. "That's the baby. I bets you any money." Rebel stared at her, frightened, her lips quivering.

"You . . . you think it is, Cristabel?" she asked hesitantly, and the girl nodded.

"I know it is," and she reached out her hand. "Come on, you've washed enough. I'm gonna take you back to your room, and then I'm gonna send someone after the doctor. The governor's gone to the other side of the island, and he ain't gonna be back till late afternoon." Rebel stood up, taking her hand, then left the tub and dried off, but she didn't put her nightgown back on. Instead she slipped into the long flowing dress, wearing nothing beneath it, and put the necklace about her neck. Her bare feet made a soft padding noise as she let Cristabel help her down the hall. She lay down on the bed in her room while the young girl left to get the doctor.

Rebel stayed quiet, waiting for another pain, but none came. So after a few minutes she got up and walked out onto the balcony, into the hot morning sun, feeling it warm on her face. Then, without warning, another pain came, this time stronger than the other, and she felt dizzy and sick, as if she were floating while the pain took over her whole body. She managed to hang onto the rail until it was gone, then sighed with relief at its passing and headed once more for the bed. Her crotch felt moist and sticky, and suddenly something began running down her leg. She gasped as she stepped into the room, and pulled up her dress.

By the time Cristabel returned with the doctor, Rebel was sprawled on the bed, her long blond hair spread haphazardly about her frightened face, the beautiful silk bedspread covered with blood and her hands clawing into her pillow for some relief.

All morning the pain went on and on, until Rebel thought she was going to die. There was no relief, except the doctor who wiped her forehead. Dr. Matthew Wilder sat beside her now, holding her hand, his eyes intent on her face. He was a solid man in his early thirties, quiet and unassuming. Rebel had been a mystery to him from the moment he'd met her. She was hauntingly beautiful, her violet eyes suggesting a passion that was held severely in check, her warm, full mouth stingy with its smiles. She was proud and could be haughty at times, yet there were times when she didn't seem to care what she did or said.

He hadn't liked her at first; she'd seemed hard and callous, but he'd soon recognized it as a facade, and as he held her hand, watching her suffer, he felt ashamed because he knew that now he cared more than he should. He should have taken his first impression of her, kept it, and let it go at that, but he hadn't.

Rebel looked over at the doctor, watching his eyes. He had eyes the same color as Beau's eyes, cool deep green. She had noticed it before when he and his wife, Miriam, came to dine, or for a visit, and she'd sit next to him and they'd talk and talk about so many things. Funny he should have eyes like Beau's. He was older than Beau. Maybe a year or two older than Brandon, but his eyes were nice. It was nice having him around, and she squeezed his hand as another pain came.

He kept her panting with each pain, trying to lessen it, but it did little good.

"How . . . how much longer?" she asked him breathlessly as she felt another pain start, but he shook his head.

There was no real way of knowing, and all he could do was stand by to help when the time came.

About four in the afternoon Brandon returned, hearing the news as he walked in the door, but instead of going right to her room, he fortified himself with a brandy first, getting the taste of the island's sandy soil out of his mouth. He hated these islands, with the heat, the bugs, the black people, and the constant smell of spices. But he'd stick it out because he was looking for bigger, better things.

He swallowed the last of the brandy and left the downstairs salon. He could hear Rebel's wailing moans, coupled with an occassional yell, long before he reached her room, and now he stood outside her door with his hand on the knob. He shouldn't feel like this, but he did, and for a moment it shocked him. He loved Rebel more than he'd ever loved any woman. She was a weakness with him, and he'd cursed himself for it a thousand times, because although he'd made her his wife and now she was even having his child, she wasn't completely his and he knew it. Not really. At first when he made love to her she'd stiffen in his arms, pretending to go along with him, pretending she cared, but as his passion for her rose, it soon became apparent that she wasn't giving the love he wanted or needed. She was holding back. A situation he couldn't and wouldn't tolerate.

The past few weeks he'd had to leave her alone, doctor's orders, but now she was having his child, and maybe with the baby's birth she'd treat him the way a wife should. Maybe the pain she was suffering now was her punishment for not letting him take her completely, for holding something of herself from him.

He opened the door and stepped inside, then casually walked to the bed. His hands tightened on the riding crop he carried. She had been wearing that godawful dress he'd told her not to wear, and now it was thrown across the chair, blood spattered all over it, and there was just a sheet covering her. But she still had on that necklace of ugly seashells Cristabel had given her.

He looked into her face, streaked with sweat, her lips bruised where she'd bitten them, but he saw none of it. All he saw was her defiance. Even now. Why did she do things like

220

this to irritate him? She was between pains, her breathing unsteady as he leaned toward her.

"Why, Reb?" he asked, puzzled. "Why did you have to put that dress and those beads on? Why now?"

She tried to smile, her lips becoming more of a sneer with the pain. "I did it for you, Bran," she whispered hoarsely, her voice almost lost in a groan. "I put them on for you because you hate them and because you made me pregnant. You did this to me! You, do you hear? I didn't want your baby. I never wanted your baby . . . Oh, God!" Another pain hit, even stronger. "I hate your baby, do you understand!" she screamed, staring at him in agony. "I hate you and I hate your baby. I hope it dies!" and tears flooded her eyes as Brandon stared at her, his face white.

Matt Wilder looked over at him, frowning; then he spoke. "You'd better leave, Brandon, it's only upsetting her," he said. "She doesn't really mean it, believe me. I've seen more than one woman curse the man who made her pregnant during birth. It's a natural thing to do."

Brandon stared at Rebel, but he didn't feel pity and he didn't feel concern; all he felt was anger. She was his wife. What right did she have to say these things? She should be proud to be having his child.

He turned and walked from the room, his face livid with rage, and Matt turned back to his patient. He didn't like the way it was going. He stood up, pulling the sheet up from the bottom so that her breasts were still covered, and he began to examine her stomach, his hands pressing gently, while Cristabel, the only one of the servants Rebel wanted in the room, stood aside waiting to help.

"Come here," he ordered her, and she crept over gingerly, waiting beside the bed. "Go pour some scalding-hot water in the basin I put on the dresser," he said quickly, "then go fetch me some goose grease, as much as you can. If you can't find goose grease, get me anything else to use as a lubricant, any oil, but hurry!" and the girl did as he said, then was out of the room in no time.

He walked from the bed, stripping off his coat and shirt, and picked up some soap, washing his hands thoroughly in the basin, clear up past his elbows; then he went back to the bed.

Rebel was exhausted. She felt like giving up, but he leaned over, looking deep into her eyes. "Come on, now, I've got one trick left," he said soothingly, his soft green eyes gazing into hers, his voice deep and resonant. "The baby's coming

221

out wrong, I'm going to have to turn it. It's going to hurt, but if I don't, you'll die."

"But I want to die," she cried helplessly, and he shook his head.

"No, not really. Not you. You don't want to die."

The pain started again, and she cried aloud, shutting her eyes; then everything began to grow hazy, and she felt like she was floating.

Cristabel rushed back into the room and held the dish of goose grease out toward the doctor, who smeared it on his hands all the way past the elbows; then he leaned over the bed. Pulling Rebel closer to the edge of the huge bed, and half-kneeling on it, with one foot still bracing himself on the floor, he reached up inside her with both hands, working slowly, deftly, moving and pushing while Cristabel watched, fascinated, and he continued working for what seemed like an eternity, until he felt the top of the baby's head in his hand; then he smiled, relieved, and pulled his hands back, letting the sweat drip from his forehead into the soft, curling hairs on his bare chest.

He spread Rebel's legs apart on the bed, bending her knees, then leaned up close to her ear, as he grabbed a towel and wiped the blood and goose grease from his hands. "Bear down now, Rebel," he ordered softly. "Don't hold back, bear down," and he put his hands on her stomach, helping her push.

Rebel was worlds away now, her mind floating somewhere in a limbo. It was spring and the waves on the lake were pounding the shore and she was diving in the water, letting it cover her and submerge her in its cool depths; then Beau was there and he was reaching for her, only she couldn't come because there was a rope around her middle holding her fast. She tried to push it off, but it wouldn't go; then she tried to force it off, using her stomach muscles, but it wouldn't budge.

"Bear down," Beau called to her, his voice sweet in her ears. "Bear down harder," and she sighed.

"I am bearing down, Beau, I am," she screamed, "but it isn't doing any good. I'm going to lose you, Beau! I love you! Please, don't leave me!" The words tumbled from her mouth wildly, and Matt stopped pushing on her stomach to stare at her face.

He knew she hadn't been aware of saying anything out loud, and he frowned as her words printed themselves indelibly on his mind; then he turned quickly and pushed once more, harder, and suddenly, as Rebel strained, the top of the baby's head popped out and the doctor let out a cry, ordering Cristabel to get a blanket ready while he worked the baby the rest of the way out; then he held it by the heels, giving it a resounding slap.

Rebel was slowly drifting back. Her insides felt as if they'd been ripped from her, and she was so tired. So very tired, then she heard the baby's crying, and her eyes opened lazily as she felt a hand smoothing the hair back from her forehead.

"It's over," said Matt as he looked down at her, pushing back another strand of wet hair that was tucked into the crease in her neck. She frowned but didn't say anything, only stared at him. "You have a beautiful little boy," he said, but there was a rather strange look on his face that she couldn't quite describe.

He motioned to Cristabel to bring the baby over now that she had it cleaned up and it had quit crying, but Rebel grabbed his hand.

"I don't want to see it!" she said suddenly, her voice barely above a whisper. "I hate his ugly baby," but it was too late and Cristabel stood beside the bed, her arms holding a small face up for her to see, and suddenly Rebel's eyes widened in disbelief. The words she was about to utter caught in her throat, and tears flooded her eyes.

"Oh, my God!" she whispered softly instead, looking into the small face, its mouth making funny little noises, and she sighed.

This wasn't Brandon's baby. It wasn't. It couldn't be. His hair was jet black, and his creamy skin, with its dusky olive hue, covered a beautiful face with high cheekbones below faintly sloe eyes and a nose that showed traces of its Indian ancestors. Rebel stared transfixed, then held out her arms, tears glistening as they rolled down her cheeks, and the doctor moved aside as Cristabel laid the baby beside her on the bed, and she forgot anyone else was in the room.

"Oh, my little one," she whispered softly, her heart exploding inside her. "I'm sorry. I didn't mean anything I said before. I didn't know. I thought you were his. I didn't know," and she reached down, lifting his little hand, kissing the fingers. Then the baby began to cry again, his little mouth searching, and Matt smiled.

"You'd better feed him, mother," he said. "He's got a pair of lusty lungs, he'll wake the whole household." She looked up at him, her eyes curiously alive for the first time in months. "We don't happen to have a wet nurse," he went on, and reached down, lifting her by the shoulders, propping the pillows under her to raise her a bit. Then he pulled the sheet down as she drew the baby closer to her, and his warm hand touched her full breast, moving it to the baby's mouth. "It's done like that," he said, and she glanced up at him quickly, blushing as the baby's mouth closed on her nipple and he began to suck.

She felt self-conscious under the doctor's gaze now that it was all over, and she looked down at the baby curiously, her heart warm with love.

Matt strolled over to the chaise longue and picked up his shirt. Rebel looked up from the baby, her eyes following him. She watched the muscles in his back ripple as he pulled the shirt on, then tucked it in his pants. She hadn't realized before that he was so well-built. His clothes were always a bit big for him, and seldom neat, looking as if he'd slept in them most of the time. How strange. She watched as he sent Cristabel out with the bloody linen and towels and told her to bring back his Excellency, the governor; then he turned, catching her staring at him, and he smiled.

"Cristabel will clean you up good after the baby's through nursing," he said as he slipped on his coat, coming to stand by the bed. "I've given her strict instructions, so you do as you're told. Follow her directions exactly or you could get a bad infection. Do you understand?" His green eyes were poised, waiting for her reply.

"Yes, Doctor," she agreed, and he smiled again.

"Good. I'll be back to see you in the morning." He walked over to the vanity and picked up his small bag. Then he grabbed his straw hat and walked out, bowing slightly as he left. Brandon met him at the door.

"Leaving already?" asked Brandon, and Matt's face reddened, glad he was getting out before the governor had a chance to look at his son, but he didn't move fast enough after closing the door, and Brandon's outraged voice fell on his ears as he reached the top of the stairs.

"You slut! You goddamned slut!" Brandon bellowed at the top of his lungs from the bedroom behind him. "Where is my son?" Dr. Matthew Wilder's mouth tightened in a firm line as he closed it forcibly; then he started down the stairs.

Rebel held the baby tight against her, trying to soothe him and make him stop crying, but Brandon's yelling was only frightening him more.

"I know whose baby that is," he gasped as he stared down at her. "It was that goddamned Indian, wasn't it? That son of a bitch! When?" he asked viciously, his nostrils flaring. "When did you give yourself to him, before or after we were married? When?" But she didn't answer; she only held the baby closer, putting him to her breast again, trying to stop his crying. "I should have known," he said, sneering. "Like mother, like daughter," and for the first time since he'd come into the room, she spoke.

"I don't know what you're talking about," she said softly, her voice weak but determined. "I don't know why you're carrying on so. I have a son for you, and you don't even want to accept him."

"A son? For me?" His eyes widened angrily. "Are you trying to say that baby you're holding is my son?" he asked incredulously, and he frowned.

"How can you think otherwise?" she asked calmly, and he froze, his eyes blazing as she looked at him. "Why, you even picked out a name for him, remember?" she reminded him. "You said we'd name him after your grandfather. He's to be Colton Avery, the Earl of Grantham, future Duke of Bourland, remember?" His mouth fell in consternation. "I really think it's a nice name, don't you?" she went on, but his fist came down on her nightstand, teetering the vase of flowers that was on it, and she jumped, startled.

"That is not my son!" he roared angrily, and suddenly Rebel's eyes narrowed and she stared right back at him.

"Prove it!" she challenged, her violet eyes flashing anxiously. He turned away, his face white with rage, and stalked to the balcony, staring out into the night.

Right in front of him. Right under his nose, she was carrying on with that Indian. That savage! How was he to explain the child? One look at him and they'd know. Maybe not. Maybe they wouldn't suspect anything. He had to try, anyway. What else could he do besides denouncing her and admitting to the world he'd been cuckolded? That he'd never do. Damn her anyway! She'd pay for this!

He turned back to the room and walked over, standing next to her bed. He was composed now, his anger submerged beneath an air of indifference. "All right, if that's the way it has to be," he said, conceding her victory. "May I take another look at the child you so blithely tell me I've fathered?" She stared at him suspiciously, wondering just what he was up to.

He glanced down at the baby again. There was no mistake. He could never have fathered such a child, but if that's the sort of game she wanted to play . . .

"We'll have him christened a week from Sunday," he said calmly. "You should be out of bed by that time, that's only eight days away." He turned then, his face showing little emotion, and started for the door. "Oh, I forgot," he said, turning back to face her. "I have to leave for the moment. I promised to let my subjects know when the big event occurred. I believe they're planning a celebration of sorts. Too bad you can't attend. I'll probably be home rather late, however, so don't bother to wait up," and as he left the room, she shuddered. There was something coldly sinister about the calm way Brandon had departed, and it frightened her. But when Cristabel came in, she momentarily forgot about Brandon.

There was a short tropical shower Sunday morning before breakfast, but it cleared before church services, and although Rebel's strength still wasn't what it should be, she was in a rather good mood as she got ready for church. Holding to his word, Brandon made arrangements to have the baby christened, with his secretary and one of the regiment captains standing in as proxy for the godparents, his sister and her husband, who were still back in England.

Rebel slipped on all her petticoats, then put on her dress. It was pale pink with just a shade of orange to it, making it the color of a ripe, rosy peach, but she had to hold her breath in especially long as she fastened the hook at the waist. She was still swollen and her breasts were so full of milk she had to put pads in front so they wouldn't leak through. It was annoying, but she didn't mind. She loved the baby so. He was all she had to remember Beau by. The baby and her memories of that last night before she became Brandon's wife. She thanked God for that night.

She walked over and looked down at Cole, sleeping peacefully in his cradle. If she had only known, she could have saved herself so much pain and misery.

The church was crowded when they arrived and made their way up the aisle. Rebel carried the baby and Brandon followed close behind. The services went well until Rebel brought the baby to the baptismal font and lifted the thin shawl that had been covering his head. No one had seen the baby thus far except Dr. Wilder, Cristabel, and the servants. As the vicar lifted his hand and looked down into the child's small face, he frowned. His words faltered for a moment; then, dipping his hand in the font, he continued, but Brandon had caught the vicar's surprise, and he wondered if the rest of the congregation would be as observant.

Rebel was sitting beneath a canopy near the table where the tea was being served. She had a few moments to herself while Cristabel was watching the baby, and Brandon talked with the general and one of his staff. She had let her tea cool the way she liked it, and was sipping it easily, being careful not to spill any on her dress.

"I see someone else likes tea the way I do," said a voice from her side, and she turned to Miriam, who'd slipped onto the seat beside her. Rebel liked Miriam, in a way, but she felt sorry for her. She wasn't even thirty yet, but there were times she seemed ancient. Always talking about the way her bones ached when it rained, how she had to watch everything she ate or her stomach acted up. Also, she was sure she must be going blind, because at times she saw spots before her eyes.

"She's a hypochondriac," stated Brandon one evening after the doctor and his wife had left a social gathering early because she had a headache. "It's a good thing she's married to a doctor," and everyone had laughed, but Rebel hadn't thought it was funny. It was pitiful.

Miriam could be getting so much out of life if she'd just quit thinking about herself so much. The vicar's wife was sure if she had been able to have children perhaps it would have helped. "The poor woman has too much time on her hands alone," she'd told a group of ladies at tea one afternoon. "After all, poor Dr. Wilder is gone most of the time taking care of someone somewhere on the island," and all the ladies agreed, but no one did anything to relieve her loneliness, probably because they couldn't stand to hear her complaints.

Rebel glanced at her now. She was rather attractive, her dark brown hair curled about her face, with tight ringlets over each ear, her wide-brimmed sun hat perched atop it, but the dress she wore was most unbecoming. It was a beautiful shade of blue, and expensive enough, but too cluttered with ribbons, bows, ruffles, and braiding, and her jewelry was too large and ornate. This was, however, the way in which Miriam always dressed.

"It was a beautiful ceremony, wasn't it?" she said to Rebel, her strangely topaz-colored eyes shining. "I always love christenings, and the baby's beautiful. Such dark eyes and hair . . . I told Matthew he probably inherited them from one of his grandparents or something," and Rebel inhaled. Miriam always called her husband by his given name, never Matt.

"My mother's hair is very black," Rebel explained, and Miriam's eyes widened.

"But your hair's so light."

"Like my father's."

"Oh." She looked a little disconcerted. "I was telling Matthew on the way to church this morning that I think it's marvelous you're up and about already. If I had a baby I'd probably be in bed for a month."

"I don't doubt it," agreed Rebel, "but then, I always was a strong person."

"That's what Matthew said."

Rebel's eyebrows raised. "Oh? You always discuss his patients with him?"

Her face reddened. "Well, no . . . not really, but the governor's wife . . . it does make a person curious."

"Just what did he say about me?"

"Nothing, really. Only that you were young and healthy and strong."

"You mean he didn't tell you that he saved my life?"

"Saved your life? How?"

Rebel took a sip of her cool tea. "Perhaps you'd better ask your husband that question, Miriam," she answered. "It isn't exactly the right sort of thing to be talking about at a church social." Then she turned, greeting the vicar's wife.

"The baby's a dear, your Grace," the vicar's wife gushed as she joined them. "Just a dear, but really, he doesn't look much like either one of you, does he?"

"Undoubtedly looks like his great-grandfather or something," answered Rebel casually, and the vicar's wife laughed, agreeing, telling about one of her brothers who didn't look a bit like the rest of the family, but whose son was the image of his grandfather. "It's strange how life works, isn't it, my dear?" she said. "We never really know who we might resemble," and Rebel, seeing Brandon beginning to eye her dubiously from where he stood across the church lawn, politely changed the subject by asking her about her oldest son's plans to follow his father into the ministry.

An hour later, when it was time to leave, Rebel was relieved. She disliked these social affairs. Private parties were all right, but at something like this there was no way to weed out the people she disliked and who disliked her, and it was annoying having to put up with the friendly gestures she knew were forced because her husband was the governor.

As the governor's carriage pulled away from the churchyard with Cristabel sitting in the back seat holding the baby, Brandon sighed. "Well, at least that's over," he said. "And it

228

went better than I expected. I think the only suspicious one was the vicar, but then, he wasn't sure, either."

"Sure of what?" she asked.

"Don't try to be cute, Reb," he demanded. "You know very well what I'm talking about."

She looked amused. "If you're still trying to convince yourself he's not your son, go right ahead," she said. "But you do happen to be my husband. The law says he's yours, I say he's yours, and you just had him baptized, acknowledging him as your son. So why don't you just forget it?"

He turned, glaring directly at her, his eyes dark and foreboding. "What you've done to me I'll never forget, Rebel," he said ominously, "not for as long as I live, and neither will you." He called to the driver to go faster, and the carriage moved quickly down the road toward the large tile-roofed house.

Miriam watched it disappear in the distance, then turned to her husband. "Really, Matthew, I do think they make the strangest couple, don't you?" she said. "They just don't seem well suited, do they?" and he shook his head as he watched the carriage disappear up the hill.

"I haven't thought about it," he said as he helped her into their small buggy.

"Well, I have," she went on. "Brandon's so handsome and dynamic, but sometimes she treats him so coldly. He's always smiling and friendly, and she rarely smiles. So serious all the time, and always saying such unusual things."

He settled beside her, his somewhat seedy appearance contrasting with her expensive gown, and he picked up the reins. "Like what?" he asked.

"Like today. She said you saved her life when the baby was born."

He flushed. He disliked talking about Rebel. It irritated him for reasons he hated to admit. "It wasn't anything, really," he said as they started for home.

"But she seems to think so." She tossed her head, her fingers toying with a strip of wood at the side of the carriage. "When I asked her to tell me about it, she suggested I ask you. Can you imagine . . . she said it wasn't the proper thing to talk about at a church social."

"It wasn't."

She waited for him to go on, but he didn't. "Well, aren't you going to tell me, Matthew?" she finally asked, but he shook his head.

"Not now, Miriam, maybe later, maybe not at all," he said

irritably. "You know I dislike discussing my patients with you. You have a habit of letting things slip when you shouldn't, and after all, a doctor is supposed to keep his patient's private lives private."

"That's the trouble with you," she complained, her lower lip pouting. "You always have to be so professional. Ethics! I miss out on more gossip because of them."

"And I get in less trouble," he answered. "Now, let's forget I'm a doctor and enjoy the day, shall we?" and she sighed.

Always the same, enjoy the day. He'd probably end up halfway across the island before the afternoon was over, setting some native's broken leg or something. Miriam began to hum to herself, trying to think of some way she could amuse herself while he was gone.

The baby was growing fast. He seemed to do nothing but eat and sleep, a condition all babies were born with, according to Dr. Wilder, who had stopped by some days later to check on Rebel.

"I never realized how helpless babies really are," Rebel said as she made her way upstairs with the doctor close behind. "He looks so fragile when he's sleeping, but when he's eating he feels as strong as a little ox, and sometimes it really hurts.

Matt frowned. "Maybe you're drying up already."

"But he's not even two weeks old yet."

"I know," he said as they stepped into the bedroom, where the cradle was set up beside her bed. "But it can happen. Why do you think there's such a thing as a wet nurse?" and she frowned.

"I guess I hadn't thought," she said, half-laughing. He turned from her quickly, looking at the baby, touching his hands lightly, then feeling his forehead. Cole was sleeping on his stomach, with his face to one side, his hands stretched out above his head. He looked fine and healthy.

"Are you still bleeding?" he asked her casually as he straightened from the baby's cradle, worried because she'd had a problem with heavy bleeding, and she blushed, shaking her head hesitantly.

"No," she said softly. "Not since the day before yesterday."

"Good," he said, then glanced down toward her bosom, bulging softly up from the low décolleté of the deep blue dress she wore. "I wish I knew if you were drying up or not," he said. "Because if you are, you'd better find a wet nurse or you'll be starving your son and he could become undernourished."

"But how can I tell?"

"You said he hurt. How badly?"

She bit her lip. It was awkward talking about such things with Matt. After all, he wasn't just the doctor, he was an important man on the island, and often a guest in the house. Her hand moved to her throat nervously. "Last night it hurt so badly, and this morning I was in tears by the time he'd finished."

"May I take a look?"

"At my breasts?"

"Rebel, I'm a doctor," he reminded her, and she looked at him skeptically.

"I know," she answered hesitantly, "but . . . I just don't feel comfortable about it."

"Why?"

She shrugged. "I don't know." She gazed into his deep green eyes and something stirred inside her, and she couldn't look away. "All right, I guess you'd better, for the baby's sake," she said uneasily, and turned around, letting him unhook the two top hooks on her dress.

He was very efficient, his hands touching her breasts gently as he checked them for fullness, then examined her nipples, but he had no idea what he was doing to her, not at first. His hands were soft and warm, and at their first touch a shock went through her that made her tremble. She closed her eyes and almost cried for him to stop, but she didn't want him to know.

She stared at him now as he examined her. His face was so close it made her feel strange inside. He wasn't handsome, but there was something ruggedly good-looking and masculine about him. The square jaw, straight nose, and brown wavy hair. Why hadn't she ever noticed it before? She'd been too busy feeling sorry for herself, that's why. Now suddenly his nearness stimulated her and she couldn't help herself as she felt her nipples harden beneath his touch.

Matt's hands stopped abruptly, and he removed them, his eyes moving to her face. She saw him flush. "I've seen enough," he said huskily, knowing that for the first time in his life the barrier that he'd always kept between himself and his patients had begun to fall apart. He cleared his throat nervously. "I suggest you get a wet nurse, Rebel," he said. "By tomorrow morning you won't have enough milk left for the baby's breakfast."

She turned around, slipping her breasts back inside her dress. "Will you fasten me back up?" she asked politely, and he obliged; then they took one last look at the baby and left the room.

"I don't think I'd better stay for any tea," he said, trying to forget what had just happened as they walked downstairs. "I have some other patients to see." She nodded, calling one of the downstairs servants to bring his hat. They were walking toward the door just as it opened and Brandon stepped in.

He stopped for a moment, staring, his eyes adjusting to the cooler light after the bright sunlight outside; then he saw Matt and smiled.

"Well, Doctor, and how is the patient today?" he asked blithely as he handed his hat to the butler, but Matt didn't smile back.

"She'll be all right as soon as you get a wet nurse," he answered. "She's out of milk."

Brandon glanced quickly at Rebel. "Have you sent for one?"

"Not yet," she answered. "He just told me."

"Well, hadn't you better?" he said. "The baby will be waking up for his afternoon feeding and there won't be any."

"There should be enough for today," she insisted, but he seemed to be trying to get rid of her, and this time his voice had a demanding ring to it.

"Go tell Cristabel or someone to find you a wet nurse, Rebel, please," he insisted. "I want it done now." She stared at him for a minute, then turned angrily on her heel and left the foyer.

"It could have waited, Brandon," said Matt, putting his hat on his head, but Brandon looked at him anxiously.

"But I can't wait," he said. "I had to talk to you alone."

Matt's eyebrows raised. "Oh?"

Brandon reached to open the door for the doctor, but hesitated. "Matt, I have to know," he said nervously, his breathing unsteady. "The baby's almost two weeks old. . . . Can I touch my wife yet?" Matt stared at him unsteadily, trying to be impartial, but he couldn't.

"If you're very careful the first time," he answered huskily. "Now, if that's all you wanted, Brandon, I do have other patients." Brandon, not noticing Matt's discomfiture, opened the door the rest of the way for him, hardly realizing he'd left.

Dr. Matthew Wilder walked slowly to his buggy and got in, pulling the hat down farther on his head; then he lifted the reins, flicking them harder than usual. The buggy moved out the gate and through the streets quickly, heading away from the house until it came to a long stretch of beach far out on the coast, where he pulled up in a secluded spot, dropping the reins. He stepped from the buggy and strolled to the edge of the beach, staring into the ocean. He removed his hat, wiped his brow; then, without any hesitation, he stripped off his clothes and waded into the surf, feeling its cool water caress his muscular body.

Why couldn't Rebel have been like other women who refused to let a doctor treat them? Why couldn't she have hired a midwife like most of the other women on the island? He should have refused to take women patients; other doctors did. But he hadn't, and he stood now, chest-deep in ocean water, feeling the sun on his face, and remembered the way her nipples had hardened beneath his touch. She'd been aroused; he knew it, and he shook his head, then plunged into the surf, trying to forget.

Cristabel had come back with a wet nurse shortly after Rebel had struggled through another painful feeding. The woman, if you could call her a woman, was a wee bit plump and round-faced, her dark hair cut very short and frizzed atop her head, with sad, wistful eyes.

"Her baby was born dead three days ago," Cristabel informed Rebel as she introduced her. "Her name's Hizzie and she's eighteen. She loves babies and she's got lotsa good milk."

"Doc Wilder say if I don't get ridda all the milk pretty quick, missus, that I'm gonna hurt somethin' powerful, so your child's welco.ne to it if he wants it." Rebel couldn't refuse, especially when she saw the young woman's face as she looked at little Cole.

The fact that the girl hadn't been married didn't seem to bother Rebel in the least, and Cristabel was glad.

Cole Avery! Rebel said it over and over again to herself as she stood in her bedroom that night and stared at the baby sleeping so peacefully. Wouldn't Beau be proud? She turned from the cradle and went back to the vanity and sat down, continuing to brush out her long blond hair as she looked at herself in the mirror. On the contrary, he wouldn't be proud, she thought. The baby looked too much like an Indian for him. He'd hate that.

She stood up and stretched, staring at herself in the mirror, the curves of her body visible beneath the diaphanous nightgown she wore. She was getting her figure back, anyway. Her waistline had come down almost two inches in the last few days, and it was good not to have that huge stomach in front of her.

She leaned over to blow out the light, then suddenly froze as she realized the handle to the door that separated her room from Brandon's was being turned. It had been almost two months since Brandon had used that door this time of night. The last time had been a little over a month before Cole was born. She had put him off whenever she could, but that particular night he wouldn't take no for an answer. She'd told him she hadn't been feeling well. That's one reason he'd let her take a separate room, because she'd been so sick most of the time. But that night he didn't care. He'd not only made love to her, at least what he called making love, but he had prolonged it, using her body in ways she hadn't dreamed a woman's body could be used, and the next day she'd started to bleed. Afraid her time had come, she'd had Cristabel call Matt to the house, expecting to go into labor, but when nothing happened, Matt became suspicious and he'd plied her with questions, discovering that Brandon didn't exactly use finesse in bed. The doctor made it a point to warn Brandon that if it happened again she could lose the baby. Brandon was furious at first that she'd discussed their private life with Matt, but he wanted the baby so badly that he'd swallowed his pride, for the first time in his life, and kept his distance. She'd assured Brandon that she hadn't told Matt everything, but it had been more than enough for him to see a side of Brandon that others on the island knew nothing of, and Brandon had not used the connecting door to their room since, keeping it locked after sundown.

Now she held her breath and whirled around as the door opened wide and Brandon stepped in, a goblet of wine in each hand, his bathrobe pulled tight.

"What do you want?" she asked softly.

"Isn't it obvious?"

"I can't."

"Oh, yes you can. I asked Matt, and he says it's all right."

"I lied to him."

"No you didn't." His eyes traveled beneath her sheer gown to the soft dark spot between her legs, and she knew there was no way to get out of it.

"But I still hurt," she said her voice shaking, "and I don't want to get pregnant again. Not so soon."

He lifted her hand and put the goblet of wine into it, pressing her fingers about its stem, putting it to her lips. "But

I want you to," he said sadistically as she took a sip and the cool wine slipped down her throat, turning to fire inside her. "I want you to get pregnant, Rebel, and I want you to have my son this time, and I want to see you go through the same thing for me that you went through for him. I want it to hurt you so badly you'll want to die, and then, when that baby's born you'll have another and another, and each one will be mine, and each time you have one I'm going to celebrate. Not their birth, my love. I'm going to celebrate because with each baby you have I'll be getting even with you for what you've done to me. Now"—he took the glass out of her hands and set both goblets on the vanity beside her—"shall we get started?"

"You're insane!" she gasped, her eyes wide with horror. "Insane!"

"On the contrary," he said, his hand closing about her wrist. "I'm quite sane. Angry and humiliated, but quite sane, and remember, my love, as you told me in the carriage the day of the christening, I am your husband and that entitles me to certain privileges. Now, unless you want to scream and wake the baby up, and your wet nurse, Hizzie, who's sleeping in the powder room, I suggest you come with me." He turned, pulling her reluctantly behind him, her feet shuffling helplessly across the carpeted floor. There was nothing she could do. If she tried to fight, he'd take her anyway.

He pulled her into his bedroom, shutting the door behind them, and stood her in the middle of the floor, stripping the nightgown from her, then stood gazing at her body. She was beautiful, not like those dark-skinned bitches he'd used the last few weeks while he was waiting for her. Rebel he could make love to, he could take his time, not try to get it over with in a hurry so he wouldn't have to think of what she looked like. Well, he wouldn't have to worry for a long while now.

He took her hand and led her to the bed, then made her lie down. She lay stiffly, shutting her eyes, waiting for what he'd do next, willing her body to accept whatever came, but nothing happened.

"What's wrong with you?" he suddenly asked gruffly.

He was standing by the bed naked, staring at her, making no attempt to do anything.

"What do you mean, what's wrong?" she said.

"You usually put up a fight."

"I'm sorry, I don't like fighting," she said calmly, but he still stood there.

"You don't like fighting?"

"That's right. I don't like being hurt. If you want to put that thing in me"—and she motioned toward his manhood, hot and swollen—"go right ahead, I won't stop you, but I won't help you, either. You can do whatever you want with me, and it won't matter a bit. In fact, if I happen to fall asleep before you're through, you can wake me up and I'll go back to my own bed. The fact is, Brandon, you look quite ridiculous standing there without anything on." She closed her eyes, waiting for him to say something.

Brandon's eyes grew wild as he stared at her. What the hell was she trying to do? He got on the bed and kissed her fiercely, bruising her mouth, but she didn't respond; then he reached out, touching her breasts, running his hands over them while she lay still, forcing her body to ignore him and think of something else, anything but what he was doing.

She began to hum a tune, and he grew furious. He moved above her, pushing her legs apart; then suddenly she chuckled as his hand touched her stomach.

"You're tickling me." She laughed softly, and Brandon, beginning to thrust into her, let out a moan as he felt himself begin to go down. His forehead beaded with sweat. He could do nothing! She was still laughing, and the more she laughed, the softer he went. "Oh, really, Brandon," she said as she opened her eyes and looked at him, pretending to relax on the bed, unconcerned, "for heaven's sake get it over with, will you? I would like to get some sleep tonight." His eyes grew cold and deadly as his arm moved back, and before she realized what was happening, his fist came smashing toward her, catching the side of her face with an impact that stunned her.

Her head exploded, and she tried to pull herself up from the dark pit that was closing over her, but she couldn't, and suddenly there was nothing.

11

It must have been well past midnight when Rebel opened her eyes. She was on her bed now in her own room, and it was pitch dark. She stirred, and her head felt like a thousand hornets were stinging it. God, what had he done? Then she remembered his fist, and she moaned as she reached up. The whole side of her head and jaw were swollen, and her eye was puffed twice its size. She couldn't even open it.

Suddenly she heard the baby stir. He began making little noises. Grunts and groans at first, then he began to wail as loud as he could, and she felt as if her head would split in two. She moved off the bed, fighting to stand up straight. Her head was pounding and she stumbled to the door of the small powder room where Hizzie was sleeping.

"Hizzie?" she called, her voice raspy and shaking. "Hizzie, the baby's awake," and within seconds she felt the young woman by her side.

Hizzie started to step into the bedroom, then stopped, staring at Rebel, straining her eyes in the darkness. "My Lord, ma'am, what on earth happened to you?" but Rebel shook her head.

"I'm all right, Hizzie," she said. "Just feed the baby before he wakes up my husband, please." Hizzie hesitated a minute before she went in and picked up the baby, changed his pants, and settled down on the chaise longue with him while he suckled at her breast. She stared across the room curiously at her young mistress.

Rebel made her way back to the bed and crawled onto it, realizing she was still naked. She reached down between her legs as she stretched out, then sighed. There was no new soreness, only the faint ache that had been there since the baby's birth. Evidently after hitting her, he'd given up for the night. Well, good. She felt her eye again, then ran her hand down her jaw. She knew he'd be mad, but to do something like this . . . She lay back, closing her eyes, waiting until she finally went back to sleep.

The next morning her head was throbbing painfully as she dragged herself from the bed and walked to the mirror, making sure not to wake the baby. Her face was on fire and she could see out of only one eye. She stood in front of the mirror looking at herself and felt sick. The bastard! He had no right!

She grabbed her wrapper and put it on, then walked stealthily to the door that separated their rooms and flung it open, her face wet with tears.

Brandon was almost dressed, and stood by his dresser casually putting the diamond cufflinks on his shirt sleeves.

"You coward!" she yelled at him, shutting the door behind her, and he whirled around, startled. "You dirty, filthy bastard! Look what you've done to me—look!" she screamed, and she thrust her face out toward him, seeing him turn pale momentarily; then the expression on his face became sardonic.

"The next time, my dear, you won't have any face left!" he retorted firmly. "I can promise you that." He finished fastening the cufflink and reached for his coat. "And there will be a next time, Rebel, don't be mistaken. There'll be many more next times. I meant what I said. So unless you want to look like this again, or worse, there'd better not be another repeat of your ungracious performance of last night. Is that understood?"

She stared at him, heartsick. "How are you going to explain this?" she asked, her voice shaking, and he sneered.

"You'll have to be careful trying to walk around the house alone in the dark at night, my love," he said nastily. "It's surprising what a fall down the stairs can do."

"You think people will believe you?"

"Why not? Why, I ran out of my own room when I heard the commotion and picked you up myself, my love. Now, don't you remember?"

She studied him for a minute, her fists clenching angrily.

"I'm the governor of this island, love," he went on. "Now, that in itself should take care of the whole situation." And he laughed as she had laughed at him the night before.

Her heart was pounding as she stared at him. "I hate you, Brandon Avery, you can go to hell!" she yelled, and left the room, slamming the door behind her.

They had been invited to the Wilders' house for dinner that evening, and Rebel was downstairs in the library, trying to read a book with her one good eye and think of some possible reason she could give for not going, when the butler stepped into the room.

"Beg pardon, your Grace," he announced haughtily as she looked up from her book, "but Dr. Wilder is here to see you."

"Oh, my God! Tell him I can't see him, Wesley," she blurted hurriedly as the butler stood waiting. "Tell him I'm not at home . . . tell him I'm—"

"Tell him to leave?" asked Matt, poking his head around the doorway to the library. She stood up, turning her back to him.

"You may leave, Wesley," she said stiffly to the butler, her back still to them, and the butler quietly left the room.

Matt walked toward her curiously, then reached down and

238

picked up the book that had fallen as she stood up. "You dropped your book, Duchess," he said. He held the book toward her, touching her arm with it, and she reached out, taking it, but still keeping her back to him.

"What are you doing here?" she asked irritably, her hands nervously clenching the book as she held it tightly against her pale green dress. "You were here just yesterday." He stared at her back for a minute.

At first when Brandon said she wasn't coming he'd thought it might be because of what had happened yesterday afternoon, but then . . .

"I ran into Brandon a short while ago," he explained. "He told me you wouldn't be able to come with him for dinner tonight, that you weren't feeling up to it, but when I offered to stop by, he said it wasn't necessary. You were just upset a little . . . something about having fallen down the stairs . . . ?"

"Did you believe him?"

He frowned. "Should I have?"

She turned around slowly, letting the effect hit him gradually, and watched him go pale at the sight of her face. "What do you think happened?" she asked.

"Oh, Jesus!" he murmured beneath his breath when he found his voice again. "He did that to you?"

"I fell down the stairs—"

"Rebel, please."

"That's what Brandon told you."

"Stairs don't leave knuckle bruises."

He exhaled disgustedly as he stared at her. "Rebel, what happened last night?"

"I laughed at him."

"You what?"

"You heard me," she answered angrily. "He was going to rape me, and I knew he was stronger than I was and I couldn't fight him, so I laughed at him. Have you ever seen the effect laughter has on a man, Doctor?" she asked bitterly. "It's really quite funny."

"But he's your husband."

"Oh, I know that fact very well, Dr. Wilder," she said, turning her back to him again. "That's one mistake I'll never forget. You see, he said the next time I wouldn't have any face left."

"I wish to God I knew what was the matter between you two," he stated helplessly. "Maybe I could do something."

"Haven't you done enough already?"

He looked at her, puzzled. "What's that supposed to mean?"

She fingered the book nervously in her hands. "Why did you have to tell him it was all right? You're a big help, you are!" she said furiously. "Why couldn't you have told him no? Why didn't you tell him it was too soon, or ask me first how I felt? Or maybe my feelings don't count, is that it, Doctor? I'm only a woman?"

"Don't be ridiculous!"

Her voice shook. "That's usually the way it is, isn't it?" she said. "A woman isn't supposed to have any feelings, is she? That's what all you men think, isn't it? A woman was made for a man's pleasure."

"That's not the way it is, and you know it."

"Do I?" Tears glistened in her eyes. "All Brandon thinks of is himself, his own pleasure, his own desires, never mine, and that's all Beau did was use me, he wouldn't marry me! Where is my pleasure, Matt? When do I get to feel and enjoy? I'm not made of stone, I'm flesh and blood. Why didn't you ask me first if I wanted Brandon to touch me? I'm a woman, Matt, not a toy!"

He gazed past her, out the window into the courtyard outside, where sweet-scented frangipani bloomed in abundance, its heady fragrance filling the room. How well he knew she was a woman. The fact had been haunting him for months.

"I'm sorry if I overstepped myself," he apologized stiffly, annoyed at her for having this effect on him. "How was I to know—?"

She turned to face him. "How indeed!"

His eyes caught hers. "Don't you think you're being unreasonable?"

"With Brandon?"

"With me!"

She looked at him long and hard, his baggy coat hiding the muscular frame she knew was beneath it, his casual appearance belying the strength and determination he possessed.

"I had no idea you hated him so much, Rebel," he said softly.

"So now you know."

"Let me help you, Rebel, please."

"You can't, Matt," she answered. "I should have known better," and she reached up, touching the tips of her fingers to her swollen face. "I know what I have to do. . . . I'll survive."

"How?"

"I'll just close my eyes the next time he wants to bed me, and the next . . . and the next—"

"Stop it!"

"I'm sorry, Matt, but that's the way it is. I made a mistake and I have to live with it. You'd better go now before he finds you here. I don't think he'd like it, especially if he thought you knew what really happened." She started walking toward the door.

"Put a cold compress on that eye," he said in his best professional manner as he followed her, "and if the swelling hasn't started to go down by tomorrow morning, send for me." He stopped at the doorway and reached in his pocket. "Here's some laudanum, it'll help you sleep tonight."

She drew back. "I don't need that."

He took her hand and opened it, pressing the packet into it, closing her fingers over it. "You'll change your mind during the night."

"But—"

"Don't argue, Duchess. Now, go back to your book, I'll let myself out."

"You won't say anything to Brandon?"

"I'd like to kill him."

She grabbed his arm. "Matt!"

His hand went over hers. "Don't worry, I won't say anything."

"Thank you."

His fingers pressed on her hand, and she felt the warmth from them stir her deep inside. Then he quickly let go and walked from the room without saying another word. She leaned against the doorframe and watched him leave before returning to her chair.

It was almost two weeks before her face healed enough so that she felt human. Brandon, able to look at her again, finally decided to make another try. This time there was no fighting. When he came to her room, she reluctantly submitted to him, hating every moment, letting him do with her as he wished, even forcing herself to pretend she was enjoying it so as not to anger him. Afterward, when she heard his heavy breathing and knew he was asleep, she cried herself to sleep.

Rebel was angry, frustrated, and bored. Hizzie was a big help with the baby, feeding and bathing him, and although Rebel spent as much time with him as she could, he didn't fill the void that seemed to well up inside her. The more she looked at him, the more she thought of Beau; and the more

241

she thought of Beau, the more she hated Brandon; and the more she hated Brandon, the harder it became for her to be a wife to him. Her life was becoming empty of joy and full of self-pity. It simply couldn't go on.

She stood in front of the mirror and studied herself seriously. Today, March 13, was her birthday. She was twenty years old.

"And I feel like eighty," she murmured to herself. Hizzie glanced up quickly from the chaise where she was nursing Cole and stared at her mistress. Rebel unpinned her hair and let the mass of ringlets that had been piled on top of her head fall naturally to her shoulders; then she picked up the brush and began brushing it vigorously. There ought to be something she could do with her time to make life more interesting. She took a deep violet ribbon from the drawer of her vanity and tied it loosely around her hair. Sadly she wandered to the balcony and stepped outside into the warm sun.

There were ships of all sizes in the harbor, like white birds resting on the calm, crystal blue waters, and the sun, reflecting off them, made her squint. She turned toward the island, staring at the green foliage, its dense cover like a carpet on the hillsides.

"Hizzie, how big is Grenada?" she asked suddenly, and Hizzie shrugged.

"I don't rightly know, ma'am," she answered. "But I do know there's lotsa island past the city."

Rebel glanced back down the hillside toward the city below her, then stepped back into the room. "You know, I've been here since last year, Hizzie, and I've never been beyond the city. Not even for a ride." She walked to the armoire and pulled out a huge straw hat with big yellow flowers on it. "Do you think you can take care of Cole without me for a while today?" she asked, and the girl nodded as she smiled down at Cole.

"I knows I can, ma'am," she said. "He's almost like my own, and he's such a good little fella."

Rebel envied Hizzie. She seemed so completely content just to take care of the baby, but then Hizzie was brought up in a large family with small brothers and sisters to take care of and knew nothing of what it was to ride a horse at full gallop through the woods, hair flying in the wind, or the exhilaration of being free to roam the wilderness as Rebel had done. Although she loved the baby, Rebel was restless now that she was feeling like herself again instead of like a stuffed goose, and she needed room to move in, to feel free again, if just for a little while.

She made sure Hizzie had everything she needed, then went downstairs, ordering the carriage brought around. In all the months she'd been here she'd never left the house alone. From the day she'd realized she was pregnant to the day Cole had been born, she'd been sick and miserable, not caring to go anywhere or see anyone, performing her duties as the governor's wife when necessary, then hiding herself away from the island except for a few friends Brandon had cultivated and whom she was obliged to meet with socially.

When the carriage arrived, the young colored footman, his red-and-white uniform clinging to a spindly frame, stoically helped her in, then climbed up on his seat in back and studied Rebel with his huge round eyes, rather surprised that the governor's wife was finally going out.

The driver, a hunched-over black man with white hair and a broad smile that wrinkled all over his face, turned around, and Rebel leaned forward, instructing him to go as far inland as he could so she could look over the island; then she sat back and straightened the skirt on her deep violet dress, folded her hands in her lap, and prepared to enjoy the scenery.

The carriage moved down the hill, passing homes of the wealthier inhabitants of Grenada, none of the houses of course equaling the grandeur of the governor's house; then it moved on down the hill into the city itself, passing buildings that had been up almost a century already, their weathered faces beginning to crumble. Many had been built during the French occupation, then added to by the British.

The carriage slowed to a walk as they moved at a snail's pace through the marketplace, teeming with crowds, and suddenly Rebel realized people were staring at her. She'd forgotten for a moment that she was the wife of his Excellency the governor. The streets were filled with soldiers too, and they stared at her curiously, some even covetously, taking in her petite figure, the low décolleté of her dress emphasizing her full bosom, and her big violet eyes in a face framed by a cascade of golden hair beneath the sun hat; but she looked away as if she didn't see them.

In the past few months since Christmas, almost four hundred troops had been added to the regiments already on Grenada, and Rebel knew something was brewing, but the days of idleness played heavily on the men, making them restless, and they roamed the streets on their off hours looking for entertainment—anything to while away the lonely hours.

They watched the carriage curiously as it moved out of the marketplace and onto the road that circled the bay, then headed away from the city toward the hills.

Rebel was fascinated as they moved inland. Before, the island had been a prison to her; now suddenly it began coming to life. They passed natives on their way to and from the city with produce in carts of all sizes and shapes, women in colorful clothes carrying huge baskets on their heads, people of all colors, a hodgepodge of nationalities. The strong smell of spices filled the air as they moved along. Nutmeg, mace, cloves, cinnamon, and waxy green leaves of the breadfruit plant swept close to the narrow roadway, while palm fronds tried to shade her from the hot sun, and exotic flowers of all descriptions grew wild and untamed, scattered amid the foliage.

Rebel stared in awe at the beauty around her, then frowned a short while later as the carriage came to a stop. "What's wrong?" she asked the driver, and he straightened, his sharp eyes intent on what was ahead of them.

They had taken a road that climbed high into the hills, and now Rebel cocked her ear, straining, listening. The soft rhythmic beat of drums could be heard in the distance, and she leaned forward as the driver turned in his seat.

"Beggin' your pardon, your Grace," he said solemnly, his voice barely above a whisper, "but we'd best turn back. This part of the island is rather desolate and wild, and I don't think his Excellency the governor would like it if we went on."

"Why not?" she asked. "I've heard there are plantations farther inland. I'd love to see one."

"Perhaps another time."

"Is it the drums?" She'd heard the drums before, dozens of times since she'd arrived on the island, sometimes close, sometimes far away, but Brandon would never satisfy her curiosity about them.

He glanced ahead to where the road curved as it disappeared into a maze of green, then turned back to her. "Partly, your Grace. The people inland are a strange lot, none too friendly at times. Especially if they think we're nosing around where we don't belong."

Rebel remembered something Hizzie had said the other day about strange happenings on the island. "All right, maybe we'd better go back." The driver turned the carriage around, noting the relief on the face of the young footman.

That evening Brandon was giving a party for Rebel's birthday. She had no idea why, except that he liked to show off and act important, and the party would give him a chance. Rebel wouldn't have minded so much if he'd arranged for a quiet dinner party, but he'd opened the house to half the population of the island, which included his cabinet and advisers and their wives and friends, assorted army officers, a couple of ship's captains, and some plantation owners from inland, along with his own special circle of friends.

Rebel disliked being put on display even for her birthday, but there was nothing she could do. At least she and Brandon were on speaking terms now. There was no way she could keep him from her bed, and although their relationship was impossible as far as she was concerned, she was trying her best to act like a proper wife and avoid the brunt of his anger, because she felt she had no other choice.

Guests were due to arrive in less than an hour, and Rebel was in her room dressing with Cristabel's assistance, while Hizzie swung the cradle lazily, trying to put Cole to sleep. Rebel lifted her arms as Cristabel held up the dress for her to put on. It was yards of white lace with diamante scattered about the skirt and an extra train of white lace down the back.

"Hizzie," Rebel asked as she put her arms in the sleeves and let Cristabel put it over her head, "what did you mean the other day when you mumbled something about being hexed?" Hizzie stopped, motionless for a minute, then continued swinging the cradle. "Well?" asked Rebel again as she pulled the dress the rest of the way on and stood waiting to have it fastened, the low décolleté in front barely covering her bosom. "I'm waiting, Hizzie."

Hizzie glanced over at her mistress as Cristabel began fastening the dress in the back; then she bit her lips. "I shouldn't have said nothin' ma'am. I'm sorry," she said, but Rebel wasn't satisfied.

"I heard you mumbling," she insisted, "and I want to know what it's about."

Cristabel fastened the last hook on Rebel's dress, then stepped from behind Rebel and glanced at Hizzie. "I can tell you, ma'am," Christabel said, scowling. "She told me Seldie's aunt put a hex on her."

"Why?"

"'Cause I slept with Seldie's man," answered Hizzie reluctantly.

"Your baby's father?"

"Yes, ma'am."

"But a hex?"

Cristabel's eyes narrowed. "Seldie's aunt's a mamba, ma'am," she said, "and Seldie said she was gonna make sure Hizzie wouldn't never have no baby of her own to take care of."

"You believe this, Hizzie?" asked Rebel, and Hizzie nodded.

"Oh, yes, ma'am," she said fervently. "I knows that why I don't have no baby. But I fixed Seldie. I went to the vicar's church and prayed . . . I prayed real hard. It was too late to save my baby, but the vicar's God gave me another baby to take care of instead. So I'm happy," and she looked down at Cole, now sound asleep, and Rebel stared at her, frowning.

Strange these people should believe such things. She wasn't exactly sure she liked the idea of Hizzie caring for Cole so much if there was a chance she'd teach him this sort of mumbo-jumbo as he grew up. Was that why Brandon didn't want the Negroes in the house? She straightened her dress and sat down for Cristabel to fix her hair, and she remembered the weird beat of the drums she'd heard that afternoon. She could tell there'd been three drums, each a different pitch, each a different rhythm, yet they'd blended into a spellbinding cadence. How often she'd heard it before, but paid little attention. She'd been used to drums, having lived so close to the Indians for years. She shivered for a moment, then glanced quickly into the mirror and raised her hands, helping Cristabel to arrange her hair in a new way.

She had her pull it back severely and twist it; then it was fastened above the twist with a diamond clip in a crescent shape that framed the plump chignon, and diamond teardrops were placed in her pierced ears. The effect, which made her look older and more sophisticated, pleased her.

She started to stand up, when the door to Brandon's room opened, and Cristabel turned shyly, watching the governor standing in the doorway staring at his wife. His eyes shifted over Rebel from head to toe, and he relaxed.

"You look lovely," he said softly, and stepped toward the vanity, holding his hand out to help her maneuver away from the vanity bench, but she declined the offer, slipping past him skillfully.

"I'm glad you like the dress," she said as she avoided his

eyes. "The dressmaker said white would be best, to go with my eyes."

"It certainly wasn't meant to signify purity," Brandon retorted, irritated over her rebuff, and her head jerked about quickly as she looked at him. Always the remarks, the vicious innuendos to throw at her.

He looked immaculately handsome tonight in his white suit with its satin lapels and ruffled shirt, a band of red silk across his chest from shoulder to waist with medals pinned to it. Anything to look impressive; but then, wasn't that what she'd wanted too, prestige? How unappealing it all seemed now.

He held out his arm. "If you're ready, we'd best go down," he said formally. "The guests will be arriving." She stared at him stubbornly, then slowly lifted her hand, laying it on top of his arm as she saw the flash of anger in his brown eyes.

"If you need me for anything, Hizzie, send Cristabel down," Rebel said as she turned and walked toward the door. Hizzie and Cristabel glanced at each other furtively as the governor and his wife left the room.

The guests began arriving shortly after they reached the entrance hall, and Rebel was subjected to intense scrutiny by most of them as they greeted her. Many were seeing her for the first time, and Brandon's eyes shone with pride at the pleased expressions on their faces, even though Rebel squirmed uncomfortably under their gaze.

"I certainly was glad to see you and Miriam arrive," Rebel told Matt some half-hour after greeting the last arrivals, a Dutch planter named Van Horn, his plump wife, and her brother, a sea captain who'd arrived only that day. "Brandon knows these people, but I don't. I have so little in common with them."

Matt smiled. He'd been making himself scarce about the governor's house of late. "They're a friendly sort, really," he said. "After all, you can't blame them for being curious. You've hidden yourself away since your arrival. I think some of them were beginning to think you weren't real."

"Oh, I'm very real," she replied, "only I'm not exactly sure I'm what they expected."

"What do you think they expected?"

She was sipping at a glass of claret wine, and her eyes caught his; then she looked away quickly. "Someone older, wiser . . ."

"I haven't heard anyone complain yet."

Her eyes shone as the claret warmed her deep inside.

"Matt," she asked, changing the subject, "you know a lot about the island, don't you?"

He shrugged. "Quite a bit."

She sipped at the wine again, then licked her lips. "Did you take care of Hizzie when her baby was born?"

"Now, what possessed you to ask that?"

"Well, did you?"

"Yes. The vicar asked me to."

"Was it born dead?"

"Yes."

"Why?"

He frowned. "You mean why was it dead?" She nodded. "Who knows? The mortality rate's high among the natives. They don't eat right, work too hard."

"That's the only reason?"

His green eyes watched her closely. "What are you looking for?"

She glanced about quickly to make sure they weren't being overheard. "Matt, Hizzie says a mamba put a hex on her. What's a mamba, and who's playing those drums I hear all the time? I heard them again today, and I'm sure there's some connection."

"Where'd you hear the drums?"

"I took a ride this afternoon on the inland road, but when the drums started, the driver wouldn't go any farther. What's going on on this island, Matt?"

"In Haiti it's called voodoo. Here it's . . . well, it really doesn't have a name. I guess you could call it black magic, sorcery, voodoo."

"What's voodoo?"

"It's a form of religion with spirits, an assortment of gods, and magic powers. There's usually a priest called a houngan or hungan, a priestess or mamba, and the choir leader or houngenican, sometimes called a hunsi. They thrive on what they call spirit possession, using blood sacrifices in their ceremonies, and their gods are both good and bad, depending upon the needs of the worshiper. Here on Grenada, they've added to the original and come up with a rather frightening substitute."

"And Hizzie's mixed up in it?"

He shook his head. "No, not really. I've known Hizzie for a long time. Her parents were freed slaves. She's at the vicar's church every Sunday, right in the front row, but it's hard for a native to shake the influence of black magic completely. Even some of the white folks turn pale when the hear the drums."

Rebel frowned. "Matt, the slaves on the island, are they natives of Grenada?"

"Some are, some aren't, if you consider children born on the island to slave parents as natives."

"Where did they originally come from?"

"Africa mostly, Madagascar." He nodded toward Mr. Van Horn's brother-in-law, the sea captain, a tall lean man with sharp features and piercing eyes that seemed to rake the room like a man sorting cattle. "The ship he commands is a slaver," he offered, and Rebel's eyes narrowed as she glanced at the captain.

"Does Brandon know?"

Matt's eyes hardened. "What do you think?"

"I think it's disgusting."

His face softened as he stared at her. Who would think the governor's wife, a woman most people considered an aristocratic snob, would dislike slavery?

She saw the expression on his face, and her eyes fell before his gaze, and he noticed the way the candlelight from the chandeliers overhead made her hair look darker than usual, like deep gold, softening her features.

"How does this voodoo or black magic work?" she asked as she looked up at him again, fingering her wineglass thoughtfully.

"You really want to know?"

"Yes."

"All right." He glanced around the stately room. No one seemed to be watching them. The overpowering odor of perfume, flowers, and spices, accentuated by the noise and confusion of all the people, grated on his nerves. "Let's step out in the garden first," he suggested. "The night air is a little more conducive to conversation." She smiled and led the way to the French doors that opened onto the moonlit garden.

A slight breeze filled the air, rustling the leaves in the trees overhead, and it was refreshing as they made their way toward a place where colorful flowered vines nestled in the shadows, covering the stone wall that surrounded the garden.

"Now, tell me," she said anxiously, and he sighed as he began.

"In Hizize's case the mamba would make a small doll to look as much like the girl as possible. Probably out of clay or maybe straw, whatever's available, and she'd make it with a large body, perhaps hollowing it out and putting a replica of

249

a baby inside. But the doll would have to have something of Hizzie's on it. A few strands of her hair, fingernail clippings, or maybe even a piece of jewelry or clothing that she was particularly fond of and wore often. When the doll was finished, they'd hold a ceremony and sacrifice something like a bird, or animal, spattering blood about. Haitian voodoo usually requires a large chorus of dancers, singers, and performers, but on Grenada, all that's required is a priest or priestess with magic powers and a passion for the macabre. Their religion's a conglomeration of chants, charms, and incantations taken from over a dozen African tribes and transplanted here, where it's fermented over the years into something quite nasty."

"But what happens to the doll?" she asked, thoroughly absorbed in his tale.

"They stick pins in it. If they wanted Hizzie dead, they'd stick them in her heart, but because it was the baby they wanted to harm, they'd stick them in the stomach or in the replica of the baby, willing it to die."

"That's absurd. You can't will something to die."

"Don't take it lightly, Rebel," he cautioned. "I've seen it in action, although I think there are times it's been helped along the way."

"But this is 1795. I thought the days of medieval superstitions like that were over."

"For some, yes, but there are always those who cling to the old. Just like in my profession. We're learning new things every day, yet there are supposedly civilized people who still think medical doctors are some strange cross between a madman and the devil. The people on this island would be shocked if they knew what I did when I delivered your baby. They were shocked enough when they found out you were my patient. Most women still go to midwives."

She inhaled anxiously, then turned, looking out over the wall and trees to the star-filled sky. "I guess these natives are somewhat like the Indians back home," she mused softly.

"Where's back home?"

She turned to him, her face shadowed so he couldn't see her expression. "America."

"I thought you were from England. Brandon said you were the daughter of an earl."

She reached out and plucked a leaf from a nearby bush, twisting it in her fingers self-consciously. "My father was the Earl of Locksley, but he only claimed the title the year before last. I grew up in the American wilderness, on the shores

250

of a lake called Erie. My father was what they call a back-woodsman."

"And your mother?"

"She was the daughter of an English lord."

"They're both dead?"

"Only my father. Mother's remarried now. She married an American and they're living in Port Royal, South Carolina."

"You compared our natives to your Indians. What are the Indians like?" he asked, not knowing the emotions his question would stir inside her.

She glanced at him quickly, then straightened and took a few steps from him to stand out of the shadows where the moonlight fell full on her, turning the back of her hair pale in comparison to the deep gold it had been in the candlelight inside; then she turned toward him, and for a moment he thought he saw pain in her eyes.

"Some are quite savage," she answered huskily, trying to put Beau from her mind, yet seeing his eyes before her every time she looked at this man. "They torture their enemies with an indifference that makes them seem inhuman, yet for all that, they can love as passionately and with as much feeling as anyone else. They interpret dreams and believe in signs as childishly as I suppose your natives do."

"You were in close contact with them?"

"Our house was only a few hundred yards from a village of Tuscarora."

He studied her closely, watching the rise and fall of her breasts. Something was disturbing her. She was breathing rapidly, her pulses quickening. He stepped forward, his eyes on hers. "What's wrong, Rebel?" he asked, but she closed her mind to him, and he saw her eyes grow cold.

"Nothing," she answered, his green eyes stirring the blood in her veins. She didn't want to feel like this. Not ever again, and she turned quickly, glancing at the house where she knew music and laughter awaited. Where she could talk and laugh and forget. "We'd better go in," she said anxiously, "before Brandon discovers I'm missing," and her eyes fell before his. "After all, I am the guest of honor," and she pursed her lips nervously. "I didn't mean to drag you into a history lesson about Grenada, Doctor," she apologized as they started walking slowly toward the house. "But I think I'll keep an eye on Hizzie, and Cristabel too, after what you've told me."

He fought a desire to stop her and demand to know why she had suddenly grown cold and distant, but something held him back. Fear. He was afraid of her. Afraid of the emotions she stirred within him, and instead he walked beside her, back to the house, indulging in idle chitchat as they slipped inside.

The evening was proving a tedious bore for Rebel. She knew few of the people to start with, and made matters worse by ignoring the rest. Not innocently, but by choice. Not cruelly, however; she didn't mean to be cruel, but she just couldn't stand the inane babbling and prattling that went on. General Bridlehurst's plump, swaybacked wife, who thought her husband's middle name was God, spent the evening clutching his arm, while he rubbed her hand affectionately and continued to flirt with every lady in the room, his receding hairline wrinkling as his eyebrows raised and lowered flirtatiously. He fawned over Brandon like a zealous puppy, doing everything but lick his boots, while his officers strutted like gamecocks readying for a fight.

It was close to midnight, the birthday cake had been cut, they'd danced and been entertained, and Rebel stood in the corner of the room trying unsuccessfully to blend in with the decorations, when Brandon slipped up beside her.

"You're being irritating tonight, Reb," he whispered closely in her ear. "These people expect my wife to be friendly, not treat them as if they were inferior."

Her back straightened like a ramrod and she felt deeply angry. Why did she have to be friendly to these people? They didn't even like her.

Brandon's arm went around her waist, and he pulled her toward him, cradling her head against his shoulder. "Look at me!" he demanded, continuing to whisper so no one would hear. A false smile covered the true meaning of his words, and she felt his fingers press into her waistline. She looked up into his brown eyes with the gold flecks in them dancing dangerously. "That's better, my love," he said, and she felt his hand relax on her waist. "It's time we let people see how happy we are together, how much in love we are." Fury choked her for a minute as she looked into his eyes; then she found her voice again.

"You enjoy torturing me, don't you?" she whispered. His answer was to bend and kiss her mouth possessively.

Her face reddened as he drew away from her and when she glanced across the room, she found she was looking directly into Miriam's eyes.

Miriam was still nursing the first glass of wine Matt had poured for her when they'd arrived. Spirits always upset her stomach, and she'd eaten little food for the same reason. Her topaz eyes stared back at Rebel's flushed face, and for a minute . . . What was it she saw in Rebel's eyes? Anger? Frustration? Because her husband had kissed her? How ridiculous! Miriam turned away self-consciously. It wasn't polite to stare. She reached up, touching a stray curl, putting it back into place as she stared across the room in a different direction, not really seeing anything. Oh, how she hated Rebel Avery. The Duchess of Bourland, indeed! Young and healthy, Matt had said. She didn't have to watch every morsel that went into her mouth, afraid to eat the wrong thing in fear of the gnawing pain that would grip her insides. And she didn't have to be afraid of bearing children, of being too weak and frail to live through it.

Miriam put her hand to her breast and could feel her heart flutter beneath it at the thought of going through all those torturous months of carrying a child and then having to endure the humiliating experience of birthing it. Even the thought made her weak and nauseated.

She had disliked Rebel from the start. Even though she was sickly carrying the baby and there were often dark shadows about her eyes, the girl had a haunting beauty that was irritating. She didn't have to struggle with rags at night to put curl in her hair, and use creams to keep her skin from flaking and burning in this horrible, hot climate. Her soft cloud of blond hair curled naturally and her skin was soft like a rose petal. Miriam fingered her wineglass thoughtfully, her stomach tied in knots. It was hard to pretend to like someone when you couldn't stand the sight of her. Rebel had everything Miriam had always wanted and could never attain. Even with a swollen stomach men had eyed Rebel covetously, envying Brandon, and now that the baby was born . . . Oh, to have Rebel's beauty instead of her own drab looks. To be the daughter of an earl, born and bred in society, instead of the daughter of a country squire, as her father had been. To be able to talk with men easily without stumbling about for something to say, as she always did. And to have the prestige that went with being Brandon Avery's wife. He was so charming and handsome. The kind of man any other woman would be proud to have for a husband, yet Rebel seemed indifferent to him, her attitude often cold, and it was obvious Brandon was hurt by it.

At the frequent dinner parties and on other evenings when she and Matthew had been at the house, Miriam had watched Rebel closely, noting the strained atmosphere that often prevailed between the two of them, and the somewhat bitter, puzzled looks that Brandon frequently bestowed upon his wife. Rebel was a selfish, callous woman, and just the thought of her being able to hold the love of a man like Brandon Avery sent angry blood flowing through Miriam's veins, and her face darkened as she put the glass of wine to her lips and took a sip, trying to wash the bitter taste of hatred from her mouth as her eyes fell on Matthew across the room, talking with General Bridlehurst.

Matthew . . . dear, staid Matthew. Why couldn't he have been a duke or an earl . . . or even a squire would have been better than this. When he'd said he was going to be a doctor, she'd been wary. His father had been a magistrate, and he'd decided to study law, then suddenly changed his mind and forsaken his lawbooks for medicine. They'd married as soon as his schooling was over, and it hadn't been too bad at first. He'd opened an office in London, and from the very start his clientele had been the wealthy, the elite. He'd even been summoned to serve the king's court; then, without warning, he'd come home one evening and announced that they were going to the West Indies. They'd gone to Barbados first, then migrated to Grenada, where they'd been for the past three years, and she hated it.

Why couldn't they have stayed in London? Matthew had been doing so well, and by now they would have had a beautiful home, and maybe he would have become the king's private physician and been knighted, and she could have had a place in society, even if it was a small one. But no. He had to devote his life to helping mankind. The poor and ignorant. Oh, Matthew!

Her eyes sifted over her husband, studying his features. He was carelessly handsome, in a very masculine way, not prettily handsome in the literal sense of the word. His nose was a little too long, his jaw too square, his features too broad to be handsome as Brandon was, but he had a certain charm and magnetism. If he'd only wear clothes that fit him right instead of the ill-fitting suits he continually wore, others might notice it too and admire him the way they did Brandon. Like tonight. His suit was midnight-blue velvet with a ruffled shirt and satin cravat, expensive and made especially for him, and yet it didn't fit him right. The shoulders drooped and the pants bunched at the knees before tucking into his boots. And the boots! God forbid! That was another thing. He loved to wear Hessian boots, but never bought a new pair until the current pair wore out completely and the creases on them were beyond polishing to the high gloss they should be. She often wondered why he'd become so careless in his appearance. He used to be so neat when he was younger, and he really was splendidly tall when he wasn't slouching so untidily. He just didn't seem to care anymore what he looked like. He was only thirty-three, but he was so wrapped up in his medicine. She loved him dearly, but why couldn't he be more dynamic like he used to be, like the governor? She glanced once more toward Brandon and Rebel, who were now talking to the Van Horns.

"I heard you had a bout with the weather, Captain," Brandon was saying as he kept his arm about Rebel's waist so she'd have to stay beside him, and Mrs. Van Horn's brother nodded.

"Ve caught a bad storm a few veeks ago, your Excellency," he answered, his German accent heavy. Mrs. Van Horn and her brother were German, her husband Dutch. "That's vhy ve are late arriving. But the *Freiheit* is a good ship, solid and vell-built."

Rebel eyed him curiously, her dislike of the man showing in her eyes. "Your ship is named the *Freiheit*? What does *Freiheit* mean in English, Captain?" she asked.

"It means vhat you vould call 'freedom,'" he answered proudly.

"Did you say 'freedom'?" she asked scornfully. "My word, Captain," she retorted flippantly, "what a strange name for a slave ship." As she spoke, Brandon's hand tightened on her waist until his fingers hurt, and the captain's face flushed crimson. "Well, it is a slave ship, isn't it?" she asked curtly, ignoring Brandon's displeasure as the captain coughed uncomfortably, and she stared at him, her violet eyes arrogantly alert. "Tell me, Captain, is it true that you chain those poor men and women on their backs barely a foot apart where they have to lie in their own excrement, and that they're given barely enough food to eat, and only half of them survive the voyage?"

"Those people, as you so lightly call them, your Grace, are illiterate savages," the captain interrupted angrily, "they are not human."

"Not human? How can you say that?"

"They cannot even converse intelligently."

"And you can?" she asked, laughing scornfully. "Come now, Herr Captain, you couldn't always speak English, now, could you?" she retorted. "But the English didn't consider you a savage because what you spoke was unintelligible to them. Even now I assume there are people who can't fully understand what you say. These people have a mind and

255

soul, and a language of their own, the same as you and I—"

"Rebel!" Brandon cut in furiously. "Stop it!"

"Stop it?" she replied with a lowered voice. "You people amaze me. You really do," she said. "You buy and sell people like cattle, condoning slavery, treating human beings like animals, then when someone points out the inhumanities of slavery to you, you try to hush them up and close your eyes, pretending the evils don't exist." She straightened, pulling herself from Brandon's grasp. "Excuse me, Captain, Mr. and Mrs. Van Horn," she said politely, her words clipped, "but I have been brought up to believe that all people are human beings with a right to be free to live their own lives, no matter the color of their skin, and I cannot change my opinion for propriety's sake. I'm sorry if I've offended you, but I'm afraid I'm not accustomed to being tactful, so it would be best if the conversation came to an end. You'll excuse me." She whirled quickly, spotting Matt across the room next to the refreshment table, and hurried over to him, unaware that Miriam's eyes followed her. She stopped abruptly next to him, her body stiff, eyes blazing.

"Will you please pour me a glass of wine, Matt?" she asked breathlessly, and stood motionless as he handed a glass to her. She sipped slowly, feeling the sweet liquid as it warmed her.

"What the devil happened?" he asked, his eyes on her face. She breathed deeply, trying to calm herself.

"I'm afraid I just insulted the captain and the Van Horns," she answered promptly, "and I presume at the moment my husband's crawling all over himself apologizing to them for my indiscretion."

Matt glanced back at Brandon, who was trying to soothe the Van Horns. "He doesn't look any too happy," he replied.

"He's furious." Her fingers tightened on the glass until her knuckles were white.

Matt frowned. "If he lays a hand on you . . ."

"He won't."

"How can you be sure?"

"Because I don't intend for him to. I've come to the conclusion that I can put up with his lovemaking easier than I can a black eye. I don't intend to take another beating, Matt." Her eyes shone stubbornly. "If I have to I'll seduce him rather than let him do that to me again." She bit her lip as Matt's eyes left hers, and she knew he was watching Brandon approach from behind her, yet she continued to stare at Matt.

Brandon stopped directly behind her, his body almost touching hers, his eyes dark with anger. "What the hell are you trying to do to me?" he asked, his voice vibrating emotionally. "Those people are loyal subjects. Van Horn practically controls the planters on this island." She set the wine glass down and turned. She was so close she could feel his breath on her face, and her hand moved up, touching the lapel of Brandon's white coat. She ran her finger along the edge casually. "I'm sorry, Brandon, please," she murmured seductively, her voice husky and intimate, "I don't know why I let my tongue run away with me like that . . ." Her lips parted sensuously, petulantly. "You will forgive me, won't you?" she asked as she breathed deeply, her full breasts rising and falling passionately, and Matt saw Brandon's eyes move to the ripe cleavage overflowing her bodice and saw his intake of breath as he stared at his wife, her voluptuous body already having aroused him, softening his anger.

Brandon's eyes moved to her face. "Why do you do things like this, Reb?" he asked, bewildered over her sudden change of behavior, and Rebel smiled enticingly, her eyes softening to limpid pools of deep violet as she forced herself to lean closer against him.

"Oh, Bran, why do I always seem to hurt you?" she whispered softly. "I don't know what's the matter with me. Sometimes I just feel like hating the whole world, and I could cut my tongue out for being so cruel." Her eyes fell as she ran her finger the rest of the way up his lapel to his ruffled shirt, smoothing his cravat, touching the side of his neck, and she felt him tremble against her. "Forgive me, please, darling. I won't do it again, I promise." She saw in his eyes that she had already won.

His breathing was short and labored, his nostrils flaring passionately as he swallowed hard, feeling himself hardening against her. "Rebel, we have guests," he answered huskily, his hands clasping her about the waist, trying to keep himself under control and hold her away from him. "We'll settle this after the guests have gone."

"But you do forgive me?"

"Yes, I forgive you . . . for tonight." He escorted her toward the door, unaware of the satisfied smile she bestowed on Matt as they headed for the rest of the guests, who were beginning to gather their wraps to leave.

Matt watched them move across the room and turned as Miriam walked up beside him.

"What was that all about?" she asked as she nodded toward Brandon and Rebel.

"It seems Brandon's upset because she insulted the Van Horns."

"My word, what did she say?"

"I have no idea." He took his wife's arm as he looked at her, noting again that the color of her dress did nothing for her. It was gray silk with yards of ruffles, and her small breasts were lost in the tucks and folds of the bodice, above which her ruby necklace looked out-of-place. How little she knew about styles. Even her hair. She still wore it the same way she had when they'd first married. "I think we'd better leave now, Miriam," he said as he turned her toward the door of the drawing room. "It looks like the party's breaking up."

After Matt helped Miriam into the carriage, he got in himself and sat back, sighing. It was a beautiful night, with stars clustering low in the sky so brilliantly that they looked as if you could reach out and touch them. They had used the larger carriage rather than the light buggy this evening, and Matt sat back relaxing, letting the driver worry about where they were going as they started down the road toward the other side of the bay, pulling up sometime later before a charming house set on the hillside.

There was a long veranda across the front. Moonlight turned the bright red roof tile that covered it, and the house itself into a scattered pattern of rustic brown. A profusion of flowering vines covered one end of the veranda, where well-used wicker chairs tried to hide in the shadows. Matt had fallen in love with the house when they'd first come to the island, and spent practically all the money they'd brought with them to buy it. But he'd never been sorry. For a while they hadn't even had furniture to fill it, but as the years passed and Dr. Wilder settled into the lives of the people on the island, from the poorest to the richest, they had not only filled the house with furniture, but now boasted two servants, a combination housekeeper and cook and a gardener who took over driving duties when Matt didn't feel like it himself or when Miriam went out alone.

A light went on in the house as Matt held Miriam's arm, helping her from the carriage, then up the steps to the veranda.

"Looks like Kuulie waited up for us," he said as the door opened, and he smiled at the woman who held it while they stepped inside. She was black. The dusky, dull black that looked like she'd been rubbed with coal dust, then brushed

258

off, leaving her skin dry and moistureless. She was in her late forties, with kinky gray-streaked hair pulled to the nape of her neck, generous eyes shining in a dour face, and thick lips a pale pinkish gray.

"I thought perhaps you might need me," she said as she closed the door behind them, then wiped her large-boned hands on the front of a calico dress, but Matt shook his head.

"It's late, Kuulie. We'll go right up," he said.

"I'll lock up soon's Jeeter gets in," she said, and headed toward the back of the house, where the servants slept, to let the gardener in the back door.

Miriam wasn't really tired as Matt helped her upstairs to her room. All the way home she'd been thinking of Rebel, envying her, hating her, yet wishing she could trade places, and the heated emotions had kept her from becoming drowsy. Even after Matt had lightly kissed her good night and gone through the adjoining door to his room, she continued to fight with herself and undressed viciously, staring at her naked body in the mirror.

She stood directly in front of the mirror and straightened severely, her chin thrust out, appraising herself. Her legs were too thin, and slightly bowed, the thighs shapeless. Her one nice feature was her small waist, but it only emphasized the prominent hipbones that stuck out on each side and the bony rib cage that was half-hidden beneath her sagging breasts. If only she'd fill out more, but it was hopeless. A person had to eat to put on weight, and too much food made her ill. Her hand went to her right breast and she grasped the loose skin above it and pulled the small mass of flesh up where it had once been. She turned sideways, gazing at herself, trying to capture the memory of what it was like when the nipple had stood high and firm.

Frowning, she suddenly dropped it again, to lie sagging, then closed her eyes, remembering the way Rebel's breasts had almost overflowed her dress. And Rebel had flesh on her bones, and her legs were probably straight and firm, the thighs filled out. Tears welled up in her eyes as she took her nightgown from the foot of the bed and slipped it on, feeling its silkiness caress her skin.

What would it be like if Matthew looked at her the way Brandon looked at Rebel? Matthew loved her, yes. He was kind, generous, tender, but he'd never looked at her that way. What kind of a look was it? Lustful? Passionate? Loving? It was a strong, overwhelming look, as if he'd undressed her with his eyes. No man had ever looked at her like that. Not even when she was younger and had had more flesh on her bones. It wasn't the kind of look most men gave their wives, but it was the kind of look she'd always wanted from a man, just once.

She blew out the candle and climbed into the huge bed and lay quietly in the dark, her body trembling. She was both ashamed and fascinated by her feelings. Respectable married women weren't supposed to feel like this. Only wanton, fallen women who went from one man to another were supposed to feel like this. It was wicked to lose control of your emotions, and she pursed her lips, closing her eyes, pushing the evil thoughts from her mind, praying for God to take them away.

Matt sat on the edge of his bed staring at his boots, which he'd set beneath the window. The candlelight only made the creases in them more pronounced. He finished unbuttoning his shirt sleeves, pulled the shirt off, threw it on the chair next to the boots, where his suit coat lay, and watched it land haphazardly, one sleeve dragging the floor.

How often Miriam chided him for wearing such ill-fitting clothes, asking him if he didn't realize they were too big. He'd only smile and tell her they were more comfortable for the work he had to do. How could he tell her the truth? How could he tell her he was purposely hiding behind them so he wouldn't have to go through what he went through in London. He'd probably been a fool to leave England, but it would have been impossible to stay, with three of his patients professing their love for him. That was bad enough, but the fact that they were wives of prominent men made it even worse, and then when one, a young woman in the queen's court, who was married to an old man, begged him to make love to her, swearing she'd die without him, and promptly did, when he refused, by committing suicide, he'd been repulsed. There was no chance of his staying. She'd left his office one afternoon in tears, but it had still been a surprise that evening when he'd been called to her Grosvenor Square mansion. She was dead by the time he'd arrived, and he was glad he'd gotten to the house before her husband came home, for while he was moving things about her nightstand, smelling the contents of the glass she'd emptied, he'd found two suicide notes. One to him and one to her husband, and the former had been all too revealing. All the latter said was that she had been rejected by her lover and couldn't go on.

Lover! If he had given those women encouragement, he would have felt it fitting that he pay the price. But lover? That he was not! He'd been kind and solicitous and treated

260

them as he did all his patients. The fact that they'd been married to men too old to satisfy their love-starved bodies made their secret yearnings betray them. At least that's what he'd thought at first, until that day in Barbados when he'd realized another of his patients was looking at him with a strange glow in her eyes. It wasn't how she looked at him, however, that brought him to his senses, it was what she said.

He'd treated her for an abscess on her breast, and she'd come back because the incision he had made was infected. He'd looked at the slightly reddened flesh, then cauterized where it was festered and put some salve on, his fingers dabing it across the partially healed marks of his knife, but when he'd started to move his hand away, she'd covered his hand with hers and looked at him soulfully, her eyes warm with desire.

"What . . . ?" he'd blurted, surprised, and she'd smiled.

"I like your hand on my breast, Doctor," she'd whispered passionately, and his eyes had narrowed as he stared at her, realizing for the first time that she was rather pretty. Yet, he was angry with her.

"My dear young woman," he said firmly, lifting his other hand to remove the hand that held his to her breast. "What you're suggesting is absurd. I'm a doctor and a married man!"

"And the handsomest one I've ever seen," she'd drawled slowly.

He should have known, but it was the farthest thing from the mind of a busy man. Over the years his friends had often chided him about going into the wrong profession. "With your looks you should have become a cavalier," Miriam's brother had told him shortly after their marriage, and Miriam herself had often marveled over his exquisite, muscular body, even though she'd never enjoyed it, and this, combined with what his colleagues often called his ruggedly charming bedside manner, had practically opened the door to every lonely, frustrated female who stepped foot in his office.

He continued to sit on the bed, and glanced toward the door that separated his room from Miriam's. Miriam had moved into the next room shortly after their arrival on the island, because of the fitfully hot weather, she'd complained, and the fact that his having to be summoned so many times in the middle of the night woke her and she was unable to get back to sleep, causing her sick headaches the next day.

He hadn't liked the arrangement. It had been so much better when they were in the same bed. All he had to do when he wanted her was to reach out and she was there. Now . . .

He stood up and began unfastening his pants, then stopped, thinking, trying to sort out his feelings. He stared across the dimly lit room at nothing, seeing nothing, visualizing Miriam as she'd looked tonight. Nothing about her had changed since the day he'd married her, and it was sad. He'd grown up with her brother, not realizing at first that his friend's younger sister was in love with him. She'd been pretty when she was young, if a tiny bit plump, but by the time she was through her teens, she'd slimmed out, and although not as pretty as she had been when a girl, she was still pleasing to look at.

He'd loved her as he'd loved his friend. She'd become like a younger sister to him, the sister he'd never had. He'd teased her and become affectionately attached to her as they grew up, so it was no surprise that when, at the age of seventeen, she'd suddenly become ill and the doctors gave her only weeks to live, he'd granted her the one wish she'd wanted more than anything in the world and asked her to marry him, to make her last days happy ones.

Instead of dying, however, she'd rallied miraculously, recovering completely. The doctor attributed it to her newfound happiness. His proposal had given her a reason to live. He hadn't wanted to marry her then, he hadn't wanted to in the first place, but had asked her out of pity. How could he have disappointed her and broken her heart by refusing? So he'd lived the lie, stayed engaged, and married her. The strange part of it all was that he had loved her, and he loved her still. Not the passionate love that a man should have for a woman, however, but the tender love a man has for a friend or relative.

He shook himself back to reality, removed his clothes, and extinguished the candle. He stood for a moment and stared out the open window at the night sky, feeling the balmy breeze in his face, only he didn't see the darkness outside. He saw a pair of violet eyes, warm and alive, looking into his from an exquisitely beautiful face. Her face, and it was becoming harder and harder for him to put her out of his mind. How many times he'd stood and studied her, the slender curve of her back, full breasts, ample hips. He felt the warmth begin to flood his loins, and the weak, tingling sensation that always went through him when he thought of her generous mouth with its faintly sensuous lines, and the way she always looked at him.

His hands were damp and his legs trembled as he rubbed

his palms on the side of his underwear, trying to dry them off, and he felt himself hardening. He turned slowly and walked to the door that joined his room to Miriam's and opened it cautiously, stepping into her room, then moved to the huge bed, barely visible in the darkness.

Miriam was half on her side, half on her stomach, with one hand stretched out beneath her pillow, the other curled up near her head.

"Miriam?" he whispered softly as he sat on the bed and reached out, touching her face, his hand moving to caress her neck in the darkness. "I need you, Miriam," and she moved, turning onto her back to meet his mouth as it descended on hers, covering it passionately. He kissed her deeply, his body on fire, his hand moving to her small breast, trying to bring some life into her body, to make her respond, but it was no use. How many times he'd tried to explain that it was natural for a woman to respond to a man, but her mother and society had done their work well, and he knew she'd never stop holding back. He'd have to play the game again all by himself.

He moved over her and entered her passive body, his own body hot and tormented with need, and he worked feverishly, trying to still the hurt that welled up inside him. Then, as he tried to forget her inhibitions, and his passion grew, her voice filtered through his sweating body as she whispered desperately.

"Oh, God, don't let me get pregnant!" With a faint groan he drew himself from her, grabbing the closest thing at hand, as he had so many times before, and climaxed into the wrinkled folds of the sheet as he held it against himself, while across the bay Rebel lay beneath Brandon, trying to make her unresponsive body pretend to respond, and hating every moment.

12

It had been a little over a month since Rebel's birthday party, and she'd learned a great deal during that time. She had taken the carriage out again the next day, and the next, and the next. After a week she'd realized that her husband had evidently given instructions that she was to go no farther than a one- or two-mile radius from the city, and therefore the driver refused to take her wherever she wanted to go, explaining that the governor wouldn't like it. So she had ceased her morning rides.

Finally, one morning, fed up with it, she'd called Cristabel and ordered her to find some excuse to get the stableboy. Then she dug into her armoire until she came up with her old buckskins, and slipped into them while Hizzie watched silently, Cole at her breast.

"And don't you say a word," Rebel had warned Hizzie as she tied a ribbon around her long hair. She grabbed a pair of scissors, cut the extremely wide brim off one of her fancy sun hats, and ripped the flowers from it. "If I'm ever going to find out what this island and its people are really like, it'll have to be on my own," and she flounced out of the house and downstairs, avoiding all the servants.

She found a spirited gelding and saddled him, then headed out across the back field and up over the mountainous hill the house nestled on, while Cristabel flirted outrageously with the young stablehands.

She'd learned so much since that day. Brandon, although well-liked by the upper gentry, was hated by the ordinary people, especially the Negroes, whether slaves or free, and from the tales that were told about him on the island, she could understand why. She had ridden far on her excursions, sneaking in and out of the house and stables whenever the opportunity arose, keeping to the hills, enjoying the lush greenery and exotic growth that covered everything. She kept away from the big plantations, and no one in the back regions, away from St. George, had the least idea who she was as she rode around the island, speaking French or English, whichever was appropriate, her old buckskins giving the impression that she was from one of the poorer white families, and people had talked more freely than they otherwise would have.

She was on her horse again early one morning, having slipped from the house after Brandon had left to visit one of the plantations. It had been some time since sunup, but steaming mists still rose from the tropical forests, like great clouds of fog rising to melt into the sun. She'd been riding for half an hour already, and it felt good to just be herself.

It had been a week since the last time she'd been able to sneak away. The air was clean and fresh as she rode out of a tangled patch of trees onto an old path that cut the forest in two. It was a wide, well-worn path, and she wondered where it led. There were paths all over the hundred and some square miles of island, as well as the main dirt roads that led from one village to another. She reined her horse to the right and began following the path as it snaked its way among the trees; then about an hour later she stopped abruptly as she topped a hill, and sat in the saddle surveying the scene before her.

She had reached the eastern shore of the island, and the beach, some five hundred feet below the cliff she was on, was scattered with fishermen. Some of their boats were in the water, others were being pulled ashore. Many of the men, their dark bodies shining from sweat and the salt water, were straining as they pulled in huge seines of netting heavy with fish.

"They're called ballyhoo, or bait fish," said a voice from behind her. She whirled around, then smiled, relieved, as Matt nudged his horse in the ribs and rode up beside her.

"What are you doing here?" she asked, surprised. He nodded toward the beach.

"There's a cocoa plantation a few miles from here along the coast. They sent word that one of the men was hurt."

"You travel this whole island?"

"Not quite. There's another doctor up north near Carib's Leap, but he's old and unable to move about anymore."

Rebel's eyes surveyed Matt closely. He was sitting erect in the saddle, wearing his usual worn riding boots and an old pair of pants, but the shirt, tucked into them, was full-sleeved, open to the waist, and she was aware of the muscles that rippled across his chest beneath the dark curling hair that covered it. She'd never seen him like this. Always before, except for the day Cole was born, he'd had on one of his ill-fitting suits, his shirt buttoned all the way up, the droop-shouldered suit coat hiding his broad shoulders, which were carelessly slouched. Like this, on horseback, in these casually masculine clothes, he looked so different. She felt a warm stirring inside her as his eyes met hers.

"You've been making yourself scarce lately," she said as she turned from him and looked back down to the beach, where palm trees swayed gently in the trade winds as the men gathered the fish from the nets, dumping them in wooden buckets that they carried aboard their long wooden fishing boats.

"I've been busy."

"Too busy to check on your patients?"

"You've been ill?"

"No. But I missed seeing you."

She knew his eyes were on her as she watched the fishermen, and she felt uncomfortable.

"Would you like to go with me?" he asked suddenly.

"Could I?"

"I hate the thought of you wandering around by yourself."

"I've been doing it off and on for some weeks now," she said.

"At least now I know who the mysterious lady in the funny clothes is that the people have been talking about." She smiled back sheepishly. "Come on."

She pulled her horse's reins and followed him onto the path again, where they rode side by side. "Tell me Matt," she asked, "are the stories I've been hearing about Brandon really true?"

"What have you heard?"

"That he rides through the town as if he owned it. That no one dares cross him. That he's had people whipped and imprisoned for no more reason than that they annoyed him. Is this really the way he treats them?"

"The little people, yes, I'm afraid so."

"Why doesn't someone say something?"

"They don't like black eyes either."

She glanced at him sharply. "You know how to put a point across, don't you, Doctor?" she replied. Matt shrugged indulgently.

"Have you had any more black eyes?"

"No."

"Have you crossed him?"

"Yes."

He looked at her cynically as she glanced away. "But I'll warrant it wasn't in bed."

She gave him another curious look. "No, it wasn't in bed," she confirmed, then added, "I've been the perfect wife in bed, and hated every minute."

"Sorry, Duchess," he said, his face flushing. "I didn't mean to get too personal."

"You haven't," she answered. "I'm glad I have a shoulder to cry on."

"Anytime, my lady," he offered, and nudged his horse harder.

They talked all the way to the plantation. Matt told her some of the history of the island, including the legend of Carib's Leap on the northern tip, where the Carib Indians committed suicide rather than be made slaves by the French, and she shuddered when he explained that the tribe also ate human flesh. He told her about the different flowers, birds, and animals and some of the folk legends as he knew them, and in no time at all the pungent odor of sweating cacao beans drifted out to them from among the close-knit trees.

"What's that smell?" she asked as they moved out of the trees into a clearing. He sniffed in, testing the air.

"They have to ferment the beans under banana leaves to separate them," he explained. The closer to the plantation they rode, the harder Rebel strained her ears, and Matt glanced at her cocked head. "That rhythmic clapping you hear is where they're drying the beans," he said. "The women shuffle them with their bare feet. It makes them dry quicker, and the time goes faster if they dance to the clapping."

Suddenly Rebel reined up short.

"What's the matter?" he asked.

"Maybe I'd better not go all the way in with you. I've been staying clear of the plantations. These people might know me."

"So?"

"If they tell Brandon I've been out here, I'll never get out of the house again without him. As it is, I can only get away when I know he's going to be gone all day. If he finds out . . ."

"He won't." He leaned forward, his green eyes on her. "This is the DuBois plantation, but we won't even be near the main house. The message came from the slaves' quarters."

"What if they decide to come out?"

"You don't know Madame and M'sieur DuBois. They leave everything up to their overseer. His name is Simon Gerhardt, and he's never met the governor's wife."

"You're sure?"

"I'm sure."

She thought it over for a minute, then nodded. "All right, let's go."

The slaves lived in huts with palm fronds thatching the roofs, and they were scattered some few hundred feet behind the sweating bins and drying racks. A big red-faced, blustery man met them behind the sweating bins.

"My God, I thought you'd never get here!" he exclaimed, half-walking and half-running beside Matt's horse. "I've been trying to do what I can for the poor devil, but he's really hurting. One of our best bucks."

Matt pulled his horse up and dropped from the saddle; Rebel also dismounted from her horse, and they both followed the overseer back to the road that ran between some of the huts. A huge Negro was sprawled in the dirt beside a wagon, his leg lying helplessly out in front of him at a strange angle.

Matt fell to his knees, his hands running lightly down the brown limb, feeling the broken bone pushing against the skin. "It's a clean break," he said, "but I'll need some help."

Rebel knelt down beside him. "I'll help," she said quietly. "We didn't have any doctors at the fort," she explained. "My father always set the broken bones and Mother and I helped."

He nodded, then started working. He gave the man brandy from a bottle one of the spectators was holding while he ordered two of the women to get some bandages cut into long narrow strips; then he told the overseer to find him two long flat boards he could use for splints. By the time everything was brought back to the suffering man, he was drunk enough for what Matt had to do.

Matt bent over, examining the break again, feeling with his fingers where the bone had shifted; then he motioned to Rebel. "Kneel down here and give me your hands," he said calmly and she got to her knees beside the big black's right side and stretched out her hands to him while the overseer and one of the other slaves sat behind her, one on each side by the man's shoulders, waiting for when they were needed.

Matt grasped Rebel's hands, and for a moment their eyes met and a sweet warmth swept over her as something strange passed between them. Matt looked away quickly and lowered her hands to the man's leg.

It was broken about four inches below the knee, and he moved her fingers along the skin so she could feel where the broken end stuck out.

"You're not strong enough to pull," he said, "so I'll do the pulling while you slip it into place. Can you do it?"

Her stomach turned over once as her fingers felt the weird, jutting bone against the skin, and she bit her lip nervously.

"You'll have to twist as you pull, won't you?" she said.

"Good girl." His eyes shone, pleased. "You know what you're doing." His hands lifted from hers, and he moved out to where the man's foot lay in the dirt. He grasped it firmly, and Rebel saw perspiration break out on his forehead.

"All right, now," he said slowly, and his hands lifted the foot barely a half-inch off the ground as he began to pull, slowly, easily, turning it.

"It's not twisting far enough," she gasped hesitantly. Her

fingers plied the skin, maneuvering the jagged bone beneath it. She bit her lip hard, her face turning pale as the men behind her grabbed the man's arms, holding him down. Tears filled her eyes. The bone was moving, and she held her breath as Matt twisted it slightly more to the right; then suddenly she exhaled, relieved as she felt the bone slip into place; the big black passed out.

"It's in," she murmured softly, and Matt's jaw set hard as he relaxed his hold and reached for the bandages. He praised Rebel for her help as they worked, and by the time the leg was wrapped and the splints put on, the man was conscious again and calling for another drink.

"They don't generally get good brandy," stated Simon Gerhardt as he handed the man the bottle.

"Have some of the men make a litter and carry him to his hut," Matt said as he dried his sweating forehead. "And don't let him walk until I give you the word, or you'll have a cripple on your hands." He avoided looking at Rebel as he patted the dust off his breeches and continued talking to the overseer. "And another thing, don't give him any more to drink when that wears off. Drink can make a man cocky, and he's liable to try standing on that leg when it's not ready."

The overseer gestured with his hand. "Thanks, doc, and you too, ma'am." He looked at Rebel, and Matt realized he hadn't taken time to introduce her, so made a quick stab at it, introducing her as a friend, without benefit of using a name. The overseer eyed her curiously, wondering where the doc might have found her, since it was unusual for him to have someone with him. But thinking better of being too curious, he tried not to look overly interested except to admire Rebel's figure beneath the buckskins. Besides, he had enough to worry about without worrying about what she was doing with the doc. "Well, now, if you'll step over to my place and sign the book," he said, and this time Matt couldn't avoid Rebel's eyes as he took her by the elbow and they followed the man to a small bungalow near where they'd left their horses.

Neither of them said a word, but Rebel could feel the strength of the man standing beside her as they waited at the foot of the bungalow steps for the overseer to come back out with the tally book for him to sign so the DuBoises could settle with him at the end of the month.

Matt signed the ledger, then walked back to the horses, reaching into a bag that hung from his saddle to pull out a small white packet.

"Give the man some of this," he said as he handed it to Simon Gerhardt. "The instructions are on the package. I'll be out again in a few days to check on him." Then he turned to Rebel. "Ready?" he asked, and she nodded.

A few minutes later as they rode away toward the path that led back toward St. George, Rebel glanced behind her. "These people must treat their slaves better than most," she said, noting the neatness of the huts and the slaves walking about freely. "Their living quarters seem pretty decent, and I didn't see anybody in chains."

"It's deceiving," said Matt. "They don't have iron chains, but the chains are there. Invisible ones. Gerhardt has his own methods of treating recalcitrants, and it's not very pleasant."

She looked puzzled, and he went on, his eyes darkening. "Gerhardt also has the pick of the women in the slave quarters. If you'd looked around you'd have noticed there are a lot of sandy-haired, gray-eyed Negroes running around the DuBois plantation."

Rebel frowned uncomfortably. This was something new to her. "I hadn't noticed."

"I didn't think you had."

"You mean he just picks anyone he wants?"

"Whether she's got a husband or not, and his specialty, I've heard, is breaking in virgins. Not one young girl on the place had better be touched until he's had her first."

"Oh, Matt, that's sickening! He's no better than an animal."

"My sentiments exactly. But there's nothing anybody can do about it until slavery itself is stamped out. The world is full of Gerhardts."

"The other plantations are the same?"

"Not all of them, but most. Sometimes it's the master who gets the choice women, like at the Van Horns'. Of course, Mrs. Van Horn doesn't know about it. Or at least if she does, she's closing her eyes to it."

Rebel's eyes hardened. "I hate this island," she exclaimed heatedly.

"Don't hate Grenada, Rebel," he admonished softly. "It's a beautiful place in spite of all this. You've only seen the surface. If you'll give me a chance, I'll prove it to you."

"How?"

"Come with me again the end of the week. I have to go up the coast to check on one of my patients."

Her voice softened. "But I don't know if I can get away."

"If you can, I'll be heading out the coast road shortly after

270

sunup on Friday morning. We should be back in the early afternoon."

She watched his eyes as he talked, the warm strength in his face. She'd gone farther with him today than she'd dared go by herself, not knowing her way about the island, and to be able to travel up the coast . . . Being with him had pleased her . . . yet . . . when she'd met him today, it had been by accident. If she rode with him on Friday . . .

"Do you think I should, Matt?" she asked hesitantly, and his eyes delved deeply into hers as they sat on their horses, staring at each other, and suddenly neither could look away. It was as if they were locked together in a breathless moment of time.

"No," he whispered huskily, his voice trembling passionately, "I don't think you should, but I'd like you to," and she felt her heart pounding unmercifully.

She swallowed slowly, trying to control the surge of emotion that was flooding her. "I can't promise, but I'll try," she whispered softly.

During the ride back they avoided talking about anything personal, and he continued telling her about the island. She learned that the fishermen she'd seen earlier, and a number of the Negroes in St. George, were not slaves, but free colored, having been given their freedom by the French some ten years before, when the British took over the island, and already, according to Matt, the birth rate among them was increasing their numbers prodigiously. Rebel hated to see the ride end. Except for the nausea that had gripped her momentarily when she'd helped him set the Negro's leg, she'd loved the ride and felt an emptiness afterward when Matt left her at the edge of the hill that ran down to the house.

She'd been gone all morning and was starved by the time she managed to sneak the horse back into the pasture and get into the house and upstairs to her room. She had Cristabel set up her bath as soon as possible, and she scrubbed off the horse smell, then changed into a dress of pink silk that made her feel cool and refreshed.

That evening at dinner she tried to draw Brandon out, asking questions about the island that she felt were important. About taxes, laws, and the courts, but he merely brushed them aside, stating that she was being impertinent, and that women were ill-equipped to understand what it took to govern an island such as this.

"Hah!" exclaimed Rebel as she looked at her self-centered husband, ignoring his order to cease and desist. "I suppose

Elizabeth didn't know how to rule England because she was a woman! And what of the other women in history who've ruled countries? I suppose they didn't know what they were doing?"

"But you're not a queen, my dear," he'd answered smugly. "You're only a duchess."

"So that makes me stupid, I suppose." She set down her napkin and stared at him. "I'll have you know that one thing my mother was very insistent about, Bran, was that all her children were educated, including myself." She tossed her blond hair dangerously. "And I probably know as much about politics and world affairs as you do."

"Knowing about them and executing them are two different things, Rebel," he snapped irritably. "Now, drop the subject. I'll govern Grenada and I'll govern the house, and you can take care of the baby, where you belong. There'll be no more said about any taxes I've imposed, any sentences I've meted out, any laws I've put into effect, or any plans I might have for the future, for that matter. Is that understood?"

She bit back the words on the tip of her tongue as she stared at him furiously. "I understand perfectly," she answered, her voice cold and hard, and she picked up her fork, attacking her food vigorously.

That evening as she lay on the drawing-room floor playing with Cole, Brandon announced that he was sailing Thursday afternoon for St. Vincent, an island to the north, and he'd be gone until late afternoon Saturday.

"I don't suppose I dare ask why," she said.

"I'm afraid not. It's a military matter."

She shrugged. "I figured as much."

Brandon watched Rebel, stretched on her stomach on the floor as if she herself were a child. He'd tried to make her act more like a lady, but with a mother like Loedicia, what could he have expected? At least when company came she abandoned her casualness and tried to be more sedate, and he thanked God for that. It was crazy, really, because her naturalness and unaffected mannerisms were what had made him fall in love with her in the first place. She wasn't phony like the other women. There was nothing pretentious about Rebel. At least there hadn't been when he'd first met her. She was so beautiful, and every time he looked at her he was overwhelmed by his feelings for her. He'd wanted her from the moment he'd set eyes on her, and now she was his.

He frowned, lines of worry furrowing his forehead, because deep inside he knew it really wasn't true. That last

272

wasn't right. She was his wife, but she wasn't his. Even this past month. Her actions were convincing enough. She could arouse him with merely a look and a gesture, but even though she'd assured him she'd changed, he felt something missing, and it angered him.

He glanced at the baby and a pain shot through him. He watched Cole's dark head turning from side to side while Rebel talked to him. That was another matter that still wasn't settled. His son! What travesty. He hated her for Cole's existence and hated Cole for existing, yet he couldn't help wanting her.

He stood up and walked over, staring down into the child's face. "Miriam's invited a few people over Saturday evening for dinner," he said casually, hiding his angry thoughts. "I should be back in plenty of time. We're not due there until seven."

Rebel reached out, putting her hand on the baby's stomach playfully, and he kicked his feet. "I wish we could take him with us," she said as she put her head down and kissed him. "He's growing so fast, and it's been a while since anyone's seen him."

"The baby stays here," he snapped, and walked out of the room.

Friday morning early, Rebel sat her horse lazily while she waited in the bushes at the side of the coast road, hidden from view. Brandon's ship had sailed on time the day before, and it had been so easy to slip away. But what if she'd been too late? Matt didn't say what time he'd be leaving, just that he'd be here early. She'd been waiting a half-hour already and was about to give up when she saw his tall figure ride into view, hat pulled low to keep off the morning sun when it rose full.

It was a gorgeous morning, the sky crimson red, the air salty with the tang of the ocean in it. He pulled up abreast of her, and she smiled as she dug her horse in the ribs and broke through the bushes.

"Well, well," he said, smiling back. "Am I late?"

"I've been waiting since dawn," she complained.

"Miriam was having stomach pains again this morning," he explained. "I wanted to make sure she'd be all right before I left."

"Brandon went to St. Vincent."

"St. Vincent?"

"On military business, so he says."

"When's he coming back?"

"In time for your dinner party tomorrow night."

"I forgot about that. Only it isn't a dinner party. It's an anniversary dinner for the vicar and his wife. They'll be married thirty-five years on Saturday."

"How like Miriam to do something like that," she said, and the smile lines about his eyes faded.

"Yes . . . how like her," he agreed, and Rebel inhaled uncomfortably as she saw the pain in his eyes. "Let's go," he said suddenly, and dug his horse in the ribs, bringing him to a slow trot.

She gave her horse his head and caught up, reining up beside him. They rode side by side for about ten minutes at an easy gait; then he slowed and guided their horses off the road and through the trees to a narrow path. The path ended at a waterfall carved out of the hillside, and Rebel marveled at its beauty, with ferns and philodendron hanging on the rocky cliff the waters tumbled over.

"Our public bathhouse," he explained as he moved past it and entered the steaming underbrush.

"There's no path here," she called.

"I know. I want to show you parts of the island everyone doesn't always see."

He took her to a lake in the mountainous hills overlooking St. George, a beautiful primitive lake that had once been a crater. It was early yet, and a misty cloud hung over it, as if protecting it from the heat of the sun. Then they moved down into a rolling valley thick with trees and vegetation.

Rebel stared at the mountains above her, which seemed to reach for the sky, and was reminded of the Alleghenies back home. Mountains had always given her a sense of being overwhelmed, as though if she took too deep a breath they'd tumble down and smother her.

They followed the mountain valley for some distance, then began to climb, moving over the ridge of the mountains, dropping down again a short while later, until they were moving across sandy soil to a white beach that spread out before them. Large coconut palms swayed gently in the wind that had begun to stir, and the waves, beginning to crawl farther up the beach as they broke, left froth as they melted into the sand.

It was shortly after ten in the morning when they reached their destination, a nutmeg plantation about two miles inland from the beach. Matt assured her no one would know who she was, but Rebel refused to go on in and stayed hidden among the trees at the far end of the property, resting while he went to see his patient, who happened to be an old Frenchman with a bad heart and two ornery sons who didn't help matters.

After an hour Matt returned to find Rebel leaning against a tree, her eyes shut, savoring the memory of everything she'd seen so far. She straightened as she heard his horse approaching, and hurriedly dusted her buckskins off. She didn't dare get decent riding clothes; Brandon might find out. Besides, in regular riding clothes she couldn't ride astride.

"What happened?" she asked as he dismounted.

He handed her a small bundle he'd had in his hands. "Here, eat this first," he said. She opened it to find two slices of bread, a hunk of cheese, and a banana. "You can wash it down with this," he said, and handed her his canteen.

She was starved and smiled graciously as she dug into the bread and cheese, noticing that he was edgy. She swallowed a mouthful, then took a sip of water. "What's wrong, Matt?" she asked.

"In the first place, I'm glad you didn't come in. Van Horn's in there. He dropped by on his way to St. George, and he'd have mentioned it to Brandon for sure the next time he saw him."

"And second?"

"Second, we can't leave to go back just yet. Van Horn knew I make my visit on this particular Friday every month, and he came purposely to tell me about some free colored up the beach about seven or eight miles. They've got some sickness in their village. Most of them are fishermen, and the people around here depend on them for their fish. The plantation owners up there are afraid the sickness will carry inland."

She stared at him, chewing the food slowly, her eyes intent on his face. "If we go up there . . . ?"

"If we go up there, that means we may not make it back tonight. I don't know what's wrong, what they've got, or how serious it could be."

"And if we don't go?"

"Considering how little these people know, there might be an epidemic."

She tried to swallow the cheese. "Then I guess we go, don't we?"

"What about Brandon?"

"He's gone to St. Vincent, remember?"

"This is insane." He ran his hand through his dark brown hair. "I should never have asked you to come along."

"But you wanted me here, didn't you?"

His eyes stopped on hers, and he held his breath. "Yes," he murmured softly. "God, yes!"

Her voice was barely a whisper as her eyes warmed to him. "Then I'm glad I came."

He reached out and touched her face, his fingers trembling; then he stiffened abruptly, pulling himself together. "Finish eating, then, and we'll get started," he said, and turned, fighting the urge to reach out and take Rebel in his arms.

"I'm ready," she finally said. He turned around with a lump in his throat.

Even in buckskins she was like no one else he'd ever known. "Let's go," he said.

An hour and a half later they rode through a stand of breadfruit trees into a clearing with palm trees scattered about and a circle of thatched huts beneath them with a bevy of fishing boats hugging the sandy beach some distance away. They were greeted by a babbling group of women who practically dragged Matt from his horse. After he broke through them and helped Rebel down, they followed the women into one of the huts.

Two children lay in the hut, and Matt glanced about curiously at the black-magic symbols on the wall. There was a sacred serpent on one wall, the Damballah on the other wall, and vevé signs were painted on the floor by the center post.

"Are you sure you want me here?" he asked, and the women nodded hysterically.

"The juju don't work this time, Doctor," said one of the women. "Please, make my child get better." He nodded as he moved over and knelt down beside one of the children.

He caressed the small, dark forehead of the coughing child and felt the pulse. "How long has he been like this?" he asked.

"Since yesterday morning," one of the women answered.

"Have you left the village at all during the past month?" he asked.

"We go to festival other side of island two, three weeks ago."

Matt leaned over and opened the child's mouth. "Bring a light," he said, and one of the women ran to the fire outside, grabbing a burning piece of wood, using it like a torch. Matt studied the child's throat, then moved to the other child. "They play together?" he asked as he looked in the other child's throat, and the woman nodded. He told them to get more blankets, then walked out to his horse and took down the bag that always hung on his saddle. "I need boiling-hot water, two pails full," he said when he came back in the hut, "and two clean large pieces of cloth." The women scurried about getting them for him. "I'll need your help again," he said to Rebel. "Come give me a hand," and she helped him pull a stand over between the two cots.

When the women brought in the pails of steaming water, he set one on each side of the table between the boys, then took a powder from his bag and put some in each pail, stirring it up with a spoon he carried with him.

"Now, do as I do," he told Rebel, and he leaned down, holding the child up where the fumes from the steaming pail would cover his face, and held him there while he spread one of the large pieces of cloth over the child's head to hold the steam in, like a tent.

Rebel moved to the other child and did the same, holding the slight body against her, letting the steam fill his nostrils and lungs, putting the tent over his head.

Matt ordered the native women out of the hut, promising to call them back if needed, and Rebel could hear them outside wailing and praying.

"How long do we sit like this?" she asked.

"Tired already?"

"No."

"Good, because we set here for at least an hour."

"What made you become a doctor, Matt?" she asked curiously, resting her cheek against the top of the small child's head.

"I wanted to help Miriam."

"Miriam?"

"She was extremely ill when she was younger, running high fevers, with a respiratory infection, weak and unable to eat. The doctors at that time never expected her to live, but she did . . . at least, part of her did."

Rebel straightened, puzzled. "What do you mean, part of her?"

"You know what I'm talking about, Rebel," he answered. "She's never been a complete woman. I thought maybe I could help her, but I can't. She doesn't want to be strong and healthy." His voice deepened. "There's really nothing wrong with her anymore except in her mind."

"There's nothing you can do?"

"I've tried. God help me, I've tried."

"How long have you known Miriam?"

"Since she was a girl." He looked beneath the cloth, check-

277

ing on his patient, then he went on. "She was seventeen and on her deathbed when I asked her to marry me. She recovered somehow. The doctors said it was a miracle, and she waited until I was through with my schooling."

"She must love you very much."

His eyes filled with pain. "I suppose so. . . ."

"And you . . . do you still love her, Matt?"

His eyes avoided hers as he glanced down at the vevé someone had painted on the floor. What could he say? How many times he'd asked himself the same question. "I don't know," he answered hesitantly; then his voice saddened. "I know I don't want to hurt her . . . yet . . . yes . . . I guess I do love her in my own way."

"I'm glad."

"Why?"

"Because from what you've told me I think if she ever thought you didn't, it'd probably kill her."

"Don't you think I haven't thought of that?" He leaned down and checked his patient again, making sure the steam was still hot enough; then he changed the subject, and they talked about their two young patients, the village they were in, and their ride back.

When the hour was up, they settled the boys back on their cots and wrapped them with blankets the women had brought. Matt asked Rebel to watch them, then went outside. He was gone for a short time, coming back stirring a thick poultice in a large dish and carrying some pieces of warm cloth over his arm. He handed the squares of cloth to Rebel, then pulled the covers from the boys' chests and rubbed the warm poultice on. A strong pungent smell drifted up from the poultice and filled the hut, mingling with the smell of the powder that had steamed up from the pails. He took the warm cloths from her and put them over the poultices, then covered the boys up again.

When this was finished they went outside, where the women had food ready, and they ate a meal of fish soup, fish cakes, breadfruit, and mangoes, washing it down with coconut milk.

Matt had them heat some of the coconut milk, and when he and Rebel were through eating, they took it in to the children, feeding them slowly, the heat from the milk helping to break loose more of the congestion.

They worked on the boys for two more hours, and by the time they were through, both boys were sleeping peacefully, the congestion broken, fevers down. Matt gave their mothers instructions on what to do, packed the powders back in his bag, and escorted Rebel to the horses. The native women's eyes filled with tears as they watched.

"I assume they don't pay you," Rebel said as they mounted, and he smiled wearily.

"Not with money." He reined his horse beside her, and they headed back into the forests. "These people have barely enough to live on. Their smiles are payment enough."

They'd been riding for about half an hour when Rebel glanced up at the sky. "Is it getting darker or is it my imagination?" she said. "It can't be more than three or four in the afternoon," and Matt squinted, glancing up through the trees.

"I've been watching it myself. The sun's gone and the wind feels strange. It's not usually this cool."

They were riding the mountain ridge again, and Matt rode to the top of a small crest, out of the trees, where he could see better. Rebel reined in beside him and they stared out across the valley to the sea beyond, where storm clouds were jockeying about the sky, swirling into position so they'd be headed straight for the island.

"Damn! I should have known by that sky this morning," he said. "It looks like a bad one heading this way."

"What do we do?"

"We can't beat it, and we sure as hell can't ride through it. We'll have to hole up someplace. It's too late to go back to the village."

She watched him anxiously while his horse pranced, sensing the storm; and the wind suddenly hit their faces with a new fury as the sky continued to darken.

Matt clamped his hat tighter on his head and turned his skittish animal. "Come on!" he said as the wind tried to whip his words away from her. "I think I know where we can go, but we've got to beat the rain."

The sky was rumbling, and the wind snatched at their clothes as they galloped along. They'd been riding for almost another hour, and yet the rain held off. The sky was not only dark now, resembling a deep twilight, but it had a strange yellow glow to it that made everything look eerie. "It's about fifteen minutes from here," Matt shouted. "I think we'll make it." But they didn't.

The rain hit with a driving force that almost knocked them from the saddles, and Matt yelled, "Let me take your reins." Rebel handed them to him, holding onto the front of the saddle as he started up a small hill, leading her horse behind him in the blinding downpour.

Five minutes later, drenched, Matt and Rebel and the horses entered an old shed. The roof leaked here and there, but they were out of the worst of the storm. He dismounted, then helped Rebel off.

"We'll have to get wet again for a few minutes," he said, blinking the rain from his eyes. "Are you all right?"

She nodded breathlessly.

"Good." He grabbed her hand and moved to the door of the shed, then took off running, Rebel in tow. She ran blindly after him, stumbling over the steps of the small house. He reached down and caught her before she fell, lifted her up into his arms, and carried her the rest of the way, kicking the door open with his foot.

He stepped inside, holding her against him. Rain fell from them to the bare wood floor, where it made puddles in what looked like a decade of dust. "It isn't much, but it's dry," he said. "The man who lived here said he was going to England to get a bride, and never came back. That was some fifteen years ago, when the French were still here, according to what I've heard. Nobody has seemed to want it since, and it's just been falling apart."

Rebel wiped the water from her eyes and looked around the place. It was small, only one room. The furniture was handmade, broken and full of dust; one of the shutters sagged on the glassless window, where rain was coming in, and water dripped through the roof. Only the fireplace looked like it was holding its own well, but it too was beginning to crumble.

Rebel was relieved to get out of the rain, and now suddenly she was very aware of Matt's arms holding her close against him. She didn't dare look at him as she spoke. "Are you going to put me down?" she asked, and he flushed as his arms dropped and he stood her on her feet.

"I'm sorry," he apologized. He stepped past her, walked to the fireplace, and inspected it as the rain beat a heavy tattoo against the roof and walls. "The fireplace looks all right." He motioned toward the old furniture. "If we finish breaking this up, we might have enough to last until the storm blows over." He reached out, grabbing what was left of an old chair, breaking off the arm.

Within a short time they had a fire going in the fireplace. It felt good on their hands and faces, chilled from the cold rain, but Rebel still shivered in her wet buckskins.

"We'll have to get out of these clothes," said Matt. The room was bare, not even a chest or any bedding, only an old mattress ticking on what was left of the bed. He walked over and picked it up, dusting it off as best he could, and set it down near the fireplace. He stood over it and took off his shirt, hanging it on one of the chairs he hadn't broken up yet. "We have no choice," he said softly. "The temperature always drops during a storm. If we stay in these clothes, we'll both be sick."

She bit her lip. He was right and she knew it. She was freezing, but there was nothing here to put on. "Matt . . . I can't."

"If you get sick, Brandon will get curious. Then what?"

"Isn't there anything I could wrap around me? Anything at all?"

He gestured, his hands taking in the whole room. "Where?"

She closed her eyes. "Oh, God, Matt, I can't do it," and she opened her eyes again in time to see his eyes harden.

"I won't touch you, if that's what you're worried about."

"I'm not worried about you, Matt, I'm worried about me," she blurted huskily. "Just the thought of letting you see me . . . do you know what that does to me?" Her eyes grew round and warm as she looked at him, at the muscles rippling beneath the soft mass of hair on his chest. "Do you know what the sight of you standing there right now is doing to me?" she asked breathlessly, and her pulses quickened. "Oh, my God, Matt . . . if we take off all our clothes . . ." Her voice broke on the words.

Matt's eyes softened as he stepped toward her, and she stared into his eyes, mesmerized. He reached down and lifted her arms, then pulled the buckskin shirt up over her head and tossed it to one side with his shirt. The dainty chemise she wore beneath it followed, and he stared at her hungrily, his body on fire.

Gently, very gently, his hands touched her breasts, and gooseflesh stood out on her skin as the nipples responded to him, hardening firmly. His eyes still stared into hers, and her lips parted sensuously as she let out a soft cry of pleasure.

"I want you, Rebel," he whispered softly. "Oh, Lord, how I want you!" and his hands slipped from her breasts, caressing her skin as they moved to her back, and he drew her to him, his mouth lowering to hers and he kissed her deeply, the sweet, heady feel of her lips against his burning through him like a hot flame.

Rebel melted against him, her breasts caressing his bare chest and her mouth opened to let him search it, the sensuous feel of his tongue firing her already-surging loins to a new peak of pleasure.

Matt straightened, his lips trembling from the warmth of her kiss, and his eyes were dazed, as if he were drunk. "Oh, Rebel, how long I've wanted to do that!"

Rebel's eyes too were glazed with passion as she reached down slowly, unfastening her buckskin breeches, and let them fall at her feet.

Matt picked her up and set her on the old ticking, pulling the wet bloomers from her body while she kicked off her moccasins; then he stood above her and methodically pulled off his boots and pants while she lay waiting, watching his magnificent body emerge.

He saw her shiver as he bent down, and he stretched out beside her, one hand cupping her full breast, the other moving down her exquisite body. She was a rare delight and his blood ran even hotter as she responded to his fingers when they touched the patch of hair between her legs, and he moved them down farther, exploring the deep secrets of her body.

She moved beneath his hands sensuously, and he kissed her, his kiss bringing new heat to her loins, and her arms went about his neck, then moved down his back, feeling the muscles that moved beneath her fingers. It had been so long . . . so long since she'd been able to respond to a man's touch like this. And she was responding. She loved every moment, every caress. It was like being in heaven.

His mouth eased on hers, and she felt him hard against the side of her hip. "I'm not hurting you, am I?" he asked against her mouth, and she sighed.

"Oh, no, Matt, no. You could never hurt me," she moaned ecstatically. "I need you!" and he groaned helplessly as his lips touched hers once more, sipping at them, sending sweet warmth deep inside her.

He kissed her mouth, her neck, her breasts, then his mouth opened and closed on her nipple while his tongue brought her to a new awareness of feeling. Rebel lost track of time. She didn't care anymore as his lips took her, his mouth savoring the sweetness of what he'd longed for and never had; then, when she thought she'd been driven to the ultimate in pleasure, he moved above her, his swollen manhood entering her, driving deep, making her cry for release, her body arching to meet his, driving him even deeper and his mouth covered hers again as he thrust inside her over and over again, and she climaxed, not once, but twice, her body shaking beneath him with the violence of her emotions.

His mouth moved against hers hesitantly, his breathing heavy with passion. "I can't hold back any longer, Rebel," he gasped breathlessly against her lips, "I'm going to come," and she murmured softly, her words like music to his ears.

"Then come, my darling, come," she whispered, and he let himself go, exploding inside her, his mouth covering hers again as he shook spasmodically, and for the first time in his life the sensation was so strong it lifted his body to a peak of pleasure he'd never known existed.

He shivered lightly and lay above her, relaxed and spent, his long frame warming her beneath him, his lips moving from hers as he buried his face in the warmth of her neck. He lay for long moments, unable to talk, his breathing unsteady as he felt her soft body beneath his. "Forgive me, Rebel," he whispered against the smoothness of her neck.

"For what? Making me happy?"

"You're happy?"

"If I could sleep with you every night instead of Brandon, I'd never want to get out of bed," she said, and he lifted his head, looking down at her.

He was still inside her, and it was strange, because he was still as hard as he'd been when he'd first entered her. Always before he'd gone soft afterward, but then, this was the first time since his marriage he'd been able to stay in when he came, and the sensation was more than pleasing, it was an ecstasy. He thrust his hips forward, moving inside her, and she stirred beneath him, arching herself closer to let him know she liked it.

"I like to pleasure you, ma'am," he said softly, and she smiled, her violet eyes warm as they looked into his.

"You don't think I'll catch cold now, do you?" she asked mischievously, and he kissed her as he drove inside her again, and she tingled all over.

He made love to her the rest of the afternoon and late into the night, as if he was afraid to let her go, climaxing again two more times before the rain subsided in the morning and daylight began to seep into the sky.

Rebel stirred in his arms. She had no idea when she'd fallen asleep, no idea when the rain had stopped, and no idea what time it was; all she saw was the light filtering through the trees outside.

Matt opened his eyes as he felt her move in his arms, and he gazed into her face. "I love you, Rebel," he whispered softly, and she stared at him, a shadow crossing her eyes.

"No," she whispered, "no you don't, Matt, you only think

you do because of what's happened," but he disagreed.

"I know the difference between love and infatuation, Rebel. I've loved you for months now. You must have known."

"But you can't," she insisted.

"Why not?"

She bit her lip as she pulled herself from his arms and sat up beside him, leaning her head on her knees. "Because I'm not in love with you."

"And last night?"

"You remind me of someone else, Matt, that's all," she confessed, and he reached up, running his hand down the softness of her bare back.

"Who?" he asked. "Beau?" and she looked at him, startled.

"What do you know about Beau?"

"I imagine he has green eyes, like myself and Cole. And I expect his hair is black like Cole's and . . ." He hesitated for a minute, wondering if it was wise to say it, then shrugged. "And he's probably an Indian. Am I right?"

There was a pained look on his face that brought tears to her eyes, and she swallowed hard, turning away from him, the tears falling down her cheeks.

"How did you know?" she asked, and his hand fell to the mattress as he stared at the crumbling ceiling overhead, where patches of daylight began to show.

"When Cole was coming and you were delirious, you called his name, and the morning after Brandon hit you, you told me that Beau had only used you, do you remember?"

She nodded unhappily as the tears covered her mouth, and she shook her head, licking them from her lips; then she turned and fell down against him, burying her face in his shoulder.

"I've loved him for years," she cried helplessly. "He wouldn't marry me because he's an Indian. Because his mother is one of his father's four wives. Oh, God, Matt, the night before I married Brandon, Beau came to me and . . . I wanted him so . . . that night was the only time I've given myself freely until tonight." She wiped her eyes and leaned up on her elbow, looking into his face. "You remind me of Beau, Matt . . . your eyes, the way you make love . . ." She sat up again and stared off into the empty room beyond him. "I should never have come with you."

He reached out and took her hand, holding it close against his chest. "It pleases me that you did," he said softly, and she looked down at him. "You can't stop me from loving you,

Rebel, you never will," he confirmed. "And I can't stop you from loving Beau, whoever he is, but what we've had here . . . Rebel, making love to my wife is like making love to the wall. I kiss her and there's no response. It isn't that she doesn't love me, but she's been brought up with the age-old notion that it's wicked and evil to enjoy the pleasures of her body, and she's been able to fight her feelings quite successfully. I touch her and she freezes. We've been married all these years, and last night was the first time I've come inside a woman in all that time. I've never been unfaithful until now." He squeezed her hand hard. "I never wanted to be until I met you. I can't just let it end here, with only last night to remember. Maybe you don't love me the way you love him, but you love me enough to give yourself to me without holding back. You proved that last night."

"But it isn't fair to you."

"Not fair to me? Oh, Rebel . . ." He drew her hand to his lips and kissed it. "I only want to be able to love you, and if, in doing so, I can keep on making you as happy as you said you were last night, if I can give you my love freely . . . what more can either of us ask?"

"And Miriam?"

His eyes saddened. "If she were my sister, I couldn't love her more," he whispered passionately, "but I don't love her with the force and drive that beats inside me when I'm with you. She rejected my body long ago. She'll never miss what I give you, as long as she has the rest of me."

She squeezed his hand back and bit her lip, looking down into Matt's face. "You're very special, you know that, Doctor," she said affectionately. "I'm just liable to end up really falling in love with you," and she kissed him full on the mouth.

13

It was almost four o'clock by the time Matt and Rebel reached the back hill overlooking the house. Rebel hated to say good-bye, and she clung to Matt desperately as he embraced her in the shadows of a breadfruit tree. They had no idea when they'd ever be able to be together like this again, and parting was painful.

Matt watched her descend the hill, keeping in the shadows of the hedgerows so he wouldn't be seen; then he mounted his horse and spurred it back over the crest of the hill.

It was easy to turn the horse loose into the pasture, but not as easy to get the saddle back in the stables. She managed to haul it ungracefully to the corner of the building, then had to wait for the two stableboys to disappear into the stables before she could move again. As soon as they were out of sight, she hefted it from the ground, carried it to the door, opened the door quickly, and ducked inside, hanging it on the low rack where it belonged. Then, peeking out furtively, she slipped from the harness room and moved to the old door in the garden wall.

So far she hadn't been seen, and she lifted the latch in the wooden door, opening it, creeping inside, staying hidden behind rows of scarlet bougainvillea as she made her way to the French doors off the drawing room. Tiptoeing inside, she moved cautiously to the doorway, where she peeked gingerly around the corner into the hall. No one was about, and she held her breath. Stepping lightly out of the room, she made a mad dash for the stairs, her moccasined feet silent as she ascended them two at a time and ran down the hall. She jerked the door to her room open and darted inside, shutting it hurriedly behind her. She leaned against it, relieved, then gasped, startled, as she stared into the horrified faces of Cristabel and Hizzie.

"Good Lord, ma'am," cried Cristabel, her eyes wide as saucers in her dark face, "I thought you weren't never gonna get back."

"I'll explain later," she said, trying to catch her breath. "Did anyone else know I was gone"

Both girls shook their heads. "No, ma'am," answered Hizzie. "Cristabel and me told 'em you was sick and it might be somethin' catchin', so we didn't let nobody into the room."

"They sent for Doc Wilder," interrupted Cristabel, "but naturally he weren't there."

"Who sent for him?"

"The housekeeper. She said long as the governor wasn't here, somebody had to do somethin'." Cristabel held her stomach. "She's been sendin' up chicken soup from the kitchen since yesterday noon when you didn't show up for lunch, and between that and my reg'lar meals, I feel like a stuffed pig. I couldn't eat it all, though. We told her you didn't feel like eatin' much."

Rebel stepped farther into the room. "Has the baby been all right?"

Hizzie nodded. "Oh, yes, ma'am."

"But you gotta hurry, ma'am," interrupted Cristabel again. "The governor's ship docked already, and he sent a message out to the house. He had to go to his offices first, then he wrote that he'd be along in about an hour."

Rebel frowned. "How long ago was that?"

"I don't rightly know, ma'am," answered Cristabel. "I ain't too good at tellin' time."

Rebel rushed to her armoire and pulled out a wrapper, while she ordered Cristabel to get some bathwater set up in the powder room. The girl disappeared out the door, and Rebel moved across to the dresser, anxiously yanking out her underclothes and some petticoats. She slipped hurriedly from her buckskins and rolled them into a ball, shoving them to the back of the armoire, putting on the wrapper, covering her dirty bloomers and chemise.

Hizzie eyed her warily, noting the dirt smudges on her underclothes. How strange. But then, the doctor, well, he'd never do anything wrong. There was probably good reasons why the duchess's underclothes was dirty, and she dismissed any bad thoughts from her mind, deciding not even to mention it to Cristabel. Both Hizzie and Cristabel adored Rebel, and she'd confided in them before she left, telling them the doctor had promised to show her some of the island, and both girls knew that Brandon had expressly forbidden her to go riding about without him, so they covered for her.

Rebel sank into the warm bathwater, and Cristabel washed her hair. Rebel told the young girl about the two sick children and the storm, and thanked her again for not making a fuss.

"We was real worried, ma'am," exclaimed Cristabel, shaking her head. "Especially when it started rainin' like the devil, but we didn't want to say nothin' to nobody 'less we had to. We talked it over and decided that as long as you was with Doc Wilder he'd see you got took care of real good. But I sure am glad you got back when you did, 'cause I don't know what we'd have told the governor, and I sure don't want you to get hurt again."

Rebel stepped hurriedly from the tub, wishing she could linger longer, but knowing it was impossible. "Nor do I, Cristabel." She sighed and grabbed the towel Cristabel offered her, rubbing herself vigorously while Cristabel picked up the underclothes and waited to help her mistress on with them.

Rebel twisted the towel around her wet hair, pulled on three petticoats, then slipped into the pale blue wrapper. There were tiny rosebuds in rows down the front of it, with lace inserts, and the sleeves stopped just below the elbow with wide lace ruffles. She shoved her feet into the slippers Cristabel had remembered to bring for her, then quickly yanked the door open. But instead of stepping into the hall, she froze, holding her breath in disbelief as she stared into Brandon's worried face.

His eyes sifted over her, and his mouth was drawn in a tight line. "I thought you were sick," he exclaimed with questioning eyes.

"You scared me," she blurted, trying a half-laugh that caught in her throat. "I knew you were coming home, but I thought I could get myself presentable before you arrived."

"Presentable?"

Her face flushed. "I look a mess. I've been in bed since Thursday evening. When I woke up yesterday morning, I felt miserable."

"Didn't anyone send for the doctor?"

"Yes, but from what Cristabel said, Miriam sent word back that he wasn't home and she didn't know how soon he'd be back."

Brandon reached out, taking her arm, and started escorting her down the hall to her room, while her legs trembled. "I just left him at my office," he said. "Maybe I'd better send for him."

Her heart turned over. Not yet, she couldn't see Matt yet, she might give everything away. "There's really no need," she said quickly. "I'm feeling fine now, Bran, really I am. Whatever it was seems to be over. It was probably something I ate that disagreed with me."

"I'd feel better if you'd let Matt take a look."

"No, really, I'm fine now."

"You're sure?"

"I'm sure."

"It wouldn't take long to get Matt up here."

He sure as hell was being insistent. "Look," she said beguilingly, smiling to hide her nervousness, "we'll be going there for dinner this evening, in only a few hours, and if you still insist, I'll have Matt take a look at me while we're there. I'm sure he won't mind."

"You're still planning to go out?"

"Certainly. I told you I'm all right now."

He studied her intently for a minute as she stood before him, and suddenly she saw the worried look on his face change to a look she knew only too well, and a lump stuck in her throat. Not now, she screamed to herself. Oh, Lord God, not now! But she knew prayer wouldn't help.

Brandon's eyes caressed her clean-scrubbed face. The scent of her perfumed soap filled his nostrils. He'd been gone almost three days, and the sight of her stirred him uncontrollably as he saw her breasts heaving beneath the dressing gown. He'd been upset when he'd first arrived home and the housekeeper had told him she was sick, but now, if she was better . . . He turned to Cristabel, trying not to appear too eager, and ordered her to have the powder room cleaned up and the tub emptied and refilled for his bath, then instructed Hizzie to take the baby downstairs for a while, explaining that she should take him into the garden more often, that the sun was good for him, and he made sure before they left that both girls understood there was no reason to come back upstairs again until their mistress called them. Rebel's heart sank as she watched them leave the room.

Brandon barely waited until the door was shut before he had her in his arms, his mouth covering hers hungrily, and he kissed her long and hard.

Rebel's body froze beneath his hands as he held her close, and she wanted to push him away and cry out, but knew she didn't dare. Then slowly, as his mouth caressed hers, she felt his tongue moving against her lips. She tried to fight it, but it was futile; her stomach turned as he forced his tongue into her mouth, and she started to gag. There was no way she could do it, not now, not so soon after the sweet sensations Matt had kindled in her. It was repulsive, and she forced her head back away from his grasping mouth and probing tongue, her face contorted with anger.

"I've told you before," she gasped as she stared into his hungry eyes. "I can't stand to feel your tongue in my mouth."

"My God, Reb, when are you going to grow up?" he cried furiously. "If you'd just let it stay there long enough, you'd enjoy it." But she shook her head.

"I can't help it. It's . . . it's sickening!"

He exhaled disgustedly, his arms tightening around her, his body throbbing. He wasn't about to be thwarted, not now, and his voice broke. "All right, Reb, for your sake, since you've been ill, I won't do it now," he said huskily, "but you are going to learn to like it." His voice deepened passionately.

"For now I can find other things just as tempting, so I'm still going to enjoy you." He set her back away from him and started unfastening her dressing gown, while she shuddered at the thought of what lay ahead of her.

All of Miriam's guests were there on time, and she was delighted. At least outwardly she was delighted. The sight of Rebel in a gorgeously low-cut dress of deep green velvet with an emerald necklace and matching earrings gracing her luxuriantly creamy skin made her stomach tighten into one huge knot, making it impossible to enjoy her own dinner.

Kuulie was a superb cook, and the six guests raved about the meal, retiring afterward to sit on the veranda and talk. General and Mrs. Bridlehurst were there; Rebel and Brandon; and the guests of honor, the vicar and his wife. Rebel had little in common with the women, but tried to hold her own in the conversation, beaming exuberantly when she was able to answer their questions about Cole.

When she and Brandon had first arrived, she'd been almost afraid to face Matt again. But it was so easy. His eyes spoke to her gently and his hand greeted her with a slight caress. She was grateful that he showed no outward change toward her. Miriam was overdressed, as usual, in yards of unflattering black lace that emphasized her shapeless figure and made her look gaunt, but Matt was solicitous toward her, as always, and was the same quiet, carelessly dressed doctor everyone was used to seeing. Suddenly Rebel understood something that had puzzled her. Now she knew why he dressed and acted the way he did. If Matt were to straighten out of his comfortable slouch, as he had when he was with her, and if he dressed in well-fitting clothes as Brandon and the others did, he'd outshine all the other men on the island. He was hiding. Actually hiding his virility behind a casual disregard of his appearance. But why? For Miriam's sake? Was it to keep Miriam from being jealous of women who might look at him longingly?

His eyes met hers across the veranda as he felt her staring at him. He turned abruptly as Brandon stepped up beside him; seconds later, both men strolled toward her.

"Brandon tells me you haven't been feeling well," Matt said casually.

"It's nothing really, doctor, I . . . It was probably something I ate."

He smiled as if nothing was wrong. "I can open my examining room. If you'd care to step in, I can take a look."

"I wish you would," said Brandon. "I'd feel better about it."

"Brandon's right," agreed Matt. "You can never tell about these things."

Rebel's hands shook and she tried to still them, but Brandon noticed right away.

"See that," he said, taking her hand in his. "She's shaking like a leaf. I wish you would look at her, Matt."

Matt's eyes met hers. "It'll only take a few minutes," he said slowly, and she nodded, her heart in her throat.

Her knees felt like jelly, and she was afraid they'd give out beneath her as Brandon ushered her across the veranda to the door, saying he'd wait outside for her.

Matt's office was the first door on the right as one entered the house. He opened the door so she could step into the dark room ahead of him. He started to follow her inside, then hesitated.

"I forgot a light," he whispered hoarsely. "If I don't get one right away, they're going to think something's wrong."

"Go ahead."

He walked across the hall into the drawing room and picked a lamp up from one of the stands, then returned to the office. He led Rebel into the examining room, shutting and locking the door behind them. This done, he took a deep breath and she moved gracefully into his arms. His mouth came down on hers warm and sweet, and she returned his kiss slowly, savoring every precious moment. She was no longer shaking as he drew his mouth from hers and looked deeply into her eyes.

"I've been so afraid for you," he whispered softly.

"I'm supposed to have been sick."

"You mean no one discovered you were gone?"

"Hizzie and Cristabel did a beautiful job of covering for me."

"I'm surprised they didn't panic."

"They knew I was in good hands, so they said."

His arms tightened about her. "That's something I don't like. I wish they hadn't known we were together."

She reached up, playing with his earlobe affectionately, her body pressed close to his. "They won't say anything. To them it's all quite innocent. Besides, they hate Brandon and they know he gave me that black eye. I told them they didn't dare tell anyone where I went because if just one other person knew and told Brandon, he'd kill me. By the way, speaking of Brandon, he said you were down at his office . . ."

He nodded, his eyes darkening. "I got home a few minutes after a message arrived from him asking to see me right away. I changed clothes and went down."

"And?"

"Brandon's going to raid French-held Tobago, Rebel," he said irritably. "There are more troops up at St. Vincent, and they plan to join forces, attacking three weeks from tomorrow."

"On Sunday?"

"Brandon figures they'll catch most at church and that on Sunday the military won't be as alert."

She eyed him warily. "Why did he tell you all this?"

"He wants me to go with them."

"You?"

"The surgeon that came with the troops died of a heart seizure two weeks ago, if you remember. There's one surgeon with the troops at St. Vincent, none for the ones here."

Her voice hardened. "What did you tell him?"

"It wasn't a matter of telling him anything." His arms dropped from around her, and he walked to the window, staring at the bamboo shades. "I told him I wasn't going; he said I was. He's the governor and we're at war with France; it's as simple as that."

She walked over and touched his arm. "Matt, what if . . . ? I couldn't bear for anything to happen to you."

He turned around and took her hands in his. They were cold, and she was shaking again. "I'll be all right, don't worry."

She squeezed his fingers. "But I will worry."

He bent and kissed her. "We'd better go out soon or they'll be getting suspicious," he whispered as his lips moved from her mouth to the sensitive spot on her neck just below the ear.

"And what's your diagnosis of my mysterious illness, Doctor?" she asked playfully.

"Not the one your husband wants."

"What one is that?"

"He hopes you're pregnant." He lifted his head and looked down at her again, half-smiling. "But you're not."

Her eyes sparkled impishly. "Unless . . . last night . . . ?"

His smile faded and his eyes looked pained. "Oh, God, I hope not."

She put her hand to his lips. "Don't be foolish. I'm not Miriam, Matt. I'd be proud to have your child. Rather yours than Brandon's."

Voices drifted in to them, and Matt realized everyone had stepped into the house. He tensed. "We'd better go out," he said.

"When will I see you again?"

He kissed her softly, then released her and reached down, picking up the lamp. "That's just the trouble," he answered helplessly. "I don't know."

"I can always say I'm sick again."

"A healthy specimen like you?" He smiled. "We'll work it out somehow, but for now, just remember I love you."

They joined everyone in the drawing room, and Rebel hoped her face wasn't too flushed from Matt's kisses.

Miriam was standing across the room listening to the vicar's wife when Rebel and Matt stepped through the doorway, and suddenly, as her eyes fell on her husband, she didn't hear a thing the woman was saying. She stared at Matthew, a sick feeling grinding into the pit of her stomach. There was something about the way he was looking at Rebel . . .

"Did you hear me, Miriam?" asked the vicar's wife, and Miriam blinked her eyes as she realized she hadn't heard.

"Oh, I'm sorry. What was it you said?" She drew her eyes reluctantly from her husband, wondering exactly what had gone on in his examining room.

The rest of the evening she rarely let her thoughts wander from Matt. She watched him furtively, but the look never returned to his eyes, and she began to think perhaps she'd imagined it. Then, as the guests were leaving, she saw Rebel glance at Matt for a moment, and she looked from one to the other sharply. It was dark out, but the look that passed between them made her cringe. She hadn't been imagining it, and she felt her insides tremble.

"Did you find out what was wrong with Rebel?" she asked Matt nervously as they stood on the veranda watching the carriages disappear from sight down the road.

"An upset stomach, from what I could see. She seems all right now."

"Matthew," she asked, "what did Brandon want you for this afternoon?" He squeezed her shoulders affectionately.

"Military matters," he answered. "I'm sorry. He's sworn me to secrecy."

"That's silly."

"Not to him."

"I bet Rebel knows."

He looked at her again and noticed a tightness about her

mouth as they stopped in the doorway to the drawing room. "Now, what is that supposed to mean?"

"You wouldn't understand."

"Try me."

"Why do some people have to have everything?"

"Who has everything?"

Miriam stepped into the drawing room and walked about picking up empty glasses and straightening pillows. "You're not blind, Matthew," she said as he watched her from the doorway. "A woman like Rebel, what does she have to worry about?" She held the glasses together with her fingers inside them as she walked back across the room. "All she has to do is bat those big violet eyes of hers at her husband and he'd probably tell her the secret plans of the whole British Army." Her brown-flecked topaz eyes looked directly into his as she brushed by him on her way to the kitchen. "You don't even discuss your patients with me."

"I told you before," he answered, following her, "you have a careless way of forgetting what I told you was confidential."

She went into the kitchen and set the glasses down, giving Kuulie instructions to make sure everything was cleaned up before she retired, then joined Matt again in the hall. She stopped in front of him, her eyes curiously studying his face.

"Matthew," she suddenly asked, touching the tight curls over her right ear, primping them up, "do you still think I'm pretty?" He stared at her for a moment; then his right hand moved to her neck and up to her chin.

"Now, isn't that a ridiculous question to ask?"

"Then why don't you ever look at me the way you looked at her tonight?"

He held his breath, his fingers motionless on her chin, his face flushed. "What the hell are you talking about?" he asked, and his hand dropped abruptly.

"You know very well what I'm talking about." She turned from him and walked down the hall, ascending the stairs with Matt close at her heels. "I'm not blind either, Matthew," she threw back at him caustically as he followed her. "And if you think I'm going to calmly sit back and let Rebel make a fool of me in front of all my friends, you're sadly mistaken." She reached the top of the stairs and walked to the door of her room, opening it, then turned to face him. "I won't tolerate it, Matthew," she snapped viciously. "I've hated that woman from the day she stepped foot on this island."

Matt frowned. "You have a strange way of showing it."

"You mean because I'm supposedly on friendly terms with her? I wouldn't be if it wasn't for her husband's position in this godforsaken place. Don't you think I haven't seen the contemptuous way she looks down at me? It's a shame we all can't be young and beautiful like she is. That nature wasn't as kind to the rest of us." She paused, and he shook his head.

"I had no idea you felt that way about her."

"Well, I do. I have to tolerate her because of who she is, but I'll never like her because of what she is, and if you ever look at her again the way you did tonight . . ." She took a step closer to him, and her arms moved up and entwined about his neck possessively. "You're my husband, Matthew, and I love you very much. I always have, and nobody's going to take you away from me, ever! I won't let them."

Matt saw tears at the corners of her eyes, but he had no idea whether they were tears of anger, hurt, or frustration. He didn't want to hurt Miriam. The last thing on earth he wanted was to hurt her. There was a physical pain in his chest as he stared into her eyes. She had said she loved him. When was the last time she'd said it? He couldn't even remember. She called him "Matthew darling" and spoke of him to others as "my dear, sweet Matthew," but to put her arms about his neck and voluntarily say "I love you"? This was something new, and he wondered what she was trying to prove and how far she'd go. Did she really love him completely, or were her words only half-truths to hang onto what she felt belonged to her? There was one way of finding out.

Matt pulled her closer into his arms. "I don't know where you get your notions or what you think you saw tonight," he said softly, holding her tightly, feeling the black lace of her dress beneath his fingers. "But whatever it was . . . you were wrong . . ." and he bent down, his mouth covering hers, and he kissed her deeply, his lips waiting for her response. Instead he felt her body tighten in his arms.

He drew his head back and stared down at her. "For a woman who says she's in love . . . you could at least return my kiss."

She licked her lips. "I did."

"Oh, hell, Miriam, I could go out and kiss Kuulie and get more response than that."

She fought tears. "What am I supposed to do?"

"Kiss me back." He felt her stiffen again, but he wasn't giving up, not yet. He had to be sure. He turned her around and pushed her bedroom door open the rest of the way, shoving her inside. She gazed at him hesitantly, the light from the candles Kuulie'd left for her on the dresser falling across his face. She bit her lip when she saw the expression on it.

"What are you doing?" she asked hesitantly. His face softened, but he didn't answer. Instead he reached out and unfastened the clasps that held the clusters of curls above her ears and took them out, tossing them onto the dresser; then he ran his hands through her hair slowly, sensuously, combing it back with his fingers.

She stared at him dumbfounded as she felt strange tingling sensations driving deep into her loins, and her heart started to pound. He turned her around gently and unfastened her dress and chemise, letting them fall to the floor.

His eyes were intent on her now as he purposefully picked her up and carried her to the bed. The silk embroidered bedspread felt cool beneath her.

"Matthew, I didn't say . . ." she gasped, trembling. It reminded her of her wedding night and the way he'd made love to her, expecting her to respond like some wanton whore. "I didn't want—"

"But I do," he interrupted. He threw his clothes aside, and she tried to put her hands over herself as best she could, cringing away from him. "You say you love me, Miriam, then prove it." He stretched out beside her and lay on his back. "Make love to me, Miriam," he whispered softly. "You say you love me, you've always loved me, then make love to me."

Her eyes widened as she stared at him, and her heart moved into her throat. "You want me to . . ."

His green eyes were intense, his breathing heavy. "I want you to forget what you've been led to believe. That a woman isn't supposed to enjoy a man's body, and I want you to show me how much you love me."

She shook her head stubbornly, swallowing hard as she lay on her side, one hand and arm covering her breasts, the other trying to hide the dark patch of hair between her legs. "I can't, Matthew, please," she whimpered. "You know I love you, but I can't!"

"Why not?"

"Because it's sinful and dirty."

He turned toward her and reached out, pulling her hand away from her pathetically small breast, and he raised up on one elbow, bending down, lifting the small mound of flesh until the nipple on it reached his mouth. His tongue caressed it gently, and he felt it harden; then he reached down, pulling her hand from between her legs, putting his own there instead, and his fingers began to move, sending even stronger thrills through her body.

"Then I'll make love to you!" he said as he lifted his mouth from her breast, and he pushed her onto her back, his lips touching hers, and he kissed her softly, while his hand moved between her legs.

Miriam was hot and burning inside, and tears sprang to her eyes. She didn't want this! She didn't want to feel what she was feeling. Her body felt like it wanted to explode, but it was wrong, all wrong!

Then suddenly, with deliberate willpower, she forced herself to think of other things, to forget what he was doing to her, telling herself it was sordid and obscene. He was a man, and men couldn't control their evil weaknesses like women could. He told her to prove she loved him. Didn't she do that every day? She saw the house was kept nice, listened to the things he had to tell her, and was a good hostess when they entertained. She even let him use her body whenever he wanted, never telling him no. That was one thing Mother had told her. "Don't ever deny him, dear, that's the easiest way to send him looking to someone else," she'd said. Why did he have to be so stubborn? Why wasn't kissing enough for him?

Matt kept up his attempt to arouse her enough to break through the age-old taboo he knew she was wrestling with. One moment he was almost sure she was going to give in and he'd feel her hips move slightly or her mouth tremble; then, as always, she'd stiffen and he'd have to start all over again.

He was angry. The more he caressed her, the more she fought him. Not physically, but mentally. She lay passively next to him, denying her body what should rightfully be hers to enjoy.

Suddenly he could go on no longer. The whole thing was useless. She'd never change. She could kiss him and say she loved him all she wanted, but he'd never believe her. She didn't love him. Not the way he needed to be loved. She only wanted to possess him. To be able to say "He's mine." She wanted a husband to show off like women show off their children.

And that was another thing. There was no reason she couldn't have had children. He'd respected her wishes in the matter because he didn't want to hurt her, but as he thought of it now he wondered if he wasn't hurt more by the lack of them than she would have been to bear them.

Weary of the whole mess, his hand lifted from her body, his mouth left hers, and he fell back on the bed. He wasn't even hard anymore. It was as if the life had gone out of him. He didn't need her. Not anymore. He'd rather go without than humiliate himself again by making love to a woman who loathed the very act itself. No. He'd take Rebel whenever the opportunity arose, but he'd never touch Miriam again unless he was really desperate.

"I'm sorry, Miriam," he said softly, and he was. He was sorry for the pitiful shell of a woman he'd married.

Thank God at least for tonight it was over, but she opened her eyes, looking at him curiously. "Are you through?" she asked softly. "Aren't you going to . . . ?"

Her voice trailed off as he lay still, staring up at the ceiling, not answering.

"Well, aren't you, Matthew?" and he slowly shook his head.

"No, Miriam, I'm through," he whispered softly, and started to rise from the bed.

"Aren't you even going to kiss me good night?" she asked as he stood up, and he turned toward the bed, startled. "Don't look like that, Matthew," she said sweetly. "You know you always kiss me good night," but instead of kissing her, a half-strangled laugh issued from deep inside him, and he turned, picking up his clothes, and he disappeared through the door that adjoined their rooms, still laughing bitterly as she stared after him, innocently wondering what she possibly could have said that was so funny and made him laugh so strangely.

14

For the next three weeks everyone on the island was tense, like a pregnant woman waiting impatiently to bring her child into the world. Rebel managed to see Matt off and on during that time, mostly when others were present, occasionally alone, when she could talk to him for a few minutes, but moments like that were hard to come by without making people suspicious, and all that could pass between them were a few stolen kisses.

Brandon was in and out of the house all hours of the day, and there was no chance for them to meet secretly and spend any real time together. Two British men-of-war had docked in the harbor a few days after Miriam's dinner party, and the docks were busy as supplies were carried on board. Everyone knew something big was in the wind, but only Brandon, General Bridlehurst, Dr. Wilder, and Rebel knew where they were headed. Brandon, however, had no idea that Matt had confided the secret to Rebel.

As the days went by, Rebel realized more and more that Brandon practically ignored the baby. He never held him or cuddled him like most fathers did, and he resented it when Rebel spent what he considered too much time with him.

"You'll have the child spoiled," he said one afternoon as she played with him on the sitting-room floor.

Brandon's temper had become short of late, and Rebel stayed out of his way as much as possible, but his appetite for her in bed had become more frequent. She was certain he was hoping to get her pregnant. So far there were no signs of his having succeeded.

It was four days before sailing time. Brandon opened the door to Rebel's room without knocking and stepped inside. It was barely light outside, and he walked softly across the room and stood looking down at his wife asleep in the big bed. He hated having to leave her again. He sat down on the edge of the bed and touched her arm, shaking her lightly. "Reb, wake up," he said. "Rebel, I have to talk to you."

She stirred, sighing, and opened her eyes, then sat up abruptly. "What is it?" she asked, half-asleep.

"A messenger came a few minutes ago. There's a small ship waiting at the dock, and I have to go to St. Vincent. There's been some trouble that has to be taken care of. I'll be back as soon as I can."

She yawned and stretched. "When is as soon as you can?"

"I know I can't get back by tonight. If all goes well, I should be back tomorrow afternoon."

"You're so secretive about everything, Bran," she said. "You have two ships, and over four hundred soldiers ready to sail on them, and still nobody knows where you're headed."

He smiled. "I have no way of knowing if there are any French spies on the island," he answered. "So I take precautions."

"With your wife too?"

"The less you know, the better," he said importantly. "Now, I've got to leave. I'm not going to wake any of the servants, I'll just slip out quietly. I came to tell you good-bye. I doubt you'll worry, but I can hope."

She studied his face. She couldn't love this man. He was handsome enough . . . but it was the eyes, the twist of his mouth, the cruel way he had of treating people, as if they were there for him to walk on. Sometimes she wondered how he had the capacity in his heart to love her. It wasn't a normal love, however, it was a cruel possessive love. The kind that smothered and dominated and left no room for simple warmth and affection.

He kissed her good-bye, enjoying her full breast with one hand as his lips pressed her mouth, and she watched him leave with a strange, uninhibited feeling. Tomorrow, he'd said. That meant she'd be alone tonight, all night. But she couldn't sneak out again like before. Hizzie and Cristabel were on her side, but if they knew or even suspected she and Dr. Wilder were more than just friends . . . she couldn't risk it.

She glanced quickly at the empty place where Cole's swinging cradle had been. He was in his own room now across the hall with Hizzie, and she no longer had to worry about waking him. Slipping from the bed, she walked to the balcony and watched the sun begin to peep over the horizon. There was another ship in the harbor, all right. It wasn't as big as the men-of-war, its lines clean-cut, sails furled, waiting for its passenger.

She stood on the balcony and waited until she saw its sails unfurl one at a time. After the ship cleared the harbor, she went back in the bedroom, her mind already made up. She quietly let herself into Brandon's room. It would be at least an hour or more before the maid would come to make the bed. The pale gold light of dawn filtered into the room as she walked over to the desk he had by the French doors.

He never kept this desk locked. The one in his office downstairs had keys to every drawer, but this one was for his personal correspondence. She opened the small drawer in the middle and looked in. There was stationery he'd brought from England with the Bourland crest on it, and she picked up a piece, fingering it nervously. She searched the rest of the drawers until she found what she wanted. It was a letter she knew he'd written to a friend but hadn't sent yet. She'd interrupted him last night to ask him something as he was finishing it, and he hadn't taken time to address or seal the envelope, merely shoved the letter in and stuck it in the drawer.

She walked to the doors and made sure they were both locked, then sat down at the desk. Half an hour later, when she was finished, she held the note up and read it. Satisfied, she folded it and put it in the pocket of her wrapper, put everything back in its place, unlocked the doors, and went back to her own room. Slipping into the hall, she went downstairs and found the housekeepr.

"Did the governor wake you before he left?" she asked calmly.

"No, your Grace, I gave him the message the man brought, then returned to bed. I didn't know he left."

Rebel sighed, relieved. "Well, he had to leave, and he gave me this note for you to have someone take to Dr. Wilder," she lied, and handed the woman the folded piece of paper.

"I'll see one of the boys takes it over as soon as possible," the housekeeper assured her, and there was a smile on Rebel's face as she went back upstairs.

Matt was on his second cup of tea when the stableboy from the governor's house came to the door.

"It's a message for you," said Kuulie as she came into the dining room and handed it to the doctor, and Miriam glanced at him curiously.

"Who's it from?"

He unfolded it and read it, then looked up, scowling. "It's from the governor."

"Well, what does he say?"

"He's been called to St. Vincent . . . some kind of trouble. Won't be back until tomorrow afternoon."

"What has that to do with you?"

"I can't tell you everything, Miriam. I've told you that."

"Everything? You don't tell me anything except that the governor's ordered you to accompany him on this escapade, whatever it is."

"You're not the only one left out," he explained. "Only Brandon, General Bridlehurst, and I know where we're headed. The others will find out after we've left shore." He stood up, leaving the note on the table, where he'd set it while they talked, and he headed out into the hall.

He was no sooner out the door than Miriam snatched the message up and unfolded it, reading it aloud to herself. "Matt, there's been some trouble in St. Vincent and I have to leave. I'll be back sometime tomorrow afternoon, hopefully. Will tell you about it when I return, Brandon." There was nothing unusual about it that she could see, so she folded it back the way it was and set it down on the table, meeting

301

Matt in the doorway on her way out as he remembered the note and came back for it, stuffing it into his pocket.

He kissed her good-bye, and she went back to her breakfast, surprised a short while later when Kuulie interrupted her again.

"Another message for the doctor," the woman announced as she approached the table, and Miriam held out her hand.

"He's left already, I'll take it." She unfolded the message and read it, her face bewildered, then stared at it perplexed. She sipped at her breakfast tea slowly as she shoved the message in her dress pocket. "Now, why on earth would Brandon send two messages just alike?" she mused aloud to herself, shaking her head, wondering, and it wasn't until some hours later that she understood, and her face paled as she took the message again from her pocket, read it, then crumpled it angrily in her hand until her knuckles were white, knowing what she had to do.

The day had been full for Matt and he was glad as he made his way about St. George in his small buggy. He would have gone crazy waiting if he hadn't been able to keep busy, and that evening he was anxious as he waited until he was sure Miriam was asleep. Before he left, he opened the door to her room easily to make sure she was all right. He saw the vague lump beneath the covers and closed the door satisfied, then left the house. He saddled his horse quietly and headed toward the other end of the bay.

He'd often left in the middle of the night like this, summoned by someone hurt or sick. They used to have to wake up the servants in order to reach him, but now he had a small bell mounted inside his room with a rope that led to a pole in the yard below. If he was wanted at night, all that was necessary was to ring the bell, and within minutes the doctor was at the window. At first he'd left notes on his pillow for Miriam explaining where he was, but she rarely seemed to worry about him, so for a long time now he'd just gotten up, gotten dressed, grabbed his bag, and left. His hand moved to the bag hung on his saddle. It had been a necessary precaution in case anyone saw him.

He reached the road that led to the beautiful stucco house and traveled it some distance before pulling into the thick woods that covered the hillside. A short time later he was on the hill overlooking the back pasture. The front of the house overlooked the bay, and there was an iron fence beyond the front lawn, running the length of it, with a gate, kept open in the daytime and shut at night. Two guards were posted at the gate at all times, but the back of the house was unguarded, and it was easy to climb the fence. There was the pasture gently sloping toward the house, the stables, servants' and slaves' living quarters, and the high wall enclosing the back lawn and gardens, giving them privacy.

He tethered his horse to a tree on the hill and went down the slope on foot, following the hedgerows at the edge of the pasture. Not a soul was about. It was a little after eleven, and dark as pitch, not even a light on in the house as he made his way to the walled garden, then pressed himself against the wall, heading toward the front of the house. Frangipani trees grew on the lawn close to the house, and their fragrance filled his nostrils as he inched stealthily along, hugging the side of the house, keeping in the shadows. He reached the corner and stopped, then stepped around cautiously, looking about, assuring himself that he wasn't being observed, and his eyes moved upward toward the balcony off Rebel's room.

Inside the house Rebel paced her bedroom floor anxiously. What if Matt hadn't understood what she was trying to tell him? What if he thought the note was really from Brandon? Oh, God! Why didn't he come? It must be well past eleven already, and her body ached for him.

She walked to the French doors and stood looking out onto the balcony, her diaphanous nightgown catching in the balmy breeze that blew up from the bay. It hugged her legs loosely as she stared into the darkness. She strained her eyes, standing on tiptoe, and looked out over the front lawn and drive toward the gate, where the two soldiers stood at attention, their redcoated uniforms only faintly visible in the moonless night.

He was certain to come to the balcony first; then she could sneak downstairs and let him in; but what if he'd been called somewhere else and couldn't come? She had to see him tonight. It was their only chance to be together before the ships sailed for Tobago. She turned to walk back to her bed, then suddenly stopped, her ears straining. She heard a slight scraping noise, then his voice came to her softly from close by, as if it were an echo on the wind.

She turned, trying to see him, but it was too dark. There was a latticework of strong vines, sturdy enough to hold a man, and they clung to the house, going all the way to the roof, and now she watched breathlessly as he extricated himself from them cautiously and swung over the top of the wrought-iron railing onto the balcony, landing only a few feet from her.

"Oh, Matt," she murmured breathlessly, her body trembling. "I thought you'd never come!"

He stepped toward her, shortening the space between them, and stood looking at her for a moment, then pulled her hungrily into his arms. His lips found hers in the darkness, and he kissed her deeply, making her tingle to her toes; then he picked her up in his arms and carried her to the bed, standing her up beside it, his hands beginning to caress her body as he slowly stripped the nightgown from her.

She shivered longingly, then melted onto the bed and lay back, stretching out seductively, waiting for him. He was beside her in minutes, and there was no more need to wait.

The long days of needing each other and being unable to touch only made them more aware of each other than they already had been. His hands caressed her as her fingers roamed the secret places in his magnificent frame, and he felt sensations long forgotten. She was making love to him as he had asked Miriam to do. Her hands and her lips teased him, and she used her body erotically, responding to him with such violent, uninhibited passion that for a moment it took his breath away.

He was on his back now, and it was she who was bending over him, kissing his mouth, her tongue pleasuring him, running her hands through the dark silken hairs on his chest, then moving down his body. She ran her fingers across him, and he felt himself hardening even more. He grabbed her, pulling her down, burying his face in her breasts, smelling the deliciously fragrant smell of her hot body.

"Now?" he asked softly. She whispered her reply as she leaned backward. He rolled her onto her back so that he was above her, and when he entered, she was hot and moist, waiting for him, arching feverishly to meet him.

Afterward, she lay still in his arms for a long time, and neither of them spoke. Then suddenly, reluctantly, she wriggled from him, moved to the edge of the bed, and stood up, walking slowly across the floor, feeling the patch of moisture between her legs that cried out to her, branding her for what she'd become.

Matt watched her standing forlornly, leaning her head on the frame of the French doors as she stared off into the night. He slipped from the bed, walking to her, standing behind her, letting the nearness of her body soothe him.

"What is it?" he asked softly as he touched her shoulder, and he felt her quiver beneath his fingertips.

"I . . . Matt, what have I become?" she said softly, her

voice almost lost in the darkened room. "I call the planters on the island animals for lusting after their slaves, and I accuse Brandon of being depraved and a beast for wanting me, yet I craved your body tonight so violently that I barely even took time to say hello when you came into the room. I could hardly wait to feel your body taking mine. I'm no better than they are!"

He touched her hair, feeling its silken texture, his hand moving to the nape of her neck, where he pulled the hair back and kissed it softly. "I love you," he whispered, and she turned around slowly, her hand touching his bare chest.

"That's another thing," she said, her voice low and husky. "I'm not in love with you, Matt. I care for you . . . I care a lot. More than I should. There's something about you . . . I don't really know what it is, but I like it, I always have. Even months ago, when I was feeling so sorry for myself and making myself miserable, I always enjoyed having you around to talk to. When you and Miriam came to visit, I used to try to get you to myself, but I'm not in love with you. Even though I know I'll never see Beau again, I still love him. I can't help it, and if he walked in right now and asked me to go with him, I'd go."

Matt felt her words cut him deep inside. They hurt terribly, yet he knew they were true. She was being honest with him, and he loved her all the more for it. How had he come to love her in the first place? It had been a gradual thing. As she said, the talks they always had, the few moments together. In time, perhaps what she felt for him would grow the same way, become even stronger, until she forgot the Indian who'd broken her heart.

His arms went about her and he drew her warm body close to him as he looked down at her and spoke. "Have I demanded that you love me, Rebel?" he asked, and she looked into his face, trying to distinguish his features in the darkness. "Have I ever said, 'Rebel, I won't ever make love to you, I never want to touch you, until you can love me in return the way I love you'?"

She shook her head. "No."

"And I never will." His voice deepened. "I'm happy just to be with you, my love. And what we have . . . what we feel—"

"It's wrong," she interrupted, whispering, her voice breaking. "I told you once before that I had made a mistake. I did, a big one, but that doesn't justify my making another. We're both married, Matt, and my conscience is getting to me." She leaned her head against his chest, feeling the soft curling hair against her cheek. "What right have I to take what belongs to someone else? When I lay in your arms before, my body throbbing contentedly from the love you'd given me, I suddenly thought how lonely Miriam must be without it."

His hand moved up her back, and he held her tightly against him. "Rebel," he began as he held her, and she could hear his heart pounding in her ear, "the night of Miriam's dinner party for the vicar and his wife, Miriam and I had an argument. She accused me of looking at you the wrong way. I probably did, but that's beside the point. The point is that for the first time since our wedding night, Miriam put her arms around my neck and told me she loved me. I was shocked and amazed, and I thought maybe . . . just maybe she was beginning to feel . . . to come alive, so I forced the issue. I wanted to find out just how far she'd go. For over an hour I tried every way I know to make her surrender to her feelings and become the wife she should be, but it was useless, and I'll never try again. I know I should feel guilty being here with you, but I can't. For the first time in years I'm alive again. If it's wrong to be alive, then I ask God to forgive me."

Rebel had listened to him intently, and she'd felt him tremble when he spoke of making love to Miriam, as if he remembered it with distaste.

"Has she always been like this?" she asked.

"Since our wedding night. I'll never forget that night. She accused me of being a savage and treating her like a wanton when I tried to touch her. I made excuses for her because I realized her mother had managed to keep her ignorant. Can you imagine, she thought kissing was as far as she'd have to surrender herself. She was horrified when I explained what I was going to do, but she loved me enough and let me have my way, until I came inside her, that is. When she felt it, she asked me what was happening. I told her it was the way people made babies, and she went into hysterics. You know the rest."

He gave her a gentle hug, then walked back toward the bed. He began to dress.

"What are you doing?"

"I don't want to hurt you, Rebel," he said. "If it's going to be too much for you to handle . . . I don't feel guilty, but you do. Guilt can be a terrible thing. I've seen it destroy people. I can't do that to you."

"Don't go," she whispered softly. "Please, Matt, don't go. Not yet . . . I don't know what to do . . ."

He hesitated and straightened, his senses reeling. He should finish what he was doing and leave, but . . .

"Please," she begged, and there was a sob in her voice. "As long as you're already here, let us have tonight, Matt, and if . . . if I never feel your love again, at least let me have tonight."

"What of your conscience?"

Her voice throbbed. "It can wait till morning, Matt," she cried passionately, "I can't!"

Later, in the darkness just before dawn, when he kissed her good-bye and silently left the room, leaving the way he came, she cried. Not for herself, but for Matt, because she knew he was hurting inside, and she hadn't wanted to hurt him. This, she knew, had been their last night together.

By the time the sun streamed into her room, she knew her life was going to be anything but easy. She cared for Matt, but at least now she wouldn't have to feel the horrible pangs of guilt whenever someone mentioned his name or whenever she saw Miriam.

Brandon arrived home on schedule, but Rebel learned nothing from him, and plans went on as usual. French-held Tobago was about forty miles southeast of Grenada and about twenty miles north of Spanish-held Trinidad. Brandon had made his plans with care. They were leaving in the middle of the night so they'd be off the coast of Tobago by dawn, making the surprise even more complete, and he had kept their destination secret, even from the ship's captains. Their sealed orders were to be opened after they'd set sail.

As governor he was under no obligation to accompany the troops, but he was bold and conceited enough to want to watch what he was sure would be an easy conquest, and he stood at the rail as the ships weighed anchor and glanced up the hillside toward the house where he'd left Rebel after a few stolen hours with her in bed. He could see the faint light and wondered if maybe she was on the balcony watching their departure. The night was still moonless, a time of month he'd purposely chosen. The air was warm in his face as he watched the sails continuing to unfurl while they cleared the harbor. He breathed a sigh as he saw the signal light from the ship from St. Vincent that was joining them at the mouth of the bay. They were together now, a force of some six hundred men.

Matt slept during most of the night, but now he was aroused by the cabin boy as the ships cut sail off the coast of Tobago and dropped anchor. The island was smaller than Grenada, only about one hundred and sixteen square miles, but the weather was hotter and Matt felt the sweat beneath his clothes as he joined Brandon on deck.

In about half an hour's time, dawn would begin to break, and the people of Port Louis, on the southern tip of the island, would wonder what hell had broken loose. Matt stood next to Brandon now, watching him as he leaned on the rail studying the sleeping town. In minutes he'd order the longboats into the water and the first wave of men would move in stealthily, to climb onto the docks and rid them of anyone who would sound an alarm.

Matt had mentioned nothing to Brandon about having known he'd been gone, and now suddenly Brandon turned and addressed him. "That trouble up at St. Vincent was spies," he said as he straightened, and Matt's eyes were on him full. Now, how did he know Matt was aware of his absence? Rebel had sent the note. Maybe he just assumed Matt had heard it from the general.

"Spies?"

"Frenchies! They knew the destination, but not the time or day."

"But how?"

"We never found out. Unfortunately, the one we managed to catch had lost a great deal of blood, and our questioning was too much for him."

"The one you caught. There was more than one?"

"There were two others. We surprised them at their rendezvous, and they started shooting. One was fatally shot, we captured the one, and the other fell off the cliff into the sea, but I doubt he survived. He was wounded badly, so there isn't much chance he's alive."

"Do you know who he was? A name, anything?"

"We have a name, fictitious of course, and a description." Brandon thought over the description once more as he told Matt. "Deep emerald-green eyes, the woman at the inn said, with wavy hair so black it almost had a blue cast to it. 'His olive-skinned face was quite handsome, Governor,' she said when we questioned her." The more Brandon thought of it as he told Matt, the angrier he became.

Matt wondered why Brandon's eyes were so intense. "Are you afraid he may have managed to survive and reach someone?" he asked, but Brandon smiled viciously.

"If he's the man I think he is," he answered maliciously, "I hope to God he did survive so I can kill him myself." Suddenly Matt understood, and he turned, looking back out over the water toward the sleeping city as Brandon checked his watch, then signaled for the longboat. A strange feeling crept over Matt. One he wasn't sure he liked.

The first wave of troops encountered little resistance on the wharves, and none from the Dutch merchant ships anchored in the harbor. The town was still asleep, but by the time the three men-of-war sailed in and the rest of the men climbed ashore, the battle was raging.

British soldiers were strung along the waterfront behind buildings, packing boxes, overturned carts, and they seemed to be making little headway. Brandon ordered Matt to stay on the ship. He said that the wounded would be brought aboard, and Matt accepted it, waiting for what he knew had to come, yet something in the back of his mind was bothering him. There'd been no French ships in the harbor, only two Dutch merchants and a few small fishing boats and sloops that were now in flames, their crews jumping overboard. There should have been at least one French ship. It wasn't natural.

He shrugged, forgetting about his uneasiness as the wounded began coming in. A few at a time at first, then more and more when batteries of cannon began to bombard the waterfront and the French moved farther inland.

Brandon had thought taking the French would be easy, but their men fought fiercely, giving little quarter. The battle continued throughout the day, and still by nightfall of the first night the British were no farther than the immediate vicinity past the waterfront. Frenchmen hugged the foothills and dug into the slopes, defending the city with determination. During the night sporadic fighting went on. The moonless sky from the night before was replaced tonight by a slim sliver of the new moon.

Brandon strode the deck of the ship, supervising the general's decisions, keeping his anger to himself, and revealing only a determined face. He slept little and conversed frequently with the men, keeping abreast of the battle as best he could.

Late in the afternoon of the next day he stood near the mizzenmast with his spyglass, watching the fighting, trying to spot anything on the hillside that might help turn things in their favor. He studied the mountains and hills, then turned abruptly at a noise behind him. Some of the orderlies were setting a wounded soldier on the deck, while a man stood directing them, telling them where to put him. It had become extremely hot, and the man stood with his back to Brandon, bare to the waist, muscles rippling across his broad back. Brandon frowned, wondering who the devil it was, then stared in surprise as the man turned toward him. It was Matt. His brown pants were tucked into his old Hessian boots, but he wasn't slouching in his familiar stance. He was standing tall and erect, his usually neat hair ruffled, biceps working rhythmically as he pointed to more orderlies placing wounded men, and Brandon's frown deepened as he studied him. My God, he hadn't even recognized him!

He watched Matt moving about the deck from one soldier to another for the longest time, his thoughts miles away. He and Rebel had been on the island almost a year, and he thought he'd learned to know Matt during that time, but as he watched him, he seemed more like a stranger. Something inside Brandon's head clicked as he thought over the past year, and suddenly his teeth clenched tight as he turned away from the man he'd considered his friend, and he shoved the suspicions to the back of his mind, thinking once more of the battle.

Things weren't going too well. They were still no farther than the waterfront, the sun was dipping low in the sky, and the wounded were piling up. Then, with the sun hanging midway on the horizon, there was a shout from one of the men and Brandon's spyglass scanned the horizon out to sea. His face hardened and his fingers twitched nervously as he made out four ships.

Three were French frigates, but one—the one in the lead—had familiar lines. She rode low in the water, her jib boom extra long, her lines made for speed. It was the *Golden Eagle*, and he knew damn well now for sure who that green-eyed son of a bitch had been on St. Vincent.

The ships were bearing down on them fast, and if the wind held, they'd be on them in no time. He glanced quickly toward shore, then turned to where Matt was tending the wounded.

"How many casualties so far?" he asked as he approached Matt, who was trying to stop a soldier's leg from bleeding where an artery had been cut.

"Too many. Haven't had time to count. Too busy," he snapped. "But I'd give an estimate at close to a hundred on board ship, plus I imagine there's more haven't been brought

310

on, and there's no way of counting how many are lying out there dead."

Brandon grimaced, then straightened. He had no idea how many men he might have left, and the ships bearing down on them probably carried reinforcements. He didn't want to give up, but there was nothing else they could do. They were like sitting ducks here in the harbor.

He called for the general, and within minutes the sounds of retreat echoed through the streets of Port Louis and men spread the word, "Back to the ships!" Men straggled wearily aboard, running like the devil as the French frigates sailed closer with each minute. Brandon held off as long as he could, then ordered the other two ships to intercept while the command ship with himself and the general aboard waited for the rest of the men who were fighting their way back from the hills that surrounded Fort Louis.

Matt reached down and touched his fingers to the eyes of the young man who lay on the deck before him and closed them in final sleep. He was a young lad, not more than eighteen or nineteen, and he kept begging Matt not to let him die.

"I won't die will I, sir?" he'd gasped more than once, moments before he'd taken his last breath. "I got my girl back home, and she's waiting for me, true to her word." Matt stared at the dead soldier.

All this for nothing. All this because Brandon Avery, the Duke of Bourland, Governor of Grenada, wanted to make a name for himself. He glanced over and saw the sails unfurling on their two escort ships and shook his head, wondering how the devil two ships were going to hold four ships at bay long enough to get the rest of the men aboard.

The ship's sails filled easily, and they lurched forward, moving from the wharves, pulling out into the harbor, and Brandon put the spyglass to his eyes, turning it toward the approaching Frenchmen.

At the sight of the men-of-war moving toward them, the French turned about, sweeping broadside of the bay to lie in wait. For the next half-hour, while men scrambled aboard, Brandon watched the two men-of-war play a deadly game of hit and run with the four ships, until finally he could no longer stay and hauled up the gangplank, yelling for the captain to put out to sea.

Occasionally shots and shouting sounded here and there along the waterfront, but the men who hadn't made it were on their own now. Brandon watched grimly as the sails overhead unfurled and the ship slowly moved from the wharf into deeper water, but instead of joining its sister ships in the battle, he commanded the captain to stay close to the shore and try to steer clear; then he cursed as he saw the *Golden Eagle* turn from its attack on one of the British ships and head straight for them.

They were at full sail now, and the wind was strong, but Brandon remembered what the *Golden Eagle* was capable of. She could outsail anything afloat, and her crew was excellent. The *Golden Eagle* was gaining on them rapidly as they cleared the harbor; then suddenly an explosion from the sea battle still raging drew his attention, and Brandon saw one of the frigates begin to go down, her insides gutted when a lucky shot had hit the powder magazine, and the ship that had scored, although badly battered, turned her guns on one of the two remaining frigates in an attempt to help its sister ship, who was sadly torn but managing to hold her own.

It was three against three now, but the odds were still against them as Brandon saw that the *Golden Eagle* was still moving dead ahead on its course. The captain was pushing his ship to the limit, and they were barely keeping out of range now as the *Golden Eagle* kept up its relentless pursuit. Then once more a loud explosion carried across the water, and Brandon put the glass to his eye again and strained to see which ship was going down, and to his surprise and relief, he saw flames cannonading up from the deck of one of the other French ships. Now it'd be two against one, and if he had the captain turn his ship about, it'd be three against two. The odds were getting better. They couldn't outrun the *Golden Eagle* and he knew it. They didn't have a chance in a million on their own against it either, but at least if they circled and joined the others . . .

He was turning, ready to call his decision to the captain, when one of the men called down from the crow's nest, and he glanced back toward the *Golden Eagle*. She was heeling about in the water, turning back, and he stared in relief. She was going back to help her ally, giving up the chase. It was over. The whole damn thing was over. He'd lost hundreds of men, and now, with the *Golden Eagle* turning back, he knew the other two ships didn't have a chance. The *Golden Eagle*, with Captain Thunder commanding, could knock out anything in the water. She could sail just out of range of her enemies and score hit after hit with the special guns mounted on her.

The next time, he thought as he stared back at her sails,

getting smaller and smaller on the horizon, and remembered the cannon on her decks with the extra long barrels, the next time maybe the *Golden Eagle* wouldn't have the advantage, and he clenched his teeth together viciously. He turned away, walking briskly toward his cabin as the ship headed for St. George.

15

Rebel tried to keep busy. Brandon had told her moments before he left what their destination was, and she'd tried to act surprised. He was so sure the time was right.

"And after we take Tobago," he'd said confidently, "we'll go north into St. Lucia and Martinique and the other islands, and south into Trinidad, and eventually the whole West Indies will be under British rule," but she'd only sighed, pretending she cared little about who ruled what. She knew if he actually could accomplish what he was setting out to do, it'd be easy for him to ask the king to let him govern the territories, and once established, he'd rule them as if he were king.

She'd spent most of Sunday in the garden playing with Cole and in the library reading. She wrote a long letter to her mother and one to Teak in England, even though he hadn't answered her last one as yet. Oh, well, boys were boys, and he had only turned sixteen in January. She wondered how he liked being the new Earl of Locksley. He was probably buying hats two sizes larger to fit his swelled head. It seemed strange that Teak had taken so readily to luxury, because he'd really been at home at Fort Locke and had been as comfortable in the wilderness as an Indian.

Indians! She stood at the French doors to her room, then stepped out onto the balcony, gazing down at the harbor, and thought of Beau. Beau with his stern hard face, shutting himself off from the world and all its hurts. Trying to pretend his heart was made of stone, yet she knew the softness that lay beneath the veneer of callous indifference he wore. Like Matt, he was astonishingly tender and affectionate. She wondered where he was right now and if Heath was still all right.

Heath with his gorgeous good looks. She smiled as she remembered how she always used to tease him about being so handsome. Oh, what she wouldn't give to know they were both all right.

She turned from gazing down at the harbor and walked back into the room as Cristabel came in carrying some freshly laundered and pressed dresses over her arm.

"I've been waiting to put on the blue," she said. The young girl extricated a blue silk one from the middle of the pile, hanging the others in the armoire, and handed it to Rebel, who slipped it over her head, then turned to be fastened up the back.

This done, Rebel moved to the dresser and opened one of the drawers, pulling out some fresh stockings. They were rolled into a ball and she loosened the end to unroll them, then watched curiously as something fell to the floor. She reached down by her bare foot and picked up a tiny feather no longer than her little finger. It was white, but the quill end had been dipped in something red.

"Well, what on earth is this for?" she exclaimed.

Cristabel's face was animated, her eyes filled with alarm as she stared dumbfounded at the feather Rebel was holding.

"What's the matter, Cristabel?" Rebel asked. "What is it?" and Cristabel's voice was hushed, wavering as she spoke.

"They goin' to kill you!" she answered.

"Kill me?"

Cristabel nodded. "When you gets a feather like that, that means you got a enemy what wants you dead."

Rebel tried to laugh it off. "Don't be silly." She fingered the silky feather uncertainly. "In the first place, I don't believe all that black-magic mumbo-jumbo, and in the second place, why would anyone want me dead?"

Cristabel shook her head and pointed to the feather. "Don't know why, ma'am," she answered, "but if that was me what got the feather, I'd sure be careful."

Rebel crumpled the feather up in her hand and went outside, throwing it off the balcony, then came back in and sat down, putting her shoes and stockings on, ignoring what the girl had said, and when Cristabel was finished fixing her hair, she went downstairs to dinner, dismissing the whole thing from her mind.

It was the next morning after breakfast when she walked into the library and found the package on the chair where she usually sat to read. It was wrapped with yellow paper, tied with a scarlet ribbon and had her name written on the top with what looked like red ink. She picked it up gingerly and shook it, but it made no noise. Curious, she sat down and put it on her lap, untying the ribbon and tearing off the paper to reveal a pretty flowered box. She took off the lid cautiously. Whatever it was, it was wrapped in a piece of soft white cloth, and she lifted the corners, looking down inside the box.

Her face paled and she gasped. Inside the box was the bloody body of a small chicken the islanders called a banty rooster. Its neck had been severed partway and its carcass was caked with blood, but that wasn't all. It must have been dead for some time, because maggots were crawling all over it and the sight was hideous.

She closed the lid tightly as she stood up, her face losing its pallor and becoming red with rage as she rang for the housekeeper, who was at her side in minutes. "Where did this come from?" she asked, trying to control her anger.

"I don't know, your Grace," she said. "I never saw it before."

"Has anyone come this morning? Anyone been in the house who doesn't belong?"

"No, ma'am. Not to my knowledge."

"Take this," Rebel said firmly, "but don't look inside, and have one of the boys bury it, box and all, and have it done right away, understand?"

"Yes, ma'am," the woman said, nodding. "But it seems a shame to destroy such a pretty box."

"What's inside, I'm afraid, is not very pretty," Rebel snapped sternly. "Now, please, do as you're told."

Rebel sauntered to the window and stood looking into the garden, ablaze with color. The sky was blue, with a brisk warm breeze filling the trees, and everything looked so peaceful. It didn't seem at all the setting for what the contents of the box had signified, and she wondered: Why? Who?

By afternoon she had almost forgotten the incident, and by bedtime, after an early visit from the vicar and his wife, she had scoffed it off, coming to the conclusion that someone was just trying to frighten her, and it had completely slipped her mind.

After her guests left, she played with Cole, tucking him in to sleep at bedtime. She read until rather late, and was quite tired as she trudged upstairs to bed. She had been wondering all day what was happening to the men who had sailed for Tobago. Anxious to know, yet dreading the news that might come back. Bran said he had no idea how long they'd be gone, but expected to be able to take the island in less than a week's time, if all went well. Men and war! It seemed like they always found something to fight about, and it was usually because of someone's greed. This time Brandon's.

She thought of Matt as she stood in the candlelight and put on the sheer nightgown she'd worn the last night they'd been together, and she remembered her decision. Would she be strong enough to keep it? Already she could feel the stirrings inside her at the thought of him.

She blew out the light and settled back into bed, feeling the breeze coming in at the French doors lulling her uneasy mind to sleep.

It must have been well past midnight when she woke suddenly, unable to find a reason for the fact that she was wide-awake, her eyes shifting about the room as she stared into the darkness. Something had awakened her, but what? She lay still for a few minutes, trying to comprehend what was going on, and her eyes moved across the room to the French doors. A chill ran down her spine and the hair at the nape of her neck raised. They were closed! She had left the French doors open so she'd be able to feel the warm brisk breeze as it blew up from the bay, but now they were closed, and she shivered, feeling the gooseflesh rising on her skin.

Then she heard it, the soft flap of wings, then more and more, and high-pitched squeaking, and suddenly something dived at her out of the darkness, almost hitting her head, followed by another and another, and she shrieked at the top of her lungs, plunging her head beneath the covers, shrieking and screaming breathlessly for what seemed like an eternity, until she felt someone grab her shoulders firmly and begin to shake her.

"Rebel! Rebel!" Brandon was shouting as he pulled the covers back from her head, and at the sight of him her eyes widened with relief and she clung to him. "They're gone now," he said as he held her against him. "There's nothing to worry about," and as he held her, she relaxed, then lay against him, for the first time in her life willingly staying in his arms.

Strange, she thought as she lay against him, his arms felt strong and comforting for a change, but then, she'd been so frightened. "What were they?" she asked hesitantly against his chest as tears of relief rolled down her cheeks, wetting the front of his dirt-streaked white shirt.

"Bats. There were five or maybe more. I shooed them outside. They must have come in during the day and slept hanging behind the curtains or something and couldn't get out because you'd shut the door."

"But I didn't," she whispered hoarsely, "I didn't shut the door, Bran."

"Are you sure?"

"Positive. I wanted them open so I could feel the breeze." She straightened, pulling herself from his arms, and stared at the foot of her bed, where Cristabel, Hizzie, and the house-keeper stood, their eyes wide, watching her.

Brandon stood up and turned to them, ordering them out, ushering them to the door, then shut it after them and came back to her bed and sat down on the edge of it.

"I just realized," she said, bewildered, trying to compose herself. "What are you doing here? When did you get back?"

"We sailed in a short while ago. I came home as soon as I could."

"And?"

His eyes darkened, his face sullen. "We lost . . . we lost the first round, but there'll be others." His fists clenched. "I made a mistake. I had no idea Port Louis was so well forti-fied. I should have used my own spies. The next time we'll do it differently. We'll take the northern and western ends of the island first, and Port Louis will be last. That way we'll be in the hills where the advantages are, and they'll have their backs to the sea and we'll be waiting for them on the water as well." He stood up as he talked, and she realized there was something else wrong. It wasn't just that he lost—there was a grimness about his mouth . . .

"You intend to go back?"

"As soon as I can get the men and ships ready."

"Bran, do you think it's worth it," she asked, "all this kill-ing?"

He looked at her sharply. "You and Matt. That's what he said." Then he stood staring at her, his face curiously inquisi-tive. "Speaking of the good doctor," he said as he came back and sat on the edge of the bed. "Did you ever notice any-thing strange about our friend?"

She gazed at him innocently, her eyes projecting surprise. "What are you talking about?"

"Come now, Reb, he delivered Cole. Surely you noticed it then."

"Noticed what?"

"That when he's lost in his work, forgetting his surround-ings, concentrating on the problems at hand, he loses his staid, scholarly manner and it's as if he becomes a different person. He stood on the deck of that ship, and I didn't even recognize him."

"For heaven's sake, I never heard of anything so absurd," she said. "How could you not recognize Matt?"

"He always gives the impression of being older than his years and somewhat stuffy at times, but the man who was on that ship taking care of those wounded soldiers was . . . I can't explain it, but he just wasn't the Matt I've known. He didn't slouch, he wasn't slow or casual, and he's built like . . ." His eyes looked into hers. "I thought maybe you might have noticed since the two of you always seemed to get along so well, and then him having delivered Cole."

She shook her head. "I never noticed a thing," she lied, shrugging, and Brandon stood up nervously again. Something was still bothering him. "Now what is it?" she asked.

"Has he been here?" he asked abruptly, and she gasped.

"Who . . . Matt?"

"No, not Matt! Don't be stupid, you know who the hell I'm talking about. Has that Indian been to see you secretly?"

"Now, why in heaven's name would you ask a thing like that?"

"Has he?"

"No!" Suddenly she sat straight up, her eyes wild. "You've seen him, haven't you? That's why!" she cried. "Oh, my God, Bran. You've seen my brother and Beau!"

"It's that bastard's fault that we lost our foothold," he blurted angrily, his eyes blazing. "He was up at St. Vincent, and we thought we'd killed him—"

"You went up to St. Vincent to kill Beau? You let me think—"

"I didn't go to kill him," he interrupted furiously, then explained the whole thing to her, including the chase from Port Louis. "We probably lost the other two ships to that bastard too," he conjectured. "But it won't happen again. The next time, I'll be ready for him."

Beau had been so close. So very close.

Brandon walked over and stood looking out the French doors, which were open again. "If he ever tries to come here after you, I'll kill him with my bare hands," he said viciously. "Do you understand? You're my wife and you'll stay my wife, and I'm sick and tired of him interfering in my life. I have to raise his damn bastard of a child, isn't that enough!" He marched back to the bed and stared down at her. "I'm going to get myself a ship and I'm going to have guns put on it. Special cannon made to my specifications, and I'm going to find a crew to man it and a captain to sail it and by God we'll see how long your precious Indian manages to stay afloat!"

Her heart was in her throat as she wished to God he hadn't come back with his ship. A few moments ago when he'd held her in his arms and tried to comfort her, she thought maybe there was a chance she could salvage something from her marriage after all. For a few minutes she'd felt safe and secure in his arms. But when he looked at her like this, it frightened her.

"Maybe it won't matter," she said vindictively, wanting to hurt him as he always hurt her. "Maybe I wouldn't be here anyway, even if he did come around. And maybe I won't even be alive for the two of you to fight over anymore. Maybe that'll satisfy you!"

"What are you talking about?"

"I'm talking about those bats, that's what I'm talking about! I didn't close those doors, Bran, somebody else did. And the other day there was a white feather in the drawer with my stockings, and somebody sent me a dead chicken, gift-wrapped!"

The hatred and anger were suddenly gone from his eyes. "Tell me from the beginning," he said anxiously, and she told him what had happened and what Cristabel had said.

"But that's nonsense. Who the devil would do something like that?"

"Somebody who doesn't like me."

"People don't threaten and scare someone simply because they don't like them."

"This island's full of strange things, Brandon," she said. "Matt told me about the natives and some of the things they do. He says he's seen people actually get sick and die when there was no logical reason why they should, except that someone willed it."

He reached out and picked up her hand. It was cold and he held it in both of his. "If anything happened to you, I'd go out of my mind," he said slowly. "I know I'm hard to live with, Rebel, and I know I'm not an ideal husband, but I do love you in spite of everything. If I didn't, I'd have sent you packing the moment I laid eyes on Cole, but I can't. I know I probably show my love in strange ways." His mouth tightened grimly. "But sometimes a man fights the only way he knows how, even though it may not be the right way. I can't help hating Beau and I can't help hating the son you gave him, but I'll never hate you, although sometimes I try."

She stared at him, studying his face.

"That surprises you?" he asked. "It shouldn't. I married you because I loved you, because I had to have you above all other women, but you married me for a title and for spite. I know it. I knew it from the start, and it's not the easiest thing to live with. It can frustrate a person into doing things he doesn't want to do. I want to hate you and despise you and make you suffer for what you've done to me, and sometimes I do, but it doesn't help. Nothing helps, because I go right on loving you in spite of myself."

She let her hand lie limply in his as he talked, and for the first time she could understand what she'd done to him. Brandon was never a nice person in the sense that he was thoughtful of others, kindhearted, and sincere. He always was and always would be a tyrant, conceited, arrogant, and cruel, but he did have feelings and she'd twisted those feelings into a warped existence that was frustrating beyond what anyone should have to endure.

"I'm sorry, Bran," she said softly. "I guess I'm not a very good person."

"But you're still my wife and I'll not have someone threatening you."

"They probably only mean to frighten me," she said.

"I'll see if I can find out what's behind it," he said softly, then leaned forward, his hand reaching out to touch her shoulder, then move to her neck, and he looked deep into her eyes. "I missed you," he whispered softly, and she felt a familiar stirring deep inside.

She tried to fight it, shove it away, force herself not to respond, but her body wouldn't listen. It had been days since she'd been with Matt, and her body was ripe for taking.

He leaned over, his mouth touching hers lightly at first, then harder, and she felt a warm tingling sensation sweep over her. He had caught her off guard. Her body was responding to his touch, and she didn't want it to. This wasn't right, she hated him, but for the first time in her life she was unable to think. He was being gentle and romantic instead of crude and lustful, and it wasn't fair. He wasn't being fair! This was something new. Brandon had never thought of her feelings, he had always pleased only himself; now suddenly he was touching her softly, his hands stroking her body as they moved beneath the covers and underneath her sheer nightgown.

This was madness! He stroked her sensuously, his hands caressing her as they had never done before, and she wanted

320

to cry out, yell for him to stop, but she couldn't. Her body was on fire. She hated it, yet craved it even though she fought against it. Her body wouldn't listen. It swelled to new feelings of pleasure. Maybe she shouldn't keep fighting, she told herself reluctantly. Maybe it wouldn't hurt just this once to give in to him. It might still the ache in her loins she'd had when she came to bed tonight, and maybe then she wouldn't be tempted to go to Matt again.

She'd never know unless she tried. Yet it didn't seem right! She hated him for what he was, what he'd done to her, and what he was doing now, but the heat of passion was stronger than her hate, and suddenly she couldn't fight him anymore. He'd caught her when her body had been yearning for Matt, when she was vulnerable, and she closed her eyes in one last effort to resist, then surrendered to him, and the first time since their marriage Brandon waited for her to come first, then reached his own fulfillment.

Afterward, Brandon didn't go back to his own bed, and his clothes stayed on the floor by her bed where he'd dropped them. She lay beside him, his arms around her as he slept peacefully, and she cried softly to herself. She didn't love him and never would. Her body had betrayed her. She had hoped to still the ache in her loins, and her body had tried, but it was still there even stronger, and she knew why. She needed love to still it. What she had felt a few moments ago beneath him had been only a mild taste of what she knew it should have been. Even though her body had surrendered to him her heart had not, and it made the whole thing shallow and meaningless.

For the next week things were anything but ideal. Brandon's defeat at Port Louis lay heavily on him, and the loss of men was whispered about by everyone on the island. The other two ships had never returned, and this too added to his problems.

Matt had set up an infirmary in one of the buildings on the waterfront, and much to his surprise, Rebel showed up one afternoon, volunteering her services.

"Does Brandon know you're here?" he asked, and was surprised when she answered yes.

"When I mentioned it, he said maybe it would look good for the governor's wife to lower herself to such menial tasks."

"Typical," said Matt. "I knew he wouldn't let you come out of the kindness of his heart."

She spent the next few weeks running herself ragged, tending to the cries of the wounded men, and it felt good being

321

useful. A number of other women were there to help too, and the days went fast. Matt had evidently decided to forgo his former habits and was no longer hiding himself in his self-imposed cocoon of scholarly casualness. His drooping suits lay at home in the armoire and his slouch disappeared. He hadn't seen Brandon since their return until one afternoon, a little over a week after Rebel had come, when he came to the door of the building where the men were kept.

It was late afternoon when Brandon walked in. Matt was changing bandages on the leg of an amputee with Rebel's help. The man was still in agony, and Brandon watched silently from the doorway as the two of them worked. Rebel anticipated every move Matt made, and they worked together with few words passing between them, as if words weren't needed. Other women were puttering about here and there, and he wondered why Rebel was helping him and not one of the others. Then as he watched her look at Matt, there was something about the way their eyes met and the look that passed beween them.

He straightened, bristling angrily, yet trying not to let it show as he walked over to them. "I thought I'd drop in and see how things are going," he said, tapping his riding crop against his knee irritably, and Matt answered.

"We've been having a terrible time keeping infections down. This place is none too clean, for all we've tried, and we lost three more this morning."

The building was long and low, once having been a warehouse, and the inside was dingy and dirty, even though it had been scrubbed. The putrid smell of decaying flesh and old blood mingled with body odors, and the foul smells that seeped from the chamber pots was sickening.

"We've tried to bathe the men," he went on, "but I could use a few orderlies. I've only got two, and they can't work around the clock. The women are a big help, and I appreciate their coming, especially Rebel, she knows what she's doing. I can tell she's taken care of wounds before, but I can't keep her here twenty-four hours a day, and if these men are going to get back on their feet, it's what they need. Constant care."

Brandon glanced about the building and looked it over, his back rigidly alert; then he turned back to Matt. "I'll see that the general sends you eight more men. Will that do? Two more for your day crew, four for late afternoon and early evening so the women can go home, and two to stay all night and give you a break."

"I don't get any breaks, Brandon," he said. "I don't dare go home. If I'm needed, a lot of good I'd do them halfway up the hillside. I'll do as I've been doing and sleep here."

Brandon looked at him curiously. "Suit yourself then, but it might do you good to get away for a while. Why don't you and Miriam come over for dinner this evening? It'll do you good to relax."

"All right. What time?"

"We'll eat about seven," said Rebel. It wasn't usual for Bran to do anything on impulse, yet she knew the invitation had been just that, an impulse.

Matt tied the bandage on the man's leg and straightened, rubbing the small of his back.

"Well, I'd best get back to my papers," Brandon said as he turned to walk away. "We'll see you tonight, Matt, and I'll see you at home," he said, addressing Rebel.

"Now, that was a strange one," Rebel said abruptly as they walked away from the cot the soldier was on. "He didn't even take time to talk to any of the soldiers, to try to make them feel better or anything. It was as if they weren't even around."

"To him they probably weren't."

"How can he be so callous? This is the first time he's been anywhere near the place, isn't it?"

"I don't think he really cares . . ." Matt hesitated. "And I have a strange feeling about today's visit."

"What's that?"

He shrugged. "Just an uneasiness. The casual way he walked in, the invitation to dinner. It wasn't Brandon."

She went back to the table where the bandages were, and Matt followed behind her. She hadn't told him about her surrender to Brandon. It was something she didn't even want to admit to herself.

"What's the matter?" he asked as he saw the strange faraway look on her face.

"Everything."

"Care to talk about it? You always said I had a good shoulder to cry on."

"That's the trouble, Matt, your shoulder's too good, and I cry too easily."

"Maybe you need more than my shoulder."

She trembled as she saw the warmth in his eyes. "Shall I tell you how perceptive you are, Doctor?" she asked, then took a deep breath. "But I'm afraid since I made a decision to behave myself, I'd better decline your offer, although it sounds enchanting. . . . Besides, I think it'd be rather hard to find the time and place."

His mouth closed tightly. He wasn't angry, she knew, he was holding himself in check, because his eyes caressed her lovingly. "Then shall we continue our bandaging?" he said as he reached out and picked up the strips of white cloth and salve, setting a large roll of bandage in her hand. "And perhaps sometime in the future we could discuss the matter further."

She smiled sheepishly, a warm lump in her throat. "Perhaps," she said softly, then looked out over the long rows of wounded men. "Now, who's next?"

They worked beautifully together as a team, and even the vicar's wife noticed it as she helped feed the men their lunch and washed their hands and faces. She'd never seen the doctor laugh quite so much as when he had Rebel at his side. Of course the young woman was prone to having a witty tongue, and she was young, yet there'd been a change in Matt since his return with what was left of Brandon's men. He was so different. He still wore the same suits when he wasn't at the infirmary, but he must have had them fixed, for they no longer drooped at the corners, and he stood tall and straight. He'd always looked so tired before. Surprising what war does to men. She even mentioned it to the doctor's wife one day, and Miriam had said she supposed he'd finally decided to take her advice and try to dress more fittingly. Whatever it was, the vicar's wife was sure it was an improvement, and she smiled for a moment as she watched the doctor and the duchess finish bandaging one patient and move on to the next.

Rebel felt self-conscious all through dinner that evening. She was wearing the dress she'd worn the day of the christening, and the ripe peach color brought a glow to her complexion. During the day, while working at the infirmary, she'd worn her hair pulled back severely and fastened in an attractive twist to keep it neat, but tonight she'd merely let it fly loose so it was a halo of gold about her head. She glanced furtively at Miriam as she watched her finishing her dessert, and an uneasy feeling crept over her.

For the first time since she'd known her, Miriam had changed her hairstyle. Her usually tight curls were no longer clustered over each ear. Her hair had been combed full, then pulled high and a curled bun set atop the crown of her head, with the hair billowing out full around it, and it gave her face an illusion of being filled out, even though she hadn't gained a pound. Her dress was new, a beautiful shade of bright yellow that deepened her topaz eyes, instead of the dull-colored, cluttered monstrosities she'd always worn before, and the tucked bodice made her bust appear larger, while the drape in the back and full skirt made her figure look fuller, the billowing sheer sleeves covering her scrawny arms.

The meal went well, with much small talk, and when the dessert was over the men retired to the library for a glass of port, while Rebel took Miriam to see Cole.

"I want to thank you for inviting us," Matt said as he sat down. "I guess I get a little too absorbed in my work for my own good. Miriam was pleased I took the time off."

"I had a rather ulterior motive," Brandon said abruptly. "I hope you don't mind, but it was something I don't like discussing in front of others, and it's been hard trying to get you alone lately."

Matt fingered the wineglass as he stretched out his long legs, the new boots he wore polished to a high shine. Damn, thought Brandon as he glanced at Matt, the doctor was actually good-looking. Strange he hadn't noticed it before. He brushed the thought aside and came to the point.

"Matt, I want to know something about this black-magic nonsense that goes on on this island. I've known it's there, but I've sort of left it be. Van Horn says it does nobody any harm, and so do most of the other planters, but now I'm not so sure. I asked my secretary and some of the cabinet members. They can't help me, although the mere mention of the words 'black magic' seems to put fear into their eyes. What's it all about?"

"What happens if I tell you?"

"What do you mean, what happens?"

"If you don't like it, are you going to try to stop it?"

"You're damn right I am!"

"It can't be stopped."

"What makes you say that?"

"It's a religion, and like most religions, it'll go underground and it'll make things worse. It'll still be there, but you won't know it, and neither will I, and it'll be harder to cope with."

"All right, what is it?"

Matt explained the fundamentals of the religion that the majority of natives on Grenada practiced, and he watched Brandon's eyes harden angrily.

"Matt," Brandon said when Matt finished, "someone's trying to use this so-called black magic on Rebel."

"You're sure?"

"I'm damn sure. She didn't catch the last one, I intercepted

325

it." He told him about the feather and the chicken and the bats. "And she has no idea that anything else has happened. This afternoon, before I saw you two, I went home for some papers and stopped on the way and bought a little something for her. I took it to her bedroom, and usually when I have a gift for her, I slip it under her pillow so she finds it when she goes to bed. Today when I slipped my hand under her pillow, there was a note there written in what looked like blood, and it said one word, 'Die!' "

"You have no idea where it came from?"

"I questioned all the servants, although I didn't show them the note."

Matt rubbed his chin. "How has she been feeling lately, all right?"

"As far as I know. Has she complained to you?"

"No . . . only I remember something. The day before last she was late in the morning. She usually shows up early to help feed the men breakfast. That particular morning she said she started to get into the carriage she always uses and she fell. The top step gave way. She said if the footman hadn't caught her she'd have had a nasty fall."

"Coincidence?"

"I doubt it."

"But who?"

Matt glanced at Brandon surreptitiously. "I'm sorry to say this, Brandon, you and I get along all right together, but you haven't made yourself too popular with most of the people on this island. They could figure this was a way of getting even."

Matt was right, of course. There were always people who disliked authority, but how could he pinpoint one person on this whole island?

"I'm going to double the guard around the grounds," he said firmly. "We've always just had two at the front gate. I'm going to post them at intervals around the place. And I'll have someone by Rebel's side every minute she's away from the house."

"And keep her a prisoner?"

"It's for her own safety."

"You know Rebel won't stand for that."

"Are you trying to tell me how to handle my wife?"

Matt's face reddened. "Your wife happens to be a patient of mine, Brandon," he said. "I think I know her pretty well by now, and I don't think she'll go for it."

"Then what's my alternative?"

"Look, I've taken your advice and decided to stay home at

night instead of sleeping in the old office. If the men want me, they can send for me. How will it be if I tell Rebel that since I have to go in town anyway I'll ride over and pick her up in the morning and bring her home again at night?"

"Why does she have to go at all? Why doesn't she just stay here? When she mentioned helping out, I thought a day or two helping feed the men or something would be all right. I didn't think you were going to try to make a doctor out of her."

Matt laughed. Sometimes Brandon could be likable in spite of himself. "I'm not making a doctor out of your wife, but she knows a hell of a lot about taking care of people who've been hurt." He wasn't sure Brandon was going to like his next statements, but he didn't much care. "She said she was raised on the American frontier and she and her mother helped her father take care of the wounded when there was fighting. From what she says, the Indians out there can play pretty rough." He saw the disconcerted look on Brandon's face. "I need your wife down there with those men," he went on. "Those other women are fine for feeding and washing them, but it takes somebody with guts and stamina to help cauterize and drain infections and change bandages."

Brandon spread his legs and leaned forward, letting his hands, holding the wineglass, dangle between them, reluctant to say yes. He wasn't sure he liked Rebel being with Matt so much anymore, especially since he'd become so dapper, and especially after watching them work together this afternoon. But Matt was the only real friend he had on the island.

"You know, there's something I've been meaning to ask you," said Brandon as he glanced up at Matt, realizing that since he no longer slouched he was about half an inch taller than he was. "What the hell happened to you, anyway?"

Matt's glass was to his lips, and he swallowed a taste of the wine. "I beg your pardon?"

Brandon eyed him curiously. "Matt, when I first arrived on this island, and every day up until we went to Tobago, I had the impression you were . . . how should I say it . . . ?"

"A seedy, slouch-shouldered old relic?" offered Matt.

"Exactly. So what happened?" He gestured with his hand at Matt's appearance. "Suddenly I find myself confronting a very confident gentleman with not only impeccable taste, but the looks and charm to go with it, and Miriam as well. I certainly was surprised when she walked in tonight. It's the first I've seen her in weeks. She looked lovely."

Matt smiled, straightening his lapel. "I guess after all these years I finally decided to take Miriam's advice," he said.

"She's always been after me to stand up straight and get clothes that fit me."

Brandon stared at him skeptically, then shook his head. "Come now, Matt. I can't accept that." He eyed him soberly, his voice lowering. "What's the real reason?"

Matt stared at him, debating, then took a deep breath. "All right, you want the real reason, I'll tell you, but for God's sake don't ever tell my wife or she'll make me go back to what I used to be."

Now Brandon was really curious. "Go on," he said, "I won't breathe a word to Miriam."

"All right." He finished off his wine, then toyed with the empty glass, rolling it back and forth between his hands as he talked. "When I first opened my practice, I dressed like this," he said, indicating his clothes. "Then one day I discovered some of my women patients were more interested in me than in my ability to cure them. Matters became rather sticky and I found myself in an impossible situation through no fault of my own, mind you. I love medicine, and being a doctor to me is the most thrilling, rewarding job I could ever want. It's a challenge to try to make people better, to be able to help them survive when the odds are all against you, and I wasn't about to give my practice up simply because there are some silly women in this world who can't help becoming infatuated with their doctors. So I tried to make myself as unattractive toward the ladies as I could. Miriam never knew why I did it, and at first I think she was even ashamed to be seen with me."

Brandon sat back in his chair and studied Matt openly, noting the broad shoulders, the deep voice and quiet mannerisms. Yes, the ladies would find him charming, and what of Rebel? Did she find him charming too? "That's all there is to it?"

"If you were a doctor, you'd understand."

"Maybe . . . but what I don't understand is . . . why revert now, why not go on the way you were?"

"Because I'm tired of trying to be something I'm not. Besides, I think I'm settled firmly enough on the island now that I don't think the deception's a necessity any longer."

"Possibly," said Brandon. "But what about your wife? Why the sudden change in Miriam?"

"I guess maybe she feels if I can change, so can she. I was surprised myself when she came down tonight just before we left, and I can't help telling you I was pleased. Maybe when the ladies on the island see how attractive my wife really is, I won't ever have to worry anymore," and he smiled, hoping it looked convincing, but something about his deep voice and the way he said it didn't ring true to Brandon, and he wasn't sure, he wasn't sure at all.

In the other room, where Rebel and Miriam were playing with Cole, Rebel was also wondering why Miriam had suddenly decided to change her hairdo and wear an attractive dress. If she was doing it for Matt, it was a pity, because she was just a little too late, and Rebel knew it was going to take more than a new hairdo and a dress to undo what Miriam had done to her marriage.

It was another month before the men were really well enough to close the infirmary. Brandon conceded reluctantly to Matt's suggestion when Rebel threw a fit over being treated like what she considered a child, and every day he let Matt drive Rebel to town and back again. The rest of the time when she had to go out anyplace Brandon was with her or she didn't go, but there were no more notes, and after a while they began to think the whole thing had been only a hoax to frighten them, and gradually the guard about the house relaxed and things went back to normal. For everyone except Rebel and Matt.

She had enjoyed working in the infirmary because it gave them a chance to be together. Not the way she would have liked, but they could talk and enjoy each other's company. Once when she was in the old office where Matt used to sleep when the infirmary first opened, and where now all the medicine was kept, she'd turned abruptly to walk out the door and bumped into him as he came in. He'd stared at her intently for long seconds, then closed the door quietly behind him, took her in his arms, and kissed her until she almost melted to the floor. It was their only kiss, but it had kindled a fire inside her that Brandon had been unable to quench, and each time she saw Matt it became worse.

Rebel spent most of her time with Cole, now that the infirmary was closed. He was a lively baby of six months and kept all three women—Rebel, Hizzie, and Cristabel—hopping. Mornings they could be found in the nursery feeding, bathing, and playing with him. Afternoons, while he napped, Rebel spent reading or trying to concentrate on embroidering, which she hated. When he woke again she'd take him into the garden and play with him until Brandon came for dinner, then Hizzie'd take him upstairs again, sometimes for the rest of the evening if company was expected. If not, he'd come down shortly before bedtime and Brandon would rebel at playing the dutiful father as he had since the day the child was born.

By September Rebel was ready to go out of her mind. Except for rain that fell in short showers almost every day, the weather was the same from one day to the next. Nothing ever changed. There were no seasons, no deviations of any sort, and the days became as boring to her as the weather.

Brandon was still keeping guards at the back of the house as well as the front now, so there wasn't even a chance to sneak away for a ride anymore. Sometimes she felt like a prisoner, and it was a relief when company came or they went out to dine. She had few chances to see Matt, and missed him terribly. When he and Miriam did come to dinner, there was never a chance to be alone with him, not even for a minute.

Finally, one day she couldn't stand it any longer. Instead of crawling out of bed, she rolled over, watching the sun climb farther in the sky, waiting for someone to wonder why she wasn't up and about. She'd never faked being ill before, but there was always a first time; besides, Brandon was still hoping she'd get pregnant, so he'd probably be elated if he thought it was a possibility. It was Brandon who was first to poke his head in the doorway. She was usually downstairs to breakfast by now, and he eyed her curiously as she complained of a stomachache, and like a dutiful husband who was hoping for the heir he felt he'd been cheated of, he promised to send one of the servants for the doctor before leaving for town.

The waiting seemed like forever as Rebel propped the pillows up behind her and nestled against them, counting the flowers in the fancy wallpaper on the wall. Funny they should have wallpaper in the West Indies, she thought as she separated the blue flowers from the pink ones, then tried to figure out how many would be under the painting that hung above the commode. Wallpaper was a rarity yet even in America, but here was wallpaper on this remote island, out in the middle of nowhere.

She tired of counting the flowers and closed her eyes, trying to remember what it was like to ride through the woods when she was a girl, galloping along the riverbank, and feel the wind in her face, blowing her hair like a golden train behind her. She opened her eyes again. Oh, if he'd only come. Just to talk to him for a while. To laugh and see him smile.

It was an hour and a half after Brandon left that Cristabel

ushered Dr. Wilder into the room, then stepped to the side of the bed, waiting.

"You may go now, Cristabel," said Rebel, trying to look as if she were hurting, but the girl hesitated.

"Maybe Doc Wilder's gonna need me, ma'am," she said anxiously.

"It's all right, Cristabel." He set his bag on the floor beside the chair he'd pulled up to the bed. "I think she'd rather not have anyone in the room while I examine her."

"Well, just remember, I'll be right outside," she offered.

Matt stood in front of the chair and looked down at Rebel, a smile playing about the corners of his mouth. "I think I've diagnosed your ailment already, Duchess," he said conspiratorially. "Should I lock the door now or later?"

Rebel straightened in bed, her eyes warm and alive. "Now," she whispered softly, and he moved to the door Cristabel had just closed, pushing the bolt easily so as not to make any noise, then to the door that led to Brandon's room, and made sure it was secure. When he returned, she was sitting cross-legged on the bed, her breasts straining against the sheer nightgown that barely covered them.

"I must say you revive quickly, madam," he teased in his best professional manner, and he sat on the edge of the bed, his eyes looking deeply into hers. "However," he went on softly as his hand slowly moved up to encircle her neck and he pulled her head closer, "I think you could use just a little more treatment," and his lips touched hers, lightly at first, then more ardently as his passion rose. "My God, Rebel," he sighed breathlessly moments later as he drew his mouth from hers, "do you know how I've missed you? It's been agony."

She kissed him brazenly, her lips sipping at his slowly. "Matt, what am I going to do?" she said between kisses. "I go crazy shut up in this house . . . I don't dare go out alone . . ." She stopped kissing him and leaned her head back, sinking onto the pillows. "Sometimes even Brandon looks good to me, then afterward I could kick myself because it's not the same and I only ache for you all the more."

He reached down and picked up her hand, kissing it softly. "If we could have just one day."

"But we can't! We have only a few minutes for me to look at you and let you know how terribly much I miss you."

He took her in his arms and kissed her, wishing he could climb in bed with her and give her the love he knew she needed, because he needed it too. The life of a celibate wasn't exactly his cup of tea, but he wasn't about to force himself on Miriam anymore. Nor was he going to find a substitute as Brandon had when Rebel wasn't available. There was too much chance of infection; besides, he didn't want anyone else, he only wanted Rebel.

"I'm sorry, Matt, I should have left well enough alone," she said softly. "I was just so damn lonely and bored."

"Don't be sorry. I enjoy every moment I can glean with you, but I'd better get those doors unlocked before Brandon or someone tries barging in."

She pulled the covers up and he leaned over, kissing her full on the mouth.

"Matt?" she said as he drew his mouth from hers and looked down at her. "I don't want you to think that all I'm interested in is what your body can do for me . . . I just like being with you, Matt, and I think . . . I think maybe I'm falling in love with you."

He looked pleased, then pained. "There isn't much future in it, though, is there, love?" he said, and she smiled wistfully.

"No, but I wanted you to know."

He gave her one last long kiss, went to the doors, and unlocked them; then he walked back to the bed and sat down on the chair, winking at her as he called for Cristabel.

His diagnosis was an upset stomach, and he stayed awhile talking while Cristabel buzzed about the room, then he stopped off at Brandon's office in town to inform him that his wife wasn't pregnant, merely suffering from a stomach complaint that should clear up in short order with a few meals of hot chicken broth.

Brandon was disappointed. He'd been hoping by now something would have happened. He thanked Matt, however, then turned as the doctor left the room and walked to the window of his office and gazed out at the harbor in front of him, admiring the ship that was making its way toward the wharf. He watched it pull in, its sleek lines resting comfortably in the water, its sails furling as it docked; then he read the name on the side, and a slow, wicked smile eased the tense corners of his mouth.

Today was the day. A new beginning. By God, it wouldn't be long now before his revenge was complete, and a sweet revenge it would be, too. He walked out the door to greet the ship that was to be the nemesis of Captain Thunder.

16

It had rained early in the morning, a short shower about dawn, but now the sky had cleared and Rebel sat in the carriage beside Brandon, wearing the deep violet dress that matched her eyes. She watched another cannon being removed from the deck of the ship he'd named the *Eagle Hunter*. The ship had been bought with money from his estates back in England and had arrived two weeks earlier. The jib had been made longer and the rigging changed to accommodate extra sails, and now the cannon were being removed in preparation for the specially designed guns Brandon had ordered.

"I'm pleased that I took such pains to inspect the guns on the *Golden Eagle* when we sailed aboard it, my love," he said as he sat beside her and watched the activity on the ship. "When I'm through with it, the *Hunter* will be equipped with cannon superior to your Captain Thunder's." Rebel wondered if perhaps he wasn't right.

The first new cannon had arrived the day before, and Bran had purposely made sure he brought her down to see it. The barrel had extended at least a foot farther than those she had remembered seeing on the *Golden Eagle* and it handled more powder, which would enable the shot to travel farther. She wished to hell it'd blow up in their faces instead.

She turned to Brandon. "May we leave now?" she asked wearily. "It's quite boring watching men dragging cannon about."

"If you wish."

"I do."

He told the driver to move on, and the carriage made its way through the streets to Brandon's office. He had stepped from the carriage and was about to tell her good-bye and have the driver take her home, when the thud of horses' hooves made them both look down the dusty street. Matt galloped toward them.

"I'm glad I caught you together," Matt said breathlessly as

he dismounted. "It's urgent. Can Rebel come with me?" he asked abruptly.

"Go with you where? What are you talking about?"

"Bondie just rode in and said there's been a fire up at the Frenchman's. The slave quarters burned to the ground during the night, and everyone was caught sleeping. It's a hell of a mess, and I'm going to need help up there."

"But that's over ten miles up the coast!"

"I know where it is."

"She can't go up there with you!"

"She's the only one I can take. Nobody else on this island can do what she can do with her hands. I can't take the whole load on by myself. Bondie says there's over a hundred burned, including children."

Brandon was adamant. "But I can't let her go off with you alone."

"Then come with us!"

"I can't do that either."

Matt's patience was running thin, and his face reddened with anger. "Dammit, Brandon, I'm not taking her up there to seduce her, I'm taking her there to help people who are hurt and dying. I'm taking men to help clear things up, and some have volunteered to help if they can, but they'll probably pass out at the first sight of a half-burned body." His voice lowered. "Please, Brandon, if we're going to save anyone, I have to have your wife's help."

Brandon stared at Matt. He wanted to help, but to send Rebel into the hills . . .

"Brandon," said Matt forcefully, "as governor of this island it's your responsibility to see that things are done for the good of everyone. Swallow your stubbornness for heaven's sake and say yes."

Rebel leaned forward, her eyes on Brandon's. He was wavering. "Bran," she said softly, "if I can do anything . . . anything at all . . ."

"All right! All right!" he answered harshly, and he glanced quickly at Rebel. "But if you get hurt . . ."

"I'll see she doesn't," answered Matt. "You'd better take her home to change. I have some more men to round up. We'll be leaving in half an hour."

"You're riding overland?" asked Rebel. "You can ride, can't you?" he asked, and she smiled.

"I certainly can." Half an hour later she waited anxiously in the drawing room, a saddled horse out front, while Brandon protested about the clothes she had on.

She was wearing a pair of pants she'd confiscated from one of the stableboys and the pink satin blouse that went with the mauve velvet riding suit she'd bought before leaving London. The blouse did have a petticoat attached, but she'd had Cristabel cut it, and the ragged end was tucked into the black pants that were fastened about her waist with a rope. The riding boots were her own, shiny black ones that she'd worn when she'd ridden in London, and the hat was her own, a wide straw hat she'd bought to wear when she played with Cole in the garden.

"You look ridiculous!" stated Brandon angrily. "I don't know why you can't ride sidesaddle. You have that nice riding suit."

"I told you before. That sort of thing is all right for show, but we'll no doubt be traveling fast from what Matt says. I don't want them to have to slow down because of me."

"I ought to go with you," he fumed irritably.

"Then why don't you? Matt asked you to come along. Maybe you could give the men a hand."

"I don't dare. I'm in the middle of a hassle with the cabinet. We're having a meeting this afternoon, and I'm expecting a couple of men down from St. Vincent for dinner this evening. I hope you'll be back in time."

"In time for what?" asked Matt as one of the servants ushered him into the drawing room.

"In time for dinner this evening. I'm expecting two important men from St. Vincent."

Matt stared at him, disconcerted. "Brandon, I don't know. We may have to stay up there until sometime tomorrow. I have no guarantee I can get her back tonight. It's almost noon already."

"And where do you plan for her to spend the night?" he asked.

"Well, where the hell do you think she'll spend it?"

Brandon flinched at the steely look in Matt's eyes, and he cleared his throat self-consciously.

"I told you before," assured Matt, "this isn't a pleasure trip, Brandon." His voice lost some of its anger. "The main house is still intact, as far as I know. I imagine they'll let her stay there."

Brandon felt foolish, yet he wasn't at ease about the whole thing. Any man could be a threat to him, and he knew it, because Rebel had little love for him. She'd surrendered to him, yes, but not willingly. He knew she disliked the fact that her body had learned to respond to his, and knew his conquest of

335

her still wasn't truly complete, so any man that so much as looked at her became a potential danger.

"We'd better leave," said Matt, consulting his pocket watch. "The others are out front waiting."

There were fifteen men, saddled and mounted, waiting in front of the gates as Rebel and Matt rode out to meet them. Rebel turned and waved good-bye to Brandon, who stood on the steps as they rode off.

The ride was a rough one, unlike the easy ride she'd enjoyed earlier in the year with Matt. The men rode long and hard, resting little. They kept to the road, but it narrowed down and moved inland and at times seemed to disappear. It took them a little over two hours to reach the plantation, and when they did, the sight was sickening.

The main house was intact, as were the buildings where the nutmeg was readied for market, but the rest of the buildings, where the slaves had been quartered, were still smoldering, the smoke from them filling the once-spicy air with the smells of burning death. The slaves had been asleep when fire broke out, and their shacks had gone up like kindling wood. Survivors who weren't hurt had stacked the bodies of the dead in an open field away from the smoldering ruins, and the wail of the injured could be heard long before they reached the plantation.

Matt set to work immediately separating the people by the severity of their burns. There had been close to three hundred slaves on the plantation and now there were sixty-eight dead, a hundred and fourteen burned, thirty of those hundred and fourteen practically beyond hope of being kept alive much longer, and the entire facility that had housed them was a twisted, ruined, smoldering mess.

The Frenchman had two sons, Armand and Henri, both of them married to women who were useless in an emergency. Rebel tried to get them to help, but they both threw up at the first sight of the crisply burned skin, and Armand's wife, who was pregnant, fainted, so she sent them back into the house.

The men Matt had brought with them were little better when it came to the injured, and Matt finally gave up and sent them off to dig graves and clean up. With the help of some of the slaves who'd survived, he and Rebel worked far into the night, bathing, bandaging, and applying ointments Matt made from plants he had the natives collect for him.

It was three in the morning. They'd lost thirty-two more—two children, fourteen women, and sixteen men—but the ones left were holding their own. Matt finished bandaging the last burned leg and stood up, rubbing the small of his back.

"I think I could sleep standing up," he said, and Rebel sighed.

"Me too."

"Your face is dirty," he said.

"So's yours."

"But you look like an angel."

"Shall we go for a walk?"

A walk might relax him some, yet he was so tired. He set the lantern on the table they'd used to hold the bandages and medicines, and they walked away from the agony of the past few hours.

"I wonder if the day'll ever come when they'll have medicine to help poor devils like those back there?" he said as they walked into the shadows of the nutmeg trees that surrounded the open field where the injured were stretched out in rows. "I imagine in a few hundred years from now they ought to be able to come up with something to make a man whole again." He put his arm around her shoulders and they walked slowly among the cool trees. "I feel so inadequate when something like this happens," he went on. "All I can do is give them some laudanum to make them sleep and ease the pain, and put on ineffective salves to try to relieve the burns, hoping they won't scar too much. If only I could help them grow new skin instead of the scars they'll have to wear if they survive."

"Your work is so important, Matt," she said. He hugged her tighter to him.

"You know, I became a doctor through circumstances, but from the first sliver I took out of a patient's finger, the work grew on me. Only, this island is too much for one man, especially now with the only other doctor on the island unable to travel. I wrote to London last week, to a friend of mine. If I can persuade him to join me . . ." He stopped and took a deep breath.

"Ironic, isn't it," he said softly. "Here we are alone, with no one to bother us, and I'm too damn tired to do anything except kiss you." He pulled her into his arms, his mouth covering hers, and the kiss was full of love and warmth, stirring her deep inside. His arms eased from about her, and his mouth moved against hers as his body responded instantly to her nearness. "I guess I'm not as tired as I thought I was," he whispered, his lips caressing hers.

"What if someone sees us?"

"They won't!" He picked her up in his arms and carried

337

her farther away from the open field, beyond the trees, to where the land sloped and another stand of trees began. He moved among them, away from the moon that tried to follow, until the ground beneath him felt like a soft cushion; then he gently laid her beneath one of the trees, clumsily unfastening the rope that held her breeches. He pulled off her boots and set them aside, then pulled off her breeches, and his hands trembled as they touched her. It was so dark she couldn't even see his face, but his caresses were filled with love.

For a few minutes his hands left her, but she could hear him moving about, and she unbuttoned her shirtwaist, waiting, then suddenly he was beside her and she could hardly breathe, her body on fire.

"I love you, Rebel," he whispered softly, and buried his face in her breasts, "I love you so much," and she sighed with delight as he kissed her again, his tongue parting her lips, and she knew that once more she'd feel the rapture of his body as he took her. The decision she'd made that night in her room was forgotten.

When they returned to the smell of the burning flesh and the cries of the injured, it was to stroll slowly among them as if they hadn't even been gone.

"You're really tired now," Matt said as he reached out for Rebel's hand, "and so am I. Let's go up to the main house."

The household had been up all night, too, unable to sleep with all the commotion, and Matt had kept them busy cutting sheets and anything else they could get their hands on into bandages, and he'd need more again before long. It was almost four-thirty by the time they came in. Armand's wife was resting, so Henri's wife showed them each to a guestroom. Rebel's room was one door over from the room where Matt was to sleep, and she made him promise to wake her up when he got up, which was to be in about three hours; then she collapsed on the bed in her room.

The sun had come up with a violence, only Matt hadn't been awake. Now he stirred reluctantly as he heard knocking on his door. Henri was efficient, and it was barely seven o'clock as Matt lifted his head from the pillow and stumbled off the bed. He pulled on his boots and stretched, blinking his eyes at the world outside, then opened the door and joined Henri in the hall.

"The governor's wife must really be sleeping sound," said Henri as Matt started for the stairs, and Matt stopped. He'd promised to wake her, but she'd been so tired.

"Let her sleep awhile," he said. "If she's not up by nine, let me know," and he went down the stairs and on outside.

The graves had been dug and the burials begun, to the accompaniment of the slaves' chanting, as body after body was lowered into the ground. He left the veranda and headed for the rows of victims stretched out in the open field, and he stopped suddenly, his eyes dangerously alive. When he and Rebel had headed for the house in the wee hours of the morning, he'd given the men instructions to stretch makeshift shelters over the burned victims so they'd be in the shade instead of out in the open when morning came. It hadn't been done, and now his voice bellowed across the yard as he chewed out the men and set them to work moving the people into the shade of the nearest trees until shelters could be erected.

He worked all morning on the shelters, side by side with the other men, taking care of patients between hammering, until suddenly he stopped and glanced at the sun, then took out his watch.

He excused himself and handed the hammer he was using to the man next to him, then headed for the house. He went directly for the room where Rebel was sleeping. The door was still shut, and he opened it slowly.

Rebel lay on her back with one arm over her head, the other dangling off the bed. He stared down at her, then reached down, lifting her hand, caressing it.

"Hey, sleepyhead," he said.

He lowered himself until her arms went about his neck, and he smiled back. "I let you sleep late, Duchess, but I have a strange feeling you're going to be glad."

"How are my patients?"

"We lost four more."

"Oh, no." Rebel felt so sorry for these people. "Isn't there anything more we can do for them?"

"Beyond prayer, no. Except change bandages again." He bent down and kissed her. "Come on, your Grace, it's time you earned your keep." He grabbed her arms from about his neck and pulled her to her feet.

Rebel snatched a sweet roll a few minutes later as Matt ushered her through the kitchen, and they joined the others outside, where they resumed their duties of the day before, rebandaging, redressing, and trying to soothe those they knew were suffering the most, using laudanum liberally but carefully.

By the time their late lunch came at almost two o'clock, they were both tired but pleased. It was brought to them on a tray, and they sat on the veranda eating, where they could keep watch of everything. Two more patients had died that morning, but the rest seemed to be stable.

"When do you think we'll be able to leave?" she asked.

"I'm sending you back in the morning with some of the men."

"Without you?"

His eyes caught hers. "I think it's best."

"But why?"

"I think I can handle it now, and if we go back together, Brandon might start having doubts. If I send you back and stay up here another four or five days, he'll have nothing to complain about. Why do you think I've been having you show those native women what to do all morning? It makes sense, now, doesn't it? He'd kill both of us if he found out there was anything between us."

"And tonight?"

His voice lowered. "Our rooms have connecting doors, or hadn't you noticed?"

Her eyes shone. "I hadn't noticed."

Their hands met across the table, where no one was likely to see, and she felt warm all over as his fingers entwined in hers. They finished their meal and continued checking and bandaging patients.

Out of one hundred and fourteen injured, seventy-six had survived, and later, toward evening, when Matt sent her to the house for the night, stating that she was tired and he and the native women could finish up, Rebel stood on the veranda and watched the sun go down, brushing her hand across her forehead, smoothing her hair back, watching the Negro women caring for the burn victims who had made it so far. Their moving back and forth beneath the tentlike shelters was an awesome sight. They made her feel small and insignificant in comparison, for they were a magnificent people and the long-legged women would have been majestic in their native land. Most of them were taller than average, shiny black, and even being slaves couldn't diminish the proud way they carried themselves. What a shame that people had to enslave each other.

Henri's wife came onto the veranda behind her as the sun disappeared over the horizon and darkness began to fall. She asked Rebel if she'd like to have a warm bath before retiring, since she'd not taken time for herself since she'd arrived. Rebel accepted the offer, assuring her it would feel like heaven, and followed her into the house, where they stood talking in the dining room.

Rebel then followed Henri's plump, brown-haired wife to the staircase that led upstairs.

Night shadows had already crept into the house as Henri's wife made sure the tub set up in Rebel's room was not too hot; then she went to her own room and brought back a nightgown. "You'll sleep better in this," she said, handing the sheer lawn nightgown and a wrapper to her. Rebel was thankful she could get out of her dirty clothes. She'd been in the same clothes since leaving St. George—even sleeping in them—and it'd feel good to get clean again. The dirt and grime from the charred ruins seemed as if it had become a part of her skin, except for her hands. Her hands had been kept clean to lessen infections while she helped Matt.

Henri's wife left, and Rebel stripped, taking advantage of the time to soak generously. She washed her hair first, then piled it atop her head while she scrubbed the rest of her. When she finally climbed from the tub some half-hour later and toweled herself dry, slipping into the nightgown, she felt like a new person.

She dried her hair vigorously and brushed it, using some toilet articles that were on the dresser in the room, then put on the green silk wrapper and went to the top of the stairs.

The men were still below in the dining room, and she could hear their voices raised. The Frenchman, in his broken English, was trying to keep peace with the two brothers, who could never seem to agree on anything constructive.

Rebel knew it wasn't proper to wander about in night-clothes, but there seemed to be no servants around, so she descended the stairs, then walked gracefully into the dining room, her bare feet noiseless on the carpeted floors.

Matt had come inside and joined the men for a brief cup of tea after having settled his patients for the evening. He looked at her hungrily as she stepped into the room, his body aroused by her clean, scrubbed look, and the other gentlemen, sensing her presence, turned toward her.

"I'm sorry to interrupt," she said, clutching the wrapper tightly at her throat, "but there aren't any servants about, and I'm finished with the bathwater."

Henri stood up, his mildly freckled face reddening. "I'm sorry, your Grace," he apologized, "the house is not its usual self at the moment . . . the servants, I'm afraid, are upset also. I will see to it at once," and he called to his wife, who gathered the servants together and had them move the tub from her room, putting it in the doctor's room at his request.

At first the Frenchman and his sons felt strange talking

with the governor's wife, who was also a duchess, but they were soon relaxed as she sat at the table with them drinking tea and nibbling on some biscuits. Matt watched her closely as she talked. Without Brandon to intimidate her, she was relaxed with these people, asking questions, giving her opinions, not forcefully, but logically.

"My stepfather has a plantation," she said as she sipped her tea. "He raises indigo and cotton, but he has no slaves. At least, not as you do. He buys slaves, then gives them a wage comparable to what a paid worker would receive for the same type of job, and they work off their sale price. When they've paid back his original debt, he gives them their freedom and they have a choice of staying and working for wages or leaving to start on their own. Most of them stay. They work twice as hard for him as they would if they were merely slaves, and consequently he makes more money in the long run than his neighbors. His neighbors resent him for what he's doing, but he's proved it can be done. The slaves who are free, yet stay on, live in small places they rent from him and keep up themselves, growing their own food, taking care of themselves, and removing the burden from him. Some planters pay outrageous sums for slaves, then have to feed and clothe them. And let's face it," she added, "to get the best work out of a slave, he has to be fed right. You can't expect a man to keep up his strength by living on half-rations, yet some men try it, hoping to save money. They end up having to use two men to do the work one man is capable of, and it's an added expense."

The Frenchman eyed her curiously, his small hard eyes intent on her face. "You do not believe in slavery?" he asked.

"No, I do not, *m'sieur*," she said softly. "I think every person is entitled to be free to work at his own choosing and live his own life." She looked the wiry Frenchman directly in the eye. "Tell me, *m'sieur*," she said firmly, "would you like it if, while we are sitting here, a group of men were suddenly to come through the door"—and she pointed toward the kitchen—"and drag you away from your family, separating you and your loved ones, and take you to a land far away, where you'd be forced to work for the rest of your days with a whip at your back, a chain around your ankle, and your life would no longer be your own?"

The Frenchman stared at her, his eyes unwavering. "But that will not happen, your Grace."

"All right. You will not concede that, then concede this. My husband is the governor, and as the governor his word is law on this island. Suppose he were to impose his will on all of you. You could no longer come and go as you pleased. You'd be forced to stay on your own land, and all moneys you earned were to be turned over to him, and if your land didn't prosper, you'd be punished severely. If you spoke against him or tried to rebel in any way, you'd be flogged or killed. Suppose he forced you to work from before sunup to long past bedtime without proper food, and the only pay you received for your troubles was a dilapidated roof over your head and a lumpy floor to sleep on, instead of the beautiful house you have here. Even now most of the people on the island are complaining because my husband's raised taxes on the lands and put a higher tariff on the goods that leave the island. You feel he's unjustified. I've heard people complain that soon they'll be working for practically nothing. What about the slaves on this island? They've been working for nothing for years, yet they're expected to enjoy it. And the women. How would you like it if my husband had the pick of the women on the island? If he could bed your wives and sisters anytime he wished, and you had to accept it or be beaten for daring to protest?"

The men's faces reddened. Matt watched her, a smile at the corners of his mouth.

"We do not speak of these things, your Grace," gasped the little Frenchman, but Rebel wasn't intimidated.

"Oh, I know you don't, *m'sieur*," she agreed, "but it does exist, and I doubt any of you would let your wife be used by my husband without a fight, yet slave women are subject to that very fate. Yes, gentlemen, I detest slavery. For one man to own another is wicked and cruel. Authority is good, there must always be leaders and there must always be laws and men to enforce them, and a good day's work never hurt anyone. Life must have a purpose, but let each man decide for himself whether he wants to work in the fields or fish in the sea or take care of the sick," and she glanced for a moment at Matt, then back to the three Frenchmen. "And let each woman decide for herself what man she will allow to lay his head beside hers. If she chooses wrong, then let it be of her own doing, don't let so intimate an experience be forced upon a woman, with no regard to her feelings. Those people outside in your yard are human beings, and the pain they've felt tonight is as real to them as it would be to you if you were lying in their place. When they're better, remember that they have feelings. Ask yourself if you'd like being owned by another human being, and if you still insist that slavery is right, then I pity you." Her eyes dropped self-consciously as the men stared at her. "You'll excuse me, *m'sieurs*, if I've taken advantage of your hospitality, but at times I get carried away, especially when I'm tired. Forgive me if I've offended you in any way. We all have opinions, and I guess I'm rather verbal in mine, much to my husband's dismay, I'm afraid." She glanced back up at the Frenchman again. "If you'll excuse me now *m'sieur*, it's probably best I retire," and she pushed her chair back, excusing herself to all of them, including Matt, and went to her room.

"Now there is truly a woman," said the little Frenchman admiringly as she walked out. "What poise, what fire and passion behind those eyes. The governor must be quite a man, *mon ami*," he said, addressing Matt. "It takes a real man to tame such a one," and Matt smiled as he stood up.

"I think you'd better take a closer look, my friend," he said. "I believe the young lady is far from being tamed." The Frenchman frowned as Matt went on upstairs to prepare for bed. The doctor was right, of course. If she had been tamed, she would never have voiced her opinion so openly. Ah, to be thirty years younger with a woman like that around, and he sighed as he began once more discussing the fire with his sons.

Rebel shut the door and bolted it, then blew out the candle on the dresser and walked to the window. Lights moved here and there across the field beneath the shelters, and the moon was beginning to rise in the distance. The scent of nutmeg and mace began to fill the air again and mingle with that of the charred wood, and she wrinkled her nose in distaste at the odors as she unfastened the wrapper and slipped it off.

She stood for a long time at the window, watching everything below, rather abstractedly, and for some reason it all seemed so unreal. Here she was, Rebel Locke, only it wasn't Locke anymore, it was Rebel Avery, the Duchess of Bourland, and she was waiting for her lover. She remembered her mother's words so clearly the night she protested her marriage to Brandon.

"What happens if you fall in love?" her mother had asked.

"I won't let myself," she'd replied, and now she laughed bitterly. Strange how sure we are of things we know nothing about. Would her mother condemn her for what she was doing, or would she understand? Rebel didn't really understand herself. She knew she still loved Beau. She'd always love him, and she hated Brandon, but she also knew Matt was a special part of her life, and she couldn't give him up, not altogether.

As she thought of Matt, she turned, hearing the door that adjoined their rooms opening slowly, and she could vaguely make out his form as he entered and stood looking at her. He wore only his underwear, and his bare feet were silent as he came toward her.

"Hello, love," he whispered softly. He smelled clean from his bath, and she smiled, stepping into his arms.

His kiss was sweet and deep, and she melted against him. His hands caressed her back as he held her close, and she sighed with longing as his lips left hers and he scooped her up in his arms, carrying her to the four-poster bed in the middle of the room. The covers were pulled back, and he set her down, stripping off her nightgown; then he removed his underwear and crawled in beside her, pulling the covers up as he took her in his arms and held her close. She could feel his heart beating wildly, and she trembled at his touch; yet all he did was hold her as if he were afraid to let her go.

"How glorious it would be to have you all to myself like this every night," he said as he began to stroke her, his hand moving sensuously along her hip. "Sometimes when I'm near you it's all I can do to keep from forgetting about everything and taking you in my arms. You're like a fire in me that never dies. How cruel life is to give us so much, yet so little."

She moved closer in his arms, feeling his bare skin against her body. "At least we have tonight," she whispered softly. "Give me a night to remember always, Matt," and his mouth came down on hers, her lips parting to meet him. Without fear of discovery, with the whole night ahead of them, she surrendered wantonly, bringing him a love he never dreamed could exist for him.

They alternately slept and made love all night, as the moon slowly rode the heavens, and as it dipped out of sight with the first rays of dawn, Rebel stirred in his arms. His eyes were on her as she woke, and she stared at him longingly.

"I don't want to go," she said softly. "I don't want to leave you. I have a strange premonition about tonight."

His hand moved up to caress her neck as she lay against him. "What kind of premonition?"

She was suddenly afraid. "Matt, hold me close and kiss me," she begged, and he did as she asked, not only kissing her, but he rolled on top of her again and entered her, his body pleasuring her sweetly, until they both clung to each other in a peak of ecstasy. He took a deep breath, his body still tingling from the force of his release, and he looked down into her face as he heard a sob escape from deep inside her.

"What is it?" he asked.

"I have a feeling that this is the last time for us, and I can't shake it. As if something's going to happen."

He kissed her to still her fears. "Hush," he whispered against her mouth. "We know it may be a while before we can ever be together like this again, but it's not the end, my darling, not for us. Even though I'm not with you, I'll love you always, and whenever it's possible, like now, we'll be together." He kissed her again. "I'll go downstairs now. Wait about half an hour or so, then come down. I'll kiss you good-bye now." Her arms went about his neck and she held him to her.

"Good-bye," she whispered softly. "I love you, Matt," and he smiled as he kissed her once more.

"Good-bye, love."

She lay for a long time in the big bed, feeling the warm spot where he'd lain; then suddenly she shivered. This was nonsense. What was wrong with her? Nothing was going to happen. Everything was all right, and she pulled the covers tighter about her, staring at the golden sunrise that was filtering into the room.

Even so, later, as she dressed and ate breakfast, then afterward when she was mounted on her horse, bidding everyone good-bye, she still couldn't shake the foreboding that something was going to happen, and her eyes were drawn to Matt's seconds before she dug her horse in the ribs and headed out of the yard with the men who were escorting her back. In that split second as their eyes met, fear gripped her. Fear unlike anything she'd ever known before, and she wanted to cry out; but instead, she shut her eyes to hold back the tears, and turned, giving her horse his head, and galloped away with a lump in her throat.

17

Rebel arrived home shortly before noon, and Brandon was surprised to discover that Matt was still at the plantation. The two men from St. Vincent had stayed over a few days and were somewhat shocked at the sight of Rebel's unusual attire, but congratulated her on her willingness to help, their eyes showing their appreciation later that evening when she was bathed and elegantly dressed for dinner in a beautiful dress of burgundy velvet that enhanced her figure and showed her flaxen hair off to good advantage. They made it a point to let Brandon know what an extremely beautiful and clever wife he had. After all, it was good diplomacy to show people he cared, and that evening at bedtime Brandon made sure Rebel knew he agreed with his guests' admiration of her, and he made love to her, kindling a response from her body as it remembered Matt's lovemaking that morning.

The next morning the guests left to return to St. Vincent, and during the next few days Rebel discovered that Brandon was preparing another attack on Tobago. This time, however, he'd have more men, more ships, and his strategy would be far different. The ship he'd been preparing to sail out after the *Golden Eagle* was almost ready. All that held them back was the arrival of the last of the special cannon. Brandon had given up boasting of it to her, and she was glad, but its presence in the bay was a constant reminder of his vicious promise.

It was two days after her arrival home that the fear she'd felt when parting from Matt began to take on the form of reality. The guards around the house had been relaxed, since no more threats had been received, and Rebel had begun to think the black magic had been no more than a practical joke.

She'd played with Cole as usual, then sent him up to bed while she and Brandon sat in the library reading. They retired at the same time, and she thanked God that tonight he didn't seem to be in an amorous mood.

Cristabel had left the lamp lit on the dresser and the room looked soft and comfortable as she stepped in and began to undress. She put on a pink nightgown, brushed her hair, then pulled back the covers before blowing out the lamp. Her heart skipped a beat.

At first she couldn't believe her eyes. She stared at the pillow transfixed. It wasn't her imagination, it was there; she couldn't take her eyes from it, and the hair at the nape of her neck tingled frighteningly.

Resting in the center of her pillow was a small doll. The hair on its head was made from bits of blond hair that had obviously been pulled from her comb or brush. The eyes were painted violet in a white-painted face, and a piece of leather from her buckskins had been used for its clothing. Rebel's face paled as she continued staring at it, but she didn't scream. She reached out gingerly and picked it up, examining it closely, her hands shaking. There was one large pin in the doll's heart and two pins in the stomach, and she shuddered as she stared at them. Who? How?

She dropped the doll back on the bed and ran to the armoire, rummaging in the bottom for her buckskins. Sure enough, a large piece was cut from the shirt near the waist-line, and she swore as she shoved them back out of sight. And her hair! Where else would they get her hair but from this room?

She marched back to the bed and picked the doll up again. Now she was angry. Her fingers pulled at the pins sticking out of the doll's stomach, but they wouldn't budge. This was silly. They were only pins. She struggled with them, but the pins wouldn't move, and she came to the conclusion that someone had purposely fastened them in so they couldn't be removed.

Her first instinct was to show Brandon; then she hesitated. If she showed Brandon, he'd put the guards about and treat her like a prisoner again, and she'd never get to see Matt, not even for a few snatched minutes of conversation. And besides, what proof did she have that Brandon wasn't behind all this? Maybe he was the one who'd put it there or had it put there. After all, pretending to protect her could be a way of turning suspicion from himself. Had he found out about Matt? No! There was no way he could have. If he was doing it, there was another reason.

She sat on the edge of the bed and studied the doll again carefully, noting every detail; then she made up her mind. She'd wait until Matt returned and see what he had to say. It was foolish anyway to worry. After all, what harm could a doll do? It was a bunch of nonsense, and she wasn't going to let it scare her. She stuck the doll in the bottom of one of her dresser drawers and walked over to pour herself a glass of cool water from the pitcher on the stand beside her bed. She blew out the light and climbed in bed, but she slept fretfully.

Matt didn't return for four more days, and during that time Rebel really began to worry. Her first inkling of something wrong was the morning after finding the doll. A short while after breakfast she began to feel sick. Not miserably sick, just a gnawing nausea that seemed to come and go, and her bowels were loose. By afternoon it was gone and she felt somewhat better, but her mouth was extremely dry and she

d nothing but drink water all day, feeling bloated by bed-
me, but without a stomachache.

The next morning when she woke up she felt fine again, so
e dressed and joined Brandon at breakfast, only to have the
me thing happen again shortly after he left the house. This
me the nausea was worse, and she was so dizzy Cristabel
d to help her up to her room.

At first she thought she might be pregnant, but then, it
asn't the same sort of nausea she'd had during her preg-
ancy with Cole, and the same dry feeling filled her mouth
gain today as she drank glass after glass of water. By bed-
me she seemed much better, except that her bowels were
ill loose. Brandon had wanted to send for Matt, but she as-
ired him it was probably only a stomach complaint again,
nd the people at the fire needed him more.

The next day was a repeat of the day before, but by the
urth morning when she tried to open her eyes she was so
ck she couldn't even hold her head up and her tongue felt
vice its size, her throat sore, like raw flesh. She could barely
lk, and her body was so weak she couldn't even move from
e bed.

This time Brandon took one look and sent for Matt with-
ut even telling her. It was afternoon when he arrived, and
randon could tell he'd been riding hard.

"How is she?" Matt asked the minute he came through the
oor, brushing past the butler, addressing Brandon in the
ownstairs hall. Brandon stared at his anxious face, not ex-
ctly pleased with what he saw. Matt's eyes were too intense.

"See for yourself." He barely got the words out when Matt
eaded up the stairs, taking them two at a time.

Brandon followed him closely, unable to grasp Matt's un-
sual concern. As they entered the bedroom, he saw nothing
nusual in the manner in which Matt began to examine
ebel, so he shrugged off his suspicions.

Matt bent over the bed, looking into Rebel's eyes closely,
en leaned over, his head on her chest while he listened to
er heart for some minutes. He lifted her wrist and felt her
ulse, then opened her mouth, sniffing her breath.

"What's she been eating?" he asked Brandon, who watched
rom the opposite side of the bed.

"Not much of anything, but Cristabel says she's been
rinking a great deal of water."

Rebel was relieved as she watched Matt above her through
er fevered, half-closed eyes, and she tried to talk. The pain
as so bad in her stomach, and she felt so weak and sick.

"Matt . . ." Her voice was almost inaudible, and he put his finger to her mouth to quiet her rasping, but she moaned loudly and tried to gather more strength. "The drawer . . ." she murmured helplessly, and her mouth felt like it was stuffed with cotton. She tried to lift her hand, and managed to get it halfway off the bed, pointing toward the dresser, but it fell as a nauseous pain filled her, making her dizzy and weaker.

"What about the drawer?" he asked, and saw her lips try to move again. He bent down, his ear to her mouth, and held his breath, listening.

"In drawer . . . doll . . ." she gasped, and he sat up slowly, then suddenly stood up and moved to the dresser, pulling open one of the drawers.

"What are you doing?" asked Brandon, watching him tossing things about as he searched the drawer, and Matt's mouth tightened.

"There's something in one of these drawers," he said angrily. "Stay there, I know what I'm looking for," and he moved from one drawer to the next hurriedly, his hands feeling among the delicate lingerie and feminine attire. Suddenly his face went white as he pulled a small object from the bottom of one of the drawers. He glanced at it only a moment, then turned toward the bed and saw the faint flicker of relief in Rebel's eyes.

"Your wife's being poisoned, Brandon!" he cried angrily. Brandon could have sworn he saw tears in Matt's eyes as he set what looked like a small doll down on her nightstand.

Matt glanced at the stand where he'd put the doll, while Brandon stared at him incredulously. Matt lifted the pitcher of water that was sitting there, bringing it to his nose, sniffing deeply; then his hand dipped into the pitcher and his fingers probed about, but there was nothing. Still, when he lifted his hand from the pitcher, he touched one of his fingers to his tongue and tasted, then made a face. He stood up and took the pitcher and glass with him and headed for the door.

"Stay with her and let no one in," he said firmly, "and let's hope we're not too late. I'll be right back."

Brandon stared at Rebel and saw tears at the corners of her eyes. He walked over and stared down at the funny-looking doll Matt had put on the stand, and he remembered the conversation he'd had in the library with Matt when he'd found the note under Rebel's pillow. His jaw tightened angrily as he looked down at her pale face again.

"You won't die, Reb," he cried heatedly, "I won't let you ie," and he held her hand.

Matt returned carrying two glasses. One was a large glass of milk, the other a glass of water with something yellow in t. "Grab the washbasin," he ordered. Brandon walked over nd took the basin from the commode, bringing it to the bed. Matt set the glass of milk on the nightstand, then sat on the edge of the bed and gathered Rebel gently in his arms. He put the glass with the yellow liquid to her lips and forced ome down her throat.

"What's that?" asked Brandon.

"Dry-mustard water. It should make her vomit anything she's taken in the past few hours." He forced the whole glass of mustard water into her, and suddenly she began to gag, and he reached for the basin Brandon was holding. When she was through vomiting he wiped her mouth, then began giving her the milk. Milk dribbled down her chin, but he paid little heed as he forced it down her throat.

She gagged and choked again, but it went down and stayed down; then he gently laid her back down and turned to Brandon.

"Things like this usually need help," he said, picking up the doll. "And someone's been doing a job of it. The water in that pitcher had poison in it."

"But who?"

"That's what's so bad. These people will die before they'll turn against one of their own."

Brandon glanced quickly at Rebel. "If she dies . . ."

"She won't, at least not if I can help it. The only food I want to pass her lips is food I bring her myself from here on in. Where are Cristabel and Hizzie?"

"In the nursery with Cole."

"Go get Cristabel for me," he said.

"Don't worry, darling," Matt whispered softly in her ear after Brandon left, "you're going to be all right," and Rebel relaxed.

For the next two days Matt left her bedside only to get her food, which consisted of milk right from the cow, whipped egg whites, and a thin gruel he'd prepared himself. He sent a message to Miriam that he was needed at the governor's house.

The first night Matt plied Rebel with as much warm milk and whipped egg whites as he could get into her, and in the morning he began with the thin, starchy gruel, alternating it with more milk. Cristabel relieved him at Rebel's side, with

orders to feed her nothing while he fixed her food in th
kitchen. At night he kept his vigil on the chaise lounge, where
he sometimes dozed, but only for short periods.

Brandon was in and out of the room constantly, checking
on her and threatening to hang every person he could find
who was practicing black magic.

"Don't be absurd," countered Matt as he bathed Rebel'
face with cool water one morning while she lay quietly, he
breathing labored. "If you do a stupid thing like that, you
days on this island are finished. Almost every slave on Grenada believes in black magic, and over half of the free population. If you'll keep your soldiers out of the way until Rebel'
on her feet, I'll find out who did it."

"How?"

"I'm a doctor. I know what kind of poison was used, and
know where the supplies are on this island."

Brandon stood firmly, his elegant gold brocade coa
catching the sun as it streamed in through the French doors
his tawny hair combed back fashionably above his prettily
handsome face.

"And if you don't find out who did it?"

"I will."

"But if you don't?"

"Then you can do as you like and suffer the consequences."

Brandon pursed his lips thoughtfully. "All right, I'll wait
but by hell you'd better find out, because if you don't, I will
one way or another." And he turned on his fancy polished
boots and left the room.

When Brandon was gone, Matt called Cristabel to bring
him warm water, soap, and towels, then showed her how to
give Rebel a bath without having to get her out of bed. His
hands were gentle as he turned her this way and that, and
Cristabel glanced at him curiously a few times. There was
something about the way he touched the duchess, something
caressing about his hands, and there was a contented look on
the duchess's face. Maybe she and Hizzie had been too naive
in their assumption that the doctor didn't like the ladies. It
was easy to see that he liked the duchess. She watched him
closely, then shrugged, paying closer attention to what he was
saying, pushing her crazy thoughts to the back of her mind.

"I want you to do this for her every morning until she's
able to wash herself," he said. "It's better if you do it than
me."

Matt had questioned both Cristabel and Hizzie, plus the

kitchen help, about the food Rebel had been eating, but they could tell him nothing, and he came to the conclusion that the poison had always been put in the pitcher of water she kept on her bedside stand, and it was probably done sometime in the evening, either before she reached her room or while she was sleeping.

By the fourth day, Rebel was alert and getting her strength back, and Matt knew the crisis was over; but to make sure it didn't happen again, he made Cristabel and only Cristabel responsible for the food Rebel ate, allowing nothing else to go into her mouth.

As soon as Matt knew Rebel was well on her way to recovery, he had given Cristabel her orders, then sent her from the room for a few minutes so he could talk to Rebel alone. He sat on the edge of the bed and looked into her face.

"I have to go now," he said softly.

"When will I see you again?"

His eyes misted over. "I don't know. Maybe tomorrow, but I don't dare stay all the time like this anymore or Brandon will get suspicious. I've already seen him staring at me rather strangely." He reached out and took her hand, bringing it to his lips to kiss her fingertips. She still looked pale, and there were shadows beneath her eyes. "Take care now and don't eat anything unless Cristabel brings it, and that means no water during the night, either."

"Yes, Doctor," and her mouth tilted into a teasing grin.

"Oh, my God," he murmured hoarsely, and he leaned forward, his mouth covering hers, and she was in his arms again and he was kissing her passionately, unable to let her go. Neither was aware of Cristabel, who'd returned from her errand and opened the door, then closed it quickly.

Matt hadn't gone straight home when he left Rebel; instead he'd ridden to the beach and gone for a swim. He sat on the beach for a long time, until evening shadows began filtering through the trees. He thought over his behavior of the past few months. In all his years of practice no woman had ever been able to entice him. They'd tried. Even the sloppy appearance he'd forced himself to accept hadn't always been a deterrent, but he'd never succumbed until Rebel. A girl of only twenty, and another man's wife at that.

He gazed out over the water and thought of Miriam. Of the mess he'd made of his life. He felt sorry for her, truly sorry. She could have been loved so deeply if she'd only given love in return. But Miriam didn't know what it was to love, not truly love. He was her possession. He belonged to her, but it wasn't love that made her keep him, not the passionate love he needed. Miriam was afraid of passion. Her body wanted it, he knew, but her convictions were against it, and nothing would change those convictions, yet he had to go home and face her.

Miriam stood in her bedroom and looked in the mirror once more, making sure everything was all right. Her hair was brushed down loose and waved about her shoulders; she had a touch of perfume behind each ear. What was it Kuulie had said, sometimes you have to fight fire with fire? Her breast was pounding. Maybe tonight he'd come home. Oh, God, but she was scared. Twenty-eight years old, married all these years, and she was scared. She had gone too far already. What did one more sin matter? She folded her hands, and her eyes looked up toward heaven beseechingly.

"Oh, dear God," she whispered. "Forgive me for what I've become." Then her eyes gleamed unnaturally bright as she looked once more in the mirror, wondering if surely he wouldn't notice the weight she'd put on in the past week. Even she could see a change already.

The nightgown she wore was a new one that emphasized her breasts, making them look larger, and the gold color made her eyes look prettier, she was sure. Hadn't the dressmaker said it would? She took a deep breath, then sighed, wondering if tonight would be the night.

She turned slowly and walked to the dresser, blowing out the lamp, but instead of climbing into her own bed, she walked to the door that separated her room from Matt's and opened it, stepping into the room that was already too dark with shadows to see anything but vague outlines. She took a step toward the bed, then stopped, hesitating for only a moment. With her mouth frozen in determination, she continued toward the empty bed, pulled back the covers, and climbed in, stretching out to wait for Matt's return, as she had for the past two nights.

When Matt arrived, Kuulie was the only one up, and he was relieved as he greeted her en route to his room. He opened the door and closed it softly behind him, then walked over, setting the lamp on the dresser. He hadn't glanced at the bed when he came in, and his back was still to it as he undressed.

He sighed wearily, then turned and cupped his hand about the chimney of the lamp to blow out the candle, when suddenly he froze, his eyes glued to the bed.

Miriam was staring at him from the bed. It was a seductive

look, and when she spoke, her voice was low and sensuous.

"I've been waiting for you," she said. "I'm glad you finally decided to come home."

He straightened, trying to figure out what the hell she thought she was doing. "What are you doing here?" he asked, and he saw her lips quiver slightly.

"I told you. I was waiting."

"Why?"

She smiled. "Now, why does a woman usually wait in bed for her husband?"

Now he was puzzled, and instead of blowing the candle out, he lifted the lamp, carrying it to the bed, and stood looking down at her. "Do you really know why?" he asked abruptly.

"You haven't come to me for a long time, Matthew," she said softly.

"Have you given me any reason to?"

Her heart was pounding, and she held the edge of the sheet tightly in her hands to keep them from shaking. "I'd like to give you a reason," she answered.

"You what?"

"Matthew, will you make love to me?" she asked, and all he could do was stare.

She gazed at his long muscular body, at the scattering of hair across his chest, and a strange warm feeling crept over her. She started to fight it, tensing up, then remembered what she was supposed to do, and instead of fighting it, she relaxed and let it take hold of her. "Will you?" she asked again.

"Why?" he managed to gasp huskily, and she relaxed farther back on the bed, her body suddenly enjoying this new sensation that filled it.

"Because I want you to."

"You . . . ?" He swallowed hard, unable to believe his ears. "You want me to kiss you?"

"And get up over me and let me feel what I should have felt years ago. Matthew, please!"

He stood stock-still. He'd never expected to hear her say these things. She'd never even discussed it with him except to refer to it as "oh, that," with a distasteful look on her face. What was she up to? Was this some kind of a game she was playing with him again, like the night she put her arms around his neck and told him she loved him? He'd called her bluff that night, and he stared at her now, anger seeping through him. If she thought she was being funny . . .

"Please, Matthew," she begged.

"You're sure you want me?"

"Yes, Matthew."

"And you won't hold back?"

"No!"

"Take off your nightgown," he said slowly, and she sat up, pulling the nightgown up until it came off over her head.

He'd see just how far she was willing to go this time. "Move over," he ordered, and she slid over to the other side of the bed and lay on her back with her arms above her head, her small breasts uncovered.

He set the lamp down and unfastened his underwear, stepping out of it, and he realized she hadn't aroused him as yet. Then he blew out the lamp and climbed in beside her. He lay on his back, muscles tense as he spoke. "I'm going to need some help," he whispered, and he heard her quick intake of breath. This was it. She'd never do it. He might as well just close his eyes and go to sleep.

Then suddenly he felt her hand, warm and caressing, and he was so startled he didn't know what to do. She stroked him sensuously; then she was above him, her lips on his, and she kissed him with an urgency that surprised him. He felt himself hardening beneath her hands.

She whispered, "Why didn't you tell me I'd feel like this, Matthew?" but she gave him no time to answer as she kissed him again.

Then slowly she drew the covers from him and began caressing him all over as she kissed his chest, her tongue flicking out as it moved down the taut skin across his stomach; then he gasped as he felt something warm and moist on him and realized what she was doing. My God! Where did she ever . . . ? He'd never done that to her. Rebel, yes, but not Miriam. He didn't think she'd ever understand, and now she was doing it to him. He didn't understand it, he didn't care to understand it, all he knew was that it felt good.

By the time he moved above her, she was like a starved animal, but there was something unnatural about the way she mumbled into his ear. Her voice was hysterically high, and the words she flung at him caressingly were crude words, the kind used by women of the streets, and even though she was no longer holding back, even though her body was totally his for the first time in his marriage, he felt a revulsion, and the desire to take her began to subside. This was nothing like it had been with Rebel, like it should be between people who loved each other. There was no warmth behind her surrender, only an animal instinct that seemed to be driving her.

Matt wanted to die inside as he felt himself softening, but there was nothing he could do.

Miriam stopped moving beneath him, and her voice was strained. "What is it, what happened?" she gasped. "Matthew, please, why are you stopping?" and he didn't know what to say. All he could do was push himself off her and climb to the side of the bed, where he sat dejectedly staring into the darkness.

Miriam sat up, her body throbbing with desire. She had never felt like this before. It was such a wild, untamed feeling that filled her. No wonder whores were pleased with their profession. She reached out and touched Matt's bare back, running her fingers down it as she whispered to him strangely, begging him to come back, but the more she talked, the more wary he became at the tremor in her voice.

What was it that he was unable to put his finger on? Why did he feel so strongly that something was wrong? "I'm sorry, Miriam," he said as she tried kissing the back of his neck to arouse him. "I don't know what's the matter."

She reached out in front of him, then drew her hand back abruptly, her voice frightened. "You're soft . . . my God, you're soft!" she yelled. "What good will you do me now?" and a sob broke from her as she sat on her knees on the bed behind him, her body trembling for release. "You wanted me to give myself to you, and now, when I do, you don't want me!"

He stood up, grabbing his underwear, and slipped it on, then turned toward the bed. He could barely make out her body as she hugged herself, rocking back and forth.

"I'm sorry," he said again. "I don't know what else I can say," and he felt disconcerted. "I guess it's just too late, Miriam. What was there, what I felt once, is gone," and he turned from her, walking to the window, staring out. "You ignored me so much that it isn't there anymore."

Miriam sat on the bed behind him rocking for a long time; then suddenly she stopped, and her body trembled with anger and frustration. "It's her," she said vindictively as she climbed off the bed. "Don't think I don't know what you've been up to. You're in love with her, aren't you?"

He whirled around. "What are you talking about?"

"I'm not blind, Matthew." Her voice was shaking uncontrollably. "I know you and Rebel have been sleeping together. I've known it for a long time. What a fool you are; the governor's wife! I lowered myself for you, and yet you'd rather have another man's wife!" Her voice rose in volume as she leaned closer, and the pale moonlight coming through the window fell on her face. Her eyes were wild and unusually bright. "I drag myself down into sin for you, and you prefer that tramp!"

He grabbed her shoulders and stared at her, at the sardonic look on her face. "What are you talking about?" he asked harshly, his hands gripping her fiercely. "What do you mean, you sinned for me?"

Her eyes narrowed with loathing and her mouth trembled. "I asked Satan to let my body feel what you wanted it to feel and to help me to like it, to enjoy it. I promised him I'd do anything to get you back, even let you take my body like some wanton whore, and now you tell me it's all for nothing! She should have died!"

He shook his head slowly, then suddenly went cold inside. "Oh, no, you couldn't," he said breathlessly and his hands tightened on her shoulders as her eyes stared at him bitterly. "You didn't, Miriam, say you didn't," he pleaded, and suddenly she laughed, her maniacal laughter filling the room, pounding in his ears, and tears rolled down her cheeks.

Then she stopped laughing abruptly, as if she'd never even started, and her mouth softened, pouting as she looked at him. "Say I didn't do what?" she asked innocently, and he shuddered.

"You tried to kill her, didn't you?"

The smile was still on her face.

"Didn't you?"

The smile broadened. "Wouldn't you like to know?" she teased coquettishly, and wrenched herself free of his hands as she strolled to the bed and lay down, her body sprawled, legs spread apart. "Aren't you going to come over and finish making love to me, Matthew?" she invited. "I do so want you to finish. I'll enjoy it as much as she did, I promise." Her voice became light and airy. "Please, Matthew, it's all right now. I've come over to your side, Matthew, you see," and she looked up from the bed in time to see Matt dressing.

She shot up in bed, her eyes wild, leaning toward him, snarling viciously. "You think she'll want you, don't you!" she yelled hysterically as he opened the door to go out. "You think you can go back to her, don't you? Well, go on! What are you waiting for? Go climb into her bed, but make sure her husband isn't in it first!" She began to laugh again, and Matt closed the door, shutting his eyes, wishing he could shut out the sound of her voice as easily as he could the look on her face. Miriam was mad, insane. Somewhere along the way her mind had snapped, and now he knew what had bothered him when he'd tried to make love to her. He shivered involuntarily as he went downstairs, her voice trailing after him, screaming obscenities.

It took only minutes to wake Kuulie, and he took her to his office, giving her some laudanum, instructing her to see that Miriam took it. "I can't do it myself," he said, his voice breaking. "I have to get out of the house for a while and try to figure things out."

"You go right ahead, Doctor," Kuulie said solicitously. "Don't worry about Mrs. Wilder, I'll see she's all right. Poor child." He left the house, getting his horse from the stables, not knowing where he was going or what he was going to do.

He rode back to the beach and sat for a long time thinking, trying to understand. Had he done this to Miriam? Was her insanity his doing, or had it been unavoidable? He thought back to her actions over the years. She had always been emotional, and he remembered her hysteria on their wedding night. If he had hurt her, it would have been understandable, but he'd been kind and gentle with her. The hysteria was uncalled-for. And there was the fact that she'd never changed her hairdo for years and the dresses she wore—then the radical change in her appearance when his appearance had changed. Was that when she'd learned about Rebel? Had she been trying to make herself more attractive for him?

It was about the same time that the threats had come, but it didn't seem possible. Even if Miriam hated Rebel, how could she possibly have done all those things? He shook his head. It was a physical impossibility. Whoever had poisoned Rebel had gotten into her room at night, probably the same way he had, by climbing the vines that clung to the house. Miriam wasn't a strong person. . . . No, she couldn't have.

All night Matt sat on the beach, tormented between his love for Rebel and his loyalty to Miriam, blaming himself and cursing the destiny that had brought him to this.

He had fallen asleep in the grass sometime in the early hours of the morning, and now he stirred, waking to the sun in his face and the shrill cawing of the terns skimming the breakers that slapped the sandy beach. He stretched stiffly and wondered what the hell time it must be, pulling the watch from his pocket. Good Lord, it was well past ten o'clock.

His horse was nearby, still grazing contentedly, when he climbed into the saddle and started for St. George.

There were two apothecaries in St. George. The first one had sold arsenic to two people in the last few months, the gentleman who owned the warehouse down the street and a plantation owner from up north, both planning to use it on rats. The second apothecary was more revealing.

"The only one ever asks for arsenic, Doc, is you," he said as he looked curiously at Matt. "Why, I sold some to Kuulie just a while back, said you needed it for some medicine you were making up."

"You sold it to Kuulie without a slip of paper?" he asked, and the man grinned sheepishly.

"She said you forgot to give it to her and she didn't want to go all the way back for it."

Matt's heart was heavy as he left the man's shop, and he stood for a minute thinking. When it hit him, he shook his head in disbelief. Kuulie! Kuulie was strong, she could climb those vines, she was devoted to Miriam . . . and he'd left Miriam with her! Kuulie!

The sight of Doc Wilder galloping through town would have caused little stir except for the look on his face. He was usually in a hurry anyway, but people knew something dreadful must have happened this morning, because as he rode through town toward his house on the hill overlooking the bay, he looked as if the devil himself were after him.

Matt almost fell off his horse as he reined up in front of the veranda and stumbled up the steps two at a time. "Kuulie!" he yelled as he stepped into the hall, but there was no answer.

He ran to the kitchen and stopped in the doorway, staring at the colored woman, who was calmly sitting at the table cutting vegetables into a dish in front of her, acting as if she hadn't even heard him.

"Why didn't you answer?" he asked breathlessly. She stared at his tall frame for a minute, then looked back down at the vegetables she was cutting. His tired eyes were on fire. "I asked you a question, Kuulie!" he shouted through clenched teeth. But she began to hum, ignoring him, and he stared at her, a sickening feeling filling his stomach. He ran up the stairs, throwing open the door to Miriam's room. It was empty! He hurried through it and opened the door to his own room, knowing in his heart that he'd find it empty too; then he ran downstairs, not stopping until he stood over Kuulie, his face white with rage.

"Where's Miriam?" he asked. Kuulie smiled as she looked up at him.

"She went out, and I don't ask her where she goes, Dr. Wilder," she answered sarcastically.

"I told you to give her some laudanum."

"I know you did, but she didn't need none."

"Didn't need any?"

"Why, no, she came down them stairs after you left last night just as fine as could be," Kuulie answered. "Would have been a shame to keep her doped up with that stuff. 'Course, I've heard tell lotsa men done that to their wives when they wanted them out of the way."

Matt had been trying to control his temper, but now he reached down, pulling the woman from her chair. "Where is she?" he asked furiously. Kuulie smiled, unintimidated.

"Like I said, I don't rightly know, sir!"

"Kuulie, I know you bought that arsenic," he said, his eyes steady on hers, "and I know you're a strong, agile woman. Did my wife know you tried to kill Rebel?" and Kuulie snorted, laughing.

"You out of your head, Doctor," she answered flippantly. "There ain't nobody on this island gonna believe I done that. You see, I'm a mamba." She saw the doctor's eyes widen. "That's right, Doctor, I'm a high priestess, and there ain't nobody on this island gonna do nothin' to me."

"Isn't there?" he asked viciously. And suddenly Kuulie's eyes swelled and fear came into them as the doctor's hand tightened on the scarf about her throat and she felt her air being cut off.

She struggled and fought him, but he knocked the knife she was using from her hand; then, as if realizing what he was doing, he drew in a quick breath and threw her from him.

"Don't be here when I get back!" he shouted. He stood for a moment catching his breath, then glanced toward an empty spot on the wall. His pistol was gone! He swallowed hard and was shaking his head in disbelief as he once more mounted his horse and galloped down the road.

Rebel had gotten out of bed for the first time. She felt so much better, but she was staying in her room and hadn't bothered to get dressed. She was wearing her blue satin night-gown with a satin-and-lace wrapper over it, and her feet were tucked into a pair of new silver slippers Brandon had bought for her.

She'd done everything Matt told her to do, and for the first time in days she was feeling more herself. She lay on the chaise longue reading when Brandon came in.

"Are you well enough for visitors?" he asked.

"I guess."

"Good, then," and he gestured toward the door, ushering Miriam in. "I think she could do with a bit of cheering up at that," he said. Miriam walked ahead of him and smiled as her eyes fell on Rebel.

"Matthew says it's all right if I visit you, that it'll probably do you some good," she said.

"I'll go downstairs and leave you ladies to talk," said Brandon from where he stood by the door, and Miriam assured him there was no need. "On the contrary," he said apologetically, "I have a dozen things to catch up with. You two have a nice visit. I'll be up later."

As Brandon closed the door, the smile on Miriam's face started to fade, and she reached around slowly, bolting the door behind him.

Rebel frowned as she watched from the chaise. "Why did you do that?" she asked, and Miriam turned to her, a quizzical look on her face.

"Why did I do what?"

"You locked the door."

"I?" Miriam's hand moved to her breast. "My dear Rebel, you're seeing things," she stated boldly, and Rebel stared at her, about to protest again, when something in Miriam's eyes told her to beware.

Rebel studied the woman closely as she walked toward the French doors. She looked quite pretty today in a new russet dress, tucked lightly to her thin figure, the skirts billowing gracefully, and her small straw hat made her new hairdo very chic, but there was a subtle tension beneath the friendly veneer she'd presented when she'd first walked into the room. She was clutching her new russet reticule nervously, as if it were trying to jump out of her hands.

Suddenly she turned from the open French doors, her face flushed, topaz eyes dancing dangerously. "Why didn't you die?" she asked strangely through clenched teeth as she leaned toward Rebel. "You were supposed to die, why didn't you?" and Rebel eased the book she'd been reading onto her lap, her fingers trembling as she stared, dumbfounded.

"I . . . ?"

"All my plans for nothing. Everything I've done for nothing." Miriam's voice sounded eerie, unnatural. "My hairdo, the clothes, even last night . . . Why couldn't you leave him alone?"

Rebel's hand moved to her throat. Miriam couldn't know. How could she possibly know? Yet she went on.

"Why couldn't you be satisfied with one husband, why did you have to go after mine too?"

Rebel finally found her voice. "What are you talking about?"

Miriam's fingers tightened on the reticule until her knuckles were white. "Don't try to lie out of it and say you don't know what I'm talking about, because I saw you with my own eyes." She straightened as if trying to hold herself in check. "I know you sent that note to Matthew that time your husband went to St. Vincent, because the governor had a note sent to him. The boy brought it half an hour after yours arrived. At first I couldn't understand what was going on, and the fact that there were two messages bothered me. It wasn't until some time later in the day that I realized who'd sent the first message. I didn't even have to follow Matthew that night, Rebel, all I had to do was find a vantage point where I could watch your balcony."

Rebel stared at Miriam, her voice lost in her throat.

"I wanted to kill you that night." Her face was pale. "I would have, too, if Kuulie hadn't stopped me when I went back to the house for the pistol. I shouldn't have listened to her, I should have done it right away." Her eyes saddened and tears misted them. "You don't know what it's like to know that your husband's going to another woman. . . . You don't know!"

Rebel's voice was breathless and unsure. "If you felt that way, then why did you treat him like you did? Why didn't you let him be a man? If you had given him the love he wanted, he'd never have needed me."

"You're trying to say it's my fault?"

"Well, isn't it?"

"I never denied him . . . not once in all the years of our marriage did I deny him."

"No, you didn't deny him. You did something worse, didn't you—you told yourself that what he was doing was sinful and evil, and whenever he touched you, instead of accepting him, you made him feel like an intruder and gave nothing to him in return."

"You think you know everything, don't you? Well, you don't, because I tried. Last night when he came home, I knew it didn't matter anymore. I'd already committed one sin by trying to kill you, so what difference did it make if I committed another? I waited for him last night. I gave myself to him. I did what he'd been wanting me to do, I played the harlot!" Her eyes were wild, intense. "He didn't want me, Rebel, do you hear that? He couldn't even stay hard for me!" Her voice broke on a sob. "You say I gave him nothing? I gave my soul to Satan for him, and he didn't want me because of you!"

Suddenly the sound of heavy feet could be heard on the stairs, then coming down the hall, and someone tried to open the door.

"Rebel, what's going on in there?" yelled Brandon, and Miriam answered as she reached into her reticule, her back to the open French windows.

"Rebel's all right," she yelled, her voice unnaturally shrill. "We're only talking!"

"Miriam!" It was Matthew. "Miriam, let us in," he called as Brandon pushed against the door, but she only laughed.

"Why? So you can spoil it like you did before? You weren't supposed to make her better, you were supposed to let her die!"

Rebel stared, transfixed, tears in her eyes, as Miriam drew a pistol from her reticule and cocked it, pointing it directly at her.

Brandon's shoulder was against the door as he turned to Matt. "She may not have locked my door," he whispered, and both men lunged for the other door as Miriam shouted hysterically.

"This time she will die!" she yelled viciously. "I won't let her have you, Matthew . . . I won't—"

Suddenly she drew a quick breath as the door to her right flew open and Brandon and Matt burst in from the governor's room. She had forgotten about the adjoining door.

Rebel took those few seconds when Miriam was off guard to stand, and started toward them, her legs trembling, as Miriam waved the heavy pistol back and forth in front of her. Miriam was crying freely now, tears streaming down her face.

"Stop!" she cried. "All of you stop!"

"Miriam, you're sick. Let me take you home," coaxed Matt, and held his hand out toward her, but she shook her head, shrinking away from him.

"No! You don't want me, you want her. I know what's been going on between you! I know why you took her with you when they had that fire! I heard about the long walks you took!"

Brandon's eyes narrowed as he glanced quickly at Rebel, then to the man beside him. "What's she talking about?"

Miriam laughed. "Tell him, Matthew," she said spitefully. "Tell him how you made love to his wife beneath the nutmeg trees, and tell him you had adjoining rooms, only yours was empty all night, tell him, love!"

Matt's face was livid, and Rebel paled as Brandon stared at them, anger surging through his veins.

"You wonder how I know, don't you?" Miriam rattled on, seeing the shocked looks on their faces. "That's something you'll never find out, ever! I have my friends too. But it won't do you any good, Matthew, you can want her all you want, but you'll never have her. The poison didn't work, but this will," and she waved the pistol toward Rebel, and Matt saw her finger squeezing the trigger.

"No, Miriam!" he shouted, and jumped between her and Rebel as the pistol discharged. Rebel screamed in horror as he stopped in midair, gasped loudly, then slumped awkwardly to the floor.

Brandon was rooted to the spot as he watched Rebel fall to the floor beside Matt, her eyes wide with horror, tears streaming down her cheeks, her hands touching his face tenderly as he looked up into her violet eyes.

"I . . . I love you . . . Rebel . . ." he gasped, the words gurgling from his throat; then his body went limp.

Rebel stared helplessly at his lifeless form, her tears falling onto his cheek, and she shook her head in disbelief. "You killed him," she mumbled beneath her breath, touching his cheek, wiping away where her tears had dropped. "My God, you killed him!" she wailed, and her head sank onto his chest. "Oh, Matt, Matt, you can't die," she begged softly through tears. "I need you! Please, Matt, don't die!" but his body lay still beneath her head.

"I . . . I didn't mean to . . ." stuttered Miriam, her eyes wide with terror, the empty pistol still pointing at Rebel. "I wanted you dead, not Matthew!" She shook her head. "I didn't want it to be him!" She screamed agonizingly, her eyes wild and glazed. "Oh, God, it wasn't supposed to be Matthew. It wasn't, it wasn't!" Then suddenly she began to laugh, a high maniacal laugh that forced Rebel's head from Matt's chest to stare at her.

Brandon took a step toward Miriam.

"Stop!" she shrieked. "Don't touch me!" Her eyes darted quickly about the room as Brandon stood motionless. The woman was insane. Her eyes stopped on Rebel, who was still

365

on the floor beside Matt. "Maybe it's better this way," Miriam cried hysterically. "This way you'll never have him, he's still mine, he'll always be mine. He sold his soul to the devil when he took you to his bed, and I sold my soul to the devil to keep him! To keep him, do you understand? And I shall keep him. He's mine now for all eternity. We'll be in hell together . . . I've won after all," and before Brandon could reach out and grab her, she turned, with the pistol still in her hand, and ran blindly out the French doors onto the balcony, hitting the wrought-iron railing, spilling over it head-first, her scream echoing into the room as she crashed to the lawn below, her body sprawling in a broken heap.

Neither Rebel nor Brandon moved for long moments, their ears still vibrating from the shrill cry as she fell; then slowly Brandon walked to the balcony and looked down, shuddering at the sight.

He straightened angrily, trying to compose himself, pulling at the sleeves of his green brocade frock coat. He stared at his wife, still prostrate beside the body of the man he'd thought was his friend. Slowly he walked toward her as he heard activity out in the hallway, and he stood looking down into her tear-streaked face.

"That's two I owe you for," he said savagely as his eyes met hers. "Cole and Matt! And I'll get even, Rebel, you can bet on that. Somehow, some way, I'll make you pay," and he walked toward the door to let the servants in while he tried to think of an explanation.

18

Paris, October 1, 1795

It was strange to see people walking in the streets again without fear. Paris was beginning to get back to some normalcy, and Beau shuddered as he thought of the first time they'd set foot in the city. The revolution was at its peak, and the shrieks of the mob as the guillotine descended were enough to turn a man's stomach, yet the people kept right on cheering up until the day their own leaders were guillotined, including Robespierre himself. Perhaps the convention that was meeting now would mean a new France free of the dreaded bloodshed and tyranny that had enveloped it the past few years.

Beau straightened the tails of his burgundy frock coat, then glanced away from the window that overlooked the street into the mirror that hung above the dresser and made sure his cravat was in place before he turned toward Heath.

"Aren't you ready yet?" he asked as Heath sat on the bed pulling on his shiny boots.

"Does it look like it?"

"I never saw anyone who took so long to dress. If you were a woman I could understand it."

Heath stood up, straightening his white breeches, flouncing the ruffles that cascaded down the front of his shirt. He grabbed his cravat from the bed and fastened it about his throat, putting the sapphire stickpin in the center, then slipped into his blue velvet frock coat.

"You're sure we won't be mistaken for the enemy?" he asked Beau as he made sure the coat fit well. "I know the guillotine has been quiet lately, but it doesn't take much to start it up again."

"Thank God it's over," remarked Beau. "Maybe now some sense will come out of all this mess."

"Those people amaze me," said Heath as he made a last-minute check of his appearance in the mirror behind Beau. "A few years ago anyone even remotely related to nobility hid the fact so astutely that no one could wring the truth from them. Now they're having these *bals à victime*, which is only another way of admitting they're related to the nobility. And the extravagance is shocking. Two years ago we'd have been guillotined for wearing these clothes, now we probably won't be fashionable enough."

Beau took a good look at Heath's blue velvet coat with its mother-of-pearl buttons on the wide cuffs and the satin braiding edging them, then reached over and grabbed the plumed hats that were the trademark of Captain Thunder and his first mate. The blue ostrich feather rippled tremulously as he tossed Heath's hat to him. He grinned at the golden earring Heath always wore in his right ear.

"Don't worry, my bucko," he said, smoothing the huge red ostrich feather in his own hat. "One look at your splendid clothes and the ladies will swoon. After you," and he bowed, motioning toward the door.

They had arrived in Paris that morning, having docked in

Le Havre three days before, and had been invited immediately to the home of Count Paul DeBarras, president of the National Convention. Beau knew the reason. Although the dinner they were to attend was supposedly a social affair, it was also a chance for one of France's most successful privateers, Captain Thunder, to account to the men who helped finance his latest voyages.

"And what do we have to tell him?" complained Heath in the carriage on the way to the count's home.

"I think we've had a rather successful trip. The loot was small this time, but thwarting an attack on Tobago should be worth something."

"How's your shoulder?"

Beau hefted his left arm, circling it in the air, then shrugged. "Fit as a fiddle again."

"How you managed to swim all the way to the longboat is beyond me. I swear you lead a charmed life."

Beau leaned back and closed his eyes, remembering his short sojourn on St. Vincent. Their contact from Grenada had given them the information he'd needed and all was going so well until one of the men had been spotted by an old shipmate who knew he wasn't supposed to be there. It had been one of those unfortunate coincidences, but had meant the death of two good French agents, and he'd come close to losing his own life. One thing he had to say about Brandon Avery, he left little to chance, and Beau could hardly wait to tell the count the new plans the governor of Grenada was making.

The count lived in the better section of Paris, and the stone house looked warm and inviting in the cool October evening as Beau and Heath were ushered inside and relieved of their hats and cloaks.

"*Mon capitaine,*" said the count as he greeted them a few minutes later in the main salon, "we have been waiting patiently. You're late." Beau made their apologies.

"Your streets are not as bare as they were a few months back, *m'sieurs,*" he said in French as he shook hands around. "I believe the people of Paris are finally learning what freedom is really all about."

The count smiled. "To be sure." They greeted some old acquaintances; then the count introduced them to a few men that were new to them, one in particular, a rather short man who studied Beau intently.

"May I present Brigadier General Napoleon Bonaparte, Capitaine. I have just given General Bonaparte the defense of

368

the city, and of the convention," he explained. "He is second in command of the Interior Forces. Napoleon, I can only introduce you to the gentlemen as I know them, Capitaine Beau Thunder, and his first mate, M'sieur Heath."

"You have no other names?" asked the general, displeased.

Beau's eyes darkened. "They're not needed."

The general's face was rather soft and boyish, although he had to be in his middle or late twenties, but his eyes were hard as steel. "I dislike men who are evasive," he retorted smoothly, but he was assured by all those present that the two men were quite trustworthy.

"In fact, I believe you may as well report now," suggested the count, to put his new general at ease, and Beau bowed congenially.

"If you wish." He accepted a glass of wine from his host and turned to the men, giving an account of the ships plundered, prisoners ransomed, and loot divided among his men. "Then, in the month of June," he went on, "the governor of Grenada in the West Indies launched an invasion of the island of Tobago. Fortunately, because of our agents on Grenada we were able to thwart the attack before a foothold was secured; however, lives were lost and the residents of Tobago are uneasy." He straightened, brushing a speck of lint from his sleeve, his handsome, swarthy face unsmiling. "I happen to know, m'sieurs, that the Duke of Bourland is planning, not only another attack on Tobago, which this time I fear would be successful, but he's also prepared to continue from Tobago, taking all the islands of the Caribbean before he's through."

"Mon Dieu!" The count looked abashed. "It is impossible," he cried. "The man is a dreamer."

"No!" General Bonaparte addressed the count emphatically. "Not a dreamer. A strategist. It could be done, if done right," He addressed Beau. "How did he fail in his attempt on Tobago?"

"He underestimated the ships we had in the area. He thought they were still at Martinique, where they would have been if it hadn't been for us."

"That was his only mistake?"

"No." Beau eyed the general knowingly. "I think he's also learned the advantage of hill fighting."

The general nodded. "He will no doubt learn by his mistakes, as do most men." His eyes flickered over Beau, then moved to Heath. Brothers? Perhaps. Americans, he was sure, even though their French was flawless. "Do you have any suggestions on how to stop him?" he asked Beau, but Beau shook his head as he sipped his wine.

"That I'll leave to you gentlemen," he said, and his eyes moved to the count, who shrugged.

"I see only one recourse," he said. "We will eliminate the governor," but Napoleon put his hand on the count's arm.

"*Non*. That is too obviously not what to do." He straightened, trying to look taller, but it helped little. "If you kill the governor, another will only take his place. It seems England wants the Carribean. The obvious thing to do is to be in a position to control the gentleman."

The count's eyes lit up. "Aha! Why did I not think of that?"

Napoleon smiled. "Because you are not a soldier, Paul."

"And how do you intend to accomplish this amazing feat?" asked Beau, and the general smiled.

"Tell me, the governor's married?" he asked. Heath's mouth tightened as he watched the expression on Beau's face, but it was unreadable.

"He's married," answered Beau.

"Happily?"

"I'm afraid I'm not that close to the gentleman, General," he answered, and Napoleon smiled again.

"What I meant, Capitaine, was if you had heard whether the gentleman's marriage was one arranged by his family or a marriage of his own choosing," but it was the count who answered.

"If I remember right, Napoleon, when the *capitaine* first became interested in the duke's little adventure in the West Indies, my London agents brought him a great deal of information concerning the gentleman, and none of it mentioned a marriage, but it was learned later that his bride-to-be accompanied him and they were married on the high seas on the way to Grenada, the duke having been quite smitten with the young lady while in London."

"You keep referring to him as the duke," said the young general. "Exactly who is the governor of Grenada?"

The count smiled. "At one time he was an aide to the British minister to France. When war was inevitable, he resigned and bought a commission in the army. At the death of his uncle, who was childless, he inherited the dukedom and is now officially the duke of Bourland. His christian name is Brandon Avery."

"And his wife?"

"She's the daughter of the Earl of Locksley. A title the earl put claim to when he returned to England from America a short while before the young lady's marriage."

Napoleon was pleased. "Then from all accounts, the governor is no doubt in love with his wife. Good! Many men have been manipulated through the women in their lives," he said, and he held his glass out for the count to refill. "With the governor's wife in our hands, we could make sure the gentleman forgot all about his conquest of the West Indies." He watched the count fill his glass, then addressed the group. "What say you, gentlemen?"

Beau straightened, his eyes dark, intense. "I dislike using women as military ploys, General," he said. "It seems a dirty way of fighting."

"There's an old saying, all's fair in love and war, Capitaine. This is war."

"I realize that, but what you suggest—"

Napoleon's sharp eyes stopped him. "I suggest we kidnap the governor's wife and hold her here in France. I'm sure the governor would then find it convenient to keep his feet at home."

The count's eyebrows raised. "You think it will work?" he asked.

"Many women have changed the destinies of empires in the past," answered Napoleon. "I say it's worth a try."

Beau studied the rest of the men, who were mumbling among themselves. "And the rest of you?" he asked.

The answers were in agreement with the general, and he knew the die had been cast. "Then I'll concede to the general," he agreed, hardly daring to disagree. "Only, may I ask where the lady will be incarcerated during her stay in France?"

"Why not here?" suggested the count. "My home is large enough, and she might be interesting company."

Beau knew the count's reputation with women. He was known to be a lecher, and his escapades were scandalous. The thought of Rebel staying here was out of the question. "I think, Count, since it's obvious the governor will make some attempt to free the lady, you'd be wise to keep her at a less conspicuous place," he suggested, and Napoleon conceded this time.

"A wise presumption, Capitaine." He addressed the count. "It would be best, Paul, if she were taken to a quiet place in the country somewhere where she could be well guarded," and the count reluctantly agreed. "Now," continued Napoleon, "all we have to do is kidnap the lady." His eyes settled on Beau. "I presume, Capitaine Thunder, since you seem to know Grenada, that you and your men would be the logical persons to entrust with the mission." He turned to the count. "Does that meet with your approval, Paul?"

The count sputtered hesitantly at the general's suggestion. "You think they could accomplish it alone?"

"You did say Capitaine Thunder was an unusual man, Paul," the general said as he gazed once more at Beau, then let his eyes roam to Heath, who seemed to be a silent partner of the Capitaine's. He noted the earring in Heath's ear and the solidly handsome looks of the quiet young man. His black curly hair and suntan made him look much like a Spaniard, and although he said little, his sharp eyes never missed a detail as they looked from one man to the other, then back to the general. "But so that there will be little chance of failure, I suggest Capitaine Thunder's ship be escorted to Grenada by two frigates. In case of trouble, they would be able to cover the shore party successfully." He downed the wine in his glass. "Does that meet with your approval, Capitaine?"

Beau studied the general. "Then you've selected me to do the dirty work."

"Since you're more familiar with the Indies, and undoubtedly know the agents you'd be working with, it seems the best idea."

"And the pay?" asked Beau.

"It will be more than sufficient," answered the count. "You'll do it?" he asked.

"I dislike kidnapping women, Paul," he stated harshly, "but if you're sure the price is right . . . then, yes." He glanced quickly at Heath. "Heath and I will deliver the Duchess of Bourland to you," and Napoleon smiled as the count relaxed more comfortably among his friends and cohorts, opening the doors to escort them to dinner.

Heath sidled close to Beau as they watched the general and the count walking ahead of them to the dining room. "The little general thinks he's somebody special, doesn't he?" announced Heath, and Beau watched closely as the general was greeted in the hallway by a beautiful dark-eyed woman with shining black hair. She was an exotic beauty in a somewhat transparent mauve dress with deep red ribbons crisscrossing the bodice.

"I was surprised to see him here," said Beau. "When we arrived in Le Havre, I learned that some three weeks ago his name was crossed off the French military list. I guess the count's influence has really increased lately, and if you'll notice who's latched onto the general and note the gleam in Paul's eyes at the successful way Josephine's manipulating him, I think you can understand that Paul probably has him in his debt, and he's going to make sure he keeps him that way."

"He'd let that little pipsqueak have Josephine? His own mistress?"

"Shhh," cautioned Beau, "as the general himself said, many men have been manipulated by the women in their lives, and the general's eyes give away his feelings where the lady's concerned." Beau smiled sardonically as he watched Josephine de Beauharnaise, whom they had met before at the home of Paul DeBarras and knew to be his mistress, flirting with the count's new protector. "But don't worry, Heath, the count's made sure you have a lady for the evening." Heath's face lit up as he caught the eye of a young lady at the door to the dining salon, recognizing the woman who'd entertained him the last time they were in Paris.

After a superb meal in the company of a bevy of beautiful women, the men retired to the library, where plans were made for the coming venture, then all except Beau and Heath joined the ladies once more in the game room. Beau made excuses to the count, and rather than stay on his own, Heath followed Beau out the door, complaining to him about leaving so early.

"Should I hail a carriage?" asked Heath. "It's gotten pretty windy," but Beau shook his head.

"Let's walk."

Heath jammed his fancy hat tighter on his head as he fell in stride beside Beau. "What the hell's eating you, friend?" he asked as they strolled off down the darkened street. "Clotilde looked daggers at me when she saw we were leaving."

"You could have stayed."

"Not without you."

"I don't like it, Heath," he said slowly as he kicked a stone aside with his foot. "The whole plan sounds too simple. Besides, I don't like putting Rebel in danger."

Heath glanced quickly at Beau and sighed. How obvious could a man be? He denied vehemently having any love for Rebel, yet the sound of her name brought fire to his eyes, and although it had probably been months since Beau had taken a woman, Heath could be sure it'd be months longer unless the captain happened to run across a woman who had blond hair and reminded him of his lost love. He could deny it all he wanted, but the facts remained.

"I thought you'd be glad to see her again," said Heath, watching him out of the corner of his eye.

"It's not that. It's . . ."

"You think she'll be in danger? She'll be with us."

"Only until we return to France." He stopped, and Heath stopped beside him. "Let's face it, Heath," he said, "Paul De-Barras will take one look at your gorgeous sister and forget all about sending her into the country. Especially now, with Josephine out of his bed."

"Maybe by the time we get back, Josephine'll be back in his bed. Besides, Rebel wouldn't sleep with the count."

"You forget, Heath, women don't always have a choice, and another thing. I don't trust that little Corsican. Paul's giving him too much say, and he's power-hungry."

"Then why did you say we'd do it?"

"If we didn't, they'd only get someone else. We'll go get Reb because with DeBarras and his new general breathing down our necks, we have no choice, but dammit, I'm not turning her over to anyone until I'm sure of the whole deal."

"And don't forget to warn the crew of the *Eagle*," said Heath. "I'd hate for one of them to make a slip. If Paul or any of his men discover we not only know the governor's wife, but that she's my sister, I don't think they'd let us go after her, and I'd hate to think of what might happen to Reb if they left the job to someone else."

They left Paris that evening, arriving at Le Havre before any of DeBarras' men could contact any of the crew. Most of the men had been with the *Golden Eagle* for as long as she'd sailed under Beau's colors, so it was an easy matter to swear them to secrecy. As far as they were concerned, their captain's word was law, and although there were times when his decisions puzzled them, he'd never failed them, so during the next few days, while preparations were being made and supplies hauled aboard, the crew of the *Golden Eagle* went about their business as usual, as if this was just another assignment, while back in Paris the count's little general, as Beau liked to refer to him, proved his worth by quelling a near-riot of royalists.

Two days later, on October 7, the *Golden Eagle*, with two French frigates as an escort, sailed out of the harbor at Le Havre into the channel, leaving the wintry French coast behind. Beau stood on the bridge fuming as they made for the open sea. At the last minute, the count, with a prod from his new general, insisted on installing a contingent of soldiers aboard the *Golden Eagle*, in case of trouble.

"From whom?" asked Beau as he and Heath stood on the forward deck watching the soldiers milling about the ship. "I don't think that little Corsican trusts me."

"I heard tell he trusts few Americans."

"I don't like the whole rotten mess, Heath," he complained. "When I told Paul my ship was at his disposal for a price, that didn't mean it belonged to him."

Heath knew how Beau felt, and he didn't like it either. Heretofore they'd always been independent, but with the Frenchies aboard, Beau's command was weakened, and the rest of the trip saw both men in foul moods, especially with the military, who were under the command of an arrogant captain named Gautier.

The crossing was uneventful and tedious, and three days before Christmas, close to midnight, the *Golden Eagle* with the two frigates at its side dropped anchor off the northern coast of Grenada and waited for the signal from shore, then sent a longboat in with a message arranging for a meeting the next evening. When the longboat returned, the three ships disappeared again into the night, reappearing on the southeastern coast at ten on the evening of December 23, a balmy moonless night. The *Golden Eagle* left its escort ships drifting out at sea while it slipped into a quiet cove on the southern tip of the island, furled its sails, and dropped anchor.

Beau and Heath stood on deck straining their eyes and ears in the darkness as the signalman stood next to Beau, a smuggler's lantern in his hand, with the beam pointed toward shore. He signaled, then waited, then signaled again, but nothing.

"What time is it?" asked Heath, whispering in the still, dark night, and Beau checked his pocket watch in the light from the lantern.

"Two minutes to ten."

The lantern signaled again.

"There!" cried Heath softly, and an answering signal flashed intermittently from the dense foliage above the beach, and Beau called for the longboat.

He and Heath took eight men, leaving the soldiers on board, much to the consternation of Captain Gautier. The captain kept insisting that General Bonaparte gave him orders to accompany them ashore, but Beau wouldn't listen and threatened to have his men shoot the first soldier who tried to leave the ship; then he'd picked his men carefully, knowing how dangerous the mission was. As the longboat moved silently toward the shore, his hands were sweaty on the oars and his stomach had tightened into one huge knot at the prospect of seeing Rebel again.

It had been almost two years since he'd made love to her in the cabin of the *Golden Eagle* the night before her marriage to Brandon, and the memory of that night still haunted him. He'd tried so many times to forget her, but nothing could shake her from his thoughts, not even the arms of other women. He wondered if she'd changed. Were her eyes still fiery, yet warm with passion? Was her hair still like a cloud of golden silk, and was her mouth still provocatively exciting? Was she still so unpretentious and vivaciously alive, or had Brandon managed to destroy her? God forbid!

He was jolted back to reality when the longboat hit the beach. As they climbed out, pulling it ashore, Beau's head jerked upward when a man moved stealthily from the shadows and confronted them.

"Capitaine?" he said in French, his voice hushed. "Here," and Beau stepped forward, shaking the hand that was proffered him. "My name is Henri, *mon capitaine*," he introduced himself. "I was surprised at your instructions. This is the first time you have set foot ashore."

"Have my orders been carried out?" asked Beau, and Henri nodded.

"Oui. My brother, Armand, is in St. George at this very moment, and at exactly eleven-thirty he will set fire to the office of the governor. A strange request, but it will be carried out."

Beau nodded. "Good." He turned to Heath. "This is my first mate, Heath." The men shook hands as Beau continued. "I've brought eight men with me. How long will it take us to get to the governor's house?"

"Almost two hours. The path is good, but on foot . . . it will slow you down." He studied Beau in the darkness. "You did not say in the message what your mission is, Capitaine."

"We're here to kidnap the governor's wife," he said, and he heard Henri's quick intake of breath. "Is anything wrong, *m'sieur?*" asked Beau, and Henri shook his head.

"Non, only I'm afraid the governor won't take what you do lightly, *m'sieurs.* He is quite fanatical when it comes to the duchess. Of course, I can't blame him, seeing as what's happened, but—"

Beau frowned. "Something's happened to her?"

Henri shook his head as they turned from the beach and began moving inland. *"Non,* not to her exactly, but . . ." He led the way up a small incline, then into the underbrush onto a well-worn path, with all the men following, and both Beau and Heath listened intently as he talked. "What happened was tragic, really," he said as he pulled branches aside while they walked. "We had a doctor on the island named Wilder. Dr. Matthew Wilder. A good doctor, young, friendly. One day his wife shot him, then jumped from the balcony of the governor's house, killing herself. The governor hushed it up, but he hasn't been the same since. Watches his wife like a hawk now."

"What does his wife have to do with it?" asked Heath, and the man acted as if the answer should have been obvious.

"Why, the doctor was her lover, naturally," said Henri, and Beau stopped dead in his tracks. One of the men almost bumped into him before he moved again, and he felt a sick feeling in the pit of his stomach as Heath grabbed his arm, pulling him along.

"How do you know this?" Heath asked cautiously, still holding Beau's arm, knowing he was ready to challenge the man, and Henri answered casually, unaware of Beau's anger.

"I saw with my own eyes, *m'sieurs*. Don't get me wrong, I like the duchess, she's one hell of a woman," he said, "and most of the people on the island believed the governor's trumped-up story about the doctor's wife going berserk, but I still say otherwise. After all, I know what I saw."

"And that was?" asked Heath."

"We had a fire at our place up north, slaves' quarters burned down, and Dr. Wilder came up to give us a hand. He brought the duchess with him. Seems she did a good job nursing the soldiers after the attempt on Tobago, so he figured she'd be helpful, and she was a big help, but while they were there, my wife, at the doctor's request, mind you, gave them the first rooms at the top of the stairs. Adjoining rooms. During the night one of the patients needed the doctor, but when I knocked on his door, I got no answer. I was rather worried, and fortunately, or unfortunately for the doctor, we happen to have some secret passages in the old house, one going to his room. You can imagine what I thought when I entered and found his bed empty. The door was bolted from the inside, and I figured there was only one place he could have gone. When I opened the door to the adjoining room, there they were. I could see them in the moonlight curled up together sound asleep." He shrugged as he walked, picking his way along the darkened path. "How long it had been going on, I don't know, but I do know they were in the bed together that evening, and I also know that a woman doesn't shoot her husband without a reason. Since then, the governor hardly lets the duchess out of his sight. He even had a soldier whipped last month because he dared talk to her when she went into St. George one afternoon with her little boy. From what I hear, the soldier was just trying to be friendly. Had a little boy of his own back home and meant no harm."

Beau had listened to the story, his jaw tightening angrily, his mouth dry. "She has a son?" he asked, trying not to let his feelings creep into his voice, and Henri nodded.

"Cute little fella. She takes him everywhere she goes."

A son! He'd forgotten. Roth had mentioned that Rebel was pregnant, but he'd forgotten all about it. Maybe because the thought of Rebel having Brandon's child sickened him, but then, what could he expect? He'd pushed her into Brandon's arms. She'd loved him, and he'd turned her away. How much had she changed? He trembled inside as they made their way along the trail.

It wasn't quite two hours later when they reached the top of the ridge and, concealed by the trees, looked down toward the harbor of St. George far below. Flames still were lighting up the sky as they made their way down the hill at the back of the house and crept along the hedging that bordered the pasture.

Henri stayed back on the hill where he couldn't be recognized while Beau and Heath led the men in, working their way past the stables and through the door of the walled garden, hiding among the flowering shrubs and bushes. Henri said the only ones they'd probably confront would be the housekeeper, the butler, the duchess's private maid, Cristabel, and the baby's nurse Hizzie.

"The rest of the servants sleep in the slave quarters over the stables," he'd said, and Beau remembered his instructions as he crept toward the French doors. The doors were easily opened with the knife he carried in the sheath on his belt, and he put it back, then hefted the pistol from its resting place at his waist and nodded for the men to follow as he cocked it, swung the doors open, and stepped inside. There were lights in the house, but most of them came from the kitchen, and he sent part of the men in that direction while he, Heath, and the two crew members remaining moved cautiously up the stairs.

"I just hope Brandon stayed in St. George," Heath whispered softly to Beau as they reached the top of the stairs. "The count might not like it if we had to kill him." Beau put a finger to his mouth, motioning for Heath to be quiet as the door on their right, in one of the front bedrooms, opened partway and they could hear voices.

"I still think you should get back to bed, ma'am," said Cristabel as she stood inside the room with her hand on the doorknob. "They ain't nothin' you can do, and who knows how soon the governor'll be back?"

The last words were Beau's cue. He pressed against the wall, and the others followed as he tiptoed to the open door; then, when Cristabel stepped out, his hand went over her mouth and he pushed her back inside, the others following closely behind.

Beau stopped inside the room, one hand over the black girl's mouth, with the back of her head pressed against his chest, the cocked pistol in his other hand, and he stared silently at the woman standing across the room from them, her beautiful violet eyes widened in shock.

The candlelight from the lamp on the vanity cast a warm, rich glow on her creamy skin, and her hair, loose, falling past her shoulders, was a golden mantle, soft and luxurious. She wore a pale blue wrapper with lace inserts, and a nightgown to match, the lustrous silkiness clinging to her body showing every smooth, seductive curve.

Her full lips parted to scream, then suddenly froze open, and a look of profound joy filled her eyes. "Oh, my God!" she gasped, trembling. "Beau! Heath!" A sob broke from her, and she ran toward them as Heath stepped past Beau and held out his arms, wrapping his sister in them, holding her close as he stroked her hair and hugged her to him.

Beau's hand eased on Cristabel's mouth, but he didn't take it away, and he held the pistol where she could easily see it. "Don't make a sound," he warned softly.

Rebel clung to Heath desperately, and he had to force her to let go as he pushed her back so he could get a good look at her. Tears rolled freely down her cheeks, and she reached up, touching the side of his face with her hand; then her eyes moved to Beau, and a shock went through her, weakening her knees as their eyes met.

They stared at each other, neither saying a word for long moments, and Beau wanted to die inside. She was lovely, so lovely, and he felt himself tremble.

"Tell the girl not to cry out," he finally said gruffly as he indicated Cristabel, and Rebel did as he asked, her voice shaking tremulously, and Beau took his hand from Cristabel's mouth, releasing her. She moved over beside Rebel, hunching up close to her for security. Beau walked farther into the

379

room, moving to the French doors, and peeked from behind the curtains out onto the balcony, where he could see to the harbor, where the fire was still raging.

Rebel grabbed Heath's arm, and her eyes danced behind the tears. "I don't understand," she whispered softly and his hands covered hers as he squeezed tightly. "Whatever possessed you . . .?"

"We've come for you, Reb," he said softly. "There isn't time to explain now." He touched her wrapper. "Do you have a dress you can slip into?" She stared at him dumbfounded. "A dress?"

Beau turned toward her, his face hard, green eyes darkening. "We don't have time to argue, Reb," he stated flatly. "Either you come with us peacefully or we'll have to carry you."

"You . . . what is this?"

"We have orders from the French, Reb," Heath tried to explain hurriedly. "If you don't come with us, they'll only send someone else."

"You mean you're kidnapping me?" and Heath's face reddened. She looked quickly at Beau, fire in her violet eyes, her mouth quivering. "Of all the nerve! Just who do you think you are—?"

Her words were cut short as Beau walked to her armoire and threw open the door, pulling out one of her dresses, and threw it at her. "Put this on and hurry it up," he said anxiously, and she started to protest. "I said put it on!" and angry tears bounced into her eyes.

"Well, you don't have to yell!" She moved to the dresser and opened one of the drawers, pulling out her underthings. "Where'll I change?" she asked as she stared at him defiantly.

"Dammit, Heath, she won't have time to change. They could be back any minute." Beau reached down in the bottom of the armoire, pulling out a quilted portmanteau, turning to Cristabel. "Grab some of your mistress's clothes and throw them in this," he said, tossing it to the girl, and he took Rebel's black cloak off the hook on the armoire door. "Wrap this around you for now," he said softly, "and let's get out of here." He whirled the cape around Rebel, resting it on her shoulders, and began tying it at the neck, pulling the hood up over her hair.

"But I can't go without the baby!"

"The baby?"

"Yes!" Her eyes glistened brightly beneath the tears. "Oh, God, Beau, I have to take the baby," she pleaded. "I can't leave him here, please?"

Beau glanced at Heath, then back to Rebel. "Where is he?"

"Across the hall."

He motioned to Heath, who slipped out the door, quietly followed by one of the men; then he told the other privateer to take the portmanteau from the black girl and tie her up. Moments later, when Beau ushered Rebel into the hallway with the other privateer close on his heels, leaving Cristabel tied up to the bedpost with the curtain sash around her and one of Rebel's scarves gagging her mouth, they ran into Heath and Hizzie, followed by the other crew member carrying a bunch of baby clothes wrapped in a sheet. Hizzie had a big bundle in her arms, cuddling it close, and was determined not to let go.

"She insists on coming with us," explained Heath, and Beau's eyes flashed.

"All right, but let's get out of here. We've got a two-hour trek through the woods yet and I don't want anyone catching up to us."

They made their way down the stairs and into the drawing room, where the rest of the men were waiting after having tied the butler, housekeeper, and one of the maids to chairs in the kitchen. They all quietly slipped out of the French doors into the garden and moved along the shadowed hedge up the back hill.

It was pitch dark, and Rebel cursed as she stumbled, almost breaking the heel on her slipper, pulling the cloak tighter about her. "I still don't know why you're doing this!" she stated angrily as she marched along behind Beau, but he didn't answer, only hurried her on.

Henri met them at the top of the hill, and Rebel was astounded. "So you're the spy Brandon's been unable to catch," she said as he grinned at her in the darkness. "You're an elusive man, Henri."

"Not elusive, Duchess, careful," he said, then addressed Beau. "Let's get out of here as soon as possible, *mon capitaine*." His eyes darted back toward the house. "Once the alarm is given, this place will be swarming with soldiers." And he started across the top of the ridge, with the others close behind.

The trail was pitch dark, and Rebel could barely see Beau ahead of her as she stumbled along in her flimsy slippers. Heath, following behind her, was having a time with Hizzie. The poor girl was near hysteria. She'd been awakened out of a sound sleep and dragged along, knowing little of what was happening and wondering why her mistress talked to these men as if she knew them, and wondering where they were going. She half-cried and half-mumbled most of the way, glancing back occasionally with dread at the rest of the fearsome crew that followed.

The baby woke up some half-hour along the trail, having sensed Hizzie's fright, and when she tried to quiet him, he only fussed all the more.

"Here, give him to me," said Heath as Hizzie bounced him around in her arms, trying to still his fears. She looked at Heath sharply, holding the baby all the tighter.

"No sirree, you ain't gettin' this little darlin'!" she cried. "Ain't nobody gonna hurt this baby."

"I'm not going to hurt him. I only want to hold him."

"I can hold him . . . shush, Cole, honey . . . shush," she cooed softly, kissing the baby's cheek. "I ain't gonna let the nasty man take you."

"For heaven's sake, Rebel," Heath called to his sister in exasperation, "will you please tell her to let me carry the baby so we can make better time? His yowling can be heard a mile off, and besides, he's too heavy for her to carry so far." Rebel and Beau stopped long enough for her to persuade Hizzie that Heath wouldn't hurt the baby.

Hizzie could barely see Heath's vague outline as she reluctantly relinquished her hold, handing Cole to Heath.

Back at St. George, Brandon stood still, gazing into the flames, watching them lick up what was left of the side of the building, eating away at the wood. He knew there was no use trying to fight it anymore. He thanked God the building sat more or less by itself here on the waterfront, because if it hadn't the whole city could have gone up in flames, and he shuddered to think of what it would be to replace it. But the government building was set apart, the closest building to it being some two hundred feet away, and they'd been able, by being alert, to contain the flames.

"I still wish I knew how it started," he said to one of his cabinet members as they stood to one side, watching the flames devour the last of the building, and the man shrugged, unable to give him an answer, then walked off to see what else could be done.

Half the town was awake watching the building burn, and Brandon sighed as he walked over to the desk and filing cabinets someone had had the foresight to carry from the burning building.

General Bridlehurst coughed, the heavy smoke clogging his

lungs, wiping his forehead with a blackened handkerchief as he approached. "I don't know what to make of it, Governor," he said. "Neither guard saw or heard a thing. If somebody started it on purpose, they sure as hell knew what they were doing."

"What I can't figure out is why," said Brandon. "Even if those papers were destroyed, there's nothing really valuable here except land records and general business. The important papers are up at the house, locked in my desk in the library. This is just ordinary government business."

The general looked at him quizzically. "You don't suppose it'd be a diversion to get you away from the house, do you?"

Brandon stepped back from the fire and glanced up the hillside toward the house. The light was still on in Rebel's bedroom, and he knew she was still waiting up, but other than that it looked peaceful; then suddenly they heard hoofbeats, and glanced down the road as one of the general's men reined up.

"Beg pardon, General, sir, but there's something I think you should know," he said breathlessly. "I've been with that detail you sent to the other side of the island to set up watch since our attempt on Tobago, and one of the men said he was sure he saw three ships earlier this evening off Prickley Point. It was dark already and he wasn't positive, so he didn't say anything right away, but it kept bothering him until he finally said something to the sergeant, and he decided to take a look to make sure everything was all right. He had some of the fishermen take him out in one of their skiffs to reconnoiter, and he says there are two French frigates lying off the southern coast as if they're waiting for something, and the third ship isn't anywhere to be seen."

"Where is this man?" asked Brandon anxiously.

"He's back at camp, sir."

"Did he say exactly where those ships were?"

"No, sir," he answered, his eyes wandering toward what was left of the building as Brandon slipped on his coat, "but the natives said there are several lagoons inland, with paths leading from them. One path leads over the ridge a short way behind your house, sir, and all the paths lead to someplace here in St. George. The sergeant figured I should come let the general know. We didn't know about the fire."

"Maybe you're not far wrong, General," Brandon said anxiously as he mounted his horse. "Those papers in my desk have the names of enough British agents on them to make the risk worthwhile. Are you coming with me?" The general yelled for his horse and followed a short distance behind Brandon with a detail of soldiers at his heels.

Brandon could hear the troops behind him and he spurred his horse faster as he made his way up the winding dirt road ahead of them, but when he reached the gates, the guards were still on duty and everything looked fine. He reined up, hesitating briefly at the gate. "Everything all right?" he asked, and both soldiers saluted.

"All's quiet, sir," they echoed in unison. Brandon relaxed and rode up the drive more slowly, studying the house in the darkness. He dismounted cautiously and walked up the steps, not quite sure what he was expecting to find, then swung the door open and stepped into the entrance hall.

The house was quiet, but then, it should be. The slaves were either down fighting the fire or asleep in their quarters above the stables; the housekeeper and butler had probably gone to bed in their rooms off the kitchen since there was nothing they could do to help with the fire. Brandon went back to the door to meet the general and his men on the front steps.

"Everything seems all right, General," he said. "False alarm. We'll sleep on it, and maybe you could take a ride to the other side of the island in the morning to check things out. Maybe my ship the *Eagle Hunter* has been giving them some trouble and they're hoping to catch sight of her. One thing, if they were on the island, they're probably far gone by now. No use worrying tonight, but we'll have to strengthen security over there." The general agreed, bade him good night, and Brandon closed the door and headed wearily for the stairs.

What a waste, he thought, as he slipped off his coat and hung it over his arm. The spies the French had on the island had really bungled this time. Risking their necks to burn down a building that was really of no value to anyone except the people on the island. Thank God he kept the really important papers here at the house.

He stopped at the top of the stairs and stared toward the light filtering out from Rebel's room, where the door had been left ajar. Strange she hadn't come out when she heard him come in, but then, she probably fell asleep waiting. He'd just go in and blow out the light. No use wasting candles.

The coat on his arm slipped into his hand, and he bundled it together with his fingers as he pushed the door open; then he froze, his fingers tightening on the smoke-blackened frock coat. Dresser drawers were pulled half-open, their contents cattered about, Rebel was nowhere in sight, and Cristabel, er eyes round and tear-filled, was tied to the bedpost, a scarf n her mouth muffling her sobs.

Quickly he moved forward, dropping his coat on the floor, nd practically ripped the gag from her mouth, his face conorted with rage.

"Where is she?" he demanded breathlessly, and poor Cristabel's knees shook uncontrollably as he worked on the urtain sash to untie her.

"They took her away!" she gasped between sobs. "They ome and got her and took her away!"

"Who?"

"Some men. She knew who they was. She called them Heath and Beau." Brandon straightened, his face livid.

"How long ago?"

"Hours ago."

"Hours?"

"Well, it seem like hours." She rubbed her wrists, trying to ase the circulation into them as she pointed toward the vanty. "They said to make sure you saw that," she said. His eyes ested on a big white envelope on the vanity.

He stepped over and snatched it up, his fingers trembling with fury as he opened it, read it, then crumpled the paper in his fist and walked quickly to the balcony, leaning over the ail toward the front gates.

"Guard!" he called, his voice echoing across the front awn. "Guard!" and one of the guards stepped from behind he stone pillar that held up one side of the gate.

"Yes, your Excellency!"

"Grab my horse and go after the general. Tell him to get ack here, they've kidnapped my wife!" He turned back oward the shaking girl, his face seething with anger as the guard headed down the road to intercept the departing genral.

"They'll pay," he whispered softly to himself as his fist clenched on the crumpled piece of paper in his hand. "By God, I'll see they pay!"

Rebel's feet were sore, and the bottom of her blue silk nightgown was covered with dirt as she started down the loping hill toward the beach, her feet sliding in the sand.

"Here, let me help," said Beau, and grabbed her hand, trying to help her keep her balance, but she fell against him anyway in the darkness.

She could feel his hard muscular body against her, and a

385

sweet pain shot through her as his arm encircled her waist holding her against him. He helped her the rest of the way down the slope onto the sandy beach; then his arm eased from about her waist.

"Listen!" he said quickly, his breath close against her cheek, and she strained her ears, trying to hear above Heath's gentle cooing to the baby as he and Hizzie made their way down the slope behind them. "Listen, Heath," commanded Beau, and Heath put his hand on the baby's mouth lightly, trying to quiet him as the men behind him froze.

Faint shouts and the sounds of horses floated easily on the night air, and Beau tensed, his heart pounding. "Hurry, come on." He practically dragged Rebel through the sand as the rest of the men scrambled hurriedly down the slope and made a break for the longboat concealed in the bushes.

Henri helped the men pull the boat out, then turned to Beau, who'd picked Rebel up in his arms to deposit her in the boat.

"I will leave you, Capitaine," he said softly. "I do not dare get caught," he said, grabbing Beau's shoulder, squeezing it in a friendly gesture. "Good luck." Before Beau could answer, the man melted into the darkness.

Beau set Rebel in the boat, then turned, helping Heath with Hizzie and the baby as the shouts grew louder and the sounds of the horses came closer.

He took one last look as they shoved the boat from the beach into the water, and the men jumped in, dipping the oars in, beginning to row to where the ship was hidden in the darkness. As they cleared the shore and moved into the lagoon, Brandon rode onto the beach, his horse's hooves scattering sand, his eyes straining to see them, but it was pitch dark and he could see nothing. He could, however, hear the unmistakable dip of the oars in the water, and he cursed knowing the longboat was moving farther and farther away.

Beau held his breath while the oars dipped rhythmically and the ship emerged out of the dark night ahead of them. In minutes they pulled up alongside, scrambled aboard, and Beau quietly gave orders for full sail. As the last man climbed on deck and the longboat was secured, he could hear the men on shore shouting and cursing as they finally spotted the vague outline of the *Golden Eagle* in the middle of the cove, but there was nothing they could do.

The gentle night breeze filled the sails that were unfurling one by one, and the ship slowly began to move.

"Take the prisoners down to their cabin," Beau told Heath

nxiously as they stood on deck, feeling the ship begin to move beneath them, but the French captain had other ideas.

"Thank you, Captain Thunder, but that will not be necessary," he said boldly, confronting Beau. "I will take charge of the prisoners now that they are aboard. You did your task well." But Beau stood firm, paying the man no attention.

"I said take them below deck, Heath," he ordered again, but again the captain protested, stopping Heath with a hand on his arm.

"They are my prisoners, sir," he repeated. "I have orders from the general to take charge of the prisoner the moment she sets foot aboard, and that's what I intend to do."

"I beg to differ with you, Captain Gautier," Beau answered angrily, removing the captain's hand from Heath's arm. "They are my prisoners, and until we reach the shores of France, you'll do well to remember that."

"You forget, Captain Thunder," reminded the captain haughtily, "you are in the pay of the French people, and as a soldier I take command here," but Beau laughed viciously, his dislike of the French captain plain.

"Is that so?" he asked, his feet planted solidly on the deck, "Well, it might surprise you to know, sir, that Captain Thunder takes orders from no one," he said. "This is my ship, not the French Navy, and as such it's under my command. You're merely along for the ride. I'll tell you again, sir, the prisoners are mine and will be treated as I see fit. I heard you and your men discussing what should be done with the lady, and I prefer my orders to yours. She and the others with her shall have free access to the ship, to come and go as they please, once we've cleared these waters, and until then they will occupy the cabins I wish them to occupy. They'll not be locked in the hold, nor in the brig, which I know was your intention. Have I made myself clear?"

"Might I remind you, Captain, that my men and I are armed."

"And might I remind you, Captain," Beau said, "that my men outnumber yours, and they are also armed. The command of this ship is mine sir," he stated boldly, "until I deem to relinquish it, and that shall be never, sir. Now, if you will excuse my first mate," he continued, "he will carry out my orders and direct the prisoners to the cabins below deck. Heath?" and he nodded toward Heath, who had settled the baby back in Hizzie's arms when they'd reached the deck, and Heath gestured to them to follow him.

Rebel hesitated for a moment as Brandon's voice drifted

out to them across the water from the darkness of the cove.

"I'll get even with you, Beau Thunder!" he yelled viciously at the top of his lungs, his fists clenching angrily toward the vague outline of the disappearing ship. "I'll kill you if it's the last thing I do!" Rebel put her arm about Hizzie's shoulders and followed Heath below deck, her husband's outraged voice still ringing in her ears from across the dark lagoon.

19

The passageways were dark as they moved below deck, and Heath opened the door to the cabin, ushering the two women inside. He pulled the curtain across the window and took the cover from the lamp on the wall. All lights had been covered on board while the ship waited, to make sure no one spotted them.

Heath stood rooted for a moment as he stared at the squirming bundle in Hizzie's arms. It had been so dark on the trail that he hadn't been able to see the child clearly. All he had been able to distinguish had been a mouth, nose, eyes, and hair, but now the baby's features were clear and precise, and he studied him intently. He looked at Rebel quizzically as she turned toward him.

"Does Beau know?" he asked in mild shock.

"Know what?"

His eyes moved to the baby. "I'm not blind, Rebel."

"I don't know what you're talking about," she said, her violet eyes telling him to tread softly.

"All right. If that's the way you want it." He nodded toward her portmanteau and the bundle of baby clothes. "You can unpack what you need. You have this cabin and the one next door. You and your maid can make your own sleeping arrangements, but you'll stay below deck for the rest of tonight, until we're well out of the area." Then he bowed slightly. "Ladies . . ." and he turned, walking out the door, shutting it firmly behind him.

Rebel sighed as she lowered herself slowly to the bed, sitting beside Hizzie. So much had happened so fast, and now she sat quietly, her heart pounding, remembering again those moments she'd looked into Beau's eyes when he'd entered her bedroom, and the violent emotion that had surged through her.

"Ma'am . . . your Grace," asked Hizzie softly from Rebel's elbow. "Who are those men, and what's we all doin' here?"

"That man who just left is my brother, Hizzie," she answered. "Well, my half-brother, anyway. We had the same mother. The other man . . ." She hesitated and bit her lip. "That, Hizzie, is the famous Captain Thunder you've heard the islanders talk about. The man my husband said the *Eagle Hunter* was going to blow out of the water, and we, I presume, are on our way to France."

Heath joined Beau on deck, watching silently as the ship cleared the lagoon, heading toward the frigates waiting a good distance off shore. The two stood side by side, yet neither of them spoke for a long time except to talk about the business of the moment, seeing the ship reach safety. They joined the frigates which took on full sail alongside the *Golden Eagle*, and within half an hour all three ships were on course for France, mission accomplished.

Heath waited until they were well on their way, then turned to Beau. "You ought to go down and see Rebel," he said softly, not wanting the crew to hear. Beau looked at him sternly, then glanced away again. "I mean it, Beau," he advised. "In the first place, you'll have to tell her about us before she talks to any of Captain Gautier's men or the crew, and in the second place, there's something you ought to see."

"Like what?"

Heath put his hand on Beau's arm. "Beau, believe me," he said seriously, "it's something . . . I can't tell you. You're going to have to see for yourself."

Beau exhaled disgustedly. He was tired, but he might as well get it over with. His stomach felt like it was full of lead, and there was a ache in his chest. "All right," he answered. "I'll go see her."

"Take a good look at her son while you're at it, too, Beau," Heath said as his friend walked away. "He's a cute one." Beau nodded, gesturing irritably toward Heath.

He didn't want to see Rebel. Not again. Seeing her standing in the bedroom of her house wearing that silk nightgown had been enough to tear him apart inside, and then, when she'd fallen against him back there on the beach . . . My

389

God! How could one woman do this to a man? It wasn't right. He knocked on the door softly and waited for a response.

Rebel opened the door, and her eyes fell quickly under his gaze as she let him in.

"I know it's late," he said as he entered. It was well past three in the morning. "But there are some things I want to tell you before you go on deck tomorrow."

Rebel had composed herself some, but her hands still trembled at his nearness. "That is?"

He took a good look at her. She had removed the cloak, but was still in the blue wrapper and nightgown, and he tried to concentrate on what he was saying, yet was too conscious of her presence. "No one in France knows you're Heath's sister," he explained curtly, fighting his emotions. "If they found out, it could go badly for both you and Heath."

"And yourself?"

"And myself." His face reddened. "We're supposed to turn you over to the agents of count Paul DeBarras, who's taken over the leadership of the National Convention in Paris. They intend to force Brandon to stop his attempted conquest of the West Indies by keeping you in France."

"And they think it'll work?"

"You don't?"

"Brandon has an obsession where I'm concerned, I know, but he'll stop only until he gets me back; then he'll start again."

"And if he doesn't get you back?"

"You should have gotten to know Brandon better, Beau," she said sardonically. "He's a very determined man. What he can't get one way, he gets another. What he can't coerce, he buys, and what he can't buy, he eliminates. And he never gives up."

Beau studied her as she stood in front of him. She hadn't changed, not in looks anyway. In fact, she was even more beautiful. But her eyes. There was a hardness about her eyes. A barrier that was impersonal. For a moment back at the house when he'd first seen her, the veil had lifted, but now it was there again as she looked at him coldly.

"In any event," he said, "we'd rather no one know about our relationship. Your brother and I'd dislike having our heads roll."

Rebel's hand moved to her throat, and her lips parted sensuously. "Don't worry. I won't tell them," she said, then turned as the baby made a noise, and Beau, who'd paid no attention to the girl holding the baby, glanced casually at Hizzie. Then suddenly his face paled.

The girl Rebel called Hizzie was sitting on the bed, her arms wrapped about a healthy boy of almost a year. His dark green eyes, beneath coal black hair, studied Beau curiously as he chewed on his little fist. The slight almond shape of his eyes made the bridge of his nose look even broader, and in the warm glow from the lamplight the dusky hue of his skin was even more apparent.

Beau's mouth went dry as he stared at the baby, and Rebel turned back to him, swallowing hard as she watched the look on his face.

"Why didn't you tell me?" he asked in disbelief, his voice barely above a whisper, and Rebel shook her head.

"I don't know what you mean." But his eyes moved from the baby to her face. He could see it in her eyes, and he knew.

"Why?"

Rebel turned away from him toward Hizzie, her hands trembling. "Hizzie, here," she said, taking a blanket from the pile of clothes they'd brought in the rolled sheet. "Take the baby to the cabin next door and see if you can get him to sleep." Beau stopped the girl for a moment so he could get another look at the baby he was certain could only be his son; then he turned back to Rebel as the door shut behind Hizzie.

"Well?" he asked, and her eyes flashed cynically.

"How was I to tell you? I didn't even know where you were."

"You could have written to your mother. We get to Port Royal whenever we can sneak in."

"Oh, yes. Tell my mother," she said bitterly. "Wouldn't she have loved that? Mother I'm married to Brandon, but I had Beau's baby."

"She'd understand."

"Would she?"

"How about Heath?"

"She was married to Roth when she got pregnant with Heath."

"But she wasn't married to your father when she got pregnant with you!"

She fumbled about, frustrated for words. "Well . . . at least he married her!" His eyes narrowed as she went on. "What difference would it have made if you had known?" she asked heatedly. "Would you have taken me away from Brandon and married me yourself?" His eyes hardened, and she laughed bitterly. "I thought not!" Tears sprang to her eyes. "At least this way he has a name."

"What is it?"

"He's Colton Avery, the future Duke of Bourland."

"And a half-breed!"

"He's only partly Indian."

"You think people will believe that, with his looks?"

"You should have thought of that a year ago."

"Oh, now I suppose it's all my fault!"

"Well, I didn't carry you to your cabin, you carried me, remember? It was your idea to show me what love was all about, not mine."

"I suppose you'll deny throwing yourself at me."

"When I was sixteen, yes, I was a fool!"

"I'm not talking about when you were sixteen. I'm talking about when you were nineteen and we captured the ship you were on. You were engaged to Brandon, yes, but you know damn well you made sure I knew you were around."

"Oh, did I, now?"

"A man can take just so much, Reb."

"You had no right to make love to me!"

"You wanted it, didn't you?"

"No!"

"Then why didn't you fight? Why didn't you cry rape?" His eyes raked over her, stopping at the luscious curves of her breasts, visible beneath the thin nightgown. "You didn't because you wanted it, that's why. Because you enjoyed it as much as I did. So don't say it's all my fault. It takes two, Reb."

She stared angrily, then lowered her eyes before his smoldering gaze and turned away. He was still so damn good-looking, and the sight of him stirred her violently, but she couldn't let him know. She could never let him know that she had welcomed the fact that Cole wasn't Brandon's.

"Why did you have to come back into my life?" she asked softly, her voice trembling. "I never wanted to see you again."

He stood behind her, the scent of the perfume she was wearing filling his nostrils as he studied the back of her hair where it cascaded from her shoulders in a golden cloud. He wanted to take her in his arms and rain kisses on the soft shoulders and smooth neck hidden beneath that hair, and see her eyes melt beneath his once more as he made her feel the love they'd known together. But he stiffened as he remembered Henri's story, and he fought the desires that were about to overwhelm him. Henri had called her and the doctor lovers. Maybe that was what was behind the cold look in her eyes. She had married Brandon, yet turned to another man. Wasn't one man enough? He could forgive her for marrying Brandon, because he knew she had done it to spite him, that she'd never loved her husband, but the doctor was something else.

"I didn't ask to come back into your life, Reb," he said huskily, his anger surfacing at what he felt was her betrayal. "You were merely an assignment. One I would have turned down except for the fact that Heath and I have been friends for a long time. I'd planned to wash my hands of you when we reached France, and let you take your chances, since you seemed to survive with Brandon so well, but now . . . the boy makes a difference. Whether I like it or not, I have no choice but to make sure nothing happens to you . . . regardless of what I feel for you, he is my son."

She whirled around to face him. "Oh, don't let a little thing like that bother you. We've done fine without you until now."

"Don't be ridiculous!"

"Ridiculous? Don't trouble yourself, Beau Dante. I'm used to taking care of Cole and me. You think Brandon accepted Cole as his? Now you're the one who's ridiculous. It's one thing to marry a man, another to give him someone else's son, but I survived. The way all women survive when there's no other way. Frenchmen are no different from other men, Beau, so don't worry—Cole and I'll survive. We don't need you to protect us, we never did, in France or anywhere else. So don't do us any favors!"

He flinched at the bitterness in her words and the callous way she'd thrown them at him. Her lower lip unconsciously quivered as they stared at each other, her breasts rising and falling with each breath. She was so near . . . His arm started to move out; then he caught himself, thought of the baby in the other cabin, and remembered the doctor. His pride got the better of him, and he turned without saying another word and left.

Rebel stood motionless, staring after him, watching him shut the door behind him. Tears rolled down her cheeks. What had she expected, anyway? Had she expected him to vow his undying love and ask her forgiveness for what he'd done? She should have known better. Indians didn't do things they'd be sorry for. They didn't have hearts. They were savages, heartless savages. She bit her lip, leaned her head against the small window in the cabin, and cried because she still loved him. Savage or not, she knew she still loved him.

Beau let the cool night air fill his lungs. It'd be morning soon, and he had to get some sleep, but at the moment sleep seemed so unimportant. He closed his eyes, remembering the face of the chubby baby Hizzie held in her arms. There was no way to deny it. The child looked more Indian than he had ever looked, and he tried to imagine how Brandon had felt when he first laid eyes on him. Was that why Rebel looked so cold and indifferent? What had Brandon done to her to make her seek a lover? Or had she changed so much that she didn't care? Had his rejection of her made her into a heartless woman?

But he couldn't have married her. She didn't understand. He hadn't wanted to fall in love. It had been wrong from the start, but how did you tell your heart to stop feeling, stop loving? There was no way. Even now . . . He cursed softly to himself as he finally returned below deck to his own cabin and dropped across the bed in an exhausted sleep.

The next morning, with only a few hours' sleep behind him, Beau was back on deck running the ship in his inimitably stern way. He smiled little, avoiding everyone as much as possible, and if Captain Gautier had thought him a hard captain on the initial voyage, the return voyage was even more unpleasant. Even the men who ordinarily took his quiet orders unemotionally found themselves the brunt of his quick temper.

Beau avoided direct contact with Rebel as much as possible, yet watched her furtively whenever she was on deck, a fact that Captain Gautier found most interesting as the ship made its way back to France. He approached Rebel on deck one afternoon, determined to find out why. After all, General Bonaparte had given him a job to do. Rumors had reached him that Captain Thunder had personal reasons for accepting this mission, and his job was to ferret out the truth and act on it if necessary.

"Good afternoon, Duchess," he said in French as he approached where she stood at the rail, watching their progress. She was wearing a pink dress that made her eyes vividly alive, and although her hair was pulled back severely, its golden sheen was softened in the warm afternoon sun, and wisps of silken hair caught in the breeze, playing about her face. "You seem to be enjoying your ocean voyage," he remarked, and she glanced at him suspiciously.

She'd seen him watching her all morning and wondered what was on his mind. "I've always been one to make the most of the situation wherever I am," she answered calmly, also in French. "It'd do me no good to fuss and cry now, would it? I could not imagine your Captain Thunder turning the ship about and returning me to Grenada merely because I cried and had a tantrum."

"Logical," he conceded. "But tell me . . . why does the captain seem to hold you in such high regard, your Grace?" he asked. "Giving you one of the best cabins and the freedom of the ship. After all, you are a prisoner."

"Captain Gautier, you amaze me. Where on earth could I escape to here in the middle of the ocean?" she asked, gesturing out across the deep blue waters.

"The point is, madam, that prisoners should be treated as such."

"And you think I should be in chains?" She shook her head sadly. "My, what happened to the chivalrous Frenchmen I always used to hear about, don't tell me they were all guillotined?"

"You're not being amusing, madam. General Bonaparte told me to take over the care of the prisoner once on board ship. I dislike being forced to disobey orders!"

She smiled cynically. "Then why don't you try to carry the orders out, sir?" she replied. "I imagine Captain Thunder's men would enjoy the exercise; they've had so little excitement this trip."

He studied her, his eyes narrowing. "You know the captain, don't you?" he asked suddenly, but she looked at him curiously—the surprise at his blunt question hidden beneath an expression of innocence.

"Know him? I've known of him. Who hasn't heard of the notorious Captain Thunder!"

"That's not what I mean. You know the captain personally. I've seen you talking to his first mate as if you were on intimate terms, and the looks that pass between you and Captain Thunder tell me something strange is going on."

Rebel smiled flirtatiously. "If you must know, I find the man attractive, Captain," she answered, "that's all. As I imagine do most women. But he's so aloof and unfriendly. His first mate, however, is rather a gallant, don't you think, and every bit as handsome, if not quite as intriguing."

"You must not talk like this, you are a married woman, madam," he reminded her sternly.

"You are too serious, Captain." Her voice was low, provocative. "Just because I have a husband does not mean my heart is dead." She rolled her eyes at him. "I would wager the acquisition of a wife would not stop you from accepting the right woman's favors. Now, would it?"

"I am a man, madam. With men it is different. As a woman you should know that."

She threw her head back and laughed seductively. "You are so naive," she whispered. "As are all men where women are concerned, Captain." Then she leaned closer to him so the scent of her perfume drifted up to him. "I know that all women are not cold and unfeeling, that there are women in the world with fire in their blood to whom affairs of the heart are a part of living." The French captain's eyes widened in horror as she continued, murmuring softly, "I believe, Captain Gautier, that Captain Thunder could steal my heart away quite easily if he were to try."

"Madam," he blurted, his face flushed at her confession, "you have gone too far. You are supposed to be a lady of quality. To talk like this—it's shocking!"

She let her eyes linger on his square-jawed face, noting the twitch at the corner of his wide mouth; then she looked up into his intense brown eyes. "Why, Capitaine, I honestly believe you're blushing," she exclaimed coyly. "I didn't mean to make you feel uncomfortable, but you did ask what my interest was in Captain Thunder." She sighed. "I think he's a devilishly exciting man and I only wish I did know him better." Her eyes took on a dreamy look as she glanced away across the horizon, where clouds streaked the afternoon sky. "Perhaps before the voyage is over . . . Who knows?" With that, Rebel turned and walked away.

She went toward the bow of the ship, where she could watch the rise and fall of the jib boom and glory in the spray from the water as they hit the waves. She caught Beau staring her way. He stood by the helmsman, his white full-sleeved shirt open to the waist, revealing his bronzed skin, his black wavy hair glistening in the sun. His eyes bored into hers, and her heart turned over as she wrenched free of his gaze and finished her walk along the rail. In the weeks they'd been at sea, he'd talked to her rarely, and then his conversation was stilted, indifferent, even when there were occasions when they were caught alone. Sometimes he was even downright nasty and rude, yet his eyes always caressed her with a passion that made her terribly uncomfortable, and she was at a loss to understand it.

She reached the jib and felt the cool and refreshing salt

spray in her face. Soon they'd be in colder waters. It was still winter in France, and the farther north they sailed, the colder the air, so she took advantage of the weather, enjoying the warm day. She felt almost carefree, wondering what Brandon was doing back on Grenada and silently thanking God for rescuing her from the prison he'd made of her life. Matt's death had tempered her emotions, and she'd felt dead inside, giving in to Brandon's love, letting him possess her, willing her body to respond to his lusts because there was no reason to care anymore. First Beau, then Matt, lost to her. What did it matter who had her, whose body took her? The feelings were the same, empty animal instincts without the softness and warm spark of love. She was a thing to be used, and she'd let Brandon use her, but now she was free again. At least for a while. Free to taste the wine of life, to give or hold back as she chose, and it felt good.

That evening, as usual, she had dinner in Beau's cabin with Heath and Beau; and as usual, Beau was quiet, letting Heath carry on the conversation with her. One of the few times they could talk freely with each other without the fear of Captain Gautier's men overhearing was at mealtime. Heath was a marvelous storyteller—colorful and vivid. He had really grown up since leaving Fort Locke, and there were times Reb wondered whether she liked the results or not. He was cynically sure of himself, whether it was women or war. Not really conceited, but proud, knowing he was extremely handsome, with an abundance of charm when he decided to use it, and using it often, with results. Most of the time, however, with outsiders, he was like a silent shadow beside Beau, backing him up when necessary and working as if he were his right hand, yet dominating Beau's background quietly.

They were more like brothers than friends, and at times, as older brothers often did, Beau overlooked Heath's preoccupation with his appearance and with women. But during mealtime he let him entertain his sister all he wanted, and although he showed not a sign of even listening, secretly he enjoyed hearing their chatter.

Tonight, as Rebel stood up to leave and Heath started to rise, Beau put his hand on Heath's arm and stood up himself. "I'll escort Rebel to her cabin tonight, Heath," he stated casually, and Heath relaxed back in his chair, but his eyes held a question Beau didn't answer.

Beau opened the door for Rebel and ushered her out silently, the black frock coat he wore tonight seeming austere against the delicate pink of her dress. Cristabel had shoved four dresses in the portmanteau for Rebel. The violet dress that matched her eyes, a pale green peau de soie, an emerald-green velvet, and the pink silk she had on.

They reached the door to Rebel's cabin, and Beau opened it for her to go in. She swept her skirts aside as she entered, then turned abruptly to say good night, but he stood his ground.

"I'd like to talk if you don't mind," he suggested.

"It's your ship." She walked farther into the cabin, and he followed, closing the door behind him, while she stood with her back to him, looking toward the window.

"What were you and Captain Gautier talking about this afternoon?" he asked. So that's what he wanted. She turned slowly.

"The captain had a strange notion that we were previously acquainted," she said, and watched the expression on his face.

"What made him think that?"

"You shouldn't watch me so much, Beau," she teased, half-smiling. "He thinks there's something going on between us."

He didn't smile back. "What did you tell him?"

"I told him you were my son's father, why?"

He grabbed her wrist. "Be serious!"

"All right." Her jaw tightened stubbornly. "If you must know, I let him think I was flirting with you. I told him I thought you were one of the most fascinating men I'd ever met."

"I said be serious."

"I am serious. I had to think of something." She pulled her wrist from his grasp. "He so much as told me he thought we were old friends, maybe more. What else could I do?"

"Did he believe you?"

"By the time I was through with him, I think he did. I'm afraid I shocked him somewhat, though. Your French captain thought it was terrible that a married lady of quality would stoop to have an affair."

"You told him we were having an affair?"

"Don't be silly." She looked directly into his deep green eyes. "I merely let him know I'd be willing if you made the overtures."

"You think that was wise?"

"No. But what else was I to do? It was the only thing I could think of on such short notice."

"Why didn't you just deny everything?"

398

"Your French captain may be stuffy and stodgy, Beau," she answered, "but he's not stupid. How could I deny something that was so obvious to him? Besides, did you have a better idea in mind?"

He shrugged. "I guess your explanation is as good as any. At least it's consistent."

"With what?"

She saw the tense stiffening of his jaw as his eyes hardened. "With women like you. Tell me," he asked coldly, "did we drag you away from your current affair, or hadn't you found anyone to replace the good doctor yet?"

"What are you talking about?" she asked slowly.

"Don't be coy with me, Reb. I heard all about him, and he probably wasn't the first, either, was he? How many lovers have you had? Two, three . . . ?"

Her hands went to her throat as she stared at him, unable to believe the anger and hurt in his voice and the ugly words he was hurling at her.

"Who told you about Matt?" she asked breathlessly.

"You met our agent Henri. Your doctor wasn't too discreet when the two of you spent the night at his plantation."

"But he couldn't—"

"Old houses have secret passages," he explained quickly. "Someone needed the doctor in the middle of the night, and Henri went after him."

Rebel stared into Beau's eyes, trying not to remember, wanting to forget, yet unable to. Beau's eyes and Matt's eyes, so much alike, deep green, both of them. Matt! Dear, sweet Matt, who'd made her forget what she couldn't have, what life had become to her. What right did Beau have to accuse her?

Her chin thrust out stubbornly. "You have no right," she resented. "You weren't there. What do you know of my life?"

"I know you had a husband and he had a wife!"

"Oh, tell me more!" She turned her back on him briskly and walked to the window, pushing it open to stare into the night, but he didn't answer her challenge, and she turned back to face him. "Well, what is it, Beau? Why don't you answer? I thought you knew all about it."

"I know enough!" His eyes condemned her.

"You know enough." She laughed bitterly, tossing her golden hair in agitation as she marched back to stand in front of him, her voice lowered. "What do you really know? What do you really know about me, Beau? You haven't been around to know. You weren't there when I needed you. I

399

didn't have you to make love to me, your arms to hold me, your lips to bring me comfort and satisfy my desires. I had Brandon to give me nothing, to make me feel used and degraded. I'm his wife, yes, but I'm his possession. There's no joy for me in his arms."

"So you went to someone else!"

"Yes!"

"You said you loved me."

"I do."

"And that's how you show it? By giving yourself to someone else?"

"I needed Matt. I needed his love. Don't you understand?" She tilted her head back defiantly. "How many women have you had in the past two years?"

"That's different."

"What's so different about it?"

"Women don't need men the same way men need women."

"Oh, don't they, now? Who told you that, another man? Maybe some women don't need men. Matt's wife was like that. She not only didn't need him, she didn't want him. Not that part of him, anyway. She thought anything beyond kissing was for whores and doxies. My mother told me that loving a man and sleeping with him was natural and good, a part of living." Her voice lowered. "You showed me she was right. You made me come alive, Beau. Do you remember what you told me when I asked you why?" Tears welled up in her eyes. "You told me you wanted to be the first because you wanted me to know what lovemaking was really all about, how wonderful it could be. You taught me well, Beau. Too well. Then you took it away from me. I had to find it again someplace with someone." Her eyes lowered before his gaze, and she walked slowly back to the window. "You condemn me for having a lover . . . yet you've had other women. And Matt was the only one, Beau. He reminded me of you. Brandon's lovemaking left me empty and dead inside. Matt made me live again for a while, something I though I'd never do again. I needed Matt as much as you needed the women you had."

"You're wrong. That's what I meant when I said women didn't need men the way men need women," he said bitterly. "I never loved any of the women I slept with. They were there and I found a physical release, but that's all. My heart still ached afterward for you." He stepped toward her, his eyes smoldering. "If a woman needs a man like a man needs a woman, then Brandon's body would have been enough for you, but it wasn't. That's the difference between us, Reb. For me to take a woman doesn't have to have anything to do with love. It can be instinct alone. Unfortunately, a man can be aroused easily, merely by a woman, any woman, pulling up her skirts. Why we're that way, I don't know, but we are." His eyes continued to smolder, but a warmth crept into them. "But a woman needs something more." He reached up and toucher her earlobe, then ran his finger down her throat and trailed it over her skin to where the low décolleté of her dress revealed the separation of her full breasts, and he felt her shiver. "A woman needs soft caresses and warm kisses," and he leaned forward, bending down to kiss her just below the ear, letting his lips follow the same trail his finger had traced on her skin, and she trembled passionately at his touch.

His breathing quickened and her heart was pounding. "A woman needs love." His arms went around her, drawing her close against him, his mouth covering hers, and he kissed her deeply, sensuously. His lips parted hers, and she moaned ecstatically as his hands fumbled at the back of her dress, and he undid it, slipping it off her as he continued to kiss her.

He had wanted to do this from the moment he'd set eyes on her standing before him in her wrapper, the soft curves of her body visible beneath the silk nightgown, but he'd fought with himself, telling himself she'd betrayed him by falling in love with someone else. She'd gone to Matt willingly, and it hurt deep down inside. Now, here he was forgetting everything but his need for her. A need that hadn't been fulfilled since the last time he'd held her in his arms, even though there had been dozens of women.

Her dress fell to her feet, and his hands completed removing her underthings; then he lifted her, his arms about her waist, and carried her to the bed, his face buried in her full breasts, the warm sweet woman scent of her filling his nostrils as he set her upright on her knees in the middle of the bed.

Rebel looked up at him, her body thrilling to the wonderful sensations that surged inside her. This was Beau, the man she loved. She knelt before him on the bed and ran her hand down his chest while he pulled off his frock coat and shirt and tossed them aside, then kicked off his boots and wriggled from his pants. He stood before her, his marvelously muscular body taut and firm, his eyes devouring the intoxicating rise of her breasts as she spoke his name.

"Oh, Beau, I thought I'd never see you again." She sighed

breathlessly, and he knelt on the bed before her, his hand grasping the soft flesh of her hips, and he bent down, his tongue teasing her pink-tipped nipples, then moving to her mouth as he began to caress her, making her tingle deep down inside, until her loins began to ache.

They fell as one onto the bed, stretching out, their bodies entwined in an all-consuming passion, and Beau moved over her, feeling the moist warmth of her on his swollen manhood, and he knew all his good intentions were lost. She was another man's wife, but he didn't care. Not at the moment. All that mattered was that she was here and he loved her and wanted her, and she sighed ecstatically as he entered slowly, savoring the sweetness of her body. She arched to meet him, her body on fire, her senses reeling.

"I love you," he whispered huskily as a thrill shot through him, and she floated to heaven on a cloud of pleasure as he thrust into her over and over again until her whole body exploded to sensations that made her cry out, and pulsated through her one after another as if they'd never stop. Then, as he too came, his mouth covered hers and he was swept up in the rapture of a pleasure so strong it left him weak and breathless.

"Oh, my God," he whispered against her mouth.

"Oh, Beau . . ." She shivered happily. "I love you. I've wanted you for so long."

He kissed her again, feeling the silkiness of her body against his; then suddenly, as his lips sipped at hers, Cole's soft, faint crying from the cabin next door touched their ears, penetrating their senses. Beau's lips stopped their loving and Rebel felt him stiffen, his muscles tense.

Her hand moved up his back into his hair, and she tried to pull his mouth back to hers, but he held himself in check.

"No," he whispered sharply, his voice breaking. "No, Reb . . . what the hell am I doing here? Oh, Lord . . . I hope I haven't gotten you pregnant again," he whispered huskily.

"I don't care."

"Well, I do!" He lifted his body from hers, and she groaned agonizingly as she felt him leave her, and he slipped from the bed. "It's bad enough one of my sons is carrying your husband's name . . . how could I have been such a damn fool!" He cursed as he put on his clothes, then glanced back at Rebel as she lay in the dim light from the flickering lantern that hung on the wall.

She'd pulled the sheet up over her naked body, and her hands clung to it desperately, clenching it to her breast, and there were tears in her eyes. He knew why he'd been so foolish. One look at her told him. She was like a drug with him. He loved her beyond all reasoning, but she wasn't his to love, and he knew it, yet she was the only woman that could do this to him. It wasn't fair.

"Beau," she whispered softly, "please don't leave me. I'll die."

He reached for his frock coat but stopped and moved to the bed instead, sitting on the edge, looking down at her. "Don't make it harder than it already is, Reb." he murmured softly. "Do you think I want to leave? Do you think it's easy to walk away from you?"

"Then don't."

"I have no choice. You're another man's wife, or have you forgotten?"

"I'll leave Brandon, we don't have to go to France. We can go away together, just you and I. . . ." She moved up, throwing her arms around his neck, her violet eyes sparkling wet with tears. "I love you, Beau!"

He pulled her into his arms again and kissed her long and hard, and she melted against him, but he knew it was no good, that no matter how much they loved each other, the facts were still the same, and reluctantly he ended the kiss, pulling his mouth from hers forcefully.

"It won't work, Reb," he gasped breathlessly as he untwined her arms from about his neck, his face flushing warmly from the sight of her bare breasts and the longings they aroused within him. "There's nothing for us together. I told you that a long time ago," and he stood up, grabbing his frock coat, fighting to keep himself in control. "I'm taking you to France, and when I'm sure that you and the baby are safe, I'm saying good-bye. I won't touch you again," and he turned, walking out of the cabin.

"Beau!" she called "I hate you, Beau Dante!" and he was gone.

She lay back on the bed, her body still aching for his touch, her heart torn to pieces inside; then she rolled over onto her stomach, buried her face in her pillow, and cried herself to sleep.

Captain Gautier stood in the shadows at the end of the passageway and watched Captain Thunder leave her cabin. Captain Thunder stood for a moment with the door shut behind him, touching his mouth as if savoring some pleasant taste; then he straightened his clothes here and there and moved toward the stairs, disappearing above deck. Now, that was strange. Only this afternoon she'd voiced her desires where the man was concerned. Had he succumbed to her charms already, or was General Bonaparte right in his suspicions? He'd watch closely during the rest of this unusual voyage, and he did watch, but saw little.

Captain Thunder still watched the duchess from afar, and the duchess still spent hours on end talking and laughing with the first mate. The first mate was a handsome young man, yet the looks that passed between the duchess and him were never intimate and intense as were those that passed between the duchess and Captain Thunder. And Heath also seemed to enjoy the duchess's baby, playing with him, carrying him on his shoulders, and generally acting inane, like most people do around a baby.

And that was something else that bothered the captain. The governor's son looked rather strange for the child of English parents. He looked more like . . . well, it was hard to say exactly, but never having seen the governor, he wasn't at all sure what to expect. The child looked almost Oriental or Indian, and the fact bothered him.

At first Rebel had made up her mind to hate Beau, but her good intentions didn't last very long. One look from his eyes and she knew there was no hate in her where he was concerned, only love. There always would be. He was part of her, whether he wanted to be or not, and no words to the contrary could change it.

Each day was a torture for them both as the ships made their way toward France. They longed to be in each other's arms, yet knew the futility of their desires, but even this didn't make it any easier, and Rebel made matters worse. She flaunted herself at him with every opportunity, until Beau wanted to thrash her; anything to ease the pain in his loins.

By the time they reached Le Havre his emotions were held in check by a fine wire ready to snap at the first opportunity. It was barely after sundown on a crisp evening at the end of March when they dropped anchor in the harbor at Le Havre and prepared to go ashore. They stood on deck, Rebel in her violet dress with her cloak pulled about her shoulders and Hizzie beside her, holding a fussy Cole, who saw little to be happy about, since it was past his bedtime.

Heath and Beau stood with them, dressed in their flamboyant uniforms, their plumed hats at a rakish angle, and they watched Captain Gautier apprehensively as he assembled his men for disembarking, then strolled toward them.

"And now, Captain," said the French captain, "since we've

reached the shores of my country, do you intend to relinquish the prisoners to my command?"

"Since you have given me no written orders, sir, and since when I accepted this job I was given explicit instructions in the matter, I will carry them out," Beau announced. "If you wish to accompany my first mate and me, that's up to you, but the prisoners are still mine." He gazed about at his men scattered around the deck, their hands resting uneasily on their pistols.

"Very well, Captain, if that's the way you want it," he answered angrily. "I'll take my men and report back to my superior officer and let him handle your arrogance."

"Was that wise, Beau?" asked Rebel.

"Hell, I don't care if it was wise or not, this whole thing is getting under my skin. Something's just not right, but come on. Let's go. I've got orders."

Beau had been given instructions about where to take Rebel on his arrival in Le Havre, but now, as the carriage he'd hailed made its way through the streets of the city, he became wary. He leaned forward suddenly and called to the driver, telling him to take them to a different address than the original one he'd given him. Then he leaned back against the seat, frowning in the darkness of the carriage.

"What's wrong?" asked Heath. Beau motioned behind them with his head.

Heath leaned over and glanced out the window of the closed carriage, and Rebel heard a sharp intake of breath.

"I saw the carriage while we were leaving the ship, and whoever was inside was talking to Gautier," Beau said.

"That's one of the prison carriages," said Heath.

"I know," answered Beau. "That's why I'm going to deposit Rebel where she'll be safe until we find out what this is all about."

"Where are you taking me?" she asked.

"To the American embassy," he answered casually.

"Are you crazy, Beau?" said Heath. "She's the wife of a dignitary from a country at war with France. They'll never take her in."

"They will if they're convinced she's an American citizen."

"Then I tell them who I am?"

He shook his head. "Heath's right. There's too much chance they might turn you over to the French."

"Then who do I say I am?"

"You're the wife of Captain Thunder, privateer and American." He turned to Hizzie. "Do you understand that, Hizzie?" he asked.

"Yessir," she said, and Beau smiled.

"Good. Let me do the talking. I don't like this whole setup. If we hadn't had those Frenchies aboard and those two frigates beside us I'd have never even come back to Le Havre," and Heath knew why, even if Beau wouldn't admit it.

The carriage pulled up in front of the embassy and Beau jumped out, hurrying Rebel and Hizzie inside with Heath's help as the carriage that was following pulled up outside and the men in it watched. The secretary at the embassy was surprised to see visitors so late, but he welcomed Beau and Heath, whom he seemed to know, and ushered them into one of the salons, where they were joined by a tall, pleasant gentleman in his late thirties who smiled warmly as he saw the two privateers.

"Heath, Beau, now what kind of trouble are you in?" he asked as he greeted them.

"I've a problem, Jim," said Beau.

"You usually do."

"This is an extraordinary problem."

"Not what have you gotten yourself into?"

"I'm glad you're here and not at the embassy in Paris," Beau said. He turned, and his eyes caught Rebel's, warm and clear, and the look that passed between them was more than revealing. "Jim, this is my wife and son. Most people didn't know I was married, but Paul DeBarras and his new general found it out. They want to get their hands on my wife and force me to continue my privateering, which I've told them I intend to stop. I want to keep her here until I can figure a way to get her out of France. Can she stay?"

James Monroe looked at Rebel thoughtfully. Captain Thunder married? No wonder his reputation as a ladies' man was wanting, even though the ladies were willing, and he could understand why, with a wife like this around. But where'd he been hiding her? He wasn't quite sure he believed the young upstart, but then again . . . the look in the lady's eyes when she gazed at the captain was far from platonic.

"Can she stay?" asked Beau again, and Jim finally acquiesced.

"Yes, certainly. I'll see she's made comfortable."

"Heath and I have to leave for a while," explained Beau. "Only a few hours, possibly less, but by no means let her leave the embassy with anyone except Heath or myself. Some men may come here and try to get you to let them take her. They'll probably say she's not my wife and make up a far-fetched tale about who she really is, but don't believe them, whatever they say. They'll try anything to get their hands on her, and I can't let that happen."

James Monroe, American minister to France, assured Beau. "Don't worry, Captain, she'll be waiting for you when you get back." Beau thanked him then turned to Rebel.

"We'll be back as soon as we can, Reb," he said. "You're not to worry. Mr. Monroe will take good care of you." He looked back at the ambassador. "If by any chance neither of us does happen to return by tomorrow evening, will you try to smuggle her aboard a ship for America?" he asked, surprising him. "Her parents are there, they'll take care of her."

"Is it that serious, Beau?" he asked.

"I'm afraid my days of friendship with the French are drawing to a close, Jim," he said, "and I don't want Rebel and my son to pay for my indiscretions."

The ambassador nodded. "All right, Beau. But I'm sure you'll return. Now, you'd better kiss her good-bye and get out of here if you intend to make it back tonight," and Beau glanced quickly at Rebel.

He hadn't counted on this. Not kissing her. But if he didn't? Was Jim testing him? he wondered.

He turned to Rebel, his eyes intent on her face, and he reached out, pulling her against him, and his hand moved up onto her neck, where he buried it beneath her hair. Her eyes were like pools of deep violet, and he was drowning in them as he lowered his mouth to hers.

He had meant to kiss her lightly, tenderly, only a short kiss to please the ambassador, but once she was in his arms it was like being caught in a whirlwind. He couldn't let her go, and Hizzie tried to hide her suprise as James Monroe glanced away embarrassed at the intimacy between them. Beau kissed her with all the pent-up passion of the past few weeks. If the ambassador had had any doubts at all that the lady was not who Captain Thunder claimed her to be, they vanished when the woman entered the captain's arms.

Rebel's face was flushed and warm, her body on fire as Beau released her and looked down into her face. "Be careful, Beau," she whispered softly.

"I'll be back as soon as I can." He and Heath said good-bye to the ambassador, then left the room.

"That's quite a husband you have there, Mrs. Thunder," said Jim as the door shut behind them.

"Yes, I know." She swallowed hard, then noticed the look on the ambassador's face as he studied the cranky baby in Hizzie's arms. "But my name isn't Mrs. Thunder, Mr. Monroe," she said. "That's not Beau's real last name. I can't tell you what it really is. He doesn't want anyone to know, but Thunder is the English translation of his Indian name. He's three-quarters Tuscarora Indian and one-quarter French, sir," she said softly, and watched the puzzled expression on his face change to one of relief.

"Indian, you say," he muttered. He glanced again at the baby, and led Rebel and Hizzie from the room with all doubts cleared from his mind. Rebel heard him mutter "Indian" again, and he shook his head as he led them to a room where they could rest.

Beau's eyes were like fiery emeralds as he brushed by the footman in the spacious house in another part of the city and confronted Paul DeBarras' agent, Maurice Rambeau, and the two men standing with him.

"I want some questions answered, and I want them answered fast," Beau ordered as he braced his feet in a wide stance before the man.

Maurice was a spare man in his middle thirties with thin hair and the disposition of a weasel; his acid smile brought Beau little pleasure.

"I think perhaps we are the ones to ask the questions, Capitaine," Maurice countered coldly as he stared at Beau. "It seems General Bonaparte has discovered some interesting facts about the lady you pretended to be unwilling to kidnap." He looked at Heath standing quietly behind Beau. "Tell me, Heath, is it true she's your sister?" he asked, and his smile broadened. "And if Capitaine Gautier's observations on your return trip are right, I believe, Capitaine Thunder, we could refer to her as your paramour, am I right?"

Beau's jaw tightened as he ignored the man's questions. "Why was the prison carriage waiting when we arrived at the dock?" he asked boldly. "I was to bring the lady here and she was to be escorted to a place in the country. Why the prison carriage?"

"The plans were changed after you boarded your ship for Grenada, Capitaine," he answered. "It was decided that the lady would be taken to the prison, where she would remain in a cell under guard, where there would be no chance of her escaping, and that's where she shall be when we have her in our hands."

"And that shall be never!" cried Beau. "Not as long as I can stop you!"

He and Heath started backing toward the door, but it was too late, as Maurice's hand wound around the bell pull. The doors behind the two privateers flew open, and Captain Gautier, sword in hand, plunged through, followed by half his men. Beau glanced quickly at Heath, who nodded his head, and both of them plunged directly at Maurice and his friends, taking them by surprise, knocking them over. When they reached the French doors directly behind the downed men, they didn't even wait to open them, but covered their faces with their arms and broke through. Glass flew in every direction as they reached the balcony, and within seconds they'd catapulted over the railing to the ground below. A high wall surrounded the garden they'd landed in, but they weren't stopped by it. Beau knelt down hurriedly, while Heath leaped onto his shoulders; then he stood up and Heath grabbed the top of the wall, pulling himself up. When he reached the flat surface, he lay down, bracing himself, and grabbed Beau's hand. Beau joined him on the wall in seconds.

The shouting from the house behind them was filled with curses as Captain Gautier and his men poured out the front door and emerged in the side yard, headed for the walled garden. Heath bounded to his feet, and Beau grinned as both of them gave the captain an arrogant salute, then disappeared over the side of the wall.

Beau had been sure something of the sort would happen and he'd been prepared. The carriage they'd arrived in was waiting out of sight around the corner, and they dashed down the street to reach it. Beau gave the driver an address as they climbed inside, and Heath turned to him in surprise.

"Madame Bouvier's at a time like this?" he asked, and Beau glanced quickly behind them to make sure they weren't being followed.

"I think I know how we can get Rebel and Hizzie to the ship," he said as he leaned back on the seat to relax and catch his breath. Heath listened intently.

It was close to ten o'clock when the men watching the embassy saw a carriage return with Heath and Beau, but the privateers weren't alone. With them were four of Madame Bouvier's most beautiful girls, laughing seductively and wearing cloaks to ward off the cool night air.

Heath and Beau swept their hats from their heads gallantly, bowing as the ladies emerged from the carriage, and they all ascended the steps to the front door.

"What in the world . . ." exclaimed James Monroe as the privateers ushered the four ladies of the evening into the salon. Beau didn't answer the question in his eyes; instead he asked his own question.

"Is Rebel all right?"

"She and her maid have had some food, and right now they and the baby are resting." He smiled as he looked at Beau. "You were right about the tales they'd tell," he said calmly. "A command of soldiers arrived, and their captain said she was the wife of the governor of some island and that I was to release her at once to his custody. I don't think he was any too happy when I refused." He looked at the women again and asked Beau about them once more, then nodded approvingly as Beau told his plan.

"You can wake your wife—she's in the room at the right directly at the top of the stairs," he said, and Beau took the stairs two at a time.

A dim lamp was the only light in the room as he opened the door and stepped inside. Rebel lay on the bed, but she wasn't asleep. "Who . . . Oh, Beau." She sighed in relief. "Is Heath all right?"

He nodded. "Reb, we're going to try to lose the men out front," he explained as he looked down into her face. "I've brought four ladies with me on purpose. The men out front will think I'm going to use them to try to sneak you and Hizzie and the baby out, and that's just what I want them to think. Instead, Heath and I are going to change clothes with a couple of Americans who work here at the embassy, and they'll leave in our place to make it look like we're leaving. We'll stay here; then, after the others leave, we'll go out the servants' entrance and head for the ship. I think it'll work. If it shouldn't, we may be in for a rough time of it, but if all goes well . . ."

"Why did you change your mind, Beau?" she asked softly, and he pulled her up into his arms.

"You should know that without my telling you," he said. "Besides, they were going to put you and Cole in a filthy cell." He kissed her hair before releasing her. "Now, let's wake up Hizzie and the baby and get downstairs. We haven't much time. We have to get to the ship before it's swarming with French soldiers."

By the time they arrived downstairs, Heath had already changed clothes with the ambassador's secretary, and another man was waiting to change clothes with Beau. They disappeared into one of the other rooms and emerged a few minutes later.

"Now remember," said Beau to the man, "it's dark out and I don't think they'll notice you're not wearing my sword." He was strapping his sword on over the suit he was wearing. "But they will notice other things, so sweep the hat from your head as the ladies enter the carriage, but keep your back to them if you can."

The ladies from Madame Bouvier's tittered, laughing among themselves at the sight of the two men in Heath and Beau's flamboyant clothes.

"They fit well," said Beau, and he was right. It would be difficult in the dark to differentiate between the men from the embassy and the real pair. Beau grabbed a pillow from one of the sofas and handed it to one of the women. "Hold this as you would a baby," he said as he stuffed it into her arms.

"But I have never held a baby, nor wanted to, m'sieur," she said in surprise.

"Then try to pretend. You've seen women with babies." He pointed at Hizzie cradling Cole in her arms. He was fast asleep, and she held him tightly against her breast. The woman shrugged as she held the pillow against her, trying to imitate Hizzie, and she rolled her eyes.

"This is ridiculous, m'sieur," she protested, giggling, but Beau didn't smile.

"I'm paying you ladies well to do as you're told," said Beau as he looked the woman over, then pulled the hood of her cape over her head to hide her fancy hairdo. "Madame Bouvier has the money waiting back at her place if you do your job right," he said. "Act natural, laugh, talk." He moved to another woman about the same height as Rebel and pulled the hood of her cape up to conceal her hair too. "You two," he said, addressing the two women with the hoods pulled over their heads, "don't do any talking, let the others talk. In fact, make sure your hoods are pulled as far forward as possible, as if you're trying to hide who you really are, but you"—and he looked at the other two women—"pretend to talk to them as if nothing was wrong. We have to make this work."

"In other words," said one of the women, a tall redhead, "you want someone to think they are leaving, am I right, m'sieur?" she asked as she gestured toward Rebel, Hizzie, and the baby.

"Exactly."

"We will get in trouble?" she asked.

"How could you? All you do if anyone stops you is say

411

you're entertaining the two gentlemen accompanying you and being paid well to do it. What charge can they make?"

She sighed. "I know you're a friend of Madame Bouvier, *m'sieur,* so I will do it," she said, "but I am not sure I like it."

"Don't be a goose, René," the one carrying the pillow said, "Just the other day you were complaining because your life was dull. So we have a little fun, and get paid for it. So quit complaining." The other girls agreed. Life had been tedious lately, and this escapade was just what they needed to relieve the boredom.

Outside, Captain Gautier, in a carriage with two of his men, had joined the prison official. It was a moonlit night, but the moon was playing hide-and-seek with some scattered clouds, and it was during one of these dark moments that Beau had the four girls leave with the men accompanying them.

He watched eagerly from a crack in the drapes by the front door as the men strolled jauntily down the steps, pretending to be carefree, and the women did a beautiful job of looking furtive while pretending not to be. Beau watched the prison carriage follow them, with Captain Gautier's carriage close behind.

He and Heath lost little time as they gathered Rebel, Hizzie, and the baby together and ushered them through the servants' quarters and out the back door to where the ambassador had another carriage waiting. Both men thanked James Monroe, and as he watched their carriage disappear into the night, he hoped they'd make good their escape. He'd always liked these young men. They were brash at times, and a bit reckless, but they were Americans. The new breed.

The ride to the waterfront and the *Golden Eagle* was at breakneck speed, and even at that they arrived just in time. The carriage stopped long enough to deposit them at the gangplank, then had barely disappeared around the corner when Captain Gautier's carriage lumbered recklessly into sight.

Beau, Heath, Rebel, and Hizzie stumbled hurriedly up the gangplank while Beau shouted orders on the way to the crew, and the gangplank cleared the dock moments before Gautier reached it, sword in hand, shouting as the sails began unfurling.

He had followed the other carriage only a short distance before overtaking it, almost killing its occupants before realizing Beau's deception. He'd been infuriated and headed directly for the waterfront, missing his quarry now only by

econds. He ordered the men with him to fire on the ship, but
heir efforts were futile as the ship continued moving out into
he harbor. Gautier ran toward one of the escort frigates and
oarded her, shouting for the captain.

Beau had Heath take the women below while he ordered
he men to battle stations, and the ship moved, inching its
vay, toward the mouth of the harbor. He watched as one by
ne the sails unfurled on one of the original escort ships and
t heaved to, starting its pursuit.

Heath came back on deck and took the helm, while Beau
ept his eyes on the frigate. They manuevered through the
ark night, through the bay, out into the channel, hugging the
oast. The wind was cold and the channel rough as they
nade their way steadily toward the open sea. The *Golden
Eagle* was fast, possibly the fastest ship afloat, but she
ouldn't move at full sail until she cleared the channel. She
ad to keep close in shore. Going too far out into the channel
vould mean taking the risk of running into the British, and at
he moment Beau wanted to avoid a skirmish at all costs, es-
ecially with a frigate on their trail. Once the ship was into
he open sea, they could easily leave the frigate behind.

It was pitch dark and Beau ordered all lights covered while
hey moved through the water like a ghost ship, silent and
eadly. Later, toward morning, when the open sea loomed
head of them out of the morning mists, everyone on board
ejoiced.

"I never did trust them Frenchies," said one of the crew to
Beau as he strolled the deck, watching the first rays of dawn
ome up over the horizon.

"Neither did I. At least not Gautier, but it was a living."

"So what do we do now, cap'n? Since we can't work for
he Frenchies anymore, and the British sure ain't gonna want
us." Beau smiled, patting the man on the back.

"Who knows?" he said. "We'll worry about that when we
each the states." And he went down below to try to get some
leep, but half an hour later he was back on deck.

The day that had looked promising was now as dark as
night, and lightning flashed off the starboard bow, with thun-
er rumbling across the water. "It'll be a bad one," said
Heath from beside him as they watched the waves swelling
igher and higher.

Beau cursed. "We're riding right into it, and we don't dare
urn back."

The rain hit with a savage force, driven by winds that
ashed at the ship furiously. It was as if a wall of water had

413

been unleashed on them by some unseen hand. Men's backs strained against the relentless onslaught, trying to control the wet lines, slipping on the rain-slick deck, the cold rain and saltwater spray soaking them to the skin. All day they fought the storm, using brute force to keep the ship afloat in one of the worst spring gales to hit the Atlantic, while below the quarterdeck Rebel and Hizzie prayed as hard as they could trying to keep their stomachs from turning inside out.

Beau cut sail to minimize damage, but the *Golden Eagle* still rode the raging ocean hard, and when dark came and the storm finally gave way to a misty drizzle, the ship was far off course and her men exhausted. Beau worked until late getting things back to normal, then finally left Heath in charge.

Beau was shivering with cold as he started for his cabin. He suddenly hesitated as the door to Rebel's cabin opened. She stood before him, her hair tousled, the blue silk nightgown clinging to her, and in the dim light from the passageway she looked warm and inviting.

"You look tired," she said softly.

He was tired. Tired and cold, yet as he looked at her, his blood began to warm inside him and the tired feeling was replaced by a vibrant yearning. "Not too tired," he whispered. He walked toward her, and kicked the door closed behind them. He reached out and pulled her into his arms, and his mouth covered hers in a deep kiss she felt clear to her toes.

"What am I going to do with you?" he finally asked passionately as he gazed into her flushed face.

"Make love to me."

"I should toss you to the sharks." His usually hard eyes were soft and warm. "But I don't think they like fallen women."

"Oh, Beau, what are we going to do?" she asked. "I love you so."

He held her tighter against him as he looked into her eyes. This was madness and he knew it, but he didn't care, not tonight. "I don't know," he whispered softly, "and at the moment I don't much care. I can't fight it any longer. All I know is I love you, Reb, and I need you, tonight and forever." He lifted her in his arms and carried her to the bed, and as he made love to her, neither of them spoke of the future, because in their hearts they knew there was none.

20

Loedicia opened her eyes, then snuggled closer against Roth, running her hand across his bare chest, feeling the softly curly hair. "Roth, wake up," she said anxiously. "Darling, please," and he opened his eyes slowly, then pulled her hard against him and kissed her lazily.

"What are you doing waking me at this hour, my lady?" he whispered softly. "It's barely breaking day."

She put her fingers across his mouth. "Shh! Listen," she said, and they strained their ears, picking up shouts and laughter that filtered in from the open French doors that led to the balcony overlooking the river. "Something's going on down at the wharf," she said.

"Then let's take a look."

They left the bed hurriedly. Roth put on his quilted robe and she slipped into a yellow silk dressing gown. They walked across the soft green carpeting to the balcony, staring across the broad expanse of lawn to the river some distance beyond, and to the pier where he kept his boat docked. The first rays of the sun had yet to come up, and night was just beginning to fade, lifting the early-morning mists from the river.

"It's the *Eagle*!" cried Dicia, her face wreathed in smiles as she saw the ship against the pier. "It's Heath and Beau, they've come home again," and she turned to Roth. "Now, aren't you glad I woke you!"

Roth stared at her amazed. Dicia never changed. Wild and tempestuous, vivaciously alive. She loved to tease him and was as unpredictable as the weather, yet there was a grace about her that made men envy him, that turned all eyes her way when she entered a room. Age hadn't found her, and youth hadn't deserted her, and the result often took his breath away. Each day he thanked God for letting her love him.

He pulled her into his arms and kissed her. "Then I guess

we'd better hurry," he said, smiling, "unless you want them to catch us in bed."

They didn't even take time to wash, but slipped into their clothes and headed downstairs. Dicia had put on a plain gold dress of watered silk and tied her hair back with a gold ribbon, while Roth slipped into a pair of tan pants, his old riding boots, and a white shirt. The house was finished now, and Roth was proud of it, smiling to himself as he followed Dicia down the stairs that led to the foyer. It was as beautiful as any of the other plantations along the river, and the finishing touches Loedicia had added gave it a sparkle of elegance. Like the crystal chandelier in the dining room and the beautiful paintings that hung in all the rooms.

He followed close behind her through the house, to the walk that led to a landing where the servants had already gathered to greet the newly arrived ship. It was barely dawn. Suddenly Loedicia stopped and stared, not sure of her eyes in the early-morning light.

"Roth, am I seeing things, or is that Rebel walking beside Beau?" Roth stared too, his eyes straining in the dim light.

"I think you're right," he said in disbelief. "In fact, I know you're right."

"I wonder what . . ." she said, but never finished as she let out a cry and ran the rest of the way to meet them. They were all talking at once as they met. Loedicia hugged Heath and Beau, then clung to Rebel for a long time, tears streaming down her cheeks.

"Well, you could have given us some kind of warning," she said, wiping away the tears as she looked at her daughter, then turned to the woman with frizzy hair who was cuddling a sleeping baby on her shoulder.

"This is Hizzie," explained Rebel. "She was Cole's wet nurse, I wrote you about her in my letters."

Dicia smiled at the young woman, who looked like she too was half-asleep; then she glanced about hesitantly. "And Brandon?" she asked.

"It's a long story," said Beau as he glanced first to Heath, then Rebel.

"One you can tell us over breakfast," suggested Roth as he shook hands with Beau and hugged Heath.

Loedicia had one of the servants show Hizzie upstairs with the baby, who had kept right on sleeping in spite of the commotion. The rest of them sat about the dining-room table eating breakfast while Beau, Heath, and Rebel told their story.

"Then Brandon thinks you're in France?" asked Roth.

"Yes."

Dicia saw the strained look on Rebel's face, and she frowned. "I have a strange feeling," she said calmly, "that you don't necessarily care if you see Brandon again. Am I right, Reb?"

Rebel looked quickly at Beau, then dropped her fork and left the table hurriedly, tears welling up in her eyes.

Loedicia excused herself and followed her daughter into the sitting room.

"Rebel, can I help?" she asked softly, but Rebel shook her head.

"No one can help me, Mother," she cried, tears cascading down her cheeks. "The damage was done the day I married Brandon. I hate him and I don't want to go back to him, but I know I have to. I know he'll find out where I am and come after me." She wiped her eyes with the back of her hand. "I've made such a mess of things, Mother," she said helplessly. "If I'd only listened to you." She threw her head back and straightened her shoulders. "You might as well know the truth, Mother, all of it. Cole's still sleeping, so you haven't had a good look at him yet, but you will, so I'll save you the shock." She bit her lip, keeping her back to her mother, unable to face her as she talked. "Cole isn't Brandon's son, Mother. Cole is Beau's son, and anyone looking at him who knows Beau's part Indian can tell. Brandon knows, and I've suffered for it."

Dicia's hand flew to her breast as she watched her daughter's shoulders sag unhappily. "When?" was all she asked, and Rebel answered meekly.

"The night before I married Brandon, but he wouldn't marry me, Mother." She turned to face her mother at last, and her face was wet with tears. "He has some strange notion that being Indian makes a difference. He's in love with me, but he wouldn't marry me. And I love him and now . . . now . . ."

Loedicia walked over and took her daughter's hands, which were cold and trembling. "Now what?" she asked softly, and a new flood of tears welled up in Rebel's eyes.

"I think I'm pregnant again, Mother," she said softly. "I've missed three times, and . . . I haven't told Beau yet. I don't know what he'll do . . . and when Brandon finds out . . ." She flung herself into her mother's arms and clung to her, burying her face in Loedicia's shoulder. "Oh, Mother, what am I going to do?" she asked, sobbing. "What am I going to

417

do?" and tears came to Dicia's eyes too, because she didn't have an answer.

"Are you sure it's Beau's and not Brandon's?" she asked. Rebel nodded, unable to talk, so Loedicia held her, cradling her in her arms, trying to soothe her any way she could, trying desperately to think of something, but there was no simple solution. Not now. Finally she released Rebel and set her away from her, smoothing the hair back from her daughter's face, wiping her own tears away with her fingers. "For now, Reb, there isn't too much we can do except sit back and wait," she said. "No one here at Port Royal knows how long you've been separated from Brandon, so if you are pregnant, there'll be no questions asked."

"But Beau knows, Mother. And he'll know it's his." She laughed bitterly. "It looks like I'm destined to have only Beau's babies, doesn't it? All that while married to Brandon, and I never got pregnant. And then there was Matt. You didn't know about Matt, Mother," she said thoughtfully. "I loved Matt because he reminded me of Beau. He was a doctor on Grenada and . . . he was in love with me, Mother. I knew it was wrong, but his wife gave him nothing . . . it was as if I had Beau with me again." Her eyes grew misty. "His wife shot him, Mother," she whispered. "She tried to kill me, but he jumped in the way. She went crazy and tried to kill me. Dear, sweet Matt . . . But it took Beau to make me pregnant, Mother. It's always Beau . . ." She straightened her shoulders stubbornly as she turned and looked out the window again. "Tell me, Mother, how did I manage to make such a mess of my life?"

"Ah, Reb, love can do strange things to people, I know. And there's no simple solution, there never has been, but don't worry. You're still my daughter, and Roth and I'll help all we can."

Rebel turned toward her and tried to smile.

"Now dry your eyes," Loedicia said as she smiled back. "Maybe Brandon will let you go."

"Oh, Mother, that's the one thing I can't count on. He's in love with me," she said. "He'll never set me free, his pride won't let him, and besides, Beau would never marry me anyway, his pride won't let him! I'd like to shove their pride right down their throats!" She flicked her hair back angrily with her hand. "Sometimes I think the world would be better off without men," she said viciously, and Roth caught the words as he thrust his head in the doorway."

"Does that include me too?" he asked.

"No, not you, Roth," she said. "The only trouble is there aren't any more like you."

"How can I help?" he asked.

"Go ahead, tell him, Mother," Rebel said. "He has to know," and she walked to the sofa and sat quietly listening while her mother explained everything to Roth.

When she was finished, Roth sat thoughtfully for a few minutes holding Dicia's hand. He looked at Rebel, and his heart went out to her. "One thing for sure, Reb," he said, "crying won't help. It'll only make you sick." He went over and brushed the tears from her cheeks. "Look, for now let's just bide our time and see what happens, all right? Maybe we can think of something." He took her hand, holding it tight. "Babies take nine months, and you've got six to go, and anything can happen in six months, so for now dry your eyes and come back into the dining room. Beau was in there talking about maybe buying some land along the river if there's any available. Said he'd decided to turn the *Golden Eagle* into a merchant ship, and I told him I'd help him all I could. Life has a way of evening out sometimes when we least expect it."

"I don't see how it can."

"Shall we just give it a wait?"

She shrugged. "I haven't really much choice, have I?"

"Come on, now, let's go back in there. Annie's come downstairs, and we want you to meet her." They walked back to the dining room, where Rebel met the young girl her mother and stepfather had brought back with them from the wilderness.

She was all of seven years old now, and the dark sloe eyes reminded Rebel of Beau's sister, Little Fawn, when she was young, only Annie's hair was light brown with a golden hue. She was delicate, and her warm smile lit up her whole face. But when she moved, it was with a catlike grace, every movement fluid and controlled, and Rebel wondered if this small fragile girl could ever truly be a child. She gave the impression of being much older, yet her laughter was warm and natural, and the gaping hole where one of her teeth was missing in front betrayed her age only too well. She was self conscious of the missing tooth and covered it as Beau and Heath, who'd met her on their previous visits, teased her affectionately.

Later in the morning when Cole woke up, Annie fell in love with him and she and Hizzie became fast friends. Rebel stood on the terrace shortly before lunchtime watching them playing in the yard beneath one of the magnolia trees, and she sighed as she looked away, down past the long expanse of lawn and gardens to where the *Golden Eagle* was anchored next to Roth's ship, the *Interlude*. The ship wasn't flying any flag now, and the men were buzzing about, working feverishly to change the lettering on her. Rebel wondered what her new name would be.

"Do you have any suggestions?" asked Beau from behind her, and she whirled around, startled. "At first I thought of naming her the *Rebel,* but I'm afraid that was a little too obvious, so I think I'll call her the *Duchess* instead."

Her eyes studied his face intently. They'd spent the crossing in each other's arms, and the love that flowed between them now was even stronger than it had been before.

"What do we do now, Beau?" she asked, her voice trembling, and she saw the sadness in his eyes.

"I guess we pretend it didn't happen," he said huskily. "It was a dream, Reb, something we knew couldn't last." He stepped close to her, stared down into her violet eyes, and lifted his hand to touch her silken tresses. "I'll always love you, nothing will ever change that, but you're married to someone else and I'm still an Indian, and nothing will ever change that either. Brandon will come to take you back, and I'd rather kill him than let him do that—but if I did we'd have the law after us the rest of our lives." He buried his hand in her hair. "I made myself a promise that I wasn't going to touch you once we reached here," he said softly. "It's going to be bad enough for you when Brandon shows up, but I only hope I can resist, because I'll tell you, lady, you do things to me no woman should be allowed to do."

"Why can't we go away?" she begged anxiously. "We could disappear, Beau. He'd never find us. We could take Cole—"

"No!" She saw his eyes darken. "I won't live with you like that, watching every shadow, afraid he'd catch up to us. Letting Cole grow up without a proper name, and you . . . Do you think I could take the chance on someone finding out? I couldn't shame you like that. Besides, you forget who I am, Reb, I'm the son of a Tuscarora—"

"And your father has four wives and eighteen children and I don't give a damn!" she burst out angrily. "That's all I've heard from you from the first time you kissed me back at Fort Locke, that we live in two different worlds. That you're an Indian. Well, I don't care, but if that's the way you want it, then why don't you go find some Indian maiden and marry her? Marry ten of them. I don't care! You're allowed to have as many wives as you want, aren't you? So why don't you go get one? Get two, three, get as many as you want if it'll make you happy. You keep reminding me it's your heritage!" She turned from him so he wouldn't see the tears in her eyes.

"Reb, please . . ."

She threw her head back stubbornly, shutting her eyes, trying not to cry. "I hate you, Beau. Just leave me alone," she whispered angrily. "Go away. I don't ever want to see you again," and she stood motionless, waiting for him to say something but he didn't, and when she finally turned around to find out why, he was gone, and she sank down on one of the wrought-iron chairs on the terrace and let the tears fall unchecked down her cheeks.

The next few days were strained. Rebel talked to Beau only when necessary, spending all of her spare moments with Cole; and Beau, who'd become fond of playing with Cole during the crossing, watched from a distance as she shut him out. In retaliation he tried to hibernate on board ship, but Roth wouldn't let him.

Roth liked Beau in spite of the man's stubbornness, and he was determined to try to help any way he could, so he dragged Beau with him about Port Royal, showing off the land and pointing out its advantages. At first Beau looked things over reluctantly from his horse's back; then one afternoon when they'd ridden upriver, he found himself standing on the banks of the river looking out across what was the most beautiful setting he'd ever seen. It was more than wild and untamed. It was as if the land were a part of him, and the next afternoon Roth took Heath and him into Beaufort and introduced them to Alec Templer at the bank, who was only too glad to carry the mortgage for Beau.

Most people in Port Royal, Beaufort, and Charleston had known Roth for some years, even before he'd settled there permanently. They knew that he had recently married Loedicia, but since Heath had seldom visited Port Royal, the fact that he was Roth's son had never been brought to light. Now the common misconception concerning his identity was revealed in a remark by Alec Templer.

"Your uncle's a man to be proud of, Mr. Chapman," the banker told Heath as Beau finished signing the papers. "Did you hear he's to run for Congress this fall?"

"I'm not his uncle, I'm his father," corrected Roth simply, putting a possessive arm about his son's shoulder, and once more went into his long explanation.

421

Soon the whole world will know, he thought later as they left the bank, and there won't always be all this explaining to do. He was very pleased as he proudly walked beside his son.

Beau swung into work on his land with a flourish, and Heath was right beside him, determined to help. They used the crew from the *Golden Eagle*, and the first thing they did was build a dock where they could moor the ship. At first the crew was disgruntled. After all, here were men used to violence and killing. Greedy men who thought fighting for something was easier than working for it, and suddenly they were working, and for what? What was there in it for them?

"I'll tell you what's in it for you," said Beau as they finished work the first night and sat around the deck of the ship tired and sweaty. "A share in the profits, and we won't have to risk our necks for it." He pointed toward shore to a stand of trees along the bank. "See those trees up there?" he asked. "Those trees have to come out if I expect to build a house and plant fields, and there's enough timber there twice over to give every one of you a good profit." He saw a few men scowl. "So you work some, and you sweat some, but it isn't forever, and you'll make twice as much as we made privateering. I still need a crew for the ship, men, but I need help with her first cargo. That timber has to be taken to market, but first it has to be cut down. If you won't help me, I'll get a crew that will. One that's not afraid of a little hard, honest work. I'm getting tired of looking over my shoulder every place I go, with one hand on my sword, and I'm tired of risking my neck for a few pieces of silver. With a ship like this we can sail the seas unchallenged and won't have to worry about getting our goods to market like ordinary merchant ships. Shipping is big business if you know what to ship, and if you grow what you ship, you've got an even bigger profit, and any man who stays with me in this will never regret it. You can leave if you want, or stay, it's up to you. It's your choice, but I'll tell you now, if you stay, you'll never be sorry!" and the men stayed.

It was strange to see these big burly seamen felling trees, pulling stumps, and clearing land, but Beau and Heath worked side by side with them, even though Heath complained that he'd rather be sailing. They slept on board ship and many nights went to bed exhausted, but slowly the land was taking shape.

A week after they'd begun to clear the land, Beau and Heath met Rachel Grantham, the dowager Duchess of Bourland, Brandon Avery's aunt. She arrived unannounced one afternoon, and their first sight of her was a blur of frothy blue approaching them across the rutted field that led from the drive they'd cut with a scythe through the woods. She was holding her skirts up, picking her way to where they were working.

"What's that?" asked Heath as they both stared toward the apparition.

"I do believe it's a lady," answered Beau as the rest of the men stopped their work and looked up. His jaw tightened as he realized who it had to be. Roth had warned them about Rachel.

She smiled coquettishly, her hazel eyes admiring them as she held onto her straw sun hat to keep the breeze from whipping it off her head. "I daresay you are the new owners, aren't you?" she asked politely, and Beau wiped his brow, nodding assent.

"I am, ma'am, Beauregard Dante, and my friend Heath Chapman, at your service. And may I ask whom we have the pleasure of addressing?" and Rachel's eyes stopped on Heath, frowning; then she looked back at Beau.

"I'm Rachel Grantham. I own River Oaks plantation downriver," she answered lightly, then looked again at Heath. "Your name is Chapman?" she asked.

"Yes, ma'am."

She studied him more intently as the smile on her face faded. "Then you're Roth's son, aren't you?" she asked, and Heath nodded. Her eyes narrowed, and the early-afternoon sun turned them almost a golden gray as she stared at Heath; then she shrugged flippantly, as if dismissing the matter, but Beau was sure he saw a hardness in the smile she gave them. "To be sure," she acknowledged warmly. "And now, the reason for my visit. I'm having a ball at River Oaks a week from tomorrow, and as new neighbors, you're both invited." She tilted her head, letting the breeze catch her hair, curling it about her face. "It's a political affair, really, in honor of Senator McLaren. All the local politicians will be there, including your mother and father, Heath. I'd be pleased if you'd attend. It isn't every day we have such a distinguished gentleman settling in this part of the country. He and his charming wife bought a home in Beaufort. Their other home is in the capital at Columbia, and it can get dreadfully warm there in the summer."

They listened to her chatter for some quarter of an hour before she finally started back toward her carriage.

"Oh, one more thing, Mr. Dante," she said. "Word travels

so fast along the river. I am right in assuming that my nephew Brandon's wife arrived on your ship, am I not? I know she's in Port Royal, Mr. Dante," she went on coyly, "and I know that Brandon isn't. What puzzles me, sir, is why."

"I suggest, ma'am," he stated with great finality, his voice lowered, "that you ask the lady herself. Good day." Beau and Heath stood watching Rachel's carriage as it disappeared down the drive.

Rachel sat back in the carriage and closed her eyes, wondering just who Beauregard Dante was. He looked French, an aristocrat perhaps, but his English was too fluent. Dante? The name wasn't familiar at all, and she bounced it around in her mind; then suddenly a cold chill ran through her as she remembered the day of her arrival in Charleston almost two years ago. Roth had talked of the captain of the ship that Loedicia was on. And Brandon had mentioned his name too. He was a French privateer, Captain Beau Thunder, Beau! Beauregard? Could it be? It had to be!

She smiled wickedly as it all came back to her, and she rubbed her arms, settling the gooseflesh that had risen. Beauregard Dante, Captain Beau Thunder. Now, what were he and Rebel doing together? Tonight she was going to write a letter to Grenada, but first she was going to pay a visit to the Château. It might be interesting to hear what Rebel had to say about the matter. She leaned forward in the carriage, instructing her driver, then settled back with a smile on her face.

Loedicia was surprised as she greeted Rachel in the sitting room. There was no love lost between the two women, and Dicia made no attempt at friendship, although when the occasion arose, she treated Rachel civilly.

"You and Roth are coming to the ball next week, aren't you, Loedicia?" Rachel asked.

"You know very well we're coming," she answered calmly. "Roth is as anxious to try to sway Senator McLaren to his side as you and your friends are to pull him the other way. We wouldn't miss the chance." She eyed Rachel skeptically. "But that wasn't the real reason you stopped by, now, was it?"

"Well . . . if you must know," she said. "I heard that Rebel's here, and I was wondering why you've been so secretive about it. After all, Brandon is my nephew, even if it is only by marriage . . . and I thought it strange I wasn't told."

"I'm sorry, Rachel, we probably should have told you, but it's a long story. One I'd rather not go into if you don't mind. Rebel is here. If you'd care to say hello, I'm sure she won't mind, but she's had a trying time the past few months, and I'd rather you kept any questions to yourself."

"Why isn't Brandon with her?" asked Rachel, ignoring Dicia's request.

"That's what I mean," countered Dicia. "You ask questions Rebel won't or can't answer."

"Why don't you let her be the judge of that?"

"Because I don't want her upset."

"Loedicia, what are you trying to hide?" she asked callously.

"All right, Rachel! If you must know, Rebel was kidnapped from Grenada by the French."

"Ah, yes, Captain Thunder, Beauregard Dante. You see, I'm not exactly stupid, Loedicia."

"Good," she said firmly. "Then you can understand why she's here. Beau rescued her and brought her to America, where she'll be safe. Now, since the French would love to get their hands on her and since there are still French agents in this country, may I ask your cooperation in not revealing whose wife she happens to be? And may I also ask you to keep silent about Beau's identity? It could mean his life and Heath's too. The French aren't pleased that she's slipped through their hands."

Rachel laughed. "I knew something was going on," she said smartly, "but I had no idea it was so intriguing. Roth certainly did get himself into a peck of trouble when he married you didn't he, Loedicia dear?" she said. "I wonder if he's had second thoughts yet. But then, he'd be the last to admit it, wouldn't he, being the gentleman he is. At least to your face, anyway." Dicia turned crimson and clenched her teeth angrily, unaware that Roth had stepped into the hall just outside the door and heard every word Rachel had spoken.

"I don't think my feelings in the matter are any business of yours, Rachel," he said as he stepped into the room. "But to put your mind at ease, since you seem concerned, I have never had any second thoughts about marrying Dicia, and I never will, no matter what problems we may have to face together." He stepped up behind his wife, putting his arms about her. "My only regret is that I couldn't have married her sooner."

Rachel studied the two of them for a minute, then straightened, her eyes distantly cool. "That was a pretty speech, Roth," she said, composing herself, unwilling to admit defeat. "But you always were good with words. That was always one of your virtues, knowing just what to say and how to say it. It's the reason you'll probably make a good politician, only it's too bad your wife hasn't learned to recognize the difference between guile and sincerity. But then, maybe she likes being played for a fool."

"Get out, Rachel," he ordered angrily, his face white. "We don't need your little games."

Rachel laughed. "Oh, I'll leave, Roth," she replied, pleased with herself as she headed for the door. "I'll be glad to leave, but don't forget dears," she added languorously, "if you don't appear at the ball next week, people will begin to wonder, and we wouldn't want any unhealthy gossip about the Chapmans now, would we?"

Dicia stared after Rachel, her hands trembling, trying to shut out the woman's voice. She hated her. Not only because she had once seduced Quinn Locke, but because since living next door she'd tried every way she could to subtly undermine the love she and Roth shared, to drive a wedge between them by dropping little hints here and there, sly innuendos to try to make her doubt Roth's love. It was a cruel game, and Rachel played it well.

"Hey," Roth said as he took Dicia by the shoulders and turned her to face him, "you're trembling. What's the matter, love? She's not getting to you, is she?"

Dicia looked into his dark, warm eyes. "Oh, Roth," she cried helplessly. "Why won't she leave me alone? Why?"

"Because she knows I love you and she can't stand it. Rachel's the kind of woman who has to have her way with men, and when she can't, it eats at her insides. She wanted Quinn and went after him. She wasn't in love with him, she just wanted him. She thought she had him that night he got drunk, but when he sobered up, he went right back to you. It was a blow to her, and now it's the same thing all over again. She wants what you have again, only it's worse this time, because she wanted me a long time before she knew I was yours, and she doesn't want to take no for an answer. Why do you think she bought the place next door? She knew I'd gone after you. I even told her to go back to England, but she didn't." He stroked a stray hair back on her forehead as he talked. "I admit, at one time I showed her some attention, but I never told her I loved her. I tried to love a lot of women while I was trying to forget you, but I couldn't."

He pulled her into his arms and held her close, his lips on her hair. "I love you, Dicia, I always will, and I'll never regret marrying you." He eased her away from him and cupped her face in both his hands. "Without you my life is nothing.

426

Call them pretty words or whatever, but it's the truth, and you know it. I love you," and he kissed her deeply, his mouth covering hers until there were no more doubts left to haunt her.

The night of Rachel's ball was hot and humid and the air was filled with the smell of cape jasmine and magnolias. At the last minute Rebel decided to go with Roth and Loedicia, since gossip of her presence had already traveled far and wide, although no one seemed to know where she'd come from, only that she was Loedicia's daughter by a former marriage. At least Rachel was keeping her mouth shut, a feat quite unlike her, and Loedicia wondered why.

The ballroom at River Oaks was brightly lit from hundreds of flaming candles in the chandeliers overhead, and people were arriving in droves.

Rachel's business manager was greeting guests at the door. She'd hired a man with an excellent business sense to help her run River Oaks, and the results had been that although she knew little of the actual business end of running a plantation, she did manage to make a good profit. Her manager was a tall gangly man named Alan Minyard, the last in a long line of aristrocrats who'd once owned land in Virginia, but lost it by being on the wrong side during the revolution. Instead of fleeing to Canada or New Orleans as did most Tories, he merely lost himself in South Carolina, working for a banking house and various lucrative endeavors until eventually ending up at River Oaks. His past, however, was lost in the shuffle as far as anyone in Port Royal knew, and since he was rather good-looking, in a jaded fashion, and safely in his middle forties, no one bothered to question his beginnings.

His deep blue eyes coveted Loedicia openly as she stepped into the ballroom wearing a dress of deep green satin with bared shoulders, her hair piled atop her head, held in place with cape jasmine that enhanced the cologne she wore. Small emerald teardrop earrings hung from her ears, matching the delicate lavaliere that rested above her full breasts.

Beside her, Roth, in the new tight-fitting long white pants that were becoming all the rage, and wearing a velvet coat of deep russet, his cravat tied meticulously, was reassuring Rebel her appearance tonight would in no way affect his political future.

"You look enchanting," he assured her as he glanced at the pink lace dress he and Loedicia had bought her, with yards of ruffled skirts and a bodice low enough to reveal her full breasts, made even fuller by her pregnancy, which was not yet apparent in the rest of her body. Her hair was styled much like her mother's, with pink camellias entwined amid the curls, and her only jewelry was a single strand of her mother's pearls and pearl drop earrings.

Roth's arm moved about Loedicia's waist possessively as he spoke to Rebel. "I'm sure you'll enjoy yourself, Rebel, so don't worry. All anyone has to know is that you've come for a visit." He turned to Alan Minyard and shook hands, then introduced Rebel.

"I can see she's your daughter, Loedicia," Alan said as he smiled at Rebel, his thin face studying her appreciatively. "Except for the coloring of her hair, she's an exact duplicate." His smile broadened, almost forcefully. "I do hope you'll enjoy your visit. Mrs. Avery, isn't it?" he queried, and Rebel smiled back self-consciously.

"Yes, Mr. Minyard," she answered, trying to be polite, "and I'm certain I'll enjoy the visit." She glanced away from him while he made small talk with Loedicia and Roth, then excused himself to greet some new arrivals. "So that's Rachel's manager," Rebel mused. "I don't think I like him."

"That makes three of us, dear," Loedicia agreed wholeheartedly as she took Roth's arm and they joined the crowd that was converging on the punch bowl.

Senator Victor McLaren and his wife arrived some halfhour late, their ride from Beaufort having been delayed by a last-minute visit from one of the senator's aides.

Rachel squired the senator and his wife about, introducing them to everyone. Victor McLaren was a paunchy man in his late forties. Unlike Roth, who'd kept himself in shape, the senator had spent too many years behind desks and at banquet tables and parties, and the years showed, not only in the excess weight he carried, but in his iron-gray hair, sagging jowls, and lined face.

His first wife had died three years earlier, and it was no surprise that the second Mrs. McLaren was some twenty-odd years his junior. Cora McLaren, it was rumored, had been a good friend of the senator's before his first wife's death, but there were always rumors of that sort, and nothing had ever come of them. Besides, Cora was gay and witty, and the senator seemed completely happy with her, even though she did spend money lavishly.

She stood beside the senator now, her honey-brown hair dressed to perfection, with diamonds peeping here and there among the curls, and her huge brown eyes were made to look

en deeper by the apricot color of the sheer organza dress
at sheathed her voluptuous figure, baring an extreme
décolleté, where pear-shaped diamonds clung to her throat.
he was not really a beautiful woman in the sense that men
ared when she entered a room, but she was attractive in a
ensuous way, her pretty face made prettier by the right
lothes. The senator, standing next to her in his gold bro-
ades, reminded Rebel of Brandon.

The senator seemed pleased with the turnout in his honor.
He knew many of the men. Statesmen, politicians, local offi-
ials, landowners, merchants; but some were new to him, as
vere many of their wives. He'd visited Charleston off and on
ver the years, but lived in Columbia, the capital. He'd never
met Roth Chapman.

"And this is my neighbor Mr. Roth Chapman of the
Château, his wife, Loedicia, and Loedicia's daughter, Rebel
Avery," Rachel said as she introduced them. The senator
smiled as he shook hands with Roth and bowed to the
women.

"So you're one of the young upstarts who's trying to help
push through a bill to stop the slave ships," the senator said.
"We need do-gooders like you in politics, young man," he
blustered energetically. "It gives us old-timers a chance to get
our teeth into a good fight. Makes us look good with the
people. Helps them take sides. Puts spice into things, but just
don't overdo it."

Roth smiled cordially. "I'm afraid you've been misled, Senator," he corrected. "In the first place, I'm not in this for fun.
The men who are backing me are as serious as I am over the
slave-ship issue. And in the second place, you're mistaken if
you think I'm a young upstart. I'm flattered, but I believe if
reports are right, sir, we are both of the same age, and political intrigues are not new to me."

The senator stared at Roth, taking a quick glance at the
slight frost at his temples and noting for the first time the
deepening lines that were beginning to frame his warm dark
eyes. He would never have dreamed . . . The man looked
ten years younger. "Incredible, sir," he remarked, and Roth
acknowledged his flattery.

"Hard work," answered Roth to the senator's unspoken
question, and the senator laughed, putting his arm about his
wife, introducing her to them proudly.

Loedicia noticed a strange, thoughtful look in the eyes of
the senator's wife as she stared at Roth when they were introduced, and she was sure the woman's face had paled slightly,

then flushed as Roth greeted her. Roth's expression neve
changed in any manner to indicate that anything was wrong
so she shrugged it off, blaming it on Rachel's damaging ac
cusations. After all, Roth was extremely handsome.

Rachel could cause more trouble with her wagging tongu
than a dozen women, and Dicia wouldn't allow it to get th
best of her.

Heath and Beau arrived while the Chapmans an
McLarens were talking. "I hate being late," Heath com
plained. He'd been staying with Beau on the ship, anchore
at his property upriver. "The men could have taken care o
the mare without our help." Beau disagreed as he followe
Heath into the crowded ballroom.

"Not a one of those sea dogs knows a thing about foaling
mare, Heath, and you know it," Beau said.

Beau had bought a mare that was ready to foal. It was ou
of season and he'd gotten her for a reasonable price, bu
she'd picked tonight to go into labor, and since none of th
crew knew a thing about horses, they'd had to stick around t
see it through.

Heath smiled as he looked at Beau. "It's just that wheneve
we're late for anything like this, I always miss out on the en
tertainment because the eligible young ladies are usuall
taken already."

"Poor lad," sighed Beau. "If I know you, you'll make uj
for it." He nodded toward one end of the ballroom, where
group of people was collected. "There's your mother and fa
ther with some other people. I suspect that's the senato
they're talking to. At least he seems to be the center of atten
tion, so I assume that's who it is." Heath glanced in the direc
tion where Beau was motioning, and he started to sa
something, then stopped dead still, staring.

"My God, what's the matter, Heath?" asked Beau. "You
look like you've seen a ghost."

Heath's mouth opened slowly. "Tell me I'm not dreaming
Beau," he whispered softly, "but that woman talking with m
mother . . . Beau, that's Cora!"

Beau studied the woman's face. Cora? Back in 1791, whe
he and Heath had left Fort Locke in search of Roth, they'
surprised some Indians raiding a farmhouse and had rescue
seventeen-year-old Cora Richmond, the only one left alive
She'd accompanied them to Philadelphia, and although sh
was two years older than Heath, uneducated, and rathe
coarse, she'd initiated him at the age of fifteen into the art o
lovemaking. When he and Heath were shanghaied and lef

Philadelphia behind, they'd left Cora too, with not even a chance for a farewell. Cora Richmond, whose taste in men was quality and who'd vowed to Beau that someday she'd be somebody.

Beau and Heath watched the senator's arm grace Cora's waist affectionately, and neither said a word for a long time. Heath watched the rise and fall of her breasts as she spoke, and the quick laughter in her brown eyes. He followed the line of her dress, taking in the curves barely visible beneath its sheer organza folds, and the way her hands gestured gracefully as she talked to the people around her. He remembered a young girl in a secondhand dress with a straw hat on her head hugging him about the waist as they rode into Philadelphia. And he also remembered vividly her soft body yeilding to him in her bed in the tiny room off the kitchen at the Blue Anchor Inn.

"What do we do now?" he asked Beau, finally finding his voice.

"What do you want to do?" he asked slowly, and Heath looked away from Cora to the crowd of people around them.

"Do you think she'll recognize us?" he asked.

"Not on purpose, she won't," he answered. "If she's the senator's wife, she won't want anyone to know about her humble beginnings. My bet is that the senator himself doesn't even know, so play it by ear, friend," he advised, "and I suggest you make up your mind what you're going to do damn quick because the dowager duchess has spotted us and she's motioning us over."

Heath took a deep breath and swallowed hard as he moved across the floor, propelled by Beau's occasional nudge. His eyes rested directly on Cora, who was still talking with Loedicia and hadn't spotted him.

When she finished what she was saying, she laughed, looking toward them, and suddenly she frowned, her eyes faltering, lips frozen momentarily as she looked directly into Heath's eyes. Slowly the blood drained from her face, and her lips began to tremble; then, abruptly, catching herself, realizing everyone was greeting the newcomers and no one had noticed, she grabbed her husband's arm as if for support.

"These are our new neighbors to the north upriver," Rachel was saying. "Young men with young dreams," and she introduced Heath and Beau to the senator and his wife.

"Chapman?" questioned Cora, her voice strained and a fraction too loud. "That's your name too, isn't it?" she asked

Roth. He smiled and proceeded to go into his long explanation about how they happened to be father and son.

"Well, indeed," said the senator boisterously as Roth finished. Further conversation was forgotten as Rachel interrupted, reminding the senator that as honored guests he and his wife were to start the first dance.

The evening went fairly well considering that Rachel had thrown together men who were on opposite sides of the slave-trade issue, which was one of the biggest issues of the coming election; and with the added weight of Loedicia's dislike for her hostess, Heath's quandary over Cora's sudden appearance, and Beau and Rebel's strained relationship, it was a wonder really that it went off at all. In spite of the undercurrents and tension that ran through the guests, everyone seemed to be enjoying himself, even Beau, who danced with Rebel more often than he should, thrilling to the feel of her in his arms and watching covetously whenever she danced with someone else.

It was almost eleven. Heath had purposely avoided Cora, afraid he might give himself away, and instead he'd paid court to a young thing whose parents owned a plantation on Hilton Head across Port Royal Sound. She was pretty, but shy. So much so that he had to force the conversation, and now he stood alone outside near the carriages, getting a much-needed breath of fresh air.

He fanned his face, then pushed a lock of hair back from his forehead and leaned back against one of the trees, closing his eyes, feeling the warm breeze on his face. The ballroom had been so stuffy. He relaxed for a long time, listening to the music that drifted out across the lawn, then stretched and started to straighten when a sound made him turn abruptly, and he lowered his arms slowly as Cora stepped from behind one of the carriages.

"It's been a long time, hasn't it, Heath?" she said hesitantly.

"I thought maybe you'd forgotten, and I didn't want to push it in front of your husband," he answered unsteadily, wondering why he was making excuses. He didn't have to. After all, she was nothing to him anymore. "A senator's wife," he mused. "How'd you manage that?"

"With no help from you," she answered flippantly; then her voice lowered. "The least you could have done was said good-bye."

"Beau and I were shanghaied."

"Oh!"

"Did you think I cared so little for you?"

"I didn't know what to think."

"But you thought I'd deserted you."

"I watched for you all that night and the next day and the next week. Polly kept me on with her. She let me work for her, and I practiced the reading and writing you taught me. But Polly died and I had no one again. She treated me like a daughter, though, and left the inn to me because she had no relatives, so I sold it and used the money to buy myself some fancy clothes and paid a lady to teach me to walk and talk properly." Her eyes lowered. "A girl has to live, Heath," she said softly, "and I wasn't about to starve. Not Cora Richmond. I wanted something better than being a serving girl and spending my days in an inn cooking and making beds. I met the senator at a party one of my gentleman friends took me to, and when his wife died . . ." She shrugged, then raised her eyes to his again as if daring him to condemn her.

"Are you in love with him?" he asked.

"What do you think?"

He was close to her and the sweet, heady fragrance of her perfume drifted up to him, stirring him deep inside. It had been five years since he'd held her in his arms. Five long years since she'd let him use her body to discover all the secret's a woman's body held. He'd been fifteen then; now he was twenty and there'd been dozens of women in between, but somehow it had never been the same. Maybe because she was the first, he didn't know. He wasn't even sure he'd even loved her; it was something else maybe, a bond between them, an intimate sharing.

She was beautiful, he had to admit, warm and sensuous, and her huge brown eyes melted him clear to his toes. "I don't think you are," he whispered softly.

He knew what she wanted, what she needed. One look at her husband told him, but he wasn't quite sure he wanted to give it to her. He disliked fooling with another man's wife, but then, this was Cora. The girl he'd been forced to leave behind on the streets of Philadelphia, the girl who'd caused him many a sleepless night for weeks and months when he'd ached to hold her, and she was a woman now.

Without thinking, Heath's arms went around her, and he drew her close; his mouth covered hers and he forgot he was no longer fifteen and she was no longer his to hold, and he kissed her with a violent passion that surged from the very depths of his soul.

21

The Fourth of July passed with the usual celebrations, an the dog days of August gave way to the easy warmth of Sej tember's golden harvests. Crops were good along the botton lands, and the river traffic kept the markets full t overflowing.

Beau denied himself the luxury of Rebel's love and threw himself into his work. He devoted all his time to the lan he'd bought, wearing himself out, while Rebel hibernate pacing the floors at the Château, wondering if she should te him about her pregnancy. She dreaded the day Brandon woul arrive and everyone would know.

Loedicia accompanied Roth about the countrysid watching him give speeches and cheering him on as he can paigned for Congress. She tried to ignore the barbs Rach threw her way, and lived down the rumors that had obvious originated on Rachel's tongue.

Meanwhile, Rachel waited impatiently for word fro Brandon. She used her friendships with Roth's opposition t her own advantage in the hopes she could ruin his marriag On her own plantation, under the sadistic treatment of h manager and overseer, her slaves seethed and smoldered wit hatred.

In secret, Heath found himself desperately entangled in love affair he hadn't wanted, but couldn't seem to end.

By the end of October, with elections drawing closer, em tions in not only Port Royal but also Charleston, Beaufor and surrounding areas were running high. Most of the plant tion owners were content with life as it was, but men lik Roth and his constituents wanted something better for th South. They wanted prosperity. Not for just a chosen fev but for everyone, and they felt the only way to accomplish was to abolish slavery altogether and create jobs for th many. Yet they knew the country wasn't ready. They'd hav to take small steps first, and the first step was to try to rid th as of the ugly slave ships that still raided foreign shores, ringing back their half-dead cargoes.

Although most people avoided association with the men who sailed these ships, they thought nothing of picking over the pitiful men and women brought back on them as if they were no better than cattle, and the appearance of Roth and his sympathizers at the auctions whenever a slave ship docked always caused a stir, because Roth seldom bid, preferring to talk about annoying people with his presence. When he did bid, he was never outbid, and people resented it because they knew that within a year or two, maybe less, the slaves he bought would be roaming about the country free. And now Beau Dante, newcomer to Port Royal, began echoing Roth's sentiments.

His first addition to the small house he and his crew built was a plump black woman and her husband. They'd have been separated on the auction block if Beau hadn't bought them, and when he explained that they'd work out their sale price, then be free, they couldn't do enough to make life pleasant for him. Liza was a good cook and Job took over the care of the horses, and slowly Beau's land began to take shape. But it was the big Watusi warrior Beau acquired that proved the best idea.

The slave market had been crowded that day with the men and women dragged from the holds of a slave ship that had docked the night before. They'd been cleaned hurriedly so they'd pass inspection, but one huge man refused to cooperate, and his strength, even after the nightmare crossing, was still that of a young bull. When Beau spotted him he was being beaten with a cat-o'-nine-tails, and still he had the courage to rain oaths on his tormentor.

When Beau, after outbidding everyone for the man, left to take him back upriver to his small plantation, people thought he was crazy, warning him that the man needed a strong overseer to whip the fight out of him, and predicted he'd run away first chance he got. But Heath knew what Beau was doing and explained to Roth on the way home that one of Beau's crew had been born a Watusi. He'd been captured by a slaver and sold to a sugar plantation on the island of Jamaica, but he'd run away from his owners, and Beau had found him unconscious on a beach one night. They'd nursed him back to health and he'd become a permanent member of the crew. They'd called him Jamaica, nicknamed him Jamie, and within a week, under Jamie's tutelage, the man Beau had bought, became a willing worker. He was also a born leader, and by election time Beau was cultivating him for the job of overseer.

His work was going well, but two things troubled Beau greatly. Rebel and Heath. He hadn't seen Rebel for almost two months. He'd had occasion to visit the Château to see Roth's overseer, Silas Morgan, for various reasons, and had dropped in with Heath several times, but he'd never had so much as a glimpse of her. The last time he'd seen her, they'd argued as usual. Why couldn't she see his side of it? It wasn't that he didn't want her. On the contrary, he wanted her so much he went to bed at night aching for her, and during the day he was restless and stony-faced, eating his heart out for her.

"You ought to come into Beaufort with me," said Heath one evening as he dressed.

"I'd just as soon stay here."

"It'd do you good." Heath straightened his cravat in the mirror over the sofa on the far wall. "You've been cranky as an old bear lately. I think you need a woman's touch."

"Forget it."

Heath stared at him. "What do you think you are, superhuman? I could find you a woman . . . blond if you want," and Beau stood up, eyes blazing.

"I said forget it!" He walked to the window that looked out over the river and pulled the curtain back. "If I want a woman I'll find one of my own," he said. "By the way, I've been meaning to ask you, what's the attraction in Beaufort lately, Heath?"

"Ladies, naturally."

"Or is it one lady in particular? Heath, if you're messing around with Cora . . ."

"And if I am?"

"For God's sake, Heath, her husband's a senator."

"And twenty-five years older than she is."

"She should have thought of that before she married him."

"Like Rebel should have thought before she married Brandon?"

Beau's jaw tightened.

"It's all right for you, but not me, is that it?" Heath went on heatedly. "I know what went on between you two during the crossing, Beau, I'm not blind."

"Rebel and I are different."

"How? Because you've had a son together? She's still another man's wife!"

"I don't have to be reminded."

436

"Neither do I!"

"Heath . . ." Beau exhaled wearily. "You're playing with fire. If the senator ever found out . . ."

"Don't worry," soothed Heath with his inimitably charming smile. "We're very discreet. And Beau," he said, "nothing's going to happen." Beau stared after him for a long time, then called to Liza in the kitchen.

"Put some bathwater out for me, Liza," he called, "I'm going to go out tonight."

As he rode up the drive to the Château later in the evening, he wondered what he was doing here. All the way downriver he'd kept telling himself it was for Heath, but now as he pulled up to the front door, he wasn't quite sure, and his stomach began to tighten, his loins tingling with a sweet, savage ache.

"Mr. and Mrs. Chapman ain't home this evenin', Mr. Dante," advised the girl who opened the door. "Miss Annie's sleepin' already, but Mrs. Avery's sitting out on the terrace in back."

Beau stepped inside and handed her his hat. "Don't announce me," he said quietly.

The night was cool and clear, with a profusion of stars overhead, and Rebel reached down to pick up the shawl she'd dropped on the chair when she'd come out on the terrace a short time ago, but as she turned, she stopped, staring at the open French doors as Beau walked through them. There was no time to hide, no time to even pull the shawl about her, and she stood before him, her face drained of color as she saw his eyes move to the thick bulge beneath the waistline of the pale green dress she wore.

He stared for a long time, then stepped the rest of the way onto the terrace. Neither of them spoke as he walked across the flagstones and stopped so close to her she could smell the familiar scent of him, clean and masculine. He continued to stare at her, then reached out, putting his hand on her stomach intimately, his eyes warm with love.

"Why didn't you tell me?" he asked huskily, and her eyes misted with tears.

"Would it have helped?"

His arm went about her waist, and he tried to pull her closer, but she held her hands on his chest, feeling the warmth of his body beneath her fingertips.

"Beau, it's no good," she said softly. "You're right. I'm another man's wife."

"And you're going to have my child."

She half-laughed. "It's nothing new."

"What fools we are," he whispered, "especially me. I should never have left Fort Locke. I should have married you in spite of everything." This time when he pulled her close she let him. "I love you, Reb," he murmured against her mouth, "I want you more than anything on this earth," and his mouth covered hers as her arms went about his neck. He kissed her deeply, savoring her body in his arms.

"My, what a cozy scene," said a sharp voice from the other side of the terrace. There stood Brandon, his brown eyes deadly, feet spread arrogantly.

"Well, well, well, Mistress Slut, playing her little games again, I see," he said viciously, and he looked at Beau. "I assume, as usual, you're the father?"

Beau stepped in front of Rebel to shield her from Brandon's wrath. "I want you to give Rebel her freedom."

"You're a bigger fool than I thought," he snapped. "The ceremony explicitly said until death do us part, and I'm still very much alive, Mr. Dante, and as long as I'm alive, Rebel will remain my wife, is that understood?"

"Even though she hates you?"

"Hates? That's a strong word," he said, his voice a little too calm and reserved. "She didn't hate me when she shared my bed on Grenada. In fact, I think Rebel's happy sharing any man's bed. A price I have to pay for marrying a woman of her temperament, I suppose, but then, one can't have everything."

"I won't let her go," said Beau angrily. "I should never have let her marry you."

"But you did, and she's my wife, and I've come a long way after her." Brandon walked toward them. "I arrived only a short time ago on my ship, the *Eagle Hunter*, and I've a carriage outside waiting. We're stopping at Rachel's——"

"She's not going!" insisted Beau, and Rebel started to scream as Brandon grabbed for Beau, but Roth's voice bellowing from inside the house stopped him.

"What's going on here?" Roth demanded angrily as he marched onto the terrace, Loedicia at his side. "What are you doing in my house?"

"I've come after my wife."

"Well, you can leave without her!"

Rebel wrung her hands nervously. They were all three on the verge of killing each other.

"I don't think Rebel wants to go with you, Brandon," Loedicia said, trying to keep her voice steady.

"What Rebel wants is immaterial," he said coldly. "The fact is, she is my wife legally, and as such she'll answer to me. I'd hate to have to bring the authorities into it, but I will if it's necessary. My ship docked not an hour ago and I've made arrangements with Rachel. We'll stay there until it's time to return to Grenada." He turned, looking at Rebel, who stood at Beau's elbow. "Get your things, Rebel," he ordered, but Beau put his hand on her arm.

"You're not going anywhere, Reb," he said firmly, and Brandon started to protest, only to be cut off by Roth.

"Beau's right," Roth said angrily. "Rebel's staying here. I had no right to stop you from taking her with you when we were in Charleston, Brandon, but she's my stepdaughter now and I say she stays. There's no law that says she has to go with you."

"She's my wife!"

"But not your slave!"

Brandon's eyes narrowed. "You can't get away with this," he said, his face red with frustration. "No one has a right to interfere with a man and his wife!"

"Since I'm well-acquainted with the authorities hereabouts, I don't think we'll have any problem," answered Roth. "Now, I suggest you leave."

Brandon was breathing heavily, anger smoldering behind his deep amber eyes as he stared at Roth, then glanced quickly toward his wife and Beau. He was no match for either man, and he knew it. Trying to take her by force would be useless. He needed time.

"All right," he conceded suddenly, straightening his brocade frock coat. "If that's the way you want it, that's the way it'll be. But I'm warning all of you," he said, his eyes sweeping over them, "the law's on my side. You'll see," and he smiled coldly. "Good evening," and he turned abruptly without saying another word and walked away, leaving a dead silence in his wake.

Loedicia was the first to speak as she looked up at Roth, her voice breathless. "Roth, what do you think he'll do?" she asked, and Roth frowned, wondering.

What would Brandon do? Carry out his threat and bring the authorities? For sure he wasn't going to give in this easily. And just how far could they go in denying him his wife?

"I don't know," Roth answered. "I wish I did. But first thing in the morning I'm going into town and find out what course Rebel has to take to extricate herself from the man."

Rebel leaned against Beau, her knees trembling. She'd been

so afraid. Not for herself, but for Beau. They didn't know Brandon the way she did. He hated Beau, and it would have been so like him to conceal a weapon beneath his coat, with the intention of ridding himself of the man who'd made his life so miserable. Roth spoke of her divorcing Brandon, but it wasn't that easy, and as Beau turned toward her, his arms trying to comfort her, she shook her head, turning to Roth.

"You can't go into town tomorrow, Roth," she told him unhappily. "It won't do any good. Brandon will never let me go. We all know it. You heard him." She straightened and pulled away from Beau. "Besides, if you go into town and start asking questions, people are bound to start wondering. As things are now, everyone thinks I'm carrying Brandon's child. If the truth comes out, it'll create a horrible scandal, and the election is so close . . . I don't want you losing the election because of me, Roth."

"I won't lose it."

"But there is a chance you could. Isn't there?"

Roth didn't want to answer, but felt Loedicia's hand squeeze his. There was no way he could fool them. "There's always a chance," he finally said. "The opposition would like nothing better than to get hold of something like this," and Rebel nodded.

"I thought as much. Then for now let's just leave things as they are, please," she said. "If Brandon goes to the authorities—which I don't think he will just yet, because I know Brandon . . . he's too proud, he'll try to think of something else first—but if he does, then I don't care what we have to do to get me out of this mess. But for now, until after the election, let's not do anything, please. Elections aren't that far away, and I couldn't live with myself knowing I was the cause of Roth's losing his bid for Congress."

Beau reached up and touched Rebel's shoulder, turning her to face him, and the love in his eyes was so intense it made her cry out. "Please, Beau," she cried softly. "We'll have the rest of our lives to be together, but this country needs men like Roth to run it. I'd feel horrible if I took my happiness at the expense of others."

"It's what you want?" he asked.

Rebel frowned for a moment, then studied the face of the man she loved more than life itself. "I think it's what we both want. Isn't it?" she asked, and she was right. A scandal like this could do irreparable damage to Roth, and as much as they loved each other, neither of them wanted that. So it was settled. Unless Brandon made the first move, they'd go on about life as if he hadn't arrived, until after the elections.

In spite of their decision, Rebel was uneasy. She didn't trust Brandon. The look in his eyes just before he'd left had been frightening. She knew he was capable of anything. But when the first couple of days went by with no word from River Oaks, she relaxed a little. Maybe Brandon was finally going to concede defeat. She had thought by now he would have at least tried another visit to persuade her, or sent a message, but nothing.

It was late one afternoon not quite a week after Brandon's unannounced arrival. Rebel, Hizzie, and Loedicia had a habit of taking Cole out for buggy rides after his afternoon nap, but this particular afternoon Loedicia wasn't along. She and Roth had gone to Beaufort to a political rally. So Rebel, with Hizzie along, and against Silas' and Jacob's wishes, was enjoying the warm afternoon, dreaming of what it would be like to spend the rest of her life with Beau, and she paid little attention as three men on horseback approached the buggy from across an empty field.

Suddenly one of the men called to them. She stopped the buggy and shaded her eyes against the lowering sun, wondering who it could be. It wasn't until the men were only a short distance away that she recognized the captain from Brandon's ship, the *Eagle Hunter*, with two of his crew but now it was too late and her heart began to pound.

She tugged frantically at the reins, trying to pull the buggy about, but the men were quicker. They spurred their horses alongside. One grabbed the horse's halter while another dived onto the seat, grabbing the reins, pushing Hizzie and Cole to the floor.

"Stay there!" he shouted to Hizzie, and she hugged Cole to her, staring wide-eyed at Rebel, who was looking into the barrel of a pistol the captain had leveled on her.

Rebel reached out and put her hand on Hizzie's head as the poor girl crouched awkwardly on the floor with the baby. "Do like he says, Hizzie," she whispered softly, and felt her heart sink to her feet.

The man handed her back the reins, then stuck a pistol in her ribs, and within minutes they had swung off the road across the field and were heading for a stand of timber some distance away, the captain still on horseback in the lead. He was sandy-haired, tall, and lean, with a narrow face that reminded Rebel of a weasel, and his henchmen were just as unsavory.

Sometime later Rebel was forced to draw rein in front of an old tumbledown shack, and once more the captain took command.

"Inside," he ordered, and Rebel was pushed from the buggy, helping Hizzie with Cole the best she could when one of the men tried to make them move faster.

"It won't work," she said angrily, her eyes blazing. "I know what he's trying to do, but it won't work. Beau will come after me."

The captain smiled wickedly, waving his pistol sweepingly as he shoved them through the door of the shed, then gave orders to one of his men to go after the governor. It was dark by the time Brandon arrived to take them with him to River Oaks.

Rebel sat quietly in a corner of the closed carriage as it pulled away from the shed, her blond hair a pale outline in the darkness, while Hizzie sat opposite her, still clutching Cole in her arms. It had been ten months since Heath and Beau had spirited them away from Grenada, and now things she'd tried to submerge about her life with Brandon all came flooding back again.

"Why so quiet?" he asked cynically. She didn't know what to say, so she didn't answer. "I don't blame you," he said. "Adultery is a sin that isn't easily forgiven."

"For a woman, you mean," she snapped angrily. "That is what you meant, isn't it, Brandon? I bet you had your fair pick of women after I was kidnapped from Grenada, didn't you? Probably the same ones you used while I was pregnant." She heard his indrawn breath. "You thought I didn't know. You've had so many women, it's a wonder you don't have your own bastards running all about, but I guess that's because you can't father anything, isn't it? It's the only reason I can think of why you never got me pregnant. You certainly did try hard enough, didn't you?"

"Shut up!" he said.

"What was that you told me?" she went on. "You were going to keep me pregnant so I could suffer." She laughed again, louder. "You couldn't even do it once."

"I said shut up!" His hand lashed out, and he caught her on the side of the head. She bit her lip as pain shot through her ear, exploding in her brain. But she didn't care. She'd scored a victory and she shut her eyes until the pain subsided, while Hizzie watched, petrified.

The rest of the ride was in silence except for Cole's whimpering and Hizzie's attempts to comfort him, and Rebel was still silent when they reached River Oaks and she was separated from her son and led to her room. She might have known Brandon would do something like this.

Rachel's household was far different from the Château. Her servants were quiet, their eyes grave as they prepared a bath for her and laid out some clothes. Brandon had brought her things from Grenada, and she finished her bath, then put on a pink nightgown one of the girls brought to her, never questioning the silent way they had of doing their work. At the Château everyone was always chattering happily. Here it was like entering a tomb.

The bedroom was huge, with gold draperies and a carpet patterned with deep blues and golds. The heavy ornate furniture was cushioned in blue plush, with pale blue netting curtaining the large bed. Rebel sat in front of the vanity mirror brushing her hair, wondering what to expect next, when Brandon walked in.

At first she thought he was over the worst of his anger because he was casual as he walked to the bed undressing. Then suddenly, as he stepped from his buff pants and threw them aside, he turned and looked at her, his eyes hot, like amber coals.

"Stand up and come here," he ordered boldly, and she stopped, the brush halfway down her hair. "Come here!"

She set the brush down and stood up, her knees shaking and heart pounding. She stopped a few feet from him, and her eyes lowered before his steady gaze.

"Take off the nightgown," he said, calmly this time. "Take it off. I want to see how much damage that son of a bitch's bastard has done to you."

"No. You can see without that!" and she put her hand on her stomach.

He reached out and grabbed the nightgown, his hand forcing the material, and she cried out as the straps pulled against her shoulder; then it gave way, ripping from her body.

He made her stand naked in front of him for a long time, hands at her sides as he stared at her, his eyes covering every curving swell of her stomach; then suddenly his face went white with rage.

"Bastard!" he screamed hoarsely, and her eyes opened wide as she saw his fist coming at her. The impact took her breath away. She tried to scream for help. "Whore! Slut!" he yelled viciously, then a tirade of obscene descriptions flowed from his mouth as he called her every name he could think of over and over again, and with each word his fists drove into her body and she tried unsuccessfully to defend the swollen stomach he was using for a target.

Pain burst from her insides, exploding into her loins as his fists ground into her flesh. She gasped for air, screaming, shrieking for help, but no help came. She tried to back away, but there was nowhere to go, and she fell across the bed gasping, begging him to stop. But he was like a madman, fists hitting her swollen stomach over and over again.

Her stomach was on fire, and pain choked her. He hadn't touched her face, only her stomach, but it was enough. She couldn't stop the vomiting. Suddenly his fists stopped as she choked the foul-tasting bile onto the beautiful gold bedspread, but he didn't help her.

She lay on the bed sobbing, then gasped for breath as her pain-racked body began to convulse.

Brandon put on his robe and called for one of the servants. The woman who came in was small, with dark piercing eyes and a forced smile.

"Take care of my wife," he ordered haughtily. "She picks the most inconvenient times to become ill." He left the room, closing the door firmly behind him.

The woman stood still until she could no longer hear him; then she moved slowly to the bed to see what was going on. The forced smile left her face quickly as she saw the gasping woman on the bed and the fine trickle of blood between her legs that was beginning to stain the bedspread.

She lifted Rebel's head up and wiped her face, then ran her cool hand across her forehead. She looked anxiously at Rebel's stomach. The black-and-blue marks became deeper as each minute passed, and she mumbled under her breath as she grabbed for the bell pull beside the bed.

Two young girls joined her, and the three of them worked with Rebel, doing everything they could, but it was hopeless. They knew who she was. They'd seen her on the night of the ball and they were well aware of who her stepfather was. They tried their best, but Brandon had done his work well. At three in the morning of October 28, 1796, Rebel had another son, born dead, a birth that was never recorded.

Heath had been pacing the floor in the drawing room of the Château for over an hour now. He stopped and glanced at Beau who sat back in one of the armchairs, eyes shut, face filled with pain. Heath had to do everything except physically tie Beau down to keep him from riding to River Oaks and

emanding to see Brandon. After all, they weren't even sure
rrandon had her.

Heath looked up, relieved now that Roth and Loedicia had
nally arrived home.

"What is it? What's happened?" asked Roth as they hurried
nto the room, and Beau left the chair, muscles tense, mouth
drawn.

"Rebel's disappeared," he said.

"She and Hizzie took Cole out for a ride and they never
came back," explained Heath. "Jacob found the buggy at the
side of the road. The horse was still harnessed, grazing, and
not a soul around."

"Oh, my God!" Loedicia's hand flew to her breast.

"Beau thinks Brandon has her," said Heath.

Roth frowned. "Are you sure?"

"No, we're not sure. But who else would do something like
this?" asked Beau.

"But we can't be sure."

"I can. He'd do anything to get her back."

"We have no proof."

"I'd have had proof if Heath hadn't stopped me."

Heath shook his head. "He wanted to go storming over
and demand to see Rebel. They'd have thrown him out."

"I wasn't going to demand to see her. They wouldn't even
have known I was there."

"You think they'd let you sneak in? If Brandon does have
them, he's bound to have them well-guarded, and how would
you get inside the house without being seen?"

"Heath's right," said Roth. "Besides, what if he doesn't
have her? What if something else has happened to her? The
river brings a lot of violent men to Port Royal. I've warned
her before about riding around alone."

"We have to find out," said Beau.

Loedicia put her hand on his arm. "I'll find out," she said,
and they all looked at her. "Well, I will," she confirmed,
glancing up at her husband. "Tomorrow I'll take a ride to
River Oaks."

"You think Brandon's going to admit he kidnapped her?"
asked Beau.

She shook her head. "No. I think Brandon will make up
some story about Rebel changing her mind or something of
the sort. But I think he'll tell me whether she's there or not."

Roth wasn't sure. "I don't know."

"I do," she answered. "He's too proud not to. He always
has been the kind to rub salt in a wound."

"And if she is there?" asked Beau.

"If she is," answered Loedicia, "once he has her back there isn't much we can do, short of kidnapping her again, to get her from him. After all, he is her husband."

Beau turned abruptly and walked to the window, staring out. Nothing they could do? Well, there was something he could do, and he'd do it, too, if he had to. He turned back to face them again, and they made plans for the following day.

The next afternoon Loedicia walked into the sitting room at River Oaks.

"Where's Rebel?" she asked angrily as she stopped in the middle of the elaborate room, staring at Brandon, and he smiled warmly, trying to show some of his old charm, never indicating that her question was at all unusual.

"She's resting," he said casually. "Last evening was tiring for her, I'm afraid. It's been a long time since we've been together . . ."

"I'd like to talk to her if you don't mind."

"Oh, but I do," he objected. "I wouldn't want to wake her. Perhaps another time."

Loedicia's violet eyes studied him warily. He was too calm and self-assured. "I want to know what she's doing here," she demanded, and Brandon gloated.

"She changed her mind."

"I don't believe you."

"Why don't you come back another time, then?" he suggested. "I'm sure she'll be rested and feeling better in a few days."

"Then let me see Cole and Hizzie."

"I'm afraid I can't do that. The baby's asleep."

Loedicia watched Brandon's eyes as he talked of the baby and the look in them gave her gooseflesh.

Brandon smiled that forced smile again. "Don't let it worry you," he said politely. "As I said when I was at the Château, we have everything ready and they'll be well taken care of," he assured her. "Now, would you care for some tea? Rachel's busy this morning, but I'd enjoy some myself. . . ."

She declined, her heart pounding as she finally managed to get away from him and leave the house, but she saw him watching from one of the windows as the carriage moved down the drive.

When she reached the Château she ran into the house. Beau, Heath, and Roth were in the library trying to keep busy, discussing the cost of some repairs to the cotton mill, when she burst in, her face pale.

"My God, what's the matter?" Roth asked.

"Roth, something's dreadfully wrong!" she gasped breathlessly. "I know it is. Rebel's there. I knew she would be, but he wouldn't let me see her, and when I mentioned Cole, he looked so strange. Roth, I think they're in danger."

He stood up as she sank down in the chair in front of his desk. Heath poured her a brandy from the liquor cabinet. "Here," he said, and she sipped it nervously, explaining everything that happened.

"I can feel it," she said. "I've seen men's eyes before when they've lost their sense of reality. Roth, Brandon's planning something horrible, I just know it."

"I say we break in," said Beau.

"We can't," argued Roth. "Not without some kind of proof. If we broke in and found out Rebel wasn't hurt or in trouble, we'd all sit in jail."

Tears welled up in Loedicia's eyes. "But we have to do something," she cried desperately.

Roth grabbed her arm as she stood up. "You don't have to do anything foolish and put yourself in danger." He sent for his overseer, Silas Morgan. "Do you know anyone at River Oaks, or do any of the men know anyone we could get information from?" he asked Silas.

"I could find out. Something's going on at River Oaks, though, I'm sure," he answered. "Of course, none of our men will admit it, but Alan Minyard and that overseer Mrs. Granham has hired are the worst along the river. Even slaves can take just so much."

"An uprising?" asked Beau.

"I don't know . . . but I wouldn't be surprised. I feel it. You work with them long enough, you can sense things like this."

Roth sighed as he looked at Loedicia. "I think you and I had better go back to River Oaks," he said.

They were greeted this time by an extremely nervous Rachel, who wasn't pleased at all to see them.

"Why, Rebel woke up and she and Brandon went for a ride," she explained quickly. "You just missed them."

Dicia eyed her curiously. "Brandon said Rebel wasn't feeling well."

"She felt much better after her rest."

"Well, then, may we see the baby?" but again she was thwarted. "They took the little dear with them," Rachel said sweetly, "and naturally, where the baby goes, the nurse insists on going."

There was nothing they could do but take her word for it although Roth tried. "I'd like to stay until they return, if you don't mind," he said. "I'd like to find out what suddenly made Rebel change her mind and come to River Oaks."

But again they were rebuffed.

"The girls are cleaning right now, and I'm expecting guests shortly, Roth," she said. "If you don't mind, I'd rather you left. Another time, perhaps." There was nothing they could do but leave the house.

Rachel watched them go, then walked hurriedly to the room where Brandon sat with his feet propped on the library desk. "I think this is stupid, Brandon," she said angrily. "They know you brought her here by force. If they find out what else you've done . . ."

He stood up and looked down at her, his brown eyes amused. "I told you, Rachel, I couldn't help it. She kept badgering me, throwing it up to me that she was having his baby. I guess I hit her too hard, but she'll live. It isn't like I killed anybody."

"How about her baby?"

"She miscarried, that's all. After all, how much am I supposed to take?"

"All right, I'll cover for you, but what about the colored nurse and the baby? Why won't you let them at least see the baby?"

"Nobody sees that baby," he said viciously. "Nobody, do you hear? Since he's supposed to be my son, I'll do with him as I wish, and I don't want anyone to see him. I'm going to find a special place to keep him where no one can set eyes on him." He stalked off toward the stairs, his boot heels clicking on the marble as he headed down the hall toward Rebel's room.

Rebel lay back on the pillows, her hair disheveled, face pale. She'd lost a great deal of blood and was too weak to talk. She'd fainted when the servant told her the child was born dead, and now as she heard Brandon talking to her, telling her how much he loved her and asking her forgiveness for hurting her, she prayed for God to let her die. She'd rather be dead than have to spend the rest of her life with him. Later in the afternoon when she woke up, Brandon demanded that she write a letter assuring her mother everything was fine. She did as she was told, then closed her eyes again, trying to forget.

Almost two weeks went by, and so did the elections, and Roth, in spite of the opposition, won his seat in Congress, but

re was little to celebrate. Brandon sent word that Rebel
d miscarried, and when Loedicia was finally allowed to see
r, Brandon was at her side watching her every move. She
d lost the baby, yes, but Brandon was treating her fine, she
d her mother. He forgave her for what happened, es-
cially when she told him it was all Beau's fault, that he
·ced himself on her, but there was a false ring to her voice
she said it, and when Loedicia left, she was far from con-
·ced.

"She's afraid," she told Roth that evening at dinner. "I
ow she's afraid, and I don't think she lost that baby
·ough natural causes."

Roth didn't want to worry Loedicia any more than he had
 but he knew she was right. Word had filtered back
·ough the grapevine, and Silas had told him that Brandon
d beaten her until she miscarried. Roth had been trying to
d some legal way to stop Brandon from taking Rebel back
 Grenada with him before Beau did something drastic, but
·e answer was far from a simple one. As Rebel's husband,
· had every right to do what he wanted, and what jury of
·n would convict a man for beating an adulterous wife?

It was late. Rebel sat at the window in her darkened bed-
·om and watched the lights flickering off and on at the
·ves' quarters. They weren't bright lights. Usually there
·re no lights at all, but tonight the lights would flicker for a
·w seconds, then go out as quickly as they'd come on. Three
·ys. This morning Brandon had told her they were leaving
· Grenada in three days.

She didn't want to go back, but there was nothing she
·uld do. He kept her a virtual prisoner. Her rights meant
·thing. As a woman she was bound to him the same as those
·or creatures out in the fields that Alan Minyard and the
·erseer abused regularly were bound to Rachel Grantham.
·en her body wasn't her own, and last night Brandon had
·me to her bed and proved that too.

She remembered how it had been on Grenada after Matt's
·ath, those last few months before Heath and Beau had kid-
·pped her, and when she remembered last night, tears rolled
·wn her cheeks. She couldn't go back to that. Not again. No
·tter what the law said, she couldn't! Somehow she had to
· away, get out of this house and take Cole and Hizzie with
·r.

How could she get away? She couldn't go anywhere. Some-
·e was always about, and everyone had orders not to let her

leave the place. And poor Hizzie. She was so afraid of Bra
don; but then, who wouldn't be? One minute he was
sweetness, the next like a madman. On the surface
pretended to be forgiving, but Rebel knew what he w
feeling. He'd never forgiven her for Matt, and the way
looked at Cole sometimes frightened her, because he'd oft
threatened that the child would never live long enough to
his heir.

If only there was something she could do. She frowned
she saw the light flicker again outside, but this time it did
go out. In fact, it was getting bigger. She stared, puzzle
then her heart skipped a beat. Fire! The slave quarters we
on fire! She started to open her mouth to scream, rememb
ing what was left of the slaves on Grenada when the Frenc
man's plantation caught fire; then she stopped, listening.

It wasn't the slave's quarters that were on fire, it was t
overseer's house. She could hear shouts and a low mumblir
as if a crowd of people was trying to keep their voices dow
She stuck her head out the window and strained her eyes, tr
ing to see, her heart pounding.

Wild-eyed men and women were marching up the ro
that led from the slaves' quarters to the house, carryi
torches to light their way. They had clubs, axes, and pitc
forks. Here and there a sword or machete. A man with a ri
seemed to be the leader. He was short and stocky, strutti
like a bantam rooster, waving his rifle in the air, and tl
words he yelled at the crowd as they moved along broug
savage cheers that echoed in the night air.

They were still some distance from the house when a sh
rang out near the kitchen.

"All of you!" She could hear Alan's voice from down b
low. "Get back to your quarters." But the bantam roost
crowed.

"We ain't got no quarters no more. We're gonna be free!"

"And where will you go? You think you'll be free?" Al
was desperate. "How? With rewards on your head? You'll
hunted like dogs."

"That's where you're wrong!" answered the bantam roost
again, and a grin spread across his face in the firelight as l
pointed to Brandon's ship, the *Eagle Hunter*, tied up
Rachel's dock. "See that ship?" he said. "Well, right now th
ship is ours. There's guns and ammunition . . . we can sail o
of here on that ship, and no one will find us!" Rebel glanc
toward the ship and saw a light flickering on board.

"You don't even know how to sail a ship," Alan tried to gue. "How many of you know anything about sailing?"

Rebel whirled around as Brandon came through the door. e had a rifle in his hand and a pistol in his belt.

"Stupid fools," he said. A shot rang out below, and Rebel w the black stocky leader grip his shoulder where blood reamed.

"Now, get back!" yelled Alan from below her window. But istead, the torches went out and a dead silence electrified the ir. The flames from the overseer's burning house lit the land-cape.

Another shot came from somewhere, and Rebel heard glass reak downstairs. Suddenly she remembered Cole and Hizzie.

She glanced quickly at Brandon. He was intent on vatching outside, his head half stuck out the window, eyes earching the bushes and shrubbery. This was her chance. Quietly she stood up and inched her way to the door in the larkness. When the shouting got louder outside, she opened he door furtively and slipped into the hall.

Now which way? To the left. She took off her slippers and moved along the hall, but each room she came to in the dark-ned house was empty. She was frantic. Where were they?

Suddenly she held her breath as a figure moved out of the larkness toward her. Her stomach was in knots, and her legs shook as she recognized the familiar walk of the woman who'd helped her the night she miscarried. Tonight there was no forced smile on her lips; instead her face was tight, con-trolled, her eyes on fire, and she held a butcher knife in her hands.

Rebel held her breath as the woman looked directly at her; then, to her surprise, she said softly, "If you're lookin' for that baby and his nurse, honey, you'd better forget it." Her breathing was heavy, labored. "Your husband keeps them locked up somewhere special so no one'll know they're around. Brings them out so only you can see them once in a while. He told the little gal if she said anything to you he'd kill her. Cute, ain't it? I don't mind tellin' you this, 'cause I saw what he done to you, and I think you're no better off'n we are." The woman's eyes widened as she fingered the knife. "But if I were you I'd get out of here now, honey," she warned omi-nously. "This place ain't gonna be safe much longer," and she pushed past Rebel, her bare feet making only a soft padding noise as she went down the darkened hall.

Rebel's heart was in her throat. My God! Where were Cole

and Hizzie? Locked away? There were more shouts, more f[...]
ing.

She placed her feet firmly on the floor. Help. That's wh[...]
she needed, help. Someone had to help her. Lifting the he[...]
of her nightgown, she ran down the stairs as fast as sh[...]
could. When she reached the bottom, no one was about, [...]
she moved directly to the front door and started to open
when a shot splintered it.

She froze for a second; then her mind began to work f[...]
verishly. Leaving the door standing ajar, she dropped quick[...]
to the ground and lay on her stomach. Flowers and vin[...]
were on each side of the door stoop, and her body was sma[...]
She wriggled through the narrow opening, making sure sh[...]
didn't move the door again. The door shut suddenly behi[...]
her, and she heard Brandon inside asking someone who[...]
opened the door. Rachel replied she had no idea, she'd bee[...]
over at the windows in the far side of the foyer.

"Well, keep the doors shut," he ordered angrily. "Alan se[...]
for help. We have to hold out. Do you know where Rebel g[...]
to?" he asked, and she heard Rachel telling him no as the[...]
voices faded. She slid on her stomach to the side of the do[...]
stoop.

Dirt scraped her, scratching her skin as she crawled alo[...]
on her belly, only the silk nightgown between her skin an[...]
the rough stones of the drive. It would have been better if sh[...]
could have gotten her cloak first, but there'd been no time; [...]
it was, she was sure her blond hair and white silk nightgow[...]
made her stand out in the darkness. She hid behind a clum[...]
of bushes with huge white blossoms but knew she couldn[...]
stay there long.

Sporadic shots were fired here and there as men tried [...]
rush the house. One slave fell so close to her that she cou[...]
see he was dead. She had to get out of there. Gingerly sh[...]
moved forward, pulling herself along with hands and elbow[...]
staying as close to the ground as she could, her face scrapin[...]
the grass. The bushes hid her, then flowerbeds, and befor[...]
long she found herself at the side fence near the pasture an[...]
carriage house, away from where the slaves lay hidden in th[...]
yard. How she'd managed it, she didn't know. All she kne[...]
was she'd gotten beyond them.

Lifting her head easily, she caught a glimpse of the hors[...]
milling about among a small group of trees. Evidently, b[...]
cause the slaves were going to use the ship for their escap[...]
they'd given no thought to the horses. Keeping close to th[...]
ground again, she slipped under the fence, then made h[...]

way to them, whispering softly as she neared them. She crouched, rubbing the nose of one of the horses, waiting for a long moment, contemplating where to go for help. Brandon had dropped a casual remark earlier about passing Roth and Loedicia on the road heading for Beaufort, so they probably weren't home. There was only one other place to go. Thankful she'd been raised in the wild, she gave a big heave and leaped to the horse's back, straddling it, her nightgown struggling up past her knees. She grabbed its mane, pulled the horse around, using pressure where the reins would hit his neck, and dug him in the ribs with her toes. The horse let out a snort, then galloped across the pasture, taking the fence like it was flying, and Rebel hung on tight as she heard shouts from behind her.

The night enveloped her swiftly, and after a few minutes all she could hear was her own breathing, the panting of the horse, and the sound of his hooves on the road.

Beau couldn't sleep. He stretched, then got up and walked to the window. Brandon had informed Loedicia and Roth that he and Rebel were leaving for home in three days. Beau clenched his fists; there were tears at the corners of his eyes. What a fool he had been. Too proud, too self-incriminating to admit that life without Rebel was less than living. He sighed and walked out into the other room.

Even Liza and Job had each other. Hell, it didn't matter that they were slaves, or where they came from. They were in love, and as long as they could be together, anything else that happened was easier to bear. He didn't bother to dress, but stepped outside and walked around to the side of the house. It was cool tonight, and he shivered involuntarily as he stood, bare-chested, looking at the empty river. The crew had taken the ship to New Orleans with another load of timber, and he and the big Watusi he'd named Aaron were keeping things going.

He stood for a long time remembering the past, cursing himself for his stupid mistakes, and trying to figure out a way to get Rebel away from River Oaks; then suddenly he cocked his head as the sound of hoofbeats echoed on the night air. Whoever it was was riding like he was being chased by the devil. His first thought was of Heath, who wasn't back yet, and he wondered if his liaison with Cora had finally been discovered.

He watched the road curiously, and squinted his eyes as a horse and rider emerged from the darkness; then he gasped as he saw the blond hair flowing behind the rider, and he broke into a run as horse and rider pulled up in front of the door.

Rebel sat the horse, gulping huge breaths of air, unable to talk. Beau reached up and pulled her from the horse, gathering her into his arms.

"My God! Reb!" he cried as he held her close, and she went limp in his arms, clinging to him desperately.

"Cole and Hizzie," she gasped breathlessly. "They're back there. I can't find them," she wept. "Please, Beau we've got to find them. . . ."

He picked her up and carried her into the house, shouting for Liza to wake up and bring a glass of brandy. He laid her on the sofa and lit a lamp, noticing the dirt all over the fancy nightgown that was half falling off her.

"Here," he said softly, "sip this, then tell me what's happened."

She sipped the brandy quickly, then told him everything. Not just about the uprising, but about the kidnapping, the beating, and how Brandon had forced her into pretending everything was all right, and about Hizzie and Cole.

Beau sat beside her, holding her hand as she talked; then he stood up and turned to Liza, his face grim. "Tell Job I need him, Liza," he said hurriedly. "Tell him to wake Aaron and meet me out front with the horses saddled."

Rebel started to get up, but Beau sat down again beside her.

"You're staying here with Liza," he said sternly.

"You can't go there alone! You can't stop the uprising!"

"I don't intend to," he said thoughtfully. "You might say I'm joining it. I don't intend to do a thing to interfere with Rachel's slaves, but I'm going to find my son." He reached out, touching her face. "I want you here when I get back" he said softly. "And I'm never going to let you go again, even if we have to run away somewhere where he'll never find us."

He bent down and kissed her, a sweet, warm kiss; then he stood up and went to his room, pulling on his clothes hurriedly. When he walked out of the bedroom, Liza was standing by the door helping Job tuck his shirttail in.

"And you be careful," she was saying.

"Don't worry, Liza," assured Beau. "Job won't do any fighting. I just want him around for moral support."

"If you need help, Mr. Beau, I'll help," he said proudly. "Ain't every man can work for someone like you." Beau smiled as Aaron opened the door and stuck his head in.

"Horse ready," he said in his deep booming voice.

Beau moved to Rebel again and bent down, kissing her long and slow, then instructed Liza to see she got cleaned up and put to bed. He'd be back as soon as he could.

The pungent smell of wood smoke filled the air as they neared River Oaks, and now Beau brought his horse to a halt some five or six hundred feet from the house, over by the carriage house.

"I've got to get in there," he said quietly, "but how?"

Job grinned. "I could get you in," he said slyly, and Beau frowned.

"How?"

"Why, I'd just throw you in, that's all," and Beau glanced at him startled. "They throws white men's bodies all around like they's nothin' when slaves is uprisin'," he said matter-of-factly. "I seen plenty in my day," and Beau laughed.

"I see what you mean, but I think Aaron better do the throwing," he suggested. "I want you to stay with the horses." He pointed to a clump of bushes near the carriage house. "Wait over there. When we leave here, it'll be in a hurry."

He slipped from his horse, followed by Aaron, and they made their way to an open window near the front of the house. Beau had been watching it, and so far it looked empty. Pistols and rifles echoed from other windows of the house sporadically, and occasionally a torch would sail through an open window, then come sailing back again. The slaves were intent on revenge. They'd suffered at the hands of these people, and before their ship sailed they were going to make sure no one was left alive.

"Okay, now," said Beau quietly, and Aaron picked Beau up in his powerful hands, holding him aloft over his head. Beau went limp, as if he were dead. The big Watusi let out a yell and ran toward the house as a rifle cracked somewhere, and he let Beau fly through the window as he cursed all white men, then fell to the ground and melted into the shadows again.

Beau rolled as he landed, but he was still bruised. He gained his feet hurriedly, and looked around. This was the library, he presumed. He moved forward in the dark house and peeked around the open door into the next room, in time to see Brandon, not ten feet from him, firing out one of the windows. This was almost too good to be true.

Beau glanced around. Only one other man was in the sitting room; the rest of them were at strategic windows about the house. If some of Brandon's crew hadn't jumped off the ship and managed to reach the house, it would have fallen to the slaves long ago, but they had enough men and were still holding out.

Beau slipped cautiously from the library, the pistol in his hand cocked as he moved stealthily up behind Brandon, who was working to reload his gun. "Drop the rifle," he whispered viciously into Brandon's ear, and Brandon froze, his muscles tensing as he felt the muzzle of Beau's pistol in his back. "I said drop it," Beau whispered again, and the duke dropped the gun on the carpeted floor, where it made little sound. "Now," said Beau, his breath hot on Brandon's ear, "take me to where Hizzie and my son are locked up, and no tricks. Do you understand?"

Brandon nodded, feeling the gun push tighter against him. He was sweating profusely, his lips trembling as he started to move from the window.

"Tell the man at the other window that you're going after more ammunition," Beau whispered, and Brandon did as he was told. They walked from the room, Beau pressed close against him.

"They're downstairs," he said through clenched teeth as they moved to a door beneath the central staircase, and Brandon pulled it open.

Beau shoved him inside. It was pitch dark, and Brandon's breath was coming in short spurts.

"I can't see where I'm going," he said, and Beau shoved the gun harder against him.

They moved slowly down a flight of steps, inching along in the pitch dark, and Beau held onto Brandon's shoulder with his free hand, his fingers biting into him viciously. Suddenly, as they reached the bottom of the stairs and rounded a bend, a faint light showed ahead, and Beau was glad that he could see again; then his heart constricted inside him.

Ahead of them, in a crude cell dug out of the side of the wine cellar, with only an old lantern for light, were Hizzie and Cole. The girl sat on an old cot, while the baby toddled around playing on the cold floor, his clothes full of dirt. A bed of sorts had been set up for him to sleep on, and there was a table where they could eat, but other than that they had nothing.

"You bastard!" cried Beau as he shoved the duke ahead of him. His eyes blazed furiously. "Where's the key?"

Brandon pursed his lips, and his eyes went to a wooden rack that held some wine bottles. Beau saw the key hanging on a peg, but it was a mistake to take his eyes off Brandon for even a second. The duke made a lunge and caught Beau off guard, and the two of them sprawled on the floor of the wine cellar, grappling for the pistol that had flown from Beau's hand.

Hizzie watched, fascinated, as they fought. She held Cole against her and tried to shield him from the violence of these two men, but the little boy seemed to enjoy it as he pointed and stared, trying to talk.

"See," he said over and over again, "see," and Hizzie held her breath as he bantered on, repeating the few words he knew, "See . . . Daddy . . . man . . ." not realizing the significance of what was happening.

Then suddenly Hizzie gasped as Brandon's fingers closed around the handle of the pistol and he lifted it from the floor. "Look out, Mr. Beau!" she screamed anxiously, hiding Cole's eyes, closing her own too as the men rolled over again. She waited for the explosion, but there was none. Instead she heard a gurgling gasp, and as she opened her eyes, she saw Beau push Brandon's dead body aside, and he slowly began to lift himself from the floor.

Beau was exhausted from the struggle, and he breathed deeply, trying to get air into his lungs as he reached down and pulled the knife from Brandon's chest, wiping the blade across the dead man's pants. He stuffed the knife back in the sheath at his waist. He still had things to do, and he reached for the key that opened the cell.

Hizzie was never so glad to see anyone in her whole life as she was to see Beau opening the cell door. They moved slowly up the steps, using the lantern this time, but when they reached the top, Beau blew it out. He opened the door a crack and peeped out, then opened it the rest of the way, and she followed. They moved into the hall and started for the library, when suddenly someone outside shouted and the place became a bedlam of running people as troops from Beaufort and Port Royal spurred their horses down the road at a dead run.

"Come on, this way," said Beau as he pulled Hizzie, and no one seemed to pay much attention to them in the darkness. The slaves were heading for the ship, with Alan Minyard and his men in pursuit.

People were all over the place, and Beau jumped to the ground outside the dining-room window, then helped Hizzie out with Cole, and they made their way away from the fighting toward the carriage house, where Job waited, meeting Aaron on the way.

"Let's get out of here," said Beau hurriedly to Aaron, "before someone realizes what we're doing." Aaron lifted Hizzie to the horse to sit in front of him as Beau mounted. He took Cole from Hizzie, and Aaron climbed on behind Hizzie, but they didn't move fast. They moved easily at first, melting into the shadows behind the carriage house; then, when they knew they were out of earshot, they set their horses at a gallop and headed upriver, working their way along its banks, staying off the road until they were well away from River Oaks.

Rebel sat on the sofa, wrapped in Beau's quilted robe, her feet pulled up under her, and she sighed for the hundreth time.

"It ain't gonna help none, honey," confirmed Liza as she watched Rebel. "You can fret all you wants, but I ain't gonna let you go after him, and it ain't gonna make him get back no quicker."

Rebel rubbed her hands over her face and settled back. Liza certainly was determined, but then, she was a comfort, too. She'd helped her bathe, then shaken her head as she realized there was nothing for her to put on, so she'd wrapped her in Beau's big thick robe to keep her warm and fed her some hot soup. Rebel liked Liza; she was warm and good and rather pretty with her plump cheeks and round face.

Rebel was just about to sigh again when she heard hoofbeats outside. Her heart jumped into her mouth as she looked quickly at Liza. "What if it's Brandon? What if Beau failed?" Reb cried in terror, and Liza frowned as she jumped from the chair.

"Go in the bedroom," she ordered hurriedly, "until we're sure." Rebel slipped from the sofa, running barefoot across the wood floor, disappearing into the bedroom.

She climbed onto the bed, her hands trembling, and sat hunkered against the head of the bed, her eyes glued to the door. The soft murmur of voices filtered in from the other room, and she waited for Liza to tell her it was all right, but nothing happened. She waited what seemed like an eternity as the murmur of voices went on and on. She was about to climb from the bed and find out for herself when the latch on the door moved up and it started to open. She held her breath, biting her lip; then her breath tore from her in a gasp as Beau stood in the doorway, his face grave.

He stepped inside, closing the door behind him.

"Cole?" she asked softly, almost afraid of what his answer might be.

"He's in the other room."

She sighed with relief. "Thank heaven. And Hizzie?"

"She's all right too, Liza's taking care of them."

"And you're all right too?"

"You haven't asked about Brandon," he said slowly, and her eyes snapped angrily.

"I don't care about Brandon."

"He's dead, Rebel," he said, and she gasped, her hand flying to her breast. "I killed him," and she looked into Beau's eyes, seeing his very soul. "He had Cole and Hizzie locked in a cell in the wine cellar beneath the house," he explained. "He always made sure they were cleaned up before he brought them to see you, and he told Hizzie he'd kill her if she told. He also told her he was going to see to it that Cole fell overboard on the trip back to Grenada. I had to kill him," he whispered softly, and he sat down on the edge of the bed, reaching out, pulling her into his arms, holding her close. "I should have taken you from him by force long ago."

She shook her head. "It was impossible. He would have had you and Roth both arrested if you had tried and failed. But I'm not sorry he's dead, Beau. He killed the baby . . . our baby, who never even had a chance to live yet. It was another little boy, and I wanted it so badly."

His arms eased from about her, and he looked into her face. "We'll make other babies, Reb," he whispered, "as many as you want," and she leaned back, letting the sash on his robe fall away so she was naked before him.

"Can we start tonight, Beau?" she asked softly. "I need you tonight," and a low groan escaped from his throat as he lowered her down onto the bed, his lips covering her mouth; then his hands caressed her as he slipped from his clothes and crawled in beside her.

He cupped her face in his hand as he looked into her eyes. "I love you, Rebel," he confirmed, feeling her warm body next to his. "I love you so very much," and as he moved over her and entered her slowly, savoring every moment, she knew this was where she would always be.

ABOUT THE AUTHOR

The granddaughter of an old-time vaudevillian, Mrs. Shiplett was born and raised in Ohio. She married and lived in the city of Mentor-on-the-Lake. She has four daughters and several grandchildren.